WINTERCOMBE

WINTERCOMBE

PAMELA BELLE

ST. MARTIN'S PRESS
NEW YORK

Design by Diane Stevenson/Snap.Haus Graphics

Library of Congress Cataloging-in-Publication Data

Belle, Pamela.
Wintercombe / Pamela Belle.
p.   cm.
ISBN 0–312–02320–0
1. Great Britain—History—Civil War, 1642–1649—Fiction.
I. Title.
PS3552.E5334W5 1988
813′.54—dc19   88–17672

First Edition

10 9 8 7 6 5 4 3 2 1

First Published in Great Britain in 1988 by The Bodley Head.

*For Chris and Maureen, with love and many thanks
for all the years of help and friendship*

HISTORICAL NOTE

Like some of my earlier books, this story was originally inspired by a house, in this case the National Trust property Great Chalfield, in Wiltshire. Like Wintercombe, with which it has many features in common (including the listening masks in the hall and the secret way across the roof space), it suffered garrison and siege during the Civil War, though for the Parliament side. Unlike Wintercombe, however, the family inhabiting it was of little interest, and so I decided to use a novelist's license and place the house some miles away, in one of my favorite villages, and people it with a variety of characters, many of whom actually existed.

The village of Norton St. Philip looks much the same as it did in the seventeenth century, and moreover has the benefit of an unusually comprehensive survey, carried out in 1638 for the lord of the manor. Using this and the parish registers, it has been possible to work out the details of almost every family, where they lived, and their approximate financial circumstances. All the villagers and almost all the servants mentioned in the book are described as accurately as possible. The soldiers, too, with the exception of Nick Hellier, were real people. Lieutenant-Colonel Ridgeley had a reputation quite as evil as I have indicated, and his fate is suitably obscure.

In telling this fragment of the history of the St. Barbe family (a noted name in the West Country), I have enjoyed the assistance of many people. The staff of the Somerset County Record Office at Taunton kindly produced maps, books, and documents on several occasions. Mrs. Pat Lawless, of Norton St. Philip, helped me with various aspects of village history. Dave Ryan, of Caliver Books and the King's Army, supplied me with invaluable information about seventeenth-century weaponry, as well as numerous vital volumes, and the London Library once more came up trumps.

Finally, I am indebted to Steve, who has given me every encouragement and much-needed assistance with items of high and low technology: and, as always, to my mother, who has read and checked every stage of the book and offered her usual helpful suggestions. In consequence, I take full responsibility for what mistakes remain!

—P.D.A.B.
January 1988

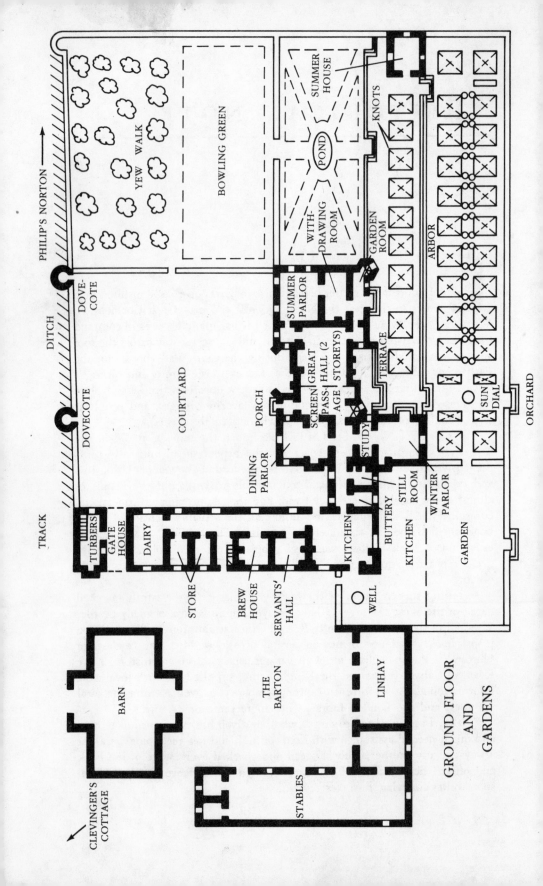

GROUND FLOOR AND GARDENS

PHILIP'S NORTON →

DITCH

TRACK

CLEVINGER'S COTTAGE →

BARN

STABLES

THE BARTON

LINHAY

WELL

DOVECOTE

DOVECOTE

GATE HOUSE

TURBERS

DAIRY

STORE

BREW HOUSE

SERVANTS' HALL

KITCHEN

BUTTERY

STILL ROOM

KITCHEN

WINTER PARLOR

DINING PARLOR

PORCH

SCREEN

GREAT HALL (2 STOREYS)

PASSAGE

STUDY

SUMMER PARLOR

GARDEN ROOM

TERRACE

WITH-DRAWING ROOM

POND

SUMMER HOUSE

KNOTS

BOWLING GREEN

YEW WALK

COURTYARD

ARBOR

GARDEN

SUN DIAL

ORCHARD

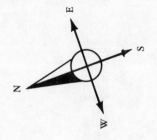

FISHPONDS
&
STREAM

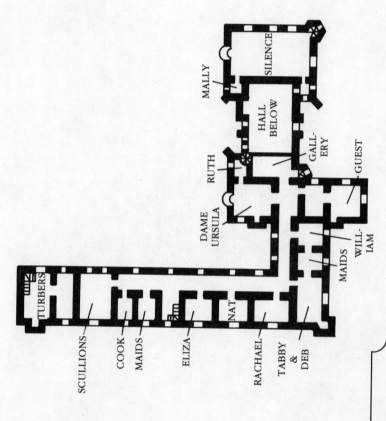

FIRST FLOOR

WINTERCOMBE, 1644

A virtuous woman is a crown to her husband.
—PROVERBS 12:4

PART ONE

THE AUTUMN-COLORED MAN

OCTOBER – DECEMBER 1644

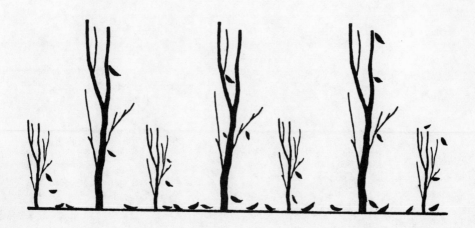

A good man leaveth an inheritance for his children's children.
—*PROVERBS 14:22*

It was unseasonably mild for late October, and the sun stole warm and welcome through her thick woolen bodice and skirts as she sat in the cozy niche in the lowest wall of the terraced, south-facing gardens. The voices of her children and her stepson, gathering early chestnuts in the orchard, came distantly, punctuated by delighted shrieks of discovery or, more frequently, of enraged argument. She did not concern herself: Nat, her stepson, could be trusted to arbitrate in all disputes between the three turbulent younger children. She closed her eyes, lapping up the sunlight with the same contented greed as her cat, Pye, who sat in the niche beside her wearing, she suspected, a very similar look of luxurious bliss on her fat black face with its startlingly asymmetrical white nose and whiskers. She put out a hand and stroked the animal's back. It was surprisingly hot, and shivered with a sensual pleasure reflected in the simultaneous rumbling purr. Pye was that rarity, a cat whose devotion was given to her lady as an individual rather than as a mere provider of food and comfort, although these were of course much appreciated.

An exceptionally loud outburst of childish rage erupted among the chestnuts. Silence—Lady St. Barbe—reflected for the hundredth time that day, as indeed she had done ever since becoming mistress of a large country household and, subsequently, mother to three healthy children in addition to the trio of young stepchildren, on the absolute incongruity of her name. But her father, a sternly religious London draper, had had strict views on the female place in the world and had named her younger sisters in similar spirit. However, since Prue was a giddy careless child, the despair of her parents, Patience a hasty young woman who was always in too much of a hurry to take thought, and Silence an inveterate delighter in words, godly Isaac Woods's hopes of rearing submissive, meek ornaments to Puritan womanhood had been sadly disappointed. The childhood of the three sisters, and their brother Joseph, had been a sad and sorry time, punctuated by frequent beatings, exhortations, prophecies of the awful fate that would surely befall them if they did not slavishly follow their father's will, and hours spent in usually false penitence on their knees. It had drawn the four remaining children (three others had not survived the harsh regimen that their father had ordained) very close. Even now, after nine years of married life in Somerset, Silence wrote to Prue, Patience, and Joseph every week. During the last two years of war, of course, letters had frequently gone astray or been delayed, but enough had evaded the hazards of the perilous journey between Philip's Norton and London for all four to be kept informed of each other's news. Marriage and children for Silence; marriage but no offspring yet for Prue; Joseph's urge to join the Parliament's army, warring with his desire to remain at home and carry on the flourishing family trade with his unwed sister Patience, all discussed with a violent swing of emotion that was characteristic of her brother. Thinking of him, Silence smiled. It would be so like Joseph to enlist in the army just as the war ended, having dithered on the brink for years. But, unfortunately, the war showed no sign of ending yet.

It had raged for two years now—two years ago last week, in fact, since the first great battle had been fought at Kineton, when the king and his fierce and bloody German nephew Prince Rupert had fought the Earl of Essex to a standstill all through a cold autumn afternoon beneath a War-wickshire hillside, and the dying froze with the dead beneath the icy moon that night. Two years since her husband, George St. Barbe, a stout man of integrity and principles, fifty years old, had taken his eldest son Sam, aged eighteen, and his servants and tenants and friends, and marched away with borrowed armor and rusty swords and patched buff coats to fight for the Parliament, leaving his young second wife and children in the care of his aged father, Sir Samuel St. Barbe, a wealthy baronet who lived at a house called Wintercombe, just outside the village of Philip's Norton in Somerset, a few miles south of Bath. And for two years Silence had had nothing of her husband save for a few battered, infrequent letters in his characteristically literal and pompous style. Guiltily she had thoroughly enjoyed the sudden and drastic change in her situation.

It had almost been perfect. Her husband's house, in the south of the county near Chard, was small, shabby, old and cold and inconvenient. There was no incentive to improve it, to introduce modern comforts, since the St. Barbe family home, Wintercombe, would one day be his. Winter-combe had glorious gardens, laid out by Sir Samuel's father in a flush of enthusiasm after diplomatic visits to Italy and France. It was also old, but very beautiful, compactly laid out in the form of a T, large enough to afford privacy, small enough to be easily managed. Sir Samuel, although nearly eighty, was a delightful man, erudite, wise in the ways of the world, full of sly jokes and sound common sense. His grandson Nat was a chip off the old block. Silence had reveled in his company, enjoyed his books, learned chess and tables and even, daringly, some card games from him, listened to his rasped but still tuneful voice singing plaintive songs from his youth, when Queen Elizabeth had repelled the might of Spain and England had known its greatest glory.

But now that voice had gone. Sir Samuel St. Barbe had been three weeks in his grave in the golden church at Philip's Norton, sincerely mourned by all, and none more so than by his son's second wife. And as she sat there at the edge of the orchard, soaking up the last heat of the year, she was unhappily aware that everything had been changed by his death and that all at Wintercombe stood at the brink of an abyss into which one false move, one unfortunate event, might hurl them.

"Mama! *Mama!*"

It was her eldest daughter Tabitha, who was eight. For once not sorry to be thus rudely awakened from her thoughts, Silence opened her eyes, blinking into the light. The child stood before her, tall for her age and slender, her great mass of ungovernable golden-brown hair turned a glorious sunlit yellow around her calm, pointed face. Her name, Silence had been told by Sir Samuel, meant "gazelle," and for such a graceful, shy, unassuming child it was especially appropriate. Now, however, there was an unwonted urgency in her voice. "Mama, William has hit Deb. Can you come, please?"

Beside her, Pye opened a jaundiced eye, yawned delicately, and went back to sleep. Wishing that she could do the same, Silence got to her feet. "Of course I will. It's late, anyway—look at the sun. You've all been here long enough, I think. How many have you gathered?"

Tabitha's hazel eyes, the image of her mother's, flashed up at her. "Not very many. I think the squirrels have been eating them too. But there'll be enough to roast on the fire tonight."

"Mama! Mama, Mama, William hitted me, he *hitted* me!" The wails of Deborah, who was four, could be heard approaching inexorably up through the trees and grass. Tabitha gave her mother one of her swift, secret smiles. Their shared sense of humor and the ridiculous was something that bound them close, and Silence was aware, with another pang of guilt, that she favored Tabitha, who was most like her, above either of her other children, or indeed her three stepchildren—save, of course, for Nat.

He was coming toward her now, a bawling child on either hand: a small, fragile-looking boy of fourteen, with an unnaturally thin face and dark hair, dressed in the sober black they had all worn since the death of Sir Samuel. When she saw her mother, Deb tore herself from his grasp and hurled herself at Silence, her small head thumping into her stomach with a force that drove the breath from her lungs. "Mama! He *hitted* me!"

Silence noted that even in her usual extravagance of grief, Deb had made sure that her complaint was adequately aired. Indeed, it would be surprising if the whole household had not heard it. She gently detached her weeping child from her skirts, seeing the absence of any genuine tears, and said calmly, "You should say 'he *hit* me,' Deb, not 'hitted me'—that's baby talk. It was very wrong of him to hit you—why did he do it?"

Deb's chubby scarlet face turned indignantly up to her mother's. "He did it for nothing!" she announced belligerently. "I wasn't doing *anything* to him and he just hitted—*hit* me!"

"I don't think that's quite the whole story, is it, Deb?" her mother asked, knowing her too well. "Nat? Did William hit Deb?"

Nat, still with the furious William in hand, considered the matter with his accustomed seriousness. Silence could only assume that he resembled his mother, who had died bearing him and his twin sister. His narrow face held no echo at all of his stout, ruddy father, save perhaps in his blue eyes. In character, he was another Sir Samuel, wise beyond his years, with the same sharp pragmatic mind. Since the departure of his father and elder brother to the wars, and more especially now since his grandfather's death, Nathaniel St. Barbe could be termed the man of the house, and Silence knew that she should not rely on him so much. But in a household composed almost entirely of women, children, and old men, in such troubled times, there was no one else whom she could really trust as she trusted Nat, whether on the farm, in the house, with the children, or among the workers and tenants.

"I'm afraid he did," Nat said now. His thin white face and frail, undersized body were a considerable contrast to the rosy sunny complexions of his half-brother and half-sisters. "Tell your mama why you hit Deb, William."

William was two and a half, and clad in encumbering petticoats that could not disguise his sturdy masculinity. Tears of rage spurted down his plump cheeks and his hands were clenched into tight fists. "Deb's got my ches'nuts! She *stole* them!"

Deb's face fell. She stared at her scuffed, worn shoes, passed down from Tabitha, and a tear dropped into the shaggy grass. Her mother sighed heavily, in a passable imitation of Sir George St. Barbe's stern paternal manner. "Oh, Deborah. Did you truly take his chestnuts? Show me."

Her expression invisible, Deb thrust out a filthy hand. Bundled inside an even dirtier kerchief were seven chestnuts, four fat and russet, and the rest so flat that not even a starving squirrel would deign to touch them. Her voice came very low. "He had *all* the best ones and he wouldn't give *any* to me."

"And so you took them from him? For shame, Deb, he's scarce more than a baby and you a great girl of four—five, next April. You can't really complain of him hitting you, now can you? But you must both say you're sorry to each other. Go on, Deb, apologize to William."

Deborah had ample faults, but this at least she had learned. Silence suspected that contrition came much too easily to her. It certainly never seemed to affect her subsequent behavior. "I am very sorry, William," she said immediately.

William glared at her, unappeased. "Want 'em back!"

Ungraciously, Deb thrust the disputed nuts into his fat sticky paw. "You're supposed to apologize too, you know, Mama said so!"

Her brother, his normally cheerful disposition abruptly restored with his chestnuts, gave her a beaming smile. "'Ank 'oo."

As further conflict threatened, Tabitha touched her mother's sleeve. "Listen, is that Rachael?"

Nat, who was standing far enough away from the terrace wall to have a view of the gardens, glanced in the direction of the distant shouts. "Yes, it is Rachael. She's coming down to us—and she'll fall if she's not careful."

Rachael was his twin sister, born ten minutes before her brother. The difficulties of the birth had left their mother, George St. Barbe's first wife, dead and Nat's health permanently affected. According to Wintercombe legend, Rachael's enraged wails at birth had been heard in Philip's Norton half a mile away, and maturity had not mellowed her voice.

"Mother—please come quick—Mother!" With a scuttering of gravel, Rachael arrived with a bump against the yellow stone balustrade just above them, her black hair escaping in regrettable rats' tails from her plain white cap.

Silence surveyed her gasping stepdaughter with her usual serenity. "Whatever is it, Rachael?"

"It's soldiers—soldiers have come!"

None of the children, except perhaps for Nat, could possibly have guessed the enormity of effort it took to maintain that look of calm, wide-eyed inquiry. But the years of her childhood, learning to keep her self, her individuality, and her liveliness beneath the subservient mask that so gratified her father, and thus escape his beatings, stood Silence well in such moments of crisis. Yet still, in the sudden and absolute quiet, she felt that they must surely hear, or see, the fierce battering of her heart against her ribs.

Soldiers! The terror that had lurked beneath the calm surface of their lives for two years now, since war had come to Somerset. Moving to Wintercombe had saved Silence and her family from penury or worse, for the county had been controlled by the king's supporters for over a year now, and the estates of all prominent Parliament men, George St. Barbe among them, had been confiscated with speed and efficiency and their owners proclaimed traitor. The aged Sir Samuel, of course, being an ancient and highly respected member of the county community, had escaped any such retribution, and with an aplomb that had disgusted his wife and secretly amused Silence, he had paid off both sides since the opening of hostilities, not caring, in his own words, a fig nor a spoon for king or Parliament so long as they left him in peace at Wintercombe to enjoy his declining years, to potter undisturbed in the sunshine or sup a tankard of beer or cider at the George.

And now a sudden seizure of the heart had terminated Sir Samuel's life, and the wolves had gathered. Silence knew why they had come, what she would say to them, what must be done to save Wintercombe from sequestration and herself and all her family from being turned out to fend for themselves as they could. She felt very much alone, and frightened.

Despite her serene mask, some of her fear had communicated itself to the younger children, who had fallen silent, their squabbles forgotten. William's small fat dimpled hand clutched her skirts, and Deb stared wide-eyed up at Rachael, who still hung over the balustrade, her hair coiling around her shoulders like some unkempt prophetess of doom. Realizing that even Nat was looking at her as if she held all their salvation in her hands, she gave herself a tiny shake and called to her stepdaughter, "How many soldiers, Rachael?"

The girl waved an arm that was splashed with dark milky stains. She had been helping in the dairy, Silence remembered. "How should I know?" she said with irritation. "*Hundreds* of them—the courtyard's full of horses." And she added, with a faintly spiteful note in her voice, "Well, are you coming, Mother, or shall I go ask Grandmother to see them?"

Since Sir Samuel's widow was crippled and had been virtually confined to her chamber for many years, this was hardly practical. Moreover, to allow such a thing to happen would be another lost battle in the long, hard-fought struggle that Silence had waged with both her mother-in-law and her stepdaughter since her marriage nine years previously. She made herself smile up at the difficult, moody, willful, stubborn child who was Nat's twin and yet his opposite, and said gently, "No need for that, Rachael. I shall come up now—and don't you go rushing back, walk with us. I want to have all of you with me when I see them."

"Why? Who? What's happening?" Deb demanded, having missed most of the vital elements of information.

Silence, resisting the temptation to snap an answer back, said reassuringly, "Only soldiers, poppet. Soldiers come to see us—but they'll soon go away, I promise, they won't be here very long. I expect they want more money, now that your poor grandfather is dead."

And they'll want more than money, she thought as, holding William by one hand and Deb by the other, she climbed the steps up from the orchard to the arbor terrace. Now the house was visible, its rough old stone, gray-gold and glowing in the sun, the large windows of the hall with their stained-glass coats of arms, the smaller panes to either side, all winking in the afternoon light. Silence drew a deep breath, her heart juddering with the realization of the depth of her love for this place and the strength of her fear that it might be taken away from them and given to rapacious strangers. Everything depended on her conduct with these unknown men now doubtless filling her hall, eyeing the furniture and the tapestries, speculating on the wealth of this old and lovely house, the farm buildings, the barn newly filled with the fruits of harvest and haymaking, the fat milch cattle and plump woolly sheep, the rich water meadows along the Norton Brook, the barrels of cider made from the small sour apples in the orchard, the horses in the paddocks, the hazel coppices up behind the house, the cheeses new and green in the dairy . . .

They will want the house, she thought, and found that her mouth was dry when she tried to swallow. They will want the house, they will know that Sir Samuel is dead and that it should be George's now, and because he's in Waller's army and Sam is with him, they will want to take it away as they did with Sir John Horner's house at Mells, and George's at Chard, and strip it of everything to feed the king's soldiers—and we will be destitute. Unless—unless I can persuade them otherwise.

Part of her, the part that had feared her father's beatings and her husband's unthinking and hurtful criticism, wanted to hide, to cower, to protest that she was not capable of such defiance, that she was only a weak and feeble woman, made of inferior flesh, Adam's spare rib, a lesser being created purely for Man's help and comfort. But as she gazed despairingly up at the mossy stone tiles and the ridiculous carved beasts that Sir Samuel's father had placed incongruously on the medieval gables, the other Silence asserted herself with quiet, confident calm. She had an unassailable argument. She had her children around her, and surely not even the rapacious lechers that popular report held to be the usual run of king's soldiers would be so heartless as to turn her and all her family out of doors, in defiance of the laws of God and man.

A hand touched her sleeve. She glanced around and saw Nat gazing at her with his characteristic seriousness. As their eyes met, he gave her a small, encouraging smile. "It'll be all right," he said. "Justice is on our side. They claim to fight for the law. They can't touch us, can they?"

"I'm not sure," Silence replied, uneasily aware of Rachael sharp-eared beside her and Tabitha, who heard everything and was unusually sensitive, just behind. But, as always, Nat's support warmed and cheered her. Turning her back on the sun, she walked with her children across the terrace, past the arbor of cherry trees, the old stone sundial whose shadow showed, sharply, that the hour approached four of the clock, and up the next flight of steps to the knot garden. The south wing of the house, built in the same rough-dressed stone as the rest, lay in shadow to their left, almost hidden beneath the weight of the huge vine that sprang from the south-facing wall of the hall and had spread in perhaps fifty years over most of that side of Wintercombe. It had only once or twice ever given any grapes, and those small and mean, too sour to eat and too few to make wine. But Silence and the elderly gardener, Diggory Barnes, had nursed and pruned and worried over it, as over some sick infant who would surely soon recover. There was a saying at Wintercombe, however, that talked of "when the vine bears" in the same way as other households spoke of falling moons or flying pigs.

On the last terrace, paved with stone and hummocked with sweet-scented thyme and marjoram and chamomile growing between the cracks, stood Eliza Davison, the chief maid, her plain horse face rigid with disapproval. "My lady, the place be all amok with soldiers, a-tramping about in the hall with their slummocky boots, and Madlin Tilley's been screaming and crying, 'tis a wonder you didn't hear her, my lady, and all the maids be afeard they'll be ravaged."

Nat snorted, and Silence fought a sudden impulse to hysterical laughter. Eliza, who gave herself airs, was always struggling to eliminate the more incomprehensible elements of her dialect from her speech, and the results were sometimes unintentionally comical. She gave her stepson a warning glance and said soothingly to the maid, who was looking somewhat affronted, "I'll deal with them, Eliza. Don't worry, I'm sure they'll soon be gone. They've probably only come for money, just as they did when Sir Samuel was alive. Can you go and calm the other servants? They must be greatly in need of a steady influence at the moment."

Gratified, Eliza bobbed a curtsy and vanished inside the house. Silence, aware of the unfamiliar sound of male voices within, took a deep breath and tighter hold of the hands of William and Deb, and stepped into the cool dimness of the hall.

The screens, dark carved oak hung with heavy red curtains, hid her from the uninvited, unwelcome visitors, but their words came to her with clarity. "Sir Thomas has been waiting for the old bugger to die for months—there'll be rich pickings here now, eh, Nick?"

"There's no plate," said the second voice, deeper, less rough-edged, but no less calculating or hard. "I wonder what they've done with that?"

"I can imagine, right enough—but still, no harm in looking, eh? An amusing way to spend an afternoon, and the lads'll be pleased. We've not had the chance of a little wanton destruction for months."

Silence, standing in the dark passageway with her children clustered around her, could feel their horror and fear. In her own breast was a cold hard knot of emotion that she recognized, with some astonishment, as rage. She had not experienced such fury since the brief, bad days when she had last attempted, at the age of ten or so, to defy her father. William whimpered, and she realized that she was clutching his hand too tight.

"A great pity, to smash such a place," said the voice of the man addressed as Nick. "But needs must, where the devil—or Sir Thomas—drives, and a quantity of plate would make any amount of pillage worth our while."

"I'm surprised you're so squeamish. The man's a proclaimed traitor, he and his son have been with the Roundheads from the beginning. We've picked his own lands at Chard bare—and now his father's dead at last, this becomes his, and therefore ours. Do you fancy quartering here, eh?"

"Better here than Bath, and besides, to my mind the women are prettier—and ripe for the taking. Did you see that bold red-haired trollop gave us the wink as we rode in? No doubt of it, Johnny my lad, there's good sport to be had here."

"I think you may be mistaken in that," Silence said, her voice holding her fury tight-leashed. As if of their own accord, her feet had moved her out from behind the screens, the children bunched around her as if to shelter beneath the wings of her rage. She saw that there were, despite Eliza's words, only two men in the high, old-fashioned room, standing before the fire, their faces turned toward her in surprise as she entered. She knew what they must see—a woman neither tall nor short, young nor old, dark nor fair, handsome nor ugly, fat nor thin, clad in sober mourning black, the habitual serenity of her expression belying the turmoil of anger and terror within. There would be no sport to be had with this woman, and it was written all too clearly on the face of the taller, fairer of the two young men confronting her. They were both dressed in the famous Taunton blue of the Bath garrison, overlaid by buff coat and sword belt. And both, as they assessed her probable identity, doffed their plumed hats and swept her low, courtly, and assuredly mocking bows.

"Mistress St. Barbe, I assume?" the shorter, darker one said. His was the voice that had so casually discussed the dishonoring of her maidservants. Silence stared at him coldly, seeing a brown face, brown hair, brown eyes, a countenance unserious and lively, seamed with paler lines where he had screwed his face against the sun and rendered peculiarly devilish by a thin dark sliver of moustache on his upper lip. He was the pattern of those brawling, swearing, wenching Cavaliers of legend, and in sudden panic she wondered if she could argue with him at all. It was the face of a man who saw what he wanted and took it.

"I am Lady St. Barbe," she said. "To what circumstances do we owe this unexpected visit, sirs?" She did not like being courteous, since they so clearly would not be, but Sir Samuel had always treated the most rapacious grasper of funds for king or Parliament with an unfailingly polite manner that had never, to the discerning, concealed his contempt for men who must be wooed by fine talk and flattery.

"To the death of Sir Samuel St. Barbe, your husband's father," the fair man said. At first sight more handsome by far than his companion, she could see at closer quarters the broken veins under the skin of cheek and nose, which in a few years would become the betraying ruddiness of dissipation and debauch. His eyes were blue and bloodshot, and he did not look as if he had slept much the previous night. "We have come to offer you our most sincere condolences on his sad demise, Mistress St. Barbe."

"And whom have I the . . . honor of addressing?"

The bite in her voice was not lost on the darker man. The corners of his mouth turned up infuriatingly, and the rebellious ten-year-old buried deep within the calm and capable wife and mother longed to hit him with all her strength. "I am Captain Hellier, and this is Lieutenant Byam. Alas, madam, sad though was Sir Samuel's death, we have not in fact come to offer our condolences."

He paused, tantalizingly. Nauseated by their hypocrisy, Silence glanced at Tabitha and saw her eyes narrowed, assessing the two men. The unaccustomed severity of her expression gave her face a mean, pinched look quite unlike the sweet-natured, sensitive child whom her mother loved so much. Up until now, thanks to Sir Samuel's wisdom, they had been spared the full horror of war, of unthinking destruction, pillage, murder, rape, the brutalizing of soldiers and civilians. Silence, seeing her beloved Tabby's changed countenance, knew with terrible foreboding that the children's loss of illusion and security this day might be only the first step down a steep and horrifying slope.

Muffled footsteps and voices came from above. She looked up to the gallery, above the screens passage, and saw the bobbing caps and curious frightened faces of a clutch of her maidservants, peering down. The brown man followed her eyes and said with every appearance of concern and consideration, "Perhaps if we may talk somewhere more privily, madam?"

"That will not be necessary," Silence told him firmly. She knew that she must win this battle, and if she did so in public, her authority over the servants, always a trifle uneasy, would be vastly enhanced. Bad enough to have her mother-in-law like an avenging Fury in her chamber, too sick to run the household but too obstinate and domineering to relinquish her grasp so tamely, without appearing weak and intimidated by a couple of soldiers. They were after all only a captain and a lieutenant. When her husband had last written, he had been raised to the colonelcy of his regiment.

"As you will, madam," Captain Hellier said formally. He came closer, and she saw that he was a little taller than herself, by some three or four fingers. Deb pressed tightly against her, while William, fascinated by all soldiers, gazed avidly at his sword.

Silence was aware of Tabitha's intense glare and the white set faces of the twins, one at each shoulder, and drew herself up. "Say what you must, Captain, and be gone—you and your men are frightening the children and the maids." And me, she could with truth have added, but did not. She would not have admitted her terror to these men for all the gold at the king's command.

"I regret, madam, that I must do a great deal more than frighten your family. Sir Samuel St. Barbe is dead, died three weeks ago, am I correct? On Saturday, the fifth day of October, in the year 1644?"

"At about five of the clock in the morning, of a seizure of the heart, if you require the finer details," Silence said, with heavy sarcasm. "And was buried in the church at Philip's Norton two days later—you may go ask Master Willis, who is vicar there, if you doubt me."

"I do not, Mistress St. Barbe. But it is my unfortunate duty to tell you that, since Sir Samuel's tragic, though not alas untimely death, your husband George St. Barbe, Esquire—"

"*Sir* George, if you please, sir—since you are so concerned to be correct. Sir Samuel was made a baronet by King James, and my husband now inherits that title—so I am *Lady* St. Barbe."

"As he has also inherited this house. And I must tell you, *Lady* St. Barbe, that all his inheritance, as a proclaimed traitor, is forfeit to the king's cause, the use and revenues thereof to be granted to Sir Thomas Bridges, His Majesty's Governor of Bath, for the support of the garrison there."

"Is it, indeed?" Silence said coolly. She could almost touch Rachael's fury; the girl was rigid with it, coruscating at her shoulder. She wanted to reach out, to give her some reassurance, but did not dare. All her energies must be concentrated on saving Wintercombe. "And so you have come to turn me out, a defenseless woman, and my five children, and my husband's mother who has not walked these eight years and is upward of seventy years old, in the king's name, and leave us with the clothes on our back and no roof over our head? Is that the king's law, and the king's justice? *I* have not fought for the Parliament, sir, and nor have these innocent children, nor my mother-in-law, Dame Ursula."

"Indeed you may not have done," Captain Hellier said. "But that, I regret, is not my concern. I have orders from my colonel, Sir Thomas Bridges, to seize this house in the king's name. No mention was made of the inhabitants of this place, madam, and other ladies in your position have in the past taken shelter with relatives or friends. In any case, you would no doubt not wish to stay while my men are quartered in the house."

Silence could hear the maids on the gallery whispering in agitation among themselves. Pitching her low, clear voice to reach them, she said, "You are laboring under a serious misapprehension, Captain. You have no rights to this house, nor has your colonel, nor the king, and I must ask you to leave at once."

That, she saw with satisfaction, had taken the wind very nicely from his sails. The brown eyes, a light, autumnal color, like William's chestnuts, widened slightly, then narrowed. "You are wrong, madam. I have the king's warrant in my coat, signed with his own hand—he is even now in Bath, though on a brief visit only. I doubt you could reach the city in time to appeal to him, and still more that he would listen to your entreaties. He has no patience with traitors, Lady St. Barbe, nor with their importunate wives."

So your gloves are off, my fine captain, Silence thought. She found that she was almost enjoying this tantalizing game, playing the man on the hook of his ignorance of the one vital fact that she had willfully withheld until now, the information that would save Wintercombe.

"There is no need for me to appeal to anyone, Captain. The law is on my side, not yours. You are mistaken in one essential particular." She took a deep breath, meeting those narrow eyes coldly, savoring her victory. "When Sir Samuel died, he left a will, as do most men at the end of their days. His lands were his to bestow as he wished, and he did not choose to leave them to his son, my husband. In his will it states plainly that Wintercombe and all the manor lands, and everything else besides of which he died possessed, goes to his wife Ursula, Lady St. Barbe, for her life, and after her death to his grandson Nathaniel, who is fourteen years old. So you see, Captain, my father-in-law has not left my poor husband a penny. This house belongs to Dame Ursula, and there is nothing whatsoever that you can do about it."

The hall was quite quiet, hushed, as Captain Hellier stared at her disbelievingly. Silence spared a quick glance for the elder children and saw Rachael exultant, Tabby's wide hazel eyes shining with delight and relief, Nat smiling. Then, abruptly, a new combatant entered the fray.

"That's taken you all aback, hasn't it, King's captain? But it's quite true, I can assure you."

As one, the faces of Silence, the children, and the two soldiers swiveled round and up to the source of the voice. Like a malignant gargoyle, the sour and wrinkled countenance of Dame Ursula St. Barbe peered over the gallery, her hands gripping its edge and her maid, Ruth, supporting her. Well pleased with the effect of her entrance, Sir Samuel's widow cackled her amusement. "There's nothing I miss in this house, Captain, as my daughter there knows full well. 'The wicked flee when no man pursueth: but the righteous are as bold as a lion.' Proverbs twenty-eight, one. I am the owner of Wintercombe and all its lands, Captain, and if you do not believe me, you may go ask Master Harley, attorney at law in Stall Street in Bath, for it was he who drew up the will." She cackled again. The sound for once did not produce the feelings of nervousness and indignation it usually inspired in Silence. "And now, *Captain,* will you be gone and leave these old bones in peace?"

The lieutenant spoke, for the first time in some while. "They're lying— they must be! Nick, you can't let them get away with it—a more obdurate pack of Roundheads never breathed. For Christ's sake, St. Barbe has been in Waller's army for *two years!* What will Sir Thomas say?"

"He has only to ask Master Harley, with whom I believe he is acquainted," Silence said, feeling some annoyance at her mother-in-law's intervention. The old lady—if that was the correct title for someone so relentlessly tough-minded, malicious, domineering, and unpleasant—had made her appearance in suitably dramatic manner and had stolen some of her own thunder. Veiled, sly comments on this unwelcome fact would probably be aired in her daily interviews with Silence for months to come, if not years. Sir Samuel, who had long shown an almost saintly forbearance in the face of his wife's godly ill nature, had been in Silence's view unnecessarily pessimistic when leaving Wintercombe to his second grandson after his wife's death. Dame Ursula had lived seventy-six years in the best of health, apart from the painful affliction of the joints that made it impossible for her to walk without assistance, and would doubtless attain her century with glee, assured of her place among the Elect in Heaven and of the certain absence of the rest of the family, saving her adored and only son George, from such bliss. She would surely see this war out, it being the crown of her hopes that the evil papist warmonger who occupied the throne would achieve his richly deserved bad end.

The soldiers stood irresolute in front of Silence. The sun, setting behind the farther hill, lit now only the high painted rafters of the hall, leaving the rest in dim shadow. The fire was dying down to red embers reflecting the glowing rays above and was in dire need of replenishment. She said, half her mind already inappropriately busy with domestic matters, "Are you satisfied? Will you now take your men from this house, Captain? Or must I go to Bath tomorrow and make the strongest possible complaint to Sir Thomas Bridges?"

The lieutenant sniggered. "That will avail you nothing, madam. Sir Thomas is most anxious to seize the property of all disaffected persons, no matter what paltry pretext they may devise."

"Pretext? My dear husband's last will and testament a pretext? May you answer in hell for that wicked insult, you blaspheming ungodly rogue!" One of Dame Ursula's claws left the gallery rail and pointed unerringly at the two men. "'As smoke is driven away, so drive them away: as wax melteth before the fire, so let the wicked perish at the presence of God.' As you will assuredly perish and burn, as will all sinners and evil-doers—be sure, your sins will find you out, as it is written in the Book of Numbers!"

Captain Hellier touched his lieutenant on the arm. "If it is indeed as they say, John, we can do nothing—yet. And since the king does not wish those who are innocent"—he mockingly inclined his head to the gallery—"to be punished, we will withdraw, for the present. His Majesty would not want such injustice to be committed in his name, after all." He turned to Silence, standing immobile in the middle of the stoneflagged hall, the children still about her. "I must bid you au revoir, madam, if not farewell, for I do not think either you or I have heard the end of this matter. Master Harley must be consulted, and all seen to be in order—and I do not think that Sir Thomas Bridges will let such a prize as this slip so lightly between his fingers." For a moment his voice became almost friendly. "So I warn you, Lady St. Barbe, you may see us again, and sooner than you might wish. Your servant, madam."

Coldly Silence watched his insolent bow, copied with an even greater flourish by his lieutenant. As they turned to go, the captain glanced up to the gallery where Dame Ursula still stood, and his face suddenly flashed bright with mischief. His parting words echoed clear and loud all around the hall. "Good-bye, Dame. You have made very free with your lines from Holy Writ—think you on the words of Paul's first epistle to Timothy, the second chapter, verse eleven. Good day to you all." And with a tramp of booted feet, the jingle of harness and spurs, they were gone.

Silence knew that quotation. It had been a part of her childhood, the exhortations flung at her because she, despite all her despairing efforts, could not fit the mold her father had made for her. But to hear it referred to by that unpleasant malignant Cavalier captain, of a blasphemous and heathen breed, was startling to say the least. Astonishingly, his words even seemed to have silenced Dame Ursula.

Nat's lips moved in a whisper, only just audible to her above the sounds of the soldiers riding away under the gatehouse arch, and back to Bath. "'Let the woman learn in silence with all subjection. But I suffer not a woman to teach, nor to usurp authority over the man, but to be in silence.'"

"You have it exactly," she said softly, knowing that Dame Ursula would be well aware of the insult. Outside, the noise of many horses died away into the distance. It was as if Wintercombe, and all within it, had been holding breath for the past half hour and only now could relax.

William said, his voice at once disappointed and relieved, "They gone? Soldiers all gone?"

"They've gone!" Rachael cried, her glee spilling over. She snatched the little boy up and hugged him. "Soldiers all gone, William—we're safe, we're safe!"

"You'd do well to hold your tongue, girl," her grandmother said from on high. "They said they'd most like be back—and they will. 'As a dog returneth to his vomit, so a fool returneth to his folly.' Nathaniel! Give me verse and chapter."

Nat tipped his head back and, as ever reliable, supplied it. "Proverbs, Grandmother. Chapter twenty-six, verse eleven."

"You have ever conned your Bible well," the ancient tyrant said, her hard gaze softening a trifle. Nat had always been her favorite, though she took good care never to show it. "You may come read to me, after supper. I grow weary, Ruth—pray assist me back to my chamber."

With her malign presence gone and the soldiers vanquished, the children exploded away from Silence, reveling in the end of danger. She stood, weak-kneed and shaking from her own reactions, watching them run out and into the porch, giving vent to the unbearable tension in shouts, whoops, and snatches of song as they charged into the courtyard. They knew better than to make such noise within the hall. There were three

squints, disguised as masks, around the upper wall, through which everything that went on below could be heard and to a limited extent seen. One,
hidden most inappropriately by a laughing face, gave directly into Dame
Ursula's chamber, and her chair stood just by it. Any transgression or
departure from her rigorous standards of behavior would inevitably be
ruthlessly detailed in the agonizing interrogations she conducted twice a
day with her daughter-in-law and her grandchildren. In the morning, as to
their planned tasks and duties; in the evening, as to the performance and
assessment of the same. Any release of childish high spirits would be severely reprimanded, and such was the force of Dame Ursula's personality,
despite her age and infirmity, that the entire household still tended to defer
to her rather than to Silence, even though Sir Samuel had made it quite
clear when she and the children had come to Wintercombe, two years ago,
that his daughter-in-law was to assume the running of the house. Much as
she loved the place, it had been a struggle to assert herself; and still more
of a battle to hold on to her hard-won authority now that Sir Samuel was
dead.

But at least she had faced up to the soldiers. She had not been cowed;
she had kept her dignity and won her argument, before her mother-in-law
had even entered the fray. She heard the whispers and scurryings that
would herald the arrival of the maids, all doubtless wanting soothing words
of reassurance, but there was one child left in the hall whose need of comfort was greater than all of them. She said softly to her troubled daughter,
"What is it, Tabby?"

The little girl turned abruptly, like a startled fawn. She was a striking
child, with that mass of abundantly curling hair that could never be fit into
any cap, the wide level brown eyes, the pointed chin and sensitive face.
One day she would be beautiful—as I never was, Silence thought, not with
regret, for vanity had never had any place in her life, but with misgivings,
for loveliness of feature was a dangerous gift, a snare for the wicked and the
foolish, and a temptation to self-love. Dame Ursula had muttered often
that those sinful curls must be cut off, as if Tabby were personally responsible for them. But Silence, whose own God was more generous and more
kindly by far, held the view that her daughter's looks were a gift from
heaven, and that therefore it would be an insult to heaven to abuse or
disguise them.

"I didn't like them," Tabitha said. "The soldiers—they were horrible!
And the way they talked—as if they didn't like us—and they didn't even
know us!"

Silence reached out and hugged her daughter, feeling the slender arms
wrap around her in response. "That's war, chicken—war does that to people. It makes them hard, suspicious, brutal, greedy. It's an evil thing, civil
war. Probably before it began they were ordinary folk, like you and me and
Father, living quietly and breeding cattle and horses, and farming their

lands—and now they can think of nothing but how best to grab the fruits of some God-fearing man's hard work." She smiled sadly. "But for the war, those men might be our neighbors, our friends—like poor Master Flower, or Sir John Horner."

"I don't think I could *ever* like them," Tabby said, her voice muffled because her face was pressed against her mother's stiff black bodice. "I didn't like the fair one at all, and the other one, the autumn-colored man, he was hateful!"

"Autumn-colored?" Silence repeated, struck by the aptness of the description. Tabby had a felicity with words that delighted her mother, and often such phrases would emerge casually, without much thought, and yet strangely poetic. In her mind's eye she saw Captain Hellier, his brown and tawny coloring, and smiled. "What a good description—'the autumn-colored man'! Much too good for the likes of him, though, chicken—you'll have to call him something foul, something more appropriate for him." She gave Tabitha a sudden, flashing grin, crackling with mischief. "Take your time, and think of a good one."

"I'll try," Tabby promised, with an answering grin the image of her mother's. She paused, the smile fading too fast, and then said slowly, "Was it true? Will they be back?"

Silence wanted to lie but could not. She thought for a moment, selecting her words with great care, and then said honestly, "I don't know. Men like that aren't so easily discouraged. We may have to pay them, as your grandfather used to do. But the house is safe, Tabby. It belongs to your grandmother now, and they can't turn us out."

"I'm glad," the child said. She shivered suddenly. "I hope they don't come back—ever, ever, ever! I hate them!"

"You shouldn't hate them—unpleasant as they were, they were only doing their duty. But I hope they won't come back as well," Silence said firmly. "And, the Lord willing, they won't."

But she could not forget the soldiers' words and knew that Wintercombe, bereft of the protective presence of Sir Samuel, would not so lightly escape Royalist attention. She watched Tabitha, her worries calmed for the moment, running out to join the other children in the front courtyard, and wondered with apprehension what the next few days would bring.

TWO

A man of wickedness is hated.
—*PROVERBS* 14:17

The soldiers, of course, were not so easily discouraged when a prize of Wintercombe's richness lay like a ripe untouched windfall in the grass, there for the taking. And the day they chose to return, nearly a week after their first visit, had begun so badly, so full of harassment, that for Silence their arrival seemed merely the inevitable climax to a more than usually disastrous series of events.

The mood of the day had been set by the weather. That unseasonable sunshine had indeed been the last flicker of summer. The following morning, Wintercombe had woken up to a depressing, relentless downpour, and it had rained more or less steadily ever since. The children, as a natural consequence, were becoming increasingly restless and fractious, given to futile squabbling and outbreaks of temper. Nat, who was taught by Master Willis, the vicar, was unable to go to his lessons. Such was the precarious state of his health that any chill or soaking might bring on a congestion of the lungs, and Master Willis, a tired-looking, perpetually hurried man in early middle age, was perforce a daily visitor, every morning earnestly taking Silence aside to ask what she could suggest for his wife's current ailment. Silence, who felt sorry for Mistress Willis, a woman brought very low by the burden of bearing nine children and losing all but one of them, did her best to oblige. Privately, however, she felt that, as Sir Samuel had been used to say, what poor Mistress Willis really needed was a good dose of happiness, pounded up with a little cheer and comfort and sprinkled with the laughter of a brace of healthy babes. Since thoughtless, busy, godly Master Willis was unlikely to provide such remedies, his wife's prognosis was not good.

The morning had been heralded by a furious argument between William and Deb as to who was to have possession that day of a much-loved carved wooden horse, which they were supposed to share. Silence, appealed to by the nurse, Doraty Locke, had settled that dispute by telling them, in time-honored fashion, that if they were to fight in such an unchristian manner over the horse that old Diggory had carved for both of them, then neither should have it. And the little nag, smooth and sleek in the cream and pink and golden colors of the yew from which he had been so lovingly and carefully fashioned, was placed well out of reach on the mantelshelf in Silence's chamber. But though William and Deb were reduced to a sulky, tearful acquiescence, the scene had not escaped the sharp ears of Dame Ursula, and the morning interrogation was more than usually unpleasant.

As usual, the children were ushered in after the morning prayers, which were held for the entire household in the hall on rising each day. It was still only seven o'clock, and dark enough for a smoky tallow candle to light Dame Ursula's chamber. She called it godly thrift, but Silence's irreverent maids, knowing the wealth and comfort of Wintercombe, and spoiled by the sweet wax in profusion elsewhere in the house, had another and less pleasant name for it.

Dame Ursula's wizened face peered at them through the rancid smell and noxious smoke. At least, Silence thought, standing behind her offspring with her hands decorously folded and her hair bestowed plainly within her starched lace-fringed cap, there was nothing at fault with their appearance. All had their hair neatly brushed, their attire was clean and tidy, and their faces wore bland and innocent expressions, schooled by long habit, and fright.

It never satisfied Dame Ursula, whose exacting standards were placed so high that no child could reach them. "You're late this morning—I have been up and reading this past hour. What was the meaning of that unseemly caterwauling I heard?"

It fell to Silence to answer this, since William did not know that a question was directed at him unless by name and Deb was too guilty to speak up. "It was a slight dispute, madam. All is quiet and settled now."

"Who were the perpetrators of that ungodly noise? You, child?"

Tabby, thus addressed, looked startled and wary. "No, Grandmother."

"Really?" Dame Ursula said with a sneer that reeked of disbelief. She detested poor Tabby, whose glorious curls seemed a personal affront to the harsh austerity she favored. "Then it must perforce have been you, Deborah, and you, William. What have you to say for yourselves, disturbing my prayers in such a way?"

"I am very sorry, Grandmother," Deb said instantly, her large brown eyes earnestly staring into Dame Ursula's glittering blue ones, as hard and penetrating as any knife. "I will not do it again, I promise."

"And you, William? Pay attention, child, or you'll be beaten as you deserve. You have interrupted my reading of Holy Scripture, a most ungodly and unchristian act. Your sister has apologized, as is befitting—what have you to say, eh?"

It was doubtful whether William understood more than one in three of her words. The tone, however, was quite plain, and he knew by heart the magic incantation that always seemed to placate his terrifying grandmother. In a toneless gabble he recited the spell. "I-am-very-sorry-Grand-mother-and-I-won't-do-it-again."

"That's better." Dame Ursula, having asserted her authority, leaned back a little in her chair and surveyed the suitably cowed figures of her five grandchildren and her daughter-in-law. "And Nathaniel—how are you to spend your day? Is Master Willis coming this morning?"

"Yes, Grandmother—if his horse can get up the hill in the mud."

Nat was the only one who showed no fear, who could give more than a plain answer, and paradoxically it was this that his autocratic grandmother loved best in him. She softened slightly. "And what are you to study to-day?"

"We are to continue with the works of Livy, Grandmother, and Master Willis has also spoken of his wish to further my knowledge of mathematics today."

Silence, listening to his words, spoken in what she feared was an ironic imitation of his father at his most pompous, was struck afresh by the change that came over all the children when in the presence of Dame Ursula. Even William and Deb put away their natural childishness, turned into wooden, frightened little puppets by the threat of her wrath and the power of her personality. She understood it only too well; she suffered in the same way herself. She waited quietly, ordering her thoughts, as Nat's catechism continued. Then it was Rachael's turn. Her sewing was called into question, her knowledge of the Book of Proverbs (Dame Ursula's fa-vorite) found wanting, her deportment criticized until the girl's face grew a fiery and humiliated red and tears of rage stood in her fierce eyes. Silence, wishing that Dame Ursula would leave her stepdaughter alone, knew that poor Rachael would be unbearable for the rest of the day.

Then it was her turn. A woman grown, a mother four times over, twenty-eight years old and the keeper of the house both at Chard and at Wintercombe for the nine years of her marriage, she stood meekly in front of her mother-in-law and stated her tasks for the day: teaching the younger children and Rachael in the morning, supervising the ritual autumn sweep-ing of the chimneys, work in the stillroom, estate business with old Tom Clevinger, the bailiff, and later, if the weather cleared, a visit of charity to the Widow Grindland, mother of one of the scullions, who had a child sick. She hated thus to itemize her duties, for no matter how detailed her intentions, nothing ever happened as she planned it, and Dame Ursula was never satisfied with her reasons for deviating from her goals, however com-pelling or justified they might be.

But at last she could find little more fault with the day, apart from a sour comment on last night's supper. "The bread was stale, and Turber forgot to water the wine again. Give him a severe reprimand, daughter. It is hardly the first time that he has been so lax. I dread to think what the servants have been doing, under his guidance."

"I shall speak to him," Silence promised with a twinge of irritation. There was no doubt of it, the footman and butler Henry Turber was becoming increasingly deaf and forgetful, but he was a willing soul, if too ancient for his duties, and she hated to criticize him for faults he could not help. It was another burden to lay upon her. Sometimes, facing Dame Ursula's implacable will, she wished with all her heart to be free of them— servants, mother-in-law, house, farm, bailiff, husband, even the children—and escape somewhere, anywhere, that might offer her the chance to be herself, and selfish, for the first time in her life.

But she could not. Her father had beaten such idle daydreams from her head years ago. The day stretched before her with children to keep calm and occupied, servants to order and cajole and correct, the bailiff to manage, and it would never end, all the days of her life . . .

She bowed her head as Dame Ursula prayed sternly for strength to overcome wickedness and the temptations of the devil and the flesh, and to live the godly life of righteousness, and heard with a flash of amusement William's infant and unpracticed tongue twisting the portentous syllables. Then, with a final exhortation, they were allowed to go—and not before time, for the growling of Rachael's healthy and hungry young belly was threatening to drown her grandmother's withered voice.

Breakfast was taken in the dining parlor. The St. Barbes did not eat in the hall unless on special occasions such as Harvest Home, or when important guests must be entertained. Another argument broke out over the last slice of white bread, which Tabby had and Rachael wanted. Silence, her calm already frayed, made them both have brown, and shared the disputed slice between William and Deb, who was being unwontedly and annoyingly virtuous. Outside, the rain streamed down the leaded panes, and the sky was too dark to promise better weather. With a premonition of continuing disaster, she contemplated the rest of the day in a mood of some gloom.

Master Willis arrived late, mired from head to foot. His clumsy old mare had slipped coming up from the village, just as Nat had foretold. He was offered a clean suit of clothes belonging to Sir George, which hung on his insubstantial frame in folds of honest russet, and as Silence plied him with mulled and spiced ale, he complained so pointedly about the appalling conditions that she gave in and suggested he need not come to Wintercombe again until the weather improved. Master Willis brightened miraculously, swallowed his ale with ungodly enthusiasm, and bore Nat off to the study to wrestle with the dubious delights of Livy. William was led away by Hester Perry, the young nursemaid, to be tended for the rest of the morning in the nursery. Despite Dame Ursula's opinions on the necessity of early education for the young, Silence knew it was of small use yet trying to instill any learning in the mind of a lively little boy of two and a half.

She must, instead, try to achieve some impression on the intellects of Deb, Tabby, and Rachael. The lessons took place, as always, in her own chamber. It occupied the whole of the eastern side of the upper part of Wintercombe, separated from the rest of the house by the two storeys of the great hall and reached by its own stairs. It had been Sir Samuel's chamber, and he had gallantly relinquished it to his daughter-in-law on her arrival two years earlier. Silence loved the room, as she loved all of Wintercombe, but with a special intensity because, amid the rambling house with its servants and children and business and lack of privacy, this part of it was hers. True, her personal maid, Mally Merrifield, had a tiny closet off in which to sleep, but she could be sent elsewhere if necessary, so that Silence might have the chance to be absolutely alone for a space.

There was small hope of that today. She settled Deb with her hornbook, Tabitha to read from a primer, Rachael to practice her handwriting, which was execrable, and then, not without some trepidation, left them under the capable eye of Doraty Locke, the nurse who had been with them since Tabby's birth, and with her maid Mally went to tackle the various problems that always beset the household.

Mally was a local girl, daughter of a Norton family that had recently been struck by disaster, when both her father and her grandfather had died within two years of each other, leaving their widows and children to weave cloth and work the family holdings as best they might. Silence, on her arrival at Wintercombe, had lacked a personal maid, her own having elected to stay with her sweetheart in Chard, and Sir Samuel, who knew everyone in Norton from Master Flower at the Manor Farm down to the smallest and humblest member of the fertile and poverty-stricken Grindlands, had suggested Mally Merrifield, newly fatherless.

It had been an inspired choice. Mally at first sight was an oddity, a girl of totally insignificant height with a beaky nose, sharp blue eyes, a multitude of freckles, and ginger hair, the mark of a Merrifield. But the short horn marked a shrewd cow indeed. Mally was resourceful and quick-witted, honest and fiercely loyal to Silence, who found in her a truer friend by far than the meek submissive girl she had left behind in Chard.

"Chimneys," Mally said, as they descended the narrow winding stair from her lady's chamber. "Don't ee disremember the chimneys, m'lady."

Silence produced a sound halfway between a sigh and a groan. "I have not forgotten them, Mally, much as I would like to. Is Walker here yet?"

"Aye, m'lady, and ready to 'gin on the hall fire. Indeed," Mally said, as they walked into the high room, to be greeted with chatter, bustle, and the sharp smell of soot, "it d'seem as if he have already."

The few pieces of furniture in the great hall had been covered with old cloths, the rush mats rolled back, the debris from last night's fire cleared away by the maids, and Walker, one of the farm workers, who was called in every year for the task of sweeping all the ten stacks that Wintercombe could boast, had his head up the chimney and his ancient and filthy clothes enveloped in a cloud of soot as he investigated some problem. The two others present, Eliza the chief maid and Leah, Walker's daughter, curtsied to their mistress. Eliza, who was of Puritan persuasion and pessimistic outlook, said gloomily, "The chimney be blocked up, m'lady, and Walker can't shift it no matter how he do try."

"Perhaps it's a bird's nest," Silence suggested as Walker, his pockmarked face entirely disguised by soot, emerged coughing from the hearth and, obviously, remembered just in time not to brush the mess from his clothes all over the flagstoned floor.

"I can't do norn with this here tun," he complained. " 'Twasn't blocked last year, m'lady."

"Do ee poke thy rod up again, Father," Leah Walker said with a smirk. "And if it don't vay, we all d'know who to blame, don't we?"

Eliza glanced at Leah with prim dislike. Walker's eldest daughter was a bold-looking girl, always neat and clean and tidy, with a sly manner and a trick of investing the mildest comment with salacious overtones merely by a wink, a lift of an eyebrow, a snigger in her voice. Her father, however, was evidently inured to it. With a resigned grunt, he poked his head once more up the chimney and then gave the rods a massive and despairing shove. There was an indistinct rustling sound and then, amid the coughs and curses of the unfortunate Walker, the entire sooty lining of the great chimney arrived with a rush in the hearth and swept out to engulf everyone in a black, evil-smelling cloud.

"Oh, dear," Silence said mildly, above Walker's most ungodly imprecations. Mally, Eliza, and Leah, coughing and spluttering, dusted themselves off with varying degrees of success. Eliza's long, rather mannish face was not improved by a random distribution of sooty smuts across her prominent nose. Silence, after one startled glance, did not dare look at her again, nor risk catching Mally's eye.

Leah, with callous vigor, applied her energy to hammering her father on the back as he choked and wheezed and wiped his streaming eyes. The water from them left long pink streaks barring his blackened face. "You girt gawk, you!" she said, with a complete absence of filial respect.

"What a lot of slummocks we must look," Mally commented with a grin. "Well, best get yourself a-going and clear this here mess, eh, Eliza?"

Eliza, still attempting to beat the soot from her starched collar and formerly immaculate attire, cast her the gloomily satisfied look of a Cassandra proved right. "I *told* en it'd come out all of a skelter," she said reproachfully. "My collar be all dirten, m'lady, and looksee at my apron, 'tis quite ruined!"

"No, Eliza," Mally said instantly, very solemn. "I don't reckon as how that'll ever be clean again."

"Be you betwitting I?" Eliza demanded with justifiable suspicion, quite forgetting her efforts to speak properly. She was notorious for having no sense of humor whatsoever, and teasing always annoyed her intensely.

Silence, judging that it was time to intervene, said hastily, "I'm sure it will clean up beautifully, Eliza—you may use some of my fine lemon soap next washday, if you like."

As the maid uttered her somewhat grudging thanks, she glanced around at the pall of thick soot that lay over every surface in the hall and thought of the hours of cleaning work that now must be done. And this was only the first chimney to be swept, though by far the largest. It was cold in the hall today without a fire. Next year, Silence thought, I shall abandon tradition and have Walker do them two weeks earlier, at the least. And then it will probably turn out warm, a Luke's summer.

With a wry smile, she walked forward, heedless of her trailing skirt in the soot—it was far from being her best—and peered at the heap of black sticks in the hearth. "It *is* a bird's nest. And more than one of them, by the look of it."

"I *told* ee," Eliza reminded them with cheerless satisfaction. "And we'll be a-sweeping of this here blatch till dimmet, I reckon."

"Nonsense—it'll only take an hour or so," her mistress said with a confidence she did not feel. "Fetch brooms and pans, and you can set to work right away, if Walker has finished?"

"Uh? Oh, aye, m'lady, the tun be all clear, I d'warnt," Walker said, rather hoarsely. He looked so comical, his face striped in pink and black, that Silence wanted to laugh. She restrained herself, and gave orders that he sweep the chimney in the dining parlor next, so that at least they might have their dinner in warmth. Then, having watched Eliza and Leah begin the laborious task of cleaning up the soot, she made her way to the next domestic crisis.

The rain had revealed a slipped tile over one of the servants' chambers in the north wing. Water had actually been dripping on to Eliza's bed, an inconvenience that she had lost no time in reporting to her mistress as soon as possible that morning. Silence noted the damp patch on the plaster ceiling and ran her mind rather wearily over the various farm workers who might be prevailed upon, for an extra jug of cider and a shilling or so, to climb a precarious ladder in the rain and replace the tile. She immediately dismissed Walker from her list. He would probably fall off and break his neck, and she doubted that the Fleur-de-Lys could afford to lose such a regular customer.

"'Twordn' be right, would en, for her to move her own bed," Mally said in her broad Somerset voice, breaking in on Silence's thoughts. Silence gave a suppressed snort of laughter. It was true, a move of the simple half-tester bed a mere six inches to one side would have eliminated the problem of the wet sheets entirely, but Eliza had a very firm idea of her own importance and would not so demean herself. Before Silence's arrival at Wintercombe she had been housekeeper, young for the role and groomed by Dame Ursula. Now the foreign second wife from London wore the keys of the house at her waist, and Eliza, after two years, could neither forgive nor forget her demotion.

"I'll do it for her—I bain't too stomachy to shift my own bed out of the wet," Mally said. She placed the back of her thighs against the sturdy frame and gave a hefty push backward. With a groan of wood, the bed moved perhaps two inches. Silence, seized by a sudden impulse of mirth, set her hands to the headboard and in two quick jerks Eliza's damp-spotted sheets were safe from further despoilation. The job done, she inadvertently caught Mally's eye. Then the two of them were giggling like a pair of silly children.

It was not right, Silence reflected, holding her aching sides. She should keep her distance from her servants, not behave with Mally, at least, as if she were with a friend of her own station. She was a lady, mistress of a great house, wife of a baronet, with a household to run and an estate to administer in her husband's absence. But she had not been bred to such a position. Her father had been no more than a draper, albeit a very rich and respected one, and his parents Kent yeomen, no less humble than Mally Merrifield's family. And her mother's father had begun by selling fish in Billingsgate. Silence had been reared in a strict and godly fashion, with indifferent success. Some of her ancestors' sturdy independence still remained, their humanity and warmth and distaste for humbug and pretension. She could cook and sew and clean; no task had been thought too lowly for her during the dreary days of her childhood. She had scoured pots and polished furniture, cleaned hearths and mended Joseph's torn hose and cuffs. With three daughters of the house to train, her father had thought it unnecessary to employ more than the bare minimum of servants: a cook-maid and a scullery boy were the usual staff, and the shop apprentices had run their errands. Silence had come to Somerset a bride of nineteen, a competent housewife, able to drive a hard bargain at market and turn out a plain but respectable meal for her husband; and had speedily found that her skills, earned with so much labor and sweat and tears, were unwanted. George St. Barbe, casting about for a second wife to mother his children and run his house near Chard, had not intended that his new bride demean herself with household tasks—after all, there were a dozen servants to do that. He had wanted above everything a young wife, one who would be more malleable than his much-loved Anne, who had had a regrettably obstinate streak; a godly girl, acceptable to Dame Ursula, able to give his three children the direction and guidance so lacking in their motherless lives and to instill some order into a household that he was too busy, and too ignorant, to supervise.

He had encountered Silence's father on one of his business trips to London, and had learned with interest that this honest, religious, and wealthy man had three daughters of marriageable age. Meeting Silence, the eldest, he had been struck at once with her decorous, seemly disposition, her neat, unassuming grace and carriage. She had had a most godly upbringing. She was young and submissive. She was not unpleasing to look at, with that serene face and modest figure. With two younger sisters and a brother, she had ample experience of looking after children and running a household, especially since her mother had been four years dead. And above all, her father was a rich man and would dower her well. Silence, too young and too frightened of her father to realize that life might hold any other possibilities, had agreed to marry this stout, middle-aged Somerset gentleman, knowing only that it brought status, security, and above all freedom from her narrow, cold, constricted life in Paternoster Row.

It had led her, instead, to the old-fashioned and inconvenient house at Chard, to a dozen surly resentful servants whom she had not the slightest idea how to direct, to three unhappy and difficult stepchildren, and to a husband who, while kind and at first quite attentive, lacked any understanding of her feelings, her bewilderment and loneliness, her isolation among people who seemed to speak a different language, and a countryside almost threatening in its richness and abundance and strangeness after the cramp and dust and noise of London, where she had lived all her life.

Yet she had managed, just. Her husband might treat her like a child, even as she bore his children with dutiful regularity and lost only one, still regretted. The servants tried to ignore or deceive or cheat her. And as for the stepchildren, Sam and Rachael were openly defiant. But she had remembered her fishwife grandmother's adage, uttered at some despairing moment of her unhappy childhood and never forgotten. "Make, do, mend, girl," old Granny Richards had said. "No regrets, no pity—just you pick up the pieces and start again." And Silence had made the house comfortable and welcoming for the husband she did not love, and set herself to manage the rambling drafty old building and obstreperous servants; had learned to understand and appreciate the richness and warmth of their dialect; and had won the trust and respect of Sam, the affection and friendship of Nat, and the grudging acceptance of Rachael. She had enjoyed no such progress, of course, with Dame Ursula, who would resent any woman wed to her beloved son who was not his dead first wife, naturally in her eyes a paragon of piety and all the female virtues. But Dame Ursula had not been at Chard. And at Chard Silence had discovered that she could cope with the life into which she had so abruptly been thrust.

And at Wintercombe, away from her husband, despite the malign presence of her mother-in-law, despite Rachael's difficulties and tantrums, despite the tortuous complexities within the servants' hall, where rivalry, resentment, backbiting, and quarreling flourished like a well-watered bay tree, she had learned a little of happiness, for the first time in her life. Sir Samuel had had much to do with it, and now he was dead. But there was the garden, and the beautiful house, and Nat, and Tabby, and Mally Merrifield, with whom she could giggle and joke as she had once done, illicitly, with her sisters Prue and Patience.

Since those days, none save one had addressed her by her given name, outlandish as it was even in this Puritan family. She was "Mother" or "Mama," "daughter," "my dear" or "wife," "madam" and now "my lady"—but only Sir Samuel had ever called her Silence.

"M'lady!"

She looked around, smiling at the aptness of Mally's interruption. The girl had spoken gently, tolerant of her mistress's occasional lapses into daydream. "What is it?"

"Someone be calling ee, m'lady, and it d'sound tarblish urgent to I."

Footsteps thundered along the passageway that ran along part of the north wing past this, Eliza's chamber, and a high desperate voice shouted breathlessly. Silence and Mally glanced at each other, exchanging a faint smile. Then the small figure of one of the kitchen scullions erupted through the doorway, all but crashing into them. It was Ned, Mally's thirteen-year-old half-brother, a boy as undersized and light-boned and red-haired as his sister, with bright blue eyes, abundant freckles, and a boundless intellect and good sense. He said gasping, abandoning all courtesies in his haste, "Do ee come quick, Darby and Sheppard, they be a-murthering each other!"

"Murdering?" Silence said. Mally was already through the door. Ned took a deep breath and grasped her arm in desperation. "Oh, yes, m'lady, Rob Sheppard, he telled Master Darby as how his sauce were too salty and Darby was despeard miffed and fetched him a girt whop with a mallet and now they be a-walloping each other, *please* come, m'lady, afore they d'slaughter each other!"

Her dignity gone, Silence ran with the two Merrifields along the north corridor, past the nursery rooms and down the narrow stairs that lay, unfortunately, just outside Dame Ursula's chamber. There would be interrogations later, but at this moment of crisis Silence could spare no thought for her mother-in-law's malevolent prying and interfering. Panting for breath, she flung herself down the steep stone steps, her skirts hitched up almost to her knees in her haste, and burst into the kitchen just ahead of Ned and Mally.

It was as the boy had said—he was an observant and truthful child—but the situation had obviously deteriorated since his dash for help. Silence, in one quick, frantic glance, took in the scene: the big stone-walled room, the two huge fires, scheduled for sweeping that afternoon, glowing between the steaming pots and cauldrons that held the noonday meal, the big worn table piled high with vegetables half prepared, a brace of hens and a rabbit, a couple of carp from the ponds, knives and implements in plenty, and the frightened faces of the two other scullions peering around the dresser by the window.

The cook, Tom Darby, a man vast in all directions with a face as flaming red as his fires, stood over his unfortunate assistant, who had had the temerity to criticize his sauces. Rob Sheppard was pinned against the great table, bent backward over it with one of Darby's fists grasping his shirt collar with a strength born of years of stirring sauces and butchering beef. His eyes were almost bursting from his skull and his mouth gasped for air like a landed fish, with a hoarse crowing sound. In his right hand, the cook held one of his meat cleavers raised threateningly above Sheppard's quailing head. And since Darby's rages were legendary, and his obsession with the sharpness of his knives almost equally so, young Ned's alarm had been amply justified.

At least there's no blood spilled—not yet, anyway, Silence thought with relief. She had half expected to find Sheppard dismembered with the rabbits and poultry. Displaying a confidence she did not feel in the least, but aware of the urgency of the situation, she stepped boldly into the kitchen and said, her voice loud and scolding, "What do you think you're doing, Darby? Let go of him at once!"

Not by one flicker of his heavy face did the cook betray that he had heard her. He strengthened his grip on the cleaver and on Sheppard's collar, and the younger man gave a despairing squawk of breath, three-quarters strangled. "I ought to chop you in little pieces, so I ought," said the cook, his voice slow and thick and menacing. "While you're in my kitchen you don't say nothing—*nothing*—against *my* cooking, d'you hear me? Nothing! Or I'll hack you in gobbets easier than that there rabbit, see?"

The frantic wobbling of Sheppard's head, still held on the stalk of the cook's fist, indicated that he did see, quite plainly. Darby gave a grunt of what might have been satisfaction, opened his hand, and walked away, throwing the cleaver down on the table. It struck with a dull thump and stood quivering in the scarred wood, but Sheppard was in no condition to notice it. He had doubled over on his knees on the flagstoned floor, coughing and retching.

Silence felt her legs shaking, both from relief that murder had apparently been avoided and with trepidation at the encounter to follow. "Darby!" she said, her voice coming out too high and nervous. "A word with you, if you please, in the servants' hall. Now." And she turned and swept out with what she earnestly hoped was a suitable imperiousness, not to be disobeyed.

The servants' hall, next to the kitchen, was a comfortable room furnished with settles, stools, tables, and a roaring fire. It was, thankfully, empty. Silence stood by the hearth, welcoming the warmth even after the greater heat of the kitchen, and kept her eye on the door. After a minute or so, too long for submissiveness, not long enough to indicate outright rebellion, it opened and Darby's overlarge bulk squeezed through it.

It was an unfortunate fact that in matters of cookery, he was an artist. Innumerable attempts had been made in the past by many of Sir Samuel's friends to lure him to their own establishments, but to no avail, Darby being, it seemed, susceptible to no inducement, however lavish. His loyalty had been given to Sir Samuel, who had seen his potential years ago as a lowly assistant in a Bristol merchant's house and had promoted him to chief cook at Wintercombe, with complete charge of the kitchen. But like many artists, Darby had a wayward and unpredictable temperament, so easily offended, so hard to please, so difficult to mollify. Sir Samuel had always been able to soothe him. Now Silence must try or face the unspoken disapproval of her household, who relished the wonders of Darby's food and could tolerate his tantrums for that reason alone.

And besides, if she could not calm him and restore order, she could imagine only too clearly what Dame Ursula would have to say about it.

"What have you to say for yourself, Darby?" she inquired coldly. He might be the creator of marvelous dishes fit to tempt a king's palate, but she was determined not to relinquish her hard-won authority. If she let him cow her, it would be common knowledge in Wintercombe within the hour, and then they would all defy her.

Darby stood just inside the door, staring at her, only slightly less menacing than when he had wielded the cleaver. Not the kind of man to be friendly with those he considered his inferiors, his origins were obscure, but Wintercombe rumor asserted that he had made his living in youth as a wrestler at fairs, and Silence could well believe it. He was above two yards high, built in proportion with massive arms and a vast unsightly belly straining his apron, and his inimical eyes were small, lost in fat like a vicious boar's, so that for an instant her imagination supplied him with sharpened tusks. But when his mouth opened, there was only the usual array of gapped, brownish teeth. "I am sorry, my lady. I do not know what came over me—the man's impossible to work with, he's always needling me, the little upstart!"

He's no more sorry than Deb ever is, Silence thought, looking at that uncomely and unapologetic countenance. "You must try to control your temper," she said, keeping an edge to her voice. "It is not seemly to quarrel thus before the scullions. Ned Merrifield wishes to follow your profession—would you place such an example before him?"

It was well known that young Ned, bright and hard-working and eager to please, was Darby's favorite. For an instant an expression that was possibly shame crossed his bovine face and then was gone. "No, my lady," he said, looking at a point past her shoulder.

"Then be mindful of that, when next you are tempted to give way to your more brutal impulses. I don't doubt that Sheppard can be difficult to work with, and I will speak to him also. But you are in charge in the kitchens, and there must be order there. Do you understand me?"

"Aye," the cook said, with slightly less courtesy, veiled but the resentment still plain. Silence, remembering his devotion to Sir Samuel, knew only too well what he must think of her. Most of the household probably did, but were more careful to hide it. To the end of her days, she would never be anything other than a foreigner, a stranger among these insular Somerset people.

Make, do, mend, Silence said to herself with determination, and dismissed him.

Sheppard was much easier to deal with. In his early twenties, he was perhaps half Darby's age, and half his size as well. Nor was he as indispensable, and knew it. Ignoring his simmering grievances, Silence gave him the kind of brisk scolding she gave to her quarreling children and sent him back to the kitchen. Then she went to see how the cleaning of the hall was progressing.

Eliza had performed miracles. Whatever her difficulties in character, she was at least capable of great industry. Leah, for once subdued under her stern gaze, had helped, as had the other maid, little Madlin Tilley, who was fifteen and had only been at Wintercombe for a few months, and the ancient tapestries had been beaten free of soot, the floor swept, the rush mats replaced, and the dust cloths removed. Now Madlin, a shy and very pretty child, was relaying the fire while Eliza stood over her, ready to correct any deviation from her instructions, and Leah, free of Eliza's attention for the moment, was idling in a corner behind the screens, leaning on her broom. Silence, ignoring the malicious gleam in the girl's eye, sent her off to help her father sweep the remaining chimneys, and wondered where Mally was.

And then Mally was there, flying down the corridor from the kitchen, her orange hair falling out of her cap, her eyes wide with alarm, so that for an instant Silence thought that Darby had gone truly mad and slain Sheppard after all.

But the reality was, almost, worse.

"They be back!" Mally gasped, all but bumping into Silence as she halted. "The soldiers, m'lady, they be back—they've come back!"

Eliza had heard her. So had Madlin, whose gasp of terror sounded frighteningly loud. I hope she doesn't give way to hysterics again, Silence thought amid the sudden rush of her own fear, or she'll set them all in a panic. At least Mally would not do so, despite her apprehension. Silence had never known her maid to be anything other than steady, resourceful, and dependable in a crisis.

"What will ee do, m'lady?" It was Mally's voice, low and urgent. "Will ee bar the door to 'em?"

"I don't know," Silence said, fighting her own panic, which seemed to rush up through her body, threatening to suffocate her, bind her limbs, and freeze her brain. "How many, Mally—how many are there? As many as last time?"

"More, I d'reckon," the girl said grimly. "There bain't any use in trying to keep 'em out, bain't there."

It was a simple statement of fact. Silence met her eyes and shook her head slowly, reluctantly. "I shall go find out what they want," she said, with much more certainty and courage than she felt. "At least the children aren't here this time, to see and hear them . . . they weren't exactly pleasant, Mally."

"Soldiers bain't, usually," Mally said dryly. Her last word was almost lost beneath the thunderous hammering on the door and Madlin's terrified wails.

Madlin, who was young and innocent and beautiful, in a fresh flowering country way. "Tell Eliza to take her out of sight—fast," Silence said to Mally, saw her look of understanding, and walked to the door alone.

The main entrance to Wintercombe, on the north side of the house, was through a porch, stone-vaulted, with an inner door and an outer to keep out drafts, and also—for the house had been built in a more violent age even than this—to delay unwelcome visitors. Both doors were oak, inches thick, studded with iron and bound with massive black strap hinges tipped by curling fleur-de-lys. The inner possessed a key that weighed the heaviest on the chain at Silence's waist. The outer had another so large that it always remained in the lock, and a great bar of wood that clasped door to stone, and looked strong enough to resist a battering ram. In these uncertain times, it was always kept bolted and barred. But no ordinary manor house such as this could hope to resist the entry of determined soldiers without much damage and injury.

Silence opened the inner door. The porch was cold, and very dark. The only light came from a little squint looking from the dining parlor that had been set into the wall as a way of keeping watch on intruders. The knocking stopped and was then repeated. She heard the cry, harsh and brutal. "Open! Open up, in the king's name!"

Using all her slight strength, Silence heaved the bar back into its slot hidden in the thickness of the wall and shot back the bolts. The knocking ceased, and she heard sounds of satisfaction on the other side of the door. She knew that this should be Turber's task, but he, old and quavering, would not be able to resist them. She might not either, but she would not have their presence soiling her beloved house, frightening her children, damaging and destroying all she held dear, without doing her utmost to prevent them. Everyone and everything in the house at her back was her responsibility, and she would not fail them without a struggle.

The key was stiff. Obviously, it had not been oiled this week. She turned it, and the twisted iron handle, and pulled the door wide.

The courtyard, usually wide, empty, neatly graveled, was full of horses, trampling and restless, a sea of brown and chestnut, gray and bay and black, so many soldiers that she had no hope of counting them. And on the doorstep, an officer she had never seen before, a caricature of a Cavalier in extravagant lace, beribboned lovelocks, fringed gloves, and preposterous bucket boots that were, she saw with a glimmer of grim satisfaction, well splattered with mud. It was still raining heavily, and the courtyard was liberally puddled with water and horse dung.

He did not bow. In her sooty old dress, opening the door to him, he must take her for a servant. "Yes?" she said, using the voice with which she had discouraged hawkers in Paternoster Row. "What do you want?"

Her hostility seemed to disconcert him not at all. He smiled menacingly, showing teeth more discolored than Darby's, but sharper. "A word with your lady, my pretty. And I'll have the proper courtesy from you, or you'll have cause to regret it."

Over his shoulder, suddenly, appeared a face she recognized: the red-veined nose and bloodshot blue eyes of the fair-haired man who had been so unpleasant before. There was no doubt that he knew who she was. Forestalling him, Silence said to the officer, "It is I who should have more courtesy from you, sir. I am Lady St. Barbe, and I demand to know what you want of me, and why you and your men have invaded my house without my leave."

"We need no leave," said the man, smiling still. "We have the king's warrant—what higher authority do you require, my *lady?*" And he gave her an insolent bow, mockingly extravagant. "Since you have no choice in the matter, I will enter."

She stood aside, her face hot with fury, because if she had not he would have shouldered his way past her. She could see it in his face. Behind him came his lieutenant, Byam she thought his name had been, and then the brown captain, the autumn-colored man of Tabitha's fanciful description, damp with rain, cloaked and booted and muddy. The rest of the men, still mounted in no sort of order in the courtyard, remained where they were, and she wondered with brief despair if there were any other officer left outside to keep them from mischief and destruction. Then, with suddenly shaking hands, she saw Mally, dependable, reliable, solid Mally, waiting in the screens passage. She left the door, knowing that the girl would shut and bar it again, and followed the three king's officers into the hall.

Fortunately, there was neither sight nor sound of Madlin, whose lovely face would undoubtedly prove a temptation to licentious men such as these; nor of Leah, who would with equal certainty encourage their attentions. The Cavaliers stood by the fire, which was still unlit, their faces as hostile as she knew hers must be. Silence clamped her hands together to stop their trembling and said coldly, "I have had the dubious pleasure of meeting these other men on an earlier occasion—but I do not know you, sir."

"Ridgeley is the name, Lady St. Barbe—Lieutenant-Colonel Ridgeley, of Sir Thomas Bridges' Foot. I also have the honor to be in command of his troop of horse."

"At present outside, trampling my courtyard?"

"At present in your courtyard, yes, my lady. Captain Hellier and Lieutenant Byam you have met before, I know. They reported that your welcome on that occasion was . . . shall we say, less than warm?"

"They came with threats," Silence said. "In the circumstances, I could not be particularly enthusiastic about their presence." Keep calm, said the still voice of reason in her head. Keep calm, for your sake, for the children's sake, for Wintercombe—or you may lose everything.

"Your husband is with Waller's army, I understand?"

"He is," she said. It was common knowledge all over Somerset, the other men had known it, so there was no point in denying it.

"And his father, the lamented Sir Samuel St. Barbe, has recently died, I understand. There seems to have been some disagreement between father and son—since this house was not willed to his heir but to his wife."

"There is no entail, he could bequeath it where he liked. You know all this," Silence said, battening down her terror and her rage beneath that old brittle armor of calm. "Tell me what you want, and I will endeavor to supply you, and then be gone. This is a house of women and children, and you have no business here."

Ridgeley laughed. He was a big man, heavily and floridly handsome, with a drinker's belly and hair so dark that his jowls showed blue, though it was only midmorning. His amusement was genuine, and utterly threatening. "Ah, that's where you're wrong, my lady. We do have business here, quite legitimate business—myself, my officers here, and those forty-three men outside." He paused, a contemptuous sneer on his face, and took a paper from inside his sleeveless buff jerkin with ostentatious slowness. As the silence crawled interminably, he unfolded it and thrust it at her. "Here, my lady. A warrant signed with the king's own hand. The manor known as Wintercombe in the village of Philip's Norton is to give shelter, assistance, and supply to Sir Thomas Bridges' Horse, without let or hindrance of any kind, on pain of forfeiture or other dire penalty, for so long as the said Sir Thomas Bridges shall think fit. There you are, madam—will that put an end to your futile arguments?"

She took it. As she read the relentless lines, in a neat secretary's hand that conveyed its message all too clearly, the full extent of their doom came down upon her, and the words blurred and wavered. Furiously she blinked the betraying tears away. She would *not* be humiliated in front of these leering, repellent, all-powerful men. She raised her head proudly to meet their insolent gaze, the sign manual of their sovereign smudged under her thumb. "There is indeed no argument," she said, deliberately omitting any mark of respect. "Where His Majesty commands, there must his loyal subjects obey."

Ridgeley smiled, vulpine. "Then you will bow to reason, my lady. I am pleased that you have made the reasonable choice."

"I did not think that I had a choice," Silence said, and was surprised at the bitterness in her voice. She was aware, at her back behind the screens, of the scratchings and shufflings of assorted members of the household, like mice creeping to listen. This time, however, there would be no argument, no dispute, no escape. The menacing Ridgeley would descend upon Wintercombe with his unpleasant officers and his forty-three undisciplined troopers, to despoil and plunder and make waste the house and gardens and lands that she loved, and held in trust for her husband and his mother— although that lady's nominal ownership was a polite legal fiction, concocted by Sir Samuel and his attorney as a means of keeping Wintercombe out of the clutches of the king.

But Sir Samuel had not thought of this, that a whole troop of roistering men and ravenous horses would be foisted on his daughter-in-law, with no means of protest or redress. She could offer them money to go. She knew that they would take it and stay. And although she could at least remain here, and try to prevent as much damage and destruction as she could, her children would be forced to witness it.

She thought of shy, sensitive Tabby, and Deb and William, whose bluster, like their father's, was only surface deep; of Nat, whose presence she suddenly, sorely needed; and of Rachael, whose difficult and explosive moods would surely not be tolerated by these men. She wanted to weep but would never give them the satisfaction of witnessing it. Instead she lifted her face defiantly. "As I told you before, Lieutenant-Colonel Ridgeley, this house is full of women and children. There are but six grown men here, apart from the farm workers who live in the village, and almost all of them are old, well past sixty. You are the king's soldiers, sir—I pray you will treat us with the same respect and courtesy that His Majesty would wish, and we will do our best to accommodate you."

Someone sniggered. She thought, seeing his sneering face, that it was the fair man, Byam. Hellier, the brown captain, stood quite still, watching her. She must have imagined the look on his face, which was gone almost before she noticed it—for it seemed to be something akin to approval.

Ridgeley laughed briefly. "We will, Lady St. Barbe, of that you can be sure." His eyes, a bold inimical blue, roved over her with contemptuous dismissal. She was evidently too old, too plain, and too dowdy to attract his appreciation, and she was fervently glad of it. "Now, madam, if you will be so good, there is much to be done. It is cold and raining outside, as

you may have noticed, and the men and horses must be bestowed as soon as
may be. What stabling have you, and lodging for the men?"

"There is the barn," Silence said, wondering how forty or fifty horses
could possibly be accommodated within the bounds of the manor. Sir Samuel's herd of cattle was so important that he had always joked that the eight
riding horses and ponies that Wintercombe housed were at least eight too
many. In this weather, all save Dumbledore, the fat round furry pony on
which Deb and Tabby were learning to ride, were safely secured in the
stables in the barton, as the farmyard on the west side of the house was
called. There were only five spare stalls, she knew. With a vision of their
riding horses being turned out into a paddock in the cold or, worse, commandeered into the troop, she added, "There is some room in the stables—
but not for fifty horses, sir."

"No matter. Horse lines can be set up anywhere. The barn, you say?
Where is it?"

With a feeling of profound relief, Silence saw Turber's hesitant, pinkly
wrinkled face appear around the screens. She said, loudly because of his
increasing deafness, "My footman, Turber, will show you all you ask." At
least, she thought, if they can be kept in the barton, men, horses, and all,
we might not fare so badly.

Turber, his kindly countenance radiating bewilderment and distress,
crept into the hall, and Silence told him briefly what was necessary. His
look of anguish wrung her heart. "Soldiers, m'lady? Here, at Wintercombe? Oh, alas-a-day! What shall we do, m'lady? Whatever shall we do?"

"Make the best of en, you dummel old gatfer" came a hoarse whisper
from behind the screens that Silence thought was probably Leah. Ignoring
it, she gave the old man his instructions and watched with a numb sense of
disbelief as he shuffled away, leading Byam and Hellier outside toward the
barton.

Silence stood listening as the front door shut behind them, unwilling to
face Ridgeley alone, wishing for another presence—Master Willis, Nat,
even Dame Ursula. She wondered whether her mother-in-law knew of this
invasion, and decided that she almost certainly did, since her chamber had
one of the squints looking down onto the hall. It was some surprise, in
fact, that she had not yet appeared. She is probably waiting to make an
entrance at another and more suitable moment, Silence thought cynically.
And she'll be quite happy to leave me here alone trying to make polite
conversation to the man who has just commandeered the roof over our
heads.

"Madam." Colonel Ridgeley's voice intruded sharply. "How many are
there in your household?"

"Fourteen servants within the house, sir," she said, knowing that most
of them were probably eavesdropping behind the screens. "And a groom,
two lads, a gardener and his boy who sleep above the stables. There is a

bailiff too, who lives in the cottage opposite the barton. And there are my children, five of them, and my husband's mother."

"Ah. The redoubtable Dame Ursula. Yes, I have heard report of her," Ridgeley said, and his smile was not pleasant. "And all these are within the house at present, Lady St. Barbe?"

"All who should be, yes."

"Then I want them gathered here, now, every one of them, man, woman and child. It is time," the Cavalier said with that vulpine, threatening smile, "that they understand who is their new master here—and what I will and will not tolerate. Do you understand me, madam? You and your servants and family are suffered to remain here only by His Majesty's good-will, and that of Sir Thomas Bridges, and it is fortunate indeed that your father-in-law saw fit to leave the ownership of the property to his wife rather than to his son, or you would even now be trudging to Bath with your children, in naught but the clothes on your backs." His gaze flicked contemptuously up and down her sooty, unalluring gown. "And if you or your family or servants do anything to cross me, or to hinder our billet here, that will yet be your fate. Understand me?"

There was no mistaking the callousness in his voice, nor the certainty of the threat he was making. Her mouth suddenly dry with fear and anger, Silence said quietly, "I think I do. We are allowed to stay under our own roof on your sufferance, and we must endure any behavior that you may choose to inflict on us, on pain of being turned out to fend for ourselves at the onset of winter. Our lives, at bottom, depend on your whim. Is that correct?"

And on Ridgeley's brutal, handsome, blue-jowled face, for the first time, she saw something of respect. His laugh, however, was as derisive as before. "Aye, you have the right of it, madam. Your life, and your children's lives, and your servants', hang on my word. The king is many miles away now, Lady St. Barbe, and you are but the wife of a traitor. No one will lift a finger to help you. All here are under our authority now—and there is nothing whatsoever that you or they can do about it."

CHAPTER

THREE

If thine enemy be hungry, give him bread to eat.
—*PROVERBS 14:22*

T hey were all there, summoned from their duties around the house, if there were any who were not already gathered in the screens passage. News of the soldiers' invasion had sped around Wintercombe so quick as thought, as the saying went. Silence, standing by the fireplace, now crackling with fresh flames, let her eye wander over them all, wondering what their reactions would be to this most unwelcome disruption of their lives.

Eliza Davison stood on the other side of the hearth, her hands folded and her horse-nosed face wearing its most sour and disapproving expression. There would be trouble there, she thought with foreboding. Eliza was of a godly disposition, undoubtedly regarded wine, women, and song as the inventions of Satan, and would have no hesitation in speaking her mind on the subject. Silence could only hope that Colonel Ridgeley's threatening and implacable manner would have a subduing effect. She planned to have a word with the senior maid in private later, but suspected that it would be in vain. She studied that grim and unrewarding face, and sighed. Eliza was younger than she was by more than a year, but no stranger would ever have thought it.

Leah posed problems of quite a different nature. She waited by Eliza, her friend Bessie Lyteman, the dairymaid, whispering something into her ear. Together the two girls presented a striking appearance, Leah with her glossy dark curls and Bessie in possession of a glorious head of rich auburn hair, inadequately covered by a cap, and a magnificently voluptuous figure. Of the two, Silence much preferred Bessie, who had a warmth and cheerful good nature that the sly, sniggering Leah entirely lacked; but both of them were eyeing the three Cavalier officers with unabashed approval.

Silence's heart sank. She glanced away to little Madlin Tilley, white-faced and trembling despite her proximity to the new furnace in the hearth. She had entered the hall timidly, trying to hide behind Leah and Bessie, and when the other girls had realized what she was doing, Leah had unkindly pushed her to the front. This had almost reduced poor Madlin to tears, but Bessie, more warm-hearted, had let her hover unobtrusively at her back, so that she was almost invisible next to the wall. Unfortunately, it was improbable that such a face could long be hidden, and Silence feared for Madlin during the coming weeks more than for anyone else, save her children.

Eliza was safe from molestation, being, as Sir Samuel had once unkindly commented to Silence, as plain as a pikestaff, if not a pike. So were the older women—Margery Turber, wife of the footman and head dairymaid, who was in her fifties, and Doraty Locke, the children's nurse, a pleasant comfortable woman who had looked after Tabby, William, and Deb all their lives. They would carry on their duties as best they might and cause no trouble. Nor would Hester Perry, the young nursemaid, a kind sensible girl who was no beauty and came of an eminently respectable Norton family.

And there was Mally, of course, reliable Mally, who shared her own sense of humor and whose robust cheerfulness in the teeth of the most overwhelming adversity would, Silence suspected, keep her sane amid the undoubted hazards to come. She gave her servant a quick smile and was rewarded by a broad Merrifield grin, doubled by young Ned at his half-sister's side. Thank God for Mally.

Her eyes flicked briefly over the men. Darby, still flushed from his earlier rage, massive and driven by moods; there were bound to be difficulties with him. Young Sheppard, scrawny and rather unprepossessing, who was hopelessly in love with Bessie, a girl lusted after by all the handsome young men of Norton. Tom Clevinger, the bailiff, who had his own cottage opposite the barton, was an elderly widower who lived alone, taciturn, deaf, and unhelpful. She could imagine the soldiers' irritation at his slow, methodical, country ways. Diggory Barnes, the gardener, almost as ancient as Turber, and gnarled like one of the yew trees that lay beside the bowling green. A placid, affable old man, he was one of the few at Wintercombe who was genuinely friendly to Silence, seeing another as enthusiastic about gardening as himself. But if they damage any of his beloved plants, she thought, then he'll do murder!

The groom, Tom Goodenough, was similarly possessive of his horses. There had already been sour looks and disgruntled words as he complained bitterly to Silence about the invasion of his barn and stables, the ejection of the carts and wagon to make way for Cavalier mounts, and the threat of requisition now hanging over all but the most stunted and elderly of the Wintercombe horses. The prospect of mediating between the callous, implacable soldiers and the dour and obstinate Goodenough was not an alluring one.

At least the boys would be no trouble. The three scullions, two stable lads, and Jemmy Coxe, the gardener's boy, were all of an age to see this invasion as an adventure, a welcome disruption of their humdrum lives, and their bright eyes and keen glances at the officers revealed their excitement.

A small, sticky hand stole into hers and clutched two fingers tightly. She looked down at William and smiled. The wide brown eyes smiled hesitantly back. "Mama," said her son—her only surviving son—in what he fondly imagined to be a whisper. "Mama, why they come back? Didn't want them to."

"It can't always be the way we want, poppet," she said wryly. "Ssh, now, Colonel Ridgeley wants to speak to us all, and it's very important that everyone can hear him." She put her finger to her lips, smiling reassuringly, and William, his own face creasing happily at this familiar game, copied her.

The children. Protect them, she found herself praying, more fervently than she had ever done in her life. Guard them from harm, shield their eyes and ears from what they should not see or hear, for they are too young and innocent to understand, and yet still they may be damaged beyond repair, like new and tender plants exposed too soon to frost and wind. I can cope with this, we will manage if we are careful, with God's help—but not the children.

"I want them to go!" Deb said fiercely, too loud, her plump angry face turned toward the men by the screens. "Why don't they go? We don't *want* them here!"

"Ssh!" Rachael hissed, scooping her little half-sister up and putting a finger across her mouth. Silence glanced hastily over at the officers, but Ridgeley and Byam appeared oblivious. Hellier, however, was looking in their direction, an eyebrow raised in ironical inquiry. Quickly she averted her gaze, noting Tabby's set, tense little face and Nat's pale, thoughtful expression. He had said very little to her in the flurry of ensuring that all the household were gathered in the hall as quickly as possible, but she had seen his care for the younger children—William's other hand was held in his—and knew without words, as she did with Mally, that she could rely on his support, whatever might befall them.

There was only one person absent: Even Ruth Spratt, her maid, was there, silent and watchful under the middle one of the three south windows, her pale strawlike hair at odds with her red face and pale eyes. Tabby was frightened of her, and even Silence found her mute devotion to Dame Ursula bewildering and her appearance decidedly sinister. She had stood by without a word as the old lady had announced to her daughter-in-law in no uncertain terms that she would not even make her way onto the gallery in order to hear the words of the evil malignant colonel. "If he wishes to speak to me, he'll come to me to do it—and you can tell him that, daughter." And she had laughed, knowing full well that Silence would not relish the task.

Nor had she. She had told Ridgeley, in the same cold matter-of-fact tones of her earlier talk with him, that Dame Ursula was old, and crippled, and courtesy demanded that he present himself in her chamber to explain his presence in her house. The colonel nodded, his thoughts elsewhere, and would have accepted her excuses had not Byam interrupted. "Is that the old beldame who harangued us from the gallery? She's no more crippled than you or I, sir!"

"She is, I can assure you," Silence had said patiently, hiding her sudden anger. "She is unable to walk more than a few steps without aid. It would be unchivalrous in the extreme to demand that she come down here—to my knowledge, apart from that one occasion, she hasn't stirred from her chamber for months."

"Then she'll have to stir now," Ridgeley had said with that sneering, mocking laugh. "Go tell your Dame Ursula that when I order all the household to appear, I mean *all*—crippled or no."

And Silence, Parson Willis indignant and fussy beside her, had repeated this to her mother-in-law, with her apologies and some trepidation. In Dame Ursula, however, Ridgeley had met his match. "He'll have to manage in my absence," she said with malicious satisfaction. "I would not go down for the king himself, and you may tell him so, daughter."

Ridgeley, informed, had sworn, muttered some threat that Silence fortunately failed to catch, and said viciously, "Very well, leave the old crone to her own devices. I'll deal with her later. Is everyone else present?"

Everyone was, massed shuffling, apprehensive, indignant or curious according to character, in the great hall. Silence gathered her children and stepchildren around her, feeling their fear and bewilderment and anger, and made room for Master Willis. So far Ridgeley had not questioned the presence of the insignificant little parson in his rusty clerical black and plain bands, and she had not drawn attention to him. She would undoubtedly need an ally who was not of the household, and the vicar, though not especially strong in character, was a man respected and liked in the village, and further afield. How far the Cavaliers would respect him, of course, was doubtful. They had all heard the stories of the notorious Royalist Sir Francis Dodington, who had shot a minister in cold blood and had also butchered his defenseless prisoners. But she was grateful for Willis's presence, even if his natural timidity precluded open support.

"Silence!" Ridgeley's voice boomed loud over the whispering, uneasy gathering, and they quieted instantly, like guilty children. Lady St. Barbe stiffened as ever at the sound of her name, which had always seemed like an admonition and was yet one more burden that her father had placed upon her. Then she felt eyes on her and glanced around. Captain Hellier was still watching her. When he saw that she had noticed, he inclined his head in a parody of gentlemanly courtesy and smiled.

Her face suddenly and humiliatingly hot, Silence whipped her gaze away, furious with herself and with the captain. She remembered how he had spoken on his first visit of some bold trollop, doubtless Bessie or Leah. How dare he look at me as if I were one of the same! she thought, longing with that disturbing flash of impotent, violent rage to punch the insolent grin from his face. Then, common sense took over. She realized that she must have reacted precisely as he had intended, for he was doubtless making game of her. She was not some light serving girl or dairymaid, but a lady, a wife and mother, unassuming, dowdy, Puritan and virtuous. With an effort she ordered her face and the angry thumping of her heart, and directed her attention to Ridgeley.

He had introduced himself, and his captain and lieutenant, quite pleasantly, but the ruthlessness was still there, though lightly disguised. Now he was explaining their presence at Wintercombe in brisk, plain words, and the tension in the hall seemed to have become a tangible, visible thing, seen in the taut faces and wary eyes, felt in the fierce grip of William's hand in hers and Rachael's tight clasp of Deb's small sturdy body.

"We are billeted on you by order of His Majesty the King and the Governor of Bath, Sir Thomas Bridges, who is colonel of this troop of horse. We have been ordered here because of the shortage of suitable forage nearer to Bath, and because it has come to the notice of Sir Thomas that the village of Philip's Norton and the manor of Wintercombe have contributed less than their fair share toward the maintenance of His Majesty's garrison at Bath, which is after all intended for the protection of this part of Somerset."

There was a pause, filled by a brief, contemptuous, and fortunately anonymous snort from the middle of the crowded servants. Silence held her breath, but Ridgeley merely sent a considering, menacing glare in that direction before resuming. "Of course, we shall require provisions, and all that we take shall be paid for, either in honest coin or in promissory notes that can be exchanged on application to Quartermaster Cox in Bath. My own quartermaster, Hodges, is at present ensuring that my men are comfortably billeted in the barn. My officers and I will be housed under this roof, of course, by gracious permission of your mistress, Lady St. Barbe."

As one, two dozen pairs of eyes swiveled in her direction, and Silence, who had naturally given no such permission, forced herself to stand still, head high, and say nothing, although within that calm haughty exterior she was alight with anger. Ridgeley doffed his hat and gave her another mocking bow before continuing, his voice suddenly hard. "You are now under military rule. That means, in simple terms, that I command here. I will have no disobedience to my orders, nor to any that my officers may give, on pain of just and severe penalty." He produced the foxy smile that Silence detested so much. "I am sure that you will all comply with my instructions. The safety of North Somerset, and the protection of these parts from Roundhead attack, may well depend on this house, as it does upon Bath, Farleigh, Nunney, and the other garrisons hereabouts. And I warn you all, here and now—any sign of dissent, subversion, concealment of supplies, or any other hindrance of our lawful duties will be punished with the utmost severity. Do I make myself clear? With the *utmost* severity."

The household stared at him in complete silence, frightened and appalled. Ridgeley paused long enough for his threats to strike home, his eyes searching them all. "Good. I see I have been sufficiently plain. So long as you bear what I have said in mind, we should be able to exist amicably together. Lady St. Barbe, pray endorse what I have said."

Abruptly the focus of attention once more, Silence swallowed, trying not to display her surprise. She took a deep breath, aware that now, as never before, the people of Wintercombe would look to her to guide them. Her voice started thinly, too high to her own ears, and she made a determined and successful effort to moderate it.

"Lieutenant-Colonel Ridgeley has the right of it—his troop is to be billeted upon us, and I have undertaken to supply them from this house." She paused, well aware that the piled provisions in barn and hayloft and storerooms were ample for a household of twenty-seven souls over the leaner months of winter but would not long sustain nearly fifty soldiers in addition. Fighting her own panic and the alarm she saw on the faces of her more intelligent servants, she added firmly, "I know that there will be difficulties and problems a-plenty, but we have no choice in this matter, and nor, I think, has Colonel Ridgeley. We must make the best of it, and manage as well as we can. It may mean that we have to go without certain luxuries, but I am sure that Parson Willis here would agree, a little self-denial is good for the soul, even if such a sacrifice benefits those whom we have previously considered to be our enemies." She eyed Ridgeley defiantly, aware that she might be provoking him, but suddenly reckless of the consequences—after all, he could hardly have her shot out of hand. "And so I will ask you all most earnestly not to make any more difficulties than those under which we already labor. If you have a problem, a dispute, carry it first to me, and I will endeavor to mediate. Remember," she added, glancing significantly at Darby, at Eliza, at the stubborn bailiff Clevinger, and at Goodenough, still angry at the invasion of his stables. "These are *soldiers*. They have swords and pistols. You have heard Colonel Ridgeley—you provoke them at your peril. Go quietly, go in peace, and we will all be the better for it. Do not forget it, ever—for your own sakes, for my sake and my husband's, and above all for the children." Her mouth trembled suddenly, thinking of them. Furious at her betraying display of emotion, she added, very low, "Thank you all," and turned abruptly to face the fire, fighting her helpless tears, which would serve no purpose now.

A muttered swell of approval rose from the ranks of the household, and a few more defiant spirits cheered, though not very loudly. She took a deep breath, brushed a hand across her eyes, and swung around to face Ridgeley, knowing that she was not now alone. "There you are, sir. You have us in your thrall. If you are a gentleman, I pray you behave as one. The house is at your disposal—but I have much to arrange, as I suspect you have, my household have their duties too, and it grows near to dinnertime. Pray excuse us, sir."

She swept him an exaggerated curtsy with a mockery the mirror of his own, and turned to the servants. "I think that is all. Remember what I have said, and what Lieutenant-Colonel Ridgeley has told you, and act upon it. You may go."

She watched the muttering, unhappy men and women leave the Hall. Most averted their gaze from the three officers by the screens. Only Leah and Bessie, their eyes bright, turned their faces toward them, and there was a spring in the dairymaid's step, a merriment on her face and a toss of that magnificent red-gold hair that brought instant notice from the men. With a sinking heart, Silence saw their response, and noticed that Rob Sheppard had also seen. It was not his lucky day, she thought sympathetically. First he had been half throttled by Darby and now the girl he loved, however vainly, was giving the glad eye to three total strangers. But how could a humble assistant cook compete, particularly if he were by no means good-looking, with Cavalier officers dripping with lace and lechery?

She had thought, briefly and naively, that she could cope with this situation, could keep the soldiers at arm's length and somehow preserve Winter-combe inviolate, undamaged. She was only now beginning to realize the depths of her error.

At least they were able to dine free of soldiers, though the meal was late, either burned or half cooked, and scanty. Darby had done his best, however, and she knew that she must speak to him and give him words of praise and encouragement. The cook would be invaluable if they were to find themselves on short commons. He had a way with sauces and dressings that could disguise the most unpalatable of meats and tempt the finicky appetites of her children.

They had always eaten well, and the sturdy figures of William and Deb proved it. White bread, fresh meat, no coarse loaf or watery broths even for the servants. She knew that she must count their blessings and give thanks for the fact that they had all been spared the rigors of war thus far, if no longer. But all she could feel as she sat at the head of the dining table, in the dark-paneled room that looked out onto the rainy courtyard, now mercifully empty of soldiers, was that rising and futile anger once more.

"Don't want it," Deb said, and pushed her plate away. The pastry coffin of the pigeon pie had been overdone and was baked hard and scorched.

Silence had already expended some effort in cutting it into small pieces to fit on the child's spoon and in her mouth. She snapped, rather more forcefully than she had intended, "You'll eat it, Deborah, and be grateful.

Now the soldiers are here, we have to feed them as well, and you'll find that if you don't want a dish there'll be no others to choose from."

There was a small silence. Deb, made uneasy by her mother's rare anger, shifted in her seat and stared mutinously at the pieces of iron-hard pastry on her pewter plate. "But there's beef. Can't I have some of the beef, Mama? Please?"

"You can have some of mine—I can't eat any more," said Rachael, sliding her two remaining slices, liberally daubed with sauce, onto her half-sister's platter. Silence saw Master Willis's shocked face and had to hide a smile. The older children were all quite capable of perfect manners in company, but in private, just the family, standards were somewhat less formal. It was typical of Rachael to ignore the vicar's presence, despite his interminable grace at the beginning of the meal. And also typical of her to combine her undoubtedly genuine love for her half-sister with a subtle defiance of her stepmother. Until the day I die, Silence thought with resignation, I shall never have Rachael's allegiance.

"Mama." It was Tabby, sitting beside Nat, her small face very serious. "Is it true, Mama? That we may not have enough to eat, now the soldiers are here?"

Silence saw Master Willis's look of pity, and knew what the parson would advise—not the plain truth, but a careful distillation of the facts, rendered fit for infant ears. She had never liked telling lies to her children, and if she started now, it would be one more crime to lay at the soldiers' door. She had always valued honesty, in most circumstances. Aware that they were all waiting apprehensively for her answer on this topic of vital concern, she said quietly, "I don't know, poppet. We have plenty of food for ourselves, all stored up against the winter. But there are nearly fifty soldiers, far more than us. They will want feeding too. We'll have to be careful not to use up too much of our supplies before the spring. If we are not too greedy—and if *they* are not either, then we won't go without food altogether. We have the garden, remember, and cattle and sheep in the fields. And besides, Colonel Ridgeley said that he would be asking for contributions from the village."

"But most of the villagers are in no condition to make any such contributions," Willis pointed out with some agitation. "I grant you, my lady, some are quite comfortable, but most have only a few cows, a close of pasture or arable. They depend on the cloth trade for their bread, and that, alas, as you know, has been miserably run down, even before this terrible war. I beg your pardon, Lady St. Barbe, but at the moment Wintercombe is much better placed to feed these unwelcome and ungodly parasites than is Norton itself."

It was a rebuke, hesitantly given, but nonetheless true. She saw the justice of it and gave him a wry smile. "It is I who should beg your pardon, Master Willis. Of course I did not intend that the poor and suffering should pay more than Wintercombe. The Flowers, at Grange Farm, are as well placed as we are, and the Apprice family is flourishing, despite the slump in their trade." She glanced at the children, who were all sitting quite still, even William, and listening intently. "We are rich, and daily give thanks for our wealth, and lend help and charity to the less fortunate. But I am afraid of the soldiers' greed, Master Willis. I can only pray that they will be reasonable—and that is not a common quality of soldiers."

"I am sure that they will be, Lady St. Barbe," the vicar said in a falsely bright tone that must have indicated at least to the older children that he was lying.

Tabby cast him a sharp glance and then said to her mother, "You didn't tell us. *Will* we get enough to eat?"

"Yes," Silence said, knowing that she herself, and many of the household, would starve themselves before the children went without. "But it may not be such luxurious fare—brown bread, or salted meat, or cabbage and beans and pottage." She smiled rather wanly at her daughter. "We have been spoiled here, eating Darby's wonderful food. It might do you good to discover what ordinary people live on, every day of their lives. And if I were you, Deb, I'd eat my pastry without complaint, for you may be glad of it in a few weeks."

There was quiet then, while the younger children addressed themselves with peculiar vigor to their remaining food. Silence, her own plate carefully cleaned but not replenished, saw that Rachael had eaten a similarly small quantity. By the white, sick look of her stepdaughter's face, she was consumed with tension, with fear and anger, doubtless plotting revenge on the men who had invaded her home. It was no use warning her. In her present mood, that would only confirm the girl's intent. With a prayer for her safety, Silence watched the younger ones finish, and rang her silver handbell to summon the fruit pies and cheese.

The hour of dinnertime proved to be a brief, illusory respite from the pressures upon her. As soon as she emerged from the dining parlor, there they were, hovering in the screens passage, the massed ranks of her suppliants. Clevinger, the bailiff, came first, white with fury, to tell her with an uncharacteristic overflow of words that the soldiers had taken a cow from the pasture behind his house, a fine beast and one of his best milkers, and slaughtered her. Even now poor Buttercup was being roasted over a fire in the barton. Before she had had time for any reaction other than instant anger, there was Goodenough, quivering with rage, complaining that two of the stable partitions had been torn down to feed the fire, and the men had laughed at his protests. "If they do go on like this," the groom said grimly, "there'll be no house left inside of a month, they'll have burnt it all on their filthy fires."

"Aye, and no kine neither," Clevinger said bitterly. Silence glanced around at the anxious, horrified faces of the children and Parson Willis, the scattering of maids, and Tom Darby, his face ruddy with kitchen heat and temper, doubtless come to complain of similar outrage. They were looking to her to provide a lead, to intervene as she had promised, and she was not at all sure that she had the courage to do it.

She bade Master Willis good-bye. He was anxious to spread the ill news among his parishioners, and she supposed sadly that if one old widow saved a heifer, or a poor family hid a couple of cheeses and a sack of corn to see them through the lean winter months, it was worth it. Then she ordered the children up to their chambers, under the eye of Doraty Locke and the nursemaid. Rachael, plainly mutinous at being thus pushed out of the way, was disposed to argue. Nat took her arm and steered her with brotherly firmness toward the stairs, and the others followed meekly in their wake. Thanking God for his good sense, she turned to her household. "I will speak now with Colonel Ridgeley. I imagine that he is in the barton with his men?"

"'Tis where I seed him last," Goodenough said, "laughing with the rest of they ungodly buggers—begging your pardon, m'lady."

"Then I will go beard him in his den," Silence said with a brisk confidence that deceived only those with inferior wits. "Mally, come with me—you too, Clevinger and Goodenough. The rest of you can go about your duties—the dinner must be cleared away, there are chimneys to sweep still, cheeses to be turned, and butter to be made. Now go, and do your work."

They went, in ones and twos, reluctant and muttering. Silence suspected that many of them would find business in rooms that had windows overlooking the barton and could not blame them. She beckoned the two men close to her, and said clearly and quietly, "How many cattle do we have at present, Clevinger?"

Whatever his difficulties of character, the man was, in his limited way, a good bailiff. He reeled off the numbers as if reciting his catechism. "Eleven yearling and two-year-old heifers in one of they meadows anent the Wellow lane, m'lady, and fourteen calves in t'other. There be seven and twenty milch kine in the close behind my house, and four head of draft oxen in the top paddock. The bulls, as you know, m'lady, be in the nether paddock. Four and fifty in all—three and fifty, now they've slaughtered old Buttercup." He heaved a lugubrious sigh. "And where will it all end, m'lady? They soldiers won't be satisfied till there be norn left of the best herd of milkers between Bath and Shepton."

"Well," Silence said, wishing that the man possessed more energy and resource—had more gumption, as the villagers called it. "We shall have to make sure that they don't. Split the cows up, Clevinger, put the best in a far pasture, as near to Wellow or Hinton parish as you can, or the closes behind the Hassage coppice. We must hide the good ones at least, or as you say, they'll have them all."

"And if they give good coin for 'em," Goodenough said grimly, "I'll turn Papist."

It had stopped raining, Silence was sorry to see. She would have preferred, warm and dry as she was, to have faced a bedraggled and soaking officer. True, the men lounging around the barton, leaning against their horses, sitting on barrels or, most wastefully, heaps of straw, were as sorry and villainous-looking a crew as had ever worn what approximated to uniform. At least their officers presented quite a dashing appearance in their Taunton blue, but the men were another matter: unshaven faces, straggling hair, patched and stained buff coats, torn muddy breeches, filthy boots were the rule rather than the exception.

As she walked into the barton, which formed a broad quadrangle alongside the north wing of the house, all activity ceased, and there was a mutter of coarse comment, openly leering glances, and raucous laughter that set her teeth on edge. Determined not to react to such crudeness, she kept her head high, but could not prevent a betraying flush from heating her face. Her bailiff at her right shoulder, her groom at her left, and Mally at her back, she stalked purposefully across the barton to the roaring fire at its center, noting with dismay the many signs of military damage already plain: the horses tethered in a dejected row, nosing at piles of good Wintercombe hay; the muddy stone cobbles, puddled and slippery, which so recently had been cleanly swept and ordered; the remains of poor Buttercup, topped by her gory and gruesome red head, piled in a bloodstained heap in a corner; and the fire with the makeshift spit above it, on which a haunch of prime Somerset cow sizzled wastefully.

Ridgeley, seated on a cider barrel by the flames, a hunk of bread and meat in his hand, watched her approach with an expression of sardonic amusement on his blue-jowled face and made no attempt to still his men's increasingly audible comments on the attributes of the two women, despite Clevinger's glower. "My dear Lady St. Barbe! You should not have troubled to visit us in our quarters! And may I take this opportunity," he added with exaggerated courtesy, "of commending your estate on the magnificent quality of its beef. Such flavor, such tenderness!"

There was a collective snigger from the troopers. Silence said coldly, "You are not eating beef. You are consuming a prime milch cow, in her fourth year, with a lifetime before her of calving and milking."

"Alas," Ridgeley said, smiling, "the poor beast has found a nobler destiny. The roast beef of England is far better fare than whey and curd cheese, eh, lads?"

The men raised their voices in assent. There was nothing that Silence would have liked better than to hew the colonel in pieces, like poor Buttercup. But shouting, rage, hysteria would avail her nothing against this callous, utterly repellent man who held all she loved so lightly. She said quietly, "I have come to ask you to see reason, sir. Kill our cattle at this rate, and you and we will starve together before summer comes. Can you not see the waste of it? You must eat, I grant you, and we have bread, cheese, beer, cider, salt beef, all manner of provisions. But do not kill the cattle, I beg you—wait until the spring, there will be calves, lambs, the animals can be fattened on new grass. At this time of year, these are poor starveling creatures."

Ridgeley eyed her, chewing the last of his meat. For a moment she thought that she had persuaded him; then he guffawed loudly. "You can't gull me so easy, Lady St. Barbe. Now is the time to kill your beef, when they're still fat from the summer. So we do but save you the unpleasant duty of culling your herd."

"We've culled them already," said Clevinger. "All sold off or slaughtered or salted—them as is left is for milk and calving, as m'lady said."

"And you have amply sufficient for your needs," Ridgeley said. He motioned to a trooper, and the man began to hack at the joint on the spit. "You won't miss one or two beasts—and they die happy, secure in the knowledge that their flesh feeds the king's cause."

There was another collective snigger. Silence, knowing that she had lost the argument, said slowly, "At least take only what you really need and give us coin for those you kill—as you promised not two hours ago."

That brought the loudest bellow of laughter yet. Ridgeley took another hunk of steaming meat, impaled upon his trooper's knife, and waved it in her face. "Alas, Lady St. Barbe, at present we have no coin. My secretary has already written a note detailing the slaughter—if it is presented at Bath, as I advised you, payment might be made. Contributions from this county have been poor and grudging in the extreme, and we are sadly lacking in money at present."

Silence thought of the cattle, the herd of sleek blood-red Somerset cows, with their heavy udders and slender horns, on which the prosperity of Wintercombe had originally been based. They were still an important part of the farm, though Sir Samuel's other manors, his sheep and clothing interests, Mendip mines and ships had long since provided the bulk of his income. Her father-in-law had loved his cattle, had named them all, bred them with care, and had known as much about them as Clevinger, if not more. If the soldiers slaughtered them, it would not spell disaster and ruin; but it was an insult to Sir Samuel's memory that Silence, who had loved him, could not tolerate. She said, without really thinking, "If you spare them, the contributions from Wintercombe might be increased."

Ridgeley gave her a sharp, considering glance. "Oh? That is news most welcome, my lady. Did you hear that, Captain Hellier? The lady is prepared to pay us more, if we will give up the chance of roast beef every day."

"I heard it," said the brown man. He was standing behind Ridgeley, his arms folded. "Any increase in contributions toward the maintenance of His

Majesty's army in the west will be most gratefully and graciously received. How much, my lady?"

Knowing that she had made a mistake, Silence said firmly, "No more, not a penny, until a week has gone by without slaughter." So clear was the picture in her mind of the estate chest in the study, its iron bindings and triple lock and the clinking bags of coin within, Michaelmas receipts of the nine St. Barbe manors, that for a moment she feared that Ridgeley might see it too. A hiding place must be found for most of it, and quickly, or the man would take it as casually as he had taken the cow.

The colonel laughed. "You seem very sure of yourself, my lady. As the wife of a rebel and a traitor, you are fortunate to have coin left to pay us. Perhaps that situation can be remedied?" He stood up, taking another bite of dripping flesh, and loomed close, so near that she could smell his sharp, unpleasant male aroma of wet leather, sweat, smoke, horse, dirt. He raised his right hand gently, so that the slender point of the knife approached her face. In terror, Silence saw the chill implacable eyes, the dribble of red bloody gravy through the dark stubble on his chin, the unassailable brutality of the man she had thought to defy, to reason with, and wondered for a second if he planned her death. She shut her eyes momentarily and opened them to find him turned away, laughing, to take a long noisy swig from the mug of cider by the barrel. So great was the relief that she felt sick, and dizzy. Mally, unseen, gave her arm a supportive touch. Both Clevinger and Goodenough were rigid and crimson with fury at the rudeness of his behavior.

She said very quietly, fearing their reaction, "Do nothing. He's trying to provoke you—don't give him the satisfaction."

"I'll have his guts on a fiddle," Goodenough said, unheeding. Fortunately his words were not loud enough to reach Ridgeley's ears.

The colonel swung around, wiping the juice and cider from his face, and bellowed with amusement. "Well, that's driven the fight from you, my fine lady! Did you think I would spit you, eh? I wouldn't waste the effort gutting a puling little Puritan like you—you're not worth the trouble. I'd sooner bed one of those lusty serving maids of yours—and if I take a fancy to one of 'em, there'll be nothing you can do to stop me." He waved the knife under her nose. With an enormous effort, she forced herself not to recoil, to stand still and straight in the face of this venomous, cruel man who seemed to delight in taunting her, and whose unpredictable actions only added to his overwhelming aura of power and menace. He studied her for a moment and then laughed uproariously. "But never fear, my lady! We have orders from the Governor of Bath—you and your household are to be treated gently, courteously, so long as you accede to our wishes. Understand me? We'll take no more of your precious cattle, for a while at least, and we'll accept with good grace the supplies you give us. The village, of course, must contribute its share, in goods and labor, and billets nearby for my men. No, my lady, there will not be fifty troopers in your barn, hand-some though it is—it would be foolish to spoil your hay and straw and corn when we shall need it to feed ourselves and our horses. And re-member, my officers and I shall require chambers in your commodious house—I trust you can oblige."

"Doubtless I can," Silence said courteously. She took a tiny step back-ward, repelled by the reek of his breath. The rotted teeth and overindulgence in half-raw flesh and new cider probably had something to do with it. "I will go make them ready—pray excuse me, sir."

And with her dignity more or less intact, her servants around her, she turned and made her way over the uneven, treacherous stones to the kitchen, ignoring the guffaws, the catcalls, and the jeers.

By evening, some kind of order and peace had returned to Wintercombe, directed by its lady in a frenzy of activity. All the chimneys had been swept, the candles and fires lit, the supper prepared. Billets in the little cluster of cottages at Lyde Green, between Wintercombe and the village, had been found, and the first contributions raised from the indignant peo-ple of Norton, who, like the St. Barbes, were naturally inclined to the Parliament side and who greatly resented the sudden intrusion of Royalist soldiers into their quiet village. To Darby's utter disgust, his kitchen king-dom had been invaded by half a dozen troopers who were under orders to assist in the cooking of food for upward of thirty hungry soldiers, and Lieutenant Byam was busy making an inventory of the supplies in barn and storerooms.

Mally had reminded her mistress of the need for a suitable hiding place for the coin and other articles of value: a few pieces of silver, some jewel-ery, and a magnificent gilt salt that was a family heirloom of great age. All were bundled up and bestowed under the hearthstone in the study, where was a hollowed-out space excavated for just such a purpose, and shown to Silence by Sir Samuel when she had first come to Wintercombe. Mally helped her to stow the heavy bags and to replace the stone. It had taken their combined strength, and an iron bar, to lever it up, and Silence had dreaded someone coming in. This secret was one that only she and her maid, whom she trusted utterly, must know. Enough was left in the estate chests to lull suspicion, she hoped. With luck, Colonel Ridgeley would not be aware of the true extent of Wintercombe's monetary resources.

After her confrontation in the barton, she had felt sick with humiliation, impotent rage and fear. The knowledge of her helplessness, that she was totally at the mercy of this terrifyingly callous and brutal man's whim, made her want to howl her frustration and fury aloud. But she was Lady St. Barbe: She must not break down, she must continue to be calm, wise, resourceful, directing and protecting her household, a leader in this time of dire trouble, a beacon of hope . . .

She shouldered the burden, as dutifully as she had all the others laid on her since her infancy, and set about making spare chambers ready for her most unwelcome guests. Ridgeley was given the suite of two rooms above the study and winter parlor, facing south over the garden. From its window could be seen, two low hills away, the gray roofs and pinnacled church tower of Philip's Norton. With a compressed mouth and resentful expression, Eliza made sure that the fire was lit and the bed freshly decked with the linen that she had only recently seen washed and stored in the huge chests in the hall, with lavender sprigs and rose water for fragrance. Leah, with a gleam in her eye, did the same office on the other side of the house, where the summer parlor, and the little withdrawing room off it, would become the preserve of Captain Hellier and Lieutenant Byam. To Silence's relief, the lesser officers, a young and surprisingly pleasant-faced cornet, the quartermaster, and various corporals, were to share the billets in the barn and at Lyde Green. Wintercombe was not so commodious that more could be accommodated without considerable inconvenience.

She smiled ruefully to herself at the thought. "Inconvenience" was a puny, banal word to describe the complete overturning of their secure, insular little world in less than a day. That morning they had been safe, naively thinking that the war which had touched them all so gently during the past two years would continue to be no more than an irritation, an annoyance.

And now it had come home to Wintercombe, roosting like an evil black crow on the chimney tops, real and more baleful by far than the grotesque fanciful dragons and griffins and wild men that crowned each gable, hissing ruin and fear and destruction with the cold wind that whipped around the house on its low hill above the little brook that fed the fishponds below the orchard. She shivered and told Mally to close the shutters against the chill, malevolent dark.

Her own chamber seemed just the same, untouched by disaster: the high-pitched ceiling, beamed and plastered; the plain stone mantel, carved with the St. Barbe arms, above a warm and glowing fire; her bed, hung with green damask and piled high with quilts and blankets; the brass lantern clock on the table, which told her that it was nearly seven o'clock, and time for supper; books, paper, pens, hornbooks littering the two walnut tables opposite the bed. She glanced at the hangings lining the walls. They were old, rather faded and threadbare, and depicted the story of Apollo and Daphne. The astonished expression on the fleeing maiden's face as she found her arms translated into laurel branches had always amused Silence. Now it did not even have the power to twitch her lips.

Mally was waiting. The younger children were already in bed, exhausted by the excitements of the day, and she had sat by Deb and William and told them one of her fishwife grandmother's stories, an old favorite about Dick Whittington. Tabby, however, had not been so easily soothed. Silence had called upon all her reserves of calm and serenity and at last, upon her fourth tale, had seen the wide anxious eyes droop and close. Her elder daughter kept too much within herself, and worried about matters that would not have given Deb a second thought, but Silence knew without need of words that the child was afraid to sleep, in case some disaster struck during the night.

With Ridgeley billeted just down the corridor, she understood only too well how Tabby felt.

"Are you ready, m'lady?" Mally said softly.

Silence cast a last, longing look around her beloved chamber, her refuge, her haven, and nodded. "Yes, Mally, I'm ready. Shall we go down?"

Trestles and boards had been set up in the hall. Ridgeley had insisted, in yet another unpleasant battle of wills, that the men who remained at Wintercombe should be fed indoors. He had put the choice forcibly: either submit to his wishes, or have the men lighting fires in the barn, with all the attendant risks. Since the big stone building contained all the stocks of hay, straw, corn, and other fodder to last the winter for cattle, horses, sheep, and household, it was a risk not worth considering. But if her house was to suffer this nightly invasion of the uncouth and raucous troopers, then she would insist on withdrawing to her own chamber to eat, rather than sit in the dining parlor with the Cavalier officers sneering at her and ogling the serving maids, while their men bellowed lewd drinking songs across the screens passage in the hall.

It was quite as bad as she had thought. Darby had labored mightily to produce an acceptable supper for them—chicken pie, rabbit pasty, spiced beef, cheese and apples, cold from their shelves in the summerhouse in the garden, where all the fruit was stored. Rachael and Nat, clean, tidy, and covertly hostile, sat at the end of the table and said not a word. The three officers occupied the middle ground, eating with noisy vigor. Silence thought, looking at Ridgeley's heavy, coarsely handsome face, his grimy hands and disregard of polite manners, that this man, despite being a lieutenant-colonel, was no gentleman born—a professional soldier, perhaps? He certainly had the appearance, behavior, and rapacity attributed to mercenaries.

Byam, making too free with the cider, was probably of good birth, from his neighing voice and well-kempt hands: the sort of idle, feckless, debauched young man who had lounged around London in her childhood and who invariably considered the height of a gentleman's achievement to be the cuckolding of some worthy citizen. She unwarily caught his eye, and looked hastily away. A man like that would put only one construction on even a fleeting glance.

Captain Hellier seemed the quietest of that unholy trio. He said little, though he drank quite as much as the other two, and once or twice she noticed him looking at the two silent children, with something—curi-

osity? enmity? sympathy?—in his face. She remembered, suddenly, what
Tabby had said to her before she slept, and wild laughter rose in her throat
at the thought.

"I called the captain the autumn-colored man," her daughter had said,
her voice trailing dreamily on the edge of sleep. "I've thought of a much
better name for him now. He can be the skummery man."

In the village dialect, skummer was mud, dirt, filth. Fortunately, Tabby
was not the sort of child to flaunt her idea. Rachael was another matter,
but the two girls were not especially friendly. And if skummery was the
worst adjective applied to the enigmatic Hellier at Wintercombe, then he
would be fortunate indeed.

Loyal toasts were drunk, to the king and queen, the Prince of Wales and
Prince Rupert, and Byam and Ridgeley grew louder. Silence, hearing the
increased volume from the hall, judged it time to retire, and caught
Mally's eye. Doraty soon appeared, to conduct Nat and Rachael to their
chambers in the north wing, above the kitchen area. They would not have
to run the gauntlet of the troopers in the hall, doubtless now far gone in
drink. Silence glanced at Mally's apprehensive, resolute expression, and for
a moment wished with all her might that she had another chamber, any
one, rather than hers, which could only be reached by its own staircase
beyond the hall.

Ridgeley saw her hesitation, and laughed. "Reluctant to leave our company, Lady St. Barbe? I wonder why. D'you think we'll steal the silver,
eh—or is it another reason?" And he nudged Byam and whispered something that made the lieutenant snigger and turn his bloodshot, leering eyes
on her with a new appraisal.

Silence kept quiet and calm with an effort, though her knees were shaking. She said with dignity, "I shall withdraw now, sir, and leave you to
finish your meal. If your men could be kept quieter, for the sake of the
children and Dame Ursula, I would be grateful. Pray excuse me, Colonel."
And she curtsied, though for a minute she feared that her legs would not
obey her, and walked, head high, from the room.

Her pride had cost her dear. As the door shut behind her, her head swam
dizzily, and she clutched at Mally for support. "Be ee faint, m'lady?" her
maid asked, and Silence shook her head.

"No—don't worry, I can manage," she told her, doubting it. She was
grateful for Mally's arm under hers, but she wanted to gather her remaining strength before entering the hall. A raucous burst of song assailed their
ears. Mally said softly, "We could slip outside, m'lady, and go along the
terrace."

It was a way out of her dilemma, but even as she nodded, the door
behind them opened, and Captain Hellier's noncommittal voice said, with
apparently genuine courtesy, "Perhaps you would appreciate an escort,
Lady St. Barbe? The men do sound a trifle . . . undisciplined."

There was a crash of metal, probably a thrown pewter plate by the sound of it, and a roar of drunken laughter. Silence said as coldly as she could, "I thank you, Captain, but I will decline."

"Then you're a fool," Hellier replied. He came to stand in front of her. In the dim light that filtered through the heavy curtains blocking the openings in the screen, she saw with surprise that his face was quite empty of laughter and mockery. "They've been given cider—I shouldn't make that mistake again. It's a potent brew, far stronger than beer by the sound of it, and they're in a dangerous mood tonight."

"Then your colonel should be there," Silence said sharply, forgetting her exhaustion and fear. "It's his responsibility to keep his men under control."

As if to taunt her, Ridgeley's voice, as loud and inebriated as his troopers, rose in song. She caught a phrase or two, and regretted it. Hellier said, his voice dry, "As you must realize, he has abdicated that duty for tonight. Are your maidservants safe in bed?"

"I sent them there when they had finished serving us," Silence said, omitting to say that Madlin Tilley had been forbidden to show her face at all, and that she had told Eliza to ensure that all their doors were bolted firmly against any would-be gallant, paying especial attention to the whereabouts of Leah and Bessie. Turber, Darby, and Sheppard had set the food in front of the troopers and made themselves scarce. All over Wintercombe tonight, doors would be barred and pillows and bolsters clamped over ears.

"A wise move," Hellier said, and another roar of drunken verse gave point to his words. "If you wish to walk through your own hall, Lady St. Barbe, instead of skulking outside in the rain, I suggest you accept my offer—I will not make another. Shall we go?"

She found her arm being taken, gently but firmly, saw Mally's nod, and realized, to her annoyance, that he spoke good sense. And then he had steered her through the curtains and into the hall.

The light, the noise, the stench, struck her like a blow. The high room was packed with men, lounging over the tables, eating, drinking, singing, wreathed with tobacco smoke. Silence almost retched from the acrid reek of it, compounded of sweat, leather, and the raw sharp-sweet appley smell of the Wintercombe cider. She saw, with horror, a trooper vomiting copiously under one of the windows, another occupied in dousing his neighbor with the contents of his tankard, and a third carving something on the board with his eating knife. As she watched, disgusted, a man lurched over to the fireplace, opened his breeches, and urinated on the flames.

A massive, overwhelming rage filled Silence. Without thinking at all, she wrenched herself free of the captain's arm and strode over to the offending trooper, who was fumbling with his buttons. "What do you think you're doing?"

The man's face, unshaven, unpleasantly scarred, gaped at her in astonishment. Then his expression changed as he realized belatedly that the furious figure in front of him was young, and female. He grinned lecherously, and his hand pawed at her. Blindly angered, she struck it away and hit him as hard as she could across the face.

There was suddenly a very dangerous quiet. The sound of the blow had stilled all talk and laughter and song. Silence stood frozen, shocked and appalled by what she had done, and felt the ugliness of their mood. The trooper seemed as amazed as she. He reeled, swearing hideously, his hand to his mouth, and one of the others leapt to his support. She said loudly, on the wings of her rage, "You are men, not animals. This is a decent house, and a godly one, and if you want to dine in warmth this winter, then I suggest that you behave accordingly. My two-year-old son conducts himself better than you do. If you want to be pigs, go live in a sty!"

There was some angry muttering. Most of them were too drunk to understand, but here and there she saw faces either resentful or, more encouragingly, sheepishly ashamed.

Then, to her astonishment, she heard Hellier's voice, raised and authoritative. "I'll second that. Any who can't act decently may go outside now, and drink themselves into the gutter in the farmyard. Call yourselves crack troops, do you, the pride of the Bath garrison? I've never seen a sorrier rabble of drunken brutes in my life."

The muttering had died away entirely. The whole hall seemed to be listening, holding its collective breath. Silence, feeling it safe to take her eyes off the man she had just humiliated, turned to stare at the captain. He stood where she had left him, just inside the screen opening, one hand resting on the hilt of his sword. He was not a tall man, slightly built compared to the large, bull-like Ridgeley, nor did his quiet coloring immediately catch the eye. And yet, she realized suddenly, without bluster or threat, using a tone of voice that was almost conversational, he had taken the edge from the situation and held that sottish crew in the palm of his hand.

She loathed him and all that he represented, she resented his help and support, which he had given unasked and unwelcome, but she could not help feeling, however grudging, some admiration for this hidden, subtle, and unexpected power.

He glanced her way and smiled. It had nothing of insolence in it, and thereby, perversely, further aroused her hostility. "My Lady St. Barbe, I bid you and your maid good night, and pleasant dreams—and I will ensure that your rest is not disturbed by any in this house. Good night, my lady."

He bowed, and she curtsied, because it seemed to be expected of her, and a voice, less inebriated than some, shouted, "Drink a toast to her, lads! To Lady St. Barbe, God bless her stout rebellious Puritan heart!"

And the cry was echoed from the thirty-odd throats around the hall, and tankards were raised, while the temporary object of their fickle admiration stood, not knowing whether to laugh or to weep or to scream with rage, by the fireplace. Remotely, one part of her housewife's mind was assessing the damage, the time it would take to clear up the mess, the likely reaction of Eliza and the other maids, who had only that morning cleaned the hall after Walker's mishap with the chimney. But above all, she wondered what Dame Ursula would have to say to all this.

Suddenly the strain was too much. She said "Thank you" to the red-faced, jovial, unpredictable men who only a few minutes before had most probably been ready to assault her, sent a look of appeal to Mally, and walked out of the hall as fast as she could while still keeping hold of her dignity. It was a long way around the side, avoiding the boards and benches, avoiding their eyes, the hands that waved overflowing tankards or clutched at her dress, but she accomplished it successfully, her head high, an expression of calm serenity masking the turmoil within. And then she was pushing aside the curtain into the little closet that led to the garden room and the stairs to her chamber, and it was over.

Exhausted as she was, she managed to climb the steps, which were narrow and spiral, set in a little turret at the southeastern corner of the house. And there, through the studded plank door at the top, was her chamber, utterly normal, quiet, peaceful, unchanged. Either Hellier's admonitions had had the desired effect, or distance had muffled the noise from the hall, but the sounds were remote and mercifully muted. Curled with feline contentment in front of the fire, now a rich cherry red and fiercely hot, was the dearly familiar figure of Pye. As her lady entered, she looked around, yawned, stretched elegantly, and strolled over, her white-tipped tail up in the air, a flag of welcome. Silence, feeling the pressure of her sturdy body as the cat wove her greeting around her skirts, found that she wanted to weep, and firmly suppressed it. She let Mally undress her, though she would rather have done it herself, for the tenets of childhood were still strong. Then the warmed nightshift was slipped over her head, and she climbed under the quilts and blankets, Pye following eagerly to curl just by her shoulder, as snug as her mistress. Finally good nights were said, Mally drew the curtains with a fortunately muffled clash of brass, and she was alone; alone with her memories of a dreadful, nightmarish day, crowded with despair, defeat, and the intolerable pressure of an insupportable burden. She curled herself tightly, feeling the hot tears burn her lids, and as she moved, Pye snuggled closer and began to purr, her whiskers tickling Silence's face.

It was comfort, small but utterly welcome, as if one of the children had hugged her. Despite her misery, she smiled into the dark, and then exhaustion overtook her, and she was asleep before the first tears had slid across her face.

CHAPTER
FOUR

"You can leave my chamber at once, you uncouth ungodly rogue, you malignant evil Cavalier, you . . ." For once words failed to leap from Dame Ursula's tongue with her usual malevolent fluency. She mouthed impotently for a moment and then fell back on her unequaled knowledge of Holy Writ. "'He that doeth evil hath not seen God,' sayeth Paul in his third epistle to John. Go, you viper, and rot in hell!"

Ridgeley stood before her, quite unperturbed, the smile fixed to his face as if it had been nailed there. "I regret that my sojourn in this house has not been welcome to you, Dame Ursula. However, despite your fine words and flowery phrases, there is nothing you can do to alter the situation, and so you had better make the best of it."

Silence, for once not the object of her mother-in-law's invective, stood unregarded in a corner and marveled. To her had fallen the thankless task of conveying Dame Ursula's peremptory summons to the Cavalier commander. With her ears burning from the diatribe she had received about her behavior in the hall the previous evening—"You wicked, foolish woman, to venture among them—I heard them sully your name with their filthy drunken lips!"—she had told Ridgeley that Dame Ursula demanded his presence in her chamber, at once, no matter what he might be doing or how inconvenient it was to leave it.

"And when the old harridan says jump, you all leap for the moon?" the colonel had said, contemptuously amused. "I am not in the least eager to meet her, Lady St. Barbe, and she may wait on my pleasure."

So it was fully three of the clock, six hours later, that Captain Hellier sought out Silence, who was with Darby in the kitchen, trying to impress on him the need for economy in their new and crowded circumstances, to tell her that Ridgeley wished now to be conducted to the old lady's chamber.

She had not thanked him for his assistance the previous night. She knew that she must, but the words stuck fast in her throat. He certainly seemed a more sympathetic, approachable person than his brutal colonel, or the sottish Byam, but she remembered the smooth-tongued serpent, beguiling Eve to her doom, and recalled also the casual manner in which he had discussed the debauching of her serving maids with Byam on their first visit to Wintercombe. She gave him a cool nod. "Where is the lieutenant-colonel now, Captain?"

"He awaits your pleasure in the hall, Lady St. Barbe," the skummery man said, echoing his superior.

Silence raised her brows, the picture, she hoped, of aristocratic unconcern. "Then you may tell him that I will be with him shortly. I have much to discuss here, and since he has kept Dame Ursula waiting for more than six hours, I doubt another ten minutes or so will dampen his ardor or further fuel her annoyance."

To her surprise, his mouth spread in a lazy, amused smile. "I doubt it too, my lady. And I shall endeavor to be as stalwart a go-between for yourself and Lieutenant-Colonel Ridgeley as you are for the colonel and your husband's lady mother. It's a duty gains us precious few thanks." His gaze sharpened. Silence, with her heightened conscience, knew what he was hinting, and decided to be perverse. He seemed, for reasons of his own unlikely to be pure or altruistic, to be seeking to insinuate himself into her good graces by presenting himself as an ally. That strategy might work on some green girl unaware of the ways of the world. She, however, was twenty-eight years old, close to twenty-nine, a wife for nine years and a mother for eight, and although she might live a quiet country life now, she had been bred in the harsher realities of London and learned early to distinguish base metal from gold.

"Then that is to the loss of us both," she said calmly. "Pray excuse me, Captain—I have much to order here."

He could little other than withdraw, and she was glad of it. She found his presence, that quiet yet ruthless air of self-possession, the hint of something quite different beneath his urbane courtesy, almost as disturbing as his colonel's naked contempt and viciousness.

She had kept her own calm, with an ease that surprised her, as Darby objected to a dilution of his sauces, a diminution of courses, and the surly, rebellious presence of half a dozen troopers to upset his routines while illicitly raiding the cider. Unfortunately, the barrels were stored in the barn and only brought into the house as required, and the key to the brew house had recently and mysteriously disappeared.

The prospect of a houseful of troopers—and officers—permanently drunk on the barrels of new, raw, and potent cider, stored in quantities intended to last a whole year, was not pleasant. Silence pushed it from her mind and dealt firmly with Darby's complaints, marveling at her boldness. Less than two days ago she had been secretly afraid of this man, his bad temper and latent violence. But last night she had faced the worst that the troopers could do and defied them. True, Captain Hellier had turned their mood at the end, but the fact that she had dared at all to stand up to their drunken behavior had enormously bolstered her confidence. And she was not imagining the new, wary air of respect with which Darby agreed at last to her suggestions.

She sallied forth with the pride of a ship in full sail and had all the wind taken from her by Ridgeley in the hall.

"You're late, madam. Kindly be more courteous in future."

Annoyed at his tone, Silence snapped, "I do not see why I should be, sir, since you so frequently are not. Shall we go up to Dame Ursula? She has been expecting you since breakfast."

In hostile silence she led him up the narrow stone stairs, announced his presence to her mother-in-law, and retired to the corner by the door as the storm broke, for once not upon her own head. Ridgeley was abused first for the delay in his arrival, then for his presence. The disgraceful scenes in the hall the previous evening—which, as Silence had suspected, turned out to have been described to Dame Ursula by her sinister servant, Ruth Spratt, watching avidly at the squint—were her next topic, and prompted a hail of invective and accusation that would have withered anyone at Wintercombe, from Silence downward. Ridgeley just stood there, his red-plumed beaver in his hand—at least he had had the courtesy to doff his hat—and let it all pour over him with an expression on his face that Silence was beginning to recognize already. She found that she was enjoying this encounter, between the two people at Wintercombe that she most disliked, and tried to reject the feeling as unworthy.

It would not go away. Dame Ursula leaned back in her chair, a bluish tinge to her lips, and Ruth slid forward with a cup of water, which was instantly and impatiently waved away. "Well, sir?" Sir George's terrifying mother asked, her eyes fixed like gimlets upon Ridgeley's dark-jowled face and insolent, callous expression. "What have you to say to your disgusting, disgraceful, ungodly behavior? You're as bad as your men, you stink of evil and corruption, you wicked spawn of Satan—well? Will you turn to God, and mend your ways?"

So the legendary king might have told the tide to turn, or the sun to rise in the west. Ridgeley laughed, a sound of genuine amusement, his eyes disappearing in the folds of skin. "You ask me that, you ranting, foul-mouthed old hag? I don't give *that*"—a contemptuous snap of the fingers—"for you or your poxy killjoy God." And as the old woman gasped at the blasphemy, he added coldly, "You have ruled this house by threats and fear, it seems. Perhaps no one in this wretched place has the wit to realize that all of it is bluff. You are too ancient, madam, you have long outlived your natural span. Look at you—a pathetic feeble old cripple, dependent on your servant for everything—and yet still you keep all about you in terrified subjection. I wish I knew your secret of command, Dame Ursula—I could rule the land with it, being young and hale and a man, whereas you are nothing but an aged and invalid old woman. How is it done? I wonder. Well, whatever your methods, I can assure you that you cannot rule me as you have manipulated these lesser creatures. You may mouth the Scriptures at me, and invoke hellfire until the roof falls in, but I shall pay you not the slightest attention. Do you understand me, you contemptible old harridan? You are *helpless*. No one will lift a finger to aid you against me. Your time has come and gone, your reign is ended, and I have the power here now. Oh, you will be fed and tended, never fear—I am not so stupid as to make a martyr of you. But I will give you no courtesy, dance no attendance upon you, pay no heed to your curses. And there you have my answer in a nutshell, Dame Ursula—take it or leave it, you can do as you please, but I will not deviate one jot from my path at your behest."

It was then that the greatest flood of abuse was unleashed, and fell dead like stones hitting a wall. As Dame Ursula screeched, "Rot in hell!" Silence saw Ruth's uncomely face twitch, whether with rage, or pain, or sympathy could not be told.

At last the old woman fell back, gasping for breath in the extremity of her fury, and Ridgeley delivered his response in a tone of false courtesy that barely disguised his contemptuous amusement. Then he turned, seeing Silence, and bowed to her. "My commiserations, Lady St. Barbe, for the appalling burden that has been laid upon you. It is not every wife who has such a gorgon for a mother-in-law. You bear it well. Perhaps it will be the less in future, and you should thank me for it. Good day to you—I have much to do." And he pushed his hat back on his head and walked swaggering from the chamber, his spurs chiming and the clank of the sword at his side providing a counterpoint.

Silence stayed where she was, unable to move. One part of her, the rebellious child, delighted in this vicious trouncing of the harsh and unfeeling woman who had instilled terror in her life, and her children's; applauded every word that Ridgeley had said; and reveled in Dame Ursula's discomfiture. The other side, the mature godly wife, shrank in horror from such barbaric discourtesy and brutal speech, and saw with distress the half-fainting old lady, trembling and abject in her chair.

The latter illusion did not last long. Ruth approached again with her cup, more purposefully, and this time Dame Ursula knocked her arm away so that water went flying and the pewter bounced with a metallic clang against the stones of the hearth. "I don't want your water, you stupid girl. Fetch me my Bible, at once—and I'll have a pillow behind my head."

Ruth, with an expression that in another might have indicated the urge to weep, scurried to do her bidding. Silence waited, knowing that she herself would inevitably be punished for her crime. She had witnessed Dame Ursula's humiliation and must suffer for it. She wanted to slip out of the chamber as unobtrusively as she could, but she knew that she had no hope of escaping unnoticed. Whatever she did, whether she moved or stayed, her mother-in-law's thwarted spleen would all be vented upon her.

But, her childish half reminded her, you do not *have* to stay still, you do not *have* to endure her maltreatment. Ridgeley defied her—why cannot you?

Ridgeley, however, was a man, a soldier, had never met Dame Ursula before and would most probably avoid doing so again. For her, it was different. She could not, in all conscience, walk out of that chamber door, never to return. Apart from compassionate considerations, there lurked always the thought at the back of her mind that one day her husband would come home from the war. He doted upon his mother, and she upon him. It was one of the rocks on which any chance of a truly successful second marriage had early foundered. Dame Ursula loathed Silence and would undoubtedly waste no time in blaming her for every disaster that had befallen Wintercombe in Sir George's absence. And then even her husband's rather belittling affection and kindness would disappear, and she would be treated as a child no longer but as an enemy.

Whichever way I turn, Silence thought, I can never win. It was the hold that Dame Ursula had over her, over the children and the rest of the household, the hidden, unacknowledged reason why they all trembled at her summons and leapt to do her bidding. Her power was not hers alone. It derived, by proxy, from her son.

"Daughter!" The harsh tone brought her attention snapping back to the distasteful present. "Daughter! Tell me where in the Good Book may I look for comfort and the knowledge of God's word in these dark times?"

It was not difficult. The lines of the Old Testament held many ferocious denunciations of wickedness and evil. Silence said at once, "In the Book of Exodus, madam, the Captivity in Egypt and the freeing of God's chosen."

Dame Ursula nodded, her fingers searching the huge pages. The great book sat ponderously on her knees, so heavy that it was all Ruth's sturdy strength could do to lift it. Silence stood, still tensely waiting for the full impact of her mother-in-law's thwarted fury to descend upon her. She surely could not escape it.

Sure enough, the clawlike, misshapen hand stabbed at her abruptly. "I see here, daughter, words that are most apt for your case. 'A virtuous woman is a crown to her husband.' Proverbs twelve, four. Remember that, when you are next tempted to consort with those filthy licentious beasts. My dearest George would chastise you most severely, did he know of your transgressions. Bear in mind, girl, I may be a feeble old cripple, but I have eyes and ears, and some not my own who answer to me. I know everything that happens in this house, do you hear me, daughter? *Everything!* And it is my godly duty to report every misdeed, every sin or blasphemy, to your husband when he returns." She leaned back, a sanctimonious smile on her face. "So beware—your sins will find you out."

"I have not sinned," Silence said, quietly angry, her voice strained, like her temper, almost to breaking point. "I have done nothing, madam, of which any wife could be ashamed, and I do not intend to change." And suddenly her fury took charge and, reckless of the consequences, she added, "If you seek words in the Bible, madam, look a little further in Proverbs, chapter twenty-one, verse nine. I also have much to do. Pray excuse me." And, trembling with rage, she turned and left before her mother-in-law could discover, or remember, the reference she had given.

"It is better to dwell in a corner of the housetop, than with a brawling woman in a wide house."

The rain stopped and the weather turned cold as November drew on. There were short days of bright sun, brisk wind, towering black clouds bringing chill stinging showers. Wintercombe, all its cozy certainties bludgeoned away, faced the worst season of the year with three dozen unasked and unwelcome guests to deplete the stores and cause damage, destruction, and mischief.

Some things were better than Silence had feared. That unspeakable Bacchanalia in the hall on the first night was not repeated. Cider was drunk, and beer, men grew loud and boisterous, but never out of control, and one of the officers, usually Captain Hellier or the young cornet, ensured that some discipline was maintained. But she was aware that the line between rowdy behavior and the ugliness of riot and mob rule was a very slender one, and that Colonel Ridgeley was quite capable of pushing the men across it on a malicious whim.

She made her excuses, however, and from thenceforth had her suppers, and the children's, brought to them in her chamber. It made extra work for the servants, of course. Mally saw the sense of it, but Eliza grumbled bitterly at the task of carrying trays up and down stairs, even if Turber or one of the scullions did most of the work. Silence knew of her displeasure, and ignored it. She was content to endure dinner with the officers in the dining parlor. They did not drink so much at midday, and their words were surprisingly moderate in front of the smaller children. She had not thought to see such evidence of common decency among these ungodly men, but welcomed it.

William, especially, was a favorite. Whenever he appeared his appealing looks, the lint-gold hair and warm brown eyes, his mischievous smiles and sturdy manner, seemed to win over the most flinty and brutal military heart. With deep misgivings she watched his growing enchantment but did not dare to protest, or to show too much disapproval. She tried to ensure, however, that his contact with the troopers was kept to an absolute minimum.

Supper, in the absence of the youngest three, was different. The end of the day to these men meant relaxation, the smoking of noxious pipes of

tobacco, the imbibing of vast quantities of beer, cider, and wine, and loud
bursts of lewd and drunken song. She could endure it at a distance, so long
as there was no actual damage done. But she would not allow her own
senses to be assailed by such uncouth behavior, still less those of the children and the maids. So the female servants ate under Eliza's sour eye in
their own hall, while the male ones, boys and men, did the minimum
service required of them and retreated hastily to sanctuary elsewhere at
Wintercombe. Silence sat with Nat and Rachael at one of the walnut tables
in her chamber, eating and talking companionably, while the candles cast
their dim glowing light onto the white damask cloth, the pewter plates,
the plain fare—cheese, eggs, bread, honey, a pigeon or rabbit pie, salt
bacon and chicken pottage—that Darby had grudgingly prepared for them.
Silence ignored both his simmering resentment and the complaints of the
children. Deb and Rachael in particular had protested at the absence of
their favorite meats, and had met not only their mother's lack of sympathy,
but Nat's.

"I wish we could have some good beef or mutton," Rachael had grumbled pointedly on one occasion, casting a meaningful glance at Silence, who
sat at one end of the table, thoughtfully putting slices of cheese upon her
piece of coarse brown bread. "We have plenty in store, Mother—why do
we have to put up with this awful broth? And it's been so long since we
had any wine—the soldiers have it, why can't we any more?"

"You had it only as a special treat," Silence pointed out.

Nat, with a grin, added, "We've had plenty of whine—yours!"

Rachael seemed disposed to sulk. Her twin went on, "If we eat up all
the good food now, there'll only be the chitterlings left by April. You must
know how the cows are fed over the winter—the worst fodder first, bean
and barley straw, and the good wheat straw and hay saved till the last. If
you did it the other way around, they'd starve, come March."

"But if we don't eat the best stores now, then the soldiers surely will,"
Rachael pointed out. She helped herself to another slice of bread, heaped
salt bacon upon it, and took much too large a mouthful, looking at Silence,
evidently daring her to object.

It had been an exhausting day, and her stepmother had other things on
her mind. She took up an apple, not one of the sour wrinkled ones pressed
into cider, but a round scarlet-flushed pippin from the trees at the higher
end of the orchard. Biting into it, she looked from one twin to the other,
struck anew by the difference of their temperaments. Rachael, as untidy as
ever, her hair in need of washing, dubious areas under her fingers and in
unregarded corners of her face, like a small boy afraid of soap, had bitterly
resented the invasion of Wintercombe. Indeed, one of the reasons why
Silence had wanted to take her supper here, with the two older children,
was Rachael's habit of uttering *sotto voce* and derogatory comments on the
Cavaliers, but especially Ridgeley, but just outside their hearing. Indeed,

from the sharp glances she had once or twice earned from Hellier, Silence thought that they might in fact have been audible, at least to the sharp-eared captain. She did not want to give Ridgeley any further excuse for unpleasantness; and so she had welcomed these quiet evenings, when Rachael's foul moods and restlessness were displayed only to those who were accustomed to her, and could tolerate them.

Here it was possible to believe that the unwelcome soldiers did not exist, had never shattered their peace and soiled the house. The meal ended, she went to sit in her chair by the fire. Although old-fashioned with its elaborate heavy oak frame, it was piled comfortably with cushions and was popular both with the little children and with Pye. The cat was curled tightly on a nest of soft damask. Gently Silence picked her up, sat down, and replaced her on her lap. A deep, loud purr was her reward. She scratched Pye under her chin, a favorite spot, and took the glass of wine that Mally brought to her. It was the new claret, rich ruby in the plain heavy English-made glass that Sir Samuel had preferred. Only a month ago his wine merchant in Bristol had sent them six hogsheads of the new season's grape, strong and rough, for winter consumption. She wondered how many weeks Ridgeley and Byam would take to drink their way through it.

A whisper to Mally, and the girl gave a glass each to Nat and Rachael, not so full, and well diluted. Silence watched the two of them, hunched over the chess game that the meal had interrupted. Nat had thanked her for the claret, but Rachael had said not a word. She would not rebuke her, although she knew that she ought to punish such rudeness. She did not have the heart to add to the girl's burden of wretchedness.

And yet, she thought, sipping her wine, enjoying the sharp tingle of it on her tongue, there was no reason for the child to be so unhappy. She was fed well, educated, treated with affection and consideration. She had had an easy and comfortable existence, and would enjoy all the advantages of her gentle birth, a good dowry, a husband of her own choosing, within limits, another household such as this to manage. Nat, sharing all these privileges, was heavily burdened by his fragile health, and yet his was the sunnier nature. His twin was made of storm and thunder, had been so all her life. Silence, first encountering this mute, rebellious, bad-tempered little orphan, five years old, had learned that the child had always been thus, with a flood of anecdote to enlighten her. At less than a year old, Rachael had bitten the wet nurse so badly that blood had run with the milk; she had kicked her father's horse when he had refused to take her up on it; she had put frogs and teasels in her poor nursemaid's bed; and, worst of all, she had spat at her grandmother and uttered a stream of shocking obscenities when restrained. Rachael, everyone had told her, was ungovernable, quite unlike her poor frail little brother.

Nat had not been so saintly, though. She had been well aware that this fragile, solemn, white-faced little boy was assessing her, the woman who had taken the place of the mother he had never known. He had asked searching, unchildlike questions, had watched her unblinkingly, coldly, for three months, and had then announced, seriously and confidingly, that he liked her. That had touched her heart, lonely and homesick as she was in the dark gloomy old house at Chard, and already pregnant with Tabitha, and from then on they had always been friends. No, there had never been any real problem with Nat, nor with Sam, the boisterous elder brother who had ridden away to war with his father. But Rachael . . .

She became aware that the twins were arguing, very quietly. It was probably to do with the game, she decided. Rachael hated to lose, but Nat was almost unbeatable at chess, having the sort of mind that ordered its thoughts and looked logically ahead. That, however, did not seem to be the cause. She heard Rachael say furiously, "I've said I'll go on doing it, and you can't stop me!"

Nat's answer was inaudible; his sister's reply was not. "I don't care if she does hear me! *I'm* not afraid to speak my mind!"

"More fool you, then," Nat said. He leaned back in his chair and studied the board. "Well? I said check—are you going to move?"

Rachael banged a castle down with some force and less thought, and hissed something. Nat, ignoring her, slid one of his bishops across three squares to take it. "And mate."

"You've won again! Why do you always win? And *don't* say it's because you think logically—you always say that and it's *boring!*" She got up with a jerk that nearly overset the board altogether, and displaced several pieces. "I'm not going to play any more. Where's my sewing, Mother?"

Silence, hiding her wry amusement, directed her to one of the presses by the oriel window. Rachael flounced over and picked up the small frame that stretched a circlet of grubby linen bearing a half-finished impression of stiff bluebells and fat, bright-green trees. She sat down in one of the window seats that looked out onto the bowling green and yew walk on the eastern side of the house, and applied herself with ostentatious industry.

Nat was left, grinning ruefully at his stepmother. "Will you give me a game?"

"I doubt it—I haven't played for weeks," Silence said. "But if Pye will let me, I'll do my best."

They were ten minutes into the game, Nat having lost two pawns and a knight, Silence the poorer by three pawns, a castle, and a bishop, when Mally came up to the table, her freckled face concerned. "If you please, m'lady—I couldn't turn him away—Captain Hellier d'want to speak with ee."

And there he was, standing just inside the doorway, dressed in a sober suit of tawny brown quite different from the Taunton blue and buff coat that was his officer's garb. It took a little while for Silence to realize what it was about him that looked strange; then she saw that he was not wearing his sword.

She got to her feet, as did Nat. Then Rachael bounced up from the window seat, scattering cushions and embroidery. "What are you doing here? This is our private place—we don't want you here! Go away!"

"Rachael!" Silence said sharply.

The girl stared at her belligerently, unrepentant. "I'm only speaking my mind. Isn't that what Grandmother does all the time? And I'm just saying what you want to say, if you had the courage." She glared from her step-mother to the unwelcome visitor, who stood there with a faint look of amusement on his face.

"There's a difference between being forthright and open rudeness," Nat said. "Don't you remember how Grandfather was always polite and courteous—especially to the people he most detested?" And he turned to Captain Hellier and bowed very low, with ostentatious correctness. "Delighted to welcome you, Captain—your servant, sir."

It was not lost on the captain, Silence saw with amusement. His lips twitched, and he bowed almost as low to her, and again to Nat. She said, wondering what he wanted, "Will you sit and take a glass of claret, Captain? I believe there is a little left in the bottle."

"That would be most pleasant, my lady," he said. As the maid poured the last into a hastily cleaned glass, Silence indicated a chair by the fire, one of a set upholstered in green damask, and not nearly so comfortable as her own. He thanked her, ignoring Rachael's basilisk stare, and moved toward it. At that precise moment, Pye rose from her comfortable sleep by the hearth, plainly too hot. She glanced around and then, with unerringly good timing, leapt up onto his seat.

A sound suspiciously like a crow of glee came from Rachael. Nat snorted with laughter. Nothing changed on Hellier's face; he surveyed the animal, now contentedly settled, and turned to Silence. "My congratulations, Lady St. Barbe—you have your cat trained surpassingly well."

She laughed. She could not help it, and was surprised to see again that slow, lazy, genuinely amused smile, as she said, "Oh, yes, Captain—we have spent night and day teaching her such tricks."

"She spits at the name of Prince Rupert," Nat informed him solemnly. "And we hope to have her dying for her Parliament before the week's out."

"A cat almost as accomplished as the prince's dog Boy," said the captain. "It must surely be unique."

"*She,*" Rachael said, at once and rudely. "Pye is *she,* not *it.*"

"Then I must beg the lady's pardon, and take another chair." Since neither Nat nor Rachael seemed inclined to move one nearer, he took another of the green damasks from its place by the wall and drew it up next to Pye's. The cat opened an eye at the noise, glared at him, and jumped off. She sat down and washed one white-tipped paw with great thoroughness, and Silence could not suppress her laughter at the captain's face. Nat was grinning as well, and even Rachael's glowering expression changed slightly.

"The might of the king's army, set at naught by an insolent feline," Captain Hellier said. He glanced at Silence, and at Mally, who was approaching with his wine. "Who's to say, if I put this chair back, she'll not leap up on the other one again? I shall take the best strategy, and occupy them both."

And that, pushing the chairs together and sitting firmly on the join, was what he did. Silence caught Nat's eye and was treated to one of his most quizzical expressions, and a wry spread of his hands. Suddenly the impulse came upon her, to give way fully to her amusement. But she could not accept this man at face value, not with his own words echoing still in her mind, not with the ugly example of Ridgeley before her. She glanced warningly at the children. Rachael had not relaxed her guard, of course, and wariness was part of Nat's nature, but she dared not risk falling into the trap of conviviality with this dangerous man, only to find him taking outraged offense at some careless word or, worse, being lightly informed of something better kept a secret. She knew exactly what was going through Rachael's mind: If willpower alone could have jerked those chairs apart and deposited Captain Hellier ungracefully on the floor, then he would already be lying there.

Nat, however, was aware of the dangers. He was steering his sister over to the table with the abandoned chess game still on it. "You take the position I left, and I'll have Mother's, and I'll wager you'll win this one."

As Rachael, unerringly, rose to the bait, Silence breathed a covert sigh of relief. She dreaded to think what Ridgeley would have said, or done, to the girl's insolence. She must have a forceful private talk with her, as soon as the captain was gone.

"I think I am being inspected," Hellier said. Pye was staring at him intently. Then she gathered her sleek muscles and leapt onto his lap. She turned around twice and then curled up neatly, her paws folded inward under her chest. He rubbed her between the ears, and a loud purr rose up in response.

"That cat has no sense of discrimination," Rachael said from the table, just loud enough to be heard. Silence decided to ignore her, and hoped devoutly that the captain was tolerant enough to do the same.

"She likes anyone who makes a fuss of her—but I am hers, first and foremost," she said, watching the thin brown hand stroking her pet's fantastically mottled back. Tabby had once said that Pye looked like a black cat who had stepped in a bowl of cream, dipped her nose and tail in it, and then splashed it all over herself. "She has owned me for five years," she added, "since she was a tiny kitten born under a hedge, and she has had seven litters of kittens herself. Some of those in the barton and the kitchen are hers, and there's a fair number around the village."

"My mother had a cat," he said, thoughtfully gazing into the deep dark-cherry glow of the fire. "A black tom, coal-colored, like a witch's cat, and as foul-tempered as the devil—you could not sit like this with him on your lap, or you risked grave injury."

"Pye is gentle, like all females," Silence said, sipping her wine. "She keeps her claws sheathed for the most part, unless, of course, you frighten her or threaten her kittens. Then, Captain Hellier, I should beware—you may be severely scratched."

"I will take great care," he said, and looked up at her. She saw that he had taken her meaning. "Whether others will be so cautious, I do not know—but I will endeavor to persuade them." His fingers had found the little white furred hollow under Pye's jaw, and tickled gently. "Of course, some cats of either sex spit and claw at all who come near—my mother's was such a one. And then, of course, it is they who should beware."

She knew that he meant Rachael, and nodded warily. "But you did not come up here to talk of cats, Captain Hellier—you said that you wished to speak with me. What is it that you want?"

He took a draft of wine, somewhat larger than her own, before he answered. "There is a problem, small as yet, but I thought that you should be warned before matters grow worse. It concerns stocks of wood for burning. They appear to be running very low."

"*Wood?* We're short of *wood?*" Silence stared at him in some astonishment. "Captain Hellier, there is enough stacked in the linhay in the barton to last beyond Christmas."

"There *was,*" he corrected her. "Unfortunately, the men have been in the habit of building fires in the farmyard and keeping them going all night. In addition, there are chambers in the house now occupied, and the hall fire has been frequently replenished. I doubt there's much more than a week's worth left, if that, and if we can't obtain further supplies, the men will begin to demolish your outbuildings or cut down your timber."

"Are you threatening me, Captain Hellier?"

"No, Lady St. Barbe, I am not. I am merely stating the facts. Think you on this—if I cared nothing for this place, I would not be here now. But wanton damage and destruction is something which I do not enjoy—"

"Why are you in the king's army, then?" Silence asked without thinking, and then sat still, a flush of anger and embarrassment flooding her face.

But he said nothing, only looked at her levelly with the narrowed chestnut-brown eyes that she had noticed at their first meeting. Then he smiled, and shrugged, and finished the wine. "I am a captain in this army for many reasons, my lady, but none that you would suspect, nor understand if you did. This house is old, but it has its own beauty and peace—your husband may be a traitor, but I do not think that is a valid reason for willful destruction which would do no one any good, or credit, least of all the perpetrators."

"He is not a traitor," she said with quiet anger. "He is a loyal subject of the king—but he believes that the dispute between His Majesty and Parliament cannot be solved in any other way."

"And if he and you believe that still, you're fools both. There has always been room for negotiation and compromise—it's just that the leaders on both sides are too stiff-necked and intransigent to see it. But we are digressing from the subject in hand. Where can more supplies of firewood be obtained?"

There was no point in hiding it from him. Better their timber than their paneling or roofs or furniture. She said, "There are three or four acres of coppice on Hassage Hill, half a mile or so behind the house. And there is also a wood in Wellow parish, which gives a lot of fallen timber at this time of year. There is no need for any of your wanton destruction, Captain—you can keep your men from idleness and send them to gather sticks and haul logs."

"They'll grumble," he said. "But they'll do it, or freeze. All the signs are here that this winter will be long and hard—not good campaigning weather."

"Not good living weather either," said Silence. "There has been much hardship in the village these last few years. So many people relied on the cloth trade, spinners and weavers, and have just a close of pasture and a cow or two to give them milk. And now with the war the trade has slumped, and then soldiers come threatening to take all they have between life and starvation. I do not know how much influence you have with Colonel Ridgeley, sir, but I ask you, for the sake of the poor in the parish, to moderate your demands as much as you can."

To her surprise, he did not mock her, nor did he laugh scornfully, as Ridgeley might have done. He said quietly, "My own family was not rich, Lady St. Barbe. I will do what I can, though it may not be enough for your liking or for my conscience." She found a rueful smile turned in her direction. "Does that surprise you, my lady? Oh, yes, there are men of conscience on our side as well as yours, although many fewer after two years of war—and you may believe that or not, as you choose." He got to his feet, gently displacing Pye. The cat settled on the chair nearest to the fire, intent only on her own comfort. "I will leave you in peace now, my lady— thank you for your courtesy, and for your excellent wine." He bowed and added, "By the way—what are those handsome young trees in wooden tubs in the room at the foot of your stairs?"

"Two bay trees, two orange trees, two lemons," Silence replied. They were her pride and joy, placed on the terrace to flower and fruit deliciously in the summer, brought in and placed in the garden room when the winter weather grew too cold for them. She could not help adding, like a boastful child, "We had three ripe oranges this summer past, and two lemons."

"Then they are not to be used for firewood, I take it?"

"For *firewood?*" She stared at him in horror. "Of course not—why? Has someone—"

"Never fear, Lady St. Barbe, your trees are safe, although one or two of the hotter spirits had some wild ideas. The prospect of oranges next summer may preserve them for a while. If they can be convinced that the trees bear an abundance of juicy fruit, so much the better."

"Instead of oranges so small and sour they're not worth the peeling," Silence said ruefully. "Like the vine, nothing bears here but in the orchard—and the peaches and nectarines and apricots in the kitchen garden." She glanced at him, wondering whether to speak further. It was very easy to converse with this man, too easy to forget that he was her enemy.

It was Nat who added his piece. He had left the chess game and his sister, and was standing close. "I ought to warn you, Captain Hellier. My mother is passionate in defense of her garden—if you harm one leaf on a single lavender bush, she'll take up arms. And Diggory too."

"Diggory?"

"Diggory Barnes is our gardener—you may have seen him," said Silence.

"Oh, I know, Old Adam with his rake and spade—yes, I have seen him muttering curses in our direction. What a very appropriate name for a gardener, Lady St. Barbe."

"As apt as is Hellier for a cavalier captain," she said, straight-faced. Nat snorted into his hand.

The captain bowed, his eyes glinting appreciatively. "Once more, thank you for your kind hospitality. I bid you good night, my lady, Master St. Barbe, Mistress St. Barbe."

And they heard his sudden soft laughter as he descended the stairs.

C H A P T E R

FIVE

Make no friendship with an angry man.
—PROVERBS 22:24

Nearly two weeks after the drastic event that Silence always referred to in her mind as The Invasion, the twins celebrated their fifteenth birthday. As if in their honor, the clouds dissolved into a blue-skied morning, sharp and crackling with frost, the windows delicately laced in imitation of Rachael's best collar and cuffs, deeply fringed with the best that the mercers of Bath could provide.

Lavish presents, of course, were out of the question. Although Bath was only half a dozen miles distant, an easy and pleasant day's outing, Silence had been deterred, both by the recent bad weather and by the arrival of the soldiers, from any expedition thence for something so trivial as birthday gifts. She felt, very acutely, that she herself was the only bulwark between Ridgeley's malice and her charge, her responsibility, her burden—Wintercombe and her family. If she left on a jaunt, even to Bath, even for a day, what might not happen in her absence?

So she had bought from one of the chapmen still plying his trade from door to door around the villages, even in these troubled times, when soldiers would have no compunction in stealing takings and purloining goods for themselves or for their wives or sweethearts, even in murdering the unfortunate pedlar for amusement. She had had to send Mally down to the Manor Farm to buy what she wanted. Word had already spread that Wintercombe was under military occupation, and no chapman of any sense would have risked his wares or his person by knocking at the door of a house full of soldiers. The maid had returned with a pair of fringed riding gloves for Nat, which Silence had then embroidered with a little running horse on the back of each, in echo of his gray mare Cobweb. For Rachael there were kerchiefs, four of them, lace-edged and of the finest lawn— much too delicate, Silence feared, to withstand her stepdaughter's characteristically ferocious sneezes. And on each of these she had sewn the likeness of a sprig of lavender, the girl's favorite flower.

The gifts were received with pleasure at breakfast. Fortunately, no soldier was present, there having been a most thorough carouse the previous night. This morning, the stink of stale tobacco and spilled wine had tainted the dining parlor so repulsively that Silence had ordered that they break their fast in the winter parlor instead. The bread, cheese, cold meats and salt herring and steaming bowls of frumenty were laid out on the semicircular, gate-legged table under one of the windows, and the set of turkey-work chairs pulled up around it. Madlin had already replenished the fire, so that it burned hot and bright, melting the icy windows and taking the chill from the room.

On such a morning as this, the hot wheaten frumenty, boiled up with milk, raisins, and a dash of new appley cider, was welcome indeed. As its steam misted the windows, a pleasurable silence fell, all the children being too hungry and too cold to waste time in talk. Only when the bowls were clean, the bread finished, and considerable quantities carved from the big hard yellow cheese were the gifts presented. Even William, his dark merry eyes glinting, had two of his precious chestnuts saved, and gave one to each twin with a beaming smile that split his chubby face in two. Tabby had made lavender bags for Rachael, out of scraps of lawn threaded with blue ribbon and filled with dried aromatic flowers from the mass of bushes and plants that lined Wintercombe's walks and terraces, and for Nat she had put together a tiny book, pieces of thick creamy paper sewn laboriously together, with a cover of stiff black moleskin. Inside, one to each page in her painstaking childish hand, were a selection of his favorite quotations, aphorisms, and sayings. And Deb, not to be outdone, had her own special gifts: a fat bunch of dried flowers for her half-sister, lavender again predominate among the flat silvery discs of honesty, and for Nat a piece of stone, the size of her fist, so pitted and marked that it looked from certain angles like a lion's face.

To all these things, each reflecting the character and interests of the giver as much as the recipient, the twins reacted with gratifying delight. Rachael seemed particularly merry on this, her special day. Silence, looking at her relaxed, laughing face, which might almost be called pretty in such a guise, wondered why her stepdaughter could not always be thus. But she remembered the confused, unhappy days of her own adolescence, the simmering fires of rebellion and resentment that had been repressed far more severely than Rachael's, and knew that the girl's swings of mood and feeling were not entirely the product of her own willful nature.

It was a beautiful day outside. Silence said, wanting to prolong the atmosphere of happiness, "Shall we all take a stroll on the terrace? It's such a lovely morning, and we haven't had the chance for so long."

The younger children, restricted to their nursery for most of the previous ten days, agreed with alacrity, and Silence made sure that collars were fastened, buttons done up, and warm scarves wrapped around necks while Doraty, the nurse, fetched hoods for the girls and firmly dismissed their protests. "You'll be despeard scrammed if you don't put en over your heads, so let's have norn of this here blather."

At last they were ready, wrapped and bundled like parcels. Silence sent Doraty back to the nursery, where a heap of William's hose and Deb's aprons awaited her needle, along with more savory objects, and opened the door that led directly on to the second of the three terraces that fell away to the orchard.

The air struck them, cold and crisp and clean after the warm, wood-smoked atmosphere within. "Race you!" Deb shouted to William and Tabby, and the three younger children pelted down the walk, dodging in and out of the formal knots with much shouting and sprays of gravel. At the end of the path lay their goal, the garden house built by Sir Samuel's father in the exuberant days of Elizabeth. Constructed in the same yellow-gray stone as Wintercombe, though more neatly and precisely dressed, it had been designed in a classical style, but frivolous details erupted here and there to frustrate the severity of the architect: curled leaves around the door frame, a charming curved roof like a cupola, and, topping it all with a flourish, a snarling winged wyvern writhing along the weathervane. This announced that the wind was from the north. The breeze blew very gently around them, hardly strong enough to lift the stray hairs around Silence's cap, or to trouble the stiff ranks of the lavender edging each knot.

With one eye on the distant laughing children, she glanced at the neat borders, the intricate clipped box in its woven patterns, the spaces between filled with colored gravel, clove gillyflowers and carnations, their spiky silvery foliage glistening with frost where the shade fell, the other flowers dull and dormant for the winter. No bulbs showed through as yet, but in three or four months those patches of seemingly dead earth would be white with snowdrops, golden with crocus and the delicate swept-back petals of the hooped-petticoat daffodil and sweet jonquils. In all the doubt and trouble and fear and confusion of her present existence, the utter certainty of her garden was a delight and a consolation. The sun would rise, true, but could be hidden by clouds and rain. Nothing would hide that joyous celebration, that yellow trumpeting of spring, and even if by some dread mischance she were not at Wintercombe to see it, there would be other flowers, other gardens. Not all the king's soldiers, not even the king himself, could stand like Canute and deny the inexorable turning of the seasons and the renewal of the year.

She knew that she should, as a good wife and mother, of the sort called Puritan, turn to God for help and comfort. And indeed her prayers, morning and night, were more fervent than they had ever been. But she had always gone for solace to her garden, and it had never yet failed her. Now she felt the tension trickle away from her body like water. She knelt to pick a freak late carnation bud, valiantly crimson amid the frost crystals, and tucked it into her bodice. Nat and Rachael had strolled on ahead, amicable for once. No stranger, seeing them together, the girl a young woman, taller than the boy by half a head or more, would ever have guessed that they had been born to the same mother, in the same hour.

Absently her fingers found a lurking, hardy weed, undiscovered by Diggory's hoe or the freezing night, and pulled it up. Almost before she knew it, she was sitting comfortably on the gravel, insulated from the cold by many layers of woolen petticoats, probing, pulling, interfering, while a small pile of weeds and disobedient twigs of box grew beside her.

"You're incorrigible," Nat's voice said suddenly. Startled, she looked up guiltily and saw his narrow pale face grinning down at her fondly. "What would the awful Colonel Ridgeley say if he were to see you now, eh?"

"Since his chamber overlooks us, he probably *can* see me—if he isn't sleeping off last night's excess, of course." Silence looked ruefully down at her fingers, now as grubby as Deb's or William's habitually were, and back up at her stepson. "You're right, of course—I *am* incorrigible. Diggory is paid good coin to keep all this immaculate, and as soon as his back's turned I'm down on my knees doing his job for him!"

"More fool you," Nat said, his voice affectionate and entirely without rancor. "That was one of the phrases Tabby put in my book, you know. 'If you would read in this book, more fool you'—on the very first page. It was a clever idea, that."

"I didn't help her at all—she thought of it herself, and kept everything a dark secret even from me." Silence got to her feet, gave her fingers an ineffectual rub together, and glanced at the heap of weeds. "Diggory will have my head on a platter—making such a mess of his nice raked paths."

"Then hide 'em—push 'em under the lavender, and with luck he won't notice for a month or two, especially if it snows." Nat watched as Silence prodded the weeds out of sight with her foot and then added thoughtfully, "It's strange—looking round at the garden, at the house, you could almost pretend that nothing has happened, that the soldiers don't exist."

"Not for long, though," Silence said dryly. "Thirty troopers in the barn and three officers in the house are not exactly invisible—or inaudible." She sighed, looking back at the gray gabled lines of Wintercombe, etched sharp against the new morning sky with the vivid clarity of winter sunlight. "But you're right, Nat, it *is* strange—how in some respects our lives carry on as if nothing at all had happened, how it's possible to pretend we are all quite safe—and yet we aren't, we sit on the edge of danger, and ignore it."

"At our peril, perhaps," said Nat. He gazed absently down the terrace to the other children, now joined by his twin, and added slowly, "It can't last, can it? They haven't stolen anything, or even damaged anything very seriously—apart from poor Buttercup, of course. They really have behaved very well, considering the reputation that Ridgeley has—Clevinger told me that he'd been the cause of much complaint in Bath last summer, and he's probably been sent here to keep him out of the way of the irate citizens." He paused, so evidently wondering whether or not to spare her feelings that she almost laughed. Instead, she nodded attentively, and he went on. "But . . . it's not likely, is it, that things will improve, or even stay the same? The king's cause rides high in the west, but nowhere else—sooner or later, Parliament will move against the Cavaliers here, there may be fighting—at the best, they will be desperate for money, supplies, horses, and then we may fare very badly."

Silence had thought the same herself, but had feared to put it into words, the certainty that this was but a brief respite, the calm before the hurricane that could blow them all, and Wintercombe, to destruction. She was not cold, but she shivered suddenly. She said quietly, "We have nowhere to go. The house at Chard is a ruin, inhabited by hostile strangers. Your Aunt and Uncle Chafin in Wiltshire can scarcely feed themselves and all their brood, let alone a pack of five extra hungry children. We would be safe with my brother Joseph in London, assuredly, but how would we get there? It would be better to stay here for the moment, despite all the dangers."

"Good," Nat said. "That's exactly my thought. At least while we're here we can do our best to prevent the worst damage. And how would the farm fare without you, or the maids, or the village? Besides," he added, his dry voice an unbroken echo of his dead grandfather's, "if we stay here we have the benefit of Darby's cooking."

"I wouldn't rely on that," Silence told him. "He's been on the point of leaving ever since Ridgeley arrived, and it's taken all my powers of persuasion to keep him here. Not only has he had to limit his ingredients according to our new circumstances, but he now has to cater for thirty extra mouths and put up with soldiers in his kitchen into the bargain. If I were in his position, I'd be in Bristol by now, in some nice comfortable merchant's house."

"There's plague in Bristol, according to Clevinger," Nat said, who was his stepmother's principal source of outside information. "You can say a great deal against Bath, but at least it's a cleaner, sweeter place than Bristol. I think Deb's fallen over."

"I'm not surprised," Silence commented, looking down the path to where her younger daughter was being competently picked up and dusted down by Rachael, her self-appointed mentor. It was one of the few points in the girl's favor, that she was, surprisingly, so very good with the little ones. "She must be all right—I can't hear anything."

There was indeed no ear-bursting wail from the child, but in the quiet and birdsong Silence heard more distant male laughter and talk—the troopers, probably making ready for further forays into Norton and the surrounding villages, seeking contributions in coin and kind. It had greatly lessened the burden on Wintercombe, which for the moment was much

smaller than she had feared. But, guiltily, she was aware that those pay-
ments, the cheeses and chickens and vegetables and oats and corn, represented the hard-earned stores of households far less able to bear the cost
than her own.

But it was her own she must look to. There was no one else to protect it.

"I felled over and I didn't cry," Deb said, arriving proudly with a hop
and a skip and a flurry of petticoats. "I didn't cry at all even though there
was blood—look, Mama!"

Silence dutifully inspected the very slight grazes on the chubby pink
palms. "What a brave girl," she said. "I know it's difficult, Deb, but *try*
not to run around shouting like a hoyden. It's small wonder you fell over."

"Sorry," Deb said at once. "I was playing a game—soldiers—I was
chasing William and he was going to shoot me so I ducked and then I
felled over and Rachael picked me up. What's that noise?"

It was a dull chunk, quite close, and unmistakably the sound of metal on
wood. It was followed immediately by a raucous cheer and loud laughter.
Silence knew instantly what was happening. Her eyes, wide and horrified,
flew to meet Nat's above Deb's untidily coifed head.

"Mama! Mama, Mama!" Tabby's voice shrieked her anguish, and Silence
turned to see her hurtling down the path, her skirts hoisted way above her
ankles, showing her stockings, and her abundant curls bouncing over her
shoulders. "Mama, *do* something, they're cutting the trees—they're cutting the trees down in the orchard!" Behind her, William ran with as much
abandon but somewhat less efficiency, scarlet-faced, until Rachael scooped
him up.

With one of the sweeping impulses that tended to overtake her at moments of crisis, Silence did not pause to take thought. "Come on," she said
to her children, and fled back along the path to the steps, nearer the house,
which led down to the lower terrace and thence to the orchard. Nat was
with her. His ill health was not so severe as to prevent him running in such
an emergency, but she heard his gasping breath falling a little behind as
she passed the sundial and came to the last steps leading to the orchard
below, where only two weeks ago Rachael had run to warn her of the
troopers' first arrival.

The land sloped away here to the little brook that ran along the tiny
valley on whose north bank Wintercombe stood. In spring and summer it
was a haven, pink with blossom, laced cream with cow parsley, lush grazing for their horses, and the clamorous resort of the bees lodged in their
straw skeps in the niches along the lowest terrace wall. Now the apples and
plums, pears and quinces and medlars and mulberries had all been gathered, the grass chewed short by a succession of pastured animals, and the
two fish ponds, intended by Sir Samuel's father for an Italian water garden
but somehow never finished, were cold and black and bleak. The trees were
bare now, the last week's gales had seen to that, save for here and there a

gold leaf still caught like a jewel in the dark webby net of branches. The troopers were easily visible, clustered around one of the largest and oldest apple trees, greeting each blow of the axe with those ugly cheers.

Too late, Silence regretted towing the children there in her impulsive wake. Too late, for Tabby had overtaken her, leaping the last two steps and hurling herself at the man with the axe.

"No!" Her voice and her mother's came together. Silence, foreseeing unspeakable horrors, followed gasping, to see her daughter, her face white and intently furious, grasp the man's arm with both hands, hanging all her insubstantial weight upon it. Such was her victim's astonishment at this unexpected assault that he dropped the axe and flailed wildly. Tabby, who had a vein of stubbornness as deep as her half-sister's, hung on grimly, shouting something. With an effort, the soldier shook her free. She tumbled backward onto the grass, skirts and hair flying, her fists clenched, and bounced up again, intent only on preventing destruction. But by this time another trooper had the axe, and a third seized hold of the child by the arms. Though she twisted frantically to gain her freedom, his grip was relentless.

"Let her go," Silence said urgently, her heart thudding so hard that it threatened to interfere with her breathing. "Put that axe down and let her go."

"She *bit* me!" the man holding Tabby complained, snatching one hand away from her arm. To Silence's horrified amazement, the blood was running down his fingers. "Why, you little hellcat, I'll teach you a lesson you won't forget in a hurry, you bitch—"

"Hit the child, and I'll shoot you where it most hurts."

It was Captain Hellier's voice, calm, implacable. It froze everyone. The trooper, his hand raised inches from Tabby's face, stared past Silence's shoulder, his expression rigid with fear. Silence realized suddenly that the officer's hold over his men was based not on sweet reason or comradeship, but on the understanding that what he said, he would do. And that the troopers knew full well that he was quite capable of pistoling a man in cold blood. It added a frightening new dimension to the pleasant, amused, and tolerant gentleman who had surprised her that evening a few days previously.

"Let the child go," Hellier continued. Without moving his face, the trooper dropped his hand, and Tabby stood free.

She did not, however, run straight to her mother, as Silence had expected. Instead, she stayed where she was, her gaze defiantly tilted upward, and directed her words sternly to the captain. "They were cutting our trees down. Make them stop!"

"They have stopped," Captain Hellier said. "And I doubt very much that they will start again."

Silence risked a glance behind her. He was standing at the top of the steps, and there was indeed a pistol in his hand. It looked heavy, brutal, and completely uncompromising. Moreover, the black hole of the muzzle appeared to be pointing directly at her. Alarmed, she stepped hastily out of the line of fire, and found Nat at her shoulder. To her relief, Rachael had the little ones safely out of the way on the terrace, beside Captain Hellier.

Tabby, astonishing Tabby, was still in danger. Captain Hellier's intervention might have saved her from injury, but she was surrounded by soldiers and directly between her erstwhile captor and the pistol.

"Tabby—Tabby, come here," Silence said, trying to keep the pleading note out of her voice. She had never known her daughter disobedient before, but then she had never seen her behave in such a way as this. The gentle, quiet, sensitive child, who thought and felt so deeply, was unrecognizable in this mulish, enraged little girl, with wide glittering hate-filled eyes, standing her ground amid the score or so of troopers.

"Make them promise they won't!" Tabby shouted. Tears of rage and fright were beginning to fill her eyes, but her voice was high, clear, and unwavering. "They're *our* trees—you mustn't cut them down!"

One of the men sniggered. "Of course we won't, little maid—of course we won't. Now you go back to your mammy."

Tabby's eyes raked him in withering contempt. "No. As soon as we're gone you'll cut them down anyway."

"They won't," Captain Hellier said, his voice cool and reassuring. "They'll have me to reckon with if they do."

"Hey!" one of the troopers shouted indignantly from the back. "The colonel told us to cut a couple of trees down, we be all but out of firewood, and 'tis tarblish cold."

"And I'm telling you that these trees are to be left. There's coppices in plenty, I'm told, just ready and waiting for your axe—all you have to do is hitch cart to horse and go and get it."

"And what if we don't want to? We bain't farmhands nor woodsmen neither, eh, lads?"

There was an unpleasant mutter of assent. Silence hooked Tabby's eyes with hers, willing the child to come toward her, out of danger, for suddenly Captain Hellier and his pistol did not seem so powerful, set against a score of hostile troopers, all armed with swords, and that axe.

Tabby might be stubborn, but she was well aware of the peril in which she stood. Silence, who knew her so well, could see it in her wide, terrified eyes, the gray-pale set of her face. She glanced around at the men, seeming very small and fragile among the hulking brutal ring of troopers, and then, her pointed chin set firmly in the air, turned and began to walk deliberately over to her mother.

It happened so fast that only afterward was Silence able to work out the exact sequence of events in her mind. The sudden lunge toward her daughter, made by the man who had wielded the axe; her own frantic screech of warning, almost drowned by the deafening crash of the pistol; Tabby dropping like a stone to the ground, followed at almost the same instant by her assailant; and the brute howl of impotent fury from the remaining soldiers.

Acrid smoke drifted down from the terrace. Her ears throbbed, her heart was numb. He has killed her, Silence thought, he has killed her, my sweet lovely Tabby is dead, oh no, not Tabby—and then, as the anguish twisted her face, she heard Deb's frantic wails and knew that the little ones had seen the murder too.

She ran the few steps to the bodies, Nat at her heels, not knowing what horror she would find, and knelt by her daughter.

And Tabby moved as she touched her, cried "Mama!" and struggled to sit up. There was no mark, no blood. Her distraught green-brown eyes, distended with fear like a cornered deer's, stared up at her mother's face as if she did not believe what she saw. Then, with a whimper, she hurled herself into Silence's arms.

The man lying beside her, she saw as she rocked Tabby to and fro, almost sick with relief and fear, was quite, quite dead.

"Lady St. Barbe!" Captain Hellier's voice was not loud, had never been so, but it cut through the troopers' mutter of fear and anger like a sword. She stayed where she was, unwilling to let go of Tabby, and he spoke again, more sharply. "My lady! I think it best if you and your son and daughter come join me here."

She could see the sense of that. She knew, with a curious feeling of remoteness, the danger that she and Nat and Tabby were in still. And if the captain only had the one pistol, and that was now discharged, what hope had he against a score or so of furious troopers bent on revenge for their comrade's death?

"Mother," Nat said, very quietly, his hand on her shoulder. "Come on, get up, carry her if you must—but do what he says, please, before something else happens."

Obediently, because Nat was sensible, Nat knew best, Nat could be relied upon, she got up. Tabby was surprisingly heavy for such a slight child, and she felt her back straining at the unaccustomed weight, but she would not let her go. And indeed she could not, for the little girl's arms were clinging to her like the curling tendrils of withywind. Very slowly, feeling Nat's presence at her side, she turned and made her way through the thick rough grass, wet with melted frost, to the steps. Behind her, no sound came, nothing stirred, no one spoke, but she could feel their eyes fixed on her in hatred, the privileged and wealthy woman, a traitor's wife, in whose protection one of their number had been slaughtered.

The steps were in front of her, familiar, worn in the middle, rounded at the edge, with gray-green lichen covering the unfrequented corners. She felt Tabby's grip tighten, and whispered, "It's all right, poppet, it's all right, you're safe."

And Nat added softly, "Just up the steps to the terrace, Tabby, and then Mama will put you down."

She would have to. Her arms, her neck, her back all ached with increasing force. But she climbed the five steps, doggedly, her eyes on the ground because Tabby's arms were dragging her head low, waiting for—what? A riot? An assault by the mob of soldiers? A bullet in the back, or a sword? She did not know what she feared, only that her mouth was dry with it, and she could barely breathe for terror.

And then her feet stepped on gravel, and Nat said urgently, "Put her down now, Mother, you're safe—Captain Hellier has his gun trained on them, they can't do anything."

But what if he only has the one, thought Silence—surely they can't be that stupid? She bent, very slowly and carefully, and set her daughter's feet on the ground. "There you are, Tabby—you're safe now, poppet, you're on the terrace. Look, here's Rachael."

Rachael's face, white, pointed, furious and fearful at once, was the mirror of Tabby's as she had faced the soldiers. Disturbed at the resemblance, which she had never noticed before, Silence unwound the child's arms from her neck and very gently separated herself. To her surprise, Tabby was not weeping. The tear tracks were dry on her face, and her expression was astonishingly calm. She looked about her, at the twins, at Deb's scarlet unhappy face and William's wide eyes.

"That man had a *gun*," the little boy said, with a mixture of fear and enthusiasm that might have been comical in another, less terrifying situation. "He had a gun and it went bang and you felled over and that other man felled over too and he hasn't got up yet." He glanced around between the balustrades and added curiously, "Is he dead?"

Out of the mouths of babes and sucklings, thought Silence. She wanted to run, to take them all back to the house, to hide them in her chamber and lock the door so that they would be safe, shielded from the horrors that they had faced that morning, gathered within her arms and beneath her wings as a broody hen protects her chicks from the marauding fox.

But it was too late for that. Had been too late, ever since the accursed Ridgeley and his crew of ruffians had ridden into Wintercombe, and ruined their secure, snug, smug existence.

"Are you all right, Tabby?" she said, choosing to ignore William's question. She did not want to think about the man lying there in his blood, the leaking neatly drilled hole in his forehead, the look of surprise already fading from his pockmarked, brutal, unshaven face. He had not been a godly man, assuredly he was one of the wicked and his soul was even now screaming in hell as the flames licked at it. But he was a man, and a moment before he had been alive, as alive as she herself or Tabby or Nat or William—or as Captain Hellier, still standing facing the rest of his troopers.

"What's happening? Captain!" It was Ridgeley's voice. Her stomach heaved suddenly, and she clenched a hand over her mouth to avoid disgracing herself. With a desperate effort, she struggled to her feet, dusting down her skirts as if nothing had occurred, and turned to look up toward the house. Hellier, she noticed out of the corner of her eye, had not moved his gaze nor his pistol from their guard over the troopers.

She owed him something, she realized suddenly. He had committed . . . an act of murder, or an act of rough military justice, to save herself and Tabby from a situation rapidly escalating out of his control, and she could foresee Ridgeley's reaction only too clearly. Hellier deserved her support, though she feared and mistrusted him. And in her situation, she in her turn needed such an ally most desperately.

So she walked boldly to the foot of the steps up to the next terrace, as Ridgeley, followed by Byam, reached the top. "I must thank you and your captain, sir, for saving my daughter's life, and my own. The men—they behaved disgracefully, Colonel Ridgeley, we could easily have been assaulted or dishonored or worse—but Captain Hellier saved our lives!"

Ridgeley stopped halfway down the steps, his chin, thrust forward aggressively. "Saved your life, madam? What is this? I heard a shot—Hellier!"

Silence found herself, to her fury, being brushed aside as the two officers strode down the remaining steps and crossed the gravel to where the captain stood, his back to them, still threatening the soldiers in the orchard. As Ridgeley appeared, they set up an ironic welcoming cheer that died away raggedly.

With a warning glance at her children huddled together a few feet away, Silence followed the two men to the balustrade. The body of the dead trooper lay below, surrounded by his live and indignant fellows. One of them called up angrily, "'Tis Hoskins, sir! Cap'n Hellier shot 'im!"

"You *what?*" Ridgeley's voice was suddenly soft and silky with menace. He turned and stared at his captain.

Hellier, a smaller man by some inches, and slighter by far, stared imperturbably back. "Yes," he said, with a calm—or callousness—that astonished Silence. "I shot him. After due warning, of course."

"Warning? You shot him in cold blood? Why, for Christ's sake?"

At the corner of her vision, Silence saw Rachael, her father's child in this at least, wince at the oath. Captain Hellier, his tone that of a man patiently and reasonably explaining the obvious, said mildly, "He was about to attack one of the children. The girl seemed in danger, and I had already warned them to let her and her mother pass in safety. Hoskins disobeyed my orders, so I shot him."

"And what was the brat doing in the orchard in the first place?"

"Trying to prevent the destruction of the trees," Hellier told him.

There was a brief, disbelieving pause. Then Ridgeley said, his voice very low, "You overstep your mark, *Captain* Hellier. It was my order they were obeying, not yours. I gave leave for trees to be cut down for firewood not fifteen minutes ago. If that traitor's brat gets in the way, that's her bad luck. Christ's blood, man, do you want the men to die of cold?"

"The trees are *apple* trees," Silence said. She stepped forward to confront Ridgeley, though her knees were shaking beneath her skirts, and her mouth was so dry that she could not swallow. "You and your men have drunk our cider very freely, Colonel Ridgeley. These trees bear the apples to make it. If you cut them down, you'll go thirsty next year."

"It's a long time away, next year," Byam said, as Ridgeley surveyed her in some astonishment. "Winter is approaching, madam, and will be here shortly. Who knows where we may be next year, and what use may your precious cider be to us by then? Our need now is for firewood, and this we will have."

"I said that you could," Silence told them. "There is a coppice nearby in need of cutting, and a wood a little more distant where you may pick up fallen timber by the cartload. You may have all of it with my blessing— why waste time and energy, cutting down perfectly good apple trees because your precious men are too idle to walk half a mile and too insolent and superior to hitch up cart to horse and go get wood that's lying on the ground?"

There was a pause, while all three men surveyed her. She avoided Byam's loose-lipped leer—a man who treated anything in skirts merely as an object of his lusts was utterly despicable—and glanced instead at Hellier. Even when facing his colonel's wrath, his self-possession had not wavered in the slightest. Unaware, she met his gaze, the chestnut-brown eyes intently watchful and alert, and saw his mouth twitch very slightly in amused acknowledgment. With a shock of surprise and indignation, she realized that he was enjoying all this.

Abruptly, Ridgeley threw back his head, the plume on his beaver dancing furiously—discourteously, he had not doffed the hat in her presence— and gave his full-throated, contemptuous laugh. "Lady St. Barbe, Lady St. Barbe, what are we to do with you, eh? One of my men slaughtered on your behalf, my orders countermanded, and in spite of all my warnings you dare stand here and defy me? Well," the colonel said, with the falsely benevolent smile of an uncle prepared to indulge the whims of a spoiled brat for the sake of a few moments' peace, "I like a woman with some spirit, eh, Byam? As long as she don't get too far above herself, of course— wouldn't do to give you an inflated idea of your own importance, my lady, now would it?" And as she stared at him, more infuriated by this patronizing tone than by anything else he had ever said to her, he thrust his head down toward her, very close, so that she smelled the stale wine and tobacco fumes on his breath. "You're lucky indeed, my lady. One of my men is dead because of you and your brat. I have you and all your traitor's brood in my power, do you realize? I could turn you and those children over to my men—they're starved of women here, they'd leap on all of you, even the smallest. I could dismantle your precious house and feed it to the flames, I could slaughter your cattle, cut down every tree in this benighted orchard of yours. I am not going to do it, Lady St. Barbe—not yet, because much though I would like to destroy you and all that is yours, I have my orders to treat you gently. Sir Thomas Bridges's father apparently had fond memories of your husband's father, and his son has old kindnesses to repay. So I will do nothing too unpleasant—yet. But let me warn you, madam. The fortunes of war may change rapidly. There may well come a time when I am no longer subject to those orders, or when I find myself able to disobey them with impunity. And then, my lady, then beware—for I will crush you and all around you, slowly, and painfully, and without mercy. It is something to which I look forward with much anticipation, and I shall derive a great deal of pleasure and satisfaction from watching your destruction. Now go, and take your squalling spawn with you, before I forget my orders. Go!"

And, terror overtaking anger, she gathered the children, and fled.

C H A P T E R

SIX

Shame shall be the promotion of fools.
—PROVERBS 3:35

"It's our only hope," Silence said, to the solemn faces that ringed her hearthside. "Our only hope of being rid of these evil parasites. Ridgeley told me himself that Sir Thomas Bridges's father was an old friend of Sir Samuel and had a kindness for us. It's by his orders that we have escaped so lightly—if you can call this situation 'light.'"

There was a murmur of assent. Each of her servants had an ample fund of unpleasant experiences to describe; indeed, had already told them to anyone, within the house or farther afield, among farm workers and villagers, who could be persuaded to listen. Silence knew them all: the trooper who had threatened Darby with his pistol and bullied even that fearsome man into parting with half a dozen chicken carcasses; another who had hit young Ned Merrifield across the face, causing a black eye and a cut lip, when the boy had taken too long to fetch a flagon of cider; Eliza's moments of terror, cornered by a drunken man in the screens passage and apparently on the point of being ravished there and then when Hellier had happened to pass. She was fortunate that it had been the captain; Byam or Ridgeley were more likely to have joined in the rape than to have stopped it. And if Eliza, with her equine face and forbidding manner, was not safe from the unwelcome attentions of the soldiers, how much more at risk was poor little Madlin, with her naive shy manner and her flowerlike face?

So Silence had sent the girl back to her parents, respectable clothiers who would much rather bear the expense of keeping their daughter idle at home than have her face the very real danger of molestation, dishonor, rape, whenever she put her nose outside her chamber door. Madlin had been glad to go, and her departure took a weight from Silence's mind, even though it meant that the other maids had proportionately more work to do. But Margery Turber was willing to help. With the onset of winter, there was much less to do in the dairy anyway.

And that, of course, meant that Bessie was frequently idle, and the devil, proverbially, found plenty for her to do. Silence had lost count of the times she had come across her dairymaid fraternizing with the soldiers, enjoying their company, giggling and laughing over lewd suggestions, or being fondled in dark corners. She knew that she should send Bessie back to her family too, but the Lytemans were very poor and could not cope without the money their daughter brought to the household. Besides, despite her moral misgivings, she liked the girl. Even now, there was something very attractive about Bessie's personality, her open, lustful enjoyment of all that life had to offer, her generous good nature, and her essential kindness. She had treated Madlin very gently, far more so than Leah, who was often downright malicious. And when required, Bessie always worked hard and took a pride in her skills.

So, despite Eliza's open disapproval, Silence had said nothing to Bessie beyond an admonition, given as sternly as she could, to leave the men alone and, if she could not, at least to take care and to be discreet. And Bessie, a glint in her lovely, amused blue eyes, had tossed her auburn hair under the neat white cap and assured her mistress that she would. "But you d'know what I be, m'lady," she said ruefully. "Somewhen I just can't seem to help myself."

"More than sometimes, Bessie," Silence pointed out dryly, and they had laughed together, understanding each other's point of view perfectly.

No, Bessie's talents in the dairy were undeniable, and far too valuable to lose for merely moral considerations. But Silence could wish, most earnestly, that the girl did not attract men like a magnet.

She did not have to, of course—every woman in Wintercombe, with the exception of Silence herself, had been propositioned before the first week was out. Even Mally, sewing now with Rachael at the table, had been leered at a score of times and been the object of numerous indecent suggestions. Nothing could be done, short of locking all the females into one room, and everyone had evolved their own strategy for dealing with the importunate soldiers. Eliza, after her narrow escape, swept by with a haughty look that effectively concealed her alarm, and had kicked another assailant so hard on the shins that word had got about that she was an unrewarding quarry. Leah pretended to discourage them, while her winks and glances told another story. Hester Perry, the nursemaid, would walk all around the outside of the house in the rain rather than encounter a trooper, and ventured outside the nursery only when absolutely necessary. And Doraty, her superior and a widow wise in the ways of the world, had developed a blistering style of speech that up until now had successfully repelled all would-be boarders.

Up until now. Silence glanced around at her female servants, all as yet, so far as she knew, with their honor intact—though with Bessie at least it was surely only a matter of time—and thought of the endless work, subterfuge, worry, and deviousness needed to keep them thus. And for how long?

It was now the middle of December. For six weeks their unwelcome guests had ruled their lives with an increasing callousness and disregard for civilized behavior. So long as they did not overstep the mark too much, any word or deed seemed to be permitted the troopers. Short of outright rape, murder, or widespread destruction, their officers were not prepared to intervene—save for Captain Hellier.

She had thought that he might be an ally. She had speedily realized her mistake. It was not that he was unpleasant, at least not openly so. By comparison with Ridgeley, and to a lesser degree Byam, he was courtesy itself. But, curiously, it was that very manner that led her to mistrust him. Not one of the women's complaints had involved him except, on at least half a dozen occasions, as their rescuer. He was polite to her, to the children, and to the servants, even to Ridgeley, who plainly detested him. He had probably saved her life, and Tabby's; he had certainly saved the apple trees, for the troopers, with rather better grace than she had expected, now made one or two journeys each week to wood and coppice for their fuel. Further, she suspected that the fact that no more cattle had yet been slaughtered was due to him. Undoubtedly their lives would be even more difficult, if not impossible, without the captain to balance and check the excesses of his men and his commanding officer.

And yet she could not bring herself to place any confidence in this man, nor to treat him in any other way but with a reserved hostility. She had pondered the reasons when she had the leisure for idle thought, generally in the long dark evenings. She supposed that she could not consider him to be fundamentally any different from his fellows, however ingratiating he might be to the Wintercombe household and to herself. How could she trust his admittedly pleasant smile, his easygoing air, when she knew that he was on terms of good comradeship with the odious Byam and indulged in those nightly drinking bouts with the other officers while Wintercombe tried to sleep, fingers in ears?

Besides, she could not forget, would never erase from her mind for the rest of her life, the moment when he had shot the trooper in the orchard. Now, weeks later, it did not seem to matter that the man had attempted to seize Tabby, for whatever vile reason of his own—his intentions might even have been relatively harmless, undeserving of that ultimate penalty. What she found most disturbing was the unthinking ease and skill with which the soldier had been dispatched by his officer, as callously as if Hellier had been killing a pig instead of a man. And afterward, quite unaffected by the slaughter, he had given every appearance of enjoying his confrontation with Colonel Ridgeley.

He may think that he can worm himself into all of our good graces, Silence had thought with righteous anger. A sweet smile and a kind word or deed, and we will do whatever he wants, which is doubtless for his own nefarious ends. But, she had told herself with a shiver of fear, he is dangerous in his own way—far more so than Ridgeley, who at least makes no secret of his menace.

But it was the shortage of supplies that had been gnawing most at her mind all these long winter evenings, when she only had Mally and the twins for company. As she had feared, the contributions from the village were given with great reluctance, and sparingly to say the least. Despite the threatening posture of the soldiers, very little had trickled into Winter- combe, and Silence strongly suspected that what did arrive was taken rather than given. Nor could she be sorry, knowing that many of the people of the village had suffered hardship for years and would swiftly become desti- tute if the troopers' demands proved too greedy.

But it meant that their own stores were being run down with alarming speed. Only today she had ventured into the barn, escorted by Mally and Clevinger, and had been horrified, not at the heaped bedding and straw at one end, which was after all only to be expected with thirty men sleeping there, but at the unexpected space at the other end where the feed for the farm's animals was stored. The cattle in their fields existed on whatever grass and herbage they could find, and additional fodder was taken out to them in the cart. The horses, ejected into the paddocks around Winter- combe, and looking very cold and miserable in these unaccustomed condi- tions, despite their shaggier winter coats, required much hay. It was the latter supplies that had suffered the most severe depletion. Grimly Clevinger had pointed out the place to which the heaps and stacks normally extended around Christmastime, and she could see the discrepancy for her- self. The barn was normally as empty as this come March, or April.

"Two month at the outside," the bailiff had said. "Two month fodder left, m'lady, and then they'll start on the straw, and the kine will starve before the spring grass comes—or abort their calves."

"And when can they be turned out into the meadows?" she had asked him, remembering Nat on the subject.

Clevinger shook his head gloomily. "If we d'get a fine spring, m'lady, after Easter, maybe. Or they'll eat the grass down to the roots and we'll have no hay for next year neither—soldiers or no soldiers."

. That had been worrying enough. But she had also made her weekly inspection of the house storerooms, noting the cheese, the bins of flour and the tubs of butter, the barrels of salt meat, sides of bacon and haunches of ham, strings of onions and garlic, the beer and cider, the wines and the honey, and the more expensive items kept on higher shelves—loaf sugar, dates and raisins and other dried fruit, herbs and spices and the jars and bottles of preserved fruits and pickled vegetables that she and her maids had labored over in happier times, not two or three months previously. Few eggs, because many of the hens had unaccountably disappeared—though no one doubted where—and those cheeses left were young and green for the most part. There was too little flour: The bin was half-empty, and another load of grain would have to be taken down to Master Apprice's mill to be ground, at his exorbitant rates. Old Apprice had always driven a hard bargain, and his son was the same. That family was one which would not suffer in these hard times, she thought sourly. Millers were never popular, but the Apprices seemed determined to live up to their proverbial reputation. And there was much less corn in the granary than there should be at this stage of the winter. If the worst came to the worst, she would have to take a little of her hidden hoard from under the hearthstone, and buy some in—again, at prices inflated both by the war and her own need.

There was the same tale in the kitchen garden. In summer it was a lovely place, fragrant with lavender and marjoram, rosemary and thyme and other sweet herbs. Now her eye wandered over rows of depressed-looking cabbages, their lower leaves turned to lacework by the attentions of the pigeons that lived in the dovecote in the front courtyard. Will Parsons, the slowest and most stupid of the three scullions, was supposed to frighten them away. He had had little more success than the scarecrow stuck forlornly on a pole, clad in a dreadful old doublet of Sir Samuel's that he had worn for fowling, and was too rent and damaged even to give away to the poor. The winter sallets, chicory and endive, had at least a net cast over them, and the leeks, fat and ready for the pot, stood to attention in the farthest bed. But for the most part the plot, large, wall lined, sheltered from the sharpest winds and frosts, presented its most barren and unpromising winter aspect, its harvest already bottled, pickled, preserved, or consumed. There would be little sustenance to be gained here for a household of twenty-six, let alone nearly three dozen unwanted soldiers.

There might be little to be gained by an appeal to Sir Thomas Bridges. She only had the word of Colonel Ridgeley, after all, that he had ordered Wintercombe to be treated kindly, and she trusted that man as she would the devil. But the prospect of hardship facing them, and the village, was looming so real, so close, that if only for the salving of her conscience, she must make the effort to beg for some mitigation of their burden. Her servants and her children looked to her for their salvation, and she was acutely conscious that some at least of her household had come to see her not as an ineffectual foreign woman, imported from the effete city of London to lord it over honest Somerset folk, but as their one bulwark against military depredation and ruin. She wished heartily that they did not have such faith in her, for she knew it to be misplaced. And her Puritan upbringing had left her with a heavy luggage of guilt, of duties reluctantly and uncomplainingly shouldered, and a deep sense of her own unworthiness. Only her love for her children was free of these complexities, the source at once of her greatest comfort and her sharpest fears.

Tabby had had many nightmares after the shooting in the orchard, the terrors of that day emerging again and again in her dreams. So dreadful and disrupted had her slumbers been that Doraty had last night taken the little girl into her bed, to comfort her. If that had no effect, Silence knew that she must do the same. Her child's peace of mind was too precious to sacrifice to convenience and convention.

And if Tabby were not worry enough, there was also Rachael to contend with: Rachael, who had taken to strolling past the soldiers, uttering low-voiced comments that might have been better left unsaid. Silence suspected that if she had not been the daughter of the house, and thus protected from assault by all but the most reckless and unregenerate trooper, she would long ago have provoked retaliation. Nat had had words with her, in his brisk sensible fashion pointing out the dangers and condemning her for a fool far more readily than Silence would. Rachael, of course, shook all the advice, admonitions, and reasonings off like a duck spilling water from its back, and went her own difficult and dangerous way—riding for a fall, as Nat said. Short of keeping her under lock and key, there was nothing that Silence could do, for any scoldings less severe than those that Dame Ursula meted out to the girl were certain to have no effect whatsoever.

Sometimes, only sometimes, Silence wished that she herself had that blistering and wholly contemptuous style of rebuke: It would make managing her children and her servants so much easier. But all her life she had wanted only to be liked, and it was impossible to change herself now. Anyway, she would never be seen as anything other than a pale and feeble counterfeit of her fearsome mother-in-law, however hard she tried.

Ironically, it was Dame Ursula herself who had finally pushed Silence into her decision to go to Sir Thomas Bridges. It was, she had realized, in the end easier to gather the courage and determination to make that uncertain journey, with its dangers, discomforts, and probability of abject humiliation, than to face another painful inquisition on her neglect of her proper duty.

So, she had gathered her principal servants here, in her chamber, to tell them of her mission and to direct their tasks for the day of her absence. Food must still be prepared, chambers cleaned, fires lit and tended; the children must be protected, amused, kept busy and out of mischief. And above all, while she was gone, they must avoid the slightest confrontation with the soldiers.

She looked around at the intent, watchful, anxious faces, some nodding in earnest agreement. She knew that they would do their best to obey her instructions, but life at Wintercombe now was a little like walking to and fro past a cave full of sleeping lions—quite safe, so long as the beasts remained quiet. She had no faith in their continued slumber. More than the journey itself, she dreaded what she might find when she came home again.

But she had committed herself now, in front of all her household. There was no going back, even when the following day dawned cold and grim, with a biting northeasterly wind. It was the seventeenth day of December, and winter had come early this year. Two or three days ago, a few hesitant flakes of snow had drifted down from a flat dark gray sky. By the look of the heavy clouds scudding above the house and crowding blue-black on the northern horizon, there would be much more today.

It would have been sensible to plead the folly of venturing out with snow threatening, and stay wrapped warm and snug in front of her chamber's blazing fire. But she knew that if she offered that excuse to herself, she would find similar on other occasions, and would never go at all. So, ignoring Mally's pointed and doubtful glances out of the window, she told her maid to get her warmest gown from the clothes closet and to lay out the thick traveling cassock coat, made of the local broadcloth, dyed a deep mulberry and warmly lined with coney fur. It was a garment essentially practical, bulky and shapeless with no concessions to fashion, and would have to be removed before she met Sir Thomas. Her cause would hardly be furthered if she arrived in his presence clad like a market woman.

On the other hand, as Mally had already reminded her, it would not do her any good if she looked too prosperous. So it must be one of her plainer collars, that with the single narrow edging of lace, and the neat but obvious repair to a tear at one corner. Mally helped to lay it over her shoulders, covering the comparatively high neck of her dark-blue gown. She had had this dress for four years, and she hoped that its plain style and rather old-fashioned high waist would look woefully dowdy to the Governor of Bath.

Finally, her mouse-brown hair was quickly arranged by the maid into its accustomed knot on the back of her head, with the side pieces left loose to wave listlessly about her face. She studied herself in the little mirror that Mally held out before her. There were lines of strain about her mouth, and a deepening crease between the thick, level brows. I am twenty-eight years old, she thought ruefully, and I look every one of them, and more. And I *feel* about a hundred and ten.

Darby, unasked, had supplied a plateful of steaming collops of bacon for her breakfast, served with eggs fried in butter, and mopped up with a big wedge of coarse brown bread. She cut up two slices of the salty bacon and shared it between the children, who had only frumenty to fill their stomachs. Then, with tender good-byes, hugs and kisses and stern instructions to be good and to obey Doraty and Hester in everything, she left the children in their nurses' capable hands and went into the hall.

Mally was there, with her cassock coat, and hood, and the beaver hat she wore when riding. There were no soldiers in evidence, but Eliza, the Turbers, and, to her surprise, Tom Darby were standing around the fireplace, looking rather embarrassed, to wish her Godspeed. Rather touched, she accepted their concern with gratitude, and thanked Darby for the bacon now warming her stomach. With Mally's help she put on her outdoor clothes carefully, so that no gap in her defenses could be left to admit the icy wind blowing in her face all the way to Bath. Then, telling them all to stay within doors if they had any regard for their health, she walked through the screens, through the two front doors that Turber opened and held for her, and into the courtyard.

The wind hit her like a hammer, on her right side. She staggered, and her well-wrapped and buttoned coat blew out like a sail. Her hat was securely tied on, which was just as well, or it would have gone bowling merrily across the courtyard like the leaves and sticks already tossed in heaps against the walls.

In the small shelter afforded by the gatehouse, Clevinger, who was to escort her to Bath, waited with the horses. She bundled her garments closely around her, waved back to Turber's anxious face with much more cheerfulness than she actually felt, and proceeded with determination across that galeswept expanse of gravel to the gatehouse.

Clevinger was there indeed, his face set in stiff lines of disapproval. And beside him, in buff coat and a long and flamboyantly scarlet cloak, was Captain Hellier, one hand holding the reins of a tall chestnut horse, while the other grasped his riding gauntlets.

She had thought that her departure had been successfully kept from the soldiers. She had no intention of having her plea for help preempted by Ridgeley. She stared in dismay at the captain, and he gave her his courtesy smile, pleasant and empty, quite unlike that slow, lazy, amused cat's grin she had seen on his face that evening in her chamber. That encounter seemed a long time ago. She thrust it from her mind and said coldly, "You are under some misapprehension, Captain. My bailiff is quite sufficient escort, thank you."

"There I think you are wrong," he said, still with that polite smile. "Whatever possessed you to choose such a menacing day for your mission, Lady St. Barbe? You'd do better to wait out the blizzard by your own hearth."

"Blizzard? What blizzard? It is but six or seven miles to Bath," Silence said. "Two hours' journey at the most, a road I know well, and my bailiff to accompany me. I do not need you, Captain—shouldn't you take your horse back to shelter?"

"You will need me," he said. "You'll need my word to take you to Sir Thomas Bridges." And as Silence gazed at him in some consternation, he added, "I make it my business to learn these things, madam, and it's common knowledge among your servants. However, I can at least set part of your mind at rest—the colonel does not know of your journey."

"He will soon enough if I stand here idly in full view," Silence said, with an asperity she normally used only with troublesome children. "Now, Captain, if you will kindly move aside, Clevinger and I can go. As you yourself said, the weather is too threatening to linger."

To her annoyance, he did not budge, although the chestnut horse ducked its head and champed noisily at its bit. Clevinger's old brown gelding, and her own fat mare, waited patiently, their eyes half closed and the wind stirring their furry flanks and blowing their manes back. "Exactly, my lady," he said dryly. "And you are not leaving without me. I shall stand here until I take root, if necessary."

Silence felt two quite contradictory impulses: to laugh and to hit him. She was Lady St. Barbe, and would do neither. Instead she said icily, "Why, sir, do you insist, in defiance of my wishes? You have no rights over me."

"No, my lady—but I do not think that you fully understand the situation. Not only may there be dangers on your journey, from the weather if nothing else, but when you reach Bath you may well find that there will be difficulties that you had not suspected."

"What difficulties? You think that Sir Thomas will refuse to listen to me?"

"He may well refuse even to see you. He has queues of petitioners, many of whom are in much worse case than yourself, with far more urgent requests. You must accept that your name alone, Lady St. Barbe, will not guarantee instant access to the governor, let alone any worthwhile response."

In her heart of hearts, she knew the essential truth of what he said, but she had her duty, and would not depart from it now. "That's as may be," she said stubbornly. "But I prefer to discover such things for myself, Captain Hellier, and always have done. Now, will you let me pass?"

Still he stood, though the smile had gone, and his face was serious. "What I am trying to tell you, my lady, is that alone you will not see Sir Thomas without trouble and, at the very least, such a long wait that you may not be able to return here today. On the other hand, if I accompany you, I can assure you that you will be able to present your case to Sir Thomas without any delay at all and be back home by dark. And that is your chiefest concern, is it not?"

Unwilling to admit her vulnerability, she refused to meet his eyes. Instead she looked at Clevinger and, to her surprise, saw him nodding at her. Of course, he probably did not share her instinctive distrust of Hellier, and the motives he might have for such an act of kindness. He saw only the obvious advantages of the soldier's presence. Safety, convenience, speed, even the success of her mission—was she to sacrifice all these merely for her own trivial suspicions?

Suddenly she heard Sir Samuel's voice echoing in her mind, speaking to Rachael after some misdemeanor. "Why so stiff-necked, girl? Unbend a little, compromise, learn to admit you're in the wrong—or you'll be as comfortable to live with as a hedgehog."

She had the greatest respect for her father-in-law's wisdom. At that moment, she would have given all she possessed to have his familiar, cynical, comforting realism at her side once more, helping her to see that the path of thorns was not always to be preferred over primroses. She took a deep, reluctant breath and turned to Hellier with as much grace as she could muster. "Very well, Captain—you have convinced me, though I still have my doubts about sharing your company."

"Well," he said dryly, "if needs must . . ."

Sir Samuel had often used that phrase. Despite herself, she almost found her mouth stretching to a smile, and had to make a considerable effort to stay it. To hide her expression, she took the reins of her mare from Clevinger, giving the broad speckled face an affectionate stroke. Strawberry was a roan of considerable age, more gray than russet now, and she had been Silence's mount ever since her arrival at Wintercombe on an overbred, badly behaved gray gelding of whom she had been secretly afraid. It had, of course, been Sir Samuel's idea to sell the gray and give her Strawberry to ride—fat, placid, amiable Strawberry, who would amble along at a comfortable yet surprisingly speedy pace all day if required, and had a broad back and a total absence of nerves or vices.

"Allow me, my Lady St. Barbe," said the captain's voice, and she found him at her elbow, his hands cupped to take her foot. She could hardly be so discourteous as to insist on Clevinger's help. Without comment, she allowed him to assist her onto the mare's back. Trying not to fumble—she still accounted herself a novice rider, having sat a horse perhaps twice during all her London years—she hooked her right leg around the pommel, found the stirrup with her left, and arranged the skirts of her gown, never intended for a riding habit, and the warm bulk of her cassock coat. The captain and Clevinger mounted their own horses, and gingerly the little cavalcade emerged from the gatehouse to cross the barton on to the rutted track, hardened by frost, that ran down the hill to the Wellow Lane, and thence to Norton.

Clevinger led the way, his shaggy sure-footed nag picking between the icy ridges, its head lowered into the wind that was blowing almost directly into its face. Behind him came Silence, concentrating on keeping her balance on Strawberry's swaying back. She could imagine only too clearly her mortification should she fall off in front of the captain. She would not turn around to acknowledge his presence behind her, but the sound of his horse's hooves, the chink of its bit, and the more gentle jingling of his sword and spurs were an unwelcome and ceaseless reminder.

Wellow Lane was too muddy to have succumbed entirely to the frost. The horses made their way through the soft, crusted mire, the puddles edged with thin sharp slivers of ice. At least the wind was less keen down there, the hills and the high hedges sheltering them. They rode past the mill, up the slope to the huddle of cottages at Lyde Green, and then followed Clevinger up the long steep lane at the edge of the village to the Bath Road.

There they were exposed to the full force of the gale. It whipped her hair free of her cap, buffeted her hat so that its strings cut into her jaw, and gleefully tore gaps in the fastenings of her coat and dress, to shiver the flesh beneath. Despite the faint-hearted soul that shrank in the cold and wished most earnestly for its own fireside, she clasped the front opening of her cassock together with one gloved hand and peered grimly at the road ahead.

"Are you regretting this, my lady?" The captain, unnoticed in this howling wind, had brought his horse up to her side. The chestnut was edgy and kept trying to turn its face from the blast, but its rider forced its head ruthlessly toward the north. Silence sent him a glance as chilly as the weather and did not deign to reply. After a while he dropped back again.

There was nobody else on the road, no one so foolhardy, not to say lack-witted. The next village, Charterhouse Hinton, was apparently deserted, only the smoke pouring flat and furious from every chimney telling a different story. It was little more than a mile from Norton, and already she felt bruised, buffeted, and above all cold. Even the thick leather of her riding gauntlets was not proof against the gale's force. But at least, so far, the air was free of snow, though the leaden color of the distant sky indicated that this good fortune would not last them long.

Progress was slow against such a wind, and the rough uncertain going, hard on top, soft underneath, was an added hazard. Silence thought of the summer, when Strawberry had been able to cover the distance to Bath in under two hours, hills notwithstanding. At least after Hinton they had some shelter, as the road descended the side of the hill to Midford. The lack of wind was almost warm, the sudden quiet deafening, though the gale still tore through the trees on the slopes above them. And again she found Hellier at her side, his horse some two hands higher than Strawberry, and thus putting him at considerable advantage. She wondered if he had deliberately chosen to ride such a tall animal to compensate for his slightness of build, and then dismissed the thought. Such a tactic would be adopted by a weak and insecure man, and that most definitely did not describe the self-assured Hellier. She could not, however, resist the comment that sprang instantly to her mind. "Comfortable on your high horse, Captain?"

"It's more windy up here," he said, with a dry sidelong glance that tempted her to laughter. She resisted it. After a moment he added, "I must beg your pardon, my lady, that I was somewhat discourteous earlier. I can only plead mitigating circumstances, and say that it was for your own good."

"You obviously have insufficient knowledge of my character," Silence told him acidly. "Otherwise, you would have learned that such a statement serves purely to arouse my antagonism. I am not some naive country wench, Captain Hellier, to be persuaded into any course under a little pressure."

"Even when it's for your own good?"

"Most particularly when it is. You would be surprised how many people say 'for *your* own good,' when what they really mean is 'for *my* own good.'"

"In my case, that is untrue. Colonel Ridgeley thinks that I am at Wintercombe and would be exceedingly unhappy were he to discover the truth—as he doubtless will, before the day is out, for there'll be no shortage of busybodies to tell him. But he has taken a dozen troopers to Wellow, the better to intimidate some obdurately tight-fisted old farmer, and so I was able to accompany you without hindrance."

"All the same," Silence said, ignoring the voice within that told her sternly that this conversation would be better left well alone, "I cannot believe that there are only altruistic reasons for your act of chivalry, Captain. All the signs are against it."

"What you mean," he said, descending from the elaborate to the direct with comical abruptness, "is that I wouldn't brave Ridgeley's uncouth fury and weather cold enough to freeze the milk in the cow, unless I had some dark design? Correct. I have business in Bath that must be completed urgently, and you and your misguided errand, my lady, provided the perfect excuse."

"Misguided?" Silence looked around at him, her hazel eyes wide and hostile. "If you had about you, sir, an ounce of sympathy and Christian concern, you would know full well that in my predicament I can do no other. Would you now do me the kindness of riding behind me, Captain? I do not wish to talk to you any further."

He opened his mouth as if to argue, plainly thought better of it, and twitched on the reins. The chestnut dropped back, and she was left once more with her own, rather uncomfortable thoughts.

The long, cold, unpleasant miles plodded past. Through Midford in its valley by the swollen Wellow Brook, up the hill the other side, more sheltered here from the wind at least, past Combe Down and Lyncombe and down the Holloway from Beechen Cliff to the bridge over the Avon. The river was in spate, hurling through the five stone arches below. From Strawberry's back, the wind still blasting full in her face, she could clearly see the livid brown water, heaving and coiling in its fury like some monstrous serpent, tossing branches and twigs on its back, the corpses of animals, dogs, cats, and the bloated woolly carcass of a sheep that had strayed too near the flood.

The gate at the entrance to the bridge was manned by soldiers, clad in the same Taunton blue cloth as those at Wintercombe. Numbed with cold, too frozen even to shiver within the heavy shrouding bulk of her coat, she realized belatedly that the rider pushing his horse past hers and Clevinger's was in fact Captain Hellier. She blew inside her gauntlets, trying to bring some semblance of warmth to her icy fingers, while the wind whipped at her garments and Strawberry stood patiently, her large head hanging, her mane and tail torn backward by the wind. A particularly savage gust snatched at Silence's skirts, revealing a length of sturdy riding boot. She tucked the wayward hem between her leg and the warm furry hide of the horse, wondering with chilled remoteness how long it would be before they reached warmth and shelter. The faces of the soldiers on duty in the gateway were blue with cold, and presumably hers was the same, or worse. There was much laughter and good-humored banter between the guards and the captain. Clevinger, his narrow sour face even more pinched than usual, turned his horse toward hers and said, "If he don't hurry, m'lady, we'll be so shrammed with the cold we won't be able to move. *And* it will be snowing."

It was indeed, very lightly, just one or two tiny flakes flung at them by the wind, so small they were scarcely noticeable. Wearily she looked up and saw, beyond the gate and the bridge, Southgate Street and the city of Bath, tiles and thatch and church towers within its yellow stone walls, behind the high ridged hill of Lansdown where the terrible battle had been fought with such great loss on both sides last year, the massed clouds a deep brownish gray, threatening not just snow but blizzards.

Someone shouted something. She looked around and saw Hellier beckoning, waving them through. The horses plodded under the gate, a makeshift affair of medieval stone and rotting wood, with a chain to raise in case of assault, and out onto the windswept bridge. The gale battered them, and the tiny motes of hard icy snow stung her face. There were few people about on such a menacing morning, none of the cheerful bustle she remembered from her previous visits to the city, the last only two months ago. The Southgate's dark entrance was obstructed by more soldiers, with perhaps a dozen citizens and travelers, and a couple of carts hurrying in or out. Once more Hellier went ahead, conversed more briefly with the guards, and then escorted his charges through.

Even under the dim archway of the Southgate, crowded with soldiers and the trickle of civilians hardy or stupid enough to be abroad in this weather, the wind shrieked and gusted. Then they were through into Stall Street, wide and straight and running from north to south, a channel along which the gale eddied and charged, whipping debris and rubbish dancing along the cobbles and whisking up into the air.

Silence had always secretly liked Bath, with its lively air of fashion and pleasure, its fine houses and prosperous citizens, the ladies and gentlemen come to take the healing waters, the shops filled with jostling crowds, and the narrow, crowded lanes. To her husband it was a place cordially loathed, to which he went only on business or to see friends who had the misfortune to live in the city. On the vaunted powers of its hot and steaming waters, he had frequently waxed contemptuous. Pity the poor gullible fools who thought that a few days up to their necks in filthy stinking mud would heal them of all ills! He had a similar opinion of doctors, apothecaries, quacks, and all who attempted by any means to alleviate the lot of the sick and suffering. Nor was he especially compassionate toward those less robust than himself. It was one of the things that Silence found hardest to forgive in her husband, that he despised Nat because of the boy's ill health.

Nat had advised her not to come here. He had known that she did not want to leave Wintercombe, but was well aware that she would ignore him. More fool you, she thought, in dry imitation of her stepson's acerbic style, and wondered bleakly if this journey would serve any purpose at all.

The presence of the Royalist Governor of Bath, Sir Thomas Bridges, whose lands lay at Keynsham, had been accepted by the citizens with the same hard-headed pragmatism that they had shown toward his predecessor for the Parliament. Sir Thomas, replacing the deeply unpopular Ridgeley, now his lieutenant-colonel a mere five or six months previously, had a house provided by the City Council, with a weekly payment of seven pounds, a further sum for linen and housekeeping, and a Christmas present of a hogshead of claret and several sugar loaves. The fact that his supporter and deputy, Henry Chapman, was a member both of the council and of one of Bath's oldest, most respectable and prosperous families doubtless had something to do with it.

The governor's house, a fine stone-built edifice of three storeys and two gables belonging to the clerk of the council, Master Wakeman, stood at the farther end of Westgate Street. Silence was unaware of this until Hellier stopped his horse in front of it. She had retreated into her shell, where the memory of warmth lingered, and was too frozen to lift her head against the wind. So she did not see the huddle of supplicants and petitioners around the door, those who, like herself, were too desperate to pay heed to the cold and wind and snow, ignored by the soldiers on guard. Strawberry would have plodded straight past had not Clevinger, more aware or less cold than his mistress, grabbed the reins and brought the mare to a halt. Silence saw that he was looking at her with some concern. "Here, m'lady, I'll help ee down."

My brains have been blown and iced witless, she thought ruefully. She accepted her bailiff's assistance and slid down from the saddle. Her legs, numb and stiff after the ride, almost refused to support her. She gripped a handful of Strawberry's mane, loath to lean on Clevinger's arm—the man was twice her age, after all. Then Captain Hellier appeared at her elbow, the soul of courtesy. "Allow me, my lady."

She sent him a glare that might have shriveled someone less arrogant and self-assured, and somehow found the strength to walk the few steps to the door of the house unaided. Seeing the cold, tired, unhappy-looking men and women waiting outside, she tried not to think of what the captain had told her. Doubtless, had he not accompanied her, she would have been left to kick her heels out here with the rest. Instead, the guards saluted, the door was opened, and she and Clevinger were ushered inside to a dark warm hall, with a blazing fire. Here a large, kind-faced woman whom she presumed to be the housekeeper bade her welcome, ordered a maid to take her cassock coat, and offered her a chair to toast herself by the hearth. Clevinger was whisked off to the back of the house, saying something about tending the horses, and she found a mug of something hot and steaming thrust into her hands. It was lambswool, hot ale with a roasted apple frothing on the top, a favorite tipple of country gentlemen. "There, my lady," the woman said cheerfully. "Feel warmer, do ee?"

She did, a little, though she could not stop the deep tremors that shook her every so often, despite the warmth that baked her from the glowing logs and the heat from the mug thawing her hands. Smiling, she thanked the woman, who curtsied and withdrew. Then she saw Hellier approach, divested now of his all-enveloping cloak, but still spurred and booted, carrying his gauntlets. He did not look as if he had done any more than walk across the street. Silence stared at him, too weary to conceal her dislike and resentment, and obtained an unwelcome smile in response. "When you are ready and rested, Lady St. Barbe, Sir Thomas Bridges will see you. In the meantime, I suggest you relax and enjoy the warmth, and your lambswool. They make an excellent one here."

Childishly, she wanted to throw the contents of her frothing mug into his face. She had not felt so exhausted, so utterly dispirited and miserable for years. It was hopeless—she had always known that it was hopeless, deep in her heart, and this insufferable man knew it too, and was laughing at her. She turned her head away, feeling the weight of the burden she had carried alone, for much too long, free the hot despairing tears from her eyes. Furious and ashamed at her weakness, she clamped her trembling mouth around the rim of the mug, took too deep a draft of the hot liquid and the hotter apple, and burned her lip.

The pewter mug dropped with a splatter and a crash to the stone flags around the hearth, and rolled away. Unable to stop the tears of pain and misery and exhaustion, too heartsick to dissemble any longer, she buried her face in her hands and tried, vainly, to prevent this sudden and deeply humiliating breakdown of the serenity upon which her whole life was based.

No one spoke; no one touched her. She heard, distantly through her sobs, the sounds of the mug being picked up, of footsteps and discreet activity. Make, do, mend, she said to herself, because it was all she could do, and took several deep, shuddering breaths, gathering the shattered pieces of her self-control. When she had calmed herself, she wiped the tears from her face and looked up.

Hellier stood on the other side of the hearth, the mug, now rather dented, in his hand. He was watching her, and his expression was serious. "Are you hurt, Lady St. Barbe?"

"No," she said. To her relief, her voice hardly shook at all. From somewhere, she found the effort of will needed to smile, albeit briefly. "I burned my mouth on the hot ale, that is all. Surely you have not cleared up the mess?"

"Why not? The housekeeper is in the kitchen, and I have two hands and my kerchief to mop it up. That is why the fire smells of ale and apples. Shall I ask for another for you?"

Stupidly, she thought she detected genuine concern in his voice, and nearly lost her composure again. Pressing her mouth together, she shook her head, and added after a pause, "No, I thank you, Captain. Perhaps later, after I have seen Sir Thomas, I will have some more. I should have warmed up a little by then."

He said nothing, only continued to study her, smiling faintly. Embarrassed by his scrutiny, she turned her head and stared into the fire, wishing herself anywhere but here, alone with this man and his disturbing mixture of courtesy and arrogance, his manner that spoke one way and his deed that indicated that there was a completely different character underneath all that impenetrable self-assurance.

"I know that you dislike and mistrust me, Lady St. Barbe," he said suddenly. Startled, she glanced up and saw that he had moved closer, to stand not three feet from her chair, his hands folded behind his back, his face unsmiling now, although she could see the fine laughter lines tracked around his nose and eyes and mouth, paler against the faded summer tan. She had the sudden sense that this was only one aspect of the man, that there were as many sides to him as one of Nat's collection of crystals, and that everyone saw him differently.

"Don't trouble to deny it," he added as her mouth opened to do just that. "You have every right and reason to do so, just as I would in your place—your home invaded, and your family threatened and abused by a rabble of ill-disciplined troopers and their boorish officers. We have menaced or attacked everything you hold dear. But you have never lost your calm, or your dignity, or your self-control."

"Until now," Silence said dryly. "My privacy, it seems, is not safe from you either, Captain Hellier."

"Then I apologize," he said, not in the least disconcerted. "I was merely, in my own rather oblique and clumsy fashion, trying to express my admiration, my lady, for the spirit with which you have preserved yourself, your family, and your household under immense difficulties and against tremendous odds."

"Then I am shortly to expect a medal?" Silence inquired tartly, and drew a laugh from him. She added, with some scorn, "You do not have to express your admiration at all, Captain, and certainly not in such pompous terms. It ill becomes you, and me, and I can very well do without it. My difficulties, as you so rightly pointed out, are quite enough for me to cope with already. And if you are thinking to place me in your debt, and yourself in my good graces, then I suggest that you think again, sir, and concentrate on your military duties."

Even that did not seem to penetrate his imperturbable manner. He smiled and inclined his head. "As you please, Lady St. Barbe. And now I should think that Sir Thomas will be ready to receive your petition."

And he turned and went out, leaving her to reflect, with some astonishment, that in that encounter at least, she had come off the victor.

Sir Thomas Bridges, into whose presence Captain Hellier ushered her a few minutes later, was not in the least as she had expected him. She had heard little of him beyond the fact that he was of an old Keynsham family, and Ridgeley's statement that his father had been a friend of Sir Samuel had led her to believe that he was of her husband's generation. But the man who rose from his desk to bow and take her hand was young, probably around her own age, with dark hair and a rather tired, peevish expression.

"Good morning, Lady St. Barbe," he said, and with punctilious courtesy led her to the comfortable high-backed chair opposite his own. Surprised, all her preconceptions shattered, she allowed herself to be settled upon the cushions and accepted wine from Captain Hellier. It was held within a goblet of Venetian glass, cut and turned with exquisite delicacy, and worth a small fortune. The claret, doubtless part of the city's gift, was young, fierce, and warming. Grateful for its sustaining fire, she sipped it, feeling her burned lips tingling, and found the captain at her elbow with a plate of cakes and sweetmeats. Not sure that she could juggle the glass and a plate successfully, she declined. Besides, her belly seemed to be all knotted up within her from tension and anxiety, and she did not feel in the least hungry.

"And what may I do for you, my lady?" Sir Thomas asked, resuming his seat behind the crowded desk. It was piled high with papers. She caught sight of one headed ominously "Order for Sequestration of Traitors' Lands," and her stomach twisted further. She was not deceived by his courteous manner. Anyone who could foist a man with Ridgeley's reputation on a harmless household of women and children was at best conspicuously lacking in imagination and intelligence, at worst a malicious and heartless villain.

Aware that she quite possibly faced a battle far worse than any encounter with her redoubtable mother-in-law, she clenched her hands round the fragile stem of the goblet, heedless of the very real risk of breakage, and said calmly, "I have come to beg a favor of you, Sir Thomas, on behalf of my husband's mother Ursula, Lady St. Barbe. As you may know, she is aged and bedridden, and cannot possibly manage the journey from Wintercombe—and so I have come in her stead."

Sir Thomas raised his eyebrows and looked at her over his hands, placed palms together and upward in front of him. They were beautifully manicured, far more so than her own, the nails neatly trimmed and the slender pale fingers adorned with an impressive collection of rings. The lace of his collar was similarly spectacular, white and intricate and lovely above the rich blue satin of his doublet, which was fastened with what appeared to be pearl buttons. Idle Court gallant, her Puritan upbringing whispered severely, and probably unjustly. To judge from the evidence of his cluttered desk, Sir Thomas worked extremely hard in his exalted position.

"A favor, eh?" the governor said, after a pause during which he had returned her critical scrutiny in similar vein. She knew exactly what he must think of her appearance, for all such men had but the one response to a woman they dismissed as plain, dowdy, and beneath their notice. "And why should the lady of Wintercombe desire such a thing of the Governor of Bath?"

The affable note had gone from his voice. She fought her rising panic and said carefully, "I have come to ask you, Sir Thomas, for the sake of past friendship between your family and my husband's, to alleviate the burden which you have laid upon us."

His eyebrows climbed further into his rather low forehead. He was not an ill-looking man, but his face lacked any trace of humor or good nature. "Friendship, madam? You appear to be laboring under a misapprehension. My father was on cordial terms with Sir Samuel St. Barbe, yes, but these are times of war, and you must realize, my lady, that past concerns are so much water under the bridge in this present emergency. And what is this burden of which you complain? You have but a single troop of horse for your garrison, and your house is a rich one and can easily afford to feed such paltry numbers. You talk of your burden—if you truly want one, my lady, I'll gladly quarter a company or two on you in addition."

Stung by his open contempt, Silence said furiously, "I think forty men camped in our barn are quite sufficient, Sir Thomas. Wintercombe can hardly feed them all as it is, let alone double the number. Would you see my children starve, and the village go hungry, for the sake of your spite?"

"You protest too much, my lady. I am told that you all eat well, if not so well as you have been used to—your orchard is intact, your maids unmolested, or comparatively so, and your cattle as yet unslaughtered. I repeat, of what do you complain? If you wish to taste the full horrors of war, Lady St. Barbe, in your smug sheltered little house, then I am sure that Lieutenant-Colonel Ridgeley will oblige. He has already had ample experience in the Irish war and is, I fear, very disapproving of my attitude toward traitors such as you, which he considers much too soft. One word from me, Lady St. Barbe, and he will create the havoc which you fear. Do you want that? I thought not. You will not object, then, to a further company of men from my own regiment. They will be foot soldiers, so you will be spared the labor and expense of feeding more horses. But if Wintercombe is to be put in a state of defense, it can hardly be garrisoned merely by an understrength troop of cavalry."

"A garrison?" Silence said after a moment, in appalled disbelief. "You cannot—you *cannot* place a garrison at Wintercombe! In all conscience, Sir Thomas—we are a household of women and children, we have no quarrel with anyone, we desire only to be left in peace—"

"But you are wed to a traitor, madam, a man who has so little desire for peace that he has taken up arms against his king, in defiance of the laws of God and man. Through cunning legal devices, your family has evaded the just penalty for treason. Think yourself lucky that you still have a roof over your head and the freedom to enjoy the revenues from your lands—those not needed for the maintenance of a royal garrison, of course." And he smiled coldly above his immaculate, tented hands.

"A company?" Silence repeated, impotent, furious, desperately afraid that the final nightmare was upon her, and no means of defense. "You *can't*—we'll all go hungry—and what will happen if the house is attacked?"

"Perhaps by your husband's forces? That would be a fine irony. There would be a siege, of course," the Governor of Bath said with a relish that he was not amiable enough to hide. "Doubtless the damage would be considerable. So I should pray for a Royalist victory, my lady traitress, for the sake of your household and your possessions, and keep your mouth shut and your head low. There are many honest loyal men and women who have suffered far worse than you, madam, and at the hands of men such as your husband. So I'll hear no more of your whining and moaning, my lady—get you back to your comfortable house, count your blessings, and await my foot company. And remember—if your life becomes too hard, you have a simple remedy. You may leave. I would be happy to sign passes for you."

"Dame Ursula can't leave!" she cried. "And my children—for pity's sake, sir, think on the children. They have not committed treason, they've done you no injury. The youngest is two years old—would you have him suffer?"

"Many just as innocent have endured far worse," Sir Thomas said mercilessly. "I grow weary of your protests, Lady St. Barbe. Perhaps it would be best were you to go, before I am tempted to increase your garrison still further."

"By your leave, Sir Thomas," said Hellier. He had been standing listening to the argument. Now he came forward, his face deferential. "With respect, sir, I think that Lady St. Barbe has some justice on her side. The house will be very seriously burdened if you increase the garrison by one company, let alone two—and as she points out, it is the innocent who will suffer most. In my opinion, it would be imprudent to stretch Wintercombe's resources at this time of year. There won't be much military activity now until the spring—why not wait until then? You can hardly fortify the place in this weather."

His commanding officer stared at him with hostility and some amusement. "You may be entitled to your opinion, Captain Hellier, but I do not remember asking for it. I should beware—you have already escorted Lady St. Barbe to Bath, which is assuredly above your usual run of duties, and now you seem to be supporting her claims. Have a care, Captain, lest you be accused of showing a traitor's family too much favor. You would not want your own loyalty questioned, I take it?"

"My loyalty has never been in doubt, as you well know," Hellier said, with a venom he could not disguise. "But I have a certain sympathy for innocent victims of brutality. You know full what Ridgeley is like—I suspect you only sent him to Wintercombe to secure him from the wrath of the citizens of Bath. It is indeed a house of women and children and old men—can you not imagine the terror he can inspire among them?"

"You forget yourself," Sir Thomas said, his voice sinking very low, almost to a whisper. Silence stared from one man to the other, bewildered at the sudden naked hostility between them, as if they were old and bitter enemies. The governor continued, furious. "I raised you, Nick Hellier, almost from the gutter, and I can cast you down like *that!*" His hand slapped on the table, making her jump. The captain stood unmoving, his eyes glittering, and his mouth a thin hard line. "If I choose, you can be plain Trooper Hellier again, and you'll not rise so fast a second time, I promise you. Under Ridgeley you won't last a week. Now get out, and take this whining woman with you—if you leave at once, you might get back to Wintercombe before dark. Good day to you, Captain, and to you, Lady St. Barbe."

She had failed. She stood shaking in the hall, her mind struggling with the realization that she had not only suffered the bitter humiliation she had dreaded, but that her journey had only increased her burden. Even if Captain Hellier did not make a full report of that terrible interview to Ridgeley, doubtless Sir Thomas's detailed account of it would be sent to him by the next messenger. And then the lieutenant-colonel's full wrath would fall upon her, and on her household and her children.

And if that were not bad enough, she had by her foolishness brought much worse to Wintercombe—the malicious imposition of yet more men to add to their misery.

She was frightened: terribly, numbingly afraid of what the future would bring.

And she could not stay there. Pointedly, no food had been offered to her. It was seven miles of exposed and hilly road back to Norton and Wintercombe, and she could see plainly through the little squares of the window that the snow had increased to a blizzard.

SEVEN

By sorrow of the heart, the spirit is broken.
—PROVERBS 15:13

"**P**lease, my lady, please." Clevinger was as agitated as she had ever seen him, his leathery wrinkled old face screwed up even more in his anxiety. "Please—us can't go back to Wintercombe to-day, not in this here storm—tarblish cold and blusterous it'll be up on they hills, and there be lodgings a-plenty here. Do ee wait till tomorrow, m'lady, when it have eased off a mite."

"And then there'll be a foot of snow on the ground." Silence stood stubbornly by Strawberry in the now-empty street outside the governor's house, which they had left in haste a few moments before. The snow whirled past her, settling on her cassock coat, her hood and gloves, speckling the roan mare's kind head with silver, frosting her mane more thickly with every minute that passed. Already it was pitching, as they said hereabouts, lying pushed into corners by the relentless wind while the cobbles of the galeswept street remained bare. "It's no colder than it was," she went on, determined to leave this place and its unpleasant associations as soon as might be, and fly back to the warmth, the dear comfortable familiarity of Wintercombe. "It took no more than two hours to come here, and it's still only a little after noon." She realized belatedly, and with a sense of shock, that the dreadful confrontation with Sir Thomas Bridges had been over in less than fifteen minutes.

And yet she would remember it with a shudder for the rest of her days.

"The going have changed," said Clevinger, who could be just as obstinate—indeed, was famous for it. "It don't look so bad down hereabouts, m'lady, but once you d'get up on they hills there'll be snow thick as butter and you won't know which way to go."

"I think I will," Silence told him. "Clevinger, I *must* return today—think of what might have happened while we've been away. And there are *more* soldiers expected, not less."

"God dang the lot on 'em," the bailiff muttered with a vicious glare at Captain Hellier, already sitting on his tall chestnut and waiting without impatience for their discussion to end, although his wide plumed beaver hat was already heavy with snow. "Very well, m'lady, we'll go back now if you d'want it. But don't say as I didn't warn you if we d'come to grief."

Such was her relief that she smiled warmly at him, despite her cold and unhappiness and terrible sense of dread. "I'm certain we won't—not with you to guide us. Let's go, before we turn into ice candles."

It was at first much easier than she had feared. She knew as well as Clevinger did the insanity of a return in such weather, and under any other circumstances would have taken the older man's advice and found a snug chamber in one of Bath's numerous and comfortable lodging houses, there to wait out the blizzard. But that vast and formless sense of urgency drove her on: the terrible fear, always present in her mind, that something appalling would have happened at Wintercombe in her absence. Not only did they lack her, to soothe and direct and intervene, but they must also do without the mysterious, enigmatic, and apparently benign interventions of Captain Hellier, who had saved so much.

As Strawberry plodded out onto the empty windswept bridge once more, the weather so bad that even the soldiers on guard duty had disappeared to warmer quarters, she pondered the problem of Hellier, now once more riding at her back. She mistrusted him still, most deeply—but he had earned his colonel's grave displeasure on her behalf, and a man with purely selfish motives for his behavior would, she thought, have avoided so doing. There remained, it seemed, the very real chance that he was acting, as he claimed, from compassion, moved by his sympathy with Wintercombe's plight. And if that were indeed so, then she had grievously misjudged him.

She had wanted him as an ally. She had never thought to like him. That added a very unwelcome complexity to the already tortuous and tangled strands of her life.

They climbed up Holloway, the stones thick and slippery with snow, the horses plodding onward with grim and weary determination. At least the wind was to their backs on the way home, and she was not forced to screw up her eyes against its stinging blast. But the snow was crusted fine and thick over Clevinger's cloaked back and over the rump of his brown gelding, and doubtless also over her own—she could feel its weight already, and poor Strawberry, who hated such weather, was constantly shaking her head and neck to rid herself of the clinging white film along her mane.

At the top, on the height of Beechen Cliff, she glanced back. Hellier's chestnut was just behind her, his scarlet-cloaked figure edged in pale thick snow. And Bath was no longer visible in the storm. All she could see was a white whirling blur.

Suddenly afraid for her own safety, for the first time, she turned her head away from that blinding snow and urged Strawberry onward.

As Clevinger had predicted, it was pitching much more thickly up here on the cold bleak down. The horses, unused to travel in such appalling conditions, stumbled and slithered in snow that was already near to covering their hooves, and lay in sweeping drifts where the wind had flung it, along the hedges. The gale seemed less, that was one blessing, but it only meant that the flakes settled in much greater quantity on the highway. Soon Clevinger's gelding was limping, obviously in distress, and the bailiff dismounted to examine the horse's hooves. The snow could be seen quite clearly, balled and compacted within, making its footing uncomfortable and treacherous. He solved the problem with a small knife, and as a precaution also cleared the hooves of Strawberry and of Hellier's chestnut.

For a while thereafter, all was well. They made their slow way past Combe Down, the wind now on their left side as the highway turned more to the east, and began the cautious, uncertain descent to Midford, snow-shrouded below them around the rushing spate of the Wellow Brook. The most difficult part of the journey was probably behind them, the exposed emptiness of the great hills that guarded the southern side of Bath. Down in the steep-sided valley, it was less cold and more sheltered, and they were well over halfway home.

Strawberry faltered suddenly on the steepest part of the slope, almost at the bottom. Silence had time to think, briefly, that the snow had balled again in her hooves, but Clevinger had drawn quite a long way ahead and was all but lost amid the heavy curtain of falling flakes. And then the mare lurched abruptly, losing her footing, her head jerked downward, and Silence, no horsewoman and taken completely by surprise, was pitched gracelessly over her shoulder.

It was a hard fall, and knocked the breath from her. For a moment, dazed and confused, she lay in the snow, wondering how she came to be there, wanting to get up and yet lacking the effort of will necessary even to move her head away from the snow that fell wet and tickling on her face.

A figure appeared, obstructing her view of the flakes spinning darker across the pale sky. For a moment she did not know who he was. Then his voice, quick and concerned, told her. "Lady St. Barbe! Are you all right?"

"I think so," she said. It was cold and wet and unpleasant, lying down there in the snow, but she felt curiously detached from herself, as if all this were happening to someone else. "But I can't seem to move."

"You took a bad fall." He was kneeling beside her. "Is there any pain? Your head? Your legs?"

"No," Silence assured him, wondering if she were dreaming this. The whole day, the journey, Sir Thomas Bridges, the snow, all seemed to have taken on the qualities of nightmare, and it was entirely in keeping that her body would not obey her increasingly urgent instructions to it. She added, puzzled, "Where's Clevinger?"

"Out of sight, and probably halfway up the next hill. I hope he'll turn around when he notices we're not behind him."

"I doubt it," Silence said dryly. "Knowing him, he'll curse me for a fool who's had her just deserts and plod dourly on to Wintercombe. He has a very low opinion of me—but then he's the same with everyone." She essayed a rueful smile. "I think I ought to be able to get up—it doesn't *feel* as if I've hurt myself."

"You can't always be sure of that," he warned her. "Take it slowly—give me your hands and I'll pull you gently to a sitting position."

With no sign of Clevinger, she had no choice but to trust him. She found she could lift her hands, and her head. Her gauntleted wrists were firmly gripped, he bent over her, and drew her up. Her head swam dizzily, and she closed her eyes. His voice, with the faint trace of accent that she had failed to identify, said immediately, "Shall I lay you back?"

"No, I thank you," Silence told him, opening her eyes with caution. "I have no wish at all to die of a chill on the lungs, and I'm wet enough already. I shall do very well soon—if you let go of my hands, I can support myself."

"Are you sure, Lady St. Barbe?"

"Of course I'm sure," she said dryly. Released, she found herself quite capable of sitting without support. She drew her knees up under the thick skirts of her gown and coat and ducked her head onto their cold wet folds. It was, as she had heard, a sovereign remedy for faintness. She took several long, calming breaths and felt almost restored to her usual self.

"There is still no sign of Clevinger," Hellier said. "I fear you were right. The man doesn't seem to be a very loyal bailiff."

"Oh, he's loyal to the St. Barbes—*was,* to Sir Samuel in particular. But I'm an interloper," Silence said, looking up. "I am not from Somerset, Captain Hellier, and so am several rungs below those more fortunate people who are natives." She added, annoyed with herself at this unwelcome impulse to confide in him, "I am ready to stand, if you will assist me."

It was easier than she had feared. Her legs felt wobbly and uncertain, but her head had stopped spinning, and apart from a slight ache in her lower back, and a sharper one in her right wrist, she seemed to be unscathed. Strawberry stood waiting unhappily a few yards away. She looked so miserable at her lamentable dereliction of duty that Silence stumbled over to give her a consoling pat and hug, rubbing her cold dripping ears. "Poor Strawberry—it wasn't your fault."

"Snow in her hooves, I expect," said Hellier. He knelt by the mare and ran his hand up her off-fore. At the familiar touch, Strawberry raised her leg as obediently as she did for the blacksmith. There was indeed hard-packed snow within her hoof. Silence watched, holding her horse's head, as the captain with swift efficiency cleaned out all four feet. "As you said, my lady, not her fault at all. She seems a safe and reliable mount, if a little lacking in fire."

"She was chosen for that very reason," Silence told him. "I was reared in

London, sir, and am no horsewoman. Strawberry is ideal for me—and I should think she would make a very poor cavalry horse."

"Don't worry—the troop would have to be in sorry case indeed before we'd consider requisitioning such as her. Although, of course," he added reflectively, "in the end it may come to that."

Silence stared at him in some dismay, the snow settling thick and fast on her head and shoulders. "What do you mean by that, Captain Hellier?"

He glanced at her, frowning, his hands absently sweeping the white flakes from Strawberry's broad mottled rump. "I mean that the time may come, next year, or the year after, when the king's army is in desperate straits—for coin, food, weapons, horses, men. Your Parliament has control of London and the north and east of the country. Bristol is the only sizable port left in the king's hands, and only here in the west is he at all secure. And who knows what the fortunes of war may be? One battle at Marston, one mistake by Prince Rupert, lost him all the north in a single day. I should pray, Puritan lady, that the West Country does not become the refuge of all the desperate Cavaliers, for then it will be one great battlefield, and your sufferings now will be as nothing to those in the future."

Suddenly afraid, she leaned her head against Strawberry's wide brow, hoping that tears would not disgrace her again. But she felt curiously bleak, empty, calm, as though the worst had already happened and that after this dreadful day, nothing else could be so bad. It was quite untrue, of course, and she knew it, but at least she was once more in control of herself.

She looked up and was surprised by an expression of concern on the captain's face. Its hard angles seemed softer, almost boyish, so that she realized suddenly that he must be no older than herself. To disguise her thoughts, she said abruptly, "We mustn't stand here all day, Captain Hellier, or Clevinger will find us white and frozen solid like statues when—if—he comes back. Please can you help me mount?"

"Are you quite sure that's wise, my lady?"

The alternative was to ride pillion behind him, on the bare back of that high and uncertain-looking chestnut. It was not a prospect she relished in the least. "Of course I'm sure," she snapped, and moved around to Strawberry's side.

After a moment's pause he smiled, the lazy relaxed grin that was perhaps his most pleasant attribute. "I salute your courage, Lady St. Barbe. Many women of my acquaintance would have a screaming fit at the very thought."

"Then your female acquaintance must be limited indeed—or very substantially wider than my own," Silence said pointedly. She retied the strings of her hood and hat, which had come loose in the fall, and waited by the stirrup.

Hellier joined her, grinning more widely. "Every time we speak together, I am reminded of just how narrow my experience of ladies has been. Not many have had the wit to bandy words with me, and those who have, assuredly do not wear sober black, nor are they mother to five children."

"Mother to three, stepmother to three," she corrected him. "*Are* you going to assist me, Captain, or do I have to clamber aboard unaided?"

Briskly, with far less effort than Clevinger, he hoisted her into the saddle. The ground seemed a long way off. She glanced away from the tumbled snow, which showed with humiliating clarity the impact of her fall, gathered up her wet slippery reins, and said, smiling, "Thank you, Captain. Shall we go on?"

Clevinger met them at Midford, his face stricken with guilt, his relief at the sight of them quite evident. He had indeed been halfway up the hill on the other side of the valley before he had realized that his mistress was no longer behind him. Silence, touched by his obvious anxiety, forbore to rebuke him. And, through increasing snow, they rode the rest of the way back to Wintercombe without incident. At least the route was plain, if not clear, and the wind easing slightly, but the cold was no less and Silence, soaked to her chemise, was frozen numb and rigid within the wet white shroud of her cassock coat. She never knew how she managed to stay in the saddle. Every movement of Strawberry's normally easy, unnoticed gait seemed almost to dislodge her, every stop for hoof-clearing seemed so long that she feared that they would never reach home, and warmth, and safety. She began to feel increasingly light-headed, as if she were floating remotely, without any contact with reality.

Someone was speaking, but for a moment she did not realize that she was being addressed. Only when Captain Hellier's tall chestnut appeared suddenly alongside, so close that the man's boot and spur almost brushed Strawberry's fat flank, did she return to full awareness, the unpleasant wet and heart-freezing cold. "I'm sorry, Captain—were you talking to me?"

"Are you all right? You must be chilled to the bone."

"I am," Silence said, summoning her wryest smile with an effort. "But then so are you, and Clevinger. This foolish journey was my idea, and I am not going to complain."

He said something below his breath that, astonishingly, sounded like "Bravo!" and then added, louder, "I called to you, Lady St. Barbe, to say that journey's end is in sight. That is Philip's Norton, is it not?"

And there, between Strawberry's flat unhappy ears, glimpsed only faintly through the steady fall of snow, were the gray roofs of the village.

It still took some time to reach Wintercombe. The narrow lane down to Lyde Green was treacherous in the extreme, almost impassable, and the two men dismounted. Clevinger led his own horse and the chestnut, which was docile with weariness, while Hellier took hold of Strawberry. All Silence had to do was to grasp a handful of thick mane and hang on. By now even that was almost beyond her strength, but she managed it, knowing that journey's end was almost here.

There was a watcher in one of the cottages at Lyde Green. A small figure, probably one of Leah Walker's cousins, burst from a doorway and pelted off up the lane past the mill, going ahead of them to announce their arrival at Wintercombe. So, when they eventually stumbled beneath the arch of the gatehouse and into the front courtyard, there was a small army of servants ready to take the horses, remove wet outer garments, and help her and her companions indoors.

Afterward, Silence remembered very little of that confused homecoming. Too cold and exhausted to pay heed to anything but the relief of her own discomfort, she recalled only the white face of Tabby, at once delighted and terrified, and Mally's calm, competent manner as she pushed a tankard of warm ale between her shaking lips and bade her drink all she could. Then she was helped upstairs to her chamber, and the heat of its fire was unutterably welcome, although she did not seem able to stop shivering. Mally quickly peeled her soaking garments from her, casting them into a sodden steaming heap in the hearth. She was vigorously rubbed into a tingling semblance of life with a hot towel, a warmed chemise was slipped over her head, and then, in a daze of weariness, she was helped into the cozy comfort of the bed. And there was Pye, purring her happiness, to snuggle against her shoulder and tickle her chin with those astonishingly long whiskers. Safe and warm at last, too exhausted to stay awake any longer, Silence fell instantly and absolutely asleep.

And darkness was only just beginning to fall on that long and terrible day.

She woke to daylight, so bright that even the thick curtains around the bed could not keep it out. Pye was now curled heavily on her chest. It was a little uncomfortable, but she was otherwise too drowsy to attempt movement. The warm feather bed lapped her snugly around, the sheet and blankets and quilt and counterpane kept out the cold, and she felt blissfully relaxed. Pye opened one eye, then the other, and uttered an inquiring chirrup of welcome. Smiling, Silence pushed a hand above the covers to tickle her cat's chin, and suddenly realized that her body seemed to ache all over. Gingerly she flexed various muscles, found that back, shoulders, arms, and legs all hurt, and remembered, with abrupt and humiliating clarity, the hideous events of the previous day.

Her journey had been a failure, a total and abysmal failure, and she had moreover made her situation much, much worse. And to produce this debacle, she had risked not only her own life, but those of her bailiff and of Captain Hellier.

She had not wanted the captain with her, she had been rude and ungrateful, resenting his offer of help. And he had repaid her by quite possibly saving her life. She did not like to think of what might have happened, had she been left lying for long in that snow, too shocked and exhausted to move, while deaf stubborn old Clevinger plodded on ahead, oblivious.

She had been foolish, naive, as simpleminded and witless as a babe. She had survived, but by reason of luck and another's actions, rather than her own efforts. She cast a clear and bitter eye over her conduct and found it lamentably wanting. Impulsive, foolhardy, disdainful of advice—the events of the previous day confirmed the stern judgment of her father, long ago. For a moment she could almost see him, so vivid was her memory: the tall man, grim-faced, who never seemed to speak in praise, always in rebuke, of whom his entire household—wife, servants, apprentices, children—went in awe and terror. A man whose only loving relationship appeared to be with a God as fierce, relentless, and unforgiving as himself.

He had done his best to turn his surviving children into images of himself, and his wife, the fishmonger's daughter, had covertly done her best to frustrate him—and had succeeded. To the end of his days—he had died three years after Silence's marriage—Isaac Woods had been sorely disappointed in his three daughters, all to some degree rebellious in their childhood, and in his garrulous, ineffectual, dithering only son Joseph. But he had never succeeded in beating his opinions into any of them. All he had done, Silence thought, wryly, was to make his children into little hypocrites, mouthing platitudes out of fear and too terrified to venture any opinion of their own. It had taken the wisdom, humor, and affection of Sir Samuel to begin a cure, although even now she was still reduced to her childhood stupor when faced with her awe-inspiring mother-in-law and had difficulty in dealing firmly with the more abrasive characters of the household.

At least she had tried to put her case to Sir Thomas Bridges, though with signal lack of success. She could claim to have asserted herself and to have stated her position. And much good did it do me, Silence thought, with some bitterness. But I am *not* going to lie here brooding on it—by the look of the light it's well into the morning, and there must be so much to do.

Gently she persuaded Pye to get off her and onto a softer but cooler nest on the bolster, and sat up. "Mally?" she called quietly.

Almost at once, the green-figured damask rustled and moved, and her maid's head, the orange-tawny curls bursting out from underneath her neat fresh linen cap, popped through. "Good morning to ee, m'lady. Did ee sleep well?"

"As the proverbial log, thank you, Mally." Silence paused, thinking, and then added, "Sit here for a moment. What o'clock is it now?"

"Past eight," said her maid. "You've slept it round and more, m'lady, and it bain't surprising—tarblish bad it must have been through all that there snow and ice. 'Tis past Turber's knees, and all they soldiers be out there shoveling it to and fro. Nice to see 'em doing some hard work for a change, 'stead of loppusing around in the barton." She paused and eyed her mistress intently. "You d'look summat more bobbish today, m'lady. You was main bellowsed out last night."

"I feel more bobbish," Silence said, smiling. "Oh, I ache all over, but that's only to be expected—I was stupid enough to fall off down Midford Hill. Is Clevinger bobbish too?"

"I ain't seed him yet, m'lady. But that there Captain Hellier, he be up and whipper-snapper as usual," Mally said with indignation. "Oh, you should'a heard en and Ridgeley, argufying last night—tarblish loud, 'twas, you could'a heard 'em at Norton, I reckon. About how the captain shouldn't'a gone with ee, and deserting his proper duty, and all mander o' things. I clapped my bolster over my head," she added with a grin. "I didn't want to hear norn of what they was bawling each at t'other, cursing flashes and suchlike. But I'll tell ee summat, m'lady—that Hellier, he reckon he've saved your life by going along of ee. Be that the truth, m'lady?"

"It could be," Silence said reflectively. "If he chooses to think that, then let him. Has Ridgeley punished him at all, do you know?"

"Not by the look of en this morning," said Mally. "But that don't surprise me, no how. The captain, he be all sharp and pointy as a knife, and that there Ridgeley be like a girt bludgeon, and I d'know which on 'em I'd choose to win."

Silence rather tended to agree with her. And besides, Hellier's razorlike competence was infinitely to be preferred to his lieutenant-colonel's loud and unsubtle brutality. She said apprehensively, "Was everything all right while I was gone? Was there any trouble?"

"Norn more than the usual," Mally replied. "Don't ee trouble yourself about it, m'lady. We be all on us safe and sound. Now, do ee want your frumenty? I've kept en hot in the hearth."

She had not had breakfast in her bed since the time of William's birth. She enjoyed this feeling of being pampered, lapped in a luxury that she normally never had the time or the opportunity to enjoy. When she had finished and given a hopeful Pye the milky spoon and bowl to lick, she told Mally something of what had passed in Bath and on the way home.

The maid, of course, loyally took her part, exclaiming with disgust at Sir Thomas Bridges's unsympathetic and threatening manner and appalled at the hardships and dangers of the return journey. Even when Silence admitted, wryly, that it had all been a disaster, Mally protested. "Don't ee say that, m'lady. You *had* to go, you d'know that so well as do I. No matter if it turned out bad—you didn't know that when you set off."

"But I could have guessed," said Silence. "And now I've brought another company of men down on our heads, and the Lord alone knows how we'll feed them—five loaves and two small fishes, perhaps?"

"At least they won't have horses, eating their heads off of all our best hay," Mally pointed out. "Besides, m'lady, by the look of that there snow, it'll be a long whiles afore they can march over here and give us trouble."

She was right, Silence thought later, gazing out at the blinding whiteness of the courtyard, its pristine glory marred only by the cleared path curving from the porch of the gatehouse, with a branch leading off round the side of the dining parlor to the kitchen door. Beyond the low wall bordering the courtyard, and the two half-ruined round turrets used as dovecote, lay a close of pasture, its rough grass now deeply and smoothly covered, the sheep that lodged there secured and folded within a ring of hurdles, awaiting early lambing. She hoped that someone had supplied them with a load of their diminishing stocks of hay. To the right, another close fell away down to the alders and willows along the Norton Brook, their tops sharp black points against the farther slopes, running up to the Lytemans' cottage at White Cross, and the Bath Road. The sky was gray still and held the menace of more snow, but yesterday's wind had died away entirely, leaving its legacy only in the fantastically sculptured coils and drifts and whirls all along the wall and sweeping across each corner, disguising every irregularity in the ground beneath.

Assuredly, there was no chance of a company of footsoldiers making their way here until it unfroze, as the local speech had it. They had won a breathing space, but at what cost to themselves, and more especially to the farm, she did not like to think.

In more normal circumstances, a large country house like Wintercombe was provisioned and supplied in the autumn for just such an emergency as this—especially if, as in this case, the manor in question was prone to extremes of weather. Last year too it had snowed very heavily, the road to Bath being almost impassable right into February, and the previous winter had also been cold. Moreover, in this land of small, stream-filled valleys and clay soil, fertile but heavy, a thaw always brought flooding, enriching the meadows but rendering travel, even on Sundays to the village church less than half a mile distant, an arduous and uncomfortable business.

In earlier years, they had always had full stores: salt ham and bacon supplemented by fresh fish from the ponds in the orchard, when not frozen over, pigeons from the dovecote, rabbits, perhaps an ancient hen or two, an elderly sheep culled from the flock and in need of long simmering to diminish its tough old sinews. Onions, garlic, herbs dried in the September sun or in the bread oven, hung in bunches in the storerooms, and cabbages, leeks, and roots added variety to pottage and broths. There were bins of flour, barley, peas, oats, all good warming ingredients to fill hungry bellies. Jars of honey from the bee skeps in the orchard wall, loaves of sugar, bags of dates and raisins and currants, butter well salted to keep through the winter, cheeses ripe and hard in the dairy, firewood and faggots stacked in the open-sided linhay in the barton and in a corner of the kitchen garden, candles of tallow and sweet beeswax, rushlights for the barton and courtyard and hall. She had prepared much of this herself, or directed the maids to do it. She had bought, made, distilled, salted, sorted, and stored, as a diligent housewife should, and had seen much of her hard work and careful preparation squandered by her rude, uncouth, and uninvited guests. Now, with this abrupt deterioration in the weather, they must rely utterly upon their own resources. There would be no buying of supplies from markets when no cart could move in the thick snow.

The children were the only ones who loved it. While the shepherds cosseted their woolly pregnant flocks with hay, the cattle huddled misera- bly in cleared and sheltered corners subsisting on peas and straw, their milk dried to a trickle that was not worth the effort to collect. Even the soldiers retreated gloomily to the barn, to dice and drink and sing away the short cold hours of daylight. But Tabby and Deb and William were allowed into the courtyard, dressed in their oldest and warmest clothes, to shriek and laugh and throw snow at each other. Rachael, newly conscious of her digni- fied fifteen years, did not deign to join them, but could occasionally be seen gazing wistfully from the window of her stepmother's chamber, as if regret- ting that she was no longer a child. The weather had also greatly dimin- ished her opportunity for taunting the soldiers, which was at least one advantage of the snow. Bessie Lyteman was likewise restricted and began, to the dismay of Eliza and Silence, to pay court to Lieutenant Byam, he being the most susceptible, if least personable, of the four officers.

Conscience-driven, Silence sought out Captain Hellier and offered her thanks for his company on the journey to Bath, adding that she hoped he had not suffered thereby.

"Suffered?" Hellier said, his chestnut eyes amused at the thought. "My dear Lady St. Barbe, I am not made from the stuff of martyrs. I unfor- tunately incurred my lieutenant-colonel's displeasure, as you have doubtless heard—not a mouse squeaks in this place, but you are informed of it in- stantly. We have decided not to quarrel, however, on such a trivial mat- ter—and besides, keeping the men sane and comparatively sober all hugger mugger in the barn is a task that at present requires our undivided atten- tion. And there is one problem that may have escaped your notice, my lady, since you so plainly are of the Puritan persuasion. Christmas is less than ten days away. What festivities do you keep here, at this season?"

Silence stared at him in astonishment. The hall, where they stood close by the fire, was empty save for themselves, but she could not prevent herself glancing up at the gallery and the stone mask that doubtless hid the ears and eyes of Dame Ursula, listening as she always did to the business of the house. For her mother-in-law, as for her own father, the day of Christ's birth had been as any other, with no vestige of the pagan riot of licentiousness and debauchery in which lesser men and women indulged. Isaac Woods had grimly opened his shop for business every Christmas Day, despite the shortage of custom, the taunts of other, less godly shopkeepers and their 'prentices, and the more powerful opposition of many City fathers. Sir Samuel St. Barbe, however, while not an advocate of excess, was happy to allow a quiet but joyous festival, despite his wife and son's adamant disapproval. But the celebrations were in Silence's mind completely entangled with the cheerful, cynical, humorous character of her father-in-law. Without his presence, leading the singing, relishing the beef and the boar's head, entertaining guests and wassailers, and devising games and stories around the fireside, she realized with a sense of shock that she had no idea at all what was expected of her.

And besides, her godly upbringing still had her bound. She had enjoyed those Christmases at Wintercombe because under Sir Samuel's benevolent guidance the festivities had been innocent, cheerful affairs in which there had seemed no harm at all. With a clear and pessimistic eye, she knew what would happen were she to attempt to direct the revels. Visions of drunken riot, destruction, debauchery sprang vivid to her mind. It was a disgusting, heathen, ungodly, and pagan time. Prayer and fasting were the proper adjuncts to Christmas, and no true member of the Lord's Elect would ever dream of doing anything else.

But she was not a saint, she realized suddenly; she never had been one. She had always feared and disliked her father and all he represented. She had been bored by the interminable sermons and secretly and sinfully mocked his pompous, priggish friends. She had resented the urge that all of the Elect seemed to have to control not only the deeds but the minds and souls and thoughts of their wives and children. She remembered her husband's earnest inquisitions before their marriage, as he tested his bride's godliness and received the answers that he wanted to hear. But beneath the sad-colored clothes, behind the still, serene, submissive face, below the platitudes and the parroted prayers, there lurked a different Silence, the inheritor of the independent spirit of her mother's stubborn, enterprising, individual family.

That Silence had shown herself last in those brief and bitter rebellions against her father, when at the age of ten she had first seriously questioned the drudgery and restrictions of her childhood. Her insubordination had been beaten out of her, with tears and prayers, apologies and many suppers of bread and water. But her spirit, though outwardly docile, had never been broken. She had shared a secret world with her sisters and Joseph, of insolence and laughter and mockery that her father had never suspected, and that her mother, who died when Silence was fifteen, had tolerated and even fostered. Marriage, at the age of nineteen to a widower twenty-four years her senior, had merely exchanged one strict male mentor for another. George St. Barbe had wanted a biddable girl to be a mother to his children and mother his household. Only with Nat, and more recently with Tabby, had she been able to recapture something of that secret self of laughter and freedom. In Sir Samuel she had found, for the first time, an adult who understood and could bring the hidden Silence into the open.

Since his death she had been too burdened with grief and the fears and anxieties brought by the soldiers to remember what merriment was, save one or two brief moments with Nat or Tabby. Now another choice faced her. She could bow to the memory of her father and to the unseen and terrifying figure of Dame Ursula hovering like a ghastly old bird of prey in her chamber, waiting to pounce on the very thought of Christmas and rend it to shreds with her talons. She could order a godly Christmas, and win the approval of her mother-in-law and Eliza, and no one else, and risk open flouting of her authority. Or she could let that other Silence run joyously free, and celebrate Christmas as Sir Samuel had, with a hearty dinner, the singing of carols, holly and ivy trailed above the hearth, gifts to the servants and quiet games with the children before the fire.

Suddenly she made her decision, and it was as if a shackle had snapped free in her mind. She turned to Captain Hellier, who waited patiently for her answer with an air of quizzical inquiry that reminded her a little of Nat, and gave him a smile of such delight that he could not imagine what had caused it. "I may be a Puritan, Captain, by upbringing and circumstance, but that does not mean that I do not approve of any Christmas celebration at all. Here at Wintercombe we have a beast killed—two, I think, since there are all your men to feed as well. And there are puddings to make, and pies to bake, and perhaps a little holly, and some games and diversions. Not a riot, Captain, but a joyful and moderate entertainment."

"I'm glad to hear it," he said. "Although I should warn you, the men will be expecting a quantity of beer and cider, in addition to a bullock or two."

"I said a beast, did I not? They must behave themselves, or they'll get rabbit instead."

"You'll have to slaughter your whole warren, in that case. Your courage does you credit, Lady St. Barbe."

"It does not. I enjoy Christmas, although I know I should not—but my father-in-law made it such a happy time. He had the gift of hospitality and a great generosity of spirit, and if he could celebrate Our Lord's birth with a clear conscience, why cannot I? And I know full well," Silence said, with a wry smile, "that if I did not give permission for a feast, your men would take and steal it instead. So—let them think I am generous too, and protect Wintercombe."

"For a Puritan, you are too much the realist, Lady St. Barbe."

"No, I am not. A true realist would never have gone to Bath. He might have put toadstools in the soldiers' broth, or hemlock in Ridgeley's beer, but that fool's errand, never."

"It was not," Hellier said quietly. "You knew you had to go—not because you thought that it would produce any result, but because it was expected of you. And because there was the smallest chance that it might succeed. You are speaking from hindsight."

"Am I?" Silence asked. She paused, and then added, "I hope I do not have cause, afterward, to regret my decision, Captain, and I hope too that you will do what you can to make sure of it."

"On that, you may rely," Hellier replied. And with a feeling that she had burned all her Puritan bridges behind her, Silence took her leave of him and went to find Darby and Clevinger.

Darby's reaction was, as she had expected, uncomplicated. He had been employed for his culinary abilities, not for his devotion to godliness, and was openly delighted at the prospect of putting his talents to better use than recently, despite the brevity of the notice. At previous Christmases, various farm workers had been drafted to assist with the preparation of the feast, to which they had all been invited on Christmas Eve, but he thought that the soldiers who assisted in the kitchen would suffice.

Christmas Day itself had been a quieter affair, restricted to the family and their household and perhaps one or two close friends. Small hope of that this year, Silence thought as she waited for Clevinger in the study. Just what had she let herself in for? It was as if another person, someone quite different from her normal calm sensible everyday self, had told Hellier of her plans for Christmas. She knew that she was ostensibly just continuing her father-in-law's tradition. Her position could be justified quite adequately, indeed must be to Dame Ursula, who would assuredly disapprove most emphatically. But she alone knew that this was purely an act of reckless rebellion, childish perhaps, wicked quite probably, against everything that her breeding had forced into her.

It was a frightening yet exhilarating feeling, as if she were a child younger than William, taking her first few steps on her own.

Clevinger arrived, his boots snowy and his dour leathery face even more gloomy than usual. She had to speak rather more loudly than her habit. His deafness always increased with the cold and the level of what Mally called his begrumplement. He was especially begrumpled today, having tried yet again, and in vain, to persuade the soldiers to give their horses, now stabled in the emptied linhay and at one end of the depleted barn, the poorer quality straw and peas, rather than the hay and oats intended for the cattle and the Wintercombe horses. She soothed him a little, saying that she would speak to Ridgeley, although by now neither of them had much faith in that course of action. Then, not without trepidation, she mentioned the small matter of Christmas.

To her surprise, for Clevinger had the reputation of being a killjoy, he actually welcomed the idea. "'Twouldn't do to have too much feasting, nor merrymaking neither, m'lady, what with Sir Samuel not long a-laying in his grave. But I can slaughter they two barren heifers what I marked for cull." He sighed. "And mayhap there'll be more fodder for the rest, to bring they safe through the winter. Supposing they troopers don't eat all on 'em first, of course."

"Not if you or I have anything to do with it," Silence said robustly. She added cautiously, still amazed at her own daring, "What other preparations will you need to make? Sir Samuel used to see to everything, so I have very little idea of what is required."

"Us'll need the faggot," the bailiff said, his slow rather expressionless voice gathering a quite unwonted enthusiasm. "The ashen faggot, m'lady. Do ee mind it from last year, that there bundle of logs? I'll send two men out to the coppice soon as this here snow have gone."

"It seems a lot of trouble," Silence said, more dubiously. Carols and even feasting were surely Christian, and harmless, but this custom, which she vividly remembered from the past two Christmases at Wintercombe, smacked most strongly of heathen rite. She could hardly say that to Clevinger, however. Like a snowball being rolled down a hill, her one small act of daring and defiance was rapidly gathering too much weight and speed to be stopped.

"Mummers," said Clevinger, his voice tinged with wistful nostalgia. "When I were a little lad, us had mummers in Norton . . . every ashen faggot night they did go from house to house, a-playing of George and the Dragon, and that there dragon he were a-hissing and a-smoking, and one night he catched fire and it weren't no dragon at all, it were old Tom Hunter . . . there bain't no mummers in Norton now, m'lady," Clevinger said sorrowfully. "Parson got rid on 'em all, when I were a lad, heathen popish idolatory he said they were . . . but, oh, I did like to see that there dragon a-hissing and a-smoking and a-roaring, and George all brave in his shiny armor."

For a moment, despite her assimilated dislike and mistrust of such immoralities, Silence found herself sharing his regret and yearning for an older world than this, where traditions slipped back into the mists of pagan antiquity and village life seemed to have a rustic innocence it now lacked. Church ales, maypoles, mummers, ashen faggots—all customs to be rigorously trampled underfoot by godly squires and parsons and justices, but what had the beliefs of men such as her husband and her father to put in their place? A joylessness, a faith in prayer and fasting and the scourging of mind and body, which surely could not long appeal to men and women who had only the distant and uncertain prospect of heavenly joy to sustain them through their earthly toil and misery. And for an instant her heart sparkled rebelliously, hating the self-righteous men who had stamped in the name of God on other people's small and innocent delights and given them nothing in their place.

Clevinger was talking now about Robin Hood. It was plain that he would blather along on the subject of mummers all day, given the chance. She called him back to the tasks in hand, entrusted him with all the necessary arrangements, and dismissed him, still wondering at herself and at the surprises to be found in those she had thought she knew well. Who would have guessed that begrumpled old Clevinger, deaf and dour and obstinate, could still remember the enchantment of village mummers in Queen Elizabeth's day?

By contrast, Eliza Davison's reaction was quite predictable. Her long narrow mouth downturned, she listened with barely suppressed anger to her mistress's plans and then burst out indignantly, "I thought as how you was one on us, m'lady, and don't hold with norn of this here heathen superstition!"

"I don't," Silence replied, wondering whether most ladies had to justify themselves to their maidservants—she somehow suspected they did not. "But we are not indulging in twelve days of riot and debauchery, Eliza. All we are having is a good dinner—and I'm sure you won't deny that to anyone, after the short commons of the last few weeks—and perhaps a little singing. Sir Samuel saw no harm in it, nor in a little holly and ivy, nor the old custom of the ashen faggot. And yet he was a good and godly man."

"Parson said as how that there faggot was a popish heathen thing and no godly person oughta have it in their hearth," Eliza said stubbornly. "I be despeard—*very*—sorry, m'lady, but I don't want no part of this here revel."

For a moment there eyes met: Silence's hazel, large and calm, Eliza's smaller, very dark and indignant. Then Silence said quietly, "Of course, that is your decision, Eliza—I can't force you if it goes against your conscience. But your conscience was not so troubled last Christmas, nor the one before that. Why is it different now, when all else is the same? Indeed, I don't want anything other than a very quiet celebration—out of respect for Sir Samuel's memory. And it is to remember him that I wish to continue these customs."

Eliza was studying the floor, unwilling to look her mistress in the face. She is only making a show of defiance, Silence thought wryly, because she thinks I am easy to persuade—unlike Sir Samuel, who went his own way, always, but so diplomatically that it never jarred anyone.

"It'll come to no good, m'lady, I know it," her chief maid muttered. "With all they soldiers goggling—drinking—all our cider and eating our good beef, and all on 'em drunk and fornicating too, I shouldn't wonder."

"Fornicating with whom, Eliza?"

"That there Bessie Lyteman, that's who," the maid said, completely forgetting her attempts to speak properly in her agitation. "Girt vorus-norus wench, always gallivanting with they wicked heathen soldiers. And Leah, she be another on 'em, sly gigletin wench, she d'think butter wouldn't melt in her mouth, but I d'know better," Eliza ended indignantly.

"Neither Bessie nor Leah will fornicate with anyone if I can help it—and I need you, Eliza, to keep them to the narrow path of virtue and righteousness," Silence said, loathing the sanctimonious tone of her voice, which always seemed to echo her father's, and invariably accompanied any moralizing or religious talk. "Between us we can make this Christmas a sober and orderly affair. But without your help, Eliza, I do not think that I will be able to manage."

She hated to admit it—but it was probably true, and it was certainly the only way to persuade Eliza into acquiescence. Convinced that she was indispensable, her pride suitably puffed up, the maid kept up an appearance of reluctance for a while longer and then capitulated. "Very well, m'lady, I will do as you wish."

She had now enlisted the support, with widely varying degrees of enthusiasm, of the most important members of her household. There still remained one, not so powerful as before, but yet a force to be reckoned with. In a mood of foreboding and fear, Silence climbed the twisting stone stairs to the main upper part of the house, and the chamber of her mother-in-law.

Usually she saw Dame Ursula only at the morning and evening interrogations. Theirs was not a relationship which permitted idle social calls or chit-chat. With the uncanny prescience that had once half convinced Silence that her husband's mother had supernatural powers, until she discovered her system of spies, the old lady was seated bolt upright in her chair, facing the door, one gnarled hand upon the thick polished ash stick with which she had been known to beat insubordinate children and servants. As soon as Silence entered, after her deferential knock, Dame Ursula snapped, "What's this I hear? You plan to keep Christmas in this house, daughter?"

"I do," Silence answered. "After all, it was kept here last year, and the year before, as Sir Samuel wished."

"Not as *I* wished," Dame Ursula said forcefully. "Nor as my dear husband truly wished. He often spoke of his dislike for such heathen ceremonies—but he felt that he must indulge his household. Now he is gone, I did not think that you would succumb to such wicked temptation."

"I see no harm in it," Silence said patiently. She knew, and Dame Ursula knew too, that only the force of her mother-in-law's powerful personality could change her mind. And she was utterly determined now upon her course. What sanction, after all, did the old lady have now? She had the allegiance of perhaps one or two servants, no more, and she could hardly incite the rest to mutiny. There were few among the household, as Silence had shrewdly suspected, willing to lay aside the chance of as much roast beef as they could eat, after weeks of scanty fare, for trivial reasons of righteousness.

"License and debauch, that is where it will end," Dame Ursula said, banging her stick upon the floor. "You should be ashamed of yourself, daughter, for even thinking to hold such an ungodly heathen festival. What will my dear George have to say when he returns, eh? What will you tell him then?"

"That I am merely carrying on his own father's custom," Silence replied calmly. "I plan no drinking, no debauch, no dancing—merely a good dinner for those who have been badly fed since the soldiers came, and singing of carols. I am sorry, madam, but my mind is quite made up, plans are well in hand, and there is nothing you can do to stop them. I will endeavor to ensure that your rest and prayers are as little disturbed as possible."

"Small chance of that, with those drunken wicked ungodly brutes in my hall below, singing lewd songs and raising a riot . . . you'll regret this, daughter," Dame Ursula exclaimed, and her stick shot out to poke Silence painfully in the chest. "You'll regret it, I'll swear. That company of Satan will destroy this house, and all that's in it. 'Be not drunk with wine, wherein is excess: but be filled with the Spirit,' thus sayeth the Apostle Paul to the Ephesians. Remember it well, daughter."

"I do. And I remember also that in the Book of Ecclesiastes he says, 'A man hath no better thing under the sun, than to eat, and to drink, and to be merry.' I shall keep Christmas here at Wintercombe as has always been done, madam—surely God cannot be displeased at a little innocent joy, after such hardship and travail? I give you good day, Mother."

She had, in a sense, won that encounter. Ironically, she had Ridgeley to thank for her mood of defiance. He had humiliated Dame Ursula in her presence, and somehow her fearsome mother-in-law would never seem so intimidating again.

But she could not, despite her fragile confidence, help but remember the words of Eliza and Dame Ursula. And she wondered if, in the face of all her good intentions, the soldiers would turn a quiet, pleasant, innocent festival into a riot of drunken revelry, lewd behavior, and debauch. They had had inconvenience, a little hardship, but no real horrors in the six weeks of military rule. What now had she unwittingly let loose?

WINTER QUARTERS

DECEMBER 1644 –
MARCH 1645

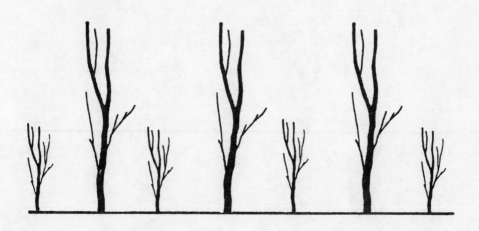

EIGHT

The wine of violence.
—*PROVERBS 4:17*

The children, clad in their best, were coruscating with excitement, quite unable to keep still, flying restlessly from chair to chair in Silence's chamber. Even Nat, usually so relaxed, seemed on edge, his normal good humor frayed by yet another plaintive query from Deb, who could get no satisfactory answer from her mother. "When are we going down, Nat? When? When? When?"

"When we're ready" was all Nat would say. And eventually, even his patience shredded. "Oh, Deb, go away and play with William—you're getting extremely tiresome."

"*I'm* ready," said Deb, twirling like a wind-blown leaf in her new russet wool dress, its cuffs and apron and collar and cap for once all sparklingly clean. She rushed over to William, seized his ready hands, and began to prance about the room, chanting tunelessly, "It's ashen faggot night! It's ashen faggot night! It's ashen faggot night!"

"Oh, don't be such a baby, Deb," Rachael said with annoyance.

Deb, her excitement changed suddenly to fury, let go of William, who lost his balance and sat down hard against a chair, and delivered a vicious kick to her half-sister's shins. "Shut *up,* you silly gawcum!"

"*Deb!*"

It was not often that Silence shouted at her children. So astonished were they that peace descended instantly, and even William, who had banged his arm, forgot to wail. Deb, realizing the enormity of her crime, stood guiltily still, her brown eyes fixed vastly on her mother's face, while Rachael, breathing noisily and holding hard to her anger, massaged her bruises.

"Three sins," Silence said, standing in front of her younger daughter, her face severe. "One, to behave like a hoyden. Two, and most grave, to kick poor Rachael. And three, to call her such names. This is the season of peace and goodwill to all. What are you going to say?"

A tear crept down Deb's fat rosy cheek. "Oh, I'm sorry, Rachael," she said, utterly and genuinely contrite. "I'm sorry, I truly, truly am. Did I hurt you?"

"Yes, you did," Rachael retorted, white-faced and furious.

"And I'm sorry I called you a silly gawcum," Deb said. "Nat does, but he says you can't help it sometimes." Then slowly she put a hand across her mouth, her eyes shooting in apprehension to her mother.

Silence could not laugh. All her authority over her wayward daughter, not to mention Rachael, depended on it. She said sternly, "That is more than sufficient, Deb. You are old enough to know what is hurtful and that you should not say it. Think yourself lucky that this is the time for good-will, otherwise you would even now be back in the nursery, with no supper. And that's where you *will* be, if you misbehave again in the slightest degree. Do you understand me?"

And Deb, mute, chastened, nodded her head.

Fortunately, Mally knocked and entered at that moment. "All is ready, m'lady. Be ee coming down?"

Quietly, the children's excitement barely contained, they descended the twisty stairs to the garden room, where Silence's precious orange and lemon trees sat in tubs to ride out the winter. They were still looking healthy, their leaves dark and glossy, meticulously watered and polished every day by Jemmy Cox, the gardener's boy. Here too were kept her own tools, a little handfork and trowel and hoe made for her by the Norton blacksmith, and the boxes of seed carefully garnered, stored dry and neatly labeled each autumn, for sowing in the spring. She wondered, hearing the wind whining miserably like a fretful child about the gables and buttresses of Wintercombe, whether spring would ever come. True, it had thawed a little, the roads were free of snow, though not of mud and icy water, and the animals could snatch a little rough grazing. But there were still white streaks deep in the hedgerows and upon the rounded slopes of Hassage Hill and Baggridge, and she was well aware of Diggory's piece of weather wisdom, that there would soon be new snow to join the old.

The hall was empty yet full of candles, hushed, waiting in the flickering light for life. The fire in the hearth had been allowed to burn down to hot glowing embers in a heap of ash, ready for the faggot, which was made of wood that burned bright even when green, although on a cold wet night like this it would undoubtedly need some encouragement to catch light. The long trestle tables were set up, with benches along each side. Two had been placed lengthways, the third, for the St. Barbe family and the officers, across the width of the hall at the opposite end from the screens. They were spread with linen cloths, not Wintercombe's best for obvious reasons. Each board boasted a host of candles, wax on the top one, tallow for the rest, and rushlights burned in their iron holders along the wall, as they did at the harvest feast and had done all through the centuries since the house was built. Every piece of pewter that the St. Barbes possessed had been brought into use, from the new service at the high table, its edges hard and smooth and gleaming, to the ancient platters and tankards, thinned and worn and battered with age, at the lowest places. There were rounds of cheese, hunks of bread set ready for each man, with great leather blackjacks brimming with the sharp rough cider, and bottles of wine, carefully decanted from their latest hogshead, stood to attention on the officers' table.

"It's beautiful," Tabby said softly, and her eyes wandered up to the high, pitched ceiling, beamed and bossed, its paint old and smoke-blurred, almost lost within the flickering shadows. "It feels as if there are ghosts up there, of all the people who used to live here—they're watching us, and they're glad."

And strangely, although she was well aware that the only unseen eyes looking down on the hall probably belonged to Dame Ursula and were far from benign, Silence felt that she was right.

A burr of sound, the tramp of feet, announced the arrival of their unwanted guests, trooping in from the north wing, where there was a door to the barton. More muddy footprints for the maids to clean, Silence thought, and followed it with the wry reflection, Why can't I ever stop thinking like a housewife?

Forty feet away at the other end of the hall, the heavy curtain concealing the entrance through the screen was briskly pulled aside, and her bête-noir, Ridgeley, stood in the entrance. He was dressed in his military gear, buff coat, brilliantly scarlet sash binding his heavy waist, the polished sword sparkling at his side. She was glad that he was not wearing the back- and breastplates he often affected when riding abroad, terrorizing simple farmers into giving up their precious winter supplies.

He saw her, and his smile bared his teeth. "Good evening, my Lady St. Barbe! I wish you a merry Christmas, and I thank you for your kind invitation to your feast—as do all my men."

"Invitation? That's rich," Rachael said quietly beside her. "They'd be roasting four of our best kine on spits in the barton if you hadn't asked them in."

"Ssh!" Nat hissed at his twin out of the side of his mouth, and followed it up with a shrewd elbow to the ribs. Rachael glared at him, caught her stepmother's eye, and smoothed her face into a properly decorous mask.

Silence, satisfied that order was restored among her turbulent brood, turned to Ridgeley and gave him a similarly polite smile, concealing a welter of fear and loathing beneath. "And I bid you welcome, Lieutenant-Colonel. If you and your officers would be seated at this table with myself and my family, your men may dispose themselves at the other boards."

In a moment the peace of the hall was shattered, as every man in the troop, all in their boots and buff coats, tramped mud onto the rush matting and scuffled for places. Silence caught sight of William's eyes, round, dark, spellbound, as the objects of his fascination jostled in front of him. It took some time before each man was settled to his own and his neighbor's satisfaction, but on the whole this seemed to be a fairly good-natured occasion. As if following her thought, Nat's dry voice said softly, "Amazing, isn't it, what the promise of a good dinner will do."

She bit back a snort of laughter, watching as Ridgeley led his officers up the aisle between the two lower tables. There was the fair-haired Byam, his face puffy and reddened by weather and drink, slouching behind, and the young cornet whose name she could never remember, Hodges, the quartermaster, and, bringing up the rear, Captain Hellier, his buff coat considerably cleaner-looking than Ridgeley's. His eyes met hers, amused lines around them, and she knew that he was aware of the latent absurdity of the situation. And then Ridgeley was bowing low with a sweep of rather dirty red plumes on his hat, and the other officers were following suit. She curtsied gracefully, seeing the bent heads of Mally and the children, and then rose, gesturing toward the table crosswise below the two masks, a king with ass's ears and a queen, that disguised the squints in the two closets leading off her chamber above. "Will you not take your places, gentlemen, and then the evening may begin."

Her own was at the center of the long board, looking down the path between the other tables to the screen, the gallery above, the laughing mask and the invisible, lurking presence of her mother-in-law. She had given some thought to the disposition of the places and had Nat on her right hand and Ridgeley, appropriately, on the side of the goats. Rachael was between Nat and Hellier, who at least would not molest her. Mally, well able to look after herself, had Ridgeley and Byam to contend with and looked, as she sat down, neat and small in her dark-blue woolen gown, as if she relished the chance of battle. On the fireplace side, where they could best see, were grouped the smaller children, under the firm eye and hand of Doraty Locke. Already William had managed to overset his tankard, half full of weak beer, and Deb had made crumbs of her hunks of bread.

There was an expectant hush, a feeling of anticipation that grew and flourished like a live thing. The hearth rustled as ash settled, and a trailing strand of ivy twisted gently in the hot rising air.

All the candles, as one, dipped and swayed in a sudden draft, and one or two went out. From behind the screen came a confused noise and bustle, and then the curtain was pushed aside to admit Clevinger, his face whipped red by the raw cold outside and a staff in his hand. He banged it on the floor and called out in his loud, rather toneless voice, "M'Lady St. Barbe! Here be the ashen faggot—shall us bring en in?"

"With pleasure, Clevinger," Silence said, smiling, and loud and raucous bellows of approval from the troopers mingled with the excited squeals of Deb and William.

Behind the screen there was much banging and scraping, cries of "Do ee shut that there door," and "Girt gawk, you, that were my foot!" Then four men came in, Rob Sheppard, the assistant cook, the groom, Tom Good-enough, the bigger and older of his two lads, Dick Stent, and the struggling bent figure of Henry Turber, the footman, bearing the ashen faggot between them.

It was a bundle of some score of new-cut ash rods, as long as Nat, and bound with seven supple strips of willow, with a rope around each end to make it secure—bad luck was unavoidable in the coming year if the faggot were to come apart before the burning. Amid shouts, cheers, and rude comments, the bundle was carried to the hearth and, with one especially loud bellow of encouragement, thrust damp and hissing into the deep embers of the fire.

Ash burned well, even as green as this. The glow began to flicker, the hissing died, and the wood started to catch. In some households it was the custom for the children each to choose a band and make a wish as it broke, or to say that the child whose withy broke first would be the first to marry. Such superstition did not hold at Wintercombe, but a yell greeted the disintegration of the first willow band. Already the blackjacks were empty as the troopers quenched their thirsts, sharpened by a grim and discouraging day spent plodding around Wellow demanding contributions in coin and kind.

Ridgeley, elaborately courteous, had filled Silence's wine cup to the brim with claret, done the same for Mally and Rachael and Doraty, and then spoiled the effect somewhat by laying a large, blunt, brutal-looking pistol, some two feet long, upon the linen tablecloth in front of him.

As Silence stared at it, horrified, he gave her his black-toothed, sneering smile. "We wouldn't want any undisciplined behavior to disrupt such a happy occasion, Lady St. Barbe. The men know what it means—a precaution only. Now, the aroma of roast beef fills the air—when will it be on our plates, eh?" And he gulped his wine in one noisy draft.

Silence decided that she liked the man even less, if that were possible, in this falsely jovial mood. She knew how quickly it could change. And she felt her confidence, so foolishly buoyant only that morning, begin to trickle down into a deep pit of foreboding. "As soon as it is ready, Colonel. In the meantime, why not take the edge from your hunger with some bread, or cheese?"

It was, however, only a few minutes before the curtains parted under the hands of Eliza and Leah to admit a procession of staggering men, bearing heaped dishes. All day Darby had labored in the kitchen to produce a feast for three times the usual number of people, and had risen to the occasion superbly. Silence, who had ventured briefly into his domain to check that all was well, had found an inferno of activity that reminded her vividly of an old crude woodcut of hell's kitchen. The heat of the two great fires, each bearing spits groaning under the dismembered weight of the two slaughtered heifers; the scullions turning and basting the joints amid the crackle of fat and sparks; pots bubbling away in the hearth on trivets, or in the huge cauldrons hung over the flames, filled with sauces and Christmas pottage, while the pans under the meat collected hot smoky dripping and gravy, to be seasoned with wine and spices; the bread ovens, heated by bundles of wood far drier, burning much hotter, than the green ash branches in the hall hearth, containing the vast pies, conglomerations of spices, meat, and fruit, traditionally served at this season. And at the center of it, Tom Darby, enormous, sweating, scarlet-faced, as much in his element as a bird in the air, directing his minions with bellows and gestures as huge as himself. Unnoticed and unnecessary, Silence had gazed at the orderly turmoil within, noted the soldiers toiling frantically alongside Sheppard and the three scullions, and had crept away again.

Now the fruits of those labors, steaming and fragrant, were borne in by every male servant Wintercombe possessed, amid riotous cheers. Every household above absolute poverty, after all, could somehow beg, borrow, buy, or steal a duck, a goose, a hen, for Christmas; but beef was beyond the purse of most, and therefore the greatest feast. And here, on the long linen-covered boards in front of every man, making nostrils quiver and mouths water with anticipation, was enough beef to fill each of them to the ears.

Foolishly, Silence had toyed with some idea of saying a Grace, but it would be like trying to restrain ravenous wolves from the kill. Abandoning her intentions, she watched with some apprehension as the meat was stuffed into mouths on the point of knife, or with fingers, and washed down with yet more cider.

Turber, his elderly arms trembling under the weight, brought their own portion: a great slab of rump, its crisped charred exterior basted with butter and dripping and dredged with fine white breadcrumbs to prevent the meat drying out. He laid it heavily in front of Silence, wiping his brow, while young Ned Merrifield and Will Parsons, a scullion as hulking and dim-witted as Ned was small and bright, laid bowls full of sauces—mustard, herbs, fruit, horseradish—along the length of the board. For those who were surfeited with beef, there were dishes of chicken, pigeon, and goose, and a great steaming tureen encircled the Christmas pottage, a glorious aromatic stew of mutton, breadcrumbs, prunes, raisins, currants, and spices. Then the servants withdrew to their own quarters, to snatch a goodly helping of the feast before returning with the second course.

Silence, as the lady of the house, was expected to carve the meat herself. It was a task she had always loathed, feeling it beyond her capabilities. However, it was part of her housewifely duties and could not be shirked. She took up the knife, eyed the rump sternly as if willing it into slices, and began.

Dame Ursula had, early in the marriage, informed Silence coldly that she herself in her salad days had been able to carve meat, however tough, thin and neat. It had been a reproof for her daughter-in-law's great ragged hunks, hacked dripping from the joint with little more science than a dog worrying at a bone. She had improved since those days. The slices were smaller, a touch more dainty. But from the looks of the hungry people on either side of her along the table, she guessed that gobbets of meat would be just as satisfactory as immaculate collops, so long as they arrived speedily on the plate.

With some effort, despite the sharp knife, she reduced the massive lump of beef to manageable portions, which Nat distributed around the board. Then at last some kind of quiet fell upon the hall, as soldiers and servants and family addressed themselves to a feast of plenty that probably would not come again for another year.

Fortunately, Ridgeley did not speak to her often, except to compliment her with a knowing smile on the quality of her beef. He was too busy satisfying his gluttony, with a disregard for the niceties of polite behavior that Silence, trying to hide her disgust, hoped that the younger children could not see. Nat, on her right, ate little but talked softly and entertainingly of the latest village scandal. Like his grandfather, he seemed to know everyone in Norton, and all their doings. Beyond him, she could see that William and Deb were at least not emulating the soldiers. This was fortunate, as the hall now echoed to increasingly inebriated merriment from the lower tables, and cheers as the last bindings of the ashen faggot burned away in a shower of sparks, releasing the half-charred remnants into the flame.

The first course, consumed, was taken away. Silence, who had given strict orders to the contrary, was dismayed to see Bessie and Leah among the male servants, collecting empty dishes, refilling blackjacks, and engaging in spirited and probably bawdy banter with the troopers. One man, bolder or drunker than the rest, pulled the dairymaid's head down to his for a smacking kiss, at the same time fumbling at her bodice. Bessie wriggled out of his grasp with a provocative and enticing smile that said as plain as words "Not now, but later," and Silence's heart sank. Leah took greater care to keep herself out of reach. She was more calculating than Bessie, though no less a mistress of bawdy comments and lewd innuendo.

"There'll be trouble in that quarter," Nat whispered, his eyes indicating the two maidservants.

At the same moment Ridgeley, already on his fourth or fifth cup of wine, belched lecherously on her other side and said jovially, "Fine-looking pair of wenches, those maids of yours, Lady St. Barbe. You keep 'em well hid, eh? Haven't seen them in the barton too often."

"They are my maids, not your men's whores," Silence said, her voice so level and calm that it took a moment or two for her words to sink in.

Then Ridgeley guffawed. "Not so mealy-mouthed, eh, my Lady St. Barbe? They'll be in demand if they're the lusty wenches they look—most of your girls have faces only fit to addle eggs. More wine? Put some good color in your whey-faced Puritan cheeks."

"I thank you." Silence had barely sipped at her claret, though normally she liked a small glass at dinner or supper. Tonight, though, she would need every shred of wit she possessed. Ridgeley squeezed some more wine into the pewter cup and refilled his own. Beyond him, Byam was three parts drunk, and a great crimson stain on the plain white cloth showed where he had poured too much into his cup.

The Christmas pies were brought in, along with more meats, and fruit, with an almond pudding and sweetmeats for the top table. By now the heat and noise and surfeit of feasting were beginning to tell on the younger children. William, flushed and drooping, stared at his slice of minced-meat pie as if he did not know what to do with it, while Deb looked exhausted but determined to enjoy herself to the bitter end. And Tabby was chewing her food as if it tasted of ashes, her clear level eyes fixed burningly on the increasingly raucous revelers at the lower tables. As Silence looked, she turned to Hellier, who was seated on her left, and asked him a question that Silence could not hear above the din. His lively brown face registered surprise. Then, smiling, he inclined his head toward her and listened, before speaking in his turn.

Silence would have given all of the mountain of food and drink in front of her to be able to hear that conversation only a few feet away, and she had at best an incomplete view of their faces. The autumn-colored man, Tabby had called him first, and later the skummery man, with the hue and savor of foul water. But, seeing her thoughtful, serious expression as she talked to the captain, Silence wondered if her daughter were not about to revise her earlier opinion of him—just as, reluctantly, she herself had had to do, in the face of friendship mysteriously yet freely offered.

William was drawn into their talk now, his urgent questions plain on his face. Then, tiredness quite forgotten, he stood on his stool and leaned over toward the captain. Silence saw Doraty looking at her anxiously, and gave a small shake of her head. Her son, thwarted, was quite capable of screaming the roof down, and she did not think that Hellier was a danger to him. If anything, it was the other way about.

The captain touched his sword and shook his head sadly. William's fiery fat face crumpled: It was obvious what he had requested. Hellier said something, and then took up his damask napkin and spread it on the table by the side of his plate. While Silence watched, as fascinated as the children, he folded it over and over again, turning it as he did so, and then suddenly reached out and dropped it onto William's silky yellow hair. He had transformed it into a neat little cap. Deb gave a shout of laughter that Silence heard, and clapped her hands. William, puzzled and a little suspicious, removed the hat, studied it, grinned, and put it back somewhat lopsidedly on his head. At once, Hellier was besieged by two clamoring children. He made a cap for each of them from their own napkins and placed them with a smile on their wildly dissimilar heads. In answer, Deb crowed with delight and Tabby's sweet pointed face broke into her swift vivid grin.

"Pray excuse me, Colonel," Silence said, unable to sit still any longer. As Ridgeley, oblivious, munched his way through his third slab of pie, she rose and slipped past the twins to Hellier's side. "I hope my children are not tedious company, Captain."

"Look, Mama, look, he made me a cap, and William and Tabby too, and he did it by magic!" Deb's voice was squeaky with excitement.

Tabby, whose head was not always in the clouds, added, "He made us caps without stitches, Mama. Please, Captain, can you show me how to do that? Can you make anything else?"

"I can make a boat out of paper—but they, alas, always seem to sink," Hellier said. His warm brown eyes, laughing, met Silence's hazel-green ones. "Will you have a cap for your head too, my lady?"

"Of course," Silence said, entering into the spirit of it. She watched as Rachael's napkin was snatched up and transformed, by deft movements much too quick for her to hold in her memory, into a little, crookedly oval cap. It sat oddly on her plainly dressed hair, being ridiculously small. Laughing, she removed it and loosened the folds, letting it dangle a plain napkin once more from her fingers. "I've never seen that done before, Captain. Where did you learn the gentle art of pleasing children?"

"A man of many talents, my captain," Ridgeley said loudly, peering down the table. "I reckon it's time for singing, Hellier—got your fiddle, have you?"

"Give me a minute to fetch it and another twenty to tune it," the captain said, "and I will play you all the music you want." He rose.

Silence, before she thought, hissed at him, "Christmas carols, not drinking songs—please!" And was rewarded by a glimpse of that amused and lazy smile, before he went in search of the fiddle she had never guessed that he owned.

It was not a gentleman's instrument, but more properly associated with taverns and bawdy-houses and long drunken evenings of the sort no Puritan could contemplate without a shudder. Silence looked at it dubiously. Sir Samuel had possessed a few musical instruments, chief among them an old and lovely pair of virginals. But music was still a mystery to her, a shadowy uncharted country that yet exerted a strange spell over her, half fear, half enchantment, much as the soldiers seemed to attract William.

Her father had disapproved of all song that did not embrace the psalms, and these he had sung in a loud, harsh, tuneless voice akin to a corncrake's. Unfortunately, she knew her own sounded similar. She remembered, also, her mother humming in the kitchen as she shelled peas on a summer day, and the tunes everywhere in the London streets, the cries and songs and dances of the City people. It was in his attitude to music that her father's extreme views showed themselves most plain. It had taken her most of her childhood to realize that even among the godly he stood almost alone, isolated by the severity of his beliefs and the uncompromising nature of his crusade against everything that, for most people, made life sweet. Even his most pious friends allowed a little innocent song and an instrument or two to be played in their families, for there was nothing in the Scriptures to deny the godly such pleasure. But Isaac Woods had been the only one to banish music and laughter from his house, and in this, as in most of his edicts, he had essentially failed.

Despite his words, Hellier tuned his fiddle quickly and easily. A blurred hush had fallen upon the hall, broken only by the sounds of eating and drinking, a belch or two, a crackle from the fire, just replenished by Turber. She wondered how he could do it, from memory and ear alone, but it was yet another aspect of the mystery that was hidden from her. Sir Samuel had had a whole consort of viols, all laid away now in a chest in Silence's chamber, mute, once loved, now useless. She had never been able to hear that low, mournful sound without a shiver. She remembered her father-in-law playing the tenor viol alone before the fire, for in his old age there was no other left at Wintercombe to make music with him, sawing his bow up and down the strings.

Although superficially similar to a treble viol, the fiddle was not held upon the knees but against the shoulder, a position that looked awkward and uncomfortable but was apparently much easier to play. A few introductory notes, light and tuneful, swooped into the thick smoky air, reeking of food and cider and sweat. Then the fiddle launched with delight into the tune that Silence recognized as "The Holly and the Ivy." With a roar, forty inebriated military throats attempted to follow, banging the time with their knives and hands on the board. Rachael kept her mouth shut tight, but her stepmother saw Nat and Mally singing lustily, and even Tabby, her eyes shining, joined in with the chorus that owed little to Christian celebration:

> *Oh the rising of the sun,*
> *And the running of the deer,*
> *The playing of the merry organ,*
> *Sweet singing in the choir.*

There were numerous verses, each one louder than the last. They seemed to know all the words, and their voices kept up, just, with the flying exuberant fiddle. Hellier played as if born to it, his eyes narrowed and distant above the swift, sure movements of the bow, as if lost within his music, seeing something else entirely from the smoke-ridden crowded riotous hall in front of him. He finished on a flourish, with two choruses, and amid cheers laid down his bow.

In the sudden quiet, Silence saw with apprehension the ungainly, unlovely figure of Dame Ursula's maid, Ruth, with whom her mother-in-law had shared a lonely meal in the eyrie of her chamber. The servant made her way up the hall, giving the soldiers at the left-hand table a wide berth, though in truth few would care to touch her, however drunk they were. Her height, her pale hair and red skin, the white lashes and strange eyes and above all the absence of life and feeling in her face, all combined to make her an object of revulsion rather than lust. She marched up to the top table, stood squarely in front of Silence, breathing heavily, and said without ceremony, "M'lady do say as how there be too much of this here rumpus."

There were several guffaws at that, and Ridgeley, his voice pitched loud enough to carry to the chamber on the other side of the gallery, said, "Tell the old crone she can go to hell for all we care!"

"Aye, tell her this is Christmas Eve!" another shouted, and was cheered by most of his fellows.

Ruth's heavy face stared impassively at Silence, and she said bluntly, "M'lady do say as how you told her there wouldn't be norn of this here randing and bingeing and such, and she d'ask you to stop at once."

"Well, we won't!" Ridgeley shouted, bringing his fist down with a thump upon the board, so that wine jumped in the cup and Tabby started with sudden fear. "You tell that joyless old hag that this is Christmastide, though she may not realize it, sour-faced Puritan as she is, and the men of Bridges' Horse don't give ground to anyone, eh, lads?"

The bellow of assent must have raised the hair on Dame Ursula's head. Silence, appalled, the situation abruptly wrenched from her control, stared at Ruth's unchanging expression. "I'm sorry," she said. "You must see—I can't do anything about it now. If you hadn't come down—"

"Come on, Hellier, give us another tune!" Ridgeley roared.

The captain, with a keen glance at the confrontation beside him, put his fiddle once more to his shoulder and said, his voice very clear in the hubbub, "'I Saw Three Ships.'"

There was no chance of any conversation after that. The noise erupted into song, and Ruth, gazing around at the scene of disorder and revelry, turned abruptly and marched back the way she had come.

The carol ended raggedly. Hellier, staring at the curtains swinging behind Ruth's broad and affronted back, said, so quietly that only Silence heard him, "A typical Puritan—suffering so greatly in the terror that someone, somewhere, might be enjoying themselves."

As she was wondering whether or not to laugh, Ridgeley's uncouth bellow blasted her ears. "Hey, Lady St. Barbe, did you hear about the Puritan whore? She charged her customers a shilling for a thoroughly miserable time!"

Amid the howls of laughter and the disintegration of her hopes for an evening at least approaching some decorum, Silence ignored him. She caught Doraty's eye and nodded meaningfully. The nurse, who had been waiting for just such a signal, got at once to her feet and spoke to Deb and William. The little boy's face crumpled with tired rage, and his shout was plain to hear even above the hubbub. "No! Don't want to!"

Fortunately, Doraty had little patience with such rebellion. She grasped William's sticky paw in one hand and Deb's in the other, and marched the two protesting, exhausted children past the bright embers of the ashen faggot and the laughing, cheerful soldiers, who all reached out a hand to pat William on the back as he was hauled screaming from the hall.

"Well, the little lad's no Puritan!" Byam shouted, on his feet, swaying, his wine trickling over his fingers as he held the cup aloft. "I'll give you all a toast, my brave boys—our youngest Cavalier!"

All over the hall cups and tankard were emptied. Silence saw that Tabby had made no attempt to follow her younger brother and sister. She had crept close to Hellier and was sitting pressed against the board, stroking the sweet curves of the violin as it lay on the white linen, the bow beside it. The captain had seen her. He bent his head and said quietly, "Don't you want to go with your nurse?"

"No," Tabby answered, her fingers continuing to caress the smooth varnished wood. "I want to hear you play some more, if you please."

And Silence, watching and listening as he took up the instrument again with a smile, was conscious of an unpleasant emotion that she identified, with some astonishment, as jealousy. Although Tabby would undoubtedly be better off in bed, out of sight if not earshot of this increasingly rowdy scene, she had not the heart to force her away.

"And now a carol for good Puritans and Roundheads everywhere!" Hellier said, and played the opening notes of a tune that brought howls of delighted approval from the troopers. As Tabby watched the movement of his hands, enchanted, her eyes glowing, her mother listened to the words the men roared out:

> *In Somerset as it befell,*
> *A farmer there that I knew well,*
> *On Christmas Day, it happened so*
> *Down in the fields he went to plow.*
>
> *As he was a-plowing on so fast,*
> *Sweet Jesus he came by at last.*
> *He said, "Oh, man, why dost thou plow,*
> *So hard as it do blow and snow?"*
>
> *The man he answered with great speed,*
> *"To plow this day I have great need.*
> *If we don't work all on this day,*
> *We should want some other way."*

Now his arms did quaver through and through,
He trembled so he could not plow.
The ground did open and let him in,
Before he could repent his sin.

His wife and children's out of place,
His beasts and cattle they're all but lost,
His beasts and cattle they die away,
For plowing on Our Lord's birthday.

Silence hoped most earnestly that Dame Ursula was in bed with a bolster over her ears. She knew, however, that it was much more likely that those ears were even now pressed to the laughing mask, listening with avid disgust to the words that mocked all her beliefs.

But worse was to come. The last notes from the fiddle had scarcely died away when Ridgeley was on his feet bellowing approval. "Let's have another ballad of a Puritan, eh, Nick?"

And Hellier, a sudden wild recklessness on his face, obliged. Silence could hardly avoid hearing the words, since both Ridgeley and Byam were bawling them at full stretch. She had never been so glad to see Doraty, who reappeared by the screens, having given William and Deb over into Hester's hands, and now returned for the other children.

It was a Puritanical lad
that was called Matthias,
And he would go to Amsterdam
to speak with Ananias.
He had not gone past half a mile
but he met his holy sister,
He laid his Bible under her breech,
and merrily he kissed her.

"I don't want to go," Tabby said, her face pale, set, stubborn, in thrall to the bright lewd music of the fiddle. "I want to hear him play some more—please, Mama, *please!*"

"Alas! What would the wicked say?"
quoth she. "If they had seen it!
My buttocks they do lie too low—I wished
Apocrypha were in it!"

"Go," Silence said in a voice that not even Rachael cared to disobey. Tabby, with one last yearning look at the oblivious man conjuring such effortless flying sounds from wood and varnish and gut, stumbled reluctantly into Doraty's grasp.

Rachael, too, was persuaded to leave with surprising ease.

Nat, however, shook his head firmly. "I'll go when you do, Mother. I've heard worse when Grandfather used to take me into the George. And I think you need some protection, don't you?"

"More fool you," Silence said, and saw his wry amusement at having his own favorite phrase turned back on him.

As Doraty, her face set in rigid lines of disapproval, hurried the two girls away, the thumping song reached its bawdy climax and exploded in roars of laughter, thrown cider, plates, and tankards battered vigorously on the table. A soldier wrenched a trail of ivy off the mantelpiece and crowned himself and his comrades amid further merriment. Silence, seeing that matters were rapidly getting out of hand, had half made up her mind to retire herself. Last year at about this time the village Wassailers, whom no censor could discourage, had visited the house, as they did most in Norton, to sing their songs and receive the customary gifts of cider and a share of the Christmas plenty. Tonight, if they had any sense at all, they would give Wintercombe and its dangerous, volatile contents a very wide berth indeed.

A fight seemed to have broken out at the end of the table by the hearth. Two men were tangled together over the board, and pewter went crashing to the floor to roll away across the flagstones to lie near the fire. Others joined in with enthusiasm, and there was suddenly a heaving mass of buff coats spreading over the table, bench, floor. Ridgeley, seeing it, bellowed something. In the general din, laughter and shouts of anger or encouragement, his voice went quite unnoticed. A candle, knocked over, lay smoking and still aflame in a puddle of wax on the cloth. And in horror, Silence saw in its fitful light a hand raised in the air and the flash of reflected firelight on a knife, before it was plunged downward.

Ridgeley lifted the heavy pistol from the table in front of him, pointed the muzzle at the dim ceiling, and fired.

The report was deafening. It reverberated massively around the stones of the hall, and a little shower of plaster from the ceiling drifted lazily down through the pungent smoke. As Silence took her hands away from her ringing ears, the colonel lowered the weapon and regarded his thunderstruck troopers with overt dislike. "God's death, I'll have none of this brawling among my men! Get back to your places, or I'll flay your backs myself."

Slowly, reluctantly, the tumble of buff coats heaved themselves apart, while Silence waited with apprehension. Sure enough, one man staggered to the bench, blood dripping from his arm. Ridgeley gestured savagely with the pistol. "Trooper Green! Who did that?"

"I—I dunno, sir," the unfortunate man said, staring down at his wound as if the arm did not belong to him. "Someone came at me from behind, dunno who 'twas."

"It were Jennings what did it, I seed him!" another man shouted, and the guilty party, so drunk or witless that he still had the bloodstained knife clenched in his hand, was thrust forward.

Ridgeley walked around the table, the pistol still dangling from his fingers. "If I had a bullet in this, I'd send it through your thick brainless skull, you stupid bugger!" Beside himself with rage, he struck the man several times across the face, following up with a vicious punch in his belly and a final contemptuous kick that laid him flat on his back, his head in the spilled ashes of the hearth, out cold.

There was absolute silence. Ridgeley, menacingly, let his virulent gaze rove across the apprehensive ranks of his troop, while the hand that was not holding the pistol fingered his sword. He indicated two men with a curt jerk of his head. "You! Wilkins! Porter! Drag him out to the barn. I'll deal with him in the morning. You lot, get back to your drinking—or I'll have the hides off you as well."

If she had not been so frightened, Silence might have laughed at the way in which all those hairy faces disappeared instantly behind their mugs. Beyond them, wide-eyed and mute, peering hesitantly around the curtains, appeared the servants, summoned by the shot. They vanished with alacrity as the two troopers, dragging the prone body of their comrade between them, stumbled toward the screen, somehow squeezed themselves together through the narrow gap, and hauled their burden away. Silence watched the curtains as the unconscious Jennings's bootsoles—worn, muddy, patched—disappeared through them, but none of the pale, anxious faces came back. They probably think he's dead, Silence thought, wondering at her calm, though inside her bones quivered. And he may well be—those blows would have felled an ox.

Slowly, his gaze still on his soldiers, Ridgeley backed up the space between the two boards. Forty pairs of eyes, riveted to him, followed his progress. When he reached the top table, he turned, cast the pistol down onto his dirty plate with a crash that made everyone jump, and laughed. "Nothing to worry about, my Lady St. Barbe—just a little bother, soon sorted out. Come on, woman, drink your wine up and I'll fill your glass— drink a loyal toast to the king with the rest of us."

Silence stared at him, her eyes huge in her chalk-white face. Hellier, watching, his fiddle forgotten in his hands, wondered at this unsuspected strength in her that held her still to that quiet enduring dignity when other ladies would long ago have fainted, or fled. She said, her voice thin but persevering, "No, I thank you, Colonel. I am weary and will retire to my chamber. I am sure your festivities will progress even better without me. Come, Nat, Mally."

"You're not going anywhere, you puling little Puritan traitor!" Ridgeley's hand shot out to grab her wrist.

Silence gasped, once, as his great hairy fist clamped around her slender bones, and then willed herself to stand still without flinching. She said, "Please, sir, let go of me."

"Not until you've drunk a loyal toast!" Ridgeley shouted, thrusting his face close to hers. The stink of his wine-laden breath wafted over her in a noxious cloud that made her eyes water, and only the force of her will kept her head from turning away.

"I cannot drink if you keep hold of me," she pointed out with patient reasonableness. On her right, Nat had moved so close that he was almost touching her. His fingers found her free hand and squeezed it gently. On the other side Mally, her face scarlet with suppressed fury, was watching Ridgeley like a hawk—as was, indeed, every other person in the hall.

"Drink it with your other hand, I don't care—I'll tip it down your throat if you refuse!"

Her mind, astonishingly, was working fast. The troopers were terrified of him—but would they stand tamely by and let her be assaulted in her own hall, at her own table? She could not rely on them. All she could depend on was the sense and support of Nat and Mally. And even they, at this moment of crisis, might well not be enough. She came to a decision, freed her hand from Nat's, and picked up her cup, still almost brimful of wine. Her eyes holding Ridgeley's, she raised it and said, loudly and clearly, "I drink a health to His Majesty King Charles. May he triumph over those who would harm his cause—especially those within his own camp, who blacken his reputation with their deeds!"

"Why, you little bitch!" The colonel, outwitted, let go of her and swung his fist. The cup went flying from her hand and careered across the table, showering wine everywhere like blood. Silence, unable to stop herself, flinched away and found Nat pushing himself in front of her. Ridgeley, his arm raised for another blow, was brought up short and stared contemptuously at the slight, frail boy suddenly standing in his way.

"Go on," Nat said, his voice high, cold, and clear. "Hit me rather than Mother. I'm smaller than she is, after all, and even less able to defend myself. At least the men you attack are your own size."

"Out of the way, brat," Ridgeley hissed between his teeth. He was so consumed with alchoholic fury that Silence, in terror, wondered if he had any knowledge of what he was doing. "I said out of my way!"

"Colonel Ridgeley." It was Hellier's voice, quiet and reasonable. "For Christ's sake, man, what are you about? You can't treat Lady St. Barbe like some drab off the streets. What good does it do?"

"Keep out of this," Ridgeley said between huge, snorting breaths. "That woman's a traitor, and the brat's no better—time they were taught a lesson."

Byam's high braying laugh echoed drunkenly. "Aye—lesson—I'll teach her a lesson too. They're all the same under their skirts, these prim Puritans—" His voice ceased abruptly as Mally, with the strength of rage and desperation, pushed him back into his chair and emptied his tankard over his head. Ridgeley, all his attention fixed upon Silence and Nat, did not even notice. Nor did he see the slight, neat figure of his captain, making his way unobtrusively around the end of the table to stand at his side, until Hellier spoke again.

"You'll regret it in the morning. I should retire now, Lady St. Barbe, if I were you."

As Silence, only too willing to take his advice, stepped backward, the colonel's hand shot out and struck Nat a great blow across the face, sending him flying back against his stepmother. "And that's for your insolence, boy—next time it'll be worse!"

"Nat—Nat, are you all right?" Silence cried. Her stepson stumbled upright, his hand to his mouth, still looking at Ridgeley. There was blood dripping through his fingers.

"You are utterly beneath contempt," he said with icy rage. "Come on, Mother, let's go now, before he turns on you again."

He took Silence's arm and steered her past the drenched Byam, the shocked-looking cornet, and all the debris of the feast, to the door leading to the little closet and the garden chamber. Silence, glancing back past Mally's shoulder, saw Ridgeley staring at them, swaying drunkenly against the table, nursing his hand, and beyond him Captain Hellier, perhaps the most sober man left in the hall, the voice of reason who would, in the colonel's present mood, probably pay dearly for his intervention. Once more she was in his debt. She met his eyes and gave him a swift look that she hoped might convey her thanks. And then, with utter relief, she turned and walked with dignity from the hall, to the refuge of her chamber.

NINE

Hope deferred maketh the heart sick.
—PROVERBS 14:12

That night, the night of peace and goodwill, Mally had barred the
door, and Nat, his cut mouth bathed and dressed with a little of
the honey, sage, and honeysuckle ointment that Silence kept in convenient
jars all over the house, for use in minor emergencies, slept on a truckle bed
in her chamber. Fortunately, there seemed to be no permanent damage.
Silence, remembering the force behind that blow, knew that he had been
lucky not to lose a tooth, at the least. Nat himself submitted to her concern and ministrations with good grace, although he was paler even than
usual, and rather too quiet. Looking at him as he sat in her favorite chair
before the fire, dwarfed by it, his dark hair falling over his forehead, the
circles blue under his eyes, and his gashed and swollen mouth, Silence felt
a rush of tenderness that she knew better than to show. Nat had an as-
tringent wit ready to rebuff all those who showed overmuch pity for his
frailty. He was fifteen, and looked four or five years younger. How could
even the vile Ridgeley have stooped so low as to strike this fragile child?

"What are we going to do tomorrow?" Nat asked her, his voice rather
indistinct and his hands curled around the tankard of spiced beer that had
been kept warm in the hearth for hours. "What is going to happen? He
won't forget that we both insulted him."

"And I poured cider all over that there lieutenant," Mally pointed out,
giving the pillows a shake. She was making up the truckle bed, kept under
Silence's own, and rarely used save for a sick child. "Don't ee fret, Master
Nat—he'll have disremembered it all come morning. He were so drunk I
doubt he'll ever bring aught of it to mind."

"I pray you're right—otherwise we shall probably be cast out," Silence
said. "Your bed's ready, Nat—how do you feel?"

"Sore," her stepson replied, taking a cautious sip of his beer. "More fool
me, wouldn't you say?"

And despite her fear and anxiety, her dread of the morning, Silence had
perforce to laugh.

Someone woke them, hammering on the door in the middle of the
night, but whoever it was soon went away again, negotiating the stairs

with some difficulty, to judge by the crashing and curses that came distantly to their ears. Eventually the sounds of revelry from the hall died away. Perhaps they've all drunk themselves into a stupor, Silence thought, as she drifted at last into exhausted sleep. And, her vengeful side added with uncharacteristic vindictiveness, I hope they all wake up with ghastly headaches.

Mally roused her the next morning, with a smile and a whispered "Merry Christmas." She added, her finger to her lips, "Come looksee at this, m'lady."

Silence, wrapped in her warm furred bedgown, tiptoed after her maid into the little closet in which she slept. It was a tiny, lovely room, stone-vaulted with whitewashed walls, the one large window looking northward over the courtyard. Opposite was the narrow squint, disguised as a king with ass's ears, that afforded a limited view of the hall below. Mally indicated that Silence should look through it, and her laughter bubbled in her face.

Wondering with some misgivings what she would see, Silence crept to the slit in the wall and peered down. The contours of the king's face rather hindered her vision, but by moving her head slightly she was able to see almost everything below her, at the eastern end of the hall. There was the top table, its cloth disfigured and stained with wine, food, dirty platters, and scattered knives and spoons. The fingerbowl was empty and the pewter salt overset. In the middle of the debris rested the quartermaster's head, dabbled with wine, one hand still clutching his cup. Even from here, his raucous snores were audible. Beyond him, a pair of legs sticking out from under the table indicated the resting place of another soldier. Silence craned her neck to look farther down the hall, toward the gallery, and was rewarded by similar scenes of devastation and debauch. She counted heads, then feet, and came to the conclusion that at least a score of men still lay in drunken sleep below. There was no sign of Ridgeley, nor of Byam, Helliar, and the cornet. They, presumably, had been able to find their beds.

A nauseous stench, compounded of stale cider, wine, wood and tobacco smoke, burned meat, and vomit, wafted up to her, and she recoiled, retching. "What a sight!"

"You'll wake 'em, m'lady—do ee let sleeping dogs lie in their own filth," Mally whispered.

Smiling despite her disgust, Silence slipped back into her own chamber. Nat was still fast asleep, a riotous tuft of tangled black hair above the blankets. She sat down by the fire, which was still giving off heat, and said slowly, "Eliza will never agree to clear that mess up."

"She will do if she have to step through it all day," said Mally. "Tarblish clean-minded, our Eliza."

Silence, visited by a sudden wild idea, said nothing for a moment. Then she gave her maid a swift, vivid grin. "Come on, Mally, help me dress—I think I know how we can solve this particular little problem!"

Perhaps ten or fifteen minutes later, those who had spent an uncomfortable, oblivious night spread over tables, under tables, on benches, and in at least one case with feet in the hearth, were poked painfully into reluctant life. They raised bleary eyes to see, standing over them, the stern-faced, neatly clad figure of the lady of the house, broom in hand. "Merry Christmas," she said caustically. "If you're going to be sick, kindly do it outside. Then you can come back and make this hall fit for decent people to eat in."

Groaning, clutching their heads, in no state to resist the brisk orders or the shrewd proddings of Mally's foot and Silence's broom, the troopers of Sir Thomas Bridges' Horse found themselves being organized. Eliza, stony-faced, dumped half a dozen leather buckets down on the flags, and told them to fill the pails with rubbish. "The bailiff's pigs will eat en, if you won't," she said, and watched with grim satisfaction as the gray-faced, unshaven, stumbling men tried to scrape plates and sweep up spilled food. Mally, seeing one of them swigging the dregs of someone else's tankard, fetched him a swift blow with her besom, and any show of resistance collapsed like a burst bladder. Silence, who had had her doubts as to the wisdom of this course of action, fitting though it was, drew a deep breath, more confident. As long as Ridgeley kept to his bed—and it was very early as yet, only half an hour or so past dawn—they would be able to keep the men, still half drunk and all feeling decidedly unwell, at work to clear up the appalling mess they had created.

With Eliza and Mally, neither of whom stood any nonsense whatsoever, to direct the soldiers, it was surprising how quickly the chaotic hall began to regain something of its former dignity. The plates and tankards and cups were cleared away and carried to the kitchen to be scoured by two of the men singled out for the task because of their slightly more responsible appearance. The linen cloths and napkins were shaken out and bundled into a big heap by the screens, ready for washing. The buckets, full of leftover food, stood beside them. Quartermaster Hodges could not be roused at all, and on Silence's instructions was dragged like a sack of meal to sleep it off in one of the closets just off the hall.

"My congratulations," a familiar voice said, as Silence was supervising the painstaking stacking of boards and trestles along the south wall, under the windows. "A feat of organization that would do credit to any general."

Silence, turning, saw Hellier standing in the doorway that led to the garden chamber. He was clad only in shirt and breeches, and the sharp line of his jaw was disguised by the night's stubble, giving him a markedly piratical appearance. His brown hair, unkempt, coiled over his shoulders, and his chestnut eyes were bright and amused. "A merry Christmas to you, Lady St. Barbe—or should I not say such things to a puling Puritan?"

"I don't mind," Silence said. "I don't think I'm a very good Puritan, anyway. Merry Christmas, Captain Hellier. Did you sleep well?"

"As well as could be expected, given the noise," he said, coming to her side. "Rather than risk coming to blows with Ridgeley, I made my excuses and left shortly after you did. Much though I'd love to sheathe my sword in his guts, it would hardly help my prospects of promotion, or favor."

Silence smothered her laughter with an effort. She knew that she should be shocked by his bluntness, but somehow she always seemed to find his comments ridiculously amusing. She said, glancing at him, "Then you do not require any of my sovereign remedy for the headache? Oil of lilies is very good."

"I do not," Hellier said distinctly, with a care that indicated that he was lying, "have any kind of megrim, thank you, my lady. You may bind their thick pates with oils and unguents and ointments if you like, but not mine." He added, grinning, "Oil of lilies, you say? I know of another excellent cure. Take one determined lady, a broom or two and half a dozen buckets, mix together with several unsympathetic maidservants, all nagging together, and there you have the remedy for headaches, sloth, drunkenness, and all kinds of similar vices and disorders. And if you try to swallow your laughter any more, my lady, you'll need a cure for the whoops."

Silence gave way, spluttering. When, with an effort, she had calmed herself and said, "I don't know why or how, Captain, but you seem to know exactly what amuses me."

"Perhaps because it amuses me too? But I was not amused last night," Hellier said, suddenly serious. "Ridgeley is a menace, notorious for it—he learned his trade in the Irish rebellion, where all niceties were cast aside, and he's too stiff-necked to change his ways. He became such a liability in Bath that Bridges was forced to send him here—a convenient way of getting rid of him and punishing you at the same time. Sir Thomas has the acquiescence, if not the support, of the Bath City Council. The things that Ridgeley did would have pushed them into outright rebellion before too much longer, and Bridges couldn't afford to risk it—or to have someone pistol him. What you saw and suffered last night, to my regret, was a very watered-down example of my lieutenant-colonel's behavior. At his worst, he'd have killed that trooper and probably done you serious harm—or given you to Byam."

Silence could not repress a shudder. Feeling the goosebumps raising the hairs on her arms, she said, "Where are they now? Safe in their beds?"

"I would hope so—but Byam, I fear, is not alone."

There was a small, shocked pause. Silence said carefully, "How do you know that, if you retired so early?"

"Not so early that I missed the arrival of your enchanting dairymaid."

"*Bessie?* She was supposed to be in her bed, with the door locked and bolted!"

"Well, she must have unbolted it again. Byam took quite a fancy to her, though he was too far gone in drink to do much about it, so her honor, if not her reputation, could still be intact."

"And she didn't cast her lure at you?" Silence asked suspiciously. Though not as tall nor as superficially imposing as his blond lieutenant, Hellier must surely present a far more attractive proposition to Bessie, despite her minimal powers of discrimination.

"She tried. I refused," the captain said, and gave her the benefit of his long, lazily amused smile. At close quarters it was thoroughly disturbing.

She felt herself flushing and wondered with increased bewilderment why Bessie had settled for Byam when, surely, with a little guile she could have had this man instead. "Your strength of mind does you credit, sir," she said with some asperity. "But that does not alter the disgraceful debauch of my dairymaid."

"Certainly it was not a deflowering," he said dryly. "And a girl such as that, not only willing but eager to be seduced—there's little you can do to prevent it. Why on earth do you keep her on in your household?"

"Because she's a good—no, an excellent dairymaid, and they're not easy to come by. And because," Silence said, ruefully, "after all's said and done, I actually *like* the girl."

"Dear God," Hellier exclaimed after a startled pause. "You most certainly are not the pattern of most Puritan housewives, are you, Lady St. Barbe? What an astonishing confession. Will you still like her when she presents you with a bouncing yellow-haired little bastard?"

"Very probably, yes," Silence told him, and had the satisfaction of seeing him dissolve into delighted laughter before she turned away to attend to a brisk and indignant Eliza, full of some tale of insult.

After the riot of ashen faggot night, Christmas Day itself proved mercifully quiet. The hall cleared and cleaned under Eliza's gimlet eye, the troopers staggered groaning back to their barn and were not greatly in evidence for the rest of the day. Ridgeley, to Silence's profound relief, did not show his face at all, not even at dinnertime, though Bessie appeared unobtrusively before breakfast, no more disheveled than usual but with a glint of bawdy triumph in her eye. Silence, reluctantly doing her duty, took her on one side. "Bessie, I hear that you didn't spend the night in your chamber."

"And what if I didn't?" the dairymaid said cheerfully. "You d'know me by now, m'lady—I can't seem to help myself. And I bain't doing nobody no harm."

"Except yourself, Bessie—what if you should fall with child?"

"Never have done yet," the girl said, with a grin and a wink and a toss of her scarlet hair. "There be ways a-plenty of stopping it, you know, m'lady. Don't ee fret for me, I'll be despeard careful." She glanced about at the almost restored hall and added softly, "Do Eliza know where I were? I were main quiet, m'lady, not even Leah heard norn."

"I don't think Eliza knew you'd gone—she has said nothing to me, and nor has Leah."

"Then 'twere that there captain," said Bessie. "About the soberest of them all, he were, and that weren't saying much. I do so like his face, m'lady, proper gentleman he be, not like that there lieutenant what's born to it—but you've got to take whatsomever you be offered, eh, m'lady?"

"I wouldn't know," Silence replied, trying to be severe, and Bessie laughed uproariously.

"Oh, yes, ee do, m'lady! Do ee think on it!"

And Silence, thinking on it much later, realized what she meant.

Ridgeley appeared at last, foul-tempered and unshaven. He had apparently completely forgotten his confrontation with Silence and Nat, and the boy, his mouth still painful and so badly swollen that he had great difficulty in eating, drinking, and speaking, kept to his chamber, attended by Doraty and Hester, and very much the hero to the other children, who had heard of his defiance from their nurses after a good gossip with Mally. Great care was taken to make no reference to the affair within the earshot of any soldier, and Silence began, amazed, to believe that all memory of it had been erased from Ridgeley's wine-sodden brain.

That night, when the children were safe in bed, surfeited with food and merriment, the wind rose and howled around Wintercombe like a coven of witches shrieking on the rooftops, and in the morning they woke to another blizzard. All that day it snowed, and for most of the following night, until two days after Christmas Silence drew back her curtains to see a white eerie world, a pale yet ominous sky, trees laden with snow so that their bare branches were barely discernible, and drifts higher than a man's waist in unsuspected corners of the courtyard. The soldiers were kept busy clearing paths and tending their horses—already, so Goodenough informed Silence with a curious mixture of sadness and satisfaction, two of the animals had died. But the house was cut off, even from the village. It took Walker nearly an hour to wade up through the drifts from Lyde Green, only just past the mill and not a quarter of a mile away, and riding was out of the question. Wintercombe, besieged by snow, settled down to endure this isolation, as it had endured many similar extremes of weather over the last two or three hundred years, buttressed by its stores and self-sufficient in the cold.

At least, Silence thought, looking out at the white wastes with a resigned eye, the arrival of Sir Thomas Bridges's threatened company would be further delayed. And even if the snow was an inconvenience and worse to the adults, the children reveled in it, and every day could be found in the courtyard, Doraty or Hester huddled in the porch to keep an eye on them, making snowballs, shrieking, throwing, sliding. Silence tried not to appear concerned when they returned dripping wet from their exertions, and reminded herself sternly that they were robust children, quite used to the cold, and had never taken harm before.

She was, however, very surprised when she walked into the barton one morning in search of Clevinger, to see William, bareheaded and soaked, exchanging a vigorous stream of snowballs with three or four soldiers. All of them were convulsed with laughter, none more so than William. As she stood transfixed at the kitchen door, one of his missiles found its target and he leapt up and down, howling with mirth, while the trooper rolled around in the dirty snow in mock anguish, clutching his arm.

At last Silence found her voice. "William!" she yelled, and her son started guiltily, turned and saw her. Not even her presence, however, could quite subdue his effervescent spirits. He scooped up a handful of snow and hurled it in a shower of silver spray, roughly in her direction. Then, still giggling wildly, he attempted to run, tripped over his clinging wet pet-ticoats, and fell flat on his face. Silence reached him at the same time as one of the soldiers. She picked him up, dusted him free of snow and horse dung and straw, and said sternly, "What are you doing here, William? I thought you were in the courtyard with Hester."

"Came to see my friends," William answered, sounding rather indig-nant. "Hester said I could."

"I don't think she did," Silence told him doubtfully. William was too young to lie with the sort of bare-faced evasion that alas characterized Deb, but Hester was a conscientious girl who knew William's wandering habits very well and would not normally let him out of her sight. "Did she really say that, Will? Did she really say you could come here?"

William's eyes dropped, and one wet scuffed brown shoe kicked at the snow. "Don't know," he said at last. "Wanted to see my friends."

Silence looked up at the three soldiers. They were all quite young, hardly more than children themselves, and wore three variations of a shamefaced and sheepish grin. "Are these your friends, William?"

"Yes," the child replied more cheerfully. "That's Harry, and that's Jack, and that's Will, and I'm Cligla."

Silence stared at him in complete bewilderment. "Cligla? What's Cligla?"

"'Tis what Captain Hellier d'call him, m'lady," the most boyish of the soldiers volunteered rather hesitantly. "Cligla, he allus do call him, or Little Boot. Dunno what he d'mean by it, though, m'lady."

"Nor do I," said Silence, looking more closely at the men. None of them had taken part in that Christmas Day cleaning, which indicated that they were either more sober or more hard-headed than some of their comrades. She added curiously, "Tell me—is my son often here?"

"Aye, m'lady," said the one that William had introduced as Jack. "Nearly every day he d'come in the barton, asking questions and looking all around—he d'love we soldiers, m'lady. And he be a nice little lad, though he d'sometimes get in our way. None of us'd harm him, he be quite safe here."

As Silence stared at him doubtfully, the one called Will added quietly, "Oh, we bain't so bad as some, m'lady. Oh, I d'know we be a drunken lolluping crew, but we wouldn't hurt a little lad—not like some as I could tell of."

"Aye—what happened on ashen faggot night, you and the colonel, that weren't right—norn of we did like it, but we was too drunken to do aught," Harry said, with endearing honesty. "Norn of we likes that there Colonel Ridgeley—Old Gallowsbait, we d'call him, or Black Jack. Your other lad, be he doing all right? He weren't hurt bad, were he?"

"He's much better," Silence said, feeling both touched and ashamed. His anxiety was so patently genuine, and she realized that perhaps she had misjudged some of the troopers, tarring them all with Ridgeley's vicious habits. "And I thank you for your concern, and for looking after William so well. Say good-bye to your friends, William."

"G'bye," the infant said, waving energetically with his free hand. The three soldiers waved in return and went back into the barn.

Silence escorted her son briskly through the kitchen and along the passage that led past stillroom and buttery to the main part of the house. At the foot of the stairs, she stopped and knelt down to face him. "William, listen. It was very wrong of you to leave Hester like that and go see your friends. Do you understand?"

William, his round red face serious, nodded solemnly.

"You mustn't keep wandering off. If we lose you, something bad might happen to you, mightn't it?"

"Didn't go near the fall-in," William said, and Silence, despite herself, laughed. Someone else laughed too. William cried happily, "Hullo!" and Captain Hellier said, just beside her,

"Hullo, Caligula."

Silence, feeling herself at a disadvantage kneeling on the cold stone floor, got to her feet and turned, her brows knitted in puzzlement. "Good afternoon, Captain. Do tell me—why do you call William 'Caligula'?"

"Me's Cligla," William said with emphasis. "Little Boot." And he began to tramp up and down on the spot, chanting a tune she had heard the soldiers whistling and that seemed to be some sort of marching song.

At that moment, Hester appeared from the hall, her face anxious. Upon seeing William she brightened at once and cried with relief, "Master William! Wherever have ee been? I've been looking for ee all over." She swooped, and before he realized what was happening William, protesting loudly, was whisked up to the nursery for a change of clothes and a hot eggy posset. Silence was left with Hellier at the foot of the stairs.

"Caligula?" she repeated, and he grinned.

"An emperor of the Romans, my lady, and commonly described as a monster of evil."

"William may be a trifle naughty at times, but I think that's going a little too far," Silence told him.

The grin became wider. "Oh, I don't call him that because of his habits. Caligula himself would make Ridgeley look like an alabaster saint. But his father was a general of the Roman army, and Caligula was brought up among the soldiers. They adored him and made him emperor in the end—a lamentable lapse of judgment. Caligula was their pet name for him—it means Little Boot, because the soldiers made little boots for him, you see."

"It seems that my education has been somewhat lacking," Silence said. "I can recite you all the kings of Israel in their proper order, *and* who begat whom unto the hundredth generation, but Roman emperors are a mystery to me, Captain. As, alas, is a great deal else."

"Then you feel your Puritan upbringing was inadequate?"

It was a remarkably public place in which to lament the limits of her childhood. She cast a covert glance around, saw no one else within earshot, and said bluntly, "Yes, woefully so. Oh, I had all the godly and house-wifely virtues dinned into me until I was ready to spew them forth again—but I was never taught the more feminine arts. I know of no cures for freckles nor recipes for cosmetics, and my garments are strictly practical." She hesitated, wondering whether it was wise to confide in this disarmingly amusing and friendly man, and then added, "They are not things which I consider important, Captain, do not mistake me—I am still a thorough-going Puritan. But it does leave me at something of a disadvantage when I converse with more fashionable ladies. I may be a lady now, but I was not bred up as one, and I am at heart nothing but an honest housewife, rearing her children, managing Wintercombe, ordering the servants. I know no other world—I have done very little, seen very little, know very little."

There was a brief pause, which gave her time to feel the first twinges of embarrassment. Not even with Nat or Mally had she been so revealing. Then, unexpectedly, he smiled. "You do yourself an injustice, Lady St. Barbe. There are other virtues, other wisdoms that you reveal, to which no court lady of fashion would ever aspire."

"I doubt it," Silence said briskly, hoping that he would not see her sudden blush in the dim light. "And now, pray excuse me, Captain—I must go find Goodenough."

His hand came out to detain her, gently. "Before you go, my lady, do explain—what is it that William calls the 'fall-in'? He's always referring to it."

"The well in the kitchen garden," Silence told him. "Doraty and I are forever telling him not to go near it or he'll fall in—so now 'fall-in' is what he calls it."

"And what is the significance of the skummery man?"

"Oh, dear," Silence said after a brief and horrified pause for thought. She glanced around at him apprehensively and saw that, although his lively face was cast in serious lines for once, the corners of his mouth had quirked upward. "Who told you about that?"

"Your daughter Tabitha, on ashen faggot night. She told me, as if conferring a great honor, that she used to call me the skummery man, but now she'd changed her mind. Then William intervened, and I never discovered what she meant by it. Can you tell me, or is it not fit for my delicate ears?"

"Then you're not a Somerset man," Silence said, surprised. "Most of the troop are."

"No—my father came from these parts," Hellier explained. "But I was bred in a foreign land—all of fifty miles distant. I gather it's not a very complimentary epithet."

"Indeed it isn't. She originally referred to you as the autumn-colored man and then decided that was much too pleasant. Skummer is foul water or dirty mud, and she thought it accorded better with your habits. She didn't know you so well then."

"I'm flattered," he said dryly. "Whatever does she call Ridgeley?"

"I haven't dared ask. But I did hear her talking about the bugaboo, which is a child's word for an evil spirit, a demon, or a bogeyman—and I think that Ridgeley was intended."

"The men refer to him as Gallowsbait, or Black Jack. Not a well-loved man, our lieutenant-colonel—and don't look so anxious, I happen to know he's in the barn checking on supplies." He paused and then added, "She has a way with words, your Tabitha—and a very great love of music."

"She doesn't have it from me—another yawning gap in my education, I fear. Her grandfather, Sir Samuel, noticed it too—he was going to introduce her to the virginals, but then he died. Perhaps I can engage someone to teach her, when we are at peace again—but I don't think my husband would approve of such extravagance."

"I could be her tutor," he said.

Silence, astonished, stared at him. "*You,* Captain Hellier? *You* teach Tabby the virginals? Why?"

"Because I have some small skill on the instrument. And because so great a passion for music argues a gift for it, and I do not care to see such things wasted. And because I like the child." He gazed at her, his face utterly serious. "Lady St. Barbe—we are not all drunken brutes and degenerate thieves. I joined the king's army because I cared about the matters involved and because I desired, I fear, a little adventure and excitement— not a particularly praiseworthy reason, but probably a common one. I did not want to rampage about the countryside raping women, robbing farmers, and terrorizing small children. Unfortunately, in a troop such as Ridgeley's, we are all, good and bad, smeared with the same skummer." He smiled briefly. "And though the military life may bring danger, adventure, comradeship, merriment—*and* debauch—there are many things I miss—the gentler arts of music, for instance, conversation, books, poetry. It's not something I would admit very readily, for I'm as wary of ridicule as anyone. But it is one reason for my offer, Lady St. Barbe, and made in all seriousness. I beg you, think upon it for a while, before rejecting my offer out of hand." And he bowed, with that easy, lazy smile, and left her, puzzled and somewhat disturbed, standing at the foot of the stairs.

She did not think he was lying. Years of dealing with the evasions of her children and servants had taught her to recognize untruth, unless most skillfully disguised. And yet it was still very difficult to accept the friendship apparently so genuinely and generously offered from someone she had once loathed and thought to be her enemy.

"Dang the man!" she said aloud in a passable imitation of the local accent, and went to see how William did.

William, warm and cheerful in fresh clothes after his unauthorized excursion, did very well. But that evening at supper he was tired, fretful, and, most unusually, reluctant to eat. Silence ordered an early bed, and watched dubiously as Doraty bore him off without protest, something almost unheard of. She fought down the sudden panic, berating herself for an overanxious mother fussing after her chick like a broody hen, and spent all evening trying not to worry.

As she was preparing for bed, Doraty came to her in some distress. "Oh, m'lady, I didn't want to disturb ee, but 'tis Master William—he've taken some fever, m'lady, and he be tossing and a-turning despeard bad, and crying out for ee—do ee come, m'lady, and see to en."

Mally buttoned up her gown again and carried a candle for her as she made her way with the nurse through the silent sleeping house. The soldiers had supped in the hall, as usual, and the great high room still held the reek of tobacco fumes, although since that disgraceful Christmas their behavior had been more decorous. There was no one about. The moon, high and full on this clear and frosty night, cast slabs of pale light over the floor and across the dimly glowing hearth. As quietly as they could, the three women slipped through the screen and up the stone turret stairs to the first floor. Immediately on their left, opposite Dame Ursula's chamber, virtuously dark, a light showed under the door of the outer of the two rooms allotted to Ridgeley and Harris, his servant and secretary. The mutter of voices came from within, and Silence hurried softly past to William's little chamber, the first of the three along this passage, once a suite for guests and now given over to the younger children and their attendants. Her son slept alone, in a bed much too large, hung with red worsted. A fortunate choice, since the color was supposed to be helpful in cases of fever. He was lying on his back, a thumb in his mouth, his long dark lashes closed on his hot cheeks and his pale hair darkened with sweat and sticking to his forehead. As Silence sat carefully down on the bed, he muttered something, opened his eyes and saw her. "Mama!"

"Yes, I'm here—don't you feel well, William?"

"Hot," the little boy said, trying to throw the blankets off. "Head hurts—make it better, Mama, please make it better!"

"I think it's only a childish fever," she said softly to Doraty. "I'll brew up a remedy at once and sit with him afterward. You watch him now, Doraty—keep him warm, and give him water if he wants it."

The day had been a tiring one, and she had been ready for bed, but all her weariness dropped away as she and Mally descended the stairs and entered the little stillroom, where were made and stored all the potions, preserves, and remedies that kept Wintercombe healthy and nourished during the long months of winter. Shelves lined the walls, under the window, and on either side of the fireplace, bearing all the paraphernalia of distillation and the preparation of medicines: alembics, glass vessels, bowls of varying sizes, a still, pestles and mortars, scales, pans, trivets, dishes, and a varied assortment of pottery jars. Even now, some months after the main labor of preserving and distilling the summer's bounty had been finished, the air smelled sweet, aromatic, and spicy.

It was very cold. Frost ferns flourished on the window, and moonlight striped the floor. Mally closed the door, lit more candles, and set to work on the fire, which had not been used for some days. Silence stood at the table in the center of the room, thumbing through her books of remedies: Gerard's huge, unwieldy *Herbal,* Master Markham's *Advice to the English Housewife,* with which she had been brought up, and the collection of recipes, cures, and simples she had amassed during her years of marriage. Sorrel water, of which she had some quantity, was excellent for fevers, but she did not know if William would like the taste. Of course, any physician would immediately prescribe a blood-letting. Bath was packed with doctors, apothecaries, physicians, and quacks of every kind, but the city was seven miles away across the snowy downs, and they could not even summon the local wisewoman, the Widow Curle, who lived right at the other end of the village. Whether it was indeed a childish fever or something more serious, she would have to deal with it by herself.

She lifted down a bottle of sorrel water, pulled out the stopper, and sniffed it. The recipe advised that it could be kept for a year, and this still smelled fresh. She put it on the table and turned the worn pages of her Markham. Was it a quotidian fever or a tertian? At least the sweat had broken out already, and that was an excellent sign. But she decided to proceed cautiously. If an illness was treated as if it were serious, very often it proved to be mild and harmless. Oil of violets and white poppy seeds, she thought briskly, and went hunting for them along the rows of jars and bottles.

William, as she had feared, disliked the sorrel water and refused to drink it, despite her urgings that it would do him good. He seemed happy, however, to have the violet and poppy-seed ointment rubbed into his back, and the pleasant fragrance of it filled the stuffy little chamber. She bade Doraty stoke up the fire and go to bed, and then settled herself down with William, in case any change should occur.

It was a restless, disturbed night. She slept hardly at all, continually aware of her son's hot little body, tossing and turning in his fever, or crying for water. Despite the oil of violets, he was no easier, and come morning, he had lapsed into delirium.

All that day she stayed at his bedside, totally oblivious to all that went on around her. Her meals appeared, borne on trays by Mally or Eliza, and went away almost untouched. Doraty helped her to sponge the child with clean water, to change his nightshirt while he struggled and shouted, to anoint his back with the violet ointment, and to hold him firm while Silence poured sorrel water down his throat. Aware that this night could well bring a crisis in his sickness, for good or ill, she tried desperately to keep awake.

She failed—and was roused by Doraty, gently shaking her. "Do ee come looksee, m'lady—he be sleeping sweet and sound, thank the good Lord."

She stumbled to the bed, hardly able to believe it, and saw through bleared, exhausted eyes that William, thumb once more in mouth and somewhat thinner than he had been, was deep in peaceful slumber. She touched his forehead, pale gold in the candlelight, and found it cool and slightly damp. "Thanks be to God," she whispered, realizing that in her desperation and anxiety she had taken no thought to pray. Guiltily she sank upon her knees by the bed, but before she was halfway through the first line of the Lord's Prayer, her head was resting on the bedcovers, and she slept.

Mally and Doraty tucked her back into the truckle bed she had used all through William's sickness, and she slept until woken by his voice, undiminished in volume, demanding loudly, "Why's Mama sleeping down there?"

"I *was* sleeping—I'm not now," Silence said, sitting up. "How are you, William? Do you feel better?"

"Want my breakfast," William replied—which was, she reflected ruefully, answer enough.

She broke her fast with William, on frumenty strengthened with cider, and sweet with raisins and dried figs and dates, a very great treat. There was nothing wrong with the child's appetite at all. He cleaned the bowl and asked for more, and Doraty brought buttered eggs with an anxious face that turned to a false bright smile as she walked in through the door.

It deceived William, but Silence was not so easily gulled. As soon as the little boy was safely engrossed in spooning the rich yellow mixture down his chest, across his face, over the bedclothes—in fact almost anywhere but in his mouth—she beckoned the nurse closer. "What is it, Doraty? Is it ill news?"

Doraty's kind mouth was twisted with worry. "I didn't like to tell ee, m'lady, not with the little master took so bad, but there be sickness in the barn. Two of they soldiers were laid low yesterday with a fever just like the little lad's, and Hester, she tell me there be half a dozen more on 'em 'smorning, and all on 'em worser than ever Master William were. And . . . and now Mistress Tabby be saying she have the megrim."

Afterward Silence was to look back upon the next week or so as the worst she had ever experienced. Her world shrank to the hot frowsty chambers where her children fought for life, gripped by a fever whose virulence seemed to increase with the age of its victims, and which roared blazing to its height in a day or two before sinking abruptly into recovery—or death.

Three of the soldiers died, so her servants informed her, with properly solemn faces that could not quite hide their glee. Only the agency of the Lord—or the devil—had saved the rest of the score or so who fell sick, for, packed as they were in that barn, they had none of the warmth and comfort offered to the children, and certainly none of Silence's precious remedies. The bodies were somehow carried by their comrades through the chest-deep drifts that the bitter northeast wind whipped up every night to cover the tracks so laboriously cleared the previous day and interred with reluctance in the churchyard by Parson Willis.

But of this Silence knew little, and cared less. All her heart, her skill, and her desperate energies were bound up with the children. She tended them herself, as she had tended William, taking it in turns with Doraty to watch and nurse while the other snatched an uneasy sleep. Mally, sturdily untainted as ever—"I've took all of they fevers and agues and all mander of what, m'lady, and I bain't likely to take no more"—ran the household, in the process mortally offending Eliza, who thought that the task should have been delegated to her.

So for once, though for the worst of all reasons, Silence was free of the never-ending, never-changing burden of keeping Wintercombe calm, nourished, warm and clean and dry. Two of the scullions, Ned Merrifield and Robin Grindland, fell sick, as did Rob Sheppard, old Turber and his wife, Leah, the two stable lads, and Jemmy Coxe the gardener's boy, so that those still healthy had not only to shoulder their fellows' duties but in addition found themselves nursing the sick. Mally gave Silence frequent reports on their progress, but Silence, beyond noting with weary remoteness that for a miracle no member of the household seemed to have died yet, hardly listened. The only lives that mattered were the children's. She had saved William—could she now save the others?

She had thought that nothing could be worse than Tabby, burning and wasted with fever, clutching at her hands with hot little claws as she begged her mother to take the pain and misery away. Tabby had swallowed every medicine without complaint, the cooling drinks, the juleps made of chicory water, syrup of violets, barberry conserve, and lemon juice, the almond milk and the violet ointment, but nothing seemed to induce that vital sweat, herald of recovery. Deb, a much more difficult patient, threshed and shouted for half a day and a night before waking cool and damp the next morning. But Tabby, her beloved, gentle, secret Tabby, fought the fever for three days and three nights, her struggles growing weaker as the sickness increased its grip.

Silence carried it all on her slight shoulders, the brewing of remedies, the desperate anxiety, the more prosaic duties of nursing, the simple acts of comfort that brought some relief, if only for a time. Deb and William had recovered and now convalesced in the little boy's chamber, watched over by a harassed but indulgent Hester. Sometimes she heard their voices raised in play or, more often, some childish squabble, but she could not yet summon any interest in their progress. Every shred of her willpower was concentrated on Tabby. And at last, on the third night, her care was rewarded, and the little girl sweated and slept, weak but at last on the way to recovery.

And then, history repeating itself like the knell of doom, Doraty told her that Nat was also ill.

It was inevitable. The frail boy had always been prey to any winter cough or cold, chill or ague, and invariably took much longer to throw them off than his more healthy brother and sisters. Rachael, indeed, prided herself on never falling sick, and this fever seemed to have passed her by completely. Rather subdued by the air of crisis within the nursery, she had lent valuable assistance to Hester and Doraty, helping to keep the three younger children amused as they recovered. Occasionally her pale, anxious face would appear around the door of her twin's chamber, her blue eyes stark with strain. And Silence and Doraty would utter platitudes and soothing reassurances that neither they nor Rachael believed, and gently urge her out before the vital heat could dissipate into the chilly corridor outside.

From the onset of Nat's illness, Silence had known in her heart that it was all but hopeless. If she had almost lost Tabby and the sturdily healthy William, how much more vulnerable was their undersized and fragile half-brother? And she and Doraty were exhausted by the days and nights of nursing, the endless worry and labor, the disturbed sleep and the hours spent brewing new cordials and remedies in the stillroom.

Since this was a task only Silence felt herself competent to perform, she spent much time there that should more sensibly have been devoted to rest, and as a consequence seldom managed more than two or three hours sleep in twenty-four. Once she caught sight of her reflection in the window at dusk, her figure divided into a score of small greenish rectangles, and wondered for a second who that skeletal old woman might be, with her pinched shadowed face and the lank mouse-fair hair dropping dully onto her shoulders. Appalled, though she had never possessed a scrap of vanity or beauty, she fastened the shutters and pulled the heavy curtains across.

They were red, like the bed hangings, and borrowed from William's chamber. Even that had not improved Nat's condition, nor could the cordials, juleps, and cooling waters make any impression on the fever. Nat himself, before he lapsed at intervals into delirium, had spoken of his enfeebled state with the resigned, wry humor he always used when on his sickbed. "Do promise, Mother, not to try out any of your more outlandish remedies. Don't go clapping half-pigeons to my feet or anything like that, will you?"

"I wouldn't dream of it," Silence had assured him with a tired smile. "I deal in remedies, not in magic—I'd have to call in the Widow Curle for that. Anyway, I've always heard it said that a bullock's milt serves much the same purpose, and with better results."

Now, sitting in the dim silence of the night, listening to her stepson's irregular, rasping breaths, his mutterings and all the other sounds of a restless, feverish sleep, she wondered with grief if that had been the last time they would ever laugh together. Over the past two years she had come to rely more and more upon Nat, on his cheerful, cynical wisdom, his enormous range of interests, the willing, serious enthusiasm with which he dealt with all sorts of problems, from farm to household to garden. Without him she felt lost, bereft, as if with his passing there would be a dark empty space and a light forever gone out of her life.

Not Nat, she prayed numbly to the silence that bore her name and threatened all around her. I know that my other children have been spared. I know that I am greedy and presumptuous to ask that this one recover too. But he is so dear to me—and I have done all I can to save him, and I don't think it will be enough. Oh, please, let him live—I couldn't bear it if he died—and what of Rachael? They may fight and argue all the time, but they are like two faces of the same coin, and she knows it. She will be even more heartbroken than I if he dies.

If. Gradually, as the night wore on and Nat's fever mounted yet higher, her shrinking mind changed that small word to "when." It was astonishing that he had survived so long. The sturdy soldiers had been struck down in two days, and here was Nat, still clinging obstinately to life on the fourth night of his sickness. Once, in one of his lucid moments, he had whispered to her, "Don't look so worried—I'm not going to die just yet."

But tonight, or this morning, or tomorrow, she knew that he would.

She was so exhausted, in mind as well as body, that she seemed to have gone past mere tiredness into a sort of dreamlike limbo where thoughts and actions came slowly, all her remaining efforts concentrated on keeping awake, if not alert. The little chamber was hot and stuffy, the fire well stoked and glowing with heat, so that she had no need of a rug or a blanket to cover herself as she sat in the chair by the table, too weary even to read or to sew by the light of the one waxen candle beside her. Every so often, principally to keep herself awake, she would rise and walk a little, very quietly up and down the chamber, her soft indoor shoes falling lightly on the rush matting. She replenished the fire, or sprinkled more twigs of dried rosemary and juniper on the logs so that the room smelled richly fragrant, the better to combat the infection. Once or twice she replaced the heavy layers of quilts and blankets that Nat had thrown off in his feverish tossing to and fro, and felt his forehead in vain for signs of the essential sweat. Each time it was still burning hot and dry. And after a while she could hardly bring herself to touch him, so urgent was her hope and so certain her dread of loss.

She stood by the mantel shelf, running her eye once more along the row of curiosities that her stepson had collected over the years. There was a jar full of feathers of all hues and textures, a few oddly shaped or colored stones, some crystals of quartz, a couple of the strange flint objects called elf-bolts, various bones and skins dried or tanned with the help of Diggory Barnes, the tiny commonplace book that Tabby had given him for his fifteenth birthday, a huge rusty key found in the garden at Chard, all so eloquent of that thirst for knowledge, the boundless interest in the world around him, that so soon would be snuffed out . . .

She heard the doorlatch lift, very softly, and a whisper of cold night air coiled about her as the candle flickered. Nat turned, and turned again, flinging out an arm from the imprisoning bedclothes and muttering something. Expecting Doraty, or Hester, she looked around, urgently telling them to shut the door, and then stopped, astonished.

It was no servant that stood there, the paneled door obediently closing behind him. It was Captain Hellier, in doublet rather than buff coat, swordless, his face bearing similar marks of sleeplessness to her own. So weary was she, so remote now from the world he inhabited outside the confines of this sickroom, that she stared at him, bemused, for several seconds before she finally found her voice. "What are you doing here?"

"I am sorry, my lady—if I am intruding, I will go away," he said softly. "But I came to see if I could be of any assistance."

"Assistance? You?" She did not mean to sound so rude, but exhaustion had stripped her words of all but the bare essentials. "How could you help?"

"I have a little skill, and some knowledge. I might be able to." He gave her a swift, tired smile, and then walked quietly over to the boy in the bed. She joined him, seeing as he did the savagely flushed face, the sore scaly hands, the small body, already undersized, wasted away to skin and bone. He stood looking down for a long moment, while Nat shifted and twitched and muttered, his breathing louder and faster, surely, than it had been only an hour before. Then he said, very low, "He is dying, isn't he?"

"No!" she wanted to cry out, denying the terrible truth with all the strength and force left to her. But she was too utterly, utterly weary to say anything other than the one, honest word. "Yes."

"He hasn't sweated yet," Hellier said. "And yet this chamber—it's like a hot thundery day in midsummer. Phew!" And to her complete horror he bent and pulled off half the mound of quilts and blankets shrouding Nat, dragging them to the end of the bed, and then went over to the window.

As she stared, too appalled even to try to stop him, he pulled the curtains briskly apart, unbarred the shutters, and opened the window. A great gust of icy, lethal night air swept in. She gasped and cried, forgetting Nat's uneasy sleep, "No! No, what are you doing, you'll kill him!"

"I doubt it," the captain said, turning, his neat-boned face demonically lit by the wildly guttering candle, so that he looked suddenly, sickeningly evil in the villainous light. "I could hardly draw a decent breath in here, so how could a sick child? And if night air were truly harmful, I'd have died years ago, and so would the rest of all the armies. He should be cooled, that'll help the fever down—all you're doing is to raise it still higher. Have you water, and a cloth?"

Silence did not answer him. Her horror had turned to rage. She stood between him and the bed, her hands clenched into fists, and said furiously, "How dare you! How dare you come bursting in here and dictate to me how I should be treating Nat! You'll kill him! Close the window, *please,* Captain Hellier, close it now, or I will."

"No—listen," he said, and she saw that the expression on his face was gently compassionate, despite the stark shadows around his eyes and under his cheekbones. "Believe me, Lady St. Barbe, I know what I am doing. You said yourself that the boy is dying. I think I can cure him, if you will let me."

The confidence in his voice gave her pause. She said, faltering, still swept by anger at his presumption, "How—how can you be so sure? Are you a physician?"

"No, I am not. But when Mally told me that the boy was like to die, I knew that I must try to save him. But only if you will let me."

Behind her, in the bed, Nat cried out and thrashed about under the lighter burden of covers. She turned, seeing his eyes wild, brilliant with fever, staring past her at something no one else could see, and the knowledge of his imminent death tore at her heart. He would undoubtedly die, despite all her loving, desperate care. And Captain Hellier's calm assurance offered her, suddenly, unbelievably, a slender sliver of hope. If he could work some miracle and snatch this beloved child from the jaws of death, it would be the answer to her fervent prayers.

She clutched at one of the boy's hands, hot and dry-skinned, and held it close. It seemed to ease his restlessness a little. Her decision made, with an inevitability and a chance of hope that terrified her, she looked around at Hellier, standing still and watchful in the center of the little chamber. "Very well," she said, her voice sounding thin and strained to her ears. "Please—do what you can."

Together they propped Nat up on the mound of feather bolsters and pillows, and she pulled off the thick woolen nightshirt, despite his feeble struggles.

Hellier fingered the heavy material as she laid it on the bed. "Were you intending to cure the boy or cook him?"

The cruelty of the remark struck her deep. She felt tears come to her eyes, and blinked them away furiously. Why had she ever thought that this arrogant, supremely self-assured man was her friend? She wanted to answer back in kind, but could think of nothing sufficiently cutting or hurtful. And besides, Nat must be her first priority. With difficulty, she swallowed her hostility and applied herself to sponging his pale scrawny body. So hot was he that she almost expected to see steam rise as she applied the cool damp cloth to his chest. He flinched away from it and tried to fight her off, crying something about cold and ice. Her heart failed her. She stood irresolute, fighting her tears, while the dripping cloth made a large damp patch on the bed.

"No stomach for it?" Hellier said, and the words stung her into action. Biting her lip to stop it quivering, she bent and rubbed Nat all over, leaving a cooling trail of glistening water all over his flushed skin. To her surprise, after that initial struggle he seemed to accept it, even to breathe a little easier. She poured a cup of sorrel water and held it to his lips. He drank a little of it, sucking it greedily in.

"Give him some of this," Hellier said.

She glanced around and saw that he held a small brown glass vial in his hand. She said doubtfully, "What is it?"

"A powder of Peruvian bark. Have you heard of it?"

She nodded slowly, staring at the vial with hungry wonder, as if it held all her hope. "But . . . but I thought it was very rare, and fantastically expensive. Is it genuine? How did you come by it?"

"You don't need to know that—let's just say that I have an acquaintance in Bath who could furnish me with a small supply at reduced rates, in return for a past favor. It's said to be a certain cure for a fever, succeeds where all else has failed—and I can vouch for its potency." He smiled at her, and she realized suddenly that he was almost as exhausted as she. "While you have been nursing your children, I have not exactly been idle either. Nearly a score and a half of the men have suffered it, in varying degrees—and the fact that so far only three of them have died can probably be credited to the Peruvian bark, rather than to my limited skills in medicine."

"You nursed them?" Silence exclaimed in disbelief, while a vision of Captain Hellier wiping fevered brows, administering potions, and comforting the sick arose to tempt her to wild laughter. "And all but three of them have recovered?"

"So far, I said. There are still four or five seriously ill, and of course the infection may not yet have run to its end. But I am hopeful that we are past the worst. And if the Peruvian bark has cured so many, I think there is a good chance that it may save your son."

"He is not my true son," Silence said, looking down at Nat. "But he is as dear to me as if he were. Please, if you think there is a chance, give it to him—how can it be taken?"

"It will dissolve in water. The taste is bitter, but it can be mixed with honey, if you have some here."

She had, in one of the jars of remedies and potions and cordials massed on the table. It was good for all sorts of illnesses, as well as being soothing to a sore throat. She took a spoonful out, and he sprinkled the powder carefully over the thick sweet golden honey, still faintly fragrant with the scent of apple blossom and the summer flowers of her garden. Then, gently but firmly, Silence pushed the spoon into Nat's gasping mouth, while the captain held him. The honey slid down the boy's throat with no trouble, powder and all. He coughed and spluttered a little, and then it was gone.

Hellier laid him back on the pillow with a gentleness and care that surprised her. She wiped Nat's mouth with a corner of the damp cloth, and touched his forehead. It did seem cooler, despite her desperate anxiety about the captain's drastic methods, which flew in the face of all she had been taught, all she had garnered from her years of treating the ailments of her family and her household.

"How long before it begins to take effect?" she asked.

Hellier shrugged. "It varies. Perhaps half an hour, perhaps less. And, Lady St. Barbe, I should warn you, it is not absolutely certain to succeed."

"You mean," Silence said at last, not looking at him or at the child in the bed, "that you have thrown the drowning man a rope just as he sinks for the third time." She could not disguise the agony and the bitterness in her voice. Suddenly her anguish spilled over with her tears, and she rounded on him. "You've come too late, haven't you, and you know it—you've had the remedy all this time, you've fed it to your precious troopers and never given a thought to the rest of us, the ones who have been feeding you and sheltering you all winter. We've had to struggle by on our own resources, while you have this cure hidden away—and William and Tabby nearly died, and now you tell me it might be too late for Nat? If it proves so," Silence said, her voice shaking with grief, "I will never forgive, or forget."

"My lady," he said, and his voice held an appeal in it that she had never heard from any man before. "My lady—I can understand your bitterness. I know how you must feel. But I only received the Peruvian bark this afternoon."

Silence stared at him. The curtains blew in the chill night air, drying the tear tracks cold on her face. She said, "I don't believe you. How could anyone bring anything from Bath, in this snow?"

"There has been a thaw, slight and only temporary, but a man was able to ride out yesterday, carrying various messages for Sir Thomas Bridges. I told him to bring back Peruvian bark, among other medical necessities, and he returned just after dinner today. And if I had known how ill Nat was, I would have brought it sooner."

The curtains flicked across the table, scattering jars. Silence ran to the window and closed it, while the captain set the pots and vials upright. She barred the shutters again, pulled the heavy scarlet folds across, and turned to face him as he stood on the other side of the table. She said, her conscience pricking her, "Please, Captain—if what you say is the truth, then I should never have spoken to you in such a way, and I am truly sorry."

His eyes met hers, and he smiled. "We all say things we regret, especially when tired—and I doubt you've had half as much sleep as I have had, if what I hear is true. And all your patients have been dear to you, whereas I can claim no such bond with those I have nursed. But neither have I been so courteous as I should, and I offer my apologies also. Are we quits?"

It was an expression Nat used. Weary, too exhausted to make any more issue of it, she smiled bleakly in return. "Yes, Captain, I think we are quits."

"Good. I do not like to be in anyone's debt, or to have anyone in mine. Now, perhaps we can see how the patient is doing."

Nat lay restless still in the bed, only partly covered by a couple of blankets and the sheet. He seemed to be trying to pull them higher, and Silence, her heart full and heavy with love and fear and grief, gently laid the bedclothes over his shrunken scrawny body. Tentatively she touched his forehead, and found it cooler—or was it her imagination, distorted by a dogged remnant of hope? It was too early, anyway, for the remedy to have had much effect. All she could do now was watch, and wait, until the die was cast, one way or the other. And of course it was only courteous, though perhaps not seemly, to allow Captain Hellier to watch with her.

I don't give a toss for what is seemly, she thought, sitting down on the chair by the bed. At this moment, I care only about Nat—and I think the house could burn down around my ears and I would not notice, so long as he recovered.

"May I pour you some wine?" Hellier said. She came back to reality with a start, and the unwelcome realization that she had probably neglected her duties as lady of the house. He was indicating the bottle and cup on a wooden tray that Mally, much earlier, had placed on the heavy oaken clothes press near the door.

"Yes, I thank you," she said. He poured with a flourish, and handed it to her with a parody of elaborate courtesy that might, at another time, have raised a smile. Too late, she remembered that there was only one cup. He caught her look of dismay and said, his voice amused, "Don't worry about me, Lady St. Barbe. I have had wine a-plenty this evening—any more and my back teeth will be awash . . . pray do not choke yourself, my lady."

"I won't," Silence said, when she could speak again. Her spluttering attempts not to laugh with a mouthful of wine had resulted in most of it being swallowed the wrong way. "I don't know why, Captain, but you always seem to be making me laugh at the most inopportune moment— and yet what you say is not especially amusing."

"Then it must be the way I say it," Hellier suggested. He had taken his seat at the table, his hands moving among her store of bottles and remedies. "You, or your maids, have been busy this year, my lady—I have rarely seen such an impressive array."

"And to such little effect," Silence said, unable to suppress the uprush of bitterness from her voice. "At the last resort, we're helpless in the face of sickness, aren't we? We bleed our patients, we fill them full of potions, we spout all manner of theories about cold and heat, dry and damp, the four humors and so on, we bind their wounds and treat their symptoms—and sometimes I wonder if we are doing any good at all. Perhaps they would recover—or not—whatever we do."

"Perhaps," Hellier said. "But it's a very defeatist view, isn't it, to leave everything in God's hands—although I know it to be a habit with you Puritans. I prefer to do the best I can to comfort and help, while eschewing the wilder realms of superstition and magic. Why do you smile?"

"Because one of the last things that Nat asked me was not to put pigeons on his feet. And I can't stop thinking of it," she said miserably, impelled by her exhaustion and the wine and the lateness and strangeness and quiet of this situation to confide in him. "I keep thinking that we will never laugh together again."

The response to that came very softly, and not from Hellier. So unexpected was it that for a moment she thought that a ghost had spoken in that almost inaudible whisper. "More fool you, Mother."

For a moment she did not move at all. She sat quite still, her eyes wide, haunted, staring at Hellier. Then, very slowly, hardly daring in case her sudden wild hope would be denied, she turned to look at her stepson.

Nat lay where she had left him, the blankets pulled neatly up to his wizened face. But there was life in it now, the vacancy of delirium had given way to the old, dear spark of intelligence and awareness. "I told you," he said, his voice hardly stirring the air. "I'm not going to die yet."

"And didn't I always say you wouldn't!" Silence said, her joy irradiating her face so that Hellier, coming to the bed, saw that its calm, rather severe lines had been made unexpectedly beautiful. She touched the boy's forehead, found it cool, and her fingers came away lightly filmed with sweat. Then, overcome with exhaustion and relief, she slid from the chair and knelt in prayer by the bed, while Nat, his smile faint and remote, stroked her hand.

Hellier stayed for a long moment, looking down at them with a curious, almost bemused expression on his face. Then, very softly, he turned and left them alone.

TEN

When he speaketh fair, believe him not.
—PROVERBS 26:25

"I *hate* February," Rachael said, glaring out at the steady, relentless rain as if the ferocity of her expression could frighten the water back up into the sky. "I hate it. I wish we could go straight from Christmas to March and miss out January and February altogether. I don't mind March, when spring is coming."

"If we avoid February," Silence pointed out, smiling, "then we also avoid the most important day of the year—to my way of thinking, at least. Have you finished your copy?"

"Yes. What's the most important day? Oh—I remember. Your birthday, Mother."

My birthday, Silence thought, wryly as her hand stroked Pye's sleek mottled fur. My twenty-ninth birthday. And of all the days of the year on which a Puritan's daughter could be born, surely Valentine's is the least appropriate.

"I suppose you'll want a present," Nat said. He was sitting by the fire, well wrapped in two doublets, cushions all about him. Glancing at him, Silence wondered whether he had gained any weight at all in the month or so since his illness. He was shrunken inside all his bundling clothes like a very old man. But he ate enormous amounts of food—Rachael was always making little digs about the size of his appetite—and seemed now to be well on the way to health, or what in Nat passed for that state. Excused study, although his nose could never be kept out of a book for long, he spent most of his days, now that he was not strictly confined to his bed, here in the warmth and companionship of his stepmother's chamber, talking or reading or writing as the fancy took him, his meals served on a tray while, down below in the abused hall, over a hundred men every night caroused, ate, and drank to excess.

The thaw had come three days after Nat's fever broke, and with it, in rain and mud, toiling and slipping to the beat of drum up the treacherous little hill from the Wellow Lane, had come Sir Thomas Bridges's threatened company, some sixty or seventy musketeers, obstreperous, down-at-heel, and led by a solid, heavy-featured captain called, rather appropriately, Bull. These had been quartered in the barn, already packed with the troopers and their equipment, and the two senior officers, Captain Bull and Lieutenant Combe, had been allotted one of the chambers under hers, while Hellier and Byam had perforce to share the other one. Silence had thought this no bad thing, since such an arrangement would necessarily cramp Byam's amorous style. Now, however, since discovering him with Bessie several times in somewhat compromising positions, she was beginning to think this a rather naive hope.

Bessie, indeed, was becoming a problem. Still working willingly and cheerfully in the house and dairy, she was yet adept at snatching illicit moments with the tall, fair lieutenant, who seemed to be following at least the first two parts of the Cavalier philosophy of excessive indulgence in wine, women, and song with boundless enthusiasm. Silence knew, indeed had been told many times by the outraged Eliza, that she ought to dismiss her errant dairymaid forthwith. But though she knew that it should have been done months ago by any truly conscientious and godly housewife, somehow she could not bring herself to turn Bessie out.

At least Leah, who was as amoral as Bessie but much slyer, much more careful, seemed to be conducting herself with some propriety. Silence, however, could not rid herself of the suspicion that the maid, with her devious cunning, had merely arranged her fornication more discreetly.

Anyway, she had more serious worries by far than the activities of her servants. The arrival of all those extra mouths had meant that everyone's food suffered. That superb, lavish Christmas feast had been, as she had suspected, their last glimpse of plenty. The dreary fare of winter, with little in the way of vegetables, fresh milk or cream or eggs, was bad enough in the ordinary way of things, although a skilled cook such as Darby knew a hundred different methods of serving salt beef or stockfish or bacon. Fortunately Clevinger's cow, old Dowsabel, who resided all winter in his stable, fed on good hay and giving milk sufficient for the household's daily needs, remained so far unmolested by the soldiers. But there were no hens left, and several of the sheep had mysteriously disappeared, quite apart from those lambs that had failed to survive the bitter weather and then this incessant rain. February Fill-dyke was certainly living up to its name this year. And the cattle, those remaining in the far pasture out of reach of the hungry troops, were according to Clevinger lean and starveling beasts, with prominent bones and shrunken udders.

Without the soldiers, this winter would have been difficult but not disastrous. The St. Barbes were too wealthy, even in these troubled times, to be greatly discommoded if cattle failed to thrive or lambs were lost. But now, with almost the entire burden of feeding a hundred and five men and forty-six horses cast upon Wintercombe, virtually isolated by the weather, times were hard. They did not go hungry, or cold, but bread, cheese, salt beef, ham and bacon, or variations on these themes, formed all their diet. Delicacies were begged, hidden, or scrounged for Nat and the other convalescents within the household, but the unfortunate soldiers lingering in the barn, cured by Captain Hellier, had no such titbits to aid their recovery. Nor did they have the benefit of Silence's sundew water, a most effective restorative, brewed in the summer months from the leaves and roots of that plant, gathered in the morning during the fullness of the moon, steeped in aqua vitae, mixed with sugar, dates, and liquorice, distilled in her alembic, and administered in beer, half a spoonful at a time. Master Markham had written that this remedy produced a marvelous hungry stomach, and that was certainly true. But she wished that her stepson's ravenous appetite would put some flesh on his scrawny bones. If not, he was in danger of falling into a consumption, though as yet he had none of the other, more ominous symptoms.

She caught his wicked eye and grinned. "Of course I shall want a present, and I shall live in daily expectation of it all through February, I should think. There's small chance of a jaunt to Bath in our present situation."

"I shan't need to go to Bath," Nat said. "I shall produce for you a kingly gift, Mother, from the infinite resources currently at my command."

"A likely story," Rachael said acidly from the windowseat. "Especially since you only have four days in which to do it."

"Not at all—unlike you, dear sister, I plan ahead." Nat gave her one of his most infuriating grins. His twin stuck her tongue out at him and returned to contemplation of the weather, her fingers drumming out an irritated, annoying beat on the glass.

After a space in which Silence exchanged wry grins with her stepson, Rachael said, "Ridgeley's going out again. They're taking . . . ten men, and that awful Byam, and our cart. Wonder who they'll be robbing this time?"

"Yesterday Wellow, Norton the day afore, Hinton afore that—it must be Beckington's turn," Mally said, looking up from her seat in one of the east windows, where she was stitching at a dropped hem on Silence's second-best winter gown. "Some of them can well afford it. Last time they went there, some old gatfer had hid his hens in the bread oven."

Nat chuckled. "And did they find them?"

"Aye, they did—trouble were, he'd forgot the oven were still a mite warm, and there were a powerful stink of burned feathers," Mally replied, grinning. "I do suppose I oughta be sorry for the old boy, but we Nortons don't get along of they snipping stomachy Beckington folk—too mean to pay for their own shrouds, my dad allus said."

"Doubtless they say the same about Norton people," Silence commented. "Like Somerset and Devon, chalk and cheese, dog and cat—the generosity and Christian good nature of Philip's Norton will never mix with the miserly puffed-up inhabitants of Beckington."

Mally, alive to the irony as Eliza would not have been, giggled. "Aye, m'lady, 'tis true. There be only one place worser nor Beckington hereabouts, and that be Charterhouse Hinton. All thieves and villains, sneaking a little patch of land here, a little bit there, and calling en part of their field when the whole wordle d'know 'tis ourn. My granfer had half a strip took, back in King James's time, and he never disremembered en. Couldn't abear a Hinton man, my granfer."

"Typical Somerset farmer—the disposition of an ox, the cunning of a fox, and the memory of an elephant," Nat said, grinning at her.

Mally took his teasing in good part, as he had intended. "The size of an oliphant too, my granfer—two yard high, he were, though you wouldn't think it to look at I and Ned. Oh, m'lady, there be Captain Hellier—shall I let en in?"

The quick double knock was one with which they had all become familiar over the past weeks. Silence, aware of the debt she and Nat owed to him, and prompted by her stepson, had encouraged him to take an interest in the boy's slow recovery, which had so far lasted a fortnight and more. He had formed the habit of dropping into Nat's chamber at least once a day, to see how he did, advise on remedies if asked, and talk to him. After several of these visits, Nat had confided in his stepmother. "You know, it's a shame Captain Hellier is a Cavalier. He's much too nice for one. And he talks of so many interesting things—he's been to Paris, and Rome, and the Low Countries, he's seen so much! I could listen to his traveler's tales for hours, even if half of them are rather tall ones—I'm sure he made up the one about the Papist priest and the dancing bear. And don't look like that, Mother—it was perfectly proper."

"I never doubted it for a moment," Silence had said mendaciously. Hellier puzzled her more and more. There seemed almost to be two people behind the warm chestnut eyes, under the earth-brown hair: the roistering Cavalier, good comrade, drinking companion, ready to swill wine and roar lewd songs with the repellent Ridgeley and the leering Byam, and the quiet, traveled man of the world, who could cure fevers, juggle words, play the fiddle, and turn napkins into hats as if these were the ordinary, commonplace accomplishments of a gentleman. Nat, it was plain, admired him, and that in itself was something of an achievement, for her wise, cynical, shrewd stepson had never hero-worshipped anyone, save perhaps the grandfather whom he so greatly resembled.

The little ones adored Hellier, especially Tabby, who always hung back where the more boisterous William and Deb rushed forward. The lessons on the virginals had had much to do with her changed view of the skummery man. True to his word, he had begun teaching Silence's beloved daughter something of music. She sat in the study, trying to cast her accounts, or keeping her inventories up to date, while next door, in the cozy warmth of the winter parlor, the Cavalier captain explained the mysteries of the keyboard to a fascinated Tabby. It was not long before the first, hesitant one-fingered tune trickled through the door, and Hellier had told Silence that the child showed an unusual aptitude for music and had a very keen ear.

There was not, of course, a lesson every day. Hellier had many duties to perform and little chance of fraternizing with the enemy when there were supplies to requisition, men to drill, messages to write, and all the other tasks that seemed to take up much of the officers' time. But perhaps twice a week or more, Tabby would slip down to the winter parlor, her eyes glowing, and return humming shreds of tunes, with a strange dreamy look on her face, as if she had visited some magical country that no one else understood. Each day, however, the captain would somehow find the time to visit Silence and her family in their refuge, her chamber, warm and safe from the ravages of the soldiers, who could be found almost everywhere else in the house.

Sometimes Silence thought that she was become as much of a recluse as her mother-in-law, who lurked bitter, vengeful, and impotent like an unsuccessful spider in her own chamber, balked of flies and nourished on secondhand news and gossip relayed to her by Ruth. The children now saw their grandmother only in the mornings, and purely as a matter of courtesy, which was rather unfair as they never received anything but abuse in return. But the chilly damp weather had brought its usual harvest of swollen and painful joints, and Dame Ursula was only one of several of the older Wintercombe inhabitants in receipt of Silence's mustard plasters and frankincense ointment.

Mally opened the door with a brief bobbing curtsy—she still did not entirely trust the captain—and Hellier came in. "Good afternoon, my Lady St. Barbe. Hullo, Nat—I have an hour or so, sufficient time for a game of chess, I think."

As Nat agreed with enthusiasm, Rachael scrambled down from the oriel windowseat with her usual abrupt lack of grace. "Pray excuse me, Mother," she said, her voice flat and hostile. "I promised I would help Margery in the dairy today." She ignored Hellier completely as she marched past him, but with her hand on the door, she added loudly, "There seems to be a noxious stench in here. Perhaps it's a rat—I should have it killed, Mother."

"*Rachael!*"

The slam of the door was her stepdaughter's answer. Silence sighed and gave Hellier a rueful, apologetic smile. "I am very sorry about that. This time she has gone too far—I shall speak to her later."

"It won't do any good," Nat said. "No one can make Rachael do anything other than what *she* wants to do—not even Father."

"She's hardly more than a child," Hellier pointed out. "And she has every right to detest me and all the rest of my ungodly comrades. I don't want her punished on my account, Lady St. Barbe—that would hardly improve matters."

"I shall speak to her on *my* account," Silence said. The sharpness of her anger had surprised her. "And it is generous of you to make allowances for her, Captain, but she is hardly a child—the twins turned fifteen in November."

"Twins?" Hellier stared at Nat, so much smaller yet so much more mature than his turbulent sister, in disbelief. "You and Rachael are twins?"

"Unfortunately, yes," Nat said, not at all disconcerted. He had long ago come to terms with his size, even if he remained a little touchy about his perpetual ill health. "I got the short straw," he added with a cheerful grin. "It comes in useful for wheedling the stallkeepers at the fair or the market. I persuade a mountain of gingerbread from them."

"You liar, Nat—you don't even like gingerbread!"

"I can tell tales as well as the next man," Nat said, bright-eyed and mischievous. "Well, Captain, will you set out the board? If my memory serves, you are a game ahead, and I am determined to have the trouncing of you this time. And I warn you, do not attempt to hand me the victory on a plate from misplaced kindness."

"Your skills are such, I doubt I could," Hellier said dryly. He placed the pieces on the heavy checkered board, making, wisely, no effort to help Nat as he struggled doggedly up from the chair and made his slow, careful way to the table. Neither did Silence, though she watched his uncertain progress with covert, anxious eyes before returning again to the cuff that she was mending. For a while a companionable quiet descended upon her chamber, broken only by the steady beat of the rain, the click of the chessmen and the soft voices of the players, and Pye's irregular, throaty purrs. The younger children were in the nursery, and Tabby practicing her music, so there was peace for once. Silence was fast losing patience with Deb's incessant harping on the subject dearest to the little girl's heart, food. Apart from anything else, it only served to increase her own hunger.

Her stomach growled, plainly audible, and she caught Mally's eye with a rueful grin. There had been but two courses at dinner, and both plainly dressed. She had risen from the table not exactly hungry but not satisfied either, a state of affairs all too common now. And how could she fill her own belly when all about her the children gazed longingly at the scant fare laid before them and wolfed down each mouthful with ravenous appetite? For that reason alone she hoped that Ridgeley and his men would return well laden from parsimonious Beckington.

"Check!" Nat announced with satisfaction. There was a brisk flurry of moves and a considerable exchange of pieces, before he pushed an insignificant pawn at Hellier's beleaguered king, backed into a corner, and locked the trap shut. "And mate. Six games all."

"I'm glad you've found a worthy opponent," Silence said as Nat laid the men back in their box. "It takes you about five minutes to overcome my feeble resistance."

"Oh, no, Mother—all of ten now," Nat said, laughing. "Thank you very much, Captain Hellier. I greatly enjoyed that." He got to his feet, glanced at Silence, and said, "Please excuse me, Mother, Captain. I have to get a book from my chamber—I forgot to bring it up this morning."

"Oh, no, ee don't!" Mally exclaimed, jumping to her feet. "Do ee tell I what you d'want, Master Nat, and I'll go for en."

"*I'll* go," Nat said, with a firmness that brooked no opposition. "I came up here this morning, didn't I? How am I going to get better if I'm mollycoddling myself in front of the fire all day? It's about time I did something for myself." He walked slowly to the door, opened it without seeming to lean too much on the latch for support, and added with a grin, "But I'll let you come and pick me up, Mally, if I fall down the stairs—just you sit and wait for the crash."

There was, of course, no sound of it. Nat's determination was such that Silence knew he would return triumphantly, book in hand, even if it were an hour later. Mally sat down again, sighing. "He won't be told, will he, our Master Nat. And I d'suppose 'tisn't no use trying to, for he allus d'go his own way."

"And we must let him, hard though it is," Silence said wryly. She put down the finished cuff and surveyed her visitor, still sitting at the walnut table in front of the empty chessboard. "What news do you bring today, Captain, of the world beyond this chamber? What outrages have occurred since last we spoke?"

"Nothing of great moment," Hellier said, getting up and strolling over to the hearth. "That cat has the loudest purr I have ever heard—was her mother a lion's daughter?"

"You could be right—she has the soul of one. But as for purring, this is not the best she can do. When she has kittens, *then* she purrs. But that won't be until the summer, so perhaps you will not hear it."

"I should think we'll still be here," the captain said. He ran his finger along the intricate carvings of the mantel. Silence found herself watching to see if he picked up any dust, and gave herself a mental kick. "It will take an army to dislodge this particular crew of limpets. Compared to the garrison of Bristol, we have things very easy here. No plague, no filth, a plentiful supply of good food and clean water, a little innocent requisitioning here, some wenching there, and no fighting. Make no mistake, my lady, these particular soldiers won't budge until Waller himself appears at the gates."

She felt the gooseflesh rise chilly on her arms, even under the thick warm woolen folds of the mulberry gown, her third best. Trying to make her voice light, she said, "Then I shall pray that Waller comes swiftly to our rescue. Where is he at present? Have you heard?"

News came regularly to Wintercombe, with more formal messages from the governor at Bath. It irked her that there was at present no other way of knowing how the war progressed. She had not heard from her husband since September. She did not even know if he had had her letter telling him of his father's death. Nor had she received any word from her brother and sisters in London since before Christmas. This was hardly surprising, since the roads must be in an appalling state after so much snow and rain, not to mention the activities of hostile soldiers, but she missed their words of cheer and the family jokes, the bold hand of Prue and the swift scrawl that belonged to Patience. Even Joseph's earnest debates, once so annoying, would be welcome now. She had written to them many times, and had a letter in hand in her writing desk that would be added to each day and sent as soon as the weather improved. But for now she must rely on tidings heavily larded with Royalist bias, if she wanted to know even a little of the situation outside the confines of Wintercombe.

The weather had isolated them often enough before, but never had she felt this sense of impotent, frustrated helplessness.

"Waller's army are in winter quarters in Farnham or thereabouts," Hellier told her. "I should imagine that your absent husband is with him. There are said to be plans afoot for him to lead six thousand horse into the west as soon as the weather improves. Your friends in the Parliament have spent their winter reorganizing their armies—and not before time, you might think, though of course my point of view is somewhat different from yours, my lady. Fairfax, the Yorkshireman, is apparently appointed general. There is little other news—this incessant rain is not helpful to campaigning, and things seem very quiet. Goring, who as you may know has a reputation even more evil than Ridgeley's, is at Salisbury. And there you have it, Lady St. Barbe—all the news at present, from the western parts, presented to you by your own speaking newsletter."

"Thank you," Silence said. She sat still for a moment, staring into the deep red heart of the fire, stroking Pye. Then she added a little hesitantly, "Captain Hellier . . . Waller was involved, was he not, in a battle some months ago?"

"He was indeed—at Newbury, it was, at the end of October, just before we arrived here. Why do you ask? Are you concerned for your husband's safety?"

"Of course I am," Silence said with some asperity. "And for Sam, his eldest son, who is hardly more than a boy. And I have not heard from my husband since before the battle."

There was a brief, taut pause. Hellier said softly, "Do you wish me to make inquiries? What rank does he hold?"

"He is colonel of a regiment of foot—it would not be difficult to find out if . . . if he were safe," Silence said carefully. "If you could do that, I would be most grateful. Although it must be done discreetly, I think. You have angered Sir Thomas Bridges enough already by helping me."

"It wouldn't harm my military career, such as it is. The king's army is awash with colonels, lieutenant-colonels, and majors who have lost their regiments and have nothing to do but kick their heels in Oxford, get drunk, and reminisce about their past exploits—no mere captain has a hope of promotion as matters stand, save over the bodies of his senior officers. And as a motive for mass murder," Hellier said, very straight-faced, "I don't think that rates particularly high, do you?"

"And you are not intent on military glory, either?"

"Hardly," he said, laughing suddenly. "My dear lady, do I *look* like a hero? I have never been careless of my life. I'll leave feats of bravery and derring-do to others, less cautious than I am, and probably a great deal more foolish. No man—or woman—of intelligence is anything other than a coward."

She thought suddenly of Sam, her eldest stepson, the true child of his father, big-boned and ruddy of face, bold and eager and aflame with the glory of it, riding off to war in a buff coat so new that it creaked, armored in his ignorance. She said slowly, "That may very well be true, Captain. But surely it takes courage, though of a slightly different order, to admit as much?"

"I doubt it. I, my lady, am an opportunist pure and simple. Life in a garrison such as this is infinitely preferable to the hurly-burly of the field army, different quarters every night, desertions, fleas in the bed, if you get a bed, bullets flying right past you or, if you're very unlucky, right through you, cold, damp, misery, exhaustion, riding until you and your horse drop . . . oh, I have experienced all these things, and believe me, Wintercombe's clean and most comfortable feather beds are pure heaven by comparison. Besides, when the enemy attacks I would much rather be safe and secure behind solid stone taking pot shots at them than out in the open with only a buff coat for protection." And he gave her the long, slow, very amused smile that stretched his mouth and curled it up at the corners, and lent a completely different look to his neat, sharp, lively face.

"Then I shall have to arrange a nice, muddy, inconvenient, and uncomfortable battle for you," Silence said as briskly as if he were a slug-abed servant. "With plenty of musket balls whistling past your ears, and rain as ceaseless as before the Flood, and preferably dark."

"Don't wish too hard—if that comes to pass, it will most likely be here."

She felt once more the claw of fear clutching at the pit of her stomach. She said, quite calmly, "But this house is not a fortress, Captain."

"Not yet. I am not supposed to tell you this, but the order came from Bath yesterday. As soon as the weather improves, Wintercombe is to be put in a state of defense."

She stared at him, appalled. He added, with some sympathy, "This is only what Sir Thomas Bridges told you would happen before Christmas. The reckoning has been delayed until now because of the snow and rain. You knew it would happen eventually."

"Perhaps," Silence murmured. She had recovered a little of her composure and was able to look up at him with some trace of her rueful smile. "But I am also aware of the certainty of my eventual decease, Captain. That doesn't make it any easier to bear, when it approaches too soon. Oh, I can remember only too clearly what the Governor of Bath told me. But after two months, during which I have had rather a lot of things on my mind, I was allowing myself to hope a little."

"Misplaced, I'm afraid," he said. "Sir Thomas is not one to forget where matters of personal animosity are concerned."

"I can imagine it," Silence said, thinking of that immaculate and entirely unsympathetic face. "Well, I suppose we must pray for a continuation of the rain, even if it does play havoc with the plowing. But if the Lord does not choose to answer our prayers, then I suppose we must do as we have done over the past months, and make the best of it. And I would be grateful if you could tell me, Captain Hellier, I am so ignorant of military matters—what exactly is meant by 'a state of defense'?"

"Walls," Nat said, entering at that moment, a little flushed and breathing fast but otherwise unaffected by his arduous journey across the house. He shut the door and came over to the hearth, his book in his hand. "Walls and dykes and fences and ditches and cannons and unpleasant things called swine's feathers—am I right, Captain? I thought so. Is that what is going to be done here?"

"Apparently," Silence told him. She turned to Hellier, trying not to show her anxiety. "Please, Captain, tell me if you can—what are they going to do? Are your men going to build all of those things around Wintercombe?"

"What she really means," Nat said, his hand resting affectionately on his stepmother's shoulder, "is are you going to dig up her garden?"

"My garden doesn't really matter," Silence said sadly. "It doesn't matter at all, beside the prospect of Wintercombe suffering siege and battle and slaughter—the danger to us all, if this house is made into a fortress. Because you can only defend what is capable of defense, can't you, Captain?

And if we are surrounded by walls and ditches, then any passing Parliament force will have to attack, whereas one small manor house in a position that isn't especially prominent might escape their notice, even if a hundred soldiers are billeted there. But they can't afford to ignore a fortress."

"Unfortunately, you are quite right," Hellier said. "I can tell you what the plans are for the fortifications—they will be obvious enough, after all, once they're dug and built. There is an old wall on the north side of the courtyard, and a ditch beyond it, skirting the track. The idea, I believe, is to raise the wall a foot or so higher, dig out the ditch, and use those two dovecotes as lookout towers."

"And where will the doves go?" Nat inquired. "Those of them that are left, of course—we've had pigeon pie too often recently for there to be many still alive."

"The doves don't matter," Silence said. "They'll roost in the ruined tower at the far end of the yew walk—perhaps some of Captain Hellier's nice kind soldiers would help to rebuild it? No? Oh, well, it was a thought."

"And what about the south side of the house?" Nat went on. "I know that attack would most likely come from the north, because that's where the road is, but foot soldiers could easily work their way along the valley, cross the stream and come up the terraces. If poor Mother's garden is not to be sacrificed, you must somehow fortify around the orchard—and it's a considerable distance to patrol."

Silence surveyed him with wry amusement. "Dear Nat, Captain Hellier is supposed to be our enemy, even if he has somehow come to be our friend as well. You aren't supposed to advise him how to defend Wintercombe with quite so much enthusiasm."

"You know me," Nat said ruefully. "If a problem is presented to me, I have an insatiable desire to solve it. Mally? Is there paper there, and ink? Thank you."

"You're going to draw him a *map*?" his stepmother asked, after a startled pause in which Nat, supplied with his requirements, sat down in one of the other fireside chairs, board and paper on his knees, and dipped his quill thoughtfully into the ink. "Nat, I don't think—"

"I know you don't want me to," Nat said gently, the pen scratching busily across the paper while Hellier, a glint of amusement in his eyes, stood behind him to watch. "But isn't this the more sensible way? We know the land, what it will bear and what we do not want destroyed. If I show Captain Hellier where to dig, your garden *and* the orchard will be safer—if not entirely secure."

"And what if, through no malicious intent of course, you tell us to dig in the wrong place?" Hellier inquired. Nat's flying quill was delineating the plan of the house and grounds, an irregularly shaped T, two sides of a square around the north courtyard, the barton to the west, the bowling green and yew walk to the east, and on the south side the lovely terraced gardens falling away to the orchard, the fishponds and the stream at the foot of the tiny valley. Beyond was pasture and meadow, sloping up again to the next low ridge hiding the cottages at Ringwell, and the gray stone tiles and golden church tower of Philip's Norton.

"No malicious intent, of course," said Nat. Silence hoped that Hellier could not see his secret, mischievous smile. "I think, Captain, that you would be best advised to dig ditches here." The quill stabbed down at the hedges and ponds bordering the lower end of the orchard. "Water is one of the best and surest defenses. Wintercombe has never had a moat—it's wrongly sited for that, on the top of the hill. But you can dig one down here—join the two ponds to the stream with an even wider channel, and make the stream broader and deeper still. You could even try damming it, which would flood the valley but leave the house and gardens dry. The lower part of the orchard would sit in water, of course, but I doubt it'll do the trees much harm. Then you dig ditches down from the barton to the pond, and from the lowest terrace to the stream, here, and you have the house encircled." He glanced at Silence, his smile a secret from Hellier at his back. "That's my advice, anyway, Captain—you can take it or leave it, as you choose."

"It's not up to me to decide," Hellier pointed out. "Colonel Ridgeley, of course, is put in charge of the fortifications, though I fear he has precious little experience of such matters and does not in the least want to reveal that fact. He might listen to me—he certainly would not listen to you."

"Well, more fool him," Nat said, and with a sudden, swift movement crumpled the map and threw it lightly onto the fire.

Much later, he explained himself to Silence in response to her puzzled questions. "I know he's in some sort our friend—but the rest of them are much, much worse. I wouldn't advise Ridgeley not to put his hand down a cannon while I lit the match. And remember, all the ground hereabouts is that heavy red clay."

"How could I not, when poor Eliza spends all her time scrubbing it off the floors for the troopers to tramp it in again?"

"Exactly. It holds water like a sponge—good for meadows, not so good for digging ditches. They'll fill with water all right, from the first turn of the spade. I've seen the ditches and channels dug for the water meadows along the Norton Brook—they're never dry, even in summer, unless there's a long drought. They'll be working up to their knees in water, and every spadeful will weigh as heavy as lead. So I thought that if I encouraged them to dig down by the stream, rather than the obvious thing, which is to fortify the terraces, they might leave your garden alone. And if Ridgeley is as ignorant and pig-headed as Hellier implied, once he starts he won't give up very readily. With luck, it'll keep all the troops out of the house, exhaust them so they've got no energy for carousing in the evening, *and* they'll take all summer over it."

"Nat," Silence said, shaking her head, "you are the most devious person I have ever met—excepting your grandfather, of course."

"Oh," her stepson said, his eyes modestly and mischievously cast down, "I only study to emulate him."

Which, Silence thought, he already did quite adequately.

For a miracle, it did not rain on her birthday, Valentine's Day, when all the birds chose their mates, and in less serious households there was much play with notes and assignations, and gifts. Such things, of course, were not seen at Wintercombe, although there was some giggling among the maids and a lighthearted exchange of ill-spelled pieces of paper. This resulted, through the machinations of Leah, in Bessie unwittingly choosing Rob Sheppard, who had lusted vainly after her for years, as her Valentine. The unfortunate assistant cook, once he had realized the trick played upon him, took such umbrage, despite Bessie's attempts to defuse the situation with her usual cheerful good humor, that he swore never to work in the company of such rogues and whores again, packed his bags, and trudged off in the cold morning sunshine to Bath, declaring his intention of becoming a soldier for the Parliament.

"But there bain't no Parliament men in Bath!" Bessie had called after him in astonishment.

Sheppard had turned and yelled back, "Then I'll take the king's coin instead—anything be better than watching ee whoring after that there Byam."

The story was related to Silence by Eliza, who always enjoyed being first with tales of disaster. She was also quite plainly expecting, with barely concealed glee, that Bessie would at last be dismissed forthwith. She was disappointed. Silence had no intention at all of turning off one of the best dairymaids in North Somerset, whatever her morals—and besides, as she pointed out to the resentful Eliza, in this particular matter Bessie was entirely innocent, as much a dupe as poor Sheppard. If anyone were to be dismissed, it should be Leah, who had maliciously caused the trouble in the first place.

"Aye, her and all," Eliza said indignantly. "And she no better than what she should be, as bad as that there Bessie she be, though she d'take good care to hide that light of hern under a girt thick bushel."

"I am as well aware of it as you are, Eliza," Silence said, disguising her stab of annoyance beneath her habitual calm shell. "And rest assured, I shall keep a very close eye on the situation."

Eliza went away muttering and dissatisfied, and Silence sighed with a mixture of relief and dismay. She knew that when Sir George returned, the maid would lose no time in airing all her various grievances to him, although he would undoubtedly regard such things as his wife's domain. It was certain, however, that he would not ignore Bessie's lewd and immoral behavior under his own roof. The reckoning was bound to come, later if not sooner, when Dame Ursula found herself transformed by her son's return from a bitter, impotent recluse to her old position as the beloved, influential mother of the master of the house.

It was not a pleasant prospect. Another woman, less bound by duty and conscience, might have wished the war to go on forever. Silence, under a dismal cloud of foreboding that entirely spoiled her day, stared out at the pale yellow sunshine and decided to lift her spirits with a walk in the garden.

It was early yet. Their breakfast was not ready, the children still were being dressed by the two nurses. Sheppard's departure had indeed been hasty, and Silence, warmly wrapped in cloak and hood and scarf, descended her stairs thoughtfully. Could they manage without him? Certainly Darby would be happier without an assistant, and there were still the three boy scullions, Ned, Will, and Robin, to chop vegetables, scour pans, stir pots, and generally keep the kitchen clean and tidy. The soldiers had of course caused a great deal of extra work, but half a dozen men had been detailed to help on a regular basis, preparing the simple, filling stews and broths and puddings and bread upon which their comrades were fed. No, Sheppard was not indispensable at all, and if his resignation led to greater harmony in the kitchen, then it might even be a good thing.

Lost in her thoughts, she wandered down the last few steps and nearly bumped into Captain Hellier, lurking at the bottom. Startled, Silence jumped back almost into Mally, who was following her. "Oh! Captain, you surprised me."

"I am sorry," he said, smiling. The look on his face had something of mischief on it, and his hands were hidden behind his back. "I have been waiting, Lady St. Barbe, to claim you as my Valentine."

"What!" Silence stared at him in complete astonishment. "Me—your Valentine? Oh, Captain, don't be so ridiculous. We don't have such customs in this family."

"Which is where your servants are perhaps more carefree and lighthearted than yourself, my lady Puritan. I can assure you, it's the custom among my friends and family, a nice diverting game to be played at the dreariest time of the year. Where's the harm in it? Or did your father think it a filthy lewd pagan festival to be shunned by the godly?"

"Well, yes, I'm rather afraid he did," Silence said. She had recovered her composure and was regarding Hellier with considerable amusement. "So I am completely ignorant of the correct behavior on such an occasion. The servants seem to draw lots—do you follow another fashion?"

"Among my friends it is the rule that their Valentine is the first member of the other sex whom they meet on this morning. A small gift is also usual—and since I understand from Tabby that it is your birthday today, you can accept it as a token of that if you would rather. I think we are good enough friends for it?"

"Perhaps," Silence said, a little warily as he brought out a small package from behind his back. "Captain, really, I am very grateful, but you do me too much honor. Not even my husband takes the trouble to buy me a birthday present."

"Doesn't he?" Hellier's winged eyebrows raised a little. "More fool him, as Nat would say. Anyway, in his unfortunate absence, pray accept this small token of my esteem."

Laughing at his extravagant tones, she took the package, wrapped in plain paper, tied with red ribbon, and sealed with wax. It felt soft and yielding—a scarf? she wondered, puzzled, sliding the ribbon off and undoing the paper with fingers that were quite calm, despite her sudden inward excitement. She had never before received a gift from anyone outside her own close family.

A pair of soft leather gloves, fringed, tasseled, embroidered, perfumed, and quite unsuitable for a sober godly housewife, lay fragrant in her hands. She turned them over, feeling their fine quality, the exquisite stitching, and realized that they must have cost a great deal of money.

They were also quite beautiful—the loveliest present she had ever received.

"Do you not like them?" Hellier inquired. She looked up, seeing his face still wearing that amused, quizzical expression, and shook her head so emphatically that her hood descended onto her shoulders.

"No—oh, no, Captain, thank you so much, they're truly beautiful—but I cannot possibly accept them."

"Well, that's a shame, for I cannot possibly take them back."

"I'll have 'em," said Mally. She had retreated to the second step, the better to see over Silence's shoulder. "I'll have 'em, m'lady, if you don't. And if you won't take 'em, then think on what Master Nat do allus say."

Silence looked round at her. "Be you betwitting I, my Mally?"

The girl exploded into sudden giggles. "No, that I bain't, m'lady. You go on and take they gloves—they be too good for the likes of I."

"It seems I will have to bow to circumstance," Silence said, and her maid burbled softly on with her laughter. "You and Mally between you have convinced me—but I don't think I shall wear them very often. They are too fine to use as gardening gloves or to ruin by riding in them. I shall lay them away very carefully in my clothes press, between lavender and rose petals, and I shall bring them out to show my grandchildren."

"By all means—they are not intended for hard wear," he said. "I am glad they will be cherished and kept safe. But will you not wear them now, at least, if you are going outside?"

She took off her plain rubbed pair that were grubby from pulling stray weeds and slid her hands into his gift. The leather was soft, warm, and lapped her fingers like a caress. Suddenly reckless, as if that earlier, despondent mood had never been, she thought happily, It is my birthday, and what do I care if it's my twenty-ninth? I have my life, my health, my children and my friends, and someone I have come to like has given me a very beautiful present. And for the moment I care about nothing else.

She gave Hellier one of her rare full smiles and extended her arm. "Since I now have your gift to parade, Captain, will you not stroll in the garden with me? It's such a lovely morning."

"Of course," he said, bowing courteously, and took her elbow while Mally unbolted the door that led from the garden room onto the terrace.

It was cold outside, and the sun had barely hauled itself above the distant eastern hill. As they walked down the steps, she saw that deep pools of shadow still filled the square knots along the terrace. The tops of the low box hedges glistened with silver frost, and the neatly raked gravel crunched like snow under their feet. Silence exhaled for the pure pleasure of seeing her breath plume into the air like dragon's smoke and took a deep draft of sharp, chilly air, still smelling of night frost and tinged with the aroma from Wintercombe's busy chimneys. "How wonderful, to see the sun on my birthday!"

"Especially since it is not the brightest time of the year," Hellier said. "What was your good Puritan mother thinking of, to bring you forth on *Valentine's* day, of all the calendar?"

"I doubt she had any choice in the matter," Silence said dryly. "Though my father, as you may imagine, had much to say about it, then and later. I think he feared it would make me lewd and light-minded."

"And was he right?"

"Half right. I think I can safely say, Captain, that I am not lewd. But I fear that especially on days like this one, when spring suddenly seems so near, I become sadly afflicted with sinful levity."

"You are a very unusual Puritan, Lady St. Barbe. Perhaps I have been misled, and you are not one at all, but a beautiful lady with curls and dimples and satin and jewels, masquerading beneath that sober garb."

"This is almost my best," Silence said, with mock indignation. "But, sir, you have indeed been misled as to the nature of Puritans. We are not all gloomy souls who wrestle dourly with their own consciences and meddle in everyone else's. Oh, I agree that my father did, but even among Puritans he was extreme. I think now that perhaps many of those he called friend actually found him very tedious and dreary company. Rather like Dame Ursula, he did not enjoy his days, and resented anyone who did."

"He sounds truly appalling," Hellier commented. "How come, then, that you emerged from such a household with your levity intact?"

"My mother was partly to blame for that. She was ill for much of my childhood, but she was a good and godly housewife who loved music and laughter, even so. And *her* mother was a merry old woman who was selling fish in Billingsgate when she was fourteen." Silence glanced around at Hellier to see how he had taken this shocking piece of information, and noted the creases of laughter about his eyes and mouth with approval. "My goodness, Captain, you do not faint away in horror at the thought of Lady St. Barbe being a fishwife's granddaughter—you can't be as aristocratic as I'd assumed."

"I'm no aristocrat, my lady—and some would vow I was no gentleman either," Hellier said. "I am not in the least shocked—it's a common enough tale, after all. And in my view, it means that your grandmother must have been a woman of exceptional spirit, intelligence, and ability."

"She was indeed, though all I have of her is a liking for common sense and a dislike of pretension and pride and fancy frills and furbelows—so perhaps I'm a Puritan because of her."

They were strolling along the upper terrace toward the summerhouse, where at this time of year garden tools and equipment were stored. Iceferns swirled across its windows and frost crowned the graceful cupola roof with silver on gold. "Such a pretty building," Silence said, her voice quiet and wistful. "My husband's grandfather laid out all these gardens in what he fondly imagined to be the Italian manner and intended this for a banqueting house. But he died just after it was finished, and held never a feast nor a banquet in it, and his son, Sir Samuel, had no patience with such fripperies. He preferred honest roast beef and beer to foreign sugary kickshaws and sweet wines, he always said, and did not use it. So it has never been employed for its proper purpose. Diggory keeps his spades and forks and barrows in it, and I sit there sometimes—it's cool on a hot summer day, and you can see all the garden. The children like to play inside it too. But I feel almost sorry for it—it's so pretty, and so useless."

"But its beauty is its purpose," said Hellier, looking up at the sweet curve of the roof against the eggshell-blue sky and the ridiculous wyvern perched uncomfortably on top, holding a shield carved with the checkered St. Barbe arms. "To denigrate it for being useless is to deny the lilies of the field their purpose—'they toil not, neither do they spin, yet even Solomon in all his glory was not arrayed like one of these.' And doubtless, my lady Puritan, you can give me chapter and verse for that."

"You have not quoted it quite correctly, but near enough—Matthew, six, verses twenty-eight and twenty-nine," Silence said. "And if I am not in the usual run of Puritans, Captain Hellier, then you are most assuredly not the pattern of a Cavalier."

"Why not? I drink wine, frequently to excess, I enjoy the company of women, and I have a mind full of song. I fear your image of your typical king's officer has been as much distorted by rumor, bias, and malice as has mine of Puritans."

"So we are quits," Silence said. With one last glance at the lovely, abandoned summerhouse, she walked down the steps beside it to the lowest terrace. Much wider than the one above, this too was full of knots in neat rows, edged with box and islanded by gravel, but down the middle marched the long arbor of cherry trees, trained and tortured by Diggory over many years into an arched walk, interlaced with scrambling sweetbriar roses that gave flowers and scent when the cherry blossom was over. The bare tangled branches threw long and fantastic shadows over the gravel beneath. With a sudden and urgent desire for summer and warmth, light and color and humming bees and the fragrance of her flowers, Silence wandered down the narrow pathway by the balustrade, glancing occasionally at the orchard below, while Hellier, apparently content to be her silent escort, strolled just behind. As a misshapen shadow moved in the ragged grass between the apple trees, his footsteps stopped abruptly.

"What's that?"

"That?" Silence peered at the shape and smiled. "Oh, that's Dumbledore—Tabby's and Deb's pony. Poor fellow, he's never given shelter, whatever the weather."

"I don't think he needs it," Hellier said, as the shaggy shape of the small fat horse emerged into fuller view. "How do you tell which end is which, when he's standing still?"

"Offer him an apple—you'll soon find out." Silence leaned on the balustrade, clicking her fingers, and called softly, "Dumble—here, boy."

The round furry bay pony shambled into something like a trot, spurred on by the possibility of food, and arrived below her with a long blubbering snort of welcome. He had burrs in his mane and mud on his bulging quarters, and his brown long-lashed eyes were hopeful and kind. Silence reached into the pocket of her apron and dropped a piece of sugar onto his broad woolly back. The pony shook it onto the ground and crunched it with satisfaction. Hellier laughed. "Another well-trained animal! Why is he called Dumbledore? What is it?"

"A bumblebee—or, alternatively, someone stupid. Poor Dumble fits both descriptions very nicely, but he's a dear gentle soul, just right for a first pony. No, you greedy old nag, I haven't got any more. You'd eat us out of sugar if you could, slobbering old gulcher—go on, off with you."

The pony, reluctant to leave a source of food, stayed close to the terrace wall, looking expectantly up, and produced a low hopeful whicker. Silence hardened her heart and turned away to look at the rows of knots. She gave a sudden cry of delight and knelt by the nearest. "Oh, how lovely—the snowdrops are out!"

They were indeed, in a pale, hesitant way, the heavy flowers just beginning to droop on the long green stalks. "They're late," she explained as Hellier came to stand beside her, looking down. "The snow and the rain held them up, but look—spring is here at last, and on my birthday!"

Very gently, she slid her fingers down the stems and picked two or three of the most advanced. "I shall put them in a little vial by my bed, to remind me that the weather outside is not so bad after all." She rose, the fragile flowers held gently in her hands, her delight glowing in her face. "I don't think I could ever be truly unhappy, if I had my garden."

Hellier said nothing. He was standing very close, looking intently at her. Her eyes met his and could not look away: They were so fierce, so hotly brown that she wondered briefly how she had ever thought this man gentle, or compassionate. Suddenly and deeply disturbed, her smile frozen to her face, she turned away, feeling a betraying, humiliating blush sweeping her face and unable to hide or explain it.

"My lady," he said quietly. "We are friends, are we not, despite our strange circumstances?"

"Friendly enemies," Silence said, keeping her face averted until she had returned some order to its expression. Now that she had noticed them, there were snowdrops everywhere, in every knot, their delicate green and white spears a small shout of triumph over the dreariness of winter.

"That describes it very well," Hellier said. "And since we are agreed on that fact, do you not think that for you to call me 'Captain' and for me to address you as 'my Lady St. Barbe' is perhaps too formal?"

"And too much of a mouthful," Silence said, trusting herself well enough now to be able to turn and face him. The intensity of his gaze had vanished so completely that she wondered if she had imagined it. He was looking at her with that familiar amused and friendly expression that she found so disarming.

"Not so much of an impediment to free speech as 'Lieutenant-Colonel Ridgeley.' But I doubt you will ever be on such good terms with him as to call him Jack."

"I hope not," Silence replied dryly. "So—you wish me to stop addressing you as Captain Hellier. What would you rather—skummery man?"

His laugh was sudden and brief. "I hope not! My friends call me Nick—will not you?"

"I will, since you have made me free of your name," said Silence. She added warily, "I should warn you—my own is one that causes me some embarrassment."

"I know—'My gracious Silence, hail!'"

She stared at him in some surprise, although it was after all quite likely that he would be aware of it—Lady St. Barbe's ridiculous Puritan name was probably common knowledge among the Bath garrison, and Sir

Thomas might well have told him. He added, smiling, "Do you know that quotation? You probably know every reference to Silence."

"Including the one from Paul's epistle to Timothy that you so rudely shouted at my mother-in-law when first you came here," she said. "I know those words only too well—my father never tired of saying them. 'Let the woman learn in silence, with all subjection.'"

"'Let your women keep silence in the churches, for it is not permitted unto them to speak.' Corinthians, I think—am I right?"

"You are. Your knowledge of the Bible is almost the equal of mine. Were your parents Puritan too?"

"Not as your father would understand it, no. But I am well acquainted with the more favored passages in Holy Writ. And with what no Puritan would countenance, namely, stage plays. The words I first quoted to you come from one called *Coriolanus,* by Master Shakespeare. Have you heard of him, my gracious Silence?"

"Only as an object of loathing abuse," she said. "I was brought up to regard theaters and masques and plays as abominations of Satan, I'm afraid."

"Then there is a world of wonder to which I must introduce you, if your conscience will allow it. Coriolanus is a Roman general, from the same land as our friend Caligula, and that is how he addresses his wife on his return from the wars. 'My gracious silence, hail! Would'st thou have laughed had I come coffined home, That weep'st to see me triumph?'"

"It sounds harmless enough," Silence said cautiously, though her mind had marked with appreciation the subtle rhythm in the words.

"Harmless! Master Shakespeare, or Master Jonson, or even those journeymen Beaumont and Fletcher can take you in their plays to Rome and Greece, France and Italy and the shores of Illyria or Denmark, far away from your small humdrum world."

"It may be so, but it suits me very well, thank you. I have heard about some of those wild tales you've been telling Nat—and he doesn't believe the half of them, I regret to say. The opposite of gullible is our Nat."

"But fascinated, nonetheless. You may not think so, my lady Silence, with your feet in the earth and your mind forever running on your household—and don't deny it, I've seen your face too often—but the world of the imagination is to be valued, hoarded, cherished. Like your garden, it can offer great comfort in times of trouble. You love words, I know—and there is so much poetry and music I can give you, if you will let me."

Silence regarded him doubtfully, wondering at his motive and ashamed of herself for so doing. Were they not friends? Why could she never quite trust him? Was she afraid of these things that went against everything she had ever been taught? Or was her reaction a response to something else?

As she stared at him, confused, he quoted softly:

A Lily of the Day
Is fairer far in May,
Although it fall and die that night;
It was the plant and flower of light.
In small proportions we just beauties see,
And in short measures, life may perfect be.

In the quiet that followed, she heard the distant voices of the waking house, a cock crowing distantly—not one of theirs, they had all disappeared into the military pot, it must be at the mill—and the ugly cawing of rooks in the coppice on Hassage Hill. She swallowed, trying to hide the sudden rush of emotion within her. She had loved the sonorous rhythms of the Bible, had always delighted in words for their own sake, had punned and joked with Sir Samuel and Nat and Tabby. But she had never dreamed that a poem could hold such beauty or clothe her own humble philosophy in glory. She said lightly, hoping he would not notice the strength of her response to it, "That was very pretty. I have some day lilies in these knots, but they flower in June or July, not May. Your poet probably wasn't a gardener."

"Perhaps not. I know that Master Jonson once made his living laying bricks, but I don't think he ever worked among flowers. You must read some of his verses. I have a volume of them in my collection."

"Thank you," Silence said. "Is there anything that might put a godly housewife to the blush?"

"Plenty, I should think—you will just have to try and avoid them. What have you seen, my lady Silence?"

For she was looking past him, past his shoulder that was not so much higher than her own, over the fat swelling pillars of the balustrade, between the wrinkled twisted trunks of the apple trees bare and sleeping in the uneven grass, to the men tramping down with pickaxe and shovel and trenching tool along the further hedge to the fishponds.

Nick followed her gaze. His eyes, when they met hers, were suddenly full of sympathy. "It was bound to happen, as soon as the rain stopped. Ridgeley has his orders, and he wouldn't lose any time in carrying them out."

"At least they are doing as Nat suggested," Silence said at last. She was struggling with a surprising and childish fury. Why did this have to be started today of all days? On her special day? Ridgeley could not have chosen a better way to upset her if he had done it deliberately. "But," she added, trying to laugh at her anger, "I do wish he'd decided to start tomorrow."

The sounds of cheerful song echoed up the orchard. It was the tune known as "Cuckolds All in a Row," the words fortunately indistinguish-able. The mood of the morning shattered, she turned abruptly away and walked swiftly back toward the house, leaving Hellier standing by the balustrade. She knew she was behaving badly, as badly as Rachael, but her fury and disappointment were such that she did not care.

She glanced back as she climbed the steps to the next terrace and saw him still there, looking up at her. He smiled, wryly, and spread his hands in a helpless gesture so comically unlike his usual self-assurance that she almost laughed, despite herself. Then he waved, turned, and ran lightly down to the orchard, and his troopers.

"Od dang it!" Silence said to herself, in imitation of Clevinger, and went briskly indoors to face whatever domestic crises her household could throw at her next.

ELEVEN

Even a child is known by his doings.
—PROVERBS 20:11

"**I** knew it wouldn't work," Nat said with quiet satisfaction. "And I think Captain Hellier guessed that I did, but did he do anything about it? No. He probably thinks I'm about ten."

"Well, you do look it, after all," Rachael said with the forthrightness that most people found too hurtful. She rubbed the dusty pane of the summerhouse window and peered closer. Her breath promptly obscured the view, and with a muffled curse she wiped the fog away with her sleeve. "How do you know it's waterlogged? I can't see from here."

"I know," Nat said in his most portentous voice. "Don't ask me how—I have my ways."

Rachael giggled. On their good days, which were rare but becoming less so, the twins were closer friends than most brothers and sisters, sharing a mute understanding of each other's thoughts, motives, hopes, and fears. This, conversely, made them more vulnerable to the other, for they knew where best to place the knife and twist it. Nat, though more good-natured, could be just as ruthless as his sister, and less emotional about it. Since his illness, however, Rachael had become acutely conscious of his tenuous hold on life. The void that would be created by his death had opened suddenly before her, and she could never forget it. Why waste time in childish squabbles, when life was so short and sweet and precious?

Her good resolution had not lasted long, of course, but she had made valiant efforts to curb her scold's tongue, to think more before she spoke, and to wreak the consequences of what she did or said. It only mattered with Nat. To everyone else she was still the same rude, graceless, unhappily bad-tempered girl. But Silence at least had marked the change in her, and was glad.

The summerhouse was cold, smelling of earth and dust and old apples. Something that Rachael thought might be a small rat or a large mouse had scuttled behind Diggory's spades when she opened the door, and she had sternly repressed a shudder. She was not so feeble as to be frightened of a mere rat!

Nat had suggested this vantage point. It was hard to be seen through the thick panes—although looking out was also difficult—and a recent and bitterly resented felling of some of the apple trees meant that a good view of the work on the fortifications could be had. A couple of hundred yards away, many small figures, stripped to their shirts despite the cold, labored in the ditches they had dug between the two fish ponds. At frequent intervals, a shovelful of mud flew messily into the air to land on the growing rampart on the near side of the trench. Standing near them, clean and warm and dry, Lieutenant Byam's tall, slouching shape could be seen, supervising his men.

"I wish I had a perspective glass," Rachael said, staring down. "Then we could have a proper view."

"Well, we haven't—but Ridgeley has. I saw him with it the other day, a great long brass thing in a leather case." Nat glanced at his twin and saw the idea forming in her mind at the same time as it leapt to sudden joyous life in his own. They spoke together.

"Couldn't we—"

"Why don't we—"

"It wouldn't be difficult," Nat said. "He's not often in his chamber. That servant, or secretary, or whatever he is, he's more of a problem, but I'm sure we could lure him away on some pretext."

"I'll take it," Rachael said, breathless with excitement. "Oh, Nat, please let me—I can be so careful, I'm sure I can—remember when I put that toad in Eliza's bed last All Fools' Day? She never ever knew who'd put it there, no matter how hard she tried to find out. No one saw me—no one at all."

Nat stared at her, suddenly dubious, remembering, as Rachael apparently had not, the unpleasantness when Leah had been falsely accused by Eliza of perpetrating the dreadful deed. Much though he loved his sister, he was only too well aware of her failings. He himself was cautious and thoughtful. He liked to plan things out in advance, to examine his strategy thoroughly for flaws and prepare for all eventualities. These were the qualities that made him such a good player of chess. But Rachael usually went rushing in with skirts flying and forethought in abeyance, completely reckless of the consequences. She could be more careful than that, he knew she was capable of it when her mind was concentrated—the toad episode proved it, although Leah might have disagreed. But he could not help having serious doubts. She would be seen, or make a noise, or knock something over.

"You don't think I can do it," Rachael accused. "You don't trust me, do you—you think I'm stupid!" The belligerent, hostile note had returned to her voice, but behind it, Nat knew, was the desperate plea for loyalty, love, reassurance from a child who had never really possessed any of these things, save intermittently from her twin brother.

Already, however, his mind was leaping ahead to the consequences of such a reckless act, even if they were not caught. He said quietly, "I'm trying to think of what will happen when we take the glass."

Rachael giggled. "Ridgeley will be absolutely *furious,* I expect."

"Yes, I expect so too. And then what? What will he do? Think about it, Rachael. He isn't like father, all sound and no fury. If he found out who'd taken it, he'd *kill* us."

"*I'm* not afraid," his sister said stoutly. "He wouldn't kill us, anyway, he wouldn't dare."

"Perhaps not—but he might do other things. He might punish Mother, or wreck the house. And what if he *didn't* find out who'd taken it? What if he thought it was his servant, or some soldier, and had them flogged, or worse? They *hang* soldiers for stealing, you know."

"I don't care. They deserve a hanging, they all do, they're horrible," Rachael said venomously. "Even if they didn't take anything from Ridgeley, they're sure to have done something *much* worse that deserves death. Ridgeley does too. Bessie told me he pistoled two men at Bath, just because they wouldn't give him the contributions they were demanding."

"Then that settles it," Nat said. "It was a good idea, but it's too dangerous to risk it. It *is,* Rachael. What if someone quite innocent were harmed, killed even, because of our little plot? It isn't worth it, not when other people could be hurt. Ridgeley's like a firecracker; you never know when he's going to explode, or how powerfully."

"You're just frightened," Rachael said resentfully. It isn't fair of Nat, she thought, to fire me up with enthusiasm and then suddenly get cold feet just when I was beginning to be excited about the idea.

"I'm not frightened," Nat replied without rancor. "I'm just . . . well, more sensible, perhaps. I think we ought to forget about it, I really do. It'd be different if it was just us who'd be affected, but it wouldn't be—it could be disastrous for Wintercombe and everyone in it."

"Over a spyglass? And I thought Deb was childish!"

"So's Ridgeley, but he's just a little more dangerous," Nat said dryly. "Forget it, Rachael, please. It's wiser. And don't," he added warningly, "whatever you do, don't go ahead and steal it anyway."

"I wouldn't be such a fool," Rachael retorted indignantly. She got to her feet, cursorily dusting her apron. "Come on, there's no point in standing here all day, and I'm cold."

But as they walked briskly back to the house, laughing over their breath plumes mingling in the cold air, her mind was seething with plans. How dare Nat call her stupid? He was just a cautious old man, fit for nothing else but to sit safe by the fire while others took risks on his behalf.

I'll show him, she thought fiercely. I'll show him who's stupid! I'll take the spyglass and hide it so well that no one will *ever* know who's had it.

*   *   *

It was one thing to dream; it was quite another to put a plan into action. For a start, she must not act for several days, so as to lull Nat's suspicions. Once or twice she caught him watching her intently, as if trying to read her mind, though he never said anything more to her on the subject. So she behaved with decorum, abandoned her practice of hanging about the kitchen and the barton and the hall muttering half-heard abuse concerning the soldiers, and spent most of her time helping her stepmother, or Margery Turber, and working at her lessons.

Silence noticed Rachael's more docile behavior and was pleased. Nat's illness seemed to have had a most salutary effect upon his twin—perhaps the narrowness of his escape had shocked her into growing up a little. She was fifteen, after all. It was a difficult age, however. Silence well remembered her own adolescence—she had been the same age as Rachael when her mother died—and the quiet, decorous girl, so serene and biddable without, so resentful and seething within, who had gone by her name. That Silence seemed very long ago, far away, almost another person now, but she could recall most vividly the fury and unhappiness she had suffered. As a consequence she sympathized with Rachael, whose only crime was that she made no effort to hide her tempestuous feelings under a repressed and hypocritical mask.

But Rachael had learned some cunning, particularly from her twin brother. The theft of Ridgeley's spyglass became an obsession, the means by which she would prove to Nat that she could be just as devious, careful, and calculating as he. Unobtrusively she noted Ridgeley's habits. He rose early and breakfasted in the dining parlor, which the officers had effectively commandeered for their meals, the family being relegated to the winter parlor or to Silence's chamber. Then he would inspect his men, issue the orders for the day, and administer summary justice to any miscreants. The least favored offenses involved matters of faulty or neglected equipment, disobedience to orders, shirking duty, or other military misdemeanors. Pilfering, wanton damage, swearing, drunkenness, and other wants of conduct appeared to go unpunished. Rachael, who had a censorious streak, was thereby assured of the righteousness of her cause. It could be no crime to purloin such a valuable piece of equipment from a man so ungodly, so lacking in all the Christian virtues, and so personally repulsive.

On most days he would ride out at the head of his troops in search of supplies. This, in the bleak sparse time of late winter, took them farther and farther afield, and the presence of the garrison at Bath, and another regiment of foot based at Farleigh Castle, only a couple of miles northeast of Norton, meant that similar parties often descended on the same village in quick succession or even, on some acrimonious occasions, at the same time. Often the unfortunate troopers would not return until dusk, weary, resentful, and the subject of blistering contempt from their commanding

officer. Rachael could not understand, after she overheard one such tirade—
it would have been surprising if the whole of Wintercombe had not heard
it too—why more men did not desert. One or two had slunk away under
cover of night, true, but the rest seemed content to submit to Ridgeley's
brutal discipline. Surely their old lives outside the army could not have
been so bad that they would endure this rather than flee?

There seemed to be ample opportunity for the execution of her plan. All
she had to do was to choose a day when Ridgeley was absent on one of his
foraging expeditions. His servant, an insignificant little man with a cast in
one eye and a limp that had obviously excluded him from military service,
was usually to be found in his master's chamber, polishing arms, mending
and cleaning clothes, or writing letters. For a man who looked as if he did
not know a hornbook from a chapbook, not to mention his visual dis-
ability, he wrote a very neat, fair secretary's hand.

The quartermaster, Hodges, was also frequently in evidence, writing out
his accounts and making lists. Indeed, the two adjoining chambers in the
little south wing, above the winter parlor and study, were not so much the
colonel's bedchamber as the headquarters of the Wintercombe garrison. But
Rachael soon found a suitable moment. The colonel out, Hodges in the
barton, the servant, Harris, disappeared in search of sand to scour
Ridgeley's back- and breastplates. Breathless with excitement and daring,
she left her own chamber where she had been blamelessly sewing, whisked
along the corridor past the nursery doors, and into the little recess outside
Ridgeley's suite. She glanced quickly around. No one was in sight, or
hearing. The coast was clear. With trembling fingers, she very gently lifted
the latch and pushed.

The door resisted, unyielding. The bastard has locked it, Rachael
thought furiously, quite oblivious to the fact that with a room full of
important documents and items of equipment, not to mention the coin
intended for paying the troops, it would have been an act of unpardonable
foolishness not to do so. She almost kicked the oak panels, and stopped
herself just in time—childish behavior, guaranteed to draw unwelcome
attention to herself. She slunk away, seething with rage, and forced herself
to think again.

The best plan seemed to be to entice the servant out of the chamber in
such a way that he forgot to lock it after him. Rachael considered fostering
an affair with Bessie, and rejected it almost instantly. The dairymaid had
other fish, in the form of Byam, to fry, and would hardly deign to share
her favors with such a runtish and unprepossessing little man as Harris.
Somehow, Rachael decided, an emergency had to be concocted so that the
man would be summoned urgently, leaving no time to lock the door behind him. Then it would be a simple matter to nip into the empty chamber and take the spyglass. She could hide it up her sleeve, or down her

bodice—the stiff stomacher would hide it—or even, failing all else, in her apron pocket.

She had it all worked out, to the last degree. She lacked only the opportunity, and spent many hours, especially before she slept, wrestling with the problem. In the end, however, it was chance that delivered the moment to her.

It was ten days after her stepmother's birthday, and raining again. All work on the fortifications had been halted for several days. To Nat's satisfaction and Rachael's glee, there had been serious trouble with flooded trenches, and the men detailed to dig them struggled sullenly amid a glutinous sea of sticky red mud and skummery water. Further rain had brought it to a complete standstill, with only a tithe of the work yet finished, and the soldiers kicked their heels in the barn, dicing and drinking and indulging in less speakable vices, or were marched around the countryside foraging for their food.

Two months ago it had been Christmas Eve. In two months' time it would be April, nearly May. The weather might have turned sunny, the flowers would be blooming in the garden, the cherry arbor a mass of palest carnation, strewing a carpet of petals on the gravellike snow. Rachael thought of it yearningly. Then the pessimistic side of her nature reminded her that April meant showers, and gales, and unseasonably late frosts, and that quite probably in two months' time it would still be raining.

She stared resentfully at the dripping panes of her bedroom window. It was two hours past dinner, and she was supposed to be conning a Bible passage for recitation to her grandmother on the following morning. She did not see why she must—the old hag was unbearable, forever shouting and insulting her, poking her painfully with that stick, and insisting that she work, so it seemed to Rachael, far harder and better than anyone else. It isn't fair, she thought mutinously. Nat doesn't have to learn it, so why should I? She had even appealed to her stepmother, but Silence had looked at her in that calm, self-possessed way that had always infuriated Rachael and pointed out that she owed a duty of respectful obedience to Dame Ursula.

That, thought Rachael, was all very well if her grandmother had been pleasant, mellow, even merely likable. Moreover, as she had tactlessly retorted to her stepmother, it smacked of hypocrisy to insist on obedience to one's superiors when at that very moment her husband was in armed rebellion against his lawful king.

Not even that riposte had brought Silence to anger. She had merely sighed and said quietly, "You are probably right. But even so, your father wrestled long and hard with his conscience before taking up arms, and did what he thought to be right. With the best will in the world, Rachael, conscience is not your motive."

Sometimes Rachael's confused feelings about her stepmother bordered on hatred. With a glare of loathing and a curtsy that was more of an insult, she had marched back to her chamber, flung herself down on the bed, and indulged in several alluring fantasies. What if Silence had died, of the fever that had so nearly slain Nat? Rachael saw herself in sorrowing black at the funeral, suddenly become the mistress of the house—there was no one else able to take charge, after all—with the great bunch of keys dangling at her waist. She contemplated, with love, the younger children: how they would look up to her, adore her, rely upon her utterly to soothe away their grief, and how she would become as a mother to them. And her mind wandered on, dreaming, to the blistering scene where she would confront Dame Ursula, exact her just revenge for all the years of misery and victimization, and announce that none of her grandchildren would come near her again until she mended her tongue. It was difficult to imagine the old woman contrite or humbled, but for the sake of her fantasy Rachael achieved it with a supreme effort.

And then . . . then she would be a wise mistress of Wintercombe, just, fair, beloved not only for herself but for the fact that, unlike her stepmother, she was Somerset born and bred, one of their own. And the war would end, and Ridgeley would be dead—she was not sure how, but was determined to have a hand in it if she could—and her father and Sam would come home. Sam would marvel at how his scrawny little sister had grown up, and her father, who had never had much time to spare for her and Nat, would look around at his clean, shiny, immaculate inheritance, and offer his wondering and appreciative thanks for all the work she had done so well.

Rachael gave a snort of humorless laughter. This was completely ridiculous. Silence was never ill, she was famous for her resilience to coughs and colds and aches and pains, never mind more serious ailments. And even if she did die, said the nagging voice of her conscience, you wouldn't be glad—you'd be desperately, heart-rendingly sorry. And as for keeping the house run smooth and immaculate—you? You can't even keep your apron clean for five minutes!

I wish I could, the child Rachael thought unhappily. I wish I could be more like her . . . everything a wife is supposed to be, quiet, tidy, gracious, hard-working, sober, gentle—and everything that I am not. Who's going to marry me, the Hoyden of Norton?

She lay dismally on the bed, contemplating spinsterhood, the inevitable fate of those too poor, or too plain, to attract a suitable husband. Then a faint, distant commotion aroused her. It sounded like hoofbeats and shouting. She leapt up and ran to her window, which looked out on to the barton. It was difficult to see through the thick glass and the pelting rain. She wiped the panes fruitlessly, gave up and with a curse attempted to force it open. Days of rain had swollen the wood; she had to use all her strength, pushing and shoving, to persuade it, and as the frame protested, groaning, she wondered if it would break. But eventually it yielded to her brute force with a savage creak and swung wide quite suddenly, almost pitching her onto the wet stones below.

A soldier, a messenger by the look of him, had just ridden in. His horse, muddy and steaming, stood exhausted in a circle of gesticulating soldiers, while its rider, holding its drooping head, was evidently conducting an argument. Unseen, Rachael hung above them, heedless of the rain beating her face, wondering what was afoot. Messengers from the Governor of Bath usually took their time, enjoying a pleasant amble out to Philip's Norton that would last all day if they were careful.

Captain Hellier came out of the barn. At this angle, he looked even shorter than the reality. Rachael suffered a childish urge to throw something at him. She had often dropped twigs and stone on the unsuspecting soldiers, closing her window so quickly that they did not suspect her. But she had nothing handy, and besides, it would give her away. She wanted to overhear this encounter.

"What is it, Trooper Stevens?" Hellier's voice carried clearly around the barton and up to Rachael. She waited avidly for the reply.

"I've a message from the governor for Lieutenant-Colonel Ridgeley. Be he here?"

"No, he's out on a foraging expedition. Can I assist?"

"I doubt it, sir. A private matter, Sir Thomas did say it were. Some papers what aren't right, or summat—perhaps Colonel Ridgeley's secretary could help, Sir Thomas told me as how he'd writ them out in the first place. But it'll have to be quick, I've got to get to Nunney afore dark."

"I'll send for him at once," Hellier said. "And have a tankard of ale to warm you while you wait. It's a hellish day."

The men dispersed at the captain's terse orders, and he disappeared with the messenger inside the house, through the kitchen door. Rachael, her heart suddenly leaping with anticipation, closed her casement with a little more care than when she had opened it and ran to the door. Very softly she lifted the latch and pulled it an inch or so ajar.

From this vantage point, she could see clear down the passage, past the two nursery doors, the recess in front of Ridgeley's suite, and the staircase, to the gallery and beyond it the high airy space of the hall. And she knew, from her observations, that anyone coming up the stairs and walking to Ridgeley's door would not notice that hers, at the end of the corridor where it bent around to run half the length of the north wing, was very slightly open. With a forgotten smile of expectation on her small sharp face, Rachael sank silently to the floor, her gaze fixed on the gap, and waited.

It did not take long. There was the sound of booted feet, and one of the young troopers who had befriended William trotted up the stairs and into her view. He halted outside Ridgeley's door, only his buff-coated back visible to her, and hammered briskly. "Master Harris! Master Harris, be ee there?"

Evidently he was. The hammering stopped, and Rachael heard a mutter of sound. The trooper said, "Messenger from Bath, concerning Colonel Ridgeley. He haven't got much time, sir, and Captain Hellier told I to fetch ee down at once."

She saw the secretary hurry out, a harassed look on his face, and follow the trooper back down the stairs. She probably did not have very long, but then she did not need much more than a minute or so. Praying that he had not locked the door behind him, she slid from her chamber and scuttled on noiseless, stockinged feet past the nursery to Ridgeley's entrance.

It was exactly opposite Dame Ursula's. She did not dare contemplate what would happen should that firmly closed door suddenly open to reveal Ruth or, worse, the baleful figure of her grandmother. The prospect was almost as appalling as if Ridgeley himself should catch her rifling his possessions. She took a deep breath, her palms sweaty, and saw that she had guessed right. She had not heard a key turn, and there was the colonel's door, not merely unlocked but a few inches ajar.

With one swift movement she slipped inside, leaving it almost closed, as it had been before. This was the outer room, where the servant slept, on the neat truckle bed in the corner. Chairs, a settle, a little table against the window that was piled high with papers, met her urgent glance. No sign of a spyglass—and no sign of her most recent fear, someone else in the room. She ran to the further door, lifted the latch, and stepped into Ridgeley's sanctum.

It was as arrogantly and sordidly untidy as himself. Clothes, armor, papers, lay in heaps in the corners, and there was a sour smell of sweat, tobacco smoke, dirt, and stale wine. The table was even more hidden by papers than Harris's, and the bed, its curtains half closed, displayed a tumbled pile of sheets. Rachael's avid eyes swept over the squalor, the almost-dead fire, empty bottles and overturned cups, spilled wine, plates of mold-furred food, confirming everything she had suspected about the uncouth colonel. So intent was she on finding the spyglass that her gaze passed right across it before she realized. *There* it was! On the windowsill, next to those books—could that awful man really read?—and still in its leather bag. She stretched across the table and very carefully lifted it off. It was surprisingly heavy. She held it grasped tightly in triumph for a moment and then thrust it into the pocket of her apron.

As she turned to go, her eye was caught by the long, flat wooden case on the windowsill by the books. She had always been told by her grandmother that curiosity was one of the greatest of her manifold sins but had, being Rachael, never taken any notice. Whatever could be in that case? It was filmed with a fine layer of dust—for obvious reasons, the maids never ventured into Ridgeley's domain—so it was obviously not well used. Very carefully, so as not to leave betraying fingermarks, she undid the simple metal catch and pushed up the lid.

Two pistols lay within, on a bed of crimson velvet. Rachael had a limited acquaintance with firearms, but one look was enough to tell her that these were beautifully made and exceedingly expensive. Less than half the size of the cumbersome horse pistols that all the officers carried in holsters at their saddle bows, the rounded, slender butts, inlaid with silver, were in a warm reddish wood that looked like walnut. Fascinated by their alluring, deadly beauty, Rachael stared down at them, struggling with temptation. The spyglass would be missed at once. But to take one of these, not an everyday weapon, in a box that so evidently had not been touched for weeks . . .

By the time he finds out, Rachael thought exultantly, I'll have it so well hidden he'll never suspect me—or anyone else in the house. She laid the spyglass, not without a twinge of regret, back on the sill and picked up one of the little pistols. It fit perfectly into her hand, beautifully balanced. Also in the case were a little leather bag full of shot, a tiny wooden ram, another bag that proved to contain paper cartridges, each holding sufficient powder for one loading, a powder flask, and the metal spanner with which to wind the pistol up. Her hand hovered over them, hesitated, and swooped. In sudden haste she tumbled everything into the wide pocket of her apron, leaving only the one weapon forlornly alone upon its velvet, the impression of its fellow beside it. Then she shut the case with trembling hands and glanced around the chamber. It lay still in the same sordid chaos as before. The spyglass seemed untouched, and there were no telltale smudges on the pistol case. Her mission accomplished, all she had to do now was to escape.

She sped back to the outer chamber, her heart banging so loud inside her bodice that the rest of the house must surely be able to hear it. Nat's words about planning came back to her. She glanced at the truckle bed, wondering if she could hide beneath it should Harris return. But outside in the passage there was no sound. Rachael listened intently, hardly breathing, alert for any noise from the stairs or the nursery. Then, hearing nothing, she took a deep rasping breath, opened the door, and dived through it.

No one awaited her frantic, guilty gaze. She was safe. She had done it, unseen and unsuspected! Fighting the wild desire to throw back her head and screech her triumph, she closed the door to within two or three inches of the frame and then turned to walk back to her own chamber, the pistol banging against her thighs with every stride.

She was Home, as in the games of tag they played in the garden in kinder weather. Home, and safe from pursuit. She shut the door firmly and sat on the bed beside the neglected Bible, hugging herself with glee. That would show them! And Nat's face when she told him! She laughed to think of it, and then reality struck her. She could not tell him. He would disapprove. He might even make her take it back (her heart quailed at the thought), or, worse, tell her to confess all to their stepmother. And then Ridgeley would find out.

No, this was her secret, and hers alone. She did not know what she would do with it, where she would hide it. Hester made her bed, tidied and cleaned her chamber daily. It would not be safe there. Then she thought of the summerhouse, the Home of their games. It was built at the edge of the higher terrace, but there was a lower storey, used chiefly to store apples, and reached from the higher one. And in one corner of that dusty, neglected little room there was a small loose stone that Sam had found on some long-ago visit to Wintercombe, when he had been ten or eleven. He had hollowed out a cavity underneath, big enough for his secret treasures, and Rachael, trailing adoringly after her big brother, had once come upon him unexpectedly and discovered his secret. Now Sam was grown, and a soldier, but she remembered it very well. That was the perfect place to hide her spoils. And if by some dire mischance they were discovered, there would be no clue to give away the thief's identity.

Only one other problem remained: to take the pistol there without rousing suspicion. To wander outside in this rain was foolhardy, to say the least, and would only draw attention to herself. No, it would have to be concealed in her chamber until the weather improved and she could find some excuse to stroll in the garden.

Hester might make the bed, but she never moved it. A big heavy oaken four-poster, it lay against the wall. Rachael took out the pistol, holding it once more in her hand to feel the sweet balance of it, the curl of her fingers around the cool smooth butt. She peered at the silver decoration, which seemed to depict some kind of military scene amid swirls and swags of engraved foliage, and traced the graceful curves with one fingertip. It seemed strange that something so beautiful could bring death.

I can kill Ridgeley with this, Rachael thought suddenly with a mixture of horror and wonder. I can put the ball and the cartridge in it, as Sam showed us before he went to war when he had his new pistols, and I can ram the shot home, and wind it up, and raise it, and aim it at his horrible ugly face, and—bang!

She pressed the trigger, but it was slack and unresisting. The lock mechanism was similar to that on Sam's weapons, needing to be wound, or spanned, with the key she had taken care to steal along with the rest. She remembered her elder brother telling her and Nat, with his usual effervescent enthusiasm, that this was the type of most modern pistols, matchlocks being impossible to manage on horseback and firelocks often unreliable. Wheellocks like this were expensive, but simple to load and fire. They could be wound in readiness and left for a while until needed. Not too long, though, Sam had said. They could wind down again and then they would fail to fire.

She laid it down on the bed with the little heavy bag of shot, the cartridges, the powder flask, and the ram. If she could remember how to load it all in the right order, as Sam had shown her, she would have a lethal weapon at her command.

It frightened her, but it was also, somehow, wildly exhilarating. She was no longer the difficult child but a lady with the power of life or death.

She found a piece of cloth in her clothes press, left over from the making of her blue gown. She wrapped the pistol and its accessories in the soft azure wool, tied a knot in the bundle, and crouched down by the side of the bed. Underneath, behind the green perpetuana counterpane that hung to the floor, was a dark and dusty cavern in which, had she been younger, she might have been wont to hide when the world grew too oppressive. She pushed the package beneath the bed, as far back as her arm would stretch, and scrambled to her feet, dusting herself off. She doubted if the escapade had taken more than five minutes from start to finish. And now she must behave as if nothing had happened.

A betraying smirk on her lips, Rachael sat down on the bed and tried with indifferent success to apply herself to learning the first chapter of the Book of Proverbs.

CHAPTER
TWELVE

Therefore shall his calamity come suddenly.
—PROVERBS 6:15

The days slid by, and March appeared, like the lamb sweet and smiling. In Silence's garden, the snowdrops and crocuses stood in massed ranks of green-frilled white and brilliant yellow, shy and lovely in unaccustomed sunshine. Diggory's robin, a cheerful bright-eyed little bird who always followed him as he dug and who had so far managed somehow to evade the murderous instincts of Pye, began building a nest with his mate on one of the stone beasts guarding the top terrace. Silence, concerned, thought that they would be lucky to rear a brood, unless Pye's interests were speedily engaged by her inevitable litter of kittens. Since the cat had already gone calling for a mate in her usual brazen fashion, it would not be long before the arrival of four or five delightful bundles of fluff, to nestle in the old kittening basket by the fire in her chamber.

Spring was here, there seemed no doubt of it. In the pots crammed on every one of her windowsills, the bulbs she had planted in the autumn were bursting with life and fragrance: hyacinths, hoop petticoat daffodils, narcissi, the fragile purple and yellow flowers of crocus. In a fortnight or so, given further warmth, the display would be matched in the garden. Here she could forget for a while the troubles that beset her: the continuing shortage of food; the behavior of Bessie, who was almost certainly sharing Byam's bed on a regular basis; the grumbles of Darby, whose threatened departure would be utterly disastrous; and the increasingly destructive behavior of the soldiers, following Ridgeley's example. Despite their busy days spent foraging or working on the defenses, they still seemed to have the energy to get drunk every night. Wintercombe's supply of cider had run out weeks ago, though they still brewed beer every fortnight, and so extra supplies were brought in from the villages to quench the men's insatiable thirst. There had been a fair amount of damage—windows broken, tapestries ripped, wood burned, pewter squashed, melted in the fire, or severely dented. At least there was nothing of real value for them to pilfer—George had taken all the precious metal off to be melted down for the Parliament, and she had hidden the silver-gilt salt and sundry smaller valuables in the study hearth. But she spent weary hours listing the destruction and loss with Clevinger, in the hope that somehow, someday, reparation would be made. No use applying to Ridgeley, who had scored tables and paneling with his knife and amused himself at drunken suppers by throwing it at the hangings and pictures in the dining parlor. Nor, she suspected, would Sir Thomas Bridges be any more sympathetic—and a herd of wild horses could not have dragged her into the governor's presence again.

She was on her own, save for Captain Hellier. It was still difficult for her to address him as Nick—the brief syllable seemed to falter on her tongue. And it was also exceedingly strange to hear her own name spoken, in his deep, rather hard-edged voice, for the first time since Sir Samuel's death. All her life she had wished she were called Anne, or Bess, or Moll, any ordinary name instead of Silence, which made her a laughingstock among those who derided Puritans. And yet now, when he used it without any mockery or disbelief, as if she were just a common-or-garden Nan or Dorothy, she could begin, hesitantly, to delight in its strangeness, the difference that marked her out among all other women. If there was another in the whole land called Silence, he had said, he did not know of it.

He lent her a book of poems by a man called Donne, with rough boisterous rhymes and rhythms, and an urgent love of life that leapt from the page. She remembered, later, that this man had died the dean of St. Paul's, just before her marriage, famous for the beauty and godliness of his sermons, even if he did approve of bishops. And at Tabby's insistence, she instructed Turber and Clevinger to carry the virginals up from the study and install them lovingly in the little clothes closet, twin of Mally's, that led off her chamber. The instrument had only just fit inside the stairs. The larger pieces of furniture, such as the bed, must originally have been brought up in pieces and reassembled.

During the day Silence hardly saw any of the soldiers. As the weather improved, they were kept extremely busy, working on the defenses about the house. The rebuilding of the wall bordering the courtyard had been easy enough, although a severe shortage of suitable stone meant that it was no more than breast high. Silence, surveying its progress from her oriel, had to acknowledge that it was not at all detrimental to the house. Indeed, it could be said to have enhanced it. The pigeons, ejected, still flew obstinately back to their old towers every evening and were as stubbornly repelled by the soldiers on watch there. They sat glumly on the wall and the tower roofs and in the yew walk, and their despondent cooing proved so infuriating that pigeon pie began to appear with increasing regularity on the dinner table.

It was in the orchard that the real damage was being done. She had not been able to bring herself to go down there for a long time. Nat reported to her regularly, not concealing his satisfaction at being proved right. Progress was slow, water a constant problem, tempers short and morale low. Apparently the soldiers would go to almost any lengths to avoid trench duty, and there were frequent punishments, beatings, and floggings. Predictably, desertion was becoming more regular. Nick had told her that they had lost three men that week. "More trouble than it's worth, Ridgeley is saying now," he had added with a very shrewd glance at her and at Nat, sitting at the table apparently oblivious to all but his Latin. "There's some talk of building a rampart on your lowest terrace instead."

There had been a small, tense pause. Nat's head did not move, but Silence knew that he was listening intently. Rachael, sewing opposite him, was more open in her interest and had fixed Hellier with a malevolent stare. In the little southern closet the faint hesitant tinkle of the virginals could be heard, as Tabby practiced her latest piece.

"They couldn't do that!" Rachael cried hotly into the quiet. "Not the terrace—they *couldn't*!"

"They can do anything they want," Silence said wearily. "They have the power, the will, and the ruthlessness. We have nothing at all."

A strange look appeared on the girl's face, a rather smug expression, as if she knew something that her stepmother did not. She opened her mouth, closed it, and applied herself with ostentatious industry to her stitches. Nick glanced at her, and Nat, and then turned back to Silence, sitting opposite him by the hearth. He said very softly, "I think Ridgeley is realizing how he's been gulled—and for that matter, so am I."

"Gulled? Whatever do you mean?"

"I am sure you know, my gracious Silence. Nat was very keen for the ditches to be dug at the bottom of the orchard, was he not? But the obvious place to fortify is the lowest terrace. You could knock down the balustrade, build a wooden fence with shot holes—oh, yes, by far the best way."

"But not one I'd volunteer, even to you," Silence said. She found that she was trembling with anger and fear. "I know all is fair in war. But I love my garden dearly—do you think I'd hand it to your soldiers on a platter, to be destroyed at their leisure?"

"No, I don't. And I salute you for trying your best to keep it safe. I would do exactly the same, in your position."

"But as you're not in my position, you're going to tell Ridgeley where he can fortify more profitably?"

"No," he said quietly. "No, I will not. Though the future of this garrison may depend upon it, I will not."

"More fool you, then," Nat said, lifting his head from his book, his eyes gleaming with amusement. "And let's hope Ridgeley is too stupid to think it out for himself."

So far, it seemed that he was—or too stubborn to admit that his original plan had been wrong. The northern side was finished, and a wooden palisade had been thrown up along the hedge running down from the barton, bordering the orchard, and a shallow ditch dug outside it. But the earth rampart alongside the fish ponds still was not finished, and the widening of the channel between them, although ostensibly completed, would not in Nat's view have stopped a rabbit.

Silence stood now at her window, looking down over her garden, through the decimated apple trees, trying to see what was being done. Nat must have a much closer vantage point, or be so accepted by the soldiers that they let him watch their work. Today was dull but dry, quite warm for the season and the fifth of March. Out in the fields around the village, the people of Norton would be taking advantage of the calm weather to plow their arable land and to sow their crops with what grain the soldiers had left them. Those with cattle—and almost every household, except the poorest, had at least one cow—would be anxiously supervising calving or turning their beasts off the hay meadows to allow the grass to grow. After the dead wet cold months of winter, the farming year was leaping into busy new life.

All through those drear past months, save when the snow and rain rendered any movement outside the house foolhardy if not actually impossible, she had visited the old and sick and poor of the village, bringing comfort and cordials and small gifts of charity, and had listened to their woes. Some, of course, had been self-inflicted: The man who complained of poverty who had spent all his money on drink, another so lazy and feckless that his crop had failed and his cow was dead of neglect. But over and over she had heard the litany of misery and repression: the people whose small hoarded stores had been ransacked again and again, who had been abused as traitorous rebels for concealing what they did not have, whose wives had been ogled and daughters molested. The richer families, the Flowers and Perrys, the Pearces and young Ned Apprice and Mistress Baylie in her farm over near Farleigh, at risk from two garrisons, could survive the depredations of the soldiers. The lesser ones could not.

She thought of the Swiftes, who had made their living spinning and weaving in their tenement in North Street, with a close of land on which they grew a little corn and peas and beans to supplement their meager income. One of the babies had died in the autumn, and the others were quiet and sickly and lay staring up with overlarge eyes in gaunt, pale faces. Ridgeley's men had taken almost everything they had, including the seed grain set aside for next year, and now they, like a score or so of the poorest households in Norton, subsisted on charitable handouts from their more fortunate neighbors or from the comparatively wealthy gentry families. She did what she could for them, as did Mistress Baylie, a competent and kindly woman in her fifties, and the newly widowed Mistress Flower. Ned Apprice, a little younger than Silence, who owned the mill and leased much land in Norton, was almost as mean as his father—a byword for parsimony—had been, and, being also the local clothier, was directly responsible for the poor prices paid to the local weavers. Not many people had more than a spit or a curse for an Apprice, though they all had to make use of the facilities offered by the mill that lay at the end of Wintercombe's little valley.

And that reminded her of what must be done this morning. The day before, Ridgeley had taken a party of men down to the mill to requisition supplies. There had been a heated argument, and the miller, Jeffery Churchhouse, had been quite badly beaten, his wife insulted, and his only daughter, a shy pretty girl of fourteen or fifteen, attacked in a manner that only just stopped short of rape. Her three older brothers, who all helped at the mill, had intervened just in time, and Ridgeley had retired vowing vengeance. Leah Walker's father had helped to see the soldiers off, apparently with the help of a pitchfork, and the maid had come to her with the news later that day. By that time it had been too late to tackle Ridgeley, who was already deep into his second bottle of wine, and so she had asked Nick to be her messenger, and convey to his superior officer that she wished to see him as a matter of urgency.

She felt more confident at the thought of facing the man on ground of her own choosing. She knew that in all probability she would receive only abuse and unpleasantness for daring to complain about his behavior, but she had promised Leah, who had for once come to her devoid of selfish intent, that she would make an issue of this latest outrage. The Churchhouse family were godly, respectable and hard-working, and besides, if she did nothing then sooner or later young Ned Apprice would ride up to Wintercombe on his expensive and handsome horse, to sit like a pale slug in this chamber and fix her with his shiny black eyes while he demanded in that soft rather sibilant voice that she do something about the gang of rogues colonizing her house and terrorizing his miller. Apprice, Nat had once said, reminded him of something found under a stone, and Silence had no wish to entertain him in her sanctum unless she could possibly help it. At least with Ridgeley, she could indulge in the luxury of righteous anger.

Mally announced him, her face and diminutive figure rigid with dislike. No refreshments were produced: He had already made too free with what Wintercombe had to offer. Silence looked at that heavy, blue-jowled face— did the man *never* shave properly?—with its air of deeply ironic satisfaction, and her heart sank. "Good morning, Colonel."

"Good morning, *Lady* St. Barbe." Courtesies, barely veiling the unbridgeable enmity between them, were briefly exchanged. Silence kept her

head high and her air of calm wrapped around her like a cloak, surprised at
the ease with which she could assume this mask—surely some of her loathing must show on her face?

She said, her voice level and neutral, "I have asked you here to discuss a
matter of some importance, Colonel. I hope I have not inconvenienced you
by so doing."

"Not at all, my lady—since I also have some bones to pick with you."
Ridgeley's small blue eyes almost disappeared into the puffy folds around
them as he smiled maliciously at her. "But I can wait. What's your complaint? I assume it must be a complaint, since you never have anything else
for my ears."

Silence ignored his tone. She said quietly, "I regret that, yes, it *is* a
grievance. It concerns the incident at the mill yesterday. I know that you
must levy contributions on the village, and I can even see that threats and
abuse, though deplorable, are quite usual. But a girl hardly more than a
child was attacked, and all but ravished, by several of your men."

"So? That too, my lady, is part of the fortunes of war. She probably
enjoyed the experience."

"She is *fourteen!*" Silence stopped, making a furious bid to control the
sudden uprush of anger, and went on more calmly. "Apart from moral
considerations, Colonel, all that you have done is to ensure that in future
all wives and daughters, as well as stores, are kept well away from your
men. If they pillage and rape and destroy, they will make no friends in this
countryside."

"Which was a hotbed of mealy-mouthed Puritan rebellion from the
start!" Ridgeley stared at her, his eyes hard. "And doubtless your precious
husband and father-in-law gave the lead. No, madam, these stingy close-
fisted peasants deserve all they get, and more. Which leads me to the next
of the matters which *I* wish to discuss. You will, perhaps, have noticed the
trenches and ramparts presently under construction in your orchard?"

"I am not blind, Colonel."

"Then you will also have noticed that work proceeds extremely slowly.
There are unfortunately not enough men available to construct the fortifications at an adequate speed, without taking others from foraging duty. And
since your villagers appear to be concealing their stores, I have decided
upon a solution to the problem. In future, all those unable or unwilling to
hand over the coin or supplies demanded will be ordered to work upon the
defenses in lieu of payment."

Silence stared at him. Her first thought was that they would never stand
for this. There would be outright rebellion—the fields must be plowed,
crops sown, cows milked, it was the beginning of the dairying season. She
said, appalled, "But you sentence them to starvation, Colonel. Those who
really cannot pay will be forced to work for you—and everything they

ought to be doing in the fields will be abandoned. Then they will have nothing to live on in the summer—and neither will you."

"We're getting little enough from them as it is," Ridgeley said contemptuously. "They all plead poverty, with a houseful of goods—pah, they make me sick! It's high time we had some use out of them. A score or so of brawny peasants will make all the difference, and then, always supposing they don't take a fancy to the military life, they can go back to their fields."

"I don't know why you wanted to discuss this with me," Silence said, her heart full of cold rage. "You have plainly already made up your mind, Colonel, and there is nothing I can do to dissuade you—beyond the fact that you can push a Somerset man thus far, and no further."

Ridgeley laughed. "What do we have to fear, my lady? Hardly a fearsome enemy, a thick-skulled slow-brained peasant with a pitchfork or a scythe. I for one shall not sleep less easy at the thought. But there is a further matter that is of much greater concern to me—and here, Lady St. Barbe, I shall expect your wholehearted assistance. Something of value has been stolen from my chamber."

She stared at him in disbelief. "Stolen? From your chamber? Really, Colonel, I thought you guarded your possessions better."

Ridgeley flushed suddenly with anger. "This is no jesting matter, madam. Some thief has entered my private room and taken items of great value. Their loss has only just been noticed, but they could have been taken at any time in the last three or four weeks. And I shall require your assistance in bringing the culprit to justice."

"Why?" Silence demanded, infuriated by his tone. "Do you think *I* took them—whatever they are?"

"Of course not, madam. But undoubtedly it was someone within the household. The troopers are not given the run of this place—though that, I warn you, may well change. And the officers I consider to be trustworthy."

How generous of you, thought Silence, staring at that unattractive yet floridly handsome face. She said slowly, "I, sir, consider my servants to be trustworthy too, and your insinuations and accusations are an insult. Most of them have been years in our employ, and I would vouch for the honesty of all of them."

"You won't, because I have no intention of taking your word for it, madam. I have lost a valuable pistol from my chamber, with cartridge and shot, and someone in your cursed household has them. D'you think I'd let that go by? God's death, woman, do you think me so stupid? I'll not risk a bullet in the back for the sake of your scruples." He thrust his head closer to hers in that threatening, bullish stance, and his face grew redder. "Listen to me, you puling Puritan. Call your servants to the hall—now. All of them, down to the gardener's boy. God's bones, I want the truth out of them, and quickly. If that pistol is not returned by dinnertime, the house will be searched. And you know full well what that means, my Lady St. Barbe."

She did. Her face felt cold, all the blood gone from it, and her hands were clamped together to stop their shaking. The plain-buttoned front of her dark-blue bodice was sprayed with his spittle. She said thinly, "You do not have to threaten me, Colonel. Thieving is a crime, whatever the circumstances. I am quite prepared to do all I can to discover the culprit, but I find your blasphemies and manner quite disgusting. Kindly leave, sir, before I forget my natural courtesy."

"In the hall," Ridgeley repeated, as if she had not spoken. "In the hall, now. By God, woman, you'll do as I say or you'll rue the day you were born! Where's that Judas-haired maid of yours?"

Mally appeared instantly from her closet, where she had been waiting. Silence glanced at Ridgeley, seeing the slobber around his mouth and his hot, savage, enraged face, and then with an air of cool contempt turned to her maid. "Mally, will you find all the people in the household and garden and stable and call them to the hall now? I wish to speak to them urgently."

If looks could kill, Ridgeley would have withered black and smoking under the ferocity of Mally's hate-filled stare. She curtsied decorously. "Aye, m'lady, I'll be so quick as light."

Her throat tight with her suppressed rage, Silence walked into the hall a few minutes later, Ridgeley at her shoulder. She knew that Hellier was on duty at the fortifications today, and she sorely missed his presence, the sense that someone not powerless was on her side. But she could not rely on his open support. He was already on bad enough terms with Ridgeley. She had had reports from the servants, who relayed to her all the military gossip they could scrape up with a variable mixture of glee or gloom according to content, of furious drunken arguments late into the night, of Nick's quiet, reasonable defiance and Ridgeley's wild blaspheming rages. She knew that only Hellier's undoubted and invaluable competence saved him from punishment, for he was too useful to be dismissed or demoted.

He was in sufficient trouble for Wintercombe's sake already. She must handle this new crisis on her own.

They were all there; Mally had performed her task with her usual swift thoroughness. She remembered, vividly, the first time they had been gathered here, when Ridgeley had harangued them all. There had been other faces present then—little Madlin Tilley, Rob Sheppard, both now left—and those who remained had all been changed by the months of occupation. It was not just Bessie, with her bold eyes and morals to match Pye's, nor Turber, who had aged ten years in as many weeks and should undoubtedly be replaced by a younger man, more resolute and less anxious. She saw her children, brought down by Doraty and Hester: saw Tabby's serious face and Rachael's naked, contemptuous fury, and felt a stab of grief. Perhaps only Deb, resolutely self-centered, had remained untouched by the soldiers' presence—and even she had seen a man killed and violence done.

Ridgeley, still radiating fury, walked forward to the long trestle table across the width of the hall, at the opposite end from the screen. He banged one of the pewter candlesticks down upon it so that all the others rattled, and even Turber jumped. He collected their attention, bewildered, angry, frightened, or curious according to temperament, and then turned to Silence. "Are they all here?"

"Everyone save for Dame Ursula," she said, having already counted heads.

"Fetch her too."

Silence stared at him incredulously. "Colonel—you can't be suggesting—my mother-in-law is nearly eighty years old, and a cripple. And she has not been well this winter—she hasn't left her bed for weeks!"

"I don't give a toss. That's her maid, isn't it, the ugly one? You, girl—bring your mistress out onto the gallery. I don't care if she's blind and senile, Lady St. Barbe, I'll have her listen as well."

Silence knew that Dame Ursula would already be doing just that—her bed had been moved to be near the squint, which must have led to some very disturbed evenings of late. But Dame Ursula, wracked with the pain in her joints that none of Silence's salves or plasters or ointments could alleviate, seemed to derive a twisted pleasure from overhearing the sounds of debauchery below.

The unfortunate Ruth, scarlet with rage or humiliation, turned and silently pushed her way through the servants to the stairs beyond the screens. Silence thought of her mother-in-law with guilt. No doubt of it, the old lady's health had deteriorated over the past few months, whether from sheer age, or the damp in her bones, or from her increasingly reclusive position in the household, Silence could not guess. Once, not long ago, she had been a formidable enemy. Now she had dwindled into a sick, querulous, and crotchety old woman who could not usually even muster the energy to shout with her former vigor.

"You cannot possibly suspect Dame Ursula," Silence said to Ridgeley, loud enough for everyone else to hear. "For shame, sir—that is despicable."

"She probably took it by witchcraft," the colonel said savagely. "I thought you Puritans were hot against such things, but I'd believe that old beldame capable of anything. Besides, her door is opposite mine—who knows, she may have seen or heard something."

"Even if she did, I very much doubt she'd tell you," Silence said.

Ridgeley looked at her, his bad teeth showing in that sinister, vulpine smile. "And have her chamber ransacked about her? I think not."

"There is but one flaw in this plan of yours," Silence told him, seeing with horror the implacable doom that was approaching as sure as night. "You are so certain that the thief is a member of my household—but what if it was not? You will have accused them unjustly, and caused much damage and destruction to no purpose. Please, Colonel, I beg you, reconsider."

"I will not, and there's an end to it. Well, girl? Where is the old harridan?"

Ruth had appeared on the gallery, looking down. Her heavy, usually expressionless face held a trace of emotion—fear? Or triumph? She said loudly, "My lady bain't leaving her chamber. She said as how you'd have to carry her out feet first. Well, Colonel Ridgeley? Do ee want to take her from her bed yourself?"

It was the longest speech that Silence had ever heard her make. Ridgeley's face acquired a purple tinge. Then he shouted up at her, "I'll rot in hell before I do—and so will she, God curse her!"

If Ruth's ears withered under the blast of blasphemous invective, she made no movement, though several of the household, notably Eliza, winced. Ridgeley paused and then added, "You can come down. You're as much under suspicion as the rest—yes, you, you clod-faced idiot! Move!"

With her customary deliberate slowness, Ruth turned and disappeared in the direction of the stairs. Silence heard a shuffling, clinking noise behind the screens and with a sinking heart knew what it portended. There were troopers out there, probably under the command of Byam, ready to search the house. She thought with horror of the likely destruction. They would not be gentle—and it was all so unnecessary, so unreasonable. What would any of her servants want with a pistol? It was beyond belief that any would have taken it—they were loyal, devoted to Wintercombe, and they knew what Ridgeley was like, what were the certain consequences of such a foolhardy action.

There was only one person now who would be able to help her, and he was out of reach, supervising the work on the fortifications.

Perhaps, not quite out of reach. She glanced at Mally, beside her, her neatly coiffed head with its riot of ginger curls barely past her shoulder. Perhaps Mally would be able to slip unnoticed into the garden room just behind her, and from there to the terraces and the orchard . . . She caught the girl's eye and held it with significant appeal.

Her maid was nothing if not quick-witted. She nodded her head, so slightly that if Silence had not been watching her intently, she would have missed it entirely, and began very carefully to creep backward.

It did not escape Ridgeley. He whipped around, warned by some flicker of movement on the edge of his vision, and bellowed, "You! Stand still!"

Everyone stood, rigid with shock and fear. Deb, cowering against Hester's apron, began to whimper. Mally's freckled face, the blue eyes wide, was a picture of surprised innocence. Ridgeley stared at her down his fleshy red nose, his lip curled. "You will all stay here until this matter has been settled. Byam! I want some men over here to guard the doorways on this side."

Silence watched, her last hope gone, as four burly troopers, their faces shut, spurs and swords jingling, tramped through the crowded servants and children and took up their position in twos, a pair standing in front of each of the two curtained-off bays that gave access to the eastern part of the house. She felt sick, and helpless, and her impotent anger raged about her heart. If I had that pistol, she thought, gazing with hate at Ridgeley's black head, the beaver hat with its bunch of grubby red plumes undoffed, I think I would use it on him myself.

The thought shocked her. Once, before the soldiers came, she had shied from violence, from argument and confrontation and anger. Now, after little more than four months, she seemed to be a different person. And yet it was not her fault. How could anyone hope to remain calm and serene while their beloved home was being torn apart?

Ridgeley banged the candlestick again, and nearly a score and a half pairs of eyes swiveled toward him, hooked by fear and loathing. A hand touched Silence's fingers. She glanced down and saw that it was Tabby, her little faun's face white with terror. She smiled at her daughter, and the child gave a small brave twitch of her mouth in return. Their hands firmly clasped for mutual support, they listened to the colonel.

"There is something missing from my chamber," he said without preamble. "Something of value—a French wheellock pistol, with shot and powder cartridges. I paid twenty guineas for it, which is more than four times what most of you scum earn in a year. One of you has it—one of you knows where it is. Who? Or it'll be the worse for you."

There was complete silence. All over the hall, people looked at each other, vainly seeking the culprit. Silence, who knew them all so well, their faults and virtues, their strengths and weaknesses, let her eye rove among them. Who had had the opportunity, the lack of scruple, the cunning, and above all the foolhardiness to plan such a coup?

Leah, perhaps—but surely Leah would have taken other things, coin or jewelry, not a pistol and shot, which argued that the thief intended to use it. The only other servant whose honesty she would question was Robin Grindland, the oldest scullion, a bright, slightly insolent lad from a very poor and fecund family. But even so, she did not believe that the boy had been able to snatch any spare moments from his kitchen duties to indulge in a little thievery. Taking surplus foodstuffs home to his family was much more in his line, and something to which she had long ago ordered Darby to turn a blind eye, within reason. True, Robin had a shifty, rather ratlike face, with small narrow eyes and a skin disfigured by the smallpox he had suffered four or five years previously. But he is a child, Silence thought, not yet fifteen. How could he possibly have had the initiative and daring to steal a pistol from under Ridgeley's nose?

She glanced at the children. Nat, seeing her, smiled grimly. Beside him, Rachael's face was as white as Tabby's, set into its habitual tense, angry mask. For the first time since the soldiers' arrival at Wintercombe, Silence regretted not sending them away. Where they could have gone, she did not know: Chard was a ruin, her husband's sister in Wiltshire as poor as a church mouse with her parson husband and a large brood of children, and she could hardly have dispatched her own five across a hundred war-shredded miles to her family in London. No—whatever happened, they were best here, under her care. But she wished, above all, that they did not have to witness the inevitable damage and destruction that would result from Ridgeley's search.

Only possessions, she thought—so long as they leave us our lives and this roof over our heads and the means to survive, then we will. But an image of Nat's mantelpiece, the humble and fragile treasures upon it, and the lovely virginals from which Tabby already could coax music of great skill and sweetness rose to haunt her. She squeezed the little girl's hand, knowing as sure as she knew her own heart what she feared.

Rachael stood, paralyzed with terror. Her tongue was dry and stuck to her mouth. She had never dreamed that it would be a nightmare such as this. She knew that she should own up to her deed, whatever the consequences for herself. Nat would have. Indeed, from the shrewd suspicious glances he had given her, she thought he might have guessed the truth. But by the same token of honor, he would not tell tales. If anyone were to reveal the truth, it must be she herself—and she could not, though the safety of Wintercombe might well depend on it.

Ridgeley was talking, in that abrupt brutal voice, about a search of the house. Thank God, she had seized the opportunity afforded by the gentle weather, some days previously, to retrieve the pistol from under her bed. She had pushed it, dust and fluff and all, into her capacious sleeve and had walked into the garden to enjoy the sun, arms decorously folded, her heart thumping with exhilaration and fear. No one had seen her enter the summerhouse, and none would have thought little of it if they had. The children were always playing in and around it. And then it had been the work of a moment to find Sam's secret place, to prise up the stone with one of Diggory's trowels, and to drop the pistol and the two bags into the space beneath. With the stone and dust carefully replaced, it did not look as if anyone had been near it. She had no fear that a search, however thorough, would find it.

"You have one more chance," Ridgeley said, and his voice had become more pleasant and yet more menacing, with a note in it that raised the hairs on Silence's arm. "One more chance to reveal yourself—or another, if you suspect them to be the thief. And if none is brave enough to speak up, I will order my men to search this house from top to bottom—understand me? Everywhere—in the mattresses, behind the paneling, in your clothes and beds and cooking pots. And I can assure you that they will be most thorough—and not in the least considerate. Do I make myself clear, you ignorant rabble of thieving peasants?"

Silence made a sound of protest, which she cut off with her hand. Rachael stared at her stepmother's face, at the dread and despair in her eyes, and almost opened her mouth to speak. But her lips would not move, and her tongue felt so thick and dry that she knew that no words would come out. She tried to tell herself that she was of gentle birth, still a child—he could not harm her, surely?

But he had struck Nat that dreadful blow on ashen faggot night for much, much less. In her heart Rachael knew that, in one blinding moment of rage, Ridgeley would be quite capable of killing her. He had pistoled recalcitrant villagers near Bath, the tale ran, before Sir Thomas Bridges had thought it expedient to send him away from the city. She could not speak; she could not.

She closed her eyes, imagining that florid face, distorted by ungovernable rage, the great black-furred fist coming out to smash her face to a pulp. Nat, it must be Nat, took her hands in his, and she began to shake with fear. And then the colonel's voice intruded, harsh and loud with rage. "You have had ample warning. Now you'll have your just deserts. Search the house!"

"No!" Silence shouted. She leapt forward, impelled by her own fury to the defense of her house. "No, you shall not! None of them are guilty—none of them! I *know* them—none would do such a thing. Look to your own men, if you would find your thief, for a more villainous bunch of robbing cutpurses I never saw!"

Ridgeley's face was crimson, implacable, like painted stone. She grasped his arm, her desperation shattering all the years of self-possession and calm, caring nothing for dignity if her actions might save Wintercombe from despoilation. "No—how dare you—I will give you money for your wretched pistol, but not this!"

"Silence, woman!" Ridgeley bawled, and his free hand swung around to strike her a great blow on the side of her head.

Her brain rang dizzily, and suddenly she found herself on the hard cold flagstones, a ring of anxious, terrified faces around her. Confused, she tried to sit up, only to fall back into someone's arms. "Don't move, Mother,"

Nat said, sensible, level-headed, beloved Nat. "Don't move. Lie still. There is nothing you can do."

Nothing I can do, she thought, and closed her eyes. Had they bathed her head? There seemed to be water trickling into her hair. Where was Ridgeley? What had happened? She said, trying to sort it out in her mind, "I don't understand . . . did he knock me out?"

"For a moment or so, m'lady," Mally said. "He've gone now, gone on his evil business. Do ee hold still, m'lady, please—let I wipe en off."

"Wipe what off?" Silence opened her eyes to see her maid, her face so pale that the freckles stood out like blemishes across her cheeks, poised with a folded handkerchief. "Blood? Did he hit me so hard?"

"Aye, m'lady—and all sin you dared to stand up to en," Clevinger said, his voice as grim as she had ever heard it. "By God—begging your pardon, m'lady—I'd swear I'll kill en myself afore too long."

"Don't," Silence murmured. Mally was dabbing at the wound with the pad. It hurt, and she tried not to wince. "Please, don't, or he'll surely burn the house down."

"He can't if he's dead," Nat pointed out from behind her. It must be his arms in which she lay. Somewhere she heard a child sobbing, and beyond that distant sounds of mayhem and destruction.

Unable to help it, overwhelmed by her sense of failure, the first tears slid from her eyes, and were wiped away by Mally with the bloodstained kerchief. The maid leaned forward until her face almost touched that of Silence, and whispered, "Don't ee fret, m'lady. I got an idea. I'll fetch the captain for ee."

"How?" Silence asked, her voice hardly more than a breath.

Mally sat back on her heels, smiling suddenly. "Don't ee worry, m'lady," she said in her normal voice. "I'll fetch en right away—if they hulking great brutes over there will let I past 'em."

She got up, moving out of Silence's field of vision. Her place was taken by Rachael, her face gray and tear-streaked. She stared at her stepmother's cut and bloody head and then burst into wild sobbing. Above the sound, Silence heard Mally haranguing the soldiers and knew immediately what she was about.

"Well, do ee let I past, you girt hang-gallows footers, m'lady d'need salve and cordial—stand aside, I tell ee!"

There was a startled pause. Certainly anyone from these parts would recognize the strength of her abuse. Silence, despite the pain and dizziness in her skull, managed to twist around inside Nat's supportive arms. As she had thought, the sight of Mally, fiery and diminutive, confronting the oversized troopers had its amusing aspects, if so much had not ridden on her success in persuading them to step aside. The girl put her hands on her hips and tossed her head imperiously. "Well? Do ee let I past, or do ee let m'lady bleed all over the floor?"

Sheepishly they shuffled to one side. "Well, thank ee kindly!" Mally said with heavy sarcasm, and marched past them, her skirts swishing angrily. With luck she would be able to slip through the outside door of the garden room without attracting their notice. Already they had turned back to fix their gaze on the crowd of anxious servants. Silence followed their eyes and saw the voluptuous figure of Bessie well to the fore, standing in a way that thrust out her ample breasts and showed off her neat, slender waist. She flicked a hand through her hair, licked her lips, and, turning her head slightly, caught her mistress's eye and winked, so quickly that Silence wondered if she had imagined it. As a tiny, surreptitious click announced her maid's escape, the lecherous attention of every soldier in the hall was riveted on Bessie.

No shouts erupted behind Mally as she shut the door very carefully and leapt down the steps to the middle terrace, her skirts held high. Unless there were men in the garden—unlikely, it was one of the few places barred to them by tacit agreement—she would reach Hellier. Like Silence, Mally had never really trusted him. It would take a deal more than a few sweet words and music lessons to win her over. But now, with Ridgeley and his men rampaging through the western side of the house, wreaking havoc, the captain was the only hope of saving Wintercombe.

She flung herself along the graveled path between the knots and down the wide steps, rounded and worn with years of feet, onto the lowest terrace. From there she would be visible to anyone looking out of the study or the winter parlor windows, but she did not care. Unless they shot her in the back—and surely even Ridgeley would not stoop so low—she had sufficient start, and enough speed, to reach Hellier before they could catch up with her.

But there were no sounds of notice, far less pursuit. She scurried down the steps into the long grass of the orchard, still brown and dead after winter frost, the new growth only a tinge of brighter green at the roots. Heedless of the dampness marring her clean skirts and her soft indoor shoes, she plunged through the apple trees toward the ponds where the soldiers could be heard digging and singing some doubtlessly lewd working song. Please God, Hellier would listen to her, and act. He surely would not let this outrage pass unquestioned.

And if I tell en how m'lady were hurt, Mally thought, shrewdly, for she was far more observant and worldly wise in such matters than her mistress, *he'll be that much quicker to put en right.*

She erupted among the workforce like a tiny avenging angel. Her cap had come unpinned in her haste, and her fiery orange hair stood out around her face like a halo. "Captain Hellier! Captain Hellier!"

The soldiers were glad of any excuse to stop work. They laid down their shovels and pickaxes and announced her arrival with whistles, catcalls, some comments that were more or less complimentary, and one or two, highly imaginative, concerning her reasons for wanting the captain so urgently.

"Mally? What is it?" Hellier asked, arriving apparently out of nowhere. He had been working alongside the men, she realized, staring in some astonishment at his mudstained breeches and shirt and the trenching spade across his shoulder.

"Oh, Captain, please do ee come quick, I reckon as how the colonel have run ramping mad—they be searching all over the house for some pistol he've lost from his chamber, and he don't care how much damage they d'make, and when m'lady begged him to stop, he fetched her a girt whop on the side of her head and knocked her down and she be bleeding all over the floor."

"What?" Hellier stared at her, his thin winged brows drawn together across his forehead. "What did you say? Ridgeley *struck* her? Is she hurt?"

"Like I said, she be bleeding despeard bad," Mally told him.

Hellier turned, all his movements suddenly quick and decisive, very different from the more languid gestures he usually employed. "Corporal Denning! Watch over the men while I'm gone—and no shirking, or I'll have your hide and theirs. Understand? Come on, Mally."

She followed him back up the terraces, toiling in his wake, sweat under her armpits and a stitch sharp in her side. Presumably he had been working in the trenches all morning—most ungentlemanly conduct—and yet he bounded up the steps like a cat. Conscious of a twinge of envy beneath her desperate anxiety, Mally hurried after him.

Nick Hellier burst into the hall, shouldering aside the bewildered troopers on guard before they could protest. He was surprised at the rage that had flooded him when Mally had told him of Ridgeley's brutal treatment of Silence. It was despicable, beneath all contempt, that any man professing to gentle birth should treat any woman thus—and the essential generosity and gentleness and warmth of the dowdy Puritan whom he had come to regard as a friend made the crime even worse. He himself had been bred in comparatively humble circumstances, but at least he knew how to behave as a gentleman should, even if sometimes it seemed as if he did not.

The servants were huddled in a fearful mass by the hearth, a buzz of talk humming among them. It died away as he entered so abruptly, and they stared at him with horrified accusing eyes—as if, he thought bitterly, they either feared another attack or blamed him for coming too late. He saw the tearstained faces of the younger children, pressed against the skirts of their kindly middle-aged nurse, and his eyes followed theirs to light upon Silence.

She sat in one of the chairs near the hearth, half hidden by her solicitous household, a twin kneeling at either side and Eliza dabbing at her face. It was chalk white, her eyes huge with strain, and there were dark, ominous stains in her matted hair and on her cap and collar. Eliza took her hand away, and he saw the great spreading scarlet bruise on her cheekbone that in a day or two would be purple, ugly, and swollen.

The rage knotted coldly around his heart. The servants stood aside for him, and he said, his voice thick with fury, "Ridgeley—did *this?*"

"Don't worry about me, I'll heal quickly enough," Silence said, struggling to her feet. "The house—he's wrecking the house. Please, stop him if you can—tell him we haven't *got* his stupid pistol!"

"I will," Nick told her, though how he, unarmed, could do anything to prevent Ridgeley's rampage was decidedly uncertain. Nick touched her hand briefly and then turned, seeking the soldiers who stood still on guard before the bays. "You! Green, Philips, follow me. And I'll have your sword, Masters—come on, hand it over."

"The colonel told we to guard this here hall," one of the men complained doggedly. "We can't leave—"

"Yes, you can." Hellier had the sword, a cheap hanger with what looked suspiciously like rust marring the blade. "Sweet Jesus, Masters, can you not clean this? Green and Philips, come with me."

Reluctantly, with dubious glances at him and at each other, the two troopers edged away from the aperture. A bawling voice from the gallery above halted them in their tracks. "In the name of Lucifer and all his angels, Captain, what the hell do you think you're doing?"

Hellier, quite undeterred, tipped his head back to stare at Ridgeley. The colonel was standing in front of the laughing mask, his large knuckles, one grazed with the blood of Silence and himself, gripping the top of the wood. Behind him, the soldiers clustered, their faces gleeful, some bedecked in pillaged garments, and one, hilarious, wearing a saucepan on his head as an impromptu helmet. By the look of them, a winecask had been broached.

Rachael, her face raw and swollen with tears, slunk backward between the servants, always keeping someone between herself and Ridgeley, although he looked as if he had eyes only for the defiant captain. She could see how this was going to end, and it was her fault, all hers, the wanton destruction and above all that attack on her stepmother. She had the means to make some amends, though, and the determination and hatred necessary to carry it through. Hellier had called away the troopers from the southern bay; her escape lay clear, more open than Mally's had been. Quite unnoticed by anyone in the hall, she slipped outside and into the cool garden.

"I intend to stop this needless damage," Nick said. Silence, staring at him, saw the sharp, hostile outline of his face, the brown hand clenched white-knuckled on the plain sword hilt, and felt a tremor of fear that he would be hurt or humiliated by Ridgeley, as she had been.

But he was a man, a soldier, and not powerless. His tone and his manner were weapons almost as effective as that undoubtedly blunt-edged sword.

The rapier against the bludgeon, he faced Ridgeley up on the gallery, and no one guessed that his blistering voice disguised a wild desire to laugh. The situation held such close echoes of the balcony scene in that play by Shakespeare—though deadly enemies, not lovers, were involved, and he meant now, goaded beyond restraint by the colonel's brutal treatment of Silence, to put an end to Ridgeley's excesses once and for all.

The colonel laughed. "You've gone too far, *Captain*." His scorn was withering. "Perhaps Sir Thomas would be interested to learn how frequently you have taken the part of these miserable traitors. Perhaps a little too sympathetic for a king's officer, eh? Oh, yes, I know about those cozy evenings with that dowdy little Puritan—and what in God's name do you see in her, man? No face, not now"—he sniggered—"no tit on her, nothing to keep a man happy. Can't get anything better, eh?"

"You come down here and repeat that," Nick said. "Come down, you stinking son of a whore—or you show yourself a scurvy coward, before the whole household."

"I say, Nick, that's going a bit far!" Byam lurched up to the gallery rail, his braying voice instantly recognizable. "He's killed men for less, y'know. Why don't you come and have a drink with us and forget it? Can't have the officers dueling in front of the men, y'know."

"No, Johnny," Hellier told him. "Once, perhaps. Not now. Well, Ridgeley? Did you hear me? Are you going to fight? Or are you going to charge on with the wits of a mad bull until some honest man poleaxes you?"

"I'll see you hanged!" the colonel shouted, leaning over the gallery. "By God, I'll see you hung and drawn like a fowl for the traitor you are. You dare, you *dare* to challenge me . . . no, I'll not taint my blade by crossing it with yours. You! Lieutenant Byam! Take six men down and seize him!"

Byam's drink-blurred face wavered and then cleared. He glanced down at Nick, standing in the center of the hall, a seemingly insignificant figure, neat and slight in shirt and breeches, the undistinguished sword balanced ready in his hand, and then turned to his colonel. "Look here, Ridgeley— he's done nothing but question your orders—he's no traitor, I'd swear it."

"You'd swear day was night if you'd got enough wine swilling inside you," Ridgeley said with contempt. "He's a traitor—take him!"

Byam's expression became surprisingly firm and resolute. Standing quite still and straight, he said shortly, "I am sorry, Colonel, but I think you're wrong. I will not do it."

"Then you'll have to come down and take me yourself, won't you, Ridgeley!" Hellier shouted, and laughed. There was a sudden wild, reckless note to it, and Silence, watching tensely, realized that he was enjoying this challenge to his hated colonel's authority.

In the summerhouse, Rachael scrabbled with frantic fingers at the pistol whose theft had caused all this. Cartridge and shot in the barrel, rammed home with shaking fingers. May that go through his horrible skull! she thought furiously. Then to wind it up, using the key, cold as death in her hand. Finally, the priming powder in the pan next to the wheel. She prayed she had not forgotten anything. Sam's enthusiastic instruction was still clear and vivid in her memory, but such was her urgency that she might well have made some dreadful and obvious mistake. She leapt to her feet and ran, the weapon clutched in sweaty hands, out of the summerhouse and back to the hall. It had taken her no more than three or four minutes. Please God, she was not too late!

There was no sound as she slid through the door to the garden room. Then she heard, distant but quite clear, Ridgeley's voice. "Trooper Day— get my horse pistols, *now*!"

"Still too frightened to meet me?" That was Hellier, taunting his superior officer. "Pistols are a coward's weapon, Colonel—what are you going to do? Shoot me in cold blood?"

"If I have to," Ridgeley said. Rachael crept into the bay and peered past the curtain and the arched entrance to the hall. There were no soldiers near. They were standing just to one side of Hellier. Her quick glance took in her stepmother, on the edge of her chair, her knuckles white on its carved arms. Nat was close by her, his arm about her shoulders. She looked down at the pistol, running feverishly through Sam's instructions, and gasped. She had forgotten to lower the flint arm so that it touched the wheel. Hastily she pulled it down, thanking God. Had she not remembered, the pistol would have failed to fire, with disastrous results. Then she walked out into the hall.

No one was looking at her, no one turned to see her moving forward, her arms folded, the pistol concealed inside her sleeve. She did not know how close she would have to get to Ridgeley to have a chance of hitting him; she did not even know if she had loaded it correctly. It was as if someone else, someone with no other thought but murder, had taken over her body, so that her mind watched, detached, as she walked into the center of the hall in front of the captain and lifted her head to face the colonel.

Hellier saw her. His hand came out to detain her, but too late. She heard, as if from very far off, her stepmother crying her name, and the captain's voice, loud with concern. "Rachael! What are you doing? Get back—get out of the way!"

She ignored him, the full force of her hatred, a beam of light and power, directed at the man standing upon the gallery, his heavy face mocking. "Yes, traitor's brat, the captain's right for once—I should get out of the way, or you'll be hurt."

"You wanted your pistol, didn't you?" Rachael asked loudly. She stood still and brought it out of her sleeve on its side, wheel uppermost, as Sam had shown her. Both hands were clenched around the butt, and the muzzle pointed unwaveringly at Ridgeley's heart. "Well, here it is, Colonel—and I wish you joy of it!"

She pressed the trigger with fanatic fervor. There was a deafening crash, screaming, clouds of acrid smoke. Rachael, flung backward by the recoil, her hands tingling painfully, stared in astonishment up at her enemy. She had not even really expected it to go off.

And Ridgeley, his face suddenly gray, appalled, stared down at his blue doublet, on which a dark crimson stain was spreading. Then, he toppled backward and out of her sight.

THIRTEEN

Whoso diggeth a pit shall fall therein.
—PROVERBS 26:27

"Wormwood," Silence murmured. "Wormwood, as bitter as I can make it. And rue . . . wormwood and rue, and verjuice. It'll either kill him or be so unpleasant that he'll make no effort to get better."

"And us d'want him safe in his bed for so long as possible," Mally said, peering into a jar of unguent. "Faugh, this have turned bad and no mistake!"

"What has?"

"The oil of swallows," Mally told her. "Reckon you'd best throw en away." She peered closer at the label, written in a crabbed hand quite unlike Silence's neat, open script. "Dame Ursula made en, so it must be all of seven or eight year old."

"Well, I certainly didn't—and besides, I haven't the time to spare for such a complicated remedy," Silence said. She reached up for a bunch of rue, hanging with other dried plants and herbs above the hearth. "I really don't know why we're doing this, Mally. I suppose it's because as good Christians we can hardly leave the man to die."

"Christians perhaps—fools for certain," her maid said dryly.

Rachael's shooting of the hated Ridgeley with his own pistol had flung Wintercombe into a chaos that it had taken all day to order. Silence must deal with screaming children and hysterical serving maids; with her stepdaughter, who had fallen into a dead faint a second after the colonel's collapse; and with the wounded victim himself.

Her priorities well ordered, she had looked first to Rachael, while Doraty tried to calm Deb and William, both of whom were sobbing. Hester, usually so level-headed and sensible, had flung her apron over her head and was wailing in a corner while Bessie and Eliza, an unlikely pairing, attempted to comfort her. Then, as Silence tried to revive her stepdaughter with cold water and burned feathers, the cry had gone up from the gallery. "He bain't dead, m'lady—do ee come quick!"

So, with Nick at her heels, she had stumbled up the twisting stairs and stared in astonishment at a Ridgeley who still lived, and breathed, in seeming defiance of justice and retribution. And her first feeling, as she gazed down at the stricken, helpless man, was of annoyance. A wound like that should have killed him—and it was so emphatically more convenient and fitting and *right* that he should die.

She had upbraided herself sternly for her wicked, evil, unchristian thoughts, but it was nonetheless true. The colonel, alive, was a menace. Dead, he represented freedom from bondage.

But despite her loathing, she had knelt by his side, while Byam, his face almost as gray as his colonel's, unbuttoned the man's buff coat, unfastened his doublet, and laid bare his broad pale chest, its bones overlaid by heavy flesh and a thick furry mat of black hair. The bullet had entered on his left side, and the blood flowed freely. She stared, numb, helpless, at the flood of reeking scarlet. Then she pulled off her apron, folded it into a small thick pad, and placed it firmly on the wound. The man groaned feebly and tried to move. "Hold him!" Hellier ordered, and two of the soldiers, who had been standing in an appalled, unmoving circle around Byam and Ridgeley, moved suddenly to help.

"Here, sir, here be the bullet!" said another trooper, thrusting it proudly under Nick's nose. "Found en in the wall, pulled en out with my fingers."

Silence stared with horror at the small, misshapen sphere of metal lying in the man's grimy palm. Blood and shreds of cloth—or flesh—clung to it. Hard to believe that something so small could fell a man as large and vigorous as the colonel, still less bring him to death.

"Well, at least I won't have to dig around inside him to find it," Hellier said dryly. "But it means two wounds, if it went right through—two holes, two chances of suppuration and fever. Have you dressed many gunshot wounds, Lady St. Barbe?"

"None at all. But I have helped to heal cuts made by a scythe, or gashes caused by broken glass or horses' hooves or stones, and once one of the scullions ran a knife into his arm when he was dismembering a chicken." Silence glanced at him, saw the hidden irony in his face, and managed a wan smile. "But I really would rather that you had the tending of Colonel Ridgeley, sir. I might be tempted to finish the process that Rachael has begun."

There was a stir and a mutter among the curious, crowded soldiers, and she realized that her words might have been better left unsaid. She added hastily, "But naturally, I must take the Christian course and do all in my power to heal him."

Ridgeley was carried, semiconscious and moaning, to his chamber, and Leah, gawping and morbidly curious, arrived with bucket and mop to clean up the large sticky puddle of blood marring the polished oaken floor of the gallery. There was so much to do that Silence had no time to allow the shock and horror of the shooting to settle like a baleful crow into her mind. The servants must be soothed and dismissed to their duties, the children calmed and sent up to her chamber with Nat, who had promised to tell them stories. They went willingly, with swollen, tear-dabbled faces, save for Tabby, whose expression was fierce and gleeful. "I'm *glad* Rachael shot that horrible man," she had said passionately to her mother. And Silence, watching her leave the hall, wondered unhappily where that once shy, sensitive, gentle child had vanished.

Mally had revived Rachael. The hall still stank of the sharp acrid flavor of gunpowder, but the bitter reek of burned feathers was woven into it now. The girl sat on the floor, supported by the maid, her black hair hanging over her face and her arms trailing in her lap. Silence, visited by a sudden and unexpected surge of compassion, knelt by her stepdaughter and gently spoke her name.

There was no response. She tried again, and touched her shoulder. It might as well have belonged to a corpse.

"Rachael!" she repeated, more loudly, and at least received some response.

"Go away," said the girl's voice, without anger, without any emotion in it save a distant, remote exhaustion. "Leave me alone."

Above her lank dark head, Mally's eyes met those of Silence. "We can't," her stepmother said, very softly. "Rachael, come on, get up—and we'll take you upstairs and you can rest."

"I won't," the girl said flatly. "Aren't they going to punish me?"

It was then, hearing the hopeless despair in her voice, that Silence felt her own shock and horror flood her eyes with tears. She knew suddenly what Rachael feared and said gently, "You aren't going to be punished. You haven't killed him."

"I haven't . . ." Abruptly Rachael's head came up, almost striking Mally on the nose. "I haven't killed him? He isn't dead?"

"No. He's sore wounded, but Captain Hellier seems to think there is some hope of recovery."

Rachael's stark blue eyes, filled with a bitterness appalling in a child of fifteen, stared into her stepmother's. "I didn't kill him—but I *meant* to," she said. "I *wanted* to—I wanted to more than anything—and then I pulled the trigger and he fell and it was so easy and then I thought, I've *really* killed him—and I don't remember any more." She paused and then cried wildly, "I should have—he *deserves* to be dead, he does, he does—and what will he do to me when he gets better?"

It was a question neither Silence nor Mally felt competent to answer. Rachael drew a deep, quivering breath and then burst into floods of exhausted tears. Silence tried to comfort her, but the girl hunched her shoulders away and would not accept it. In the end, Silence got to her feet, feeling as ancient and care-burdened as Methuselah, and said quietly, "We'll take you up to your chamber."

Rachael at last allowed herself to be helped to her feet, and led upstairs.

The pistol, small and deadly, lay on the flagstones where she had dropped it. Mally picked it up and pushed it safely into her apron, and then followed her mistress.

The soldiers had gone, dispersed by Hellier's brisk, curt orders. The wreckage they had left behind lay in every room they had visited, though fortunately they had not had time to search more than a few before Rachael had so astonishingly halted their progress. Silence left the girl still weeping on her bed, soothed by a salve of poppy seed, which did seem to calm her somewhat. Hester, now rather more composed and somewhat ashamed of her breakdown, was set to watch over her. Eliza, who had been inspecting the damage wrought by the soldiers, came with a long face to report shredded hangings, smashed paneling, broken furniture: The study and the winter parlor were the worst affected.

"Shut the door on it," Silence said, feeling that she could not just then face a sight so certain to be distressing, and went with Mally to see how the colonel did.

They had laid him on the bed, and Harris, a little bustling man with a rather fawning manner, was wringing his hands over him while Nick, more practical, was binding the wounds. The filthy, squalid chamber reeked of blood and sweat and unwashed bodies and putrefying food. Silence, who had never ventured within while Ridgeley was in residence, stared in disgust around the guest suite that had once been kept immaculately clean and neat, and put her lavender-scented kerchief to her nose. Mally, more forthright, let out a snort of contempt. "'Tis a foul fox as can't keep his own den sweet," she said with scorn.

Fortunately, Ridgeley was past hearing, or caring. He lay in the bed, a great lump of inanimate matter like a felled tree, and drew harsh moaning breaths. Silence, listening to that sound and seeing the sick pallor of the normally ruddy face behind the aggressive stubble, thought that Rachael might after all have her wish granted. She said softly to Nick, "How does he?"

Hellier glanced up at her, his hands tying a knot in the last bandage. It was a piece of ripped linen, probably one of her sheets, but she did not particularly care. "I won't lie to you, he's in a bad way. He's lost a good deal of blood, and the ball broke a couple of ribs, I think. It might have touched something more vital, but I'm not an anatomist. It's a good thing he carries so much spare flesh, or it would probably have gone through his liver. And that he certainly would *not* have survived."

"And this?"

"If it heals, if there is no putrefaction nor wound fever, then he has a good chance of recovery. But it will take a long time," Nick said, and gave her the benefit of his long lazy smile. "And it is said by some authorities that patients of a choleric nature are slow to heal and should at all cost avoid argument or anger. However, it is almost springtime, when wounds are supposed to mend quickest. We may have him hale and hearty before the month is out."

Silence tried not to let her thoughts show on her face, though Mally behind her muttered darkly, "Dear Lord, I d'hope not!"

"And the assassin?" the secretary Harris asked, rubbing his hands over and over as if he were washing them. "I trust the assassin will not escape?"

He fixed Silence with a pleading, doglike stare, and she said coldly, "Since the assassin, as you describe her, is my own stepdaughter, and hardly more than a child, I think punishment is inappropriate. Her shock and horror at her terrible act is penalty enough."

"If I know Rachael," Hellier remarked dryly, "her shock and horror can probably be ascribed to her unfortunate failure to kill him outright. My lady, I do not like to lay this duty upon you, but you will appreciate that the men are in dire need of a firm hand—and I wouldn't put it past Lieutenant Byam to incite them to further destruction, or at any rate to turn a blind eye to it. Since I am now the senior officer here, I must enforce my authority with all speed, or risk a mutiny. Will you watch over the colonel for a while? I am sure that Harris will do all he can to help. There will be salves and ointments needed, and his ribs may need strapping much more tightly."

Silence, her heart sinking, forbore to remind him that she had had some experience of healing broken ribs—her husband had once been kicked by an unruly horse—and still more of anointing wounds. "Of course, Captain," she said with a heavy irony that escaped Harris entirely but brought a sudden gleam to Nick's face. "I will do everything in my power to bring his injuries to a proper conclusion."

"That's what I thought," Hellier said, smiling again. "But make sure it's the *right* conclusion, won't you, my dear lady. I will return as soon as I can."

She had been left in that fetid, disgusting chamber with the comatose Ridgeley and his groveling servant, and had at once set to work, summoning Eliza and Margery Turber to clear the rooms and return them to some sort of order. Harris's protests rose in vain as the two women, with relish, set about their task. Wails of "Oh, please, don't touch those papers—don't—leave that alone!" drifted from the outer chamber, and Mally, a grim smile on her freckled face, lit the fire, which had been allowed to go out. Finally, when a vestige of decency had been imposed on the chaos, Silence left Harris, still complaining ineffectually, to watch his master and went down to her stillroom.

The soldiers, fortunately, had not touched it. The door was usually locked, for many of the remedies contained within were valuable, or dangerous if used unwisely, and with the foment of jealousy, rivalry, and backbiting that flourished in the Wintercombe servants' hall, ease of access to such substances as henbane or belladonna was distinctly unwise. So her rows of bottles, jars, and vials were still intact, and she and Mally could prepare, though somewhat reluctantly, a salve that with God's providence—or otherwise—would heal the stricken colonel.

"Rue be useful against a poisoned wound," Mally pointed out. "And Mistress Rachael didn't put venom on that there pistol ball, did she?"

"No—the only poison involved was probably in Ridgeley to begin with," Silence said dryly. "But a nice bitter draft will increase his agony. I don't intend to make the healing process a pleasant one, despite what the captain said. For wounds, I have an oil of John's wort, which is very good—it cured Robert Ames when he cut his leg open with a scythe last year, do you remember? The bone showed through, and yet it was healed up in ten days and he was walking freely within the month. It's in that big bottle at the end of the second shelf—the blood-colored oil."

Mally reached it down and set it carefully on the table, while her mistress threw a handful of the dried rue into the pot now seething in the hearth. She added wormwood, and some dried poppy seeds and leaves to promote restfulness. If Ridgeley could be nursed through his sickness in a state of semiconsciousness, so much the better. The acrid steam filled the room, making both women cough. Mally, who was less gentle than Silence, hoped that the brew would prove as corrosive to Ridgeley's guts as to her nose, and said so. She added, with a relish that brought the twitch of a smile to Silence's face, "Shall I heat up this here oil, m'lady? Most such go on fairish warm."

"Warm enough to raise a blister, if not the dead," Silence said. "And, yes, it *is* supposed to be more effective if applied at a painful heat—well, why not, Mally? I do try to be a good Christian housewife, but I think that tending that loathsome man stretches my principles almost to breaking point. He brought this on himself, and if his treatment proves painful, he has only himself to blame."

"Maybe," Mally said shrewdly. "But folk in that pass allus d'blame everyone *except* theyselves, don't they?"

Fortunately, the colonel, feeble from loss of blood and in considerable pain, was in no condition to blame anyone for his plight. With Mally's competent help—Harris, fussing around the bed, was no use whatsoever—his bandages were removed, a cloth pad liberally daubed with hot oil placed on both wounds, and held in place with tight strapping. To this brisk, unsympathetic treatment Ridgeley reacted with curses, abuse, and cries of pain that sounded weak indeed after his usual stentorian bellows. As a final torture, he was propped more or less upright upon a pile of bolsters and pillows, and several spoonfuls of Silence's rue water were forced between his teeth with the assistance of Mally, who simply held his nose until his mouth opened. Silence, seeing the colonel's outraged face, felt a wicked glee rising within her. How were the tables turned! She would not abuse the power she had over him now. After all, she had her godly duty to be merciful to the afflicted. But she would not be human if she did not find some amusement, not to say pleasure, in the situation.

Nick, it appeared, had come to the same conclusion. At last she had seen his colonel comfortable—or as comfortable as could be expected, given the nature of his injuries and their remedy—and had left Harris on reluctant watch. Ridgeley, under the influence of the poppy seeds, was sunk into uncouthly snoring slumber, and with luck would be so for some while.

She closed the door from the bedchamber, Nick at her elbow. Eliza and Margery had done their best, and the antechamber presented a much improved appearance. It was still cluttered, papers stacked everywhere, but the fire burned brightly, and sweet rosemary had been thrown on the wood to perfume the air and purge it of any infection.

"You enjoyed that," he said, and Silence, startled, turned a rueful and guilty face to him.

"How did you guess? It's not something I'm especially proud of, you understand . . . but I can't help it."

"And rue need *not* have been part of that drink. Poppy in almond milk is quite enough to provoke a restful sleep—and don't fall into further temptation, I for one will be exceedingly suspicious should he fail to wake up." Nick studied her, and Silence wondered if he saw the lines of exhaustion and strain that seemed to have been graven upon her face as if on stone, and showed so deep when she looked in her mirror. He added quietly, "Today's affair cannot stay a secret. Ridgeley is not dangerously hurt—if the wound does not putrefy, he should be recovered by Easter. We must talk about this, before the day is out—the governor must be told, for one thing."

Silence stared at him. He said, "You look stricken, and there's no need. I give you my word, nothing will happen to Rachael. Where will you be, in an hour?"

She thought of all the things that must be done. The list of them would surely be a yard long if written down, but at least tending Ridgeley was a considerable way down the order of priorities. Rachael, the children, the servants, dinner—it must be close to noon, and nothing done—all needed her immediate attention. But there was one matter that could wait little longer. She said, smiling tiredly, "I shall either be in Bedlam, foaming and raging, or in the study, seeing what your troopers have left of our papers. Before dinner—which is bound to be very, very late—I shall be there. Until then, Captain?"

"Until then, my lady," he said, and bowed formally. The use of each other's Christian names was for private occasions only, and Ridgeley's suite was too public, despite the fact that only Mally, whom Silence trusted as she would one of her own sisters, was actually present. Then they went to their separate duties.

Silence looked in upon Rachael, saw that her stepdaughter was sleeping soundly, and told Hester to relieve poor Nat, still entertaining the younger children in her chamber. She next spent a harassing half hour explaining the morning's events to Dame Ursula, who had convinced herself that the uproar was all her daughter-in-law's fault but was highly gleeful at Ridgeley's fate. Then she descended with relief to the kitchen, where she arranged with Darby for dinner to be served somewhat later than usual and was able to soothe the anxious fears of the servants, who had congregated under the cook's massive wing. No, she did not think the colonel would die. It was probably just a flesh wound. Nor did Captain Hellier seem to think that Mistress Rachael would be punished. And no, it was not likely that the house would be burned down about their ears by soldiers thirsty for revenge. Captain Hellier appeared to have the situation well under control, and indeed, in matters of discipline, there might even be an improvement. Since the absence of any soldiers in the kitchen, together with certain sounds from outside, seemed to indicate that the captain was even now haranguing the assembled troops in the barton, she felt safe to predict this with some certainty.

Then, having assured herself that dinner was progressing smoothly despite the delay—pigeon pastie again, and rabbit fricassee and a nice fat carp, which Diggory had netted yesterday evening from the fish pond—she gathered her skirts and her courage, and with Mally went to see the extent of the damage.

At least they had not demolished the kitchen, but the dining parlor had suffered badly. The dark oaken paneling had been knocked and split in several places, as the troopers had sought secret compartments. One of the doors of the carved court cupboard had been wrenched off its hinges and thrown at the large north window. The lead squares were bent, and several panes broken. All the leather-covered chairs had had their backs and seats ripped open, and hanks of horsehair stuffing drifted darkly about the floor. Some troopers had evidently been in a hilarious mood: The two portraits of Sir Samuel and Dame Ursula, one either side of the fireplace, had been used for target practice. Dented pewter mugs, plates, bowls, and cups lay heaped in the hearth, and the stiff, unsmiling features of her parents-in-law, sitting upon their cartwheel ruffs like two imitations of John the Baptist, had suffered numerous indignities. Only that morning it had been a pleasant, welcoming room. Now, despoiled by gleeful vandals, it was bleak, desolate, and ruined.

"Two—three hour should see it all put aright," Mally said, as Silence gazed around. "Oh, not that there paneling, that'll need a carpenter—but us'll set it all clean and neat and decent, m'lady."

Silence walked forward and picked up a pewter mug. Its handle had been flattened and the rim violently distorted by, she guessed, a collision with the mantelpiece. Almost all the utensils had suffered similar damage. She said slowly, "It's stupid, I know, to be upset over such things—they are only things, possessions, they're replaceable—and not even very valuable.

But . . . it's the wantonness of it, Mally, they didn't *need* to smash every-thing. That pistol could hardly have been hidden behind poor Sir Samuel's portrait, but still they wrecked it."

"That be soldiers for ee," her maid said. "They wouldn't be in the army if they didn't like destroying aught in sight. And that d'go for your Cap-tain Hellier as well as the colonel and all that hang-gallize white-livered crew."

"He's far from being *my* captain," Silence said, smiling, and then saw her maid's face. "Mally, why are you looking at me like that?"

The freckles and pointed jaw took on a determined, stubborn set. "I know as how 'tisn't my place to say en, m'lady, but you . . . well, maybe you can't see en so plain as what I can. Captain Hellier . . . I do like him, m'lady, he d'*seem* a nice honest gentleman—but I can't trust him, I can't. They be all the same, these stomachy Cavalier officers—sweet and gallant to a lady, and up to all manner of no good behind her back. Don't ee trust him neither, m'lady—please, don't."

Silence stared at the girl in bewilderment and some distress. "But, Mally, I do trust him—oh, I didn't at first. I thought he was like Ridgeley and Byam, but I don't think he is. He's risked too much, for our sake."

"Or for *your* sake, m'lady," Mally said. "Forgive me, m'lady, but I can't help being voreright. He be sweetorting you, I d'swear it."

Astonished, Silence gazed at her distressed face and then suddenly started to laugh. "Oh, Mally, Mally—I'm sorry, I can't help it—sweet-hearting? *Me?* Oh, really, that's too ridiculous to think of it. Look at me—I'm twenty-nine, married nine, nearly ten years, I've borne four children, I have no looks, no graces, no conversation—and you tell me a handsome Cavalier captain is paying court to *me?*"

"He chose ee for his Valentine, didn't he, m'lady?"

"And you know as well as I do that it's a joke—why, if it was a custom in this family, I would be Nat's, or William's . . . it doesn't *mean* any-thing," Silence said. "And even if he does favor me, which I very much doubt, don't you do me a disservice by worrying about it? You've been my maid for two and a half years now, Mally Merrifield—can't you trust me to be sensible?"

Mally had the grace to look a little sheepish. The freckles were flushed, and her face doubtful. She said slowly, "I didn't mean no disrespect, m'lady—but he be so smooth-tongued, so blissom—and you don't know nought of him, m'lady, nought of him at all."

That at least was true. What did any of them know of Nick Hellier, save what he himself had chosen to show them? He could command men, and handle weapons, and kill. He was efficient, not to say ruthless, in pursuing his ends. He was prepared on matters of principle to defy his superior officers, at some risk to his person and his position. And he had an odd, jumbled assortment of peculiar skills. Where had been born and bred a man who could quote the Scriptures, knew how to heal wounds and salve the sick, play the fiddle and read poetry and teach a child the virginals, enjoy chess and talk amusingly and make hats by folding linen napkins?

No, they knew nothing of Captain Hellier: his birth, his family and education and career, even his age were all alike a mystery. And yet, knowing nothing, how to explain to Mally that she knew everything that really mattered about him?

"I *do* trust him," she said. "He is my friend. And the idea that he is paying court to me is absurd, Mally, and I hope it's the last I hear of it."

Knowing Mally, it would not be. The girl was as stubborn and tenacious as any of her family. But she was loyal and would never gossip about her mistress with the other servants. She nodded at last, reluctantly, and followed Silence across the corridor to the study and the winter parlor beyond.

There Nick Hellier found her some while later. He had called all the soldiers together, his own troop and Captain Bull's company, and informed them that an unfortunate accident had, alas, befallen Colonel Ridgeley. He would be indisposed for some weeks. In the meantime, he would assume the command until the Governor of Bath could be informed.

They had not looked displeased at that. Ridgeley was hardly loved. One or two of the more unruly had even cheered. Nick emphasized that their duties would continue broadly as before, some guarding the house, some working on the defenses, the rest foraging, turn and turn about. The difference would lie in matters of discipline, for, as he pointed out, an improvement in their relations with the villagers around about would hopefully lead to a corresponding increase in the contributions they were given—and certainly there would not be such a risk of the kind of retaliatory action that had struck down the colonel. They would not expect to be loved; he had some hope that they might become known for their justice and forbearance.

Byam and several others were looking decidedly sulky and resentful, and that was only to be expected. He added, thinking of the lieutenant, that he was not forbidding indulgence in strong drink, so long as it did not lead to damage or mischief. Nor would he deny them the company of women, so long as the females in question were willing (Byam's expression grew somewhat brighter at this). There was to be no more theft, wanton damage, or rape. And the penalties he would exact for transgressions would be swift and severe.

They knew him and that he had every intention of carrying out such punishments, if necessary. The memory of the man he had killed, months ago in the orchard, lay behind their wary, acquiescent faces. He knew that most of them, certainly those who were not irredeemably stupid, were afraid of him, just as they feared Ridgeley. But he also meant, unlike Ridgeley, to earn their respect.

He certainly had their undivided attention: Over a hundred pairs of eyes stared avidly at him. He seized the opportunity to clarify certain points. They were at Wintercombe by the leave of Lady St. Barbe (a polite fiction that would deceive only Bull's company, unaware of the exact circumstances under which the garrison had originally been installed). She and her children and household were to be treated with the utmost deference and respect. The terraced gardens, the bowling green and yew walk were the family's sanctum, and not to be entered without permission. Nor was the house itself laid open to the soldiers. Those on kitchen duty, of course, were free to go to and from their work, but in general only at supper, which by the continued generosity of Lady St. Barbe would be served as usual in the hall, would the bulk of the men be allowed inside the house.

Finally, he reminded them that, after this miserable winter, the campaigning season was about to begin. Armies were stirring. Lord Goring, with a force of five thousand, had arrived in the south of Somerset, around Chard, with the intention of joining Sir Richard Grenville's men to reduce the intransigent Parliament stronghold of Taunton. Only a day or so previously, the Prince of Wales had come to Bath, commissioned by his father as General of the West, though he was only fourteen. Under his leadership, and that of the wise and experienced councillors whom the king had appointed, the Royal cause in the West was set for a triumphant march to victory.

He had never thought himself much of an orator, but his words seemed to rouse the men's approval. They were almost drowned by the cheerful roars of assent.

"So you won't have to sit here twiddling your thumbs much longer," he said when the noise had died down a little. "In a few weeks some of you will have the chance to win your own glory—and send those scurvy Roundheads yelping back to London with their tails between their legs!"

And the howls of delight that greeted these final words quite eclipsed their previous efforts, and seemed in danger of shattering the glass in Wintercombe's windows.

Silence heard the cheering from the study. She had peered apprehensively around the door of the winter parlor, taken one appalled look at the devastation in one of Wintercombe's loveliest rooms, and shut the door on it. The chaos in its antechamber, once used by Sir Samuel to store his books and work on estate business, more recently by Nat for his lessons with Parson Willis, abandoned since the soldiers' occupation, could be faced, even put in order. At least they had burned nothing; it was fortunate that today the fire had not been lit. But the documents and papers, bills and accounts and all her careful inventories, lay ripped and scattered. The drawers of Sir Samuel's desk had been flung to the corners of the room, and the ink overset. It had dried in sticky puddles, like black blood, all over the oaken table, and the rush matting was spotted with it and shredded,

totally ruined. At least rush matting is cheap, she thought blankly, looking at the destruction, the damage, and blinking back tears at the sheer
pointlessness of it all. Those books, hurled willy-nilly from their shelves,
lay in heaps on the floor, pages torn, spines broken, the fine leather bindings stamped and trampled by their muddy boots . . .

They had not, thank God, found the hiding place under the hearth. It
was the first thing she had checked. That store of coin would be needed to
repair this damage. She knew better now than to hope that compensation
would ever be paid. And the estate chest, iron-bound oak with three
locks—the keys dangled from her waist with the rest—had remained intact, though they had obviously tried to force it open. Splintered wood and
raw bright scratches across the metal plates of the lock bore mute witness
to their vain efforts. She sank to her knees amid the papers, picking up the
scattered quills that lay among them. The jar in which they had stood lay
shattered in the hearth.

"The wicked, evil crew!" Mally said viciously, looking around at the
rampant disorder. "I d'reckon as how they *enjoyed* doing of all this."

"Undoubtedly they did. Theirs is the kind of mind that can't see anything of worth, or value, or beauty without wanting to smash it to pieces
. . . Pray God that Captain Hellier can keep them under control."

"He'll need to be firm," her maid said, with some understatement. "If
they'm used to the whip and the stick, they won't answer to aught less,
m'lady."

"I don't think it would be less," Silence said, remembering the man who
had attacked Tabby, lying in the orchard, with Nick Hellier, that warm
and amusing man who offered friendship, standing at the balustrade with
his smoking pistol . . .

Ridgeley might have controlled his men with bludgeon and brutality,
but in Hellier, she knew, there was something much more subtle and more
dangerous by far. And in her arose an element that was both attracted to
and repelled by that danger.

She returned her thoughts briskly to the matter in hand. The quills went
back on the stained table, and Mally picked up the drawers of the little
desk that sat on top. They were walnut, and inlaid with a geometric pattern in different colored woods. The fineness of the work had not prevented
damage. She surveyed the smashed edges with weary sadness. So much had
assaulted her ears and eyes this day that even the unhappy fate of Sir Samuel's cherished desk did not seem to matter very much, anymore.

"He've got their goodwill, anyhow," Mally said suddenly as she coaxed
the fire into life.

Silence did not at first know what she meant. Then she heard, distantly,
the cheering. Trying to smile, she said wryly, "Well, he's either promised
them a woman and a barrel of cider each, or a good fight. And I know
which I hope it is."

She was trying to sort out the scattered papers when the knock came at the door. Mally, who had gone for cleaning materials, came in, her face severe, her apron covered with dust and sand and old ink stains, and said without inflection, "Captain Hellier, m'lady. And Eliza d'want I to help her in the dining parlor."

"Of course—and can you tell Darby when you have finished, so that dinner may be served? Thank you, Mally."

The maid went out, leaving the door open, and Hellier walked in. He had changed his attire: The muddy shirt and breeches had been replaced by the buff coat and blue suit that proclaimed him a soldier, and the long, serviceable sword hung from a shoulder belt. He doffed his hat and bowed. Silence, sitting on the chaotic floor surrounded by papers, felt amusement rising through her bleak, weary mood of depression. She said briskly, "Don't be ridiculous—and shut the door, you're making the fire smoke."

"My pardon, lady," he said, obeying her, and then looked slowly around at the disorder. "They were thorough, were they not?"

"Not especially—they failed to break open the chest." She would not mention the hiding place under the hearthstone—that was a secret she would keep from everyone save Mally, for it might one day save them from penury, or worse.

"They lacked an axe, fortunately for you," Nick said. "Don't let my presence stop you—there must be a great deal to do."

"There is. All these papers relate to the estate, the house, the farm— inventories, invoices, lists of damage—and I'll need those last, for there is quite a lot to add to them now." She glanced around at Nick. He was crouched over the heap of books, picking them up one by one, closing them properly, dusting off their covers.

"Whose collection is this?" he asked.

"The books? Oh, they were Sir Samuel's, and probably some were bought by his father—he traveled to Italy and France and laid out the gardens."

"Some are unusual for a godly man, to say the least. Here are Spenser's poems, and Shakespeare's sonnets—very profane."

"Sir Samuel, Nick, was not particularly godly," Silence said, and an involuntary smile lit her face. "Oh, he went to church twice of a Sunday, and he mistrusted a Papist as well as the next man—but he also liked a jar of ale or cider at the George, and he could sing and play songs that weren't at all pious, he enjoyed bowls and dancing and cards . . . and he always said that he was too old and too lazy to meddle with other men's consciences, he'd leave that to his wife."

"The redoubtable Dame Ursula? An unlikely bride for such a man."

"It was arranged by their parents when they were young. And my mother-in-law does have her virtues. After all, despite her age and infirmity, she refused to be cowed by Ridgeley."

"And what does she think of his present misfortune?"

"Oh, she revels in it. It's taken years off her life," Silence told him, thinking of the jubilant exulting voice declaiming the words of the seventh psalm: 'He made a pit, and digged it, and is fallen into the ditch which he made. His mischief shall return upon his own head, and his violent dealing shall come down upon his own pate.'

"It was no more than his just deserts, after all," she added. "And her estimation of Rachael has soared. Her one complaint concerns her erratic aim."

"Rachael," Nick murmured. His hands, brown and square and callused by years of holding reins and weapons, continued to tidy the books, but his warm autumnal eyes studied Silence, kneeling a few feet away, her lap full of papers. "That, to me, is the greatest puzzle of all. How in God's name did she lay her hands on that pistol? And where did she hide it? And above all, where did she learn how to load and fire it?"

"I don't know. She's sleeping—I gave her a soothing draft. She thought she'd killed him, and much though she wanted to do it, the shock of it all near enough overturned her wits. So I haven't questioned her at all, I thought it best not to. But Nat told me that they had hatched a plot together, weeks ago, to steal Ridgeley's spyglass. He thought better of it and was under the impression that he'd persuaded Rachael out of such a foolhardy idea. But probably she decided to do it anyway—very self-willed, is Rachael. Somehow, she must have found a moment when the room was empty and seized her chance. And if she came across the pistol, I can well imagine her taking it in preference to the spyglass."

"It does seem possible," Hellier said. "But how did she know how to load it, for Christ's sake?" He saw her wince, and smiled. "I am sorry, lady—I have fallen into the habit of swearing and blaspheming too much. It's the company I keep."

She regarded him steadily, unamused. "How many of the other commandments do you habitually break, Nick?"

"Most of them, I regret to say. I am a covetous, lying and murdering thief, wenching and swearing and breaking the Sabbath. I am naught but the pattern of a roistering Cavalier, my gracious Silence, and doubtless will find my reward in a much hotter place than this."

"Doubtless," she said, trying to keep her face serious. Whatever the topic of conversation, somehow in his company laughter seemed never to be very far away. "But as to Rachael—perhaps she saw the soldiers doing it and copied them."

"It doesn't seem very likely. Those little pistols of his are French wheel-locks—he bought them in the Low Countries and paid a small fortune for them. No wonder he did this, looking for them."

"No pistol is worth this," Silence retorted, indicating the wrecked room. "Or what has happened in the winter parlor, which is much worse—thank

the good Lord the virginals were moved, or they'd be kindling by now."
She added, visited by a sudden idea, "Of course—Sam. I think Sam must
have shown her how to load a pistol."

"Sam?"

"Her elder brother. My husband bought him a pair of pistols before they
rode away to war. You should have seen him, he was like a child with a
new toy—he couldn't resist showing them to everyone. I had him at my
ear explaining how to fire them, oh, five or six times. Rachael and Nat
were only twelve, but they hung on his every word. She has an excellent
memory, when she is interested enough to harness it—I'm sure that was
how she learned."

"Perhaps. It's certainly not beyond the bounds of possibility. But that
still doesn't explain how she came to hit her target with the one bullet. Or
has she been spending secret hours with a catapult?"

"Rachael's secret hours are usually spent sulking in her chamber. She was
probably aiming for his head."

Nick smiled briefly. "In which case we can be glad that she missed. A
flesh wound, a couple of broken ribs can be explained away. A lieutenant-
colonel's corpse can't, especially if the deed was done by a fifteen-year-old
girl who'd stolen his own pistol. Sir Thomas would never have been able to
hush that up, however much he would welcome Ridgeley's sudden demise."

"Then there is no love lost between them?"

"Where Ridgeley is concerned, I doubt there's *ever* been love lost. Even
his own mother probably wouldn't waste it on him. No, he's been a thorn
in Bridges's side for nearly a year now—ever since Sir Thomas replaced him
as governor. Ridgeley resented it, he wanted to fight the war in his own
way—and took out his feelings on the villages around Bath. So Sir
Thomas, beset with complaints, sent him to Wintercombe to keep him out
of earshot."

"And to remind a smug little household of Puritan traitors of the horrors
of war," Silence said, not without bitterness. "Well, we have had re-
minders aplenty, wouldn't you think? And for how much longer are we
going to suffer all this? Or will it only stop when the house is burned about
our ears?"

"It won't be, if I have any say in the matter," Nick told her. He had
finished the books; they lay on the floor in half a dozen rather uneven piles,
their bindings battered and scarred. There was another heap, less orderly,
of miscellaneous pages that had been torn or wrenched out with rough
handling. His fingers rubbed absently at a bent and scuffed corner, trying
to restore its shape. "I have told them very exactly what they may or may
not do at Wintercombe. They all understand the extent of their limits—
and they all know what will happen to them if they transgress."

"Like the soldier who attacked Tabby?" Silence asked. She had not intended to mention it, but the thought and memory had been there, unbearably vivid, and had slipped into words.

"Like that soldier, yes," he said, and there was something different on his face, something closed and cold, that made him look older and much less friendly. And Silence, despite her earlier words to Mally, was conscious of a shiver of doubt. She had thought she could trust him—but did she really know enough of him to do so? Or was she misled by a show of support and amicability and deceived into thinking that he was worthy of her friendship?

But surely she was not such a fool. She was well aware of her vices and faults—no child of Isaac Woods could have failed to know them intimately—and she did not think that gullibility was one of them.

"I must go," he was saying, and rose to his feet. "I am afraid that one result of Rachael's impetuous action will be to reduce the time I have free to spend on those very pleasant evenings with you and your family. And, I must warn you, my first duty will be to ride to Bath and make a full report in person to the governor."

His expression was still uncommunicative, almost hostile—or was she imagining it? She scrambled up, heedless of the shower of papers that fell from her lap, and stared at him in alarm. "Rachael—what will you tell him about Rachael?"

"Nothing. The blame will be put on some trooper—one who actually died of the fever, I think, and who, I will inform him, subsequently deserted. He's unlikely to hear any other tale—after all, can you imagine Ridgeley confessing to being shot by a child? It's more than his self-esteem will allow. And with all the work Sir Thomas must be doing, he's hardly going to investigate the matter in any detail. He has far more important things to worry about—the Prince of Wales, and Waller—and Lord Goring, who makes Ridgeley look like one of the twelve apostles."

The friendliness was back in his eyes. "Oh?" Silence asked, encouraged. "Which one? Judas?"

"Very possibly," he said, laughing, and took her hand in his. He bowed over it, still smiling, and his lips, warm and dry, touched her knuckles. "Farewell, my gracious Silence. I go to Bath, to beard Sir Thomas in his lair, and I do not know when I shall return. It will either be tomorrow—or never."

"I didn't know he ate his officers," she said, laughing at him. Perhaps Mally *was* right, perhaps he *was* paying court to her—but it could hardly be serious. After all, she was probably older than he was. But no one had ever done such a thing to her, not even her husband—she stifled a giggle at the thought—and, despite her down-to-earth common sense, she could not help but feel the warm glow that a little flattery brought.

"Of course he does—with mustard and horseradish, for supper," Nick replied. "And you have no need to worry. Rachael is safe, I can promise you that—I have no intention of denouncing her, and I think you'll find that every one of the soldiers here is wishing that he had pulled the trigger and been a little bit more careful of the aim. I shall take a small detachment of men—Captain Bull will be in charge while I am gone, and I don't think he'll give you any trouble—indeed, he'll have me to reckon with if he does. So, until tomorrow, or the next day, Silence—I bid you au revoir."

And he was gone. She stood in the wrecked study, her mind bewildered, jostling with the memories of the morning. Ridgeley's face, dark with fury as he shouted at her servants. Rachael, like an avenging angel, the pistol balanced deadly in her hands, her blue eyes blank with hatred, and her enemy staring down amazed at the wound she had dealt him. Dame Ursula, gleeful and triumphant, spouting the Psalms from her sickbed, and Mally, reluctant yet stubbornly doing her duty, warning her of what she saw to be Nick Hellier's intent. And Nick himself, bowing over her hand, smiling, so easily able, with a neat turn of phrase, a dry witticism, a lift of those winged eyebrows, to draw laughter from her.

She could still feel the touch of his mouth on her hand. She smiled, thanking God that she yet had the grace to laugh at herself. She would be thirty next birthday, she was a wife and mother unendowed with beauty— a plain Puritan in sober garb, to outward appearance at least. Other women, more frivolous, might have their heads turned—and doubtless he had practiced his compliments on many such. But all she looked for was friendship. And she certainly did seem to be assured of it, even if it did come accompanied by wit, poetry, and the elegant, empty game of courtship.

It was strange, she thought, looking around at the study, still in chaos despite their struggles to order the devastation. This day had brought destruction, appalling violence, and attempted murder. By all the tenets of ladylike behavior, she should now be lying on her bed, with Mally mopping her brow and administering soothing cordials. But here she was, the fishwife's granddaughter, lady of a substantial manor house that had suffered greatly at enemy hands and would probably endure still more. And yet she felt more hope, and optimism, than she had done for many months.

If that is the effect that a little dishonest flattery can have, Silence told herself wryly, then Nick can assert I'm a goddess until my ears spill over, so long as he can keep my spirits up thereby.

And with that surprisingly light heart, she went to see how the dinner did.

CHAPTER

FOURTEEN

The son in whom he delighteth.
—*PROVERBS 3:12*

"**M**'lady! Captain Hellier be back!"

Since all of Wintercombe was probably goggling out of the windows facing onto the courtyard, filled with horses and men, this statement was somewhat superfluous. Silence, standing at her oriel, gave her butler a smile that was wider than she had intended. "Thank you, Turber. But he's brought more troops, hasn't he? He only took a score or so with him, and there must be all of fifty out there."

Turber, whose eyesight was not improving with age, stared at her in dismay. "Oh, no, m'lady, not more—we can't take no more soldiers, you must tell him, m'lady, there bain't no room for them."

Silence turned back to stare down at the milling mass below her. About thirty of them bore red coats, very fine scarlet with gold lacing, and their cornet carried a richly embroidered standard. It was another still, dull, comparatively mild day, and the device was concealed in the heavily hanging folds of cloth. She looked for Hellier's tall amber horse and found it immediately, next to a handsome milk-white animal whose quality, among the somewhat tattered, spavined, and down-at-heel mounts of the Wintercombe garrison was at once apparent. Its rider was richly dressed, but seemed to be no more than a boy, of about the same age as the twins.

A boy, perhaps, but he was being treated with extreme deference and courtesy.

Silence, her heart painful within her ribs, was struck by a sudden, wild suspicion. She whipped around again to face the astonished Turber. "Did you discover who they have with them?"

"N-no, m'lady—I haven't spoke with 'em—I come straight to you, m'lady," the old man said, quavering.

"You did very well," she told him, knowing that he must be soothed or he would remember none of her instructions. "What o'clock is it—near ten? Turber, go down to the kitchen and tell Darby that he must be ready for some extra guests for dinner—and they may well be very important guests."

"Important? Who be they, m'lady?"

"I don't know," Silence said mendaciously. But, she added to herself grimly, I have a very good idea—and if Nick has thoughts of doing me honor, this is a strange method indeed.

She waited until Turber had fumbled his way out and then said to Mally, "Do I look the part?"

"Of a sober godly housewife, m'lady?" her sharp-witted maid asked. "That ee do indeed. Who be it, then? Who have the captain brung to see us?"

"Take a look," Silence said.

The girl peered through the panes at the bustle in the courtyard. "But, m'lady, 'tis only a boy—though he be dressed tarblish fine for a young lad."

"Perhaps. Think, Mally. Who has just arrived in Bath? Yesterday, in fact, if what Master Willis said is true."

Mally's mouth fell open, comically. "Not—'tis the *prince?* The Prince of Wales? *Here?*"

"Who else can it be? Well, since he's here, I suppose I'd best go and greet him—and find out what he wants."

Wintercombe was in an uproar: She could hear it even as she descended the stair, the noise of voices and feet. Her palms were sweating, and she wiped them on that part of her skirt normally hidden beneath her apron. She paused in the little bay between the garden room and the hall, to calm herself. The child in the courtyard would be the next King of England when he grew up, but he was still a boy, younger than Nat and Rachael, and surely not yet submerged by the cloak of stifling formality and rigid superiority that so notoriously enveloped his father.

She took a deep breath and walked briskly into the hall, Mally as ever at her back. As she entered, so did a great troop of officers and gentlemen through the screens opposite. Hellier, neat and flamboyant in his Taunton blue and that brilliant scarlet cloak, was at their head, and by his side the boy who must, surely, be the fourteen-year-old Prince of Wales.

She saw Master Willis, who had only that morning resumed his lessons with Nat, standing open-mouthed under the southern windows, his pupil, rather less taken aback, by his side. He saw Silence and sent her one of his secret, mocking smiles. It heartened her considerably. She returned her attention to her uninvited and exalted guest with vastly increased confidence, and sank into the deepest curtsy of which she was capable.

She rose to find Nick regarding her with some amusement. He smiled, briefly and encouragingly, and then said, "Your Royal Highness, may I present the mistress of Wintercombe, my Lady St. Barbe."

The Prince of Wales was taller than both the twins, though younger by some six months, and quite stockily built: He would be a big man. Silence recalled the stories about him, how his mother the queen had been ashamed of his ugliness. Certainly he was no beauty: His hair, long and curled, was a dense shining black, and the skin of his rather plump face distinctly swarthy. But the dark eyes were bright with life, curiosity, and humor, as he stared at her. She wondered what he thought of her, in her plain mulberry worsted gown with the mended tear at the back where her heel had caught it, the decorous collar with its narrow border of lace, and her mouse-brown, uncurled hair tucked beneath a plain cap. At least everything was clean, even if she did look like a farmer's wife instead of the lady of the manor. Certainly she bore no resemblance whatsoever to the gorgeous satin-clad and silk-skinned ladies of the Court.

"Welcome to Wintercombe, Your Highness," she said, hoping that she did not sound too nervous. Surely the prince must know that her husband was in armed rebellion against his father?

If he did, it apparently did not matter. The dark, rather heavy face split into a cheerful grin that made it at once attractive. "I must beg your pardon, Lady St. Barbe," Prince Charles said. "Coming unannounced like this, it's most discourteous. I do hope we're not inconveniencing you—I'm afraid I persuaded Captain Hellier to bring me here, and I think it was rather against his better judgment."

"It's no inconvenience," Silence said, warming at once to this direct and friendly child—was he really a king's son? "You do us much honor, Your Highness—as long as you can put up with our somewhat disordered surroundings. And of course you must stay for dinner."

"That's one of the reasons I'm here," the prince replied candidly. "I've heard all about your cook, and I couldn't leave Bath without sampling his food. Besides, I wanted to see one of the garrisons for myself, and this is the nearest. Captain Hellier was in Bath, so I suggested that I visited Wintercombe under his escort. And Sir Thomas Bridges told me that poor Lieutenant-Colonel Ridgeley would be much heartened by my presence. I understand that you've been nursing him, Lady St. Barbe—how does he do?"

"Not very well, I'm afraid, Your Highness," Silence said, feeling somewhat uneasy. "The wound in itself was not especially dangerous, but there has been some inflammation and a fever. He may be too sick to receive any visitors."

"Oh, well," the boy said. "I shall put my head round the door, all the same. Now, Captain Hellier was telling me that you have a stepson called Nat, who's the same age as me. Is he here? I am lonely for other boys since I left my brother James behind in Oxford."

"He is here," Silence said, unable to suppress a smile. "Do you require his companionship for the day, Your Highness? I'm sure he'd be happy and honored to oblige."

"Even though his father is fighting against mine?" the prince asked, his black eyes suddenly, piercingly shrewd. Nonplussed, Silence stared at him.

Then Nat's voice intruded. "He may be. I'm not. And if you'd like me to accompany you around Wintercombe, Your Highness, it would be my pleasure."

He bowed, and the prince inclined his head in acknowledgment. The two boys were almost the same age, and black-haired, but there the resemblance stopped. Nat barely came up to the prince's shoulder, and the other's sturdy frame would have made two of his frail body. His white face and dark-ringed blue eyes were in painful contrast to Prince Charles's air of rude good health, and his voice had not broken yet, whereas the prince's was already as deep as a man's. Nor could his plain everyday doublet and breeches of deep blue match the rich gold-laced scarlet satin of the king's son.

With some uneasiness, for she did not want Nat to be hurt, Silence watched the two boys, so completely dissimilar, size each other up for a brief moment. Evidently Nat liked what he saw. His pale face warmed into a smile that was echoed by the young prince. "What do you want to see, Your Highness?"

"Oh, I think the fortifications first," his guest said. "I have been hearing all about them from Captain Hellier. Did you really draw a map to show him where they should go? You must tell me all about it."

And Silence, hoping that Nat would not tell the prince every single detail concerning that map, was left standing in the middle of the hall floor, watching as all the officers and gentlemen (and, probably, lords as well) moved out in a great body headed by the disparate figures of her stepson and the eldest child of the King of England. If she had not been consumed with anxiety about how this mass of uninvited guests were to be fed, she might have laughed.

"I'm sorry," Nick said ruefully, and spread his hands. "There was no help for it—he's a strong-willed lad, and insisted. Are you aware of the honor being done to Wintercombe? You'll be able to dine out on this tale for years."

"Perhaps—but will the prince be able to dine today? That's what concerns me at the moment."

"Oh, kill a fatted calf," he said. "Remind me—I have a surprise for you later, but now I must follow them—forgive me."

"The impertinence!" she said loudly at his retreating back, and in conscious imitation of Dame Ursula—who would doubtless have something to say about this latest crisis in Wintercombe's war-ravaged existence.

She was right. Hardly had the heavy curtains closed behind Nick's unrepentant figure, when they parted to admit the flat-footed Ruth, her pale eyelashes blinking in what passed, in her, for agitation. "M'lady, madam d'ask ee to come up to her at once."

She would, thought Silence. I have the house to order, the Prince of Wales is here, tables must be set up, we probably haven't got enough pewter and not even Darby can possibly produce a dinner fit for royalty with less than an hour's warning, and my domineering old mother-in-law wants to assail my ears with, most likely, nothing more than some virulent denunciation of the king . . .

No, she told herself with resolution, no—I will not be browbeaten at command. She will just have to wait awhile, because I am not at her beck and call—I have more important duties to discharge. And something must be done about Ridgeley—he can't be allowed to tell the prince the truth of what happened to him.

Aware that she would undoubtedly rue it later, she faced the maid and said firmly, "Pray give Dame Ursula my regrets, Ruth, but I am at present too hard-pressed to spare the time. As the Prince of Wales himself has seen fit to honor us with a visit, I am sure she will understand. I will of course come up to her chamber as soon as I am able—but it probably won't be before His Highness has returned to Bath."

Ruth's inexpressive face did not move, although she must surely have been surprised at such uncharacteristic defiance. "Very good, m'lady," she said in the surly mutter with which she communicated to everyone, and turned to plod back upstairs. Silence, with a curious emotion bubbling within her, compounded of freedom and panic, went hot-foot to the kitchen.

Charles, Prince of Wales and heir to the throne of England, was thoroughly enjoying himself. Although he had been reared in the close companionship of a large family, which in these troubled times of war had been reduced to his brother James, three years his junior, his father had thought it politic to surround his eldest son with adult councillors and advisors when he took up his new position as General of the Western Association. The king's intent had been to "unboy" him, and certainly the prince was eager to attain his manhood. But he missed James much more than he cared to admit, and the company of another boy his own age was a luxury to be savored. He had not been especially impressed by Nat St. Barbe at first sight—was this undersized child really fifteen? He looked and sounded more like a ten-year-old. But he liked the rather cynical, worldly wise air about the other boy, and by the time they had walked down the terraced gardens to the orchard, a rapport had sprung up between them, founded largely on a similar sense of humor.

He was shown the fortifications, and tried to hide his surprise: They were so small, so feeble, beside the vast ramparts and bulwarks that had been thrown up around Oxford. Captain Hellier, whom he liked for his lack of fawning pretension—Charles had early developed a strong distaste for toadies and hypocrites—obviously shared his disappointment. "I'll freely admit, Your Highness, that the work is scarce begun. We have been hampered by the weather—it seems to have snowed or rained almost continuously since Christmas. We are also short of men and proper equipment."

"I hope the other garrisons under my authority are not so poorly defended," Charles said dubiously. "Would it not have been better to have placed your bulwark upon the terrace? That looks a good stout wall, and you must have a better view from there, it's easily thirty foot higher. Down here you can see nothing but the stream and the hillside."

There was a small, awkward pause. Charles noticed Nat's rueful expression. "Master St. Barbe—surely you can understand what I mean?"

"I can," Nat said. "But my stepmother would be most distressed. She prizes her garden almost as highly as her children."

"Gardens can grow again—a kingdom once lost cannot," the prince said: He had recently heard his cousin Prince Rupert saying something similar. He added, curious, "Do you have any guns here, Captain Hellier? I don't remember seeing any—and *surely* you should have one or two, even if they're only to frighten the enemy."

"Alas, Your Highness, there are few guns to be had, of any size—and they are needed for the defense of Bath and Bristol," the captain told him. "And I doubt they'd be of much use. Even placed on the terrace, it would be very difficult to aim them anywhere but at the hillside opposite or into the sky. You'd have better luck if you mounted one or two in the courtyard at the north side of the house—which is where an attack is most likely to come. Would Your Highness care to inspect the position?"

Within Wintercombe, the household was in a condition of barely controlled panic. Silence, the still center of the storm, had ruthlessly repressed her own terror and had marshaled her chaotic thoughts into a swift, precise stream of directives. Darby had promised to produce something, even the proverbial fatted calf, that would be suitable for the Prince of Wales and his high-born entourage. The common soldiers of his troop, some score in number, would have to share with the other men in the barton plain coarse brown bread and cheese, rather old and hard, and a steaming cauldron of broth based on dried peas and a piece of salty bacon.

A clatter from the dining parlor indicated that Leah and Eliza were setting the table. Silence had chosen to have the dinner in this room, rather than the chilly vastness of the hall, which seemed empty and echoing with less than three dozen in it. It would be rather a squash around the big oak table, but the smaller children could sit at the side table by the hearth, under Doraty's direction. Already the news of their exalted guest had reached them, and they were desperate to be allowed to dine in his company. And, seeing their urgent, pleading faces, knowing that Prince Charles came from a large and close-woven family himself, she could not bring herself to refuse them. Stern warnings about behavior were unnecessary: They all knew the rules of polite table manners, even William, and would not intentionally disgrace themselves on such a momentous occasion.

Rachael presented a different problem. Since her shooting of Ridgeley two days ago she had stayed in her bedchamber. The trays of food had been returned untouched, Doraty's attempts to comfort her had been met with abuse and hurled slippers, and to Silence the girl had refused to say anything at all. Only Nat had seemed to be welcome, and he, loyal to his twin, would divulge almost nothing of their brief conversations. It was noticeable, however, that his intervention had no effect at all on Rachael's black mood. And Silence had strongly suspected that the words "more fool you" had featured largely in Nat's utterances.

It would be easy enough to punish Rachael, were she not already doing it herself quite adequately. When Silence knocked on her stepdaughter's door and, as usual, received no reply, she wondered if she were not being a fool to herself. Let the girl stew in her own bile. That was what Dame Ursula, and indeed Sir George, would say. But Silence, remembering her own deep misery as a rebellious, misunderstood fifteen-year-old, could not help but feel some sympathy. If only she could penetrate her stepdaughter's hostility—but in nine years she had never completely succeeded, and she doubted sadly whether she ever would.

With trepidation, she opened the door.

Rachael sat at the table by the window, staring out. She gave no indication that she was aware of her stepmother's entrance. Silence closed the door behind her, took a deep breath and said quietly, "We have a visitor, Rachael."

There was a pregnant, inimical pause. Then the girl turned her head, very slowly and deliberately. Her face was as white and haggard as Nat's had been after his illness, and the circles under her eyes were violet with strain. To a stranger, her expression might have seemed completely hostile, but Silence, who knew her better than her stepdaughter liked, saw with compassion the terror in Rachael's eyes. She said, as if she feared the answer, "Who? What visitor?"

With sudden insight, Silence realized that she thought it was someone come to take her away, or punish her. For an act such as Rachael had committed, however great the provocation or the excuse, could earn terrible penalties for its perpetrator. She said, smiling reassuringly, "A most important one—Captain Hellier escorted him here from Bath. It's the Prince of Wales has come to see us!"

"Oh," Rachael said. Some of the tension left her body, but she looked distinctly unexcited, as if it were the sluglike Ned Apprice viewing the fortifications and not the next King of England. Silence sighed with weary resignation. She longed to shake some sense into the girl, but knew from past and bitter experience that it would do no good at all. And how would it help to dissolve the agony she knew lay behind the wall of defensive hostility?

She said instead, on impulse, "Captain Hellier told me. There is no need to worry. What happened will not go beyond Wintercombe. Ridgeley won't admit to being shot in such humiliating circumstances. His soldiers all wish they'd had the courage to do it themselves. No one else blames you."

"But *I* blame me!" Rachael cried, suddenly passionate. "I shouldn't have done it—it was wicked, a sin, I wanted to murder him—and *how* I wish I had!" There were no tears. Another, less fierce soul might have dissolved in self-pity, but though her despair and hopeless confusion showed clear on her face, Rachael did not break down. She added, more quietly, "I have been thinking and thinking about it—I know it was wrong, I ought to be punished, it's only fair—and yet I wish I'd killed him. And no matter how hard I try I can't see any way out—I *should* be punished. 'Thou shalt not kill,' the Scriptures say—and even if I didn't actually kill him, I *meant* to." Her blue eyes, distended with anguish, stared at Silence, and her last words came in a whisper. "If I am so wicked . . . will I go to hell?"

"Oh, Rachael," Silence murmured. All her own fears and sorrows seemed pale and faint beside the vivid sharpness of her stepdaughter's agony. She reached out to touch the thin rigid shoulders, feeling the shuddering tension beneath her hands. Then, suddenly, as if a spring wound too tight had snapped, the girl slumped into her chair and buried her face in her hands, sobbing as if her heart and spirit alike were broken. She made no resistance when Silence, tears in her own eyes, put her arms around her. And after a few seconds, Rachael returned the embrace.

It was the first time, in the nine years of their difficult, unrewarding relationship, that Silence had received any affection, any confidence at all, from her stepdaughter.

Much later, when Rachael had calmed a little and her tears had dried, Silence said quietly, "Why do you think you will go to hell?"

The girl's face, no longer white and sharp but red and swollen with sobbing, was still pressed against her shoulder. She said, punctuated by hiccups, "Because—because I've been wicked, and the wicked shall be turned into hell."

"But God will forgive you—just as we have all done."

"He can't forgive this," Rachael said.

Silence thought with dislike of Dame Ursula, who had tried for years to mold her recalcitrant granddaughter in her image and seemed to have unexpectedly succeeded in the worst possible way. She said, gently and reasonably, "God loves you, as He loves all of us. He looks into our hearts—He sees the reasons for what we do, as well as the actions themselves. Yes, what you did was wrong—but it was entirely understandable. I doubt there's one person in Wintercombe who would not have pulled that trigger. We're all human, we fail, we fall short of perfection. That doesn't make God love us any the less. I know that your transgression was a trifle more spectacular and dramatic than most. But it isn't so terrible when you compare it with all the other things that we've been hearing of in these troubles." She smiled suddenly, having remembered suitable biblical examples. "Think of the story of Jael and Sisera—or Judith and Holofernes. Both women killed their enemy—and used far more guile and deceit than you did. Yet they're hailed as great heroines."

Rachael's face was dubious, but there was a dawning hope there too. Silence pressed on, sensing that she was succeeding. "Who would you consider has the last word in this house, on the subject of heaven and hell?"

The girl's mouth twitched involuntarily. "Grandmother, of course."

"Would it make you feel any better to learn that she thoroughly approves of what you've done?"

"*Does* she? *Really?*" Rachael asked, still doubtful. "But I thought—I thought she'd disapprove—she always does, of everything I ever do, no matter how I try—she's always criticizing me."

"Well, to be fair, she's still criticizing you. She told me she'd have made a better job of it—'straight through his wicked ungodly black heart' was how she put it. But I think you'll find that her opinion of you has soared."

For the first time, there was the glimmer of a proper smile on Rachael's face. "Though it wasn't very high in the first place. That *has* made me feel better. What were you saying about the Prince of Wales?"

Silence told her again, and added, with more confidence, "Will you attend dinner? Darby has promised something special."

Like all the St. Barbes, Rachael usually enjoyed her food. A wistful, hungry expression crossed her face. "Do you think—could I? Does he *know?*"

"The prince? Of course not. He's a nice merry-looking lad, about your own age. Nat's with him now, showing him the fortifications. No one knows what you did, outside Wintercombe, and your secret is safe, I promise you. And, what's more to the point, Captain Hellier promises it too."

"I can't wear this," Rachael said, as if she had barely taken notice of what her stepmother had said. "This" was her oldest gown, which had been let out and taken down to allow for adolescent growth and now presented a distinctly threadbare and shabby appearance. "Can I wear my yellow? Please?"

The garment in question was her best and would undoubtedly outshine her stepmother's. "Of course you may," Silence said with heartfelt relief. It was months since Rachael had taken any interest at all in her attire, and despite her own unconcern about her appearance, it seemed to be a healthy sign in her stepdaughter. She added, "I must go—there is so much to do. But I'll ask Hester or Doraty to help you change."

"I'll need them—that gown laces up the back," said Rachael. There was animation in her face now: Take away the ugly blotches, do something about her lank unkempt hair, and there was the shadow of prettiness there. She went on, with unwonted humility, "Mother—thank you."

It was not much, but the thought, the beginnings of a change for the better between them, were there. Silence smiled. "Thank you, for listening."

She felt more cheerful by far as she closed the door. So much to do, so little time—but, cautiously, it seemed that she and Rachael were at last starting to grope their way toward a real affection.

When, perhaps an hour later, the prince and his entourage returned to Wintercombe after an exhaustive tour of the defenses and the barton—the loyal cheers of the troops had been audible all over the house—a great deal of hard work had been done in their absence. The dining parlor's two tables were dressed with glowing white linen and gleaming pewter, from which the dents had been hastily knocked by Turber and his wife. In the center, where the salt had once stood (Silence refused to bring it out from its hiding place under the study hearthstone, even for the prince), she had placed a bowl of hyacinths, brought from her chamber. Their heavy, rich scent filled the air with the fragrance of spring. There was no disguising the ruined portraits, nor the damaged paneling, though Walker had mended the window. It'll do no harm for the boy to see the evidence of the damage some of his supporters can do, she thought, smiling a little grimly, and closed the door softly on Eliza's and Leah's work of art.

She had no more idea than the prince of what was to be served on that immaculate table. She trusted Darby to fulfill her expectations as she would trust almost none of her servants—save for Mally.

Mally helped her dress. She might normally wear the plain garb of a godly housewife, but on this momentous occasion she must clothe herself as befitted her rank, even if that status was borrowed and had never quite suited her. So out of the hanging closet on the left hand side of the hearth, the twin of Mally's on the right, came her only silken gown, bought when she and George had sat for their portraits three years previously. Those portraits had been left behind at Chard and had probably been destroyed or looted with the rest of the house. She had not regretted it. The stiff, crude image of herself in unaccustomed finery was not how she wanted to be remembered by her descendants. George would undoubtedly want another to be taken, and she hoped that next time, he would choose a rather less provincial and pedestrian artist and that the whole family would be represented.

The gown itself was not pedestrian, though as it was three years old, was probably by now rather provincial. Sir Samuel's Bath tailor had made it up, and it had been beautifully done. She had forgotten the cool, slippery feeling of the heavy smooth silk, and the rich depth of color struck her afresh with its beauty. Her everyday clothes were dyed in the plain dark shades almost universal in the countryside: blue, russet, gray, mulberry. But this was tawny gold, the exact hue of her favorite wall gillyflowers, which in two months would scent the air along the terraces. It had a high waist, laced across the matching stomacher with ribbons of a darker hue, and full, wide sleeves that reached to just below her elbow.

Mally helped her to put it on and arranged her hair. Its mouse-fair color took a glow from the gown, and although there was no time to curl it into the fashionable ringlets, it fell in soft, heavy waves on either side of her face. She looked at the result in the mirror that the maid held for her. Quite a different reflection stared back: Not the harassed housewife but the lady of the manor, her pale oval face calm and assured, her skin almost as white as the broad lace-edged collar that fell from the low-necked gown. Around her neck, Mally placed a simple necklet of small, well-matched pearls that had been George's bridal gift to his second wife and had spent the last few months under the hearthstone in the study.

The overall effect was quite pleasing, she decided. She would never be beautiful, nor even pretty: Her brows grew too thick and straight, for she would not pluck them, and her eyes were not the fashionable blue but a sort of indeterminate greenish brown—like pond water, Silence thought ruefully. Granted, her nose was straight and her chin softly rounded, but her mouth was wide almost to ugliness, and lacked the fashionable droop— it was as level as her brows.

It's a good thing I've never succumbed to vanity, she thought wryly. I've never had anything to be vain about. Ordinary face, ordinary figure. This isn't so much gilding the lily as putting silk on a sow.

"You d'look tarblish fine, m'lady," Mally said, very bright and encouraging. She added, with an accusatory note in her voice, "You oughta make more of yourself. You bain't ill-looking, not at all."

"I just give the appearance of it?" Silence said. "Mally, fine clothes and lovely lace do not become me. Anyway, I'd soon have raspberry juice and dust and William's dribbles all down it, and Pye's hairs, and the lace would be torn and the necklace string would undoubtedly break and all these pearls trodden underfoot. I am *not* a gracious lady, Mally, I'm a practical housewife, and my grandmother sold fish and your grandfather would probably have thought himself above her."

"Aye, so he might," Mally said, unimpressed. "But you be Lady St. Barbe, fishwife or no, and they d'say in the village, some on 'em, that you don't dress fitty."

"They can say what they like," Silence commented. "You know me, Mally—I have too many duties to do to pay much attention to what people think. And although I'm wearing this because to dine with the Prince of Wales in my old mulberry would be a mark of considerable disrespect, I don't really give a toss for what he thinks either."

"Oh, well, please yourself," Mally said, in a cheerful voice that entirely robbed the words of their sting. "*I* d'think ee look tarblish fine, m'lady— and it d'suit ee passing well, that gown."

"That's quite enough, Mally. Do you really want a fine lady for a mistress, all soft white hands and clean linen and curled hair? You'd have so much to do, you wouldn't have time to sleep."

"Maybe 'tisn't such a brave idea," her maid said, her face sparkling with mischief. "Shall us go down, m'lady, and see if the children be ready?"

The children were ready, lined up for inspection in the Hall, with Doraty and Hester standing at once pleased and nervous behind them. Their hair neatly brushed, their faces clean and shiny with excitement, they looked enchanting: chubby, happy-natured William, strong-willed Deb, and Tabby, her lovely hair for once allowed to flow beneath her cap and her face free now of the terrible unchildish fierceness that had so greatly distressed her mother. Beside the smaller children, their hair shaded gold to tawny with increasing age, Rachael's sharp black and white seemed alien, as if she belonged to a different family altogether. Her bright marigold-colored gown would suit her in three or four years, but did not now: It made her look like a child dressing up.

Mindful of their newfound, hesitant friendship, Silence would rather have died than admit it. She smiled encouragingly at them. "You all look splendid. Doraty and Hester must have worked very hard. I'd forgotten how nice that dress is, Rachael—the color really suits you. And I needn't have any worries about whether or not you are going to behave yourselves—your manners are all beautiful."

"William's nose is running," Deb announced. "William's got an *awful* cold and he's forgotten his kerchief."

"No, I haven't," her little brother protested, fishing a pristine square from his sleeve and dragging it across his nose, which he still could not blow properly. He glared at Deb over the top of it, and then screwed it up and thrust it back into his sleeve.

Tabby said nothing, but her wide hazel eyes met her mother's and her mouth twitched slightly, her amusement subtly expressed. Silence could not stop a grin breaking out in return, from delight at having her old Tabby restored to her. "Well," she said happily, sniffing the delicious aroma wafting from the direction of the kitchen, "all we need now is the prince."

Afterward she could look back upon that dinner as a miraculous, civilized oasis in their busy, humdrum lives: two hours when the outside world descended upon Wintercombe like a gorgeous, exotic butterfly, dazzling with a life and beauty they had all forgotten. It was as if the long dreary days and months of winter, the hardships and worries and deprivation, had never been, and as if that ghastly day of violence and destruction only forty-eight hours previous was but a figment of her imagination.

To preserve the illusion, she averted her gaze from the damaged portraits and the cracked paneling, and the prince, sitting on the carved oak chair that normally graced her own chamber, made no comments except upon the quality of the meal, which even for Darby was high. Silence, smiling, making polite conversation as she had learned to do with her husband's friends and cronies at Chard, noticed with approval that he addressed his food with the normal avid hunger of a boy in his teens. He was also, it seemed, on most friendly terms with Nat. Looking at them chattering away, Silence was conscious of a twinge of guilt and sympathy for her stepson. She had never really considered that he might lack the company of other boys. He had never been able to go to school, and this last winter his activities had been drastically curtailed because of illness and the terrible weather. In the summer months he and Rachael had often been with the two orphaned children of Master Flower, who had held the Manor Farm in the village. Tom Flower, though, was a rather surly, overgrown, and not especially intelligent lad of sixteen or so, and his sister Eleanor, a year younger, a forward minx who was not at all good for Rachael. There were the three Baylie girls, who lived on the other side of the parish, near Farleigh, and their cousins the Tovies—although whether the nephews and nieces of the keeper of the George would be considered suitable friends for a baronet's son, she did not know. Sir Samuel, who liked the Tovies and had spent much time in their inn, had approved. She doubted that her husband would. It was a good thing that Nat preferred more solitary pursuits—or did he favor them only because his ill health precluded him from the kind of active sports in which the Flower boy or the young Tovies so delighted?

She concentrated on her food, and on the conversation of the amiable officer next to her, whose name she had failed to catch. The food—roast pigeons, a fricassee of rabbit, boiled carp, tansies and pies made of her bottled autumn fruit, and a syllabub of the first spring cream—was simple but delicious, the sauces perfect. William did not talk too loudly, or throw his food around, or argue with Deb, who was likewise on her best behavior. It was with great difficulty that Doraty, sitting with them on the smaller table, had managed to persuade them not to gaze fixedly at their exalted guest, talking so easily with Nat that a stranger might have thought they had grown up together. Silence had been enchanted by the prince's greeting of them: As they had curtsied (and, in William's case, bowed so low that he almost knocked his head on the floor), he had asked each one their name, told stories of his own brothers and sisters, and earned their undying allegiance in the process. My Royalist brood, Silence thought ruefully. Whatever will George say? Not to mention Dame Ursula.

At last, dinner was finished, the bones of the second course picked bare, only crumbs left of the pies, and the cheeses reduced to their rinds. The prince rose, his black eyes merry. "I regret, Lady St. Barbe, that I must return to Bath. My councillors will imagine that I have been captured by

Waller—did you know he was moving close? You may need your defenses before too much longer. But before I go, with your leave, I must do two things. I should visit poor Colonel Ridgeley, and I must pay my compliments to your superb cook."

So he was ushered into the hot, steamy kitchen, and while the amazed, whispering scullions stood in a corner, Darby bowed over his stomach and stood to receive his due reward with as much dignity as if he were himself royal. "I've never tasted better, not even in Whitehall," the Prince of Wales said, with reminiscent greed. "Pray accept this, Master Darby—as token of my appreciation. And when my father is restored to his rightful home and place, I shall summon you to cook for us in London."

"You can't do that, Your Highness," said Nat. "Darby will never leave Wintercombe. Everyone in Somerset has tried to persuade him—but he's not to be bribed."

"Well—it wouldn't be fair to deprive you, I suppose," the prince said. "But oh, how I'm tempted! Thank you, Master Darby—and perhaps you'll cook again for me one day."

And Darby was left, turning the five golden guineas around on his palm with complacent satisfaction, as if his skills had previously been taken entirely for granted.

Silence had been deeply worried about Ridgeley. She had not seen him since early that morning, when he had been restless, feverish, and unpleasantly abusive. Would he say anything to the prince? Would he reveal that the thin, almost pretty child who had sat demurely next to her twin brother at table, within touching distance of the royal guest, had only two days previously attempted murder? No chance then of discretion, of hushing up Rachael's dreadful deed.

She need not have worried. Mally, a look of smug satisfaction on her face that reminded Silence of Pye after she had purloined some titbit from the table, greeted them in the neat, fragrant antechamber, and explained that Ridgeley was sleeping peacefully. If His Highness wished to see him, he could quietly enter, but it was best not to wake the colonel, since rest was the only certain cure.

And sure enough, Ridgeley lay, resembling a felled ox, his mouth open, the unshaven stubble rendering his face even more coarse and brutal, snoring fit to rattle the glass. The chamber was hot and frowsty and smelled sharp and acrid with the remedies and salves ranked in their bottles and jars on the windowsill. The prince withdrew at once, apologizing, and took his affable leave of all at Wintercombe. They were lined up in the hall, from the ancient Turber, Clevinger, and Diggory at one end to the three scullions and Jemmy Coxe at the other. With cheering and much waving of hats from the soldiers grouped in the courtyard outside, he mounted his beautiful white horse and rode back to Bath with his gorgeous scarlet troop of horse. And his uninvited hostess breathed a huge and tremulous sigh of relief.

"I gave en extra poppy seeds," Mally whispered, her eyes glinting. "Us can't have en blathering all about Mistress Rachael to the Prince o' Wales, can us? So I made sure he were well asleep." She added maliciously, "Pity I didn't give en so much he'd never wake up, eh, m'lady?"

"Mally!" Silence said severely, but both she and her maid knew that her real reaction was quite different.

After the prince's departure, Wintercombe lapsed into an anticlimactic quiet. A fine misty rain had begun, spoiling the day as it drifted into evening. Ridgeley was still sleeping. Nat was studying in his chamber, Rachael playing with the smaller children. Silence knew that she should go to see Dame Ursula. Guiltily, she avoided the prospect. She had not even mentioned to the prince that her mother-in-law resided at Wintercombe too. Etiquette demanded that she be presented to him, but Silence had quailed at the thought of that stream of venomous abuse being directed at the future King of England. In avoiding that disaster, however, she had laid up a grim store for herself, and sooner or later she would have to pay the reckoning.

She had ordered supper to be sent to her chamber, a light meal for herself, Mally, and the children. The knock on the door could not be them, however: A glance at her clock showed that it was not yet six, although quite dark outside. The shutters and curtains were drawn, the fire burned warmly, the candles illuminated the dark with pools of amber. Pye, pregnant with the first of her season's kittens, lay on her back in Silence's lap, while she stroked the snowy white fur around the pink-flushed nipples and wondered who in the village would appreciate a sturdy young mouser. The barton here was well supplied, and Pye's offspring were much sought-after. With satisfaction, Silence noted that there were no fleas scurrying through the thick hairs. She had bathed the cat in a strong decoction of pennyroyal only last week, so there should be none for a month or so.

As contented as Pye, she tickled her under the chin, felt the vibrant purr begin, and thought about the young Prince of Wales. He was an attractive lad; far more so, probably, than his notoriously awkward and intransigent father. It was a pity indeed that the king did not share his son's affable, easy temperament. Unpleasant policies could undoubtedly be swallowed more easily when sweetened thus.

Then the knock interrupted her reverie. Mally was elsewhere, collecting linen. She bade her visitor enter.

It was, as she had thought, Hellier, still in buff coat and sword, with the long lazy smile. "Good evening, Silence. Do I find you alone?"

"Save for Pye, yes—I won't get up, in her condition she needs rest."

"She wasn't resting this morning—when we were inspecting the ditches, she was stalking a blackbird in the orchard. Unsuccessfully, I hasten to add."

"She's much better at catching mice—she and the other cats wage war in the spring and summer, around the house and barton. But she does love to try her paw at a bird occasionally—and manages it once or twice too, don't you, my female Nimrod?"

Pye, tickled, purred the louder. Nick came over to the hearth, quite at home. He said, looking down at her, "The day went very well, don't you think?"

"Considering the brevity of the notice we were given, yes, I think it did," Silence said, somewhat astringently.

"For that I apologize. But the prince, as I said, can be *very* insistent. He persuaded his councillors to let him come, and of course if he demands his own way, in the end he'll be allowed it, so long as it is on trivial matters. I know his command is only nominal, but he is a determined child, with a mind of his own. It won't be long before he is acting on his own authority."

"I liked him," Silence said. "It's hard to tell, of course, on a few hours' acquaintance, but I think he will make a good king—he seems friendly, approachable, and intelligent. And Nat likes him too."

"Then he must be all right—Nat's judgment is impeccable." Nick pulled up a chair and sat, spreading his hands to the gentle warmth of the flames. "And has his visit turned my Puritan rebel Silence into a Royalist?"

"Not in the least. But I think all the children are. Their poor father may find it rather disconcerting when he comes home."

"Ah," Nick murmured. As she looked at him questioningly, he felt in his doublet. "That reminds me—do you remember I said that I had a surprise for you?"

"No—I'd quite forgotten," Silence said, and her sudden eager hope showed on her face. "Don't tell me—have you a letter?"

"Not merely one letter, but three." He pulled them from inside his doublet and handed them to her, warm, slightly creased, and smelling of oiled leather. "I was given them in Bath—the landlord of my inn had them. I fear they have been some weeks, not to say months, in his possession, and may have taken even longer on their journey."

Three letters: three different hands, all so dearly familiar. The same inscription, three times repeated: To My Lady St. Barbe, of Wintercombe in the village of Philip's Norton near Bath. To be left at the White Hart in Stall Street in Bath, to be called for. The swift, heavily looped scrawl was that of her sister Prudence. The round hand that galloped up the page as if it had no concept of the horizontal, and then down again, belonged to her brother, Joseph. And the fattest letter, the handwriting firm, upright, painstaking, was from her husband, Sir George St. Barbe.

Pye, disturbed by her movements, leapt off her lap and began to wash herself with some indignation before curling up by the fire. Silence brushed a few stray black and white hairs off her silken skirts and laid the precious letters down, her hand hovering. She had not heard from any of them for five or six months—and now to have three at once! What news would they bring?

She longed to open Prue's first. Of all her family, Prue was the nearest to her in age and in temperament, although far more impulsive. Silence had learned moderation and sense; she wondered if her scatterbrained sister would ever attain those qualities. Prue had suffered worst of all in their childhood, the despair of their father and mentioned in all his prayers. She could hear his incongruously deep, mellow voice as if it spoke now in her ear: "Lord, grant that my daughter Prudence be turned from her wild unseemly ways and guided into the paths of righteousness." God had not obliged, and Isaac Woods had gone to his grave even more disappointed, if that were possible, in his second daughter than in the other two. Ironically, it was Silence whom he had considered to have turned out the best of his children: married at nineteen, a brilliant match, well above her station, mistress of her household, and mother to a brood of hopeful grandchildren. If he had but known the true situation . . .

With a sigh, she picked up George's missive. Nick was looking at her with something of that unnerving intensity in his gaze. He would certainly think it strange if she did not read her husband's letter first. She pushed her thumbnail under the seal and opened it.

There were two sheets. It was dated the twenty-third of December, more than two months previously. There was no indication of where it had been written. She glanced down at that round hand, so deeply pressed into the paper that the ink had spluttered. And that in itself was a little unusual.

> *My dear wife,*
>   *It is with the deepest sorrow that I must write to you with such unhappy news, but alas, the Lord hath seen fit to take away from me my dear son Samuel . . .*

She could read no further. Nick, watching her, saw all the color leak from her face, leaving it paper-white with shock. Slowly her hand crept to her mouth. Her eyes, distended in horror, tried vainly to focus on the words that George, his writing deteriorating with his distress, had used to describe to her the death of his eldest son and heir.

Sam. Sam, so bright and eager with his new pistols, talking excitedly of war. Sam, teaching his handsome chestnut to caracole like a warhorse in the courtyard, while Nat and Rachael looked admiringly on. And, a much more distant memory, the reserved, dark-haired child, twelve years old, turning to her one hot and sunny summer's day, to confide that he did quite like his new stepmother. She remembered how, when her second child, little George, had died of a fever at the age of two, it had been Sam who had offered her the greatest comfort. He had not spoken of God's will, nor had he told her that the infant's spotless soul was now in heaven. He had sat with her in a quiet corner of the garden at Chard, talking of the frail, intelligent boy whom they had both loved and for whom she had had such hopes.

As her husband had had for Sam. The son who was closest to him, his heir, bred in his image, not tall but sturdy, with the dark coloring and narrow face of his mother, the curling hair and uncomplicated nature of his father, but with a sensitivity that George lacked entirely. He was twenty years old; and now he was dead.

She was distantly aware that Nick was speaking, very gently. He must have realized that it was bad news. With a massive effort of will, she forced her tear-blurred eyes to read the rest of the letter. There was a great deal of detail, unsparing. George had poured it all out, apparently quite unaware of its likely effect on her. She made herself take it all into her quailing mind: the wound in the leg sustained at Newbury in October, not at first considered serious; the slow putrefaction, followed by the inevitable amputation, more putrefaction, fever, convulsions, and agonizing death. Though in much pain, George wrote, he had taken much comfort in his father's presence, and had perished in the certain knowledge of his eternal salvation.

It had taken him nearly six weeks to die.

The letter fell from her hands and slid to the floor. She wanted to weep, to howl her grief, but her throat was dry and there were no tears. She was suddenly conscious that the emotion surging within her was not sadness but anger. Anger, not only at the war that had so cruelly taken a young man's life, but also and chiefly at her husband, who could write in such callously gruesome detail of his son's death, without a thought for what his wife, or indeed his mother, might suffer from reading it. She knew that George did not intend to make her natural grief even worse. But, as usual, he simply had not considered anything but his own feelings.

She knew that she would never erase from her mind the terrible image that haunted her now of Sam, mutilated, dying in unbearable pain, crying out in agony. And that ghastly picture was her husband's gift to her.

"Silence."

It was Nick's voice, very soft, very gentle, so that she hardly recognized it. She raised her eyes and saw him kneeling in front of her, an expression of deep concern on his face. He said, "You have had ill news. Is it your husband?"

"No—oh, no," she whispered—her voice seemed to have disappeared. "No, he wrote the letter—before Christmas, it's taken months to reach here . . ." She took a deep breath, suddenly unwilling to put the dreadful truth into words. Her hands, she realized suddenly, were twisting together, over and over. With an abrupt effort she stilled them, lacing her fingers. It helped a little. She said starkly, "Sam. My stepson, Nat's and Rachael's elder brother. He—he's dead, he died months ago, after Newbury . . . and how am I to tell them?"

"The children?"

"And Dame Ursula—she was fond of him, so far as she could be fond of anyone, he was a nice boy . . ." Her words trailed away as she thought, anew, of how nice Sam had been, once she had breached that early reserve. Poor, deluded Sam, riding off in such high spirits to the war that had slain him, as it had slain so many others . . .

Pull yourself together, she told herself sternly. Other women all over the country have lost sons, sons of their own blood as Sam, however dear, was not: sons, brothers, fathers, and husbands. You are not unique—and you have not suffered as much as others have, so there is no call to indulge in self-pity.

Hardly knowing what she was saying, she added, "Nat and Rachael—they were very close to him . . . Oh, poor Rachael, after all she has endured . . . he was the hero of them both, but hers especially, she always followed him around—and Nat, Nat will be the heir now, which he never wanted, he wanted to be a scholar—and his father didn't want it either, he worshipped Sam, and he never had any time for Nat at all. Nat was a weakling, feeble, beneath contempt—well, he'll have to take notice of him now, won't he, because Nat is his heir." She stopped, suddenly appalled at the bitterness and anger in her words, and pressed her hands to her mouth. She could not look at Nick. After a while she added so softly that he could barely hear it, "I'm sorry—I shouldn't have said those things."

"It doesn't matter—you are distressed," he said, astonished at the desperate strength of her. Although over the months he had known her, he had become aware of its existence, this controlled endurance still had the power to surprise him. He added, addressing the bent, mouse-fair head, the hair still formally arranged, "Would it help you, to talk? I am here to listen, as always."

She raised her eyes to meet his; he was expecting grief and saw anger instead. "Talk? About Sam? About how his father carried him off to war with as much idea of what they were involved in as—as a bear goes to its baiting? About how George loved him, as we all did, and still took him away from us and encouraged him to fight? And then when he died to say it was God's will—how can, how *can* it be God's will to make him suffer like that, a dear boy with no harm in him at all—read it, go on, read it, see how he died—and don't you dare mention God's will to me either!"

He bent and took the paper that her foot thrust toward him. Silence stared at him as he read, her hands still clenched together, her whole body trembling with rage and anguish. At the end of the first page, his own face aghast under the light-brown skin, he raised his eyes to hers, shaken. "My

God, he hasn't spared you anything, has he? Why in Christ's name didn't he write a few platitudes, a few lies—you would never have known—but *this* . . ."

"George has no imagination," Silence said. The tears were beginning now, dribbling from her eyes, running down her nose and into her mouth, but she made no attempt to check them. "He never has had—it wouldn't occur to him to think that all the details might distress me—or his mother, who will certainly demand to read it. And what do I tell the children? That it was God's will that their brother lingered six weeks in desperate agony before dying?" And at last the hard-won control broke, and she buried her face in her hands, sobbing wildly.

Mally, puffing up the stairs with a bundle of fresh linen for pillows and bed, knocked briefly, bounced in with her usual brisk cheerfulness, and stopped, appalled. Her mistress sat upon the chair, her head bowed, weeping brokenly, and the captain knelt beside her, his arms about her, holding her close.

"Zuggers, what's to do here?" she demanded, deliberately loudly. Hellier, as guiltily as if caught in the act of adultery, leapt to his feet and stood staring at the maid. Mally, all her suspicions confirmed, met his eyes coolly. "I think you'd best go, Captain," she said, and with a brief, rueful smile, he acknowledged it.

"Yes. But, Mally, there has been a letter. Bad news—look after her, please."

Mally, puzzled, apprehensive and hostile, watched him leave the chamber.

Silence, still sobbing, did not seem to notice that he had gone.

C H A P T E R

FIFTEEN

A gift is as a precious stone.
—PROVERBS 17:8

"Well, that's another rebel dead—death to 'em all, that's what I say!" Johnny Byam took a deep draft of cider and banged his empty tankard on the table. "Here, Bessie my sweet, let's have some more."

His paramour regarded him with an indignant eye. "There bain't no call to talk about Master Sam like that. He were a good lad—good to me, anyway."

"Eh?" Byam peered at her through unfocused eyes, and Bessie, the jug of cider on her ample hip like a child, stared unrepentantly back. "Eh? Well, death to all my rivals in love, then. Am I better than him between the sheets, sweetheart?"

"He didn't so much as kiss me," Bessie said. "And you bain't half the man he were." She banged the jug down on the stained, smeared cloth so that cider slopped down its black leather sides and said angrily, "I've had enough of ee. I be going to my bed now—and I be going *alone*." With a flounce and a provocative sway of her hips, she turned and walked out, banging the door behind her.

Cornet Wickham, lighting his pipe with a taper from the central candlestick, caught Nick's eye and winked. Byam, his lower lip thrust out petulantly, poured himself another brimmer of cider, raised the tankard to his lips, and drained it, noisily, in one long gulp. Nick watched the Adam's apple rise up and down his scrawny throat, and could not conceal his distaste. As Byam banged the tankard back on the table and fumbled again for the blackjack, he found it whisked out of his reach.

"No more, Johnny," said his captain, putting the jack down on the little table where, earlier in the day, the three youngest St. Barbe children had sat at dinner with their nurse. "You've had quite enough. Go to bed—it must be past ten."

Ensign Parset, a neat quiet youth with dark curly hair already receding, consulted his timepiece, of which he was enormously proud. "Near half-past, I'd say."

Byam, with the obstinacy of the very drunk, stayed where he was, his bloodshot eyes glaring at Nick. His doublet stained with food and cider, his face scarlet from drink and his mouth slack and slobbering, he did not present a very edifying spectacle. Nick, his gaze cold, stared back across the table. "What if Waller's men turned up tonight, eh? You'd be worse than useless."

"They won't—not within a hundred miles of here. 'Nyway, Captain Bull's on watch and his lot don't let a cockroach past." Byam sniggered. "You didn't used to be so prim and proper, Nick—been listening to your little Puritan, have you? Good in bed, is she? Don't fancy her m'self, not enough bubbies on her."

Something in the set of Nick's face made Wickham say uneasily, "Stow it, Byam, for Christ's name, and get to bed—I don't want your spew all over the table."

"Shan't," Byam said, and belched. His mutinous tone was so like Deb's that Nick almost laughed, despite the hard knot of anger in his throat. His lieutenant's bleary eye wandered from face to face around the table, all of them his comrades, even if they could not be described as friends, meeting the eyes of men decidedly less inebriated than he and none of them approving. With a sudden swing of mood he surged unsteadily to his feet, swaying like a tree in a gale. "A' right—know when I'm no' wanned—damned crew of sober-faced Puritans, wheresh your old shpirit, eh?" And on the last word, he rocked too far backward and fell.

Wickham got to him first. "Out cold," he said with satisfaction. "Can't you send him to join Goring's men, Nick? He'd really feel at home with them."

Lord Goring's debauches were legendary. Nick Hellier stared down at the squalid snoring figure of his lieutenant, who had been quite an agreeable young man before overindulgence in wine and cider had transformed him into a much less attractive personality. "I'll not spend the effort to carry him to bed," he said. "Leave him there, and if he wakes with twice the hurt to his head tomorrow, it's no more than he deserves."

He went back to his chair. The leather had been neatly stitched by someone, probably Eliza, after the damage caused by the search for the pistol. Suddenly sickened by the war, he sat down and took a deep draft of the cider. The irony of it struck him: He disliked drunkenness in such as Byam, and yet tonight he deeply desired it for himself.

It would not do, not after his self-righteous speech just now, to drown his own sorrows in rough and potent Somerset cider. But every time he allowed his thoughts to drift, they invariably slid into a small dark fetid room where a boy with Nat's face was dying in agony.

He knew, as Silence had not, the full horror of such a death. He had seen many end in such a way, their wounds bursting with pus, the ghastly pain, the appalling stench, the fever that mounted inexorably higher until, at last, death came as a blessed relief. He had once tried, and failed, to save a friend struck down by a gangrenous finger; such a little wound, to cause such a hideous death. And yet none of those dreadful scenes that he had unwillingly witnessed had affected him so much as the thought of Sam, a boy whom he had never even met, a rebel soldier, whose end he ought to welcome as Byam had, dying in that terrible way.

"Any man's death diminishes me, because I am involved in mankind." Donne's beautiful words drifted into his head. If I am involved in mankind, he thought with sudden anger, then why in Christ's name am I involved in this dubious, pointless, agonizing war, when defeat is writ large on the wall for any man to read it, and from blindness and stubbornness and sheer stupidity they will not? And all the king's army has brought me is an illusory relief from boredom and an entirely unnecessary, inconvenient, and possibly dangerous friendship with a woman who should be my enemy, and somehow is not.

He took another draft of cider and was aware that Ensign Parset, a conscientious boy little older than Sam St. Barbe had been, was bowing, making his excuses. He nodded curtly, and the youth fled. Milksop, Nick thought, knowing that he was being unfair. Ridgeley had teased poor Parset unmercifully, and the other officers had taken their cue from him, sending the boy on useless errands, telling him to ask Atkins the farrier for a remedy for some imaginary disease, or Darby for a barrel of red herrings and a peck of green oats. It had seemed amusing at the time. Now, in his present bitter mood, he could see the stupid childishness of it all.

There was silence in the dining parlor. Wickham's smoke, more than usually pungent, assaulted his nostrils. Silence, he thought, smiling despite himself. What a name to give a child—more fitting for a character in a lampoon by Ben Jonson. But, like the absent Sir George St. Barbe, her father had obviously lacked any sensitivity or imagination.

He, unfortunately, was blessed with too much. It made him a good officer, aware of the mood of his men, able to predict the likely movements of the enemy; but also a bad one, too sympathetic toward the foe, too careful of himself. His only experience of action had been in skirmishes, brief hectic affairs where you were so busy fighting off attack that there was no time to feel fear. He knew in his bones that this year would be different. This year might see him dead—and if that were so, he wanted it to come quickly, unannounced. Not, please God, that long-drawn-out unbearable suffering that Silence's stepson had perforce endured, too strong to die easily.

Admit it, he thought. The boy's death has affected you, not for any pious altruistic reason of sorrow or sympathy but because Silence is so greatly distressed. He remembered her at dinner, the dowdy Puritan almost unrecognizable, save for the quiet laughter in her face, the amusement in those brown-green eyes. Her dress had been old-fashioned and provincial. No woman à la mode wore those high waists any more, the new shape was longer, leaner. But the tawny hue had suited her coloring, the shades of earth, brown and green and gold. And he had been conscious of a deepening feeling of desire.

It was ridiculous. He had begun his overtures of friendship partly from sheer lightness of heart, and spurred also by the challenge in winning over a woman so hostile, an implacable enemy. It might be useful. It had certainly been pleasant. He had flirted with her because plain, middle-aged and deserted wives could be more easily won over thus.

He had not expected genuine friendship, a real feeling of closeness with this unassuming, modest, not in the least elderly woman. He had never thought that his shallow motives could so greatly betray him and lead to something that, even now, he hesitated to acknowledge to himself.

It had begun purely as a diversion. Now he realized the danger almost too late, for falling in love had never been part of the plan.

Spring that year was a capricious season, one day promising sunshine and warmth, the next bringing cold, rain, even snow. The flowering bulbs in Silence's garden, alternately battered by wind and lacking in sunlight, suffered greatly, the fragile crocuses beaten and bruised, the daffodils bent and broken under the sudden weight of overnight snowfall. But at least they were there, valiant, the yellow cups and trumpets a fanfare for summer and a reminder that, though death and disaster might yet strike them all, the turning year remained, eternal.

The St. Barbes wore black, for Sam. Silence, in the first flush of her grief, had wanted to shroud her chamber, even the hall, in the funereal hangings that had announced Sir Samuel's death only six months previously. She had thought better of it. Such an act might be dangerously tactless and provocative under their present circumstances. But black garments were conventional, and quite acceptable.

Mally had never mentioned that moment when she had entered to find her mistress in Nick Hellier's arms, and Silence, deliberately, had not spoken of it either. He had been giving her comfort, that and that alone. And in her rage and sorrow for Sam and the manner of his death, she had not considered any other possible motive. She would not justify herself unnecessarily to her maid. And Mally, loyal and outspoken friend though she was, did not accuse her of impropriety again. Instead, she had given her own comfort, mixed a soothing hot posset, shed tears for the young master herself, and had stood firm at her lady's elbow when Silence told the children.

William, a tiny baby when Sam had left, had no memory of him, and Deb little more, just a shadowy godlike creature who had lifted her up onto his horse, but Tabby, aged six when her glorious big brother marched away, could remember him quite clearly, and her small elfin face was stricken as Silence spoke to her own three, telling them gently how God had seen fit to take their dear brother from them but had given him the merciful dispensation of a swift and glorious death in battle. And as she uttered the lie, with a conviction that frightened her, the cold stone of her bitterness lay grimly around her heart. She loved her children, and would spare them the truth. But George, who professed affection for her and knew her fondness for her eldest stepson, had not.

Tabby wept, heartbroken, and Deb and William, taking their cue from their sister, wailed with her, without understanding but nevertheless full of grief. She uttered more words of comfort that sounded to her own ear suspiciously hollow, a false echo of George's platitudes. They must not cry, for Sam was now in heaven, and at peace, and one day they would all see him again.

She left them still weeping, and with misery and dread in her soul went to see the twins.

They knew that there was something very wrong. They sat at the table in Nat's chamber, a half-finished game of chess between them, and stared at her, Nat calm, Rachael more openly apprehensive. They had heard the sounds of distress from the nursery. The boy said straight away, his face very pale, "Is it bad news?"

"I'm very much afraid that it is," she said, and told them.

Nat, who had more skill at hiding or controlling his feelings, sat still and quiet, staring out of the window. Rachael, always buffeted by her emotions, did all the things that Silence had dreaded and known that she would do: She wept, wailed, cried in anger and despair, and howled her hatred for the wicked Cavaliers who had slain her beloved brother. Silence, her own tears returned, tried to comfort her and was beaten away. Then Rachael turned on her twin, sitting frozen like stone in his chair. "Look at you—cold, heartless, you couldn't care less!"

"Oh, yes, I could," Nat said, suddenly angry. "And you know I do— you're not the only one to love him, you know, though you'd think it to hear your caterwauling."

"You—you filthy bastard!" Rachael screamed, normally so disapproving of foul language, and fetched her brother a great blow across his cheek. It left a vivid scarlet mark, the print of her fingers plain. She stared at it aghast, her hands to her mouth, and then, with a cry of "Oh, no, I didn't mean it, I'm so *sorry!*" flung herself into his arms.

Silence, seeing them united in grief, left softly, wiping her own eyes. She stood outside the door, Mally silent and sad next to her, gathering her courage. Then she went to tell Dame Ursula.

And that was the worst of all. The old lady, sick, humiliated but not humbled by Ridgeley, had seized avidly on his shooting and sucked new vitality from the colonel's misfortune. Yesterday and today, for the first time in months, she had left her bed and taken up her usual position next to the spy hole behind the laughing mask. She could not have failed to ascertain, as had the twins, that some kind of disaster had befallen them, but the arrival of her daughter-in-law, in her rusty black gown, served only to goad her into abuse. Before Silence had even set a foot across the threshold, Dame Ursula was in full cry, having heard from Ruth of the identity of the day's visitor. She demanded to know how Silence dared to let the ungodly spawn of that wicked king through the door, and then in the next breath lamented her daughter-in-law's discourtesy in not hauling the prince up to her chamber so that she could be presented to him, as was only her proper due and right as lady of the house. Silence, her nerves and emotions already shredded to exhaustion, stood quiet under the flood of complaint until Dame Ursula had at last run dry. She said, her voice still raw and hoarse, "Mother, I have had a letter from George."

"From George? A letter? Why didn't you say so, daughter? Give it here, if you please—I must read it."

Silence, who had taken good care to leave it locked away in her chamber, said doggedly, "Madam, I warn you—it brings bad news. Very bad news, I'm afraid—"

"Well, don't just stand there, girl—I said, give it to me!"

With the feeling that she had done her best to prepare the ground, Silence said, "The letter was addressed to me, madam. But I can give you the gist of what it contained." She tried to catch Ruth's eye, but the maid's puddinglike face never changed; she stared fixedly ahead at her mistress. With apprehension, Silence told her mother-in-law briefly and gently of the fact of Sam's death, though not the manner of it, and waited for the explosion of furious grief that must surely come.

It did. Screeching her rage, Dame Ursula raised two skinny arms to heaven and called upon her Lord to avenge her grandson's death. Even Ruth flinched at the noise. Silence resisted the temptation to clap her hands to her ears. There was no point in offering comfort; her mother-in-law did not know the meaning of the word. Dame Ursula would find solace in her thirst for revenge and in her certainty that Sam, despite his youth, had given his life nobly for God's cause and was now enshrined in heavenly bliss.

Unable to endure any more, Silence crept unnoticed from her mother-in-law's chamber and fled to the refuge of her own.

She had sought her own solace in the Bible, during the long hours of that first night, when she had been reluctant to go to sleep for fear of what she might dream. Her finger had traced the words in Ecclesiastes: "To everything there is a season, and a time to every purpose under Heaven." Once, in times of despair, she had drawn great strength from that verse. Now the beauty and the faith and, yes, the fatalism of the prophet's writings had no more power to move her.

A time to be born, and a time to die. They would all die, the only certainty that life had to offer. But who could deny that Sam's hour of death had come too late? What possible purpose had his agony achieved? And how could the imposition of such suffering be perceived as the will of a just and merciful God?

She knew that there was pain, misery, and injustice all around, and that too had always been represented to her as God's natural order. Everything, everyone in the world had their allotted place, and should ask for no more. She knew what Dame Ursula would say: that Sam was one of the Elect, marked from birth for heaven, and that his earthly sufferings were irrelevant, a mere antechamber for the eternal bliss that was his by right. The wicked, by contrast, destined for hell, might endure much sorrow and despair in this life, but that of course was the just punishment for their sins.

But if we are destined for heaven or hell, Silence thought in the long deep quiet of the night, if our place is allotted from our birth, then what is the point of trying to live a godly life? If you are one of the Elect, you will go to heaven anyway, and if not, then you might as well enjoy yourself on the road to everlasting torment.

Her thoughts frightened her. They were wicked and blasphemous, and quite probably proved that she herself was not one of the saints on earth, pious, virtuous and unstained by imperfection. It was her father's creed, and Dame Ursula's, and her husband's; but, she realized at last, Sam's death had taught her to recognize that it was not hers. She was too tolerant, too easygoing, too fond of the primrose path, too susceptible to the fleeting illusory pleasure that her house, her garden, her children, and all the world around brought to her. Oh, she would do her best to live a virtuous and sober life—not for her the giddy round of worldly delights, decadence and fashion and fripperies, but a solid existence rooted in home, family, children, the joys of the countryside. But her God was her own, a spirit of growth and rebirth, gentler by far than the vengeful, terrifying deity invoked by Dame Ursula.

She fell asleep in her chair, just before dawn, and slept dreamlessly, exhausted and yet, somehow, having achieved a kind of peace.

The tide of war washed near to Wintercombe, nearer than it had done for almost a year, and then receded. Waller, and General Cromwell, had been ordered west by the Parliament, to relieve sundry beleaguered garrisons in Dorset. Near Trowbridge, hardly more than six or seven miles from Philip's Norton, they had fallen upon the Royalist regiment of Colonel Long, inflicting severe damage and taking many prisoners. Messengers galloped in and out of the courtyard at Wintercombe, bringing instructions from Sir Thomas Bridges, taking answers away, and all the Horse, under the leadership of Captain Hellier, rode out under orders to join with other troops in the vicinity and harass the enemy intruders.

Wintercombe seemed very quiet without them. Clevinger, taking advantage of their absence, cleared out the barn and fed all the remaining store of hay, little enough, to the cattle, now approaching their calving. The grass was beginning to grow, and in the water meadows along the brook it lay a thick, lush and vivid green, eagerly grazed by the herds belonging to Wintercombe and the Manor Farm, before they were removed to allow the herbage to grow tall for hay. The earth was waking, soon Norton would embark on another dairying year, making butter and cheese and cream, and probably to no one's profit but the soldiers'.

Ridgeley had commandeered the five best of the Wintercombe horses, but Cobweb and Strawberry, the two that were spared, joined Dumbledore in one of the paddocks at the northern end of the little valley, just by the mill, their winter coats already looking somewhat patchy. There were buds on the remaining apple trees in the desecrated orchard and on the cherry arbor along the lower terrace. Lambs bleated and skipped with delight among their stolid dams, and Darby, with every evidence of pleasure, served up one of them roasted for dinner, knowing that only a few of the soldiers would be present to enjoy it. Captain Bull's company, much occupied with guarding Wintercombe and very conscious of their responsibility in the absence of the more prestigious Horse, were scarcely seen inside the house. Silence, enjoying the deliciously sweet tender meat and the sharp contrast of the spearmint sauce, hoped that Clevinger had thought to hide the other ewes and lambs well away, up on Hassage Hill perhaps, where there was an old barn at present occupied by hay, straw, cows and calves, and other temptations too vulnerable to military greed.

It was one small concern among many, much greater worries. She missed Nick. He had scarcely spoken to her since the fateful evening when he had given her the letters and seemed to be keeping his distance even before he rode away to harry General Cromwell's greatly superior forces. She upbraided herself for her foolishness, but she could not rid herself of the fear that she would not see him again.

Then there was Ridgeley, hovering between life and death. She had dreaded to see signs of putrefaction in the double wound, knowing that she could not face a death such as Sam had suffered, even if it happened this time to someone she loathed. She left the bulk of the nursing to poor Harris, venturing in to see her patient only two or three times a day. When Ridgeley was awake, she had small thanks for her trouble, and the nourishing broths and possets and cooling almond-flavored drinks and juleps were hurled aside when the colonel was strong enough. Even on his bad days, she had to summon the services of two stout musketeers to hold him still while dressings were changed, salves applied, and medicines forced down his throat. He was, as might be expected, an exceedingly bad patient. And sometimes, exasperated, she caught Mally's eye and knew the thought behind that blue glitter. How much more convenient it would be if he died.

But the colonel did not die. Kept to life by his own undeniably stubborn will and his oxlike constitution, he made slow, irregular, and hesitant progress. The fevers grew more intermittent, the abuse and oaths louder. Silence, listening in the antechamber as yet another bowl of mutton and barley broth was tipped over the unfortunate Harris, wondered fearfully how long it would be before he regained his strength and his command, and what he would then do to Rachael—although so far as she knew, he had not yet mentioned the girl's name.

But try as she might to immerse herself in the activity of the house, and of her children and the farm, and all the other anxieties, she could not forget Sam and the manner of his passing. Nat had appalled her by his perspicacity. He had turned to her, one day in the garden when she was peering up at the vine, wondering if this year it could be coaxed into fruitfulness, and said very quietly, so that Jemmy and Diggory would not hear, "Mother, tell me about Sam. Did he really die a glorious death in battle?"

Faced with such a sudden and direct question, she had no time to lie, no chance to prevaricate. She could only stare at him in distress, and Nat, his shrewd blue eyes examining her face, nodded after a while. "I thought not. It's all right, I won't tell Rachael. She still cries herself to sleep every night, thinking of him. What was it—a fever?"

"A wound fever," Silence said, even now unable to bring herself to utter the truth. It seemed to satisfy Nat; he smiled sadly and touched her hand, a brief gesture that was curiously comforting. "I wish . . . I wish so much that he could have come home safe," he said slowly, unusually hesitant. "Mother . . . I know it sounds strange to say it, but I am Father's heir now, and I really don't want to be. Oh, I'm well aware that I haven't any choice. But I'd—I'd always expected Sam to have that burden. I don't think I'd make a good Justice, and I wouldn't be able to ride around all the lands and manors—and I'm very sure that I don't want to go to London or Oxford and study law and grammar and all the other things that Father will expect of me now." He caught Silence's eye and grinned rather ruefully. "I had always somehow hoped to stay here and idle my life away in scholarly pursuits—a second son has no responsibility save to himself. And you know as well as I do what Father thinks of me. When he comes home he'll try to force me into Sam's mold."

There was nothing she could say: They both knew it for the truth. Silence, looking down at his dark head—perhaps, at last, he was beginning to grow?—felt love and great compassion for this wise child, old beyond his years. He did not pity himself; after this uncharacteristic lapse, he would armor himself once more in his usual cheerful cynicism and convince the world that he was a chip off his grandfather's old block. She touched his hand in return and said quietly, "Whatever happens, remember—I am with you."

"Even against Father?" Nat asked, his blue eyes open very wide in his narrow pale face.

"Even against your father," Silence replied, her bitter heart resolute within her. Once she had respected George, feared his careless, thoughtless, belittling comments, yet managed to feel some affection for him as her husband and the father of her beloved children. But she knew that she would never forgive him for that unwittingly cruel letter, somehow typical of his attitude toward her—she was a warm-blooded, intelligent, tenderhearted woman, not a dutiful unquestioning housewife and broodmare whose feelings were of no account.

Even the letters of Prue and Joseph, full of news and family gossip— their youngest sister Patience betrothed at last to someone suitable, Prue expecting her first baby, Joseph courting a handsome young mercer's daughter—had not lightened the sick thoughts within her. If Sir George St. Barbe were to return to Wintercombe now, she trembled to think of what she would say to him.

But of course he would not. She did not know if he was still with Waller, or if in this last winter's reorganization of the Parliament's armies, he and his regiment now served under another general. Joseph had written a confused paragraph about this plan for a new-modeled army, upon which all of Parliament's hopes were fixed, under the leadership of the Yorkshire general, Sir Thomas Fairfax. Below he had described, almost as an afterthought, the visit of his brother-in-law Sir George St. Barbe at the New Year, spoken of his sorrow at the news of Sam's death, and written about God's will in a way that suspiciously echoed her husband's letter. Joseph had always been too ready to take his cue from others. Disgusted with him, Silence nearly threw his letter on the fire.

Prue's, although bubbling with her joy at her pregnancy, was much more sympathetic, and her hasty scrawl brought tears to her sister's eyes. She spent some time writing to all of them, sitting by the fire through the long empty evenings after the twins had gone to bed, Mally stitching opposite her, the board on her knees and quill in hand, trying to give some flavor of life at Wintercombe under enemy occupation. It was difficult, to say the least, but not so hard as her letter to her husband proved to be.

She was working on that, for the tenth time, when the troop returned. It was very late, and raining. She heard the distant commotion, noise, hooves, shouting, and knew what it must be. Pye, an ear flickering crossly at the disturbance, yawned, stretched, and curled up again in the warmth. Silence had calculated, from past experience, that her kittens would be born two weeks after Easter. There was no outward sign of them yet, save the increased size and pinkness of the cat's nipples. She never had very many—five at most—and the thickness of her parti-colored fur hid any extra rotundity for the time being.

Silence stared down at the paper on her knees, a mixture of sadness, bitterness, and anger clogging her mind. She did not know what to write. She knew that she should compose the fluent, graceful phrases that were part of every lady's education and the same whether expressing feelings or concealing them. But the words stuck in her mind, ludicrously, hopelessly inappropriate to describe her real emotions, her actual reaction to the news of Sam's death. Yet they were what George would expect, indeed what he would want. He had never thought of her as an individual in her own right, and the unconventional had always alarmed and angered him.

For the tenth time, she dipped her quill into the bottle of ink secure in a hole at the top of the board and wrote, "My dearest husband."

Even those three words lied—as if, she thought, suddenly exasperated with herself, she had more than one spouse, and George the best of them. She crumpled up the paper and flung it into the fire. It bounced off a log and rolled back, unburned, at Pye's oblivious feet.

"I'll get en," Mally said, bending forward. She picked up the ball of paper and thrust it into the flames. Then she leaned back in her chair, the needle plying almost of its own accord in and out of the fine holland of one of her mistress's smocks, and said slowly, "You must write *summat,* m'lady."

"I know that, Mally—but it's not exactly easy." Silence closed her eyes for a moment. She thought of Sam, like a taller, healthier, paradoxically more childish edition of Nat, with that sadly familiar stab of grief. Then a picture of George came into her mind, stout, ruddy, with the appearance of being cheerfully good-humored, yet capable of flying into a rage when provoked by something a more tolerant man might not even have noticed; deeply suspicious of anything out of the ordinary, tenacious of his rights and firm in upholding the proper privileges of his position. It was this belief that had led him to rebel against his anointed sovereign and would inevitably bring him into conflict with Nat.

Suddenly Silence was aware of a terrible, treacherous tendril of thought that slid into her mind serpentine and would not be denied. She did not want him to return. She wanted the war to be over, peace and certainty restored to Wintercombe; but she did not want George to come back.

Shocked at herself, she dipped the quill in the ink and began again.

My dearest husband,
It is with the greatest grief and sorrow that I read of the sad death of our
beloved Samuel . . .

There was a sharp, familiar double knock on the door. Mally's head jerked up, and she met Silence's eyes significantly. "Your captain be back again."

This is wrong, Silence thought, fighting the sudden panic and the equally sudden sensation of delight. I should not, should *not* be sitting here wishing that my husband would never come home and then feeling quite unwarranted joy because some Cavalier captain is knocking at my door.

Mally, her face carefully neutral, rose and opened it. Nick stood there, a bundle in his arms, smiling the lazy smile. "Good evening, Mally. Sorry to disturb you so late—can your lady spare a moment or two? I have a gift for her."

Silence got to her feet, laying the unfinished letter down by Pye. She found, suddenly, that she did not want to meet his eyes. She said, falsely bright, "A gift, Captain?"

"A gift." He walked toward her and then stopped. He looks tired, she thought inconsequentially. I wonder—what on earth is in that bundle? Did it—did it *move?*

"Is the door closed, Mally?" he asked.

"Aye," the maid said. Behind Nick's shoulder, Silence could see her grimace and shrug her bewilderment. The captain stayed where he was; the bundle was definitely squirming. He said to Silence, "Forgive me. It has only just occurred to me that this may be a mistake. I acquired it on impulse, you see, and perhaps I didn't give the matter enough thought. And one thing's quite certain—Pye won't like it."

Indeed, the cat had woken from her slumber and was sitting bolt upright in front of Silence's chair, her eyes and ears fixed on Hellier's bundle. From the back of her throat came a low, threatening, musical growl. Silence bent to stroke and soothe her, but she took no notice; her back was rigid, her tail had begun to twitch and her fur was starting to rise.

"It's a dog," she said, suddenly sure of it. "Pye always reacts to strange dogs like that. Oh, Nick—have you brought me a *dog?*"

"It certainly wasn't a very good idea at all," Hellier said, tightening his grip on the bundle, which humped and wriggled in an alarming fashion. "I'm sorry—I'll take it back."

"Oh, no, you won't," Silence said firmly. "Pye gets on very well with most dogs, once she's asserted her superiority—and don't laugh, I'd wager on her to beat any dog on earth in a free fight—and anyway I've always wanted a dog. We never had one in London, of course, and George doesn't like them, he has no interest in hunting. Now put the poor thing down before it widdles all down your front."

Mally giggled. Hellier looked sorrowfully at Silence. "Too late, I'm afraid—it already has."

Pye, still all a-bristle, leapt for safety onto the bed as Nick knelt down, laid the bundle on the floor, and, with a flourish, whisked off the damp-stained brown cloth. A puppy, perhaps eight weeks old, shook itself so vigorously that it almost fell over, sneezed violently, and looked about itself with great interest. It was a thin, scrawny creature, with short, snow-white fur. Enchanted, Silence knelt and snapped her fingers. The puppy's ears pricked at the sound, one up, one down, and then it trotted over to her and gave her hand a liberal and enthusiastic washing.

Her joy shining in her face, Silence glanced up at her benefactor. "Nick—how can I thank you? It's delightful! I've never had a puppy—and the children will love it."

"Her," said Hellier. "I'm glad you like her—such a surprise gift is not always welcome."

"You knew it would be—your instinct was right." The puppy was now worrying her forefinger with tiny, needle-sharp teeth. She had played similar games with Pye in her skittish youth, before she became a serious matron and mother to two dozen hopeful kittens. There was a brief tussle that ended, just, without bloodshed, and the puppy sat back on her haunches, her eyes, round, dark and long-lashed, sparkling merrily and her small pink tongue lolling. "She's utterly beautiful," Silence added, rubbing her scratched and slobbery finger on her apron. "What kind is she? Where did you find her?"

"A bitch at the farm where we laid last night had a litter of seven, and this was the best. The farmer needed a little persuasion, because he'd promised her to someone else, but in the end he relented. And don't look like that, Mally, I didn't use hot coals or the rack—I meant *monetary* persuasion."

"Huh," Mally said, appeased but trying not to look as if she were. "It d'look like the skummery kind to I."

Nick caught Silence's eye and grinned. "It's the rabbit-hunting kind—a small greyhound. The dam was a little more than the height of my knee, very lean and graceful, though a brindle color. The white are reckoned the best—hence the farmer's reluctance to sell."

"She is lovely," Silence said. Still kneeling, she picked the little dog up, cradling her in her arms. The puppy squirmed, warm and smooth and wriggling under her fingers, then stretched up to wash her face.

George won't like her, she thought rebelliously. And George can say what he pleases—she is mine, and I love her already, and I shall never let her go.

A menacing wail of dissent reminded her that her acquisition was unpopular with at least one other member of the household besides her husband. Pye, on the bed, had increased to twice her normal size, spiky with hate, her ears flat and her emerald eyes, furious, locked on the puppy. Thus had she looked when first introduced to Sir Samuel's ancient mastiff, Solomon, who had passed away not long before his master. Yet within the week she had been sharing his bed and stealing out of his foodbowl from under his very nose. Silence knew that this ferocious display was but a warning: Once she had ensured that the puppy knew her, inferior, place in the hierarchy of Wintercombe, she would treat her as she had treated the elderly mastiff, with amused contempt.

Not unlike the way that George always treated me, Silence remembered, and tried to thrust such unloyal comparisons to the back of her mind. She had hardly given her husband a thought for months. Indeed, she had enjoyed life in his absence, free to direct the servants and herself as she pleased, free of his criticisms, his assumption that she restrict herself to domestic matters, and above all free of his ponderous attentions in her bed. But now, prompted by his letter and by Sam's death, he was an unwanted and ever-present figure in her mind, a threat hanging over her, the disturber of her peace and the progenitor of that hard, alien knot of bitterness and resentment that had invaded her heart.

The puppy, seeing Pye, scrabbled out of her arms and, quite without fear, went trotting over to the bed. She stood on her hind legs, front paws on the counterpane, and whined, her thin curved tail wagging hopefully. Pye dismissed this overture of friendship with an arch of her back and an increase in the volume of her growls. When the puppy refused to be deterred, she spat viciously and raked her across the shiny black leather of her sharp little nose.

There was an astonished, agonized yelp, and the puppy fled back to Silence, leaping into her arms with a trustful and endearing abandon. One or two beads of bright red blood had sprung from the track of Pye's claws. Laughing, she wiped them off with a finger. "They'll be friends soon. Once she's learned that cats can be dangerous, she'll treat Pye with more respect. Mally, can you find an old blanket that we can use for her bed? Pye always sleeps on mine, and I think it'd be in the interests of harmony to keep the puppy off."

"And it'll have fleas, I'll wager," Mally said, and disappeared into the hanging closet, from whence sounds of rummage emerged fitfully. Silence, the puppy still nestling in her arms, got to her feet and smiled at the captain. "Mally disapproves, but, like Pye, she'll be won around eventually. Thank you, Nick—you couldn't have chosen a better gift."

"I'm glad of it—especially as I thought just now that I'd made a grievous error of judgment. Though probably the farmer would have taken her back willingly. What will you call her?"

"I shall think on that. A name should be appropriate, and chosen with care."

"As you have good cause to know, my gracious Silence."

She laughed, used to his teasing. "Did you find General Cromwell?"

"No—the old fox was much too wily for us. We spent three days blundering up and down Wiltshire, Somersetshire, and Dorsetshire, antagonizing the countryside but seeing neither hide nor hair of any Roundhead." He paused and added slowly, "I had not realized how very much hated we are in the villages to the south of here. And not only the king's army, either—they spoke of the Parliament men in just the same terms. There is trouble brewing there, for both sides. They have plundered and despoiled for so long that the people have had enough. At the moment they show it with muttered oaths, surly looks, and a distinct aversion to helping us in any way, whether it's with guidance or provisions or billets. Fortunately, I had some coin with me—but there's precious little money left in the king's coffers, and none of his loyal gentry in the west have bothered to stir themselves this winter to raise any more—or men, or arms. They're too busy squabbling among themselves to remember that they're supposed to be fighting for the king. Wyndham and Hopton aren't on speaking terms, the Prince of Wales is too young to give effective leadership, and if the countryside don't like us much now, they'll like us even less when Goring makes his presence felt in the south."

There was a brief pause. Silence, her arms full of the puppy, which seemed to have fallen asleep, waited for further revelations, but suddenly he smiled and shrugged. "Ah, well, now it's my turn to say too much. Here am I lamenting the disarray and incompetence of the king's army in the west, and you are doubtless praying for the furtherance of that situation."

"It hadn't really occurred to me to do so," Silence said wryly. "My prayers of late seem to concern smaller, more personal worries. Do you think Lord Goring will move here?"

"I doubt it. He's supposed to be helping to besiege Taunton—instead, his men are gaining themselves a most evil reputation around Chard. Where there is easy plunder and an abundance of strong liquor, there will be Lord Goring—and since this part of the country is already well burdened with soldiers on free quarter, I don't think he'll come so far. Anyway, it's too near Bristol and the prince. He'll want to keep his independence."

Silence said nothing, thinking of Chard, a small, pretty town, and the inconvenient, dark old house in which she had spent the first seven years of her marriage and where all her children had been born. Now it would be a blackened, smoking ruin, looted and despoiled, the cattle and sheep slaughtered, the orchards and timber cut down and carted away for a fraction of their real value, and the contents of the house sold or stolen. She found that she could contemplate the prospect with equanimity. She had never been happy there, as she was happy at Wintercombe.

"I should think there's nothing left for him to plunder," she pointed out with asperity. "The country around must have long been laid waste. No wonder the people are desperate."

"And they'll be more desperate yet, if this war continues another year. The people of Norton don't know how lucky they are. Which reminds me, how is my dear lieutenant-colonel?"

"Sick still, and hating it. He throws broth at Harris and calls for roast beef. Everyone's in agreement—the longer he's confined to his bed, the better."

"Hence the broth and the lack of beef?"

"Exactly." Silence caught his eye and laughed. "I've continued to put rue and wormwood in his medicine. It tastes *disgusting*."

"I've very little sympathy for him. And, speaking seriously, I'm entirely with you in this. When he eventually recovers, Rachael may find herself in a most awkward situation. And he'll probably take out all his ill humor on the village. He was going to force them to work on the defenses, remember?"

"And you won't?"

"I have more sense, and perhaps more humanity. At this time of year, men can't be spared if their farms are going to prosper. And since soldiers will probably take most of what they produce, for their sake and ours they ought to be let alone to produce as much as possible."

Silence studied his face. It was not at first sight a gentle one: The lines were too sharp and abrupt, his straight nose jutted aggressively, his chestnut eyes were narrowed under lids heavy and creased with tiredness, and his flying, peaked brows and the narrow line of moustache on his short upper lip, merged into four days' worth of stubble, gave him a devil-may-care look. But though he might assert the ruthless, callous side of his character when dealing with military matters, his manner with her, and with the children, suggested quite another story. Acting on instinct, thinking aloud, she said slowly, "You've come to dislike this war as much as I do—haven't you?"

Disconcerted, his autumn-colored eyes gazed into hers, and then he laughed. "Touché, my Silence. You are right, as ever. I dislike wanton destruction, brutality, the ruination of the lives of innocent people. Perhaps it was naive of me to think that an English war would be different, especially after what I'd seen in Europe. Now I know better—but there can be no going back. And it can't have been so bad, can it, if it has brought me such a delightful friendship?"

This time she chose not to succumb to his flattery. "That's a very poor reason to allow rapine, terror, and murder—isn't it, Captain Hellier?"

He took it in good part, as it was meant. "Perhaps. I think it time to bid you good night, my gracious Silence. May 'golden slumbers kiss your eyes, and smiles awake you when you rise.'"

As the door shut behind him, Mally appeared with suspicious alacrity from the closet, carrying an old and moth-eaten blanket. She said, unnecessarily, "I founded summat."

"So I see." Silence put the puppy on the floor and watched her run about the chamber, sniffing all the new smells. Pye, settled down warily on the bed, followed her every move with bright beady eyes.

Mally watched with a look scarcely less hostile. "What for did he give ee that, eh? A-widdling in all the corners, like as not—see, what did I tell ee?"

"I'll clear it up," Silence said. "And she can be trained. Oh, I *know* it's inconvenient—but I have always, always wanted a dog. Pye is very dear, but she's not the same—she's much more independent than any dog."

"You've too many dependent on ee already, m'lady, strikes me," Mally said, unconvinced. "Can't deny, though, she be a pretty, bobbant little dog. And if she *can* catch rabbits, she might prove useful, maybe."

And, grudgingly, she dumped the blanket down by the hearth. Whether Mally liked it or not, Hellier's gift undoubtedly felt at home. She trotted over, sniffed, turned around three times, and collapsed in the warmth with a contented sigh.

As Silence had predicted, the children were much more welcoming. Indeed, they threatened to crush the puppy with affection. She had to be rescued, squealing and breathless, from William's overenthusiastic grasp, only to suffer almost as badly in Deb's. Tabby, her face glowing with wonder, was more reticent, and contented herself with a quick stroke and caress. She said, watching as the puppy wriggled and rolled on her back to be tickled by Deb, "Have you given her a name, Mama?"

"I haven't, no," Silence said. "Can you think of one?"

Tabby's small pointed face took on a dreamy, faraway look that her mother knew well. "She's small—will she grow?"

"Oh, yes—to perhaps a foot and a half high, no more."

"And is she a hunting dog, or a baiting dog like Grandfather's old mastiff?"

"A hunting dog, like a small greyhound—she'll run as fast as the wind when she's grown."

"Something white . . . and beautiful . . ." Tabby seemed barely to hear. She said suddenly, quite loudly, "Lily!"

The puppy leapt to her feet and looked about her eagerly. Tabby laughed and clapped her hands. "Look—she knows her name! Can we call her Lily, Mama?"

"It's a good name," Silence said. "What do the rest of you think of it?"

"I don't think our opinion matters very much," Nat pointed out. "She seems to have decided for herself. Lily!"

All the children took it up, calling the name, and the puppy rushed from one to the other, eager, licking, bouncing with excitement, while Pye watched disdainfully from the bed. In the hubbub, Silence caught Tabby's eye, and they exchanged that old secret look of amusement. It had been her intention to let Tabby name the puppy, as she had named Pye, and Dumbledore. The little girl had as great an affinity for words as she had for music, and could be relied upon to produce something apt and unusual.

After the dark days of the winter, they seemed to have climbed, blinking with bemused happiness, into the sunny warmth of spring, all the sweeter because Silence knew, even if the younger children did not, that it could not last. Already the war had brushed them. If all that Nick had said about the parlous state of the king's cause in the west were true, then it would not be long before it came much closer. It would not be long, either, until Ridgeley was able to resume his duties, and then they must beware.

She glanced at Rachael, hugging William. The girl's fondness for her little half-brother and sisters was one of her most endearing characteristics. She seemed to have recovered a little from Sam's death, but there was a sadness in her face that even the frisking Lily could not disperse. If Ridgeley tries to take his revenge, Silence thought with foreboding, we shall have to try and send her away—but where? Bath would be too risky—London is too far, and too dangerous. Perhaps we could find a quiet remote house somewhere . . . the Baylies at Wick Farm, perhaps.

But for now that problem could wait, although she would have a quiet word with Mistress Baylie at the church on Sunday. All her problems could wait. March was going out like a lamb, in sunshine and warm showers toward Easter. Nick was in command, Ridgeley confined to his bed, and the enemy gone many miles away. An oasis of comparative peace beckoned; and Silence, defying the inevitable, was determined to enjoy it while it lasted.

PART THREE

SO EARLY
IN THE
SPRING

APRIL–MAY 1645

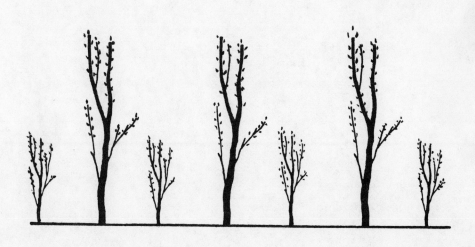

CHAPTER

SIXTEEN

The food of love.
—TWELFTH NIGHT

"I tell you, Lady St. Barbe, it is a most burdensome imposition—
it will cause terrible hardship in the village, terrible!"

The vicar, Master Willis, godly and immaculate in his best Sunday
black, drew a quivering, indignant breath. Silence, seeing that if allowed
he would run on in similar vein for some time, hastened to put her word
in. "Please do not distress yourself, Master Willis. I shall do all I can to
dissuade Captain Hellier. He is certainly a more approachable, well-dis-
posed man than the lieutenant-colonel."

"That spawn of Antichrist!" Parson Willis exclaimed, for once forthright. "And when will he be in command again? That will be an evil day!"

"I don't know," Silence replied. "He seemed to be recovering, but he
suffered another attack of fever last week, and it has left him still confined
to his bed."

"Mistress Rachael should have had better aim," Willis said petulantly.
"It can be no sin to slay a man so steeped in wickedness and vice of the
worst kind—the world would be well rid of him."

"Rachael was very distressed by her action," Silence reminded him.

Willis shrugged. "Ah, the child has a new and tender conscience . . .
only natural in one so young. How does she now? Does she pine for her
poor noble brother?"

It took Silence some seconds to realize that Willis meant Sam. She said
quickly, "Yes, yes, though she has accepted it bravely, as have all the
children."

Rachael's rather loud laugh echoed through the churchyard at that moment. Silence, looking past the vicar's shoulder, saw her stepdaughter in a
cheerful gaggle of other girls: Eleanor Flower; the three Baylie daughters,
Kitty, Moll and Bess; Susannah Parsons; and a clutch of young female
Tovies. Master Willis, turning, looked at once disapproving and wistful.
Of the nine children born to himself and his wife Anne, only Thomas, who
was the same age as William, remained alive. Every time Silence beheld

the gray, defeated figure of Mistress Willis, the misery in her face and her hopeless, desperate love for her one last child, she was moved to thank God wholeheartedly for the strident good health of her own brood.

The churchyard was crowded with villagers, glad of this chance to talk and gossip after the service. The southeasterly sun shone through the branches of the tall elms that lined the wall dividing it from Church Meadow, a large field now affording good grazing for one of the Manor Farm's considerable herds of cattle. This was the first Sunday after Easter, the thirteenth of April, and the vagaries of the weather had ensured that previous sabbaths were uniformly wet and windy, making the churchyard an unpleasant place to linger. Today was different. The sun warmed Silence's black gown, there were daffodils everywhere, and this morning, riding past the mill, they had all heard the cuckoo, harbinger of spring.

Tabby had immediately piped up in song, a tune that Silence did not recognize:

> Oh, the cuckoo, she's a pretty bird,
> She sings as she flies,
> She bringeth good tidings,
> She telleth no lies.
> She sucks on white flowers
> For to keep her voice clear,
> And when she singeth "Cuckoo,"
> Summer draweth near.

"That was prettily sung," Silence had said, and Tabby smiled, a small smile of pure pleasure.

"Did you like it? Captain Hellier taught it to me. I can play it on the virginals now, but too slowly to sing to it yet. And if I try and sing while I play, my voice gets all tangled up, and my hands do too, and I have to stop."

"Your voice wasn't tangled just now," Nat commented approvingly. "Have you been sucking wildflowers too, little Tabby-cat?"

And Tabby, suddenly embarrassed by all the praise and attention, turned very pink and quietly drew back into her shell.

Silence, smiling at the memory, soothed Master Willis, who had been under the misapprehension that Captain Hellier was going to make the villagers work on the Wintercombe fortifications, and left him to the dubious mercies of Mistress Sloper, a formidable and opinionated widow who, with her son, managed the village malting house.

The villagers were making no effort to return to their homes on this, their one day of rest in a week of toil. The Wintercombe servants, who had made their way over on foot across the fields, were taking full advantage of the opportunity to catch up with the gossip, disseminate some of their own, and greet their families. Silence studied the crowded faces, some avid, some laughing, others serious or sorrowful. Many would be discussing the sermon, which today had been a learned interpretation of the misfortunes of Job, all too appropriate in such times. In common with the other dairying villages in this northeastern part of Somerset, Norton was strongly Puritan. Every household of any standing could boast a Bible and a Book of Martyrs, even if it had no other books at all, and many men, and women, could juggle scriptural quotations and theological niceties around like the tisty-tosty cowslip balls that the village girls played with in May. Sir Samuel had often regaled his daughter-in-law with amusing, affectionate tales of evenings in the George, thick with the smoke of tobacco and the sharp aromas of beer and cider, as earnest husbandmen and weavers argued religion and politics over their tankards.

Silence, who was coming to know the villagers better, reflected that it was just as well that bad weather and Ridgeley's incapacity had prevented them from suffering the worst at the hands of the Wintercombe troopers. She remembered Hellier's comments about the ill-feeling in the south against all soldiers, Cavalier and Roundhead alike. These people, stubborn, opinionated, rooted in the land they worked, might appear of no account to such as Ridgeley, but their shabby clothes and weather-hardened faces hid enormous depths of feeling. Two years ago a skirmish in the village between Sir Ralph Hopton's Cavaliers and Waller's Roundheads, part of the campaign that had ended in the bloody battle of Lansdown, had resulted in the death of a Royal soldier, and the villagers had joined in on the Parliament side with enthusiasm, wielding pitchforks, rusty swords, and ancient halberds. She did not think that they would be any less ready to defend their own rights and property, should Ridgeley once more pose a threat.

Mindful of the colonel's resurrection, which despite this latest relapse would probably not be much longer delayed, she moved through the crowds in search of Mistress Baylie. However, she was immediately approached by a succession of villagers: Being the Lady of Wintercombe carried duties and responsibilities as well as privileges. Madlin Tilley's mother, an overbearing woman who dominated her family, wanted to know if it was true that the wicked colonel was at death's door. Silence was unable to give her the news she wanted to hear, and advised her that for the moment Madlin was best kept busy at home. As soon as the soldiers could be persuaded to leave, however, the girl would be welcome to return to Wintercombe.

Hardly had Elinor Tilley left her, somewhat disappointed, than it was the turn of Robin Grindland's widowed mother, a downtrodden, scrawny woman of indeterminate years, begging that Lady St. Barbe visit her poor little Ned, who was ailing again. Silence agreed to do so that afternoon, with a mental sigh. A visit to the tiny, squalid tenement behind the Fleur-de-Lys invariably depressed her, and the contrast between little Edward, feeble, crooked of limb and racked by coughs, and her own William, a year younger and substantially larger, always wrung her heart. She would take a basket of food as well as remedies, and perhaps a warm blanket or two and some of William's outgrown clothes.

The Widow Grindland crept away, her effusive thanks ringing in Silence's guilty ears, and was replaced by old Goody Waters, herself well into her seventies and bent over two sticks, to ask if Lady St. Barbe would visit her husband, who had suffered a bad winter and had very painful joints. Her husband would be a hundred years old in a few months, the wonder and marvel of the village, and had an inexhaustible fund of tales about the old days. He had been born in the reign of Henry VIII, seen out three kings and two queens, and possessed a typically Somerset humor, dry and laconic. Silence accordingly agreed to a visit, and promised to bring some of her camomile and frankincense cerecloths, so soothing when laid on swollen joints. Then, at last, she saw her quarry, and with relief drew her aside. "May I have a quiet word, Mistress Baylie?"

Christian Baylie, who leased Wick Farm and managed it with the help of her son Robert, was a short, stout, and very capable woman, well into her sixties, dressed in plain and sober black with a high-crowned hat tied over her cap in a rather old-fashioned manner. It was not long since her granddaughters had persuaded her to give up wearing her hopelessly outmoded ruffs. Although she was no more than an acquaintance, she had always been very affable to Silence, unintimidated by any supposed difference in station, and her granddaughters were friendly with Rachael. In the past they had exchanged recipes and remedies. Now she must ask a greater favor.

"What may I do for you, my lady?" Christian Baylie inquired. Her eyes kept sliding sideways to her middle granddaughter, Moll, a pretty, silly fourteen-year-old who was paying unsuitably close attention to young Fulke Tovie, a handsome lad who had gained a very dubious reputation.

Silence knew that she would have to be quick. She said quietly, "I take it that you have heard of the unfortunate, uh, accident that has befallen Colonel Ridgeley."

"Heard? Aye, I have—whole village too, come to that," Mistress Baylie replied. "And what a shame, eh, that he's still alive." She grinned cheerfully up at Silence, who though not especially tall stood half a head higher than the older woman. "Have your remedies not finished him off then, my lady?"

"No, unfortunately not," Silence said, grinning back. She always found Mistress Baylie's forthrightness infectious. "He'll be back in the saddle by the end of the month, alas. And when he's returned to his former self, I would like Rachael to be well out of the way."

"Ah," Mistress Baylie said, seeing her point at once. "And you'd like her to come stay at Wick, would you, my lady? Well, one more month won't make much difference, and she'll enjoy the change. And with the spring coming on apace, we could do with another strong arm in the dairy."

"She'll be only too happy to lend a hand, I expect," Silence told her. "She always liked to help our dairymaid Bessie, and learned a lot from her—of dairying, mind you."

"Just so long as it *was* only dairying," the older woman said, understanding her perfectly: Bessie's morals were as notorious as her skills were famous. "I'll be glad to have her, my lady, for as long as you want—and don't bother to send word, I'll expect her when I see her come up to our barton." Her eye slipped past Silence's shoulder again, and she whistled softly, in a most unladylike way. "Well, well, well. Look at what the cat's brought up."

Silence turned. They were standing at the west end of the churchyard, close to the tower. Beyond the low boundary wall lay the lane that led past the Vicarage toward the great South Field, once open strips but long since divided up into scores of tiny closes of pasture or arable. Along the wall were tethered all the horses that had brought those of the better sort, Baylies and St. Barbes, Apprices and Flowers, to the church, under the watchful eyes of a couple of boys paid a penny each for the task. And behind them, suddenly arrived, she saw half a dozen or so troopers, with Nick Hellier on his tall chestnut at their head. He saluted Silence with a smile, doffing his hat, while his horse sidled restlessly, champing its bit. The noise, and the turning heads, alerted the rest of the crowd. Gradually the talking died away, the scampering children stood and stared with a mixture of admiration and fear, and the separate knots of gossipers coalesced into one large, hostile mass, gentry and cloth-workers, laborers and husbandmen, old and young, all merged and joined together to face the threat.

The threat of six men, Silence thought, disturbed, against a couple of hundred people? For the first time she understood the import of Nick's words about the sullen peasants he had encountered on the expedition to find General Cromwell. The faces around her, weather-hardened, seasoned by suffering and toil and poverty, were all alike steeped in menace. She felt their hatred rise, almost a tangible thing, and despite the cool breeze in the April sunshine, a sweat broke out on her body.

"Good morning, people," Nick said affably, his voice, deep and clear, pitched to carry to the back of the crowd.

A heave and sway around Silence presaged the arrival of Parson Willis, perspiring and earnest, at her side. He shouted, his own insignificant tones sharpened by recent practice in the pulpit, "Why were you and your ungodly rabble not at prayer, sir? Are you above God's law, as you are above man's?"

"There isn't room for us all," Nick pointed out, reasonably enough, Silence felt. "But that is an issue which does not concern me now, Master Parson. I have come here for the purpose of clearing up certain misunderstandings which seem to have arisen among your flock."

The flock, a notably independent and opinionated set of sheep, stared at him resentfully. Someone, safely at the back, called out, "Bain't ee come to rob we, then?"

There was a mutter of laughter. Nick, his hand still holding his hat, which rested on one knee, smiled with what appeared to be genuine amusement. "No," he said cheerfully. "For once I have not. Oh, I don't deny that your contributions to our garrison's supply will be needed as much as ever, but that's for your own protection, to keep you from the ravages of the Parliament's army."

Silence heard the irony rich in his voice, and wondered that the villagers did not. Above the surly murmurs, he went on. "But it has lately come to my notice that a rumor has been put about alleging that men, and women, will be conscripted to work on the garrison's defenses. I can tell you, here and now, that rumor lies. The defenses of Wintercombe are all but finished, and we have no need of your assistance—particularly no need of your *forced* assistance. None of you will be asked by me to contribute any labor whatsoever to the fortifications. Is that clear?"

If he had expected a cheer, even a mutter of assent, he was doomed to disappointment. The village of Philip's Norton eyed him in a dubious and stony silence, and waited. Quite unperturbed, Nick surveyed them in leisurely fashion, in their muted colors of the countryside: the undyed grays and faded browns of the poor, more prosperous people in russets, blues, and mulberries, and everywhere the dull black of the bereaved or the godly. His own brilliant scarlet cloak, draping the quarters of his horse, seemed almost a blasphemy in the gentle spring sunshine.

In the front rank of the villagers he saw Silence, flanked by the rabbity little parson and a stout woman with the red hands and complexion of a farmer's wife. Her clear face, shadowed from the sun, stared up at him as impassively as the rest of these sullen peasants. But he had seen her mouth twitch and knew that, once again, she was closer to him than she was to the people among whom she stood.

He went on, ignoring that extremely unpromising lack of reaction. "As for the matter of contributions, as I said, they will still be necessary. But it is my wish that it will be done with all consideration. Where we can, we will pay. Where we cannot, we will take less from the poorest of you, more from those well able to afford it."

"Just like Robin Hood," said a scathing and anonymous voice from the body of the crowd, eliciting a collective snigger.

"Yes, just like Robin Hood," Nick agreed, refusing to rise to the bait. "As I said, it will be done gently. No abuse, no wanton destruction, no rape or murder. My wish, and my command. There has been too much harm done already here. I can't aspire to your goodwill—I realize that only too well. But perhaps we may coexist without too much ill feeling on either side. We will undertake to protect you from other plunderers, and enemy forces—in return, you and other villages will supply us with what we need. The country hereabouts is rich enough for all of us—there is no need for anyone to go hungry, and if there are some among you in real distress, we shall leave you alone."

He paused, seeing the grim, highly skeptical faces before him. At least they were not throwing things—although the presence of the pistol holsters at his saddle bow, and similar, sinister-looking cylinders by the knees of his men, might have something to do with that forbearance. He knew that this speech was as likely to succeed as Canute's to the tide, but at least he had made a brave, and probably quite ludicrous, attempt to heal the chasm lying between them, a far greater obstacle than the low churchyard wall and the line of dozing, somnolent horses that separated him from the resentful people of Norton, upon whom, like a leech, he parasitically fed.

"If any of my men, or Captain Bull's, cause any problem, any nuisance at all, then you can refer it to me, and I will punish the misdemeanor. I am as interested in justice as are you, and I will do my best to administer it fairly."

The sounds emanating from the crowd at these hopeful words were so redolent of disbelief and derision that Nick laughed aloud, causing several of the less sleepy horses to flick their ears in alarm. To the surprised villagers, he said recklessly, "You can believe me or not—but when the time comes, you may try me. My thanks for listening so patiently. Good-bye!"

Silence watched, trying not to reveal her laughter, as he wheeled the fiery chestnut about, the flamboyant cloak swirling with the abruptness of the movement, sunlit motes of dust around his head like a halo. The horse reared, all tossing mane and high, plumed tail and flailing hooves, and several villagers appeared disappointed that the ungodly, insolent captain failed to fall off. Then he clapped his hat on his head, and the chestnut, all four feet back on the ground, was given free rein. The soldiers, never reluctant to join a race, turned their own, less lively mounts and followed in cheerful pursuit, uttering whoops and hunting cries.

Amid the grumbles, condemnations, and fevered discussion, Silence stood, smiling wryly. Nat appeared, with young William Tovie, his own age and a head taller, to ask if he could spend the afternoon at Wintercombe. Knowing the other boy wanted to see the soldiers at close quarters, Silence agreed. If Will carried the tale back to the George, that the wicked Cavaliers were in fact moderately civilized human beings who might drink, smoke, swear, and dally with willing serving girls but who did not toss babies on pikes or engage in hair-raising orgies with droves of terrified village virgins, then it might be no bad thing.

She found her own placid Strawberry, who had pieces of grass sticking to her bit. Nat made his hands a stirrup for her, and for Tabby and Rachael, and she rode home with them, trying to think of domestic matters, the servants, dinner, the right remedies for little Ned Grindland and ancient Jack Waters: anything, in fact, to expel from her mind the bright sunlit image of an autumn-colored man in a scarlet cloak, laughing at his own foolishness, showing off his prowess in horsemanship before the people of Norton, who, as he well knew, were likely to be entirely unimpressed . . .

She visited Susannah Grindland that afternoon, taking all the things she had planned, to assuage her own guilt at having wealth, a husband, a fine house, and healthy children, and the tearful thanks she received only made her feel worse. Then she rode down South Street, Mally pillion behind her, avoiding the shrieking, laughing children who played exuberantly on the one day of the week when they would not be required to pick stones, scare birds, spin or weave or make butter and cheese. She nodded to elderly villagers sitting comfortably in their doorways to catch the first of the spring sunshine, and stopped outside Jack Waters's tenement, a small but sturdy stone-built cottage with thick, mossy thatch.

She called one of the children to hold the horse. It was Ned Merrifield, whose widowed mother lived opposite, and who had been given a free afternoon, as he was every Sunday, to visit her. Pleased to be trusted with the responsibility, he held Strawberry's bridle while the other children, already deeply envious of his position at Wintercombe, clustered around at a safe distance. Mally gave him a friendly grin, and at Silence's suggestion crossed the narrow, rutted street to see her stepmother, while her mistress ducked below the wooden lintle of Waters's door to minister comfort, as was the pious duty of any godly lady.

Jack Waters might be in his hundredth year, and creaky in his joints, but his blue eyes were as bright as a young man's in his ancient face, brown and serrated with lines like the bark of an oak tree, and his hearing was undimmed by time. He greeted her in friendly fashion, and his grand-daughter Alice fetched cool cider and bread and new, sweet, crumbly cheese, while Silence sat and listened to the old man talking about days that not even Sir Samuel had seen.

He had been to London, 'prenticed in his youth to a draper, and had seen Queen Bess crowned in her red hair, pale and slender and made beau-tiful by the love and acclaim of her people. He remembered the coming of the Armada, when beacons had leapt from hilltop to hilltop all across the West Country, a chain of fire that brought the dread news to London. But she liked best to hear him talk about the old days in Norton, so similar and yet so different. Like Clevinger, he preferred a world in which magic and mystery, mummers and revelry and the shockingly pagan maypole had all had a part: the young people going out on May morning to gather flowers and branches for garlands, the girls bathing their faces in dew to preserve their complexions and making the cowslip balls that, tossed in the hand, were supposed to foretell whom they would marry. He spoke of unseemly goings-on at church ales, when even the vicar got drunk, with the excuse that it was all in a good cause, to mend the roof or pay for a new Bible, and worse scenes at bride ales, with the bride, the supposed beneficiary, frequently the most riotous.

And once in Norton there had been rough music, the impromptu, frightening ceremony in which adulterous couples were serenaded, with much beating of pots and pans, and in this case a bonfire outside the house, topped by an effigy of the faithless wife and her cuckolded husband, crowned with horns.

The old man described it with relish. Silence, listening, found herself sympathetic toward that erring woman. Had her deluded husband been insensitive, overbearing, dull? Had he ignored her feelings and driven her heart away with his lack of consideration? And had her lover wooed her with laughter and delight, flattery and friendship, made her feel as if she mattered, as if she were a person of worth and value?

Frightened to the soul by the direction her thoughts were taking, Silence finished her bread and cheese, left her cerecloths with detailed instructions for their use, promised to visit again next week, and rode with Mally back to Wintercombe, where the only rough music was that made by the boisterous soldiers.

But at Wintercombe was Nick Hellier, a man she trusted because he had seemed to be her ally and whose friendship she needed and valued, because he was the only person among all those in and around the house who was both friend and equal, distanced from her neither by birth nor by age.

He came to her chamber that evening, to teach Tabby. It had been a week since his last visit, and Silence did not like to admit that she had missed his company. She tried to subdue the leap of her heart at the familiar double knock on the door and made herself say casually to Mally, "That must be Captain Hellier. Can you let him in?"

Mally, without enthusiasm, did so. She, it was plain, did not trust Hellier at all, though she had become accustomed to the puppy, as Silence had predicted. Pye, grown large and near her time, was also now more tolerant. She had confirmed her superior status and ignored all Lily's wagging, fawning attempts to be friendly.

Nick, entering, saw all the St. Barbes gathered in cozy domesticity, quiet in their black mourning. William and Deb were playing a solemn quiet game with Deb's two wooden dolls in a corner, and the soft, confident sounds of Tabby at her virginals filled the air. The twins, one each side of the walnut table, worked busily with paper and pen. Silence sat in her chair, sewing, and the white puppy sprawled at her feet, exhausted with play. Pye, rotund on the bed, stretched and yawned and chirruped a welcome, but did not move from her warm soft nest.

"Good evening," he said, and saw with pleasure how they all, save for Rachael, of course, put aside their various tasks and came to greet him. Lily bounced up at him, her paws on his knees, and he laughed and patted her. "She's growing apace, is she not? I think she'll be taller than her mother."

"She doesn't make messes in the corner now," Deb said with serious approval. "Mama smacked her and she knew she'd been naughty. William and I take her in the garden, don't we, William?"

William gave Nick his merry, sly grin. His nose was running again. His sister, forthright as ever, told him so and wiped it. Ignoring her, the little boy held up something for inspection. "Look, Captain, look!"

It was a chestnut, old, dull, and wrinkled. "For you," William said. "I kept it for you. 'S from the tree in the orchard."

Nick took it with grave appreciation. William's third birthday had fallen some two weeks previously, and he had found himself showered with gifts. Even some of the soldiers had given him little presents, a musket ball, an empty and broken powder-flask, and a beautifully carved musketeer in what Silence had suspected to be apple wood. Intoxicated with receiving, William had taken to giving in return, and although his own gifts were perhaps more valuable to him than to the recipient, such was his charm that they were always accepted in the proper spirit.

"You can roast it if you like," said the child, gazing up at Hellier with something that appeared to Silence, watching amused, to be alarmingly like adoration. What would George think when he returned from the wars, to find that his youngest son looked upon an enemy soldier almost as a father figure and could not remember his own?

"I might if I find myself in need," Hellier told him solemnly. "But for now I will keep it. Thank you very much, William. Hullo, Tabby—I see you have learned your pavane most excellently."

"Oh, did you hear it?" Tabby asked anxiously. No false modesty with this child. One such as Deb might have played on, deliberately showing off her skill, but Tabby had stopped her practice as soon as she became aware of his entry into the chamber. Still, he had heard enough to know that her early promise would one day be fulfilled. She played delicately, accurately, and with great feeling.

"I heard a little," he said. "Why not play some more? I expect you have been practicing hard, and I haven't had the chance to listen to you all week."

"What shall I play?" Tabby's eyes, hazel like her mother's, turned up to him, serious and a little apprehensive.

"Try everything you know you can play well, and then I'll go through a new piece with you." He watched as Tabby dived back into the hanging closet where the virginals were kept, and then crossed over to the twins, who were watching him from their table, Nat wearing an expression of lively amusement.

"Will you play chess with me later, Captain?" the boy asked.

"You're supposed to be translating your Virgil, Nat," Rachael said in a self-righteous voice that, to the perceptive Nick, hardly disguised her jealousy of the attention shown to her brother.

Nat grinned at her, apparently oblivious. "I've nearly finished it—I can surely spare the time for one game. Now hush—I'm sure the captain wants to listen to Tabby's playing."

Rachael, once more the odd one out, scowled terrifyingly and returned to her writing. Nat caught Nick's eye and winked. No longer surprised by the mature mind in the child's body, Hellier winked back and went over to the hearth as the first careful notes dropped into the quiet.

If he has done nothing else, Silence thought as Nick sat down on the chair beside her, he has given Tabby this—and it is a gift more precious than gold. She did not like to think what George would say when he found out—he did not disapprove of music for its own sake but preferred it to be sober, and in praise of the Lord. And to have it played by his young daughter would surely be repugnant to him. Was not music an instrument of seduction, frequently the skill of harlots and lewd women?

Queen Elizabeth played the virginals, Silence thought firmly, and I shall tell him so if he shows signs of being bigoted. She glanced at Hellier, surprising that strangely intense gaze, as the notes of the instrument swirled, fresh, fragile and beautiful as snowflakes, into the air.

Tabby played, slowly at first, the tunes she had learned, humming soundlessly as her small fingers stretched to find the right keys. "The Cuckoo," then a slow stately tune, surpassingly beautiful, called "Greensleeves," and a lovely thing of deceptive simplicity, running up and down the notes, that Captain Hellier had said was "Tallis's Canon." She had asked what a canon was, thinking of persons, and had been told that it was kind of round, but for instruments, not voices. So far she could only play it with one hand, but hoped to graduate to two.

Four more pieces, and she had all but exhausted the repertoire of tunes she could play perfectly. There was a surprise for him, though. She had been practicing in secret and was certain that he had no idea of her accomplishment. The music had been written on the back of one of the sheets he had given her. It had looked complicated, and she had been afraid to try it at first, but her fingers, tentatively touching the keys, seemed to take on a life of their own, their early hesitancy transformed to flight.

A forgotten smile of mischief on her elfin face, Tabby took a deep breath, put the music in front of her, and began.

As the first ripple of melody trickled from the closet, Silence saw Nick stiffen in his chair. It did not sound as if it were Tabby playing. The accurate delicacy had been replaced by quite a different mood, careless, reckless, and joyous. There were notes missed or wrong, even Silence could tell that, but it did not matter. The rhythm was there, infectious, dancing with the tune. Wondering, she stared at Hellier, saw his fingers tapping, and saw her own doing the same.

"I can't keep myself still," she said, smiling, and Nick gave her that slow smile in return. She found herself unable, suddenly, to meet his gaze. Blushing, she looked away, disturbed and confused.

The music reached a climax of delight and stopped abruptly in a cascade of notes. There was a pause, and then Tabby, flushed and intense, popped her head out from the closet. "Did you like it?" she demanded of her family and her tutor. "Was it all right?"

"It was beautiful," Silence told her, and meant it. Tabby, so sensitive, knew that she spoke the truth, and smiled vastly, her whole face lit with the delight within. "It's called 'Packington's Pound.' Captain Hellier, what's a pound?"

"A kind of dance, I should think," Nick answered. "Tabby, I didn't know you could play that—and to do it so well! You must have been practicing in secret."

"I didn't play it *very* well," Tabby said, ever the perfectionist. "I made lots of mistakes."

"But they didn't stand out—what matters is the *way* you play it," the captain said. "And that was entirely delightful."

"It certainly was, Tabby-cat," Nat said. "Well done."

Tabby, pink with pleasure and embarrassment, looked down at the floor. Nick said, "Can you play it again?"

Silence's daughter looked up, her hazel eyes flashing suddenly with joy. "Yes—oh, *yes*! And I'll try not to make so many mistakes this time." She turned, her skirts flying, and disappeared back into the closet. They heard her settled on the stool, the first notes, a false start; then, suddenly, the bright flood of sound.

"Would you care to dance, my dear lady?"

Silence, startled, looked up and saw Nick in front of her, hand outstretched. She laughed, shaking her head. "Oh, no, no—dance? I've never danced in my life."

"Then now is the time to start," Nick said. He seized her hand and pulled her upright, ignoring her protesting laughter. "No, please, no—I *can't*!"

"You're human, aren't you? Then you can dance—you can't fool me, I saw your fingers tapping. You see, you do it like this: one-two-three, one-two-three, one . . . !"

Silence found herself whirled around the broad empty space in the center of her chamber, tripping over mats and trying to avoid Lily, who was leaping around her skirts and yelping her excitement. She saw Nat's grin, and the wondering amazement of the younger children, and Rachael's white face perfectly still. But above all there was the touch of Nick's hands, warm, brown, surprisingly strong, turning her in steps that made her dizzy and breathless, resting on her arm, her shoulder, and, as the music reached a tumbling climax in which, for once, the rhythm faltered, on her waist to swing her in the air and set her back on her feet, dazed and laughing so hard that she could not speak.

"What's happening?" Tabby emerged from her closet, looking, bewildered at the faces of her family, all save Rachael's contorted with merriment.

Deb, squeaking with delight, told her, "Mama *danced,* she did, Mama *danced*!"

"She danced with the captain," William added. "And he picked her up and threw her in the *air*!"

"Well, not quite," Silence said, trying to recover her composure and her dignity, as befitted a sober and godly housewife. Her sides hurt, tears of laughter stood in her eyes, her face felt stretched with it. Then she became suddenly aware that Nick was still holding her waist, his hands resting lightly on the stiff boned bodice that concealed the warm live flesh beneath, and in haste turned her body neatly out of his grasp. Her face flushed, she added, "Thank you, Captain. I don't think I have ever spent such an energetic evening."

"Do it again, Mama," Deb cried, running up with urgently clutching hands. "Oh, do please do it again, it was so *funny*—oh, Captain, please make her do it again!"

Above the bobbing tawny-gold head of the child, Silence's eyes met Nick's, and locked and held. Oh, dear Lord, she thought in sudden terror, what is happening to me? Why has this man become more to me than any other—more even than my husband, my son, my stepson, my brother? Trying to disguise her panic, she bent down to Deb and said brightly, falsely, "I'm not going to dance any more, Deb, but why don't you ask the captain to dance with you? If Tabby will play again for you, of course."

"Poor Tabby can't see what's happening if she plays," Nat pointed out. "Tell you what, Tabby-cat—if you jump out when you're halfway through the piece, you might just catch them still dancing."

Tabby eyed her half-brother dubiously. "No, I won't. When I stop, they're bound to stop too. Why can't we move the virginals in here, Mama?"

"Nat and I can manage them," Nick said immediately, his face sparkling with the same wild reckless laughter as it had that morning, outside the church. "Come on, Nat, flex your muscles—if we lay the case on the table, very carefully, just there, Tabby can stand up to play. And with any luck we'll avoid setting it out of tune."

Silence hovered anxiously, afraid that Nat, from pride, would take on a task too heavy for him. But he managed the task with efficiency, his normally pale face flushed with triumphant effort. The wooden case, plainly decorated with classical motifs, was lifted off its stand, carried into the main chamber, and put carefully down upon one of the two walnut tables under the east windows. Tabby, hopping from one foot to the other, followed, as concerned as Silence but more, her mother suspected, for the safety of the virginals than for her half-brother's health. As soon as the instrument was laid down, she ran her fingers along the keys. Silence, unversed in music, could hear one or two false notes, but such was Tabby's excitement that she ignored them, pulling up a chair and kneeling on it, the better to play.

Silence retreated to the hearth, considering discretion here to be most valuable. "Are you ready?" asked Tabby, the dancing master.

Nick had Deb's hand in his. He glanced at Nat. "Why don't you dance with Rachael?"

"No, thank you," said Rachael. She added, in her best imitation of Dame Ursula, "Dancing is unseemly and ungodly, especially on the Lord's day." Her eyes, blue and bitter, glared at Silence. "It's sinful to profane the Sabbath with immodest dancing, isn't it, Mother?"

"Well, I hardly think that Captain Hellier dancing with Deb constitutes immodesty," Silence said reasonably.

Rachael, unappeased, continued to stare at her belligerently. "Perhaps not—but *you* dancing with him certainly did."

"Oh, don't be ridiculous," said Nat, coming to his stepmother's rescue. "Rachael, you'll turn into a pious and priggish bore if you think like that. Look at Grandmother—never happier than when preventing other people from enjoying themselves. Do you want to be like her?"

"I don't care—I think it's wrong," Rachael persisted. Ostentatiously, she turned her back and gazed out of the window at the dim, dusky garden, the bowling green, and the yew walk lost in approaching darkness.

Tabby, ignoring her half-sister's bad temper, struck up the tune of "Packington's Pound," faltering slightly as she tried to play and watch at the same time. Deb, giggling with delight, was paraded, turned, and finally, to her utter delight, tossed in the air by Nick as the music ended.

"I *can't* play any more," poor Tabby said, flexing her hands. "My fingers have gone all numb and tingly, and they won't do what I say."

"You did very well," Nick told her. "Now I think I shall play—in a soft and sober fashion, as befits the Lord's day." And his glance at Silence, as he sat down at the virginals, was wickedly ironic.

She let herself drift to the gentle sounds, wondering how he came to play so well—and without written music to help him. The fiddle was not a gentleman's instrument, but the virginals assuredly were. He spoke well, he had a wide knowledge of the cultural arts—poetry, music, wit, conversation, dance, even stage plays—he had traveled abroad, he could conduct himself with ease in royal company. Yet these undeniably civilized accomplishments sat oddly on the man who had played popular carols on his fiddle, who thought nothing of stripping to his shirtsleeves and digging alongside his men, and who showed a somewhat ungentlemanly knowledge of a physician's skill. And Sir Thomas Bridges, in that terrible interview, had taunted him with his humble origins.

He was a mystery to her, at once open, friendly, companionable, and a closed and secret book. The man who played with her children and had known her well enough to give her Lily had killed in cold blood. She could not reconcile them, and could not try. She sat and dreamed as his music washed over her, and Pye, seizing her advantage, leapt ponderously onto her lap. Stroking her, Silence found herself watching his fingers, assured and skillful, drawing the sweet sounds from the instrument while Tabby leaned on the table beside him, rapt, her chin in her hands and all her heart and soul in her eyes, entranced by his playing.

Silence saw that Mally, sitting in her accustomed chair doing her usual sewing, was looking at her covertly, and glanced away, blushing. Is my heart in my face too? she wondered in confusion and alarm. Do I gaze at him like some lovesick virgin sighing over her country swain? He is a friend, a dear friend, and no more—he must *not* be any more to me than that, or I am lost.

The pit yawned before her, peopled by grinning demons, gesturing invitingly. The temptations of lust, fornication, adultery, the most terrible sins, disguised by the longings of a lonely, isolated woman for companionship . . .

I am *not* lonely, she told herself sternly. I am surrounded by my family, my servants, I have so much to do that the day is not long enough . . . I have my garden, my cat and my dog, and above all my children, and although I know that I should not feel thus, I do not miss my husband in the least—in fact, I am happier for his absence. All I see in Nick Hellier is a friend, someone who could make me laugh, in whom I can confide a little . . . like Sir Samuel, except that he is half my father-in-law's age and more, and happens to be a Cavalier officer. . . . I will have him as a friend, and no more, whatever ideas he may have, and whatever Mally may think.

But her eyes were drawn back, irresistibly, to the swift sensitive movement of his hands on the keyboard as he played a fantastical variation on

"Greensleeves," which had always been Sir Samuel's favorite. She stared at the straight clear lines of his face in profile as he gazed at nothing, at invisible music perhaps, and the fall of his brown hair on his shoulder and back, a man so absorbed in what he did that he could notice nothing else at all.

And she thought of her husband, pompous, unsympathetic, insensitive, grown a dim and distant and resented memory beside this man's vivid presence, and acknowledged the danger she was in.

It can't do any harm, she thought fiercely. All I want is friendship, no more, no less—and so far, friendship is all that is offered.

And at that moment he glanced around, his chestnut eyes seeking hers, and his long, lazy, amused smile gave her the lie.

Beware
Of entrance to a quarrel.
—*HAMLET*

"Mother, *please* may we go to the fair?"
Silence stood in the garden room, packets of seeds and her little trowel in her hand, wearing her oldest apron, and looked doubtfully at her stepdaughter's pleading face.

Rachael added, as if to clinch the matter, "Nell Flower is going, and Tom, and all the Baylie girls and the Tovies too—*please* can we go? We went last year."

Yes, Silence thought wryly, and you had your coin stolen and saw a wrestling match and bought some exorbitantly expensive lace that fell apart when you wore it and Tom Flower gave William Tovie a black eye and Fulke Tovie was discovered in most unfortunate circumstances with Nell Flower in the Church Meadow and poor Jeffery Flower, her father, had an apoplexy from which he never recovered. Aloud, she said, "You may—but you must promise to keep close to me."

Rachael's face fell, and her lower lip came out in an expression familiar from her childhood. "Very well," she said. "I promise. Oh, I can't wait until tomorrow—can I ride over to Manor Farm with Nat this afternoon and tell Tom and Nell?"

"If, and only if, you have finished your studies," Silence told her, and watched as her stepdaughter thanked her effusively and hurried off to her chamber to copy out the passage from the Book of Daniel that Dame Ursula had insisted she recite the next morning. Then she turned and walked out onto the sunny terrace.

In two days' time it would be May, and her garden was bursting with life and color. The daffodils were nearly all over, except for the sweet-scented pheasant's eye narcissus that filled two of the knots. Their place had been taken by the fragrant wall gillyflowers, tawny and yellow and the deep rich crimson ones known as bleeding hearts, graceful fritillaries with their drooping purple heads, and her pride and joy, the early tulips, yellow and scarlet, the bulbs sent from London at Sir Samuel's instigation and expense during a lull in the fighting. The air was warm and thick with the aroma of the flowers and the humming and buzzing of the bees. The cherry trees, which only ten days ago had been naked and bare as winter, were erupting now into flower, their branches bearing a heavy fragrant mass of blossom that made the arbor look from the house as if it had suffered a magnificently unseasonable fall of snow.

By the sundial the garden boy, Jemmy Coxe, was pulling groundsel from the gravel. He scrambled to his feet and bowed as Silence approached, his mop of dark hair obscuring his face. She smiled, and greeted him. "Hullo, Jemmy. How are you this morning? Is Diggory about?"

"Tarblish well, thank ee, m'lady, and Diggory be up at the vine, he d'think it'll flower!" said the child, who was twelve and not usually noted for an excess of words and excitement.

Catching her mood from his, Silence felt a leap of her heart. "*Really?* The vine, flowering? Oh, I must see—thank you, Jemmy!"

She left the boy to his weeding, put her trowel and seeds down by the steps to the next terrace, and ran toward Diggory. He was standing on a box by the south door, near the vine, and peering up into its tangled branches. There were few leaves as yet. They were just unfurling, like fragile green hands stretching out to feel the day's warmth. The old man, as gnarled as the twisted, sturdy trunk of the vine, heard her footsteps as she hurried up the last flight of steps to the flagstoned terrace nearest to the house. He climbed down from his perch and smiled at her, revealing only one or two brownly discolored teeth. "Good morning to ee, Lady St. Barbe. Did young Jemmy tell ee 'bout this here vine?"

"Yes—is it really true?" She stared up into the twisted branches, breathless, and Diggory took her arm and pointed.

"Aye, m'lady, 'tis true enough—looksee at all they flowers there."

She peered, hardly remembering what a flower had looked like. The vine in the past had borne perhaps half a dozen in a year. But there did seem to be many, tight and tiny green bundles nestling among the new leaves. "Oh, Diggory—it's true! How on earth do you suppose we've managed it? What have we done to it?"

Diggory ruminated. His eyes, a faded gray-blue, were almost lost in the wrinkles around them, and the rest of the skin on his face was as lined and dried by long exposure to sun and wind and rain as an ancient piece of leather. He did not know exactly how old he was, but could remember, as a small child, the beacons lit to warn England of the Armada, and the bonfires and bell-ringing when it was defeated. This, by Silence's reckoning, put him at just past sixty. Soon, she supposed, he would have to be given a little cottage with, of course, a patch of garden in which he could grow the plants to feed himself in his declining years. He had no wife, no children, no family, his birthplace was some village near the Devon coast, and she had never discovered how he came to be at Wintercombe. But for the moment he was still hale enough to continue as the gardener, to train

up young Jemmy, and to impart to the boy, and to her, all the accumulated knowledge of a lifetime's love and care for the living, growing plants
around him. In the cupboard in the garden room, Silence kept a little
leather-bound book, the twin of that in which she entered her recipes and
remedies, and jotted down in it all the pearls of Diggory's wisdom and
some of his weather sayings, which would fill a volume in themselves.

"I dunno what us have done right," the gardener said, looking at her
quizzically. "Never in all my days have I seen such flowers on she—let's
hope they all turns to grapes."

"If the birds don't feast on them first," said Silence. It was deliciously
warm there. The worn flagstones beneath her feet had sweet herbs, chamomile, thyme, marjoram, planted in the cracks, and the scent from their
bruised leaves filled the air. She felt the desire to sit down on the steps and
dream the morning away, lulled and soothed by the promise of summer:
but there were seeds to sow, flowers to pick for the house, children to
watch and teach, servants to oversee . . . the list was endless. Only in the
evenings, when at last Wintercombe lay quiet, could she afford to waste
time just sitting.

Above them, a window opened with a creak of wood, and a well-remem-
bered voice said, "Ah, there you are, my Lady St. Barbe. I want a word
with you—now."

She turned and looked up, her bright happy mood suddenly dwindled to
ashes. Ridgeley's blue-jowled face leaned from his antechamber, thinner
than it had once been and still unhealthily pale. She said, her voice cool
and calm despite her knocking knees, "Why, Colonel, you should not have
left your bed yet. It is only three days since Captain Hellier last bled you."

"And he can go hang—and all of your putrid namby-pamby broths and
juleps!" Ridgeley shouted, his temper evidently on a very short fuse indeed. "Up here, madam, or it'll be the worse for you!"

Once she would have shaken and quailed and rushed to obey. Now,
however, she valued herself higher. "No, I will not," she told him in the
voice she used to Deb when the little girl was rude or obstreperous. "I'm
not at your beck and call, sir—I'll see you when it's convenient for me.
Good morning."

"Bravely said, m'lady," Diggory whispered gleefully, clapping her approvingly on the arm. "Do ee tell him, he bain't your lord and master."

She grinned at the old man. Ridgeley, still at the window, seemed to be
thunderstruck. His mouth working, he stared impotently down at the lady
of Wintercombe. Then, furious, he banged the casement shut. There was a
small, apologetic tinkle of glass—one of the panes must have become dis-
lodged, and descended through the vine to smash on the stones of the top
terrace. Silence and Diggory looked at each other ruefully.

"Don't ee fret, m'lady, I'll clear en for ee," Diggory said, and ambled off
into the house, calling Eliza, doubtless for one of her brooms. Silence

hailed Lily, who was dangerously close to the broken pane, and hurried back to the lowest terrace before Ridgeley could shout at her again.

He was well enough to emerge from his sickroom. Indeed, he had been for a week or more. She had dreaded it, the end of their quiet, comparatively well-ordered life, the return to the drunkenness, indiscipline, and brutality of the winter months. Trembling with anger and fear, she knelt by the first of the knots, well screened from the house by the arbor, and tried not to give way to her tears. Rachael must be sent to Wick Farm. She would go this afternoon, Nat could escort her, and Christian Baylie would understand the lack of notice.

She was only just beginning, belatedly, to comprehend the danger in which her stepdaughter stood. Ridgeley was not a man who would let convention, chivalry, the civilized virtues stand in the way of his revenge, and she realized that she had been foolish to think otherwise. He had pistoled recalcitrant villagers when temporary Governor of Bath. The very least that Rachael could expect was a beating, and the damage that it would do to the girl's mind, let alone her body, made Silence's blood run cold. At least if she went to Wick, she would be out of harm's way. Ridgeley had not, in her hearing at least, made any reference to the circumstances of his shooting, but she had no doubt that if, presented with the opportunity for revenge, he would take it ruthlessly.

She had Nick and Mally to thank for the fact that Ridgeley had taken so long to recover. The wounds had healed some time since and left two angry, knotted scars on front and back. But Mally had put powdered senna in his restorative drinks, with predictable result, and Hellier, speaking authoritatively about his colonel's choleric disposition and the need for rest, had further weakened Ridgeley with regular blood-lettings. Small wonder, thought Silence, that the wretched man looks a shadow of his former self. But the evil day cannot now be delayed. I will send Rachael away, and tell her that she cannot go to the fair—it will be too dangerous.

The great fair at Norton, held around Mayday, the feast of St. Philip and St. James, was usually a splendid occasion, packed with buyers and sellers: milch cows and oxen tethered all down the wall bordering Fair Close, stalls set up there and around the Market Cross in the center of the village, and the great loft that ran the length of the George given over to the bales of fine Somerset cloth that had taken the local weavers all winter to produce, from last year's fleeces. But the disruption of the war had curtailed much of the activity. Too many people feared to come, risking attack or robbery by marauding soldiers or thieves taking advantage of these lawless times. More simply had not enough to sell, their sheep or cattle slaughtered, their cloth stolen or commandeered to clothe the regiments of king or Parliament.

Last year Sir Samuel had complained that the fair was a pitiful travesty of what it had been in earlier times. Only a part of the long loft in the George filled with cloth, whereas before it had been piled all along the length of it from floor to ceiling, a paltry score of booths selling fairings, pots, pans, trinkets and similar items, few chapmen, pedlars, merchants, and farmers, and only people from the immediately surrounding villages come to buy. This year, with the soldiers lodged at Wintercombe like carrion cows hunched over a carcass almost picked bare, it was likely to be even worse. Silence thought of the rents unpaid from her husband's tenants in other villages less fortunate than Philip's Norton: tenants who had seen even their seed corn taken, their houses or cottages ransacked again and again, their cow or pig or hens stolen, deprived all means of subsistence save what they could beg, borrow, or scrape from garden or pasture. Farther south, it was especially bad. Goring had spent some time at Bruton, less than twenty miles away, where the St. Barbe family owned a considerable amount of land. Even though the villages near to Bath had so far escaped the worst effects of the war, it seemed that there would not be much of a fair for anyone to visit.

Silence had never enjoyed it, and the dubious experiences that had befallen her stepchildren last year had not changed her mind. She disliked the crowds, the noise, the people bawling their wares, even thrusting them under her nose, the beggars, cutpurses, the spavined, sharp-boned horses with their sad, fly-blown eyes, the patient oxen and frantic sheep and lambs . . . It was altogether too much like a rural version of London, and it was only now, as an adult, that she could admit to herself how much she had loathed the chaos, the frightening sounds and packed hostile mobs of her native city.

Ridgeley had spoiled the day. Planting her carefully hoarded seeds, poppies and nasturtiums and marigolds, stocks and columbine, held no pleasure for her now. She could not stop thinking about Rachael and about the colonel. After five feverish, urgent minutes during which she put the fine seeds of the tall poppy in front of the shorter nasturtiums, and had no prospect of rectifying the error, she gave up. Still using the cherry arbor as cover, she walked along the terrace to the end, up the steps to the summerhouse, and back along to the garden-room door. It was a ridiculously circuitous route, but she did not want to attract Ridgeley's notice. With any luck, however, his outburst had left him weak, sweating, and cursing in a chair, calling for good red wine. There was none: It had all been drunk, by himself and his officers (Byam must have accounted for at least a barrel on his own), and there were no more supplies from Bristol. Presumably the garrison there had cornered the market. If he wants it, Silence thought vengefully, he can ride over and get it himself, or make do with beer and cider.

Rachael would almost certainly be in her chamber. Silence went there at once, knocked briefly and went in.

Her stepdaughter was sitting at the table, scribbling furiously, the bulk of her Bible before her. She looked up ungraciously as Silence entered, and with no show of courtesy said, "Yes?"

For once her rudeness was ignored. Silence said quietly, for Ridgeley's rooms were not so far away, "I think our plans for the next few days must change. I don't think it will be very long before Ridgeley emerges from his lair. We can't keep him purged and bled into weakness forever, after all."

"I don't see why not," Rachael said, with an attempt at bravado, singularly transparent. With compassion, Silence saw that her face had turned greenish white, and her eyes were huge with terror. She added, in a desperate whisper, "Do you—do you think he'll try—try to *punish* me?"

"I don't know," Silence replied, making herself calm and rational to soothe another's fear or distress. "What I *do* know is that he's much more likely to try to do something to you if he sees you here, walking freely about. So, what do you say to a visit to Wick Farm for a little while?"

It was like telling a condemned man of a last-minute reprieve. Rachael gave a great gasp and jerked as if she herself had been shot. She said in a whisper, hardly daring to hope, "Can I? *Can* I? Go to Wick? Stay with Kitty and Moll and Bess? Oh, Mother, *thank* you!"

"It's not I you should thank," Silence said gently, disentangling herself at last from the girl's fervent embrace. "It's Mistress Baylie. I suggested the idea to her some weeks ago, and she agreed readily, good soul that she is. What's more, there's no warning needed: You'll be made welcome as soon as they see you riding into their barton. When do you want to go? Now?"

Rachael's eyes, filled with relief yet still haunted, sought hers, and she nodded slowly, as if afraid to speak. Silence smiled at her. "You can take one small bag—we don't want to arouse too much comment. And you can ride pillion behind Nat, just as if you were going to see the Flower children."

"But I won't be," said Rachael, her volatile mood already changing to one of excitement. "I'll be escaping—and he'll *never* find me at Wick!"

"I doubt he will. The place is so close to Farleigh that it supplies that garrison, not this, for all it's in Norton Parish, so of course Ridgeley never goes near it. He probably doesn't even know it exists. But, Rachael . . . remember one thing. Stay at Wick, don't come back into the village. Most of the time it will probably be quite safe, but if Ridgeley should see you . . ."

Her stepdaughter, eyes sparkling with sudden mischief, nodded agreement. "Don't worry, Mother, I won't. Can I take my sea-green gown, as it's nearly summer? I tried it on last week and it still fits, and I can let the hem down while I'm at Wick, it'll give me something to do."

In fifteen minutes she had a small linen bag stuffed with spare chemises, collars, cuffs, caps, aprons, and the sea-green gown. Nat, apprised of the situation, was all in readiness, and his gray Cobweb, burdened with saddle and pillion pad, waited below. Anything that Rachael lacked, Mistress

Baylie's three granddaughters, who with their parents also lived at Wick, could surely supply. There was no sign of Ridgeley: Silence hugged her stepdaughter in the porch, feeling once more the tentative, gentle closing of the gulf between them, and bade her be good, and behave as befitted a St. Barbe.

"Of course I shall," Rachael said indignantly. "I shan't disgrace you, Mother, don't worry. I shall do everything Mistress Baylie—*both* Mistress Baylies—tell me to."

Since the younger of the two women at Wick Farm, a Flower by birth, had been a quiet and gentle invalid for years—one reason for her husband making his home with his widowed mother—this was probably not necessary. Silence smiled at her stepdaughter. "I'll warn you—Christian Baylie wants a strong arm in the dairy. The season's just beginning, after all."

"Oh, good," Rachael exclaimed, looking pleased. "I can try and do all the things Bessie taught me last year. Perhaps I can make my own cheese!"

"If that's all Bessie's taught her," said a quiet voice beside her, as she watched Rachael arrange her russet skirts over Cobweb's round dappled rump, patchy where the heavy winter coat was falling off, "then perhaps Bessie has more discretion than I thought."

"She has," said Silence, not troubling to look around. Only one man at Wintercombe had that dry quality to his voice. "She herself is infinitely corruptible, but only where men are concerned. What she would never do is corrupt others. Leah, now, would think nothing of it. But Bessie works well in the dairy and likes to pass on her skills, especially to someone like Rachael, who's eager to learn."

Nat grinned and waved. Rachael, clutching her bulging bundle, did so as an afterthought. Silence watched as the cob ambled out of the courtyard in the sunshine and down the little hill toward the mill, and Norton, and Wick Farm, and safety. Half an hour's leisurely ride, or less: but such a little distance was surely all that was necessary.

Only when the twins' dark-hatted heads were out of sight could she allow herself to relax. Rachael was safe. Ridgeley was still sulking in his chamber, and even if it occurred to him in the next hour to avenge himself on the child who had so nearly killed him, he would not find her, not now. And in all Wintercombe, only Nat and she herself would know where Rachael was.

"Are you sending her away?" Nick asked, still in the shadows behind her. She doubted if the twins had seen him, hidden in the dark deep porch.

She nodded reluctantly. "Yes. Ridgeley cannot be held at bay any longer. He was abusing me from his window not an hour since, as I stood on the terrace—he'll be up and about tomorrow, and your tenure will be at an end. And then what shall we do?"

"Manage, as we did before," Nick said. He smiled at her. "And I shall have as much a care for you, and yours, as I always did. Some things I may not be able to prevent, but I will do my utmost, I promise. And now, my dear Lady St. Barbe, will you do something for me in return?"

She stared at him, not knowing whether to smile or not. Was he going to have the effrontery to do something like . . . kiss her? The very fact that she had thought of it meant that she recognized the possibility: even, dear Lord, welcomed it.

A blush, vivid and betraying, swept right over her face and neck and chest. She hoped fervently that in this obscure light, he would not notice. "What do you require?" she said, her voice determinedly casual.

"A small one only," he told her. "The fair begins tomorrow, does it not? The fame of Norton Fair resounds throughout the West Country, and I have a fancy to see it. Will you do me the honor of accompanying me?"

Silence stared at him, visited by an urgent desire to laugh. Her voice came out as something of a squawk. "Me? Go to the fair with you? I went last year with the children, and it was a sorry affair—oh, don't laugh, there was no pun intended—and I'd hoped to escape it this time. The fair is best for children, the village people, merchants and farmers and pedlars and chapmen, servants and . . ." She stopped. She had almost added "sweethearts," but that might be unfortunate. She went on, hastily, "And I can't come—I intend to tell the household that they can have the day off to go, if they wish. I'd envisaged being left here in lonely splendor with Eliza, Dame Ursula, and Ruth."

"None of whom, of course, agree with such things—what a golden opportunity for drunkenness, debauchery, fornication, levity, and all manner of vice—or even, simply, for enjoying oneself," Nick murmured. "From my experience of such things, however, all that tends to happen at night. During the day, they're harmless enough as a rule. And I know that the children are very eager to go, Tabby told me. She said herself she did not much care for it—she doesn't like the noise and the crowds and the animals tied up. Why are you smiling like that?"

"Because her thoughts are the mirror of mine—yet we've never disclosed them to each other. Pray go on."

"She said that Deb and William, however, had been filled full of wonderful stories by Rachael and had set their hearts on it."

"They may well have. That doesn't mean they'll go," said Silence, who did not want to be thought too indulgent a mother, particularly in her husband's absence. "In truth, Nick, this fair of ours may be famed for many miles around, but that was before this wretched war began. Now it's a poor shadow of its former glory—all the gilt rubbed off the gingerbread with a vengeance."

"You're trying your best to convince me," he said. "And failing lamentably. Besides, the children are so eager to see it—would you disappoint them?"

He had hit her, as they both well knew, on her most vulnerable point.

Silence, ruefully, caught his eye and smiled. "No—you know I would not. Are you always so devious a plotter?"

"Not invariably, no. Just usually. Well, my lady Silence, I must bid you good-bye for the moment—duty calls, as ever. So, unless we meet beforehand, until tomorrow—after dinner? I shall be waiting!"

"But Rachael, we're all going, all of us, Grandmother and Moll and Bess and me—even Father's going!" Kitty Baylie sat on the end of the big oaken bed that all four girls were to share and gazed in dismay at her friend and guest. "And only last week you were so excited about the fair, you couldn't wait to go, you told me yourself. And now you sit all scrunched up and say you've changed your mind—I don't understand!"

Rachael stared unhappily back at the eldest Baylie girl, who was short and well built, like her grandmother, and possessed of a good strong arm for the dairy—a prime qualification for any wife or daughter in this country of butter and cheese. Kitty's face was plump and pleasant, with a tilted nose, red cheeks, and straight brown hair falling under her cap. She always said what she thought, and was plainly puzzled by the more sensitive, secretive Rachael. But as the oldest of the three sisters, and the one with most sense and wisdom, she had been tacitly allotted the task of restoring their friend to her usual high spirits.

Something was wrong, though—even Kitty could see that, in the younger girl's haunted, torn, miserable face. She said more gently, "Why can't you go? Did Lady St. Barbe say that you must not?"

"Not exactly," Rachael said sullenly.

"But *why*? We all went last year—I know there was a little trouble, but that was nothing. *Why* can't you go?"

"Because if I show myself in Norton, he'll kill me!" Rachael cried suddenly, and burst into angry, frightened tears.

Kitty stared at her, comprehension dawning on her face. Something of Rachael's exploit—albeit very garbled—had of course been spread around the village for some weeks now, but her grandmother had sternly squashed all idle gossip on the subject, and Kitty and her sisters knew little more than the bare outline, the details filled in with imagination and wild speculation. She said slowly, "Who will kill you? The man you shot? The colonel?"

"Of course he will!" Rachael shouted, her thin body shaken by sobs. "Wouldn't you, if I'd tried to murder you? *That's* why I can't go into the village. Mother told me not to."

"Not even to the fair?"

"She didn't *exactly* say I couldn't go to the fair."

Kitty hesitated. She had, in fact, more respect for maternal injunction than Rachael, but she had been looking forward to the four of them going—four girls, all in their Sunday best, on two horses, the oldest and slowest in the stable so as not to attract the attention of any soldiers. She liked Rachael, despite her moods, for the girl of necessity, being a baronet's daughter, had access to a different and fascinating world. Had she not dined with the Prince of Wales himself? Kitty had been looking forward to asking her all about it, about Wintercombe and what life was really like under the eye of all those ungodly and wicked Cavaliers. And somehow, to leave her miserably behind, probably reading to the girls' fragile and bedridden mother, while the rest of the household from her grandmother to the stable boy went jaunting off to the fair, made future cozy confidences less likely. Even on two years' rather haphazard acquaintance, Kitty knew how intensively Rachael could sulk.

So she said, pleadingly, soothingly, "He won't be at the fair, surely. Isn't he supposed to be still in his bed?"

"He is," Rachael said. "Mother thought he was going to rise, but she might have been mistaken. And she didn't say I couldn't go to the fair—in fact, this morning she said I could, though that was before she thought Ridgeley was going to recover."

She was looking more hopeful, and Kitty hastily pressed home her advantage. "Well, there you are—he probably won't be up for a day or so yet! And even if he is, he certainly won't be fit enough to ride to the fair tomorrow if he's only just got out of his bed."

"I hadn't thought of that," Rachael said, considering, the tears drying on her lean, pale face. She giggled suddenly. "Leah Walker told me that Mally Merrifield has been putting purges in his broth to keep him feeble!"

Kitty laughed heartily at that, so much that tears ran down her own, plumper face. She said breathlessly, "Oh, that's a good one, that is—purges in his broth! Well, I expect Mally will give him another good dose, and it won't be a horse he'll be sitting on all tomorrow afternoon!"

Rachael howled with delight, all her blue devils vanished. She sat upright on the bed, her eyes suddenly bright with a mischief that Silence would have recognized with foreboding, and said cheerfully, "Yes, I'll come. And the best of it is, Mother won't be there either. She doesn't like the fair, not after last year, and I think she's planning to stay at Wintercombe and sit in the garden in peace."

"Good," Kitty said, who had been uneasy about the prospects of Rachael being caught in the act of disobedience by her stepmother. "So she need never know about it."

"Never!" Rachael exclaimed with gleeful and unguilty triumph.

The household servants at Wintercombe were given time off, as was customary: half of them on the first day of the fair, half on the second, as was also usual. The third, known as pack-a-penny day because that was the time when the traders, eager to be rid of unsold goods, marked their wares down to bargain prices, was always a time of noise, mayhem, and general license, even more so than normally. To be allowed time to visit the fair at all was regarded as a great privilege at Wintercombe. Certainly a chance to attend on the third day would be more fun, but on the whole the servants were glad of the opportunity to go at all.

Dame Ursula, of course, would have been happier had everyone stayed fretting and resentful at home. In previous years, her husband had always let his household attend the fair as a matter of course. Now that he was dead, she had thought, obviously, that she could browbeat Silence into putting a stop to it.

But Silence was no longer to be cowed. She stood quiet and gracious under the torrent of argument, illogic, maliciousness, and willful ignorance that characterized an attempt at what her mother-in-law fondly considered to be reasoned persuasion. She waited until Dame Ursula had come to her inevitable spluttering, gasping conclusion and was handed a cup of water by the impassive Ruth. Then she said composedly, "I am afraid that I have already informed all the household that they may spend either this day or tomorrow at the fair, as usual. It is a tradition which in my view it would be unwise, and unfair, to discontinue."

"Unwise?" Dame Ursula said in disbelief. "May the Lord witness this stupidity! The fair is like all such, daughter, a hot bed of lechery, fornication, frippery, and all manner of wickedness and vice—and you say it is *unwise* to prevent our servants attending?"

"They will resent it, if I do—and much goodwill is bound to be lost. Besides, on the whole I trust them. Pray, madam, what manner of lechery or vice are Turber and his wife likely to indulge in?"

Dame Ursula, disgusted, uttered a noise that sounded like "Bah!" She added venomously, "I'm not thinking of them, daughter. What of that forward Lyteman trollop? Yes, I've heard the tales. If I had the use of my legs she'd be turned out without a character, *and* the weight of my stick to speed her on! And the Walker hussy, she's almost as bad."

"I have already warned them of the perils of the occasion, madam, and I do not doubt that all our servants are well aware of them. Of course, if they choose to disobey my instructions in a flagrant or unpleasant way, then I shall have no choice but to punish them—by dismissal, if necessary. But that is my affair." She jangled the keys at her waist, a gentle hint. "You no longer need disturb your rest with anxieties about the household, madam."

The irony was not lost on Dame Ursula, who stared at her son's supposedly meek and biddable second wife as if she were some evil Jezebel, suddenly discovered. Her stick shot out to poke her daughter-in-law in the chest, but Silence moved back two unobtrusive steps, leaving the knobbled cane wavering impotently in the air. Deprived of her wish to inflict physical pain, the old lady banged it on the floor instead and shouted viciously, "You'll regret the day you ever thought to defy me, you hussy! Anxieties about the household, pah! Riotous suppers, soldiers wrecking, looting, fornicating, thieving—my own grandchildren show me no respect, and the maidservants share the officers' beds—and don't you dare deny it. I wouldn't be surprised if you didn't do it yourself! You're—you're no better than a brothel keeper, daughter, a procuress—evil, wicked, you'll rot in hell—as the Lord is my witness, I'll tell George everything, d'you hear me, *everything* of what has been happening in his absence, and he'll take a strap to you, you . . . light and lascivious whore! He should disown you, turn you out as you deserve—"

"For what, pray?" Silence inquired. She had gone very pale but was otherwise calm. Keep still, the inner voice of reason urged, keep your head and your temper—she rants and raves to no effect, and you know it. "What have I done, Mother? Though I'd question your right to that title of respect and honor, after what you have just said to me. Have I fornicated? No. I have kept the household running smooth, I have ensured there is food on your plate and wood on your fire and that you are unmolested. Other damage I have not been able to prevent, but I have done my best to guard Wintercombe and keep it safe for my husband against great odds. And the thanks I have from you are small indeed. I hope that George is more appreciative of my efforts on his behalf."

"He won't be—I'll see he won't be!" Dame Ursula screeched. Her lips were tinged with blue, her face distorted, and spittle foamed at the corner of her mouth.

Silence, frightened despite herself by this naked malevolence, took an involuntary step backward and stopped herself. With a huge effort of self-control, she said quietly, "You should rest, madam, and try not to upset yourself. The doctors have always advised you against undue excitement and stress. Perhaps Captain Hellier can bleed you—he has had some success with Colonel Ridgeley."

Some regrettable spirit of mischief had prompted her last words. If Dame Ursula had been angry before, now she shook with fury, the stick thrashing in the air while she spluttered incoherently. A few words— "Whore—wickedness—Satan—hell"—were discernible, which made Silence glad she could not distinguish the rest. When the sounds had dwindled somewhat, and there seemed no danger that her mother-in-law would succumb to an apoplectic fit, she said calmly, "I must leave you, madam. There is not further purpose in this conversation, if so it can be called, and I have much to do with so many absent today. Good morning to you."

She made her escape with her head held high and proud, oblivious to the venomous screech following her out of the door. "You wait, you vicious harlot—you wait until George comes home!"

Which he undoubtedly would. But somehow, that threat no longer had the power to alarm Silence. Freed by his insensitivity of the duty of affection for him, she was also freed of her fear. After Ridgeley, the thought of her stout, determined, priggish, upright husband no longer frightened her.

As if her thought had conjured him up, she all but bumped into Ridgeley at the top of the stone stairs. He was fully dressed for riding, in buff coat, boots, hat, and heavy leather gauntlets, and although his face was gray and sheened with sweat, there was a look of grim obstinacy upon it. Harris, the fawning servant and secretary, was in anxious attendance, and Cornet Wickham, a decent enough young man whom she knew Nick liked. Emboldened by this, her blood already raised by Dame Ursula, she sketched a curtsy and said with every appearance of pleasure, "Why, Colonel Ridgeley! I am so glad to see you recovered, and on your feet."

"Recovered be damned," said the colonel, glowering at her. "It's my belief that maid and cook of yours have been poisoning me—and don't deny it! I should have healed weeks ago, but flux after flux has kept me on my back—I'm certain, madam, that there was some villainy in those feeble broths and eggs and suchlike pap your women served me."

"Don't be absurd, Colonel," Silence replied, trying to hide her unease at his effortless guess at the truth. "You may not have relished those nourishing dishes, sir, but if we'd fed you roast beef as you asked, it's my opinion that you'd have been dead by now."

"Your opinion, eh? And your wish, no doubt, like that whey-faced brat? Where is she now, eh—skulking somewhere? I wish to see her at once, madam—at once, or I'll turn the house inside out looking for her."

A chill had settled around Silence's heart. The elation gone, she answered him directly. "There is no need. She has been sent away."

The pause was brief, and menacing. Ridgeley's face darkened, and his eyes glared at her hotly. "Sent away? Has the vicious little chit been punished, then?"

"Amply, sir, I can assure you," Silence said, trying desperately to sound as if she too condemned what Rachael had done. "And I have packed her off to distant relatives, so that she may repent of her wicked deed at her leisure, far from her family."

There was another pause, heavy with disbelief. Silence wondered urgently whether Harris or Wickham would give her away, perhaps without intending to. The little secretary had kept almost entirely to his master's chambers, and might not have seen Rachael. Whether he had heard her or not was another matter, for the girl's voice was lamentably loud. Perhaps he would think it belonged to one of the servants, for few gently bred maidens had voices like bullen cows. But Wickham, in and out of Wintercombe all the time, must surely know that she had been here only twenty-four hours earlier. Silence glanced at his pleasant young face, free of signs of dissipation or dishonesty, and saw him looking at her speculatively. He gave her a quick, encouraging smile and instantly schooled his face back to its usual bland blankness.

"Just as well for her," Ridgeley growled unpleasantly. "If I'd caught her, I'd have thrashed her within an inch of her life, with my own hand, the little bitch. Good day, my *lady*. You will see me later—we have much to discuss."

She heard his feet tramping heavily down the stairs, Wickham's lighter tread and the secretary's rabbity skips following, and breathed a huge, shaky sigh of relief. She had done the right thing, and only just in time. Thank the Lord Rachael was safe in hiding at Wick, out of Ridgeley's eye and reach, and with any luck would remain so until somehow this monstrous many-headed burden could be heaved off Wintercombe's back.

Perhaps this afternoon, in the continuing sunshine, she could shake off her own load of cares and just for a few hours enjoy the cheerful atmosphere of Norton Fair.

C H A P T E R

EIGHTEEN

Remorseless, treacherous, lecherous, kindless villain!
—*HAMLET*

"We're going to the fair-air! We're going to the fair-air! We're going to the fair-air! Hooray, hooray, hooray, we're going to the fair!"

It was Deb's voice, strident, tuneless, and annoying, disrupting the spring birdsong and sending at least one robin fluttering hastily for the cover of a sprouting hawthorn. The little girl sat on Dumbledore, astride, her legs sticking out almost horizontally across the pony's broad back and her new summer skirts, in a nice shade of hyacinth blue, bunched up around her. She was ostensibly controlling the pony, although Dumbledore, after years of church and village visits, knew his way into Norton as well as any of the St. Barbes. Behind Deb sat William, also astride, with his russet petticoats somehow up around his waist, revealing quantities of hose and shoe. He had not deigned to hold onto his sister's waist and was in some danger of falling off.

Tabby rode pillion behind Nat on Cobweb, much more decorously, with her legs properly to one side, her hands clasped across her half-brother's chest, and the afternoon sun turning her darkly blond curls to pure, new-minted gold. From their pony came sounds of talk, laughter, snatches of song in Tabby's pure treble, unmatched by Nat's croak. His voice at last was breaking, and the sleeves of all his summer doublets had been found to be several inches too short.

"They're happy, at least," Nick said. He rode beside Silence on his tall chestnut, the scarlet cloak artistically draped over its quarters even on this glorious sunshiney day, more like June than April. He looked happy too, she thought, glancing at him, relaxed, almost slouching in the saddle, in a tawny suit with gold lacing in what must be the latest fashion, but was rather more flamboyant than anything she had seen him wear before. To go with the clothes, his mood seemed reckless, mischievous, merry to match the children's. In such company, she could no longer shoulder her cares: She felt them, almost a real, physical weight depressing her, gradually grow lighter, melted by sun and birdsong and the laughter of children, until unnoticed the last of them trickled away and she was left smiling.

"So you don't regret coming to the fair?" Nick went on.

Silence found her smile becoming broader, stretching with delight. "Of course I don't," she said. And, for once, she spoke the pure and unalloyed truth.

The outskirts of Philip's Norton were as empty as they were on a Sunday in church time. There was no one at the mill, or working in the gardens of any of the cottages at Lyde Green. By long-standing arrangement, they left their horses under the care of the Flowers' groom at the Manor Farm, which lay, shielded by cottages and tenements, just behind West Street. The house, an imposing edifice that the late Master Flower had had rebuilt in the most modern manner, was as deserted as any other they had seen. Young Thomas and Eleanor and their mother had gone to the fair like everyone else.

The St. Barbes threaded their way through the dried mud and dung of the barton, past the cottages, and into the sudden noise and life and sunshine of Philip's Norton on this, the most important occasion in the village year.

On the other side of West Street lay Fair Close, which for most of the winter had nourished, turn and turn about, sheep and cattle from the Manor Farm. The animals had been evicted to make way for an assortment of makeshift booths, bedecked with an astonishing variety of tatty pennants and bunting, and many more pedlars and cheapjacks and chapmen selling their wares from trays. All up West Street those beasts that had survived the winter, the farmers' necessity, and the depredations of two hungry garrisons were tethered, their lowing and bleating adding to the chaotic cacophony of sound. There were horses, from sturdy draft animals to small shaggy ponies like Dumbledore, one or two wistful-looking mares with young foals at foot, and a few flashy animals with curried, shining coats, their manes and tails gaudily bound up with ribbon in an attempt to distract the prospective purchaser's eye from defects in temperament, soundness, or conformation.

If, to Silence's eye, the crowds were thinner than in previous years, the booths less crowded, the faces almost all familiar, to her enchanted children it was as if a new and enticing garden of delights had been opened out before them. Deb, for once speechless at this transformation of the normally quiet West Street, stood and stared, thumb in mouth. William, always one to act on impulse, gave a joyous leap forward into the throng and nearly fell flat, brought to an abrupt halt by the length of the hanging strings sewn onto each shoulder of his doublet and held firmly in his mother's grasp. "Want to *see!*" he wailed urgently. "Oh, Mama, please may I *see!*"

Silence, a little belatedly, realized that her son's perpetual view of legs and feet must be frustrating in the extreme. Nick solved the problem. He said cheerfully, "Would you like to sit on my shoulders, Caligula?"

"Ooh, yes, *please!*" William cried, ecstatic, and his enthusiasm was echoed by Deb.

"Me too, Captain Hellier—me too!"

"Later, but not now—I couldn't have both of you on my shoulders at once," Nick said, laughing. "I'm not Atlas, after all." And as most of the St. Barbes, all save Nat lacking any sort of classical education, stared at him in puzzlement, he swept William out of his mother's grasp and settled him on his shoulders, where the child crowed with delight at the sudden improvement in his view.

Deb, lacking hanging strings by virtue of her supposedly more mature years—she had turned five two weeks ago—was dangerously close to being lost in the crowd, her round face flushed hot with excitement. Silence hastily grasped her hand and said, quietly but seriously, "Do you remember what you promised me earlier?"

"That I'd stay close to you, Mama," Deb replied somewhat reluctantly. She was plainly unable to understand why she risked being mislaid in a place so familiar, even if so utterly transformed.

"Good," her mother said. "Then keep hold of my hand, and we'll go see what those booths have for sale, shall we?"

She had given them each a few pennies and half-pennies, worn and silvery, to spend. They had come from the Wintercombe hoard, now transferred, very quietly and gradually, to new hiding places in and around her chamber. She had reasoned that, even with Ridgeley's imminent and unwelcome resurrection, this would be the last and least in any search. It was said that those of truly gentle birth could feel the shape of a pea through the soft thickness of a featherbed. Silence, sleeping blissfully on a hundred pounds in silver and gold, had reflected wryly that this must prove her humble origins. Only she and Mally knew about the coin and its new location. She had taken care to secret it while her children and the rest of the household and Nick were all safely out of the way, and her chamber was now always kept locked if she was not within it.

The war might have diminished the numbers of both buyers and sellers, but those who had braved these troubled times, out of curiosity, merriment, or necessity, seemed to be enjoying themselves with undiminished vigor. Once, merchants, farmers, and country people had come from all over the West Country to Philip's Norton Fair, and many small pedlars, thieves, vagrants, and cutpurses from much further afield than that. The justices were always kept busy in the weeks afterward, dealing with minor felonies. But now there were no ballad singers from London, no Scottish dancers with bare legs and wild hair, no incomprehensible hardware men from the Middle Shires with knives and pots and pans to sell. There were tumblers, though, a dark and brightly dressed trio who displayed such an inhuman flexibility that Deb's eyes almost fell from her head, and Silence felt quite ill. There was a dog, dressed in a ruff, that could do all kinds of tricks, and for a finale walked a few steps on its back legs. The little ones applauded wildly, but Tabby saw its skinny ribs and haunted eyes, and the tail curled fearfully beneath its belly, and turned away.

At each step Silence was greeted by people she knew: villagers who doffed their hats humbly, and those who called themselves gentry and went through the appropriate rituals of courtesy. Many of them she had not seen for some months, friends of her husband or her father-in-law, from villages round about. She became aware, fairly early on, that Nick had quietly detached himself from her. She knew where he was, for William still sat on his shoulders and made him for once taller than anyone. And although she wanted him by her side, missed his amusing conversation and flow of hilarious comment on the life of the fair, she knew that the identity of her escort would give rise to scandalous gossip and speculation. Quiet untrue, of course—but all the same, she suddenly had no wish to draw attention to herself.

Tabby was with Nat, Mally stood as ever at her shoulder, and Deb, hot and sticky and urgent to sample yet more delights, was her excuse to move on. She bought ribbons for the children, and some pins and needles and thread, always in short supply, and embroidery silks in vivid colors; some wooden pattens, cheap because the winter mud was almost gone; laces and trimmings for new gowns; a purse for Nat from the leather stall; and on impulse a blue collar for Lily's slender pale neck. All these went into her maid's soft rush basket, or her own. The crush, the noise, the variety of goods on sale, reminded her overpoweringly of London, of walking down Cheapside or Paternoster Row, beset by hawkers and shopkeepers. She broke out into a sweat, which the hot sun did nothing to dispel, and took several deep breaths to calm herself. She was Lady St. Barbe. She would not be panicked by a crowded fair.

A shriek of raucous laughter, somehow familiar, drew her sudden attention. A knot of young people was standing by the booth selling sweetmeats and gingerbread. She recognized Eleanor Flower, her brother Thomas, the dubious Fulke Tovie with his hot wandering eyes and hands, and the three Baylie girls. Surely she had imagined it?

But no: The laugh erupted again, unmistakable. Silence made her excuses to Mistress Sloper, another capable widow with claims to gentility that the College of Arms had firmly rejected twenty years ago, and, with Deb still by the hand, walked through the press of people to where her stepdaughter Rachael was standing, in blatant defiance of her instructions.

The girl had not seen her, but Kitty Baylie had. Her face flushed with sudden alarm, she dug Rachael none too gently in the ribs and bade her turn. Silence, more disappointed than angry, surveyed her stepdaughter's defiant, chalk-white face and said softly, "Why are you here, Rachael?"

The young Flowers, who always contrived to extract themselves from awkward situations, were already slinking back into the crowd. Fulke

Tovie, his hand resting on Eleanor's shoulder, was with them. The Baylie girls looked uneasily at each other, obviously well aware of the situation. Rachael said, rather loudly, "I wanted to come to the fair, and I didn't see any harm in it."

"You disobeyed me," Silence said. She was aware that the girl deserved a beating, and George would certainly have given her a sound one, but she knew in her heart that it was no answer to the perennial problem of this difficult, wayward, moody, and secretive child. "You know the reasons for my instructions, and you disobeyed me. They were for your own safety, Rachael—not because I wanted to spoil your happiness, not from spite nor whim—but because you are in danger if you wander about the village. Can't you understand that?"

For the first time she saw a flicker of fear behind the bravado. If she could speak to her alone, she knew that Rachael would soon crack, but the presence of the other girls stiffened her defiance. "There isn't any harm in it," her stepdaughter said belligerently. "He's not here, is he? He's still in bed because Mally keeps putting senna in his broth."

One of the younger girls giggled. Rachael went on. "Anyway, I asked Mistress Baylie, and *she* said I could come. And I'm supposed to be in her household at the moment, aren't I?"

"You should go back," Silence said, feeling, as so often with Rachael in this intransigent mood, that she was banging her head against a stone wall. "You should go back now, before the soldiers see you."

"I can't go back on my own," her stepdaughter pointed out. "And it wouldn't be fair to Moll and Kitty and Bess to make them go home with me, when we've only just come." She stared at Silence, her bright blue eyes daring her to make a scene. "But I promise I'll go back as soon as we're ready, and Mistress Baylie says. And I'll be very very careful, and always stay with my friends." She gave a bright, false smile. "Thank you, Mother."

Silence, manipulated into a corner, stood staring after Rachael's willful, head-tossing figure, surrounded by Baylies, and did not know whether to laugh, or weep, or stamp her foot in a fury.

It was only then that she realized that Deb, taking advantage of the distraction afforded by her half-sister, had slipped free of Silence's loosened hand and vanished into the crowd.

For an instant a wave of blind, suffocating panic—or was it rage?— swept over her. Oh, Deb, you *fool,* you silly, disobedient, willful little girl! Then, with an effort, her usual calm achieved supremacy. She turned to Mally and said, as if discussing an acquaintance briefly glimpsed, "Did you see which way she went?"

"That I diden," Mally said apologetically. "I be despeard sorry, m'lady, I diden even see she were gone. Shall I go look for she?"

"Yes—you work that way around the close," Silence said, indicating the clockwise direction. "And I'll go the other, and we'll meet at the gate. Oh, and Mally—you have my full permission to spank her when you find her."

"I'll do en willingly when I do get a hold of that forweend little wench," Mally said with a grin, and dived purposefully into the throng.

Silence, wishing suddenly for the cheerful support of Nick Hellier, turned and made her way back through the heaving, merry, raucous crowd, in the direction they had already followed. Deb had expressed a yearning to look at a stall crammed with tawdry trinkets and beset by giggling girls and their sweethearts, and Silence had by means of timely distraction ("Oh, Deb, look at that boy walking on his hands!") steered her past. Perhaps she had gone back with the idea of spending her coins on some cheap bauble— and why not, Silence thought ruefully, when I myself gave her the pennies to spend as she wished?

But Deb was not there. Admittedly, she was only five, but she was sturdy and big for her age, and Silence was certain she had not missed her. Also, the little girl was well known to the villagers, and no one whom her mother questioned had seen her. Hot, perspiring, anxiety and annoyance mingling, she arrived at the gate of the fair close, where one of the Flower family servants was collecting the toll money from every eager entrant. He had not seen Deb either, but she did not have much faith in his powers of observation. Then Mally appeared, disheveled, her cap askew, her hands empty, and shook her head. "No sign of she, m'lady, and none I've asked have seed her either."

It was as if, thought Silence, her all-too-substantial daughter had vanished off the face of the earth. Realizing that they were blocking the entrance, she drew Mally out of the way, and found Nat and Tabby beside them, arrived suddenly and out of breath. "Will Tovie said you'd lost Deb," Nat explained. "I saw her just now, nipping out of the gate here— I'm sure it was her, I haven't seen another little girl in that particular shade of blue. And before you ask, I didn't see which way she went, the crowds were much too thick."

"Have you seen Ni—Captain Hellier?" Silence asked. "He has the misfortune to have William on his shoulders—or he did when last I saw him."

"He didn't when I saw him," Tabby said. "He had him by the hanging strings, and he was finding pennies in his ears—William's ears, I mean." Her voice had an amused, wistful quality, as if she wished that Captain Hellier, with his seemingly inexhaustible fund of unexpected and delightful diversions, would find coins in her own ears. She added, on a different note, "What was Rachael doing here? I thought she was supposed to be hiding from the soldiers somewhere."

"She's going back to the place very soon," Silence said hastily, unwilling to raise the difficult specter of her stepdaughter, threatening to spoil the afternoon. "Now, I really do think we ought to find Deb before she gets into mischief."

It was agreed that Nat and Tabby should take the less crowded road down to the churchyard, where Deb might have gone to play. Mally and Silence would make their way up West Street to the Market Cross and the George, where the crowds were thickest.

She was not particularly worried. The child was well known in Norton, obviously of gentle birth, and possessed of a stalwart pair of lungs. But she knew that Deb, who had all of Rachael's willfulness and little of her cunning, could quite easily do something foolish, something that might demean the St. Barbes—saying something rude to the vicar sprang to mind. And she had no fear, and some of those beribboned horses tied to the fair close wall were exceedingly frisky . . .

There was a great press of people at the top of West Street, where the four roads met: from Bath, from Wells, from Farleigh, and from Frome. There was the Market Cross, which so far had survived the efforts of Parson Willis to have it flung down as Papist and idolatrous, largely because Sir Samuel St. Barbe had resisted it. Here the two inns faced each other across the broad cobbles of the market place: the George, ancient, mellow, famous throughout Somerset and beyond, run by the Tovie family for generations, a respectable house patronized by wealthy travelers and the better sort of villager. Opposite, the Fleur-de-Lys, or, as invariably known in Norton, the Flower, an upstart rival rather less respectable, condemned by the vicar as a den of drunkenness and vice, and run by the Parsons family, whose morals were not above reproach—one of the daughters had produced a bastard son who, very properly, had been boarded out and now labored as a scullion at Wintercombe.

Silence and Mally came up at the edge of the crowd, out of sight of the Market Cross and before the junction with North Street. People were peering, jostling, trying to get a better view. Mally prodded the woman in front of her and said something. The woman, one of the Stents, gave her an anxious glance and said, loud enough for Silence to hear, "They soldiers be back again, but I can't hear what he do say."

"Who?" Silence asked, but she had no need of an answer: Ridgeley's stentorian tones, the words inaudible but the threat all too apparent, burst suddenly on her ears. Mally, using heels and elbows ruthlessly, gave her lady a meaningful glance and plunged into the crowd. Somewhere in that packed, dense mass was surely Deb, alone, perhaps frightened, possibly in danger. Silence, uttering a heartfelt prayer for her daughter's safety, took a deep breath and did likewise, taking the right-hand side as Mally had taken the left.

It was quite easy to thread her way through, uttering polite excuses. Those who recognized her made way for her, saying in answer to her hasty inquiry that they were tarblish sorry, m'lady, but they had seed no sign of the little maid. Gasping and hot, though this part of the crowd was in the shade, she found herself at last by the George, without Deb but with a decidedly better sight, and sound, of the Market Cross.

There were perhaps a score of troopers crowded around it, their horses sidling, restless, dangerous in such a close-packed, limited space. And on this big, heavy-boned bay, made much thinner by his illness but still exuding brutal vitality and unmistakable menace, sat Lieutenant-Colonel Ridgeley.

"Is that clear, you ignorant uncouth hobbledehoys?" His voice's power was undiminished, carrying to all save the farthest fringes of the crowd. "You seem to have plenty to sell, so we'll take our share. It's the price you pay for our protection, anyway. And remember—we serve your lawful anointed king. To resist us is to commit treason and will invite a swift and merciless response."

The stillness was total, sullen and bitter. Silence, in the doorway of the George, glanced about her at the men and women and children, poor and wealthy, who lived here and at Wellow, Charterhouse Hinton, Farleigh and Beckington, Tellisford and Hemington and Rode, who had suffered the depredations of these men all through the winter, had thought themselves reprieved, and were now angrily realizing their error. They were powerless against even so few soldiers, and no one sane would care to begin a riot when so many innocents stood in danger. But, Silence thought, her skin prickling at the fear and tension and hatred emanating from the people around her, it would only take one or two hotheads inflamed with drink, some thrown pebbles or abuse, and the match would be set to the fire with a vengeance.

Where, oh where was Deb? And Rachael, oblivious of the danger in which she stood? And Nick, who could possibly check some of his colonel's worst excesses?

Forcing herself to keep calm, Silence searched the faces in the crowd, and saw no sign of any of them. As she did so, Ridgeley spoke again. "There is another duty which your loyalty to our cause must lay upon some of you. This does not apply to those of you who are willing and able to contribute fully to our maintenance, but those who are poor, or intransigent, may instead work upon the fortifications of our garrison."

There was no hiding the murmurs of dismay and resentment. A man cried from the body of the crowd, "Your captain said as how we weren't needed no more!"

"My captain erred. My orders are quite clear. When this fair is ended, my men will be coming among you each week. Those who can pay, in cash or kind, need trouble themselves no further. Those who cannot or will not contribute to our cause in other ways will labor on the fortifications, men and women alike, on pain of severe punishment. Do you understand me?"

"Aye, we understand you well enough, you ungodly limb of Satan!" someone bawled from the center of the crowd.

Ridgeley's face suffused darkly. He dug spurs into his horse, and the animal leapt and shouldered its way forward into the mass of people. Fearful, half panicking, they pushed backward, opening up a path to a young man whom Silence could not recognize at this distance. Deliberately, Ridgeley removed the heavy pistol from his holster and pointed it down at his opponent's face. For a moment the crowd hung poised between terror and fury. There were moans of fear, and a woman cried out. Then, with a contemptuous laugh, the colonel turned the pistol in his hand and struck the young man viciously across the face with the butt. "That will teach you manners, perhaps," he said curtly, and turned his horse back toward the cross.

No one else said anything, but if looks and intent could have killed, the combined malevolence of Philip's Norton would have slain Ridgeley there and then.

For a moment he surveyed the packed, hate-filled faces, and then he laughed. "Good. Now, I'm told there are beasts for sale farther down that street. If all you people would *kindly* make way, my men and I will go investigate. I have a fancy for roast beef tonight."

Sullenly mute, they shuffled back, like a many-hued, living version of the Red Sea. And, thought Silence grimly, it would not take much more provocation for them to roll forward again, to engulf the loathsome colonel and his hated minions.

Nick Hellier, walking up West Street, still with William firmly in tow, was unaware that Ridgeley had arrived in Norton until he rounded the corner and saw the soldiers, amid a hostile, silent throng, picking their way down. His first instinct was to make himself scarce. It would not do any good to his already low stock to be seen holding the hanging strings of a traitor's brat. Then a woman, weeping, ran up to him, crying something about thievery and blood, and a man behind her added urgently, "Can't ee do summat to stop en, Captain? He'll rob us all blind and kill anyone as stands in his way!"

He had told them, outside the church a month ago, that he could help them. Now, faced with their need, he knew the futility of what he had said. Short of killing Ridgeley and thereby signing his own death warrant, he could do nothing. The man might make a show of reason, in that unpleasantly elaborate style that was more of an insult than plain words would be. But underneath the thin veneer of civility, the colonel was as ugly and implacable as a charging bull.

Nick was not, he had told Silence once, the kind of man to be reckless with his life, or his liberty. Moreover, he had William, three years old, clutching his hand. But as more people saw him and came clamoring, begging for his help, and Ridgeley's big, bad-tempered bay approached even nearer, he knew he could not refuse. He thrust William's hanging strings at the first person he recognized, which happened to be the red-haired scullion who was Mally's brother, and stepped out into the middle of West Street.

Ridgeley saw him, and laughed. Still ten or fifteen yards away, he drew rein and hailed his captain. "Well, Hellier! Enjoying the fair, eh? Why are you not at your duties?"

"I had thought them adequately provided for," Nick said pleasantly. "What brings you here, sir, so fresh from your sickbed?"

All around, people stared, anxiously whispering, at this encounter. Some of the more prudent had drawn their children back to the edge of the street, well out of harm's way, and watched from there. Nick saw with relief that Ned Merrifield had pulled William into one of the gardens that bordered the road on the opposite side of the fair close.

"Supplies," Ridgeley said concisely. "And it's high time these whining peasants were put in their place—God's death, they've had it too easy while I've been laid up. And whose fault is that, Captain Hellier?"

"You seem to think it mine," Nick said more cheerfully than he in fact felt. Ridgeley kicked his spurs into his horse's ribs, and the big animal flinched, squealed, and kicked sideways. Several unwary souls who had not put a safe distance between themselves and the iron-shod hooves now hastened to do so. They ran to join the others who lined the gardens and walls down West Street, intent on this promising confrontation between the detested colonel and his rather more sympathetic officer.

They were to be cheated of it. Ridgeley, urging the bay forward almost to Nick's feet, suddenly checked it with a savage jab at the curb bit and the animal, blood-sprinkled foam gathering at the corner of its mouth, came to a snorting, reluctant halt. The colonel stood in the stirrups and pointed past Nick's shoulder. "By God, there she is, the little bitch! Come here, you, or I'll have your hide!"

Nick, astonished, whipped around. Down the hill of West Street, edged with gawping villagers, cattle and sheep, restless horses, merchants and pedlars, women and children, people with packs and trays of wares, there stood a little group of young girls, their faces pale, aghast, mouths open; and in the center, frozen with terror, Rachael St. Barbe.

His first emotion was anger—had the stupid child no more sense than to put herself in such danger, so needlessly? And then he felt fear for her, and for Silence, who had done as much as she could to make her stepdaughter safe, but not, it seemed, enough.

"Come here!" Ridgeley roared in a voice that bounced off the stone cottages. "You stinking little bitch, come here!"

Rachael stood still for a second longer. Then she turned and plunged back into the crowd.

Ridgeley, with a howl of anger, brought his whip down on the bay's sweating quarters. The horse plunged forward again, and Nick, before he had even thought about the consequences of his action, grabbed its bridle as the animal shot past.

Silence, struggling down from the marketplace through the crowd with neither Deb nor Mally, saw it clearly. Ridgeley, shouting, appeared to be trying to beat Nick away with his whip, while clapping spurs so cruelly to the horse that bright blood streaked its russet sides. The captain, slight beside the threatening bulks of the great horse and its rider, hung on grimly as the colonel dragged the reins back, making the animal rear up. Silence stared in horror, seeing the flailing hooves, the horse almost dancing on its hind legs at the vicious jabs of hand and heel, and Nick tossed this way and that under the flashing strikes of Ridgeley's whip.

Then one of the flying hooves struck, and the captain was flung off sideways to lie in a tangle of limbs in the dust. With a yell of triumph, Ridgeley brought the plunging horse back to all fours and sent it flying down West Street, his troopers galloping after.

Rachael, running like a mad thing, heard them coming. She did not know why pursuit had taken so long, but at least she had a good start. She pushed her way rudely past two gossiping old widows standing in the middle of the road and on impulse dived left, up toward the church.

After that initial moment of terror, like a rabbit before a fox, she could think of nothing else but escape. Her lungs hurt, her legs ached, her mouth was dry with fear. She had no illusions about what would happen to her if Ridgeley caught her. For her own sake, and everyone else's, somehow she had to lose him and find her way back to Wick Farm unseen.

Easier said than done. She ran into the churchyard, gasping. Hide inside the church itself? Too obvious. Behind a tree? Don't be ridiculous. She heard shouting, hoofbeats. They must have seen her coming in here. She reached the wall dividing the churchyard from the meadow, nearly trod on a couple laying entwined in the long grass under one of the elms, and scrambled over, grazing her thumb. Years of games played at Chard and, later, on the terraces of Wintercombe, came to her rescue. She ducked down below the level of the dry, lichened stones and crawled purposefully through the grass and new nettles, cursing under her breath with words learned from the soldiers each time she was stung. Amid her fright and the wild pumping of her heart, a small voice spoke severely inside her head with words her grandmother might have used. "This is *your* fault, my girl—yours and no one else's, for disobeying your stepmother."

She could not believe they had not seen her leave the churchyard. But perhaps, she wondered with burgeoning hope, they thought she had run into the church. It was the obvious place.

Her head almost smacked into stone. She had come to the corner where the meadow joined the fair close. She glanced behind her. The field was empty, save for an assortment of cattle that belonged to the Manor Farm.

She stood up, with care, and climbed over the wall that bordered the fair close. As she did so, a cry went up behind her. "There she is! Get after her!"

Her fear was like a stab in the belly. Rachael dived under the booth nearest to her, one selling leather goods, worming her way through impatient legs, ignoring the exclamations of surprise or annoyance and at least one well-aimed kick. She struggled to her feet, hearing someone say "Why, 'tis Mistress Rachael—what be ee doing under there, maid?" She ignored him, aware with an itch between her shoulders of the pursuit behind her, and thrust into the mass of people crowded round the stall.

There were fewer here than earlier, she had time to see—perhaps they were all in West Street, following the soldiers. If she had planned to lose herself in the crowds, she must think again. Wildly she ran to the gate, stumbling over the rough ground, pushing her way past curious fairgoers, and hurled herself out into West Street past the astonished tollman.

There was a trooper riding up, not ten yards away. He let out a yowling cry more appropriate to the hunting field and clapped his spurs to his horse's sides. The nag, somewhat less fiery than Ridgeley's brute, laid its ears back, swished its tail crossly, and lumbered into a trot.

Rachael did not wait to see it. Nor did she notice the little knot of people bent over someone lying on the ground farther up West Street. She turned and fled back into the fair close, dodging among the stupid gawping villagers, whose only function seemed to be to get in her way.

There were troopers in the meadow, they must have ridden through the churchyard and jumped the wall. For an instant a vision of Parson Willis's probable expression, had he seen this, rose to choke her throat with incongruous laughter. But her mind, astonishingly, was still working hard, and her legs still plunged up and down as if they belonged to someone else, quite tireless, but it hurt to breathe and her mouth was so dry the air rasped through it like a knife. Breathless, she thought desperately, I must go where the horses can't—through the gardens.

At the top of the close there were some outbuildings—a small barn and a stable, facing up the hill. Rachael saw the low wall beside them and dived over it recklessly. She landed on her face in a soft and pungently odorous midden, rolled over, scrambled to her feet, and ran up the garden between rows of cabbage and bean seedlings and panic-stricken hens, nearly falling again over a carelessly placed spade. If I can work my way along the gardens behind South Street, she thought, perhaps I can hide in someone's barn or bakehouse, until they give up—they can't look *everywhere*—oh, dear God, I hope they don't find me—*how* I wish I'd stayed at Wick Farm!

Nearest the house, the wall bordering it was high, higher than Rachael. She came to a stumbling halt, her thin body shuddering with effort, and stared at it blankly. Could she climb it? What was on the other side? That big, half-timbered and stone building beyond was the George—no use hiding there, too many people to give her away, too many who could be punished for concealing her.

The wall was roughly made, with plenty of hand- and foot-holds. Moreover, there was a conveniently placed apple tree. Rachael, dripping dung-laden straw and sweat, kilted her skirt up to her knees, set her jaw, and began the laborious climb up. The top of the wall seemed an unending distance above her, forever out of reach. Her hands slipped and she fell back, scraping her shoulders painfully against the tree.

It was then that Rachael felt like giving up. It would be so much easier if she just lay there and waited for them to find her.

"I'm buggered if I will," Rachael said aloud, and sternly. She wiped the blood off her hands and the tears from her eyes, and tried again.

There was a narrow alley on the other side, she remembered as she struggled painfully over the wall. It ran from the marketplace to the meadow, down between this house, in which lived William Levett, a prosperous weaver, and the George. She dare not use the main street. She dropped clumsily into the beaten earth of the pathway, jarring her ankles, and hobbled back down the alley until she found the gate into the orchard belonging to the George. Somehow she would have to struggle through all the gardens bordering South Street, until she could find a safe place to cross the road and work her way around across the fields to Wick Farm. Alternatively, she could find a barn to hide in.

They're bound to look in all the buildings, she thought, hauling herself over the wall between the George and the next garden, the Widow Seeld's overgrown plot. I'll run until I drop if I have to—but I am *not* going to let that ugly brute catch me!

At first, Silence had thought that Nick was dead. He lay so still in the road, like some bundle of old clothes thrown down in the gutter, and the people around him stood and stared foolishly and did nothing, while her heart turned over and over and she shook from fear for him. With the self-discipline of years, she made herself calm, despite the terror in her soul and the sweat on her skin, and walked the long, long yards down the uneven rutted street as if she were as unacquainted with the body lying in front of her as the Good Samaritan had been with the man who fell among thieves. She knew that she ought to turn her thoughts to finding Deb, to telling Rachael to leave the village at once—pray God this had nothing to do with her—but she could think only of Nick, and how badly he might be hurt.

"Be he dead, m'lady?" someone cried, plucking at her sleeve. And then, as she came closer, a small solid body hurled itself at her, crying something incoherently, and she knelt and took her sobbing son in her arms.

"He bain't hurt, m'lady," Ned Merrifield said, his earnest freckled face bending down to hers. "But he saw all of what happened, I couldn't stop en, I be despeard sorry, m'lady."

"That's all right," she said, and, feeling the worst kind of traitor, gently disentangled William's clutching hands from her skirts. "No, sweetheart, you stay with Ned, just for a little while—I must see to Captain Hellier— *please*, William, let go."

At last, screaming, the little boy was carried away by Ned, who was quite used to children, and she was able to attend to Nick.

He lay on his face in the dust, which in this country of reddish-brown clay was brighter than his hair. Very gently, terrified of what she might find, she took his shoulder in her hand and turned him over. Willing hands assisted her, eager Somerset voices poured advice, comments, details of what had happened into her ears. She ignored them all.

He was not dead. A pulse beat strongly below the sharp clean line of his jaw. His face was bruised and split, and there was the beginnings of a truly splendid black eye, but she did not think, slipping her fingers gently through the long thick hair, that there was any other serious damage. There was a small lump, raised and sticky with blood, just behind one ear. He had probably hit it on a stone in the road, for surely those heavy metaled hooves were capable of stoving in any brainpain.

"Jesus Christ!" he said, startling her. The previously empty face, devoid of the life and laughter and character that made it so attractive, was suddenly screwed up with pain. "Jesus—what happened?"

All around her, Silence heard the indrawn breaths and tut-tuts of the godly, unaccustomed to hearing the name of the Lord taken in vain. She said severely, "There is no call for such profanity, Captain. You have had a knock on the head, but I don't think it is very serious. Lie still for a moment, and try not to talk. Do you feel sick, or dizzy?"

"How can I tell you if I'm not supposed to talk?" Nick inquired dryly.

Silence found herself shivering with relief. To disguise the sudden up-rush of emotion, she said tartly, "Yes, or no?"

"Yes to sick, no to dizzy. Ridgeley saw Rachael, did you know that? He's gone after her."

"Then I pray God he doesn't catch her," Silence said. She looked up at the ring of sympathetic, interested faces and scrambled urgently to her feet. "You all know my stepdaughter, Mistress Rachael St. Barbe. That brute mustn't catch her. Please, can you do what you can to stop him? Don't put yourselves in danger, please—but don't tell him where she's gone, if you see her—he'll half kill her if he finds her!"

There were shocked, appalled murmurs, and a woman said earnestly, "The shame of it, m'lady—a little maid like that!"

"I d'reckon as how we be in mortal danger from that man just by *living*," an old man said dryly. "I'll do as I think fit, m'lady, and I'll warrant I speak for all on us when I d'say, us'll do as much as is needful to stop that limb of Satan a-ramping all over God-fearing folk. And if that d'put we at risk of our lives, m'lady, well, I be more than willing to do en."

There were mutters of assent from both men and women. Silence stared at the brown, honest faces of people whom she knew, whom she felt had never really accepted her, to whom she had thought she would always be the foreign lady from London. Tears of gratitude and emotion filled her eyes. Overwhelmed, she said quietly, "I don't know why—I haven't earned the right to such feelings—but please, don't do anything that will bring down his wrath on innocents. He's totally unpredictable, dangerous—he's capable of firing the village if he thinks it will gain him anything."

"Why be he after Mistress Rachael, anyhow?" someone inquired, and the old man, whose name she remembered was Emmanuel Atkins, snorted scornfully.

"Bain't ee heard? Brave little wench shot en with his own pistol. Trouble were, she diden do more than wound him. Now he d'want to lay his wicked hands on her—but us 'on't let him do that, now will us?"

There was a heartfelt bellow of agreement. Silence foresaw the situation rapidly escalating out of any control. She said quickly, "Please, oh, please, be careful—be careful—I couldn't forgive myself if anyone was hurt, or killed."

"If it happen, it happen," Atkins said. "Us'll be tarblish careful, m'lady—but I'll tell ee this, us be many—and for all their guns and sharp steelen swords, they be despeard few."

"Hold your tongue, you blathering old gatfer," another said, poking him in the ribs. "There be one on 'em a-laying down there and listening to all ee have to say for certain."

"Since Ridgeley's just done his best to ride me down, I don't think you have any reason to fear me," Nick commented. He lifted his head cautiously and then sat up with care. "I hope she's got safe away—I may have given her enough start, I don't know—"

"There she be!" someone yelled, a little farther down the street. Silence whipped around in time to see the disheveled figure of her stepdaughter run out to the fair close, straight into the path of a soldier. The man gave a howl of triumph and urged his reluctant horse forward, but Rachael had seen him. She turned, and with a flash of sea-green skirt and white petticoats, sprinted back into the enclosure. More troopers came thundering back up West Street, scattering people right and left, and trotted over to the close.

"Oh, sweet Lord, let her get away," Silence said, her hands to her mouth. There appeared to be a vigorous argument going on between the troopers and the tollman: Shouts and abuse rose from the gate.

Then suddenly she saw Nat and Tabby running toward her, hand in hand, breathless. She had not thought her stepson capable of moving so fast, but these last months his body seemed to be sloughing off childhood and catching up with his mind. He shouted, as soon as he was near enough, "Ridgeley's after Rachael! Where is she?"

"She went into fair close," Silence told him. "Where's Ridgeley?"

"Trampling all over the churchyard, cursing," said Nat. "He'll be coming this way any moment—quick, we must block his path!"

"How?" Silence cried, with a vision of all the people of Norton making a human wall, which the colonel's horse was capable of demolishing quite ruthlessly.

Nat gave a crow of laughter. "You'll see. Come on, Will, Tom, you can help—quick, before he comes! And everyone else, get out of the way—go on, now!"

They stared at the child who was now, astonishingly, the heir to Wintercombe, as he gathered his friends and ran up the street to where the animals were tethered. With realization dawning, Silence watched as the boys brushed aside protest and untied the first animal tied to the close wall. It was a skittish red heifer. She lowed enthusiastically and plunged into the road. Tabby, with a yelp of glee, evaded her mother's hands and hurtled up to join them. Then more and more, mostly young people, ran to let the animals loose.

"Get back!" Atkins roared at those foolish enough to be still blocking the road. Swiftly Silence knelt down by Nick. "You must get up, Captain, or crawl, or something, or you'll be trampled."

"I'm all right," Nick said, and proved it by struggling unaided to his feet. He stood swaying for a few seconds, his face gray-white under the light-brown tan. Then, with the support of one of the village men, he stumbled the few paces to the garden at the side of the road.

He was only just in time. As he leaned gasping against the dry stone wall, the rest of the troopers, headed by Colonel Ridgeley, came trotting briskly up West Street, to trickle to a disbelieving halt at the sight of what lay in front of them.

Even at this apology for a fair, there had been at least two score of beasts for sale, mostly cattle, with a few horses and sheep in addition. Nat, with the aid of Will Tovie, Tom Flower, and Tabby, had freed at least half of them, and other willing adult hands had done the rest. The animals had been tied up all day and were restless and frisky. With much bleating, lowing, and neighing, they milled aimlessly about West Street, constrained by the walls on each side and by a mass of enthusiastic villagers, directed by Nat, at the top end. There was only one way for them to go; and to the accompaniment of shouts and whistles, the mass of hoof and hide began to move, heaving with skittish freedom, down toward Ridgeley.

Emmanuel Atkins, safely in the Horsingtons' front garden, was shouting in his cracked old voice, delight spilling over. Silence, glancing at Nick, saw his grin turn to open laughter. After a second, weak with wild relief, she joined him.

"Let me see, let me *see,* Mama!" William cried. He had somehow struggled free of Ned's grip and was plucking at her skirts. Still laughing, she whisked him up into her arms and stood him on the top of the low wall, holding tight to his hanging strings.

Directly in front of them lay the width of West Street, empty save for the usual debris of dung, hay, rubbish. To the left, up the hill, was that impenetrable sea of beasts, being driven slowly forward. To her right, Ridgeley sat at the head of perhaps a dozen troopers, utterly thunderstruck, their horses already uneasy and restless at this monstrous advancing four-footed regiment.

The animals were rapidly escaping control. A heifer broke away and tried to struggle over the wall. Amid cheers, whistles, catcalls, prods, and the crack of a whip, the rest broke into a trot, then a lumbering run. Silence pulled William into her arms and retreated to the back of the garden, by the house, as the beasts poured past. Few other people were as cautious, eager to see the most of this novel diversion.

No horse could have withstood such a tide. Moreover, with horned cattle in the front rank, they stood in some danger of being gored. Even before Ridgeley had given the order, his troopers' collective nerve broke. They wrenched their horses around and stampeded back down West Street in a panic-stricken rabble, followed by the derisive cheers of the people of Philip's Norton, and upward of two score assorted cattle, horses, and sheep.

Rachael, unaware of the efforts being made on her behalf, crept cautiously up an alley to spy out the ground, and found South Street quite empty. She dashed across it, thanking God for her good fortune, and spent an hour or so weaving through the gardens and fields on the eastern edge of the village. She saw no one save an old woman weeding her vegetable plot, and no sign or sound of any soldiers.

As the sun was beginning to sink behind the handsome ash trees that bordered Wick Farm, Rachael limped up the path that led to the barton. She was hungry, exhausted, bruised, grazed, her favorite sea-green gown was a disgraceful wreck, and an aroma of old dung hung about her like a cloud, but she was safe.

Smoke wreathed up from the chimneys, and the watchdog barked and leapt to the end of his rope, tail wagging as he recognized her. Rachael, too weary to speak to him as she usually did, plodded past, wondering apprehensively what had happened after her escape.

The door opened, and Mistress Baylie, short, rotund, uncomfortable, stood there. "Well, so you're back, are you?" she said. "Don't suppose you know the trouble you've caused."

Rachael could only stare at her helplessly. Suddenly Christian Baylie held the door wide. "I'm main glad to see you, Rachael," she said, smiling. "Come in and sit down—you look as though you could do with a good meal and a long rest, after your adventure. Oh, child, there's no need for that—you're safe now, he doesn't know you're here."

For Rachael, overcome with shame and exhaustion and guilt, was standing in the barton with tears pouring down her face. She was safe, yes, for the moment—but what had her willfulness and folly cost her stepmother, and all at Wintercombe?

NINETEEN

All dark and comfortless.
—KING LEAR

Silence walked into the center of the hall, still in her riding dress, her gauntlets clasped fiercely in her hands. Above, the westering sun cast a sliding sliver of ruddy light across the topmost corner of the wall. Then Ridgeley moved forward to face her.

The faint glow disappeared, and the hall seemed all at once colder, darker, the shadows crowding threateningly upon her. Nat and Mally stood on either side of her. The younger children, including Deb, whom Mally had finally run to earth in the smith's shop in North Street, watching a horse being shod, had been sent straight upstairs to rest after the excitement of the day.

After the rout of the soldiers by, as Nat put it, all the four-footed beasts of the earth, it had seemed expedient to return to Wintercombe as soon as possible. However, it had taken some time in the confusion to find Mally and Deb, to reassure those villagers less stout of heart than Emmanuel Atkins, and to extract Nat and Tabby from the crowd of exultant young people, made jubilant and reckless by the overwhelming success of their stratagem. She had asked and asked, but no one, after that brief glimpse of her disappearing into fair close, had seen Rachael. She could only hope and pray that her stepdaughter had shown some of the sense previously conspicuous by its absence and made her way back to Wick Farm, using a roundabout and secret route. There was no way of knowing. But she hoped that Mistress Baylie would send her a discreet message when she had news.

Nick had insisted on remaining in Norton. She did not know what he was about, but sensed that he had a plan in mind. He had been steadier on his feet when she left him, and the gray look had gone from his face, but he moved and breathed as if it hurt, and she guessed that his ribs were badly bruised at the least. But she could not persuade him without seeming to make a fuss and so, unhappily, rode back to Wintercombe with only her overexcited children, and a dryly cheerful Mally, for company.

Amid their chatter, and Tabby's sweet exuberant song rivaling the birds, she had no time, or wish, to think about what the events of this day portended. What would Ridgeley, temporarily cheated of his prey, do now? And what would happen to Nick, who had defied him in front of two hundred villagers and fairgoers?

With a quailing heart, she saw Ridgeley's glowering expression waiting for her in the hall, and was glad she had sent the little ones straight upstairs to Doraty. She faced him with a look of polite inquiry that completely masked the turmoil of fear within. "Yes, Lieutenant-Colonel? What may I do for you?"

"You lied to me, madam," he said, through shut teeth. "You lied to me—you said that little bitch of yours had been sent away—and she's here, in the village."

Silence could think of nothing to say that would not inflame his temper still further. She made herself keep calm with an enormous effort and said mildly, "I am sorry if I misled you, Colonel."

"Misled! Mis*led*! You told me an outright lie, madam, and I'll see you pay for it! Where is she? Where is the little slut, eh?" He took three steps forward to tower over her, huge, menacing, black-avised and foul.

She saw the haggard lines around his mouth, the unhealthy pouches under his eyes, and the sheen of sweat over his face, and resisted the temptation to order him back to bed, since he was plainly not well enough to be thus exerting himself so soon after his illness. She said quietly, "I am sorry, Colonel, but I will not tell you."

"Sorry? Yes, my fine lady, you'll certainly be sorry!" His eyes glared hotly into hers. For a moment she thought he was going to strike her, and braced herself. But instead he shouted over his shoulder, "Baker! Phelps! Here!"

Silence, Mally, and Nat watched dubiously as the troopers emerged briskly from the screens passage. They marched up to the colonel, still booted and spurred, their hands on their swords, and stood beside him, waiting.

"Since you're so intransigent, madam, you give me no choice," Ridgeley said savagely. "I'll make you and your feeble offspring prisoners in your own house until you relent—and I don't doubt a few days' confinement in your chamber on a scanty diet will do wonders for your cooperation. May I remind you, madam, that attempted murder is punishable by death, and that evil brat deserves everything I will give her, and more." And he laughed sneeringly.

Silence stared at him in helpless, furious disbelief. "You *can't*!" she cried desperately. "You *cannot* do this—it's inhuman, uncivilized!"

"I can, madam, and believe me, I will."

"But the children—punish me if you wish, if it will give you any satisfaction, but for pity's sake do not lock up my children—they are innocent!"

"Perhaps—but their presence will, I hope, incline you to be more acquiescent. Besides, innocent they may look, but they are still traitors' brats, and such a nest of young vipers is best kept confined—or snuffed out altogether."

Suddenly terror overwhelmed her. She cried, "They're *children*. You monster, what are you suggesting? Rachael is only a child—do you threaten her with death? And the others? Before God, you will burn in hell forever if you harm them."

"Hot words from our mealy-mouthed Puritan, eh? It is up to you, madam, whether or not your children are harmed. Cooperate, and you and they will be released forthwith. And as for your vicious young murderess— a child, madam, is not old enough to kill. Your daughter is not a child. What is she? Fifteen? Quite old enough for what I have in mind for her." He laughed, and to Silence, rigid with horror, it seemed to be the most evil sound she had ever heard. "It's a long time since I had a virgin."

"You animal!" That was Mally, normally so unruffled and sensible. Beside her, Nat had gone quite white, the pallor of his face ghastly in the gathering gloom.

Silence gripped their hands, trying to calm and support them, although how she could offer any comfort in the face of such unspeakable, implacable wickedness, she could not see. She said desperately, "You brute—you couldn't—you wouldn't dare—she's not one of your village whores, she's gently bred, an innocent, she's fifteen years old. What are you, some kind of fiend, to talk of raping children?"

There was no flicker of response on his face. She added, fighting her tears, "And you must be six sorts of fool to think I'd tell you where she is when you threaten such appalling punishment."

"On the contrary, madam," Ridgeley said. His eyes glinted, and she realized with dread that he was enjoying her torment. "That is what will happen to her if you cooperate and tell me her whereabouts. I will give you a day or so to think about it, and if you do not see sense, I will take that village apart, stone by stone and stick by stick, until I find her. And then I will do to her what I have promised—with two additions. When I have finished with her, I shall pass her on to the men. And when *they* have finished with her, which may of course take some time, I shall kill her with my own hands."

Silence did not struggle as the troopers pushed her, Nat, and Mally up the stairs to her chamber, Ridgeley following behind with drawn sword. There was no point. And besides, she was still numbed with shock at the colonel's threats. She did not doubt that he would carry them out. It was the animal cruelty and brutality, the terrible punishment to be inflicted, that appalled her and filled her with horror. Surely he could not intend it? He was a man, a soldier of the king, not some naked Irish savage or wild beast from the darks of Africa. It was Goring's crew who raped and murdered for amusement, and even they would surely draw the line at attacking a young virgin of gentle birth in such a way. Certainly Sir Thomas Bridges, unsympathetic toward traitors' wives, would shrink from such a dreadful crime—would undoubtedly punish the perpetrator.

She said urgently, "You *cannot* do that to Rachael—it's utterly barbaric! If Sir Thomas Bridges comes to hear of what you've done—"

Ridgeley made an unpleasant noise. "And how will the Governor of Bath hear of it, eh? He has other fish to fry. Here I do as I please—and matters have been too lax for too long. Get in there!"

She drew the key from her waist and unlocked the door with shaking hands. Before she could open it, the trooper beside her had kicked it back.

Pye, in her basket by the fire with five ten-day-old kittens, leapt up, startled at the noise, and her offspring, their feeding disrupted, squeaked in dismay. A hand shoved at her back, and Silence was pushed forward into the room. Nat, similarly treated, all but fell over, and Mally, indignantly protesting, joined them. They turned and gazed at Ridgeley, who had followed them into the chamber, and stood looking about as if he had not seen it before. "Very comfortable, madam—very comfortable indeed. More than you deserve, I'd say—but I'll leave you here for now, as it's convenient to guard."

"And the other children?" said Silence. "Don't frighten them, I beg you—they are so young—"

"I shall do exactly as I please with them, madam. I'll dash their brains out against the wall if I desire it." He glanced past her shoulder, and his face lit with that peculiarly cruel smile. "How charming—a cat and her kittens before the fire. Five kittens, I see—as many as you have children. So many, she will not miss one or two."

Appalled, too horrified to move, Silence watched him stride across the chamber to the basket. Pye, her ears flattened, hissed as he bent and picked up one of the tiny, mewling kittens, pied black and white like its mother, by its stump of a tail. He studied it as it squeaked and struggled, and Pye, yowling distress, jumped out of the basket. Then, casually, he tossed it into the blazing fire.

"*No!*" Silence screamed, running forward too late. She hurled herself between Ridgeley and the basket, and was brought up short as his hand shot out to grasp her wrist. It squeezed tight, until her bones shifted. Almost weeping with the pain, she cried furiously, "Let go! Let me go!"

"All in good time, madam. Have you not learned your lesson? Five children you have. If you do not give me the information I require, you might well have one less by this time tomorrow. An infant smothers easily—and who's to say it did not die of a fever? Remember this, my lady St. Barbe—you, and all yours, are utterly in my power now, and I am no longer disposed to be benevolent. What is more, it has not escaped my notice that you seem to have access to considerable amounts of money. When my men have been paid with great irregularity, and recently not at all, this does not seem fair to me. Your household has contributed too little to our cause, madam, and I intend to alter the situation. The king's army in the West is desperate for coin and supplies—why should you traitors live off your ill-gotten gains while my men go hungry? I shall search the house tomorrow. In the meantime, you can think over all I have said. I am sure that even such a hardened rebel as yourself will see reason. Good day to you, madam."

He released her with a twisting movement that flung her to the floor, knocking her hip against the heavy oak chair. She lay there, dazed with pain and fear and horror, and watched him tramp heavily out of the chamber. The door was slammed behind him, and the key turned in the lock. They were prisoners.

Mally knelt beside her, tears pouring down her freckled cheeks. Silence stared at her in surprise, for she had never seen her maid weep before. She said, wondering why she could seem so calm, "Oh, Mally, it can't be so bad as that—he can't do what he threatened, he *can't*—he wouldn't be human."

"He bain't," Mally said, wiping her sleeve brusquely across her face. "Oh, m'lady, what will happen to us? And the children? And Dame Ursula?"

"Captain Hellier is in Norton," Nat said. He had something in his hands, and on his face, gray-white with shock, there was the beginning of a smile. "He'll do his best to save us, I know. And even Ridgeley isn't all-powerful. Look."

He opened his hands. On them, somewhat singed, but moving and mewing lustily and very much alive, was the kitten that the colonel had thrown into the fire.

"How on earth?" Silence said in wonder.

Nat's smile grew. "It landed on an unburned log at the side of the fire. Pye fetched it out while Ridgeley was threatening you, and he didn't notice. I think it's unharmed, save for a burn here and there—and yes, Pye, you can have it back now."

He replaced the kitten in the basket, and Silence, her eyes overflowing, stared at it as if a miracle had been vouchsafed, while her cat washed it with such vigor that it seemed to be in more danger from that than from the flames. She said slowly, "You're right—Nick is our only hope. Though what he can do to stop Ridgeley, I don't know."

"I doubt he will," Mally said grimly. "He be one as rides with the hare and hunts with the hounds, if you ask me. There be one of him, and five score of men what'll do Ridgeley's bidding, and I reckon as how he d'know what side his bread be buttered."

"I don't believe that," Silence said, astonished at the anger her maid's judgment had roused in her. "He's been a very good friend to us, Mally, and I wish you'd remember it."

"I d'mind as how he have wormed his way into your good nature," Mally said stubbornly. "And with what intent, I can guess. I'll believe he be a true friend to ee when I d'see some certain proof of it."

It was not worth arguing with her, and besides, Silence was afraid of disturbing too much the tumultuous emotions within her. Already she felt more for Nick Hellier than was wise in a married woman. No longer could she pretend to herself that friendship was all that he asked, nor that it was all that she herself wanted. The strength of her feelings, when she had briefly thought him dead, had taught her that, and terrified her. The abyss plunged down at her very feet, and the demons of hell beckoned temptingly.

Yet, in spite of what Mally had just averred, he had offered proof of his friendship, had put his life and his position in jeopardy for her sake more than once. She must trust him now, as a ship trusted to its anchor in a storm, because she could do no other.

There were sounds outside, the key turned in the lock and the door opened to admit Ridgeley and the two troopers, dragging with them the tearful, frightened figures of William, Deb, and Tabby.

As Silence scrambled to her feet, her arms open to embrace them, the colonel spoke. "They're unharmed, as you can see—for the moment. But remember what I have said, my dear lady. You have until tomorrow to think it over, and since hunger is supposed to sharpen the wits, I do not intend to let you sup tonight. There will be a guard on the door, and his orders are to let nothing and no one pass. Good night to you, Lady St. Barbe—and pleasant dreams."

At least they were together—that was one small comfort in the dark hopelessness that overwhelmed Silence as he banged the door behind him. But she must keep calm, for the children's sake. Deb and William wept in her arms because they were frightened, but on Tabby's white and tearless face there was the old, terrible fierceness that her mother found so disturbing.

William, soothed at last, realized that he was hungry, and said so, rather loudly. Mally came to the rescue. She produced a sticky brown wedge of gingerbread from the pocket of her apron, to cries of delight from Deb and William, and divided it with care into six, giving the biggest pieces to the smallest children. There was a pitcher of water and two cups on a side table, so at least they would not go thirsty. As Nat pointed out, it could be worse.

"It could indeed," Silence said. She would not talk about Rachael, and the terrible doom that might befall her. She could not mention it in front of the younger children, and besides, she must keep up her own spirits as well as theirs. So she let the little ones stroke the kittens, though she did not tell them what Ridgeley had done with Tabby's favorite, the one that looked like Pye. Apart from some slight charring to the fine white fur on its paws and belly, and a faint aroma of burnt hairs, it seemed none the worse for its appalling experience.

There was paper and ink and books, and Nat, still pale but as calm as his stepmother, sat down at one of the walnut tables to study with what Silence thought was very commendable calm. But the preservation of some semblance of normality, for the children's sake, was a terrible strain. Silence, her nerves and emotions already stretched almost to breaking point, had to answer a stream of urgent questions from Deb. Why were they locked in? When would they be let out? Why was Colonel Ridgeley angry? Was it because she had got lost at the fair?

Silence, not knowing whether to laugh or to cry at this evidence of Deb's bewilderment, smiled down at her daughter's round, anxious face and was able to reassure her on that score. She could not, however, offer any hope on what, to Deb's mind, was the most important question of all. When was supper? And why wouldn't Colonel Ridgeley let them have any? What were they being punished for?

Such queries were impossible to answer, and certainly not to Deb's satisfaction. She was still grumbling as the sun sank lower, and the door remained firmly shut and locked.

Mally, who had been watching over the courtyard from the northern oriel, reported that the forage troop had ridden in, bringing two cows and a great deal of plunder, but that there was still no sign of Captain Hellier. It was beginning to grow dark, and the youngest children were fretful and fractious, obviously exhausted by the excitements of the day but too hungry and upset to settle easily into sleep.

There was a truckle bed on wheels run under Silence's own. She and Mally hauled it out, and piled it high with blankets, for the night was plainly going to be clear and cold, perhaps even frosty, and the fire, starved of wood, was already ebbing. Then Deb and William, protesting, were divested of their outer garments and tucked neatly into bed, feet in the middle and a head at either end. Tabby, still ominously quiet, was allowed to study alongside Nat for a little while, but there were only a few candles, and the two gave up as it became obvious that there was insufficient light.

"I don't want to go to bed," Tabby whispered to her mother. "I want to see what's happening in the hall. I can hear something going on."

Silence had not noticed it before, but now she became aware of a low buzz of noise. She beckoned to Nat and Mally, and the four of them, very quietly so as not to disturb the sleeping children, crept into the maid's closet and crowded around the spy holes behind the king's mask.

Below, the hall was full of soldiers, setting up trestles, laying out platters and cups on the top table just below them, laughing and talking. Silence could see only Cornet Wickham, standing in the corner below the opposite queen's mask, supervising them. Surely Wickham would not stand tamely by if Rachael were attacked?

She could not rely on any of them, save Nick, to take the girl's part, she reminded herself, however sympathetic they appeared. They were the enemy, and to them she was a traitor's brat who had attempted to murder their colonel. They had all turned a blind eye while Ridgeley lay on his sickbed, but now he had recovered most of his strength and regained power, they were doubtless all as terrified of him as before.

Byam came into view, the dairymaid Bessie hanging onto his arm. She sported a string of cheap beads and ribbons in her russet hair; her lover had evidently been spending coin on fairings. Something about the way she stood, the even more generous swell of her breasts above the low-cut bodice of her gown, unconcealed by any scarf or collar, made Silence suddenly suspicious. She glanced significantly at Mally, and her maid jerked her head downward. "Be ee thinking what I be thinking, m'lady?"

"I expect so," Silence said. She added wryly, "And all I feel is mild annoyance—I can't pretend to ignore her behavior any longer, and where in Somerset can I find a dairymaid as good?"

Tabby was evidently puzzled, but Nat understood. He whispered, grinning, "Is Bessie going to have a little Byam bastard, then?"

"Nat!" Silence said reprovingly with a glance at Tabby.

Her daughter, still with that pale, vengeful look, said in a low, fervent voice, "It serves her right for going with that dreadful man. Why didn't she choose Captain Hellier? He's the only nice one of all the officers."

I am so glad she did not, said Silence's traitor heart. Appalled at herself, she resolved to spend an hour or so in prayer this evening. Prayer for Rachael, for their safe deliverance from this nightmare, and above all for her own salvation from the terrible wickedness into which she was so sorely tempted, and from which she stood in danger still . . .

She knew already that her pleas would not work. Even if she did manage to keep Nick Hellier at arm's length, it was too late, for somehow he had slipped into her soul and lodged there like a burr. She no longer possessed any loyalty, any affection for her husband. His letter about Sam's death had destroyed any vestige of wifely feeling, and whatever their marriage became after his eventual return, she knew that she would be no more than a puppet, mouthing platitudes she did not feel, performing duties she had no wish for. The autumn-colored man possessed her heart, for good or ill, and now, for her own sake and her children's, she must suppress that emotion, which threatened her whole world as surely as did Lieutenant-Colonel Ridgeley.

Confused, miserable with fear and grief, she stared blindly down at the bustling hall, until someone tugged gently at her sleeve, and Tabby's voice whispered, "Mama, can I see too?"

She drew back to allow her daughter to peer downward. From this restricted vantage point, only the far corner of the screens was visible and a triangular sliver of the hall. The queen's mask in the other closet gave the opposing view, of the fireplace and the screens nearest to the front door, but identically limited. She did not know if Ridgeley was aware of the squints' existence and that everything which happened in the hall could be heard, and partly seen, by anyone in her chamber—and in Dame Ursula's.

She wondered what he would do with her mother-in-law. Ignore her, most likely. She hoped that Ruth would be able to carry up her supper on a tray, as usual, and replenish her fire. She did not in the least like the old lady, but nor did she want to see her suffer. Despite her age and frailty, she was almost a match for Ridgeley, verbally at least, and Silence could admire her indomitable spirit.

"M'lady." Mally was speaking softly. Nat and Tabby were kneeling on the floor, engrossed by the comings and goings below.

Silence turned. "Yes, what is it?"

"Have ee disremembered, m'lady? We bain't prisoned here after all! We can get out of here, anywhen we d'want—through the roof."

She had indeed forgotten. In Mally's closet, behind the green hangings in the corner, a tiny twisting stair had been built into the thickness of the wall by a past St. Barbe, obviously enthusiastic about the defense of his house. It led into the roof space above the hall. She had never been up there, but Sam had told her once that with care you could walk from joist to joist the length of the hall and come down the corresponding stair that opened into Ruth's closet, just off Dame Ursula's chamber.

It was as if a huge weight had been lifted off her mind. They could escape—although what Dame Ursula might say to her daughter-in-law's and grandchildren's arrival suddenly in her chamber, apparently out of nowhere, would probably beggar description. Silence stood, thinking hard. If necessary, they could get out—though how they would manage to carry the smaller children across the roof, she did not know. Quickly, in her mind, she traced some possible routes from Dame Ursula's chamber. Presumably it had not been thought necessary to guard it—but its door stood directly opposite Ridgeley's. With luck, judging by the preparations below, there would be a big feast that night, which would render most of the officers and men drunk and insensible. If that were the case, then it might well be quite easy to get out of the house without being seen.

But then what? Carefully she made herself consider the likely consequences. Wintercombe would be left entirely at Ridgeley's mercy, and she already knew the kind of damage and destruction he could inflict. In revenge, he might well gut the house, or even fire it. The servants, and Dame Ursula, would take the brunt of his wrath. Quite possibly, given the unbridled malevolence of Ridgeley's nature, there might be murder done. Her conscience shrank from that thought. The house and all within it were her responsibility, left in her charge by Sir Samuel and by George. She had done her best to preserve it from despoliation, and so far had had some success. To escape now would ensure her children's safety, but it would surely also sign Wintercombe's death warrant.

And where would they go? To Wick Farm, which might no longer be a haven? Or perhaps to Farleigh Castle, to throw herself on the mercy of the Royalist garrison there and rely on the chivalry of Colonel John Hungerford to protect them. Or they could go to Bath, or even Bristol—farther off, safer from pursuit, but lacking any friendly face, anyone who might take in a sad little group of abused and threatened refugees. And behind them, Wintercombe would burn.

There remained one other possibility: to send away Nat, or Mally, or both, with the younger children. If she herself remained behind, a prisoner still, Ridgeley's rage would most likely fall only on her. He would still have a victim on whom to wreak his revenge, even if balked of the children. And perhaps, somehow, possibly with Nick's help, she could prevent any further damage to Wintercombe.

Short of shooting the man, she did not see how this could be done, but at least she would not be running away. She would send her children to safety, but stay to do what she could for the house and for the people who were her responsibility.

"Did ee hear what I said, m'lady?" Mally whispered urgently, and Silence, abruptly returned to reality, gave her a quick smile, and nodded.

"Yes, I did—I'm sorry, I was thinking. Mally, can you come with me for a moment? I want to talk to you—I have an idea."

The chamber was quiet, Pye and her kittens lying by the still-glowing fire, Deb and William slumbering with the utter abandonment of small children in their truckle bed. The little boy had fallen asleep on all fours, his head on the pillow and his round rump sticking up under the blankets. Silence stared at the dim, shrouded shapes of her son and daughter, and her breath caught in her throat. Tiresome, willful, stubborn Deb, William with his open, sunny, friendly nature, both so dear to her—and Tabby, showing disturbing signs of the harm done by the presence of the soldiers, always her favorite, her firstborn, the deep, quiet, sensitive dreamer, with the gift for music that it had taken a stranger's eye to perceive. And Nat, her support, her friend in a way that none of the other children were able to be.

Ridgeley had threatened them all. It could be just that, a threat, uttered to frighten her into submission, and it had certainly made her very afraid. But she knew Ridgeley, and she could not forget the dreadful cruelty, the casual gesture with which he had thrown that kitten into the fire. By a miracle, it had survived almost unscathed. But would her own children be so fortunate?

He had spoken, with unbelievable brutality, of smothering. She simply could not afford to take the risk, to call his bluff. The most terrifying quality of the man was that he seemed quite ready, indeed eager, to carry out even the most extreme of his threats. And with the lives of all her children at stake, she would not gamble on his forbearance.

"Yes, m'lady?" Mally said softly. And Silence, her heart suddenly thudding in fear at the danger in which they stood, bent her head and whispered her plan into her maid's ear.

"I don't like to leave ee," Mally said, when she had finished. "But I can see the sense on it. And that hang-gallized fiend, I don't doubt as how he'll do just as he said. If I can bring 'em to safety, m'lady, I'll be main glad of en."

"And so will I." Silence added slowly, "My fear is for them—not for myself, but for them. If I know they are safe, I will be happier, even if I face Ridgeley's wrath by sending them away. He can hurt me most by hurting them, and he knows it. If the children are gone, what can he do to me?"

"Burn the house down, most like," Mally said dryly. "But they bain't safe yet, m'lady. We have to get 'em across that there roof first—and 'twouldn't be very secret if Ridgeley was to look up and see a foot come through the ceiling, would en?"

Despite her fear, Silence had to swallow a snort of laughter at the vision that Mally's words conjured up. "No," she said. "No, it definitely would not. And then you have to take them through Dame Ursula's chamber without my lady thinking that she's about to be murdered in her bed—and *then* you have to smuggle them out of the house somehow, without anyone seeing, and take them—where? There's no chance of obtaining horses, you'll have to walk, and it'll be dark and cold . . . I shouldn't lay such a charge on you, Mally."

"Don't ee fret," the girl said. Her eyes were shining brightly in the dim dying light from the fire, and her voice was buoyant with hope. "I d'know Norton like 'twas the back of my hand—I were born here, after all, m'lady. Why not to Wick Farm? It'll take days for that there Ridgeley to search all on the village, and Wick be so far away it be almost to Farleigh. I'll explain all to Mistress Baylie, she won't be miffed. And then all the children will be together, and maybe I can get help for ee from the castle garrison."

Silence stared at her thoughtfully. Wick did indeed lie at the farthest corner of the parish, on the border with Farleigh, and reached by a lane that led off the main highway, from which it was screened by a fine belt of timber. It was difficult to find unless by one familiar with the village, and surely, to a stranger such as Ridgeley who had no local knowledge, so isolated that he might well be entirely ignorant of its existence. And at Wick they would be sheltered and protected. Very few people, if any, in the village knew that Rachael was there, and she was certain that none would give her or the other children away. The mood in Philip's Norton had not yet spilled over into violence and riot, but she remembered, with gratitude and a strengthened heart, the words of Emmanuel Atkins. They would not attack the soldiers—yet. But they were already prepared to show open defiance, at great risk to themselves and to their possessions.

And Wick was two miles away, inhabited by people she knew and respected. She had heard little of the garrison at Farleigh, and her mind shrank from sending Mally, accompanied by four children, one of whom at least would have to be carried, and another in poor health, on the difficult, tortuous tramp up hill and down dale to Bath, where for all most people cared they could probably sleep in the streets. A dreadful vision of her beloved children, and Nat, huddled together in some doorway or begging charity from the governor, or the mayor, rose up to haunt her. Decided, she nodded at Mally. "Yes, I know it's close, but for the moment I think Wick is safest. And it's very near to Farleigh—you can flee there, if danger threatens."

"They d'say that Colonel Hungerford at Farleigh be a good man, for a Cavalier," Mally told her. "He won't hand 'em over to Ridgeley, I be certain of that, m'lady—and once I've told en what that villain have said to ee, I d'reckon as how he'll come to help ee."

A small, pale figure slipped silently out of the closet and crept around the bed to join them, her hands wound tight together. "Mama," Tabby's voice hissed urgently. "Mama, come quick—Captain Hellier's come back!"

Silence's heart gave a deep, betraying lurch; her face and hands did not move at all. She whispered to Mally, "We'll talk more about it later—we can't do anything for some hours yet." And as her maid, still with that air of suppressed hope about her, nodded in agreement, she turned and walked casually back to the closet, Tabby clinging tightly to her hand.

Nat was peering down through the king's mask. As she came softly up behind him, he turned and moved aside to let her see. In the dim light from the one small candle burning on the stool by the bed, she saw that his pale face was unwontedly grim, but he did not say anything. Suddenly apprehensive, she applied her face to the eyeholes of the mask.

Ridgeley's voice suddenly bellowed out, so loud that she jumped and knocked her head against the stonework. "At last you condescend to visit

us, *Captain*. I am waiting eagerly to hear your explanation for your unauthorized absence. If any of the men do likewise, they are flogged. What
is your excuse?"

Nick Hellier moved into her view, to stand just below the high table.
To her watchful eyes, he looked absolutely normal, although her view of his
face was from this angle a somewhat restricted one. His tawny doublet and
breeches presented a slightly more dusty appearance than they had that
morning, but he showed no other signs, bar that black eye, of the battle
with Ridgeley and his horse, and no one could have guessed that he had
spent some time lying unconscious in the dust of West Street. She could
not see his expression clearly but could imagine it so vividly, the calm, the
glint of irony, and the sudden, reckless smile of defiance.

And so his answer, when it came, was still more of a shock to her. There
was nothing but serious apology in his voice. He said quietly, "I am sorry
for my unavoidable absence, sir. I can assure you, however, that it was
undertaken entirely in the cause of duty."

Within the boned, restricting confines of her bodice, Silence's heart began to pound, slowly, ominously, like the rhythm of a passing bell. Her
hands clenched together, she listened intently as Nick added, in response
to a snort of derision from Ridgeley, "I have been conducting my own
search for the St. Barbe girl."

"Oh? Really, Captain? And what has caused this sudden change of heart?
You were very keen, as I remember, to prevent me from laying my hands
on her earlier. That is also a crime punishable by flogging, if not worse.
Since you are a commissioned officer, and supposedly a gentleman, I shall
generously grant you the opportunity to persuade me not to reward you as
you deserve."

Silence did not know very much about the habits of Cavaliers, but she
was sure that to impugn a man's honor was an insult only redeemable in
the blood of a duel. She waited, in terror, for the returning insult, the
clash of swords, and heard only Nick's voice, mild, reasonable, friendly.
"That, sir, was a ruse designed to win the acceptance of the villagers. It
worked exceeding well, to the extent that I now know where Rachael St.
Barbe can be found."

I am not, I *cannot* be hearing this, Silence thought. A tide of nausea
threatened to choke her. She felt dizzy, and her throat was filled with bitter
bile. It is not true—it cannot be true—not Nick—before God, he was my
friend, I trusted him, we all did—

All save for Mally. Mally had seen the truth and warned her, and she,
pathetic gullible fool, prey to the first smooth-tongued man to flatter her,
had paid no heed.

Below, Ridgeley leaned forward, his black-furred fists planted on the
table, his face thrust forward, unawares echoing her thoughts. "I don't

believe you. You've been a thorn in my side for months, thick as thieves with that whining Puritan bitch—planning to bed her, were you? Well, all Roundheads were born to be cuckolds. I don't blame you for wanting to set the horns on her husband's head, even if she's too whey-faced and virtuous for my taste."

"Not so virtuous, I think," Nick said, and she could tell by his voice that he was smiling. Sick to her very soul, she leaned against the cold stone, feeling its clammy chill seep into her bones, filling her veins with a miasma of utter despair.

Ridgeley laughed. "Well, you can have the woman with pleasure—I've locked her in her chamber, along with her brats, until she tells me where the girl is. And now you say you know? How?"

"As I said, by gaining the acceptance of the village people. Fine words and flattery win hearts and minds, Colonel, as I discovered long ago. They still think of you as the devil incarnate, but they see me, poor fools, as a friend. And it was in conversation with them that I discovered where the girl fled this afternoon. I presume she is still there—unless she came here?"

"God's bones, man, I doubt even one of those hell-spawned brats is so stupid! No, I don't have her—yet, but all the others are under lock and key, and the house is mine. There's store of coin here somewhere, and I'll lay my hands on it if I have to take the place apart to find it. And as for the girl . . . where is she?"

There was a pause. Someone's hand, probably Nat's, crept across her shoulders, offering a comfort that could never be adequate. Then Nick laughed, a cold, unfeeling sound that reminded Silence suddenly of the day when she had first met him and had thought him a callous, brutal Cavalier like his master. She had come to believe that he was in fact very different, and now the scales were being stripped from her eyes: for he knew, if Ridgeley did not, the significance of the masks high up on the walls above him.

She listened, her heart quailing, for the final, irrevocable betrayal, and found that the reckoning had been deferred.

"Is that wise?" Nick asked. He glanced around the hall. For an instant, she had a glimpse of his face, knew that their eyes had met, as his gaze swept arrogantly across hers. "Many unsympathetic ears may be flapping. I'll tell you in private, later, and we can plan how best to deal with her."

"Ah," Ridgeley said, and sniggered lecherously. "That I have already decided."

She could not endure any more, to listen to that inhuman, monstrous man describe in prurient detail exactly what he would do to her fifteen-year-old, virgin, innocent stepdaughter. Her hands over her ears, she turned and stumbled away from the mask. Nat was there, steadying her, and Mally, all the brightness gone from her face, took her arm and led her from the closet, away from those dreadful voices.

But she could hear them still in her mind, even after Mally had shut the door on them, and in the gloom of her chamber there was no distraction from the pictures that leered in her mind to match the words. She saw Rachael's face, white, terrified, driven screaming into madness, and covered her eyes with her hands.

She must not break down. For the children's sake, she still had to keep calm and sensible, the rock on which they could all lean. Every one of her illusions cruelly shattered, she must yet preserve the appearance of normality and plan their escape.

"Be ee all right, m'lady?" Mally whispered anxiously.

With a greater effort of will than she had needed at any time past in her life, Silence took her hands away from her face, and drew a deep, shuddering breath. "Yes. Yes, Mally, I will be fine. Let me sit down, please."

The touch of her hands on the smooth oak of her favorite chair, the soft fur of Pye, who, sensing her distress, had left the kittens and leapt onto her lap, gave her strength. She lifted her tearless face to see Mally, Nat, and Tabby staring at her. Their own fear and horror was writ plain on their faces. Tabby's cheeks were tracked with thin, silvery tears. She said furiously, "I thought he was my *friend*! And he's worse than an enemy, he's a traitor!"

"Not to his own kind he bain't," Mally said. She pulled up a stool and sat down on it, heedless of etiquette, and the children knelt on the floor beside her. "He ain't never been your friend, Mistress Tabby, and don't ee forget it. But your mother have a plan for all of ee, and she'll tell ee about en."

Very quietly, still mindful of the slumbering Deb and William in the truckle bed, Silence gave Tabby and Nat a brief description of their escape route. Outwardly she knew that she seemed quite calm, her hands still, her face unmoved, her voice level and reassuring. But behind the mask, her mind was a turmoil of grief and agony at her betrayal. She had trusted in the decency and honor of another human being, and, worse, she had trusted her fledgling emotions. She saw, with humiliating clarity, how by wooing her, however gently and wittily it had been done, Nick had demonstrated that he was not to be trusted. If friendship and help had been all that he wished to give, his integrity would have been undoubted. But the subtle attempt at seduction proved otherwise.

Did he think me such easy prey? she thought miserably, with wonder at her own foolishness. I am only a conquest to brag about in taverns and tippling houses—the cuckolding of a rebel colonel, a real medal of honor for him to wear.

Now, amid the wreckage of her misplaced belief, she could not weep, or mourn, or berate her own stupidity. Instead, for the sake of those who depended on her, she must ruthlessly suppress her feelings and try to think rationally.

It was unbearable, when all her impulses were at the mercy of the emotions within her, their power undiminished by years of control, repression, and duty. But she must bear it; and she did.

Nat, his mind as keen as ever, said as soon as she had finished, "But, Mother, what will happen to you? We can't go without you."

"You can," said Silence. "And you will—I insist on it. You are in danger from Colonel Ridgeley, deadly danger. You heard what he said to me earlier—you know what he has threatened. He may only be bluffing, Nat, but I don't think he is. And I cannot take the risk with your lives."

"But then he'll—he'll punish you!" Tabby said.

Silence shook her head. "No. He will not dare. And I cannot run away and leave Wintercombe and all the household, and your grandmother, to the mercy of the Cavaliers. I *can't,* Tabby—you see that, don't you?"

Tabby's head moved up and down, reluctantly. Then she leapt up and flung her arms around her mother, holding her so tightly that she could hardly breathe. Her mass of hair tickled Silence's face, and her voice whispered passionately in her ear. "Please—let me stay too, let me stay, I don't want to go!"

"You must, chicken, you must!" Silence felt her eyes prickle with the tears she had held back too long. Once allowed to flow, she knew that she would never be able to stop. She would weep forever, for herself, her children, the house she loved, the people whom she was duty-bound to protect; and above all for someone who did not exist, who had attained reality only within her imagination.

"Don't worry, Tabby-cat," Nat said, his voice serious. "Mother can look after herself very well, you know. And she's right—we're the ones who have to escape. Think about Deb and William—they can't protect themselves, so we'll have to do it for them."

Tabby's hold relaxed, and Silence could breathe freely again. She said, "Don't be difficult, please—I want you safe, I don't want to have to worry about you any more. Please, Tabby, go with Mally and Nat."

She had won the battle. The child drew back, slowly. She was crying harder, quietly, the tears flooding her face, but her distraught eyes held acceptance. In the light from the few candles, Silence saw her take a deep shuddering breath. Then she said, very low, "Yes. I don't want to, but I'll go. When do we start?"

"Not until they're all so roaring drunk they wouldn't notice if we walked across the tables," Nat said, with a feeble attempt at a grin.

It was Mally who kept watch by the mask, her lips tight, listening to the progress of the supper below. Silence could not bring herself to do it, to listen to the noises of debauchery, to see Nick, whom she had once erroneously thought to be different, carousing drunkenly with the rest. Nor did she want to hear again the plans for Rachael's rape, and her own, discussed with greedy, brutal anticipation in public. She made Nat and Tabby lie down on her bed, covered with blankets, and bade them try to rest. They would need all their strength later. It seemed incredible, amid all this turmoil, that Deb and William still slept, but they did, utterly oblivious. She would not wake them until all was ready.

She went hesitantly to the other closet, candlestick in hand. The night was cold. Outside, the moon would ride full and high among the stars clear and cloudless. The children wore only their thinly woven spring clothes, and they would need something extra, to warm them.

She opened the door. The noise from the hall below hurled itself at her: drunken singing, the smash and clatter of furniture and pewter, yells and talk, the smell of spilled cider and beer and tobacco smoke. Unwillingly, as if pulled by an invisible rope, she moved closer to the listening mask, disguised by the queen's head, and peered down at the chaos below.

It was as well that she could see only a little, and that was quite enough. There were women there, all known and reviled in the village as whores of a discreet kind, and several of similar sort whom she did not recognize and who must hail from Wellow or even from Bath. In varying stages of drunkenness and undress, they dallied with the soldiers strewn about the benches. The floor was littered with food, plates, tankards, and other debris, and several comatose figures. Silence averted her gaze and found herself looking at the top table. There was Byam, Bessie lolling against him, a hunk of meat in her fingers. Foolish girl, she thought angrily, to allow her child to be fathered by such an unsavory young man.

Beside her was a girl whom Silence did not at first recognize, a girl very trim and neat in a blazing red dress, her dark hair coiling around her naked shoulders, being pawed by Ridgeley. With a shock of real surprise and disgust, she realized suddenly that it was Leah.

She had never liked the maid, but she had not thought her stupid. Leah had had aims to better herself, to rise above her humble origins. Why, now, play the whore and risk a bastard, risk her position at Wintercombe and exile from her family?

I suppose she thought that I would look on it as leniently as I looked on Bessie's indiscretions, Silence thought unhappily. Then a more unwelcome and more probable reason presented itself. Perhaps Leah had decided that her mistress's reign was ended—and she could therefore cease to be circumspect.

Leah was certainly not being circumspect now. Silence, watching her entwine herself around the colonel, wondered what enticements he had offered her. The gown, for a certainty; money, jewels, a privileged position as a gentleman's mistress had probably also swayed Leah from her nicely calculated path of virtue.

If ever we return to something like normality, my first act will be to send her packing, Silence vowed to herself. She wondered where the other servants were. From this narrow viewpoint she could not see them, but that was not to say they were not there. She could not, though, imagine Eliza, Doraty, and Hester taking part in such a debauch, and hoped that somehow, perhaps under the protection of Darby and the groom, Tom Goodenough, they were safe—for the moment.

Something, some impulse to further self-punishment, made her twist her neck to see more of the high table. Nick sat next to Leah. No female hand fondled him in the appallingly wanton manner in which Leah was toying with Ridgeley—and where did she learn *that*? Silence wondered, shocked despite herself—but even in the brief glimpse she allowed herself, he seemed to be drinking as heavily as the rest. I hope his conscience troubles him, she thought savagely—if, indeed, he has one.

Sickened, she turned away from the mask, retching, and stumbled over a stool. The pain in her skin reminded her of what she must do. There was no profit in crying over what could not be altered. She must learn from that experience, dreadful as it was, and accept her punishment. She had looked upon Nick Hellier with adulterous eyes, the gravest sin, and now her wickedness had reaped its just reward. This agony, not yet come to its flowering, this pain that was almost physical in its intensity was proper retribution for her crime, and she deserved no less.

She found the clothes press, raised the heavy lid, and searched through it. Old garments, outgrown or threadbare, lay at the bottom. She picked out what she wanted, moving calmly, while her mind, remote, watched her hands sorting ancient doublets and outmoded gowns as if they belonged to someone else. And ever afterward, to the last day of her life, the scent of damask roses and orris root, laid in bags to sweeten the clothes and keep away the moth, had the power to induce bitter feelings of nausea and despair.

Burdened, she shut the lid, picked up the candle and left the closet, closing the door behind her with a swift kick. If only the agony in her soul could be so easily shut out.

The waiting was the worst. She had nothing to do but think, and she dared not let her mind dwell on the hall below. She tried to read her Bible, but the light was too dim. In the end, she sat on the floor by the dead fire, stroking Pye, her eyes open on darkness, while the children slumbered and Mally watched from the other mask.

She had not realized how exhausted she was until Mally woke her, gently shaking her shoulder, and she found that she had gone to sleep with her head resting on the seat of her chair, cushioned in her arms. Stiff, weary, unrefreshed, she stared in bewilderment at her maid's face, evilly lit by the candle she held. All the others in the chamber had gone out. "I reckon as how 'tis safe to be gone," Mally said. "They villains all be snoring drunk down there, and that Ridgeley have gone to his bed—and *he'll* be too busy to hear ought less than a thunderclap in his chamber, by my way of thinking. Shall I wake the little ones, m'lady?"

Tabby and Nat were easy to rouse. The excitement of their impending escape was still with them, lightening their sleep, and they struggled out of bed quickly and quietly, their hair and clothes rumpled and their eyes brilliant with anticipation. But waking William and Deb proved almost impossible. It seemed, after several failed attempts, that they would have to resort to violence. But at last Deb, yawning and bewildered, stood in her smock by the truckle bed, rubbing her eyes and staring at her mother and sister and half-brother. Silence knelt by her side, slipping the hyacinth-blue gown over her head, lacing it up the back with sleep-fumbled fingers, all the time explaining, slowly and clearly, what was happening and hopefully instilling in her younger daughter the necessity of absolute quiet and instant obedience.

The strangeness of it all made an impression on Deb as no mere words could have done. Her eyes vast, she nodded earnestly. With luck, she would give no trouble. Nor would William. He remained obstinately asleep, his round face angelically fair, his hair curling over his soft cheeks.

"'Tain't no good, m'lady," Mally hissed, when cold water had failed to have any effect whatsoever. "I'll have to carry en."

They stared at each other doubtfully. Silence had no idea of what the roof space looked like, whether it would be possible to carry a heavy, sleeping three-year-old across it quietly and safely. And there was only one way to find out. "I'll carry him, as far as Dame Ursula's chamber," she said.

They were all ready. She hugged Nat, and Tabby, and Deb in turn, took the comatose William in her arms, feeling the inert weight, smelling the sweet peaceful aroma of a young child. Dear Lord, she prayed with a fervor she had never felt before. Please keep my children safe. Do not punish me through them.

The stone stair was tiny, cramped, winding narrowly up in the thickness of the wall. Nat went first, a candle stub in his hand, his small size for once an advantage. Tabby followed, her skirts held well up above her ankles, a cloak bundled under one arm. Then Mally, with the best of the candles, several inches high, grasped in one hand and Deb's small paw in the other. Silence, William's head on her shoulder and his weight on her arms, brought up the rear. She had decided to help the children across the roof and through Dame Ursula's chamber, for the old woman would probably be woken by their unexpected entry. She might listen to Silence's explanations, whereas Mally would undoubtedly be brushed contemptuously aside.

There was no door at the top of the stairs, only a hole onto a vast expanse of darkness beyond the pale confines of the candlelight. The rafters were quite close together, and there was plenty of headroom below the sharply pointed roof. Amid the dust and debris, birds' nests and ancient eggs and pieces of tile and plaster, someone had laid narrow planks across to make a walkway.

Swiftly and silently, Nat set out across them, candle in hand, and Tabby close behind him, her small face crumpled with the intensity of her concentration. Mally and Deb followed much more slowly, a step at a time, the little girl wobbling uneasily on the uneven planks. And Silence, still burdened with William, shuffled in their wake. Below, men snored drunkenly in the hall that would be forever sullied with their presence. Somewhere, Bessie and Byam, Leah and Ridgeley, writhed together in fornication, as did all those other whores. And up in the rafters, unseen and unsuspected, their victims made their escape.

The hall was forty feet from one end to the other, but to Silence's taut, scraped nerves it seemed nearer to a mile. Nat and Tabby, moving as lightly and surely as cats, had reached the other end before she was halfway, and she saw them turn and smile triumphantly back from the top of the other stair. Hoping that they would have the sense to wait, she concentrated on following Mally, afraid of missing her footing. The planks were perhaps twice as wide as her hand, and her maid's remark about a foot appearing through the ceiling seemed only too credible.

At last, they were there, stone beneath her feet, and below, the dubious mercies of Dame Ursula. She indicated to Mally and the children that she should go first, and squeezed past them. With no hands free to steady herself, her descent of the narrow steep stairs was perilous in the extreme, and she moved very cautiously, Nat's candle lighting her from above and behind, feeling her way with her feet. At last a small stout oaken door appeared in front of her. Praying that it would not be locked, she shifted her son's dead weight from both hands to one and tried the latch.

It opened, slowly, stiffly, with a creak like the mouth of a tomb yawning. There were hangings beyond it, obstructing the door's progress. She fumbled her way through them and emerged breathless and apprehensive into the closet where the unprepossessing Ruth had her bed.

Nat, following on her heels, cast a much-needed light. The maid was soundly asleep, her head buried under a bolster. It would be so much easier if she were not woken. Silence put her finger to her lips as the rest pushed past the hangings, making rustling noises that seemed appallingly loud in the night's stillness. But Ruth did not stir, her sense blotted out by sleep and by the thickness of the feathers in the bolster. They tiptoed past her to the door that led into Dame Ursula's chamber. It was ajar, probably so that the maid could hear if her mistress called her in the night. Nat slid through it like an eel, and Silence followed with the others close behind her.

Dame Ursula's bed curtains, of a deep-blue damask, were tightly drawn. The room smelt frowsty, of old age and sickness. In the uncertain light from the two guttering candles, it looked quite different, a sinister dim place with huge black shadows slabbed across the walls and ceiling. The old woman's chair stood by the listening mask, and her stick leaned on the close stool next to the bed. Mally glanced around and nodded significantly at the children, her finger to her lips. It began to seem possible that Dame Ursula need not be woken either.

In single file, moving silently over the rush matting covering the floor, they crept to the farther door. Here, if anywhere, lay their greatest risk of discovery. There might be a guard outside, or someone watching from Ridgeley's chambers opposite. And there was no way of knowing without opening the door.

It was bolted, top and bottom. Evidently Dame Ursula had feared invasion. Only Silence was tall enough to reach the top bolt, and to do it, she must relinquish William. Still he slept, but increasingly restlessly. Once or twice, on their journey through the roof space, he had muttered something, and he was beginning to move within her grasp. Very carefully, for now of all times they must not risk him crying out, she transferred him to Mally's arms. He shifted and whimpered softly as she let him go, and her heart turned over in love and fear. But he settled against the maid's scantier breast with a sigh, and was quiet.

Very gently, her arm aching with the strain, Silence reached up to the top bolt and drew it back. It had been greased, and moved smoothly and soundlessly; so did the lower. Finally she lifted the latch with a click that sounded terrifyingly loud in the room. She froze, waiting for the inevitable sharp cry of anger and suspicion from the bed, but it did not come.

Her mouth was dry, she could not swallow, and the frantic thundering of her heart seemed ready to smother her. Now or never, Silence thought, and with infinite caution pulled back the door just enough to let her peer around it.

The corridor outside was empty, she saw at once. Nothing showed under Ridgeley's door, and the quiet seemed absolute. The way was clear. All they had to do now was to flee.

Very quickly she hugged them all, Nat, Tabby, small wide-eyed Deb, so unexpectedly quiet and obedient when it really mattered, Mally and William together. They would tiptoe down the stone stairs and slip out through the door to the garden. Then they would have to negotiate the steps and the knots and the gravel, under the clear blue-white glare of the moon, and somehow find their way through the orchard and across the stream without attracting the attention of any soldier who might be on guard. She and Mally had thought it the safest, if not the most direct route. It all depended on whether Colonel Ridgeley had thought to place anyone along the unfinished ramparts and ditches that separated the orchard from the field beyond. She hoped that confidence had made him careless, but it could not be relied upon. From now on, Mally's resourcefulness and courage, the children's silence and endurance, were all that kept them from capture. And she, Silence, was giving up these, her most precious hostages, to the whim of a capricious Fortune—or to the mercy of a God who might, or might not, choose a truly terrible way of punishing the sins of their mother.

They would slip through the village to Wick Farm, warn Rachael that her hiding place was discovered, and go with her to Farleigh. It was not a plan with which she was happy, but Nick's betrayal left them no choice. Before Ridgeley arrived on Christian Baylie's doorstep in the morning, they must all be gone, to the unknown mercies of Colonel Hungerford at the castle.

She could do no more. She must say good-bye, not farewell, and wish them Godspeed, and pray for their safety. She had the candle stub. She shielded it in her hand as they slunk through the door, and then shut it behind them as carefully as she could. Once more the latch clicked, but less loudly than before. She pushed the bolts home and turned to creep back the way they had come with such fear and hope.

Still neither Dame Ursula nor her maid stirred. Silence, still shielding the light with her hand, went into Ruth's closet and slid behind the heavy blue hangings, careful not to let the candle brush the material. It was not easy to pull the door open against the weight of the damask, but she managed to push her body through the narrow gap, catching the bodice of her gown on the latch. She heard the rip, but was past caring about such trifles. All that mattered now was the journey back across the roof, dangerous and utterly lonely, back to captivity and the terrible retribution that would surely befall her tomorrow. She had lied to Nat and Tabby. She knew that Ridgeley would not spare her when he found that the children had escaped. But nothing he could do, no pain he could inflict, would have the power to touch her, if only she could be certain that her children were safe.

She came to the top of the stairs, and the great dim void opened up before her. The planks seemed unbelievably narrow. Had they really crossed them safely, even Deb? She hesitated at the brink, terror suddenly, abruptly rising to paralyze her. This was ridiculous. She had done it once, she could do it again. But her body, brought to the limit of endurance, refused to obey the frantic commands of her mind. Her hands shook, her head swam. And then the candle slid from her loosening fingers, and went out.

It was curious, she had time to think, how such an unutterable disaster had the power to restore her strength and clear her mind. She stood quite still in the impenetrable darkness, ordering her thoughts. No hope of finding the scant stub, and no means to light it even if she did. So she must manage without, or molder there forever, trapped by her own fear.

She made herself recall the direction of the planks, closing her eyes and visualizing exactly how they had been placed: almost straight across to the other side, but irregular in length and side by side on the rafter where one ended and the next began. It would be madness to walk across such an uncertain route in utter darkness. She would have to crawl.

She crouched down and touched the rim of the stone. So this was how it felt to be blind: the confusion, the bewilderment, hovering on the knife's edge of complete panic. She fought it back and ran her fingers along the stone. There was the plank, rough wood jabbing into her fingers. She prayed silently, desperately for success, and put her hands down onto the splintery surface.

It seemed like hours, endless, infinite, as if she had been damned forever to crawl like a dog through the blackness of night—or of hell. Splinters rammed painfully under her nails, and she ignored them, concentrating all her mind on the plank and her painstaking progress on hands and knees. Her petticoats and skirts hampered her, but she could not cast them off. She did not want to stand up. Keeping low, she knew instinctively, was the only certain way to avoid falling.

On, and on, and on. There was no noise from the rest of the house. Surely she would hear it, if the children and Mally had been discovered? But every moment of stillness increased their chances of escape, and no cries of anger, no sounds of pursuit or capture, arose through the plaster and rafters from the hall below.

Suddenly, painfully, her hands met rough stone. Hardly daring to breathe, she felt it with her fingers. It was, unmistakably, the step of the farther door. Suddenly weak with relief, she bowed her head onto its dusty coolness, unable to move. She had done it. She was safe—until tomorrow.

She could not lie there all night. Slowly, with care, she crawled up on to the step. The stairs were treacherous, twisting. It would be easy to stumble and fall. With sore, splinter-stuck hands, she gathered up her skirts in one hand, set the other against the curve of the wall, and began very slowly to descend, blotting out everything from her mind except the next movement, and the next. It would do no one any good if she broke her ankle, not to say her neck.

She almost bumped her head on the door. She sought for the latch and opened it. She had forgotten the hangings, and it immediately swung back into her face, banging her nose. With a muffled gasp of pain, her eyes watering, Silence clapped a hand to her face and struggled through the narrow gap to Mally's closet and, beyond it, the haven of her chamber.

Somehow, in the dark, she found the bed and crawled into it, pausing only to kick off her shoes. Suddenly the impact of the day's events struck her like a blow. She began to shake, uncontrollably, and tears flooded her face. She was alone, utterly alone, for the first time in her life. But even so, she rolled over and buried her face into the pillow to stifle her wild, desperate sobs.

Something landed lightly on the bed and walked purring toward her. She was not quite alone: Pye recognized her lady's distress, even if she did not understand it, and was offering her own small comfort. Grateful, Silence let her snuggle just under the bedclothes. She stroked the soft thick fur, thinking of Lily, who had been left behind in the kitchen while they went to the fair. She hoped the puppy was all right. She could not think that anything she loved was safe from Ridgeley's retribution.

Gradually her sobs lessened. Weeping would not solve anything, even if it released the pent-up grief and bitterness and terror that she had stored up all day. And Pye, enthusiastically purring, had still her own power to soothe, as if Silence were one of her kittens. Exhaustion took over, relaxing her sore limbs, cramped with tension and studded with bruises and splinters, and the quiet and dark and warmth at long last lulled her into sleep.

And despite her fears, the Night Mare did not visit her dreams.

TWENTY

His foul and most unnatural murder.
—HAMLET

The rattle of the key in the lock woke her. The room was still dim, the shutters and curtains drawn, but it was obviously full daylight outside. Every muscle in her body ached as she moved. She became aware of intense discomfort, bruises on her legs and soreness in her hands. The key rattled again, and there was the abrupt, savage sound of the door being slammed back upon its hinges.

Memory returned. She was lying in her bed, fully clothed. The children and Mally had escaped. And Nick, whom she had thought to be her friend, had betrayed her.

She sat up, and saw him. He was standing by Ridgeley, just inside the doorway, two leering troopers at their back. The colonel did not look well. There was a gray, unhealthy tinge to his face, and the pouches under his bloodshot eyes were prominent. He saw her, and smiled. It was not a pleasant sight.

A chill settled on her soul. This was the reckoning, and it must be paid. She wanted to hide, to crawl back into sleep, to pretend that these men were not standing there in her chamber, radiating menace. But she could not. Reality had come back to roost with a vengeance, and there was no escape. Her children were safe. She had chosen to stay, and she would not flinch from the bitter path that lay before her.

Her hair was tangled, her clothes crumpled, torn and filthy with dust, but she left the bed with careful dignity and stood before them, her head high and her feet bare. "Good morning, Colonel Ridgeley. What brings you here?"

He did not answer directly. He was looking around, at the dry ashes of the fire, the cat basket in the hearth, the empty truckle bed. His words spat venom. "You know what brings me. But this chamber seems singularly empty, madam. Where are your brats and your Judas-haired maid?"

There was no point in deferring the evil hour. She said, with a small, tight smile, "They are gone."

The silence was complete. She had not looked at Hellier since he had entered the chamber; she stared instead at Ridgeley, defiant.

His face became slowly suffused with crimson as his anger grew, and his next words came sprayed with spittle. "What? What do you say? They are gone?" And as Silence nodded, he turned to the troopers. "You! Search those closets, now!"

It took perhaps a minute, no longer, before the men reappeared, shaking their heads. Silence stood quite still, very upright, her hands clasped in front of her, her calm manner at odds not only with her tattered appearance but with the quaking, terrified woman behind the wide, impassive eyes. She said quietly, "They are gone. I took them over the roof last night. There is a stair in that closet which leads up to the roof space, and you can walk across the rafters to the other side, and down a staircase there. They are beyond your reach, Colonel."

"You little bitch!" Ridgeley took two paces forward and stopped, his mouth working with rage. "By God's bones, you'll live to regret this day—and so will your murderous daughter." He paused, savoring his news, and added with that evil, wolfish smile, "Did you put your trust in Captain Hellier, my lady? Well, you can learn now how grievously you were mistaken. The captain has discovered where your daughter is hid— and perhaps the other brats by now, eh? In a little while we'll be going there to seize her. So you may have the pleasure of knowing that your intransigence will lead to the greater of the two punishments I threatened." He paused menacingly. Silence thought of Rachael, her desperate, misplaced bravado, and the silent, obedient children, creeping to safety along the dim rafters above the hall. Surely by now they would have reached Wick Farm, warned Rachael that her hiding place was known, and fled to Farleigh.

That hope gave her courage. She made herself look Ridgeley in the face without flinching and said, because he would expect her to plead, "I beg you, Colonel—she is a *child,* you cannot be so inhuman—"

"She intended to kill me," Ridgeley said. "You are wasting your breath, woman. Her fate is sealed—and so is yours." He gestured to Hellier, standing by his side. "What are you waiting for, Captain? There she is— yours for the taking."

Silence could not move. Rigid with horror, she watched as the man who had only yesterday claimed to be her friend walked across the width of her chamber toward her. The two troopers were grinning lecherously, and Ridgeley's teeth showed in vulpine anticipation. Silence, forced at last to look at Hellier's face, saw there no trace of the amusing, supportive companion who had earned, if temporarily, the respect and affection of her children. She thought of Tabby, her musical gifts forever tainted, and could have wept for the loss of their illusions. For there was no compassion now in that neat, lean, clever face, nothing but threats in the narrow, intent gaze. She backed involuntarily, and almost fell over a stool beside the bed.

A surge of anger rushed through her, the longing to assuage her own hurt by inflicting physical damage on her betrayer, as once the five-year-old Silence had plunged at her stern, uncompromising father, small fists flying, when her best efforts had been scorned and derided. She had been beaten for that. One of the blows had burst the skin of her back and given her a scar she had still. Doubtless the penalty for this act of futile defiance would be far, far worse, but the rags of her pride would not let her give in without a fight. She picked up the stool.

Ridgeley laughed. "Oh, so the little Puritan wants to defend her virtue, does she? This should be entertaining."

Silence held the leg of the stool in her hand. Nick stopped, just out of reach, his smile as wolfish as his master's. "If I were you, my lady, I would put that down. I have no patience with time-wasting tricks."

She could retreat no further, she was pressed against the bed. His smile widened. "And all you do is put off the inevitable for a moment or two. You can go nowhere, my lady St. Barbe—why struggle?"

She saw his hand coming to grab the stool and swept it hard in the opposite direction, down upon his shoulder. Wood hit leather with a satisfying crack. The captain swore viciously and wrenched the stool from her grasp. It crashed onto the floor and broke. In an extremity of terror, Silence swung her hand at his face. It was no woman's dainty slap, but a tight-fisted blow she had learned from her brother Joseph, long ago. It connected with his cheekbone, and the impact sent a tingling jar all up her arm. Then, swearing still, words that she had never heard, he grabbed both her wrists and held them in a grip like iron. There was blood on his face, she saw with satisfaction. Intent only upon doing further damage, she tried desperately to twist free and, failing, bent her head and sank her teeth into his right hand.

She drew blood there too, but he did not let go. Instead he tightened his hold and flung her backward onto the bed. Ridgeley gave a raucous, juvenile cheer as Hellier flung himself on top of her, using his superior weight and strength to stifle all remaining resistance.

It worked. Hardly able to breathe, sobbing from fear and the pain in her wrists, there was no way left for her to retaliate, and struggling would, for the moment, only make things worse. Above her head, he spoke to the colonel. "How long? Ten minutes, perhaps? I prefer to rape in privacy, if you would allow me the opportunity."

Ridgeley's laugh tore at her ears. He loomed above her, his face leering down. "On one condition, Captain—that I take over, when we've found the girl. I'm looking forward to the deflowering, but this one's got more flesh on her. Ten minutes and we ride, Captain. Is that long enough?"

"Quite long enough," Nick said. He glanced down at Silence, and she closed her eyes against the intention writ plain on his face. "My thanks, Colonel."

Something landed on the bed beside her, and Ridgeley said cheerfully, "You'll need that, to lock her in again afterward. I'll leave these two men outside, make sure you're not disturbed—and that she doesn't try to murder you. Enjoy her, Captain—as I will, later."

Still she could scarcely breathe. Too frightened to open her eyes, she made herself as still as possible. Perhaps he would think she had fainted. Maybe she could still try to escape, up the stairs and across the roof space. Her mind quailed from the prospect. She was weary, unutterably weary, of struggling. How much easier it would be to give up and drown.

The door slammed. For a little while he did not move. He was half lying, half crouching on top of her, and his hands still grasped her wrists. She lay, waiting for her fate, wondering if she had the strength or the will for further resistance.

His grip loosened, his weight came off her. She opened her eyes and saw him kneeling astride her, his face very close. He was smiling. Slowly, deliberately he moved upright, freeing her wrists.

Before she had thought what to do, she jerked up, raking her hand down the unbloodied side of his face. It was all she had time for. Almost as quick, he had pinioned her flailing arms in his own and had flung her back upon the bed, using his body to pin her down.

It was no good; she could do no more. She closed her eyes, ready for the inevitable, brutal invasion.

It did not come. Her muscles, rigid with tension, began to ache furiously, and she could take only small, inadequate breaths. Her head was starting to swim. Then his voice spoke almost in her ear, scarcely above a whisper. "Silence. Listen to me. I am not going to rape you."

Her eyes flew open in disbelief. His face was almost touching hers. She could not focus on it so close, nor could she read his expression. She said, her voice small and thin, "Why not?"

"You almost sound as if you want it," he said, and in his voice was the dry amusement that had always, to her, been one of his most attractive qualities. "But somehow I don't think you do—and I swear to you, my dearest lady, that I will do nothing with you that you do not desire as much as I do. I repeat—I am not going to rape you—and if you promise not to struggle when I let go of you, I will attempt to explain."

It was beyond belief, beyond hope. Bewildered, she stared up at his blurred face, and found that part of the reason for her imperfect vision lay in the tears seeping from her eyes. Very gently he disengaged himself and sat up. The vicious, wolfish look had vanished from his eyes so completely that she might have imagined it, but his already battered appearance was not improved by the bloody bruise on one cheekbone and the scarlet raking track left by her nails on the other.

She said desperately, "Don't play with me—tell me the truth, not lies, don't torment me, don't give me hope when there isn't any—"

"I have never lied to you," he said, and his smile was more gentle than she had ever seen it, illuminating yet another unexpected facet of his character. "I freely admit I've lied to almost everyone else—and most of all to Ridgeley. He does not know you were listening last night, but I guessed you would be. I knew how much you would be hurt, but I could do nothing else—I had to convince him that I was on his side all along, and Rachael's whereabouts were the bait to the trap."

"But you've told him!" Silence said. "He'll find her—you know what he has threatened to do—things utterly unspeakable, the man's an inhuman monster—and you *told* him where she was?"

"Yes. But I told him wrong—unless Rachael has been concealed in a tenement behind the Fleur-de-Lys, which I somehow doubt."

"No, she isn't," Silence said. She stared up at him, wondering dazedly what this meant. "So—so you didn't betray her?"

"No." His smile became wider. "I will not tell you exactly what I have in mind, in case something goes wrong. Suffice it to say that I hope you will soon be free. But for the moment I must pretend still to be your enemy, and the rape must seem to have taken place. Can you scream convincingly?"

Silence did not answer him. She was grappling urgently with this astonishing volte-face, with the realization that the betrayal that had struck at her heart, had all the while been counterfeit. It was too much to hope for. After the horror and fear of the past hours, she could not adjust her mind to the idea that he was, and always had been, her friend. She said at last, "Is it the truth?"

"The truth? My dear Silence, it is undoubtedly the truth—I would swear it on your Bible, were I not tolerably certain that you would not believe me even then. Let me convince you another way. I encountered your children, and Mally, in the garden last night."

Silence became perfectly still, her heart thudding. Slowly the tears began to slither down the side of her face, to tickle her hairline. Nick leaned forward and with a deft touch of his fingers wiped them away. Her skin shivered beneath his hands, and she blushed. She said hesitantly, "You *met* them? In the garden? What were you doing there?"

"Returning to sobriety with a stroll in the cold night air. I knew I would need all my wits about me today, but it might have made Ridgeley suspicious if I had not drunk my fill at supper. Then I saw your little band of refugees slinking through the knots. Mally thought the worst, but I managed to persuade her otherwise. She has gone to Rachael's hiding place, and they'll stay there until it's safe for them to return. There should be no need to go on to Farleigh, unless my plan miscarries." He smiled suddenly. "And in case you think I am still lying, I will say that William was still sleeping soundly, and that Tabby did not want to put her cloak on, and that Nat thought it a miracle that his grandmother did not wake when they went through her chamber.''

It was true. He had met them and let them pass to safety, unchallenged. And that, she supposed, was the proof she needed. She did not ask what his plan was, but she hoped that it would succeed. Anything, to escape from the nightmare that had so nearly engulfed them all, and might yet do so. She wanted to weep, but had no wish to give him another excuse to touch her. She said, keeping her voice low, "I can scream now."

"Excellent. A few agonized shouts of 'No,' followed by loud screams, should convince those witless ruffians outside that I have had my wicked way with you. I shall cut off your screams with my hand, so don't bite me again."

Involuntarily, her eyes went to his thumb, which sported the unmistakable crimson marks of her teeth. "I'm sorry," she said shakily. "And about your face—I didn't know—"

"Don't worry—it adds authenticity. Besides, I am so covered in cuts and bruises that another half dozen make no odds. Can you do it now?"

She nodded and shut her eyes, trying to force her mind back through those moments of agony and terror when rape had seemed imminent. Her emotions, still raw and painful, responded wholeheartedly, and her fervent cries and screams filtered through the door to assail the ears of the men outside. They grinned at each other, each wishing himself in the captain's place, lucky devil—just what the prudish little Puritan deserved!

The sounds of naked terror rose to a crescendo and were abruptly cut off. Silence, staring at Nick above his hand clamped across her mouth, experienced a wild and incongruous urge to explode into laughter. When she could speak, she whispered, "Was that good enough?"

"Undoubtedly—my ears are still ringing. It's a pity you were not bred in Court circles, my lady—your acting abilities are first class."

"I wasn't exactly acting—I was remembering," Silence said. She sat up and shivered. "And the memory is still too fresh."

He was quite still, staring at her. The look on his face spoke of affection, admiration, even tenderness, and it frightened her almost as much as his pretense of brutality had done. Her skin hot, she turned her head away.

Remotely she heard his voice, low and soft. "Silence—I am sorry that I had to subject you to such agony. I knew that you would hear, knew that you would think yourself betrayed. I deliberately let you suffer, because it was the only way to convince Ridgeley that I had come back to his side."

"And you haven't?"

"I don't know what I can do to convince you," he said ruefully. "If my plan succeeds, I think even you will believe I am telling the truth. Certainly Mally does now." He leaned forward, set his hand to her face and turned it toward him. "Silence—look at me."

Unwillingly, she did. She saw his battered, abused skin, the smooth planes of the bones beneath, the peaked brows and narrow chestnut-brown eyes, the bristly evidence that he had not yet shaved this morning. It was a face not conventionally handsome, unlike Ridgeley's, but full of a life and light and recklessness that made it very attractive. Like a plant growing toward the sun, starved of warmth, she felt the pull, stronger than ever, drawing her into wickedness.

"Trust me," he said simply. "Just for today—trust me. And I swear that I will do all I can to make matters right. Is that enough for you?"

It was too much. She nodded, mute, feeling the tears begin in earnest. He added, very softly, "Weep all you want. It will do you good, and serve to convince the soldiers. I will leave you the key. As soon as I am gone, lock the door and don't come out until I return. I shall order the guards away and pretend to lock it myself. Bull is in charge of the garrison today, but he's a purblind fool who obeys orders like a sheep, and he will do nothing that Ridgeley has not explicitly told him to. Don't worry—it will be all right, I promise."

He took her face in his hands and kissed her, very gently, just above her brow, and the touch of his lips burned her skin like a brand. Then he left her, weeping still, and went to the door. She heard it open, and close, and laughter outside. Once more she was alone.

She waited a few minutes more, until she was sure that Nick and the soldiers had gone downstairs. Then she picked up the key to her chamber. With this in her hand like a talisman, she felt, suddenly, the truth of what he had said. For this was the proof: this, and the fact that he had not raped her; he had let her children go in safety; and he had misled Ridgeley as to Rachael's hiding place.

Cautiously she crept to the door and put the key in the lock. No sound of protest erupted from the other side, and the door remained shut. She turned it triumphantly. Unless they brought a battering ram, she was safe.

Below, in the courtyard, she could hear sounds of activity. She went over to the lovely oriel window that looked over the north front and peered around the curtain. Most of the troop were preparing to ride out. There was Ridgeley, resplendent in his plumed hat, and Nick, distinguished by that brilliant scarlet cloak. The sun shone as it had yesterday, a glorious spring morning. And she remembered with a shock that it was Mayday.

The troop clattered out under the gatehouse, leaving Wintercombe temporarily at peace. Slowly, reluctantly, Silence went back to the bed and sat down on the place where, only moments before, she had lain in terror, expecting rape. It was hard to believe that Nick was, after all her agony, her friend. But she wanted to trust him, and the evidence he had given her was nothing if not convincing.

And yet she hardly dared to hope that at last, after all their suffering, they would be free, and safe. The last few months had taught her not to take anything at its surface value. She had no idea of what Nick's plan might be, or whether it would work. All she could do was trust him, as he had asked, and wait.

Lieutenant-Colonel John Ridgeley, lately of Sir Thomas Bridges' Foot, at present commanding the single troop of Sir Thomas Bridges' Horse and the garrison at Wintercombe, rode up North Street at the head of a score or so of his men. Despite the early sunshine, slanting between the houses on his left, he was feeling the cold, and glad of the thickness of his buff jerkin. There was no doubt, he had not yet recovered from the wound dealt him by that infernal girl. But very soon now she would pay the reckoning. He smiled with anticipation. He would be avenged for the two months spent lying in his bed, for the pain, the fever, the fear that he would die, the indignities of sickness, the suspicion that the remedies administered so assiduously were actually prolonging his incapacity. In a few minutes he would see that whey-faced wench, her stark blue eyes and black hair and, incongruously, the budded breasts beneath the plain garments proving that she was not the child her mother claimed. He would savor her terror, her agony, he would enjoy her virgin body, and watch as his men took their turn. And if by the end she was not dead of pain and fright, he would strangle the life from her with his bare hands.

It was no outrage. Goring and his men had done similar things, many times. Sir Francis Dodington was notorious for rape and murder, all through the West Country. These rebels, these traitors, needed to be taught a lesson, and fine words and fair promises did not work half so well as absolute severity, despite Hellier's words yesterday evening.

Hellier had certainly turned out for the best. Ridgeley had never liked the man, but he had to acknowledge his efficiency as an officer. He could never rid himself of the feeling, however, that there was a great deal more within the captain's smooth head than he allowed himself to reveal to his superiors. And after all, the colonel supposed that to be the truth. Certainly he had never suspected that the man was in fact currying favor with the rebel wife in order to procure her downfall. And now, after being a thorn in his colonel's side for months, he had saved him a great deal of effort by discovering the St. Barbe girl's whereabouts. God's bones, it almost made him like the man!

There were people around the Market Cross and more outside the George. They stared at the soldiers sullenly but did not approach. They've learned their lesson sure enough, Ridgeley thought with contempt. Ignorant, uncouth peasants, soon put to flight by a show of force, a few threats, a beating or two, an expedient corpse. He drew rein outside the Fleur-de-Lys and beckoned to Hellier. "Where did you say the girl was?"

"In the tenement at the end of the stableyard,' the captain said. There was an air of suppressed excitement about him, and his beaver crowned his head with a flourish of plumes, at an angle that was almost jaunty. "There is no exit to the rear, and only one door. A couple of men will suffice—she cannot possibly escape."

Ridgeley glanced around at the troopers, sitting curiously at his back. He had as usual told them little of the purpose of this expedition. He waved the nearest two down from their horses, and ordered Cornet Wickham to wait outside with the rest. Then he dismounted stiffly, cursing the ache of his unused muscles. That wench last night had known a trick or two, had indeed well-nigh exhausted him, but the experience had whetted his appetite and sharpened his lust. He thought of Rachael St. Barbe's untouched body and smiled greedily.

There was no one in the inn yard. Too early, he supposed. Down one side ran a row of stables, with lofts above, and on the other side and at the back more outbuildings, converted into tenements. The one at the end appeared empty, the door closed, the windows shuttered. He strode up to it, ignoring the pains in his leg and the weakness that made his head swim suddenly, and put his shoulder to the door.

It juddered but did not move. He tried again, harder, still without success. It was galling to hear Hellier say, in that pleasant, unassuming voice, "Let me try, sir."

He was at least four inches shorter than the colonel and several stones lighter, even allowing for the weight that Ridgeley had lost during his sickness. As he pushed and kicked at the obstinate planks, one of the soldiers shouted, "There, sir! At the window!"

Ridgeley, looking up, had a brief glimpse of a pale face peering down through a gap in the shutters of the first-storey window. At last! Delighted, he pushed forward to the door. "Come on, man, put your back into it!"

And suddenly, under their combined weight, there was the sound of splintering wood and the battered door gave way. The two men almost fell into the dark room beyond. Ridgeley recovered his balance first and carefully drew his sword.

It took some time for his eyes to adjust to the lack of light. He looked around at the poorly furnished chamber, seeing the rough table, half a dozen stools, a crudely made bed in the corner, a heap of cold ashes in the hearth, above which an iron cooking pot hung on its chain. There was no sign of the St. Barbe girl, but above his head something moved.

Ridgeley's lip curled upward, exposing his teeth. He turned to the two troopers, who were standing at the door, peering curiously within. "You, men. Stay there—and if that hell-spawned wench tries to escape, you're to hold her—but don't kill her, understand? Leave that to me—I want her unharmed, for the moment."

The stairs, a primitive affair little better than a ladder, led upward to his quarry. With greedy anticipation, the colonel began to climb them,

Hellier at his back. He emerged breathless into the half-lit upper chamber and peered eagerly about in the gloom.

There was no sign of the girl. Instead, three large, menacing figures rose from bed and stools and moved a little way toward him. Astonished, Ridgeley swore angrily. "God's death, what's this? Who are you? Where's the girl?"

"She isn't here," Nick Hellier said. He stood behind his colonel, between him and the stairs. "She has never been here. The face you saw belongs to Flower Churchhouse, over there."

Ridgeley stared in fury and disbelief at the girlish, unfortunately named young man standing nearest to the half-shuttered window. He did not know that it was Flower's sister Elizabeth whom his men had nearly raped at the mill in March; but the look of utter loathing on the smooth, fine-feathered face gave even the colonel pause. He swung back to Hellier, his rage rising inexorably. "You—you've lied to me! Why have you led me here? By God, I'll have you flogged for this—or shot, that's more like it, you traitor—I'll see you before a firing squad if it's the last thing I do."

"I am no traitor," said Nick. Although slighter by far than Ridgeley, the look of purpose on his face, the taut watchfulness of his body, poised at the head of the stairs, lent him a power that dominated everyone in the room. "I have done this for the ultimate good of the king's cause in the West as well as for less lofty reasons. While at Wintercombe, Colonel, you have offended all the laws of God and of man. You have indulged in brutality and debauch, you have planned and threatened murder and the rape and torture of a girl fifteen years old. For her sake, and for the lives and peace and prosperity of the people of Wintercombe and Norton, I call you to account."

Ridgeley stared at him, as if he could not believe the effrontery of what he heard. "You, you insolent hypocrite—you call *me* to account? God's bones, you'll answer for this outrage. Draw your sword, you ignoble coward, and I'll spit you here and now."

"No," Nick said. He added, in conversational tones, "If I were you, Colonel, I would turn and look behind you."

With a speed surprising in such a heavily built man, Ridgeley whipped around, his sword stabbing at the air. Young Edward Walker, brother to Leah, stood just out of its reach, his broad hands grasping a long-tined pitchfork. He said viciously, "You've debauched my sister, fornicated with her—and don't ee dare deny it."

"Your sister?" Ridgeley glared at the young man, his head thrust aggressively forward. "She didn't struggle—in fact, it was she who made the first advances, and I can tell you, you stupid prudish peasant, that she knows a whorish trick or two, so she's not the innocent you think."

"You bastard!" Edward cried, and lunged. In the confined space, there was no room to dodge, and the colonel's sword was useless, far outreached by the pitchfork. He stared in horrified disbelief as the great curved tines impaled his body with the ease of a skewer thrust through meat. His mouth opened, but no sound save a frantic gurgling came out.

With a practiced, easy twist, Edward Walker pulled the pitchfork back and out, and suddenly there was blood, bright, flowing, soaking the broad buff jerkin, dribbling from the sharp, wicked tines onto the dirty floor. Ridgeley's face had turned a ghastly gray, and his eyes bulged. Nick drew his sword and moved to face him, calm, sure, ruthless, his face as impassive as an executioner's. The colonel staggered but did not fall, his hands pressing frantically against the double wounds, blood pouring between his fingers. "Help me!" he gasped. "For God's sake, man—help me!"

"You'll have no aid from me," Nick Hellier said. "Save one dispensation only. You will assuredly die from your present hurts, Colonel, although the process will probably take some hours, if not days, of agony. You were not prepared to allow Rachael the benefit of a swift and merciful death, but I am going to give you that blessing. This, sir, is for Wintercombe, and Philip's Norton, and the St. Barbe family, and all the pain and horror and suffering that you have inflicted. This is your reckoning—and may you burn in hell for what you have done!"

The bright sharp sword drew back and lunged. For an instant Ridgeley stood, still living, gazing down at the blade which had transfixed his heart. Then, as Nick wrenched his weapon free in a torrent of blood, the colonel's heavy body shuddered, his breath rattled in his throat, and he fell backward through the stair hole. There was the sound of breaking wood and a massive crash, and nothing more.

Nick looked at the blood on his rapier, the puddles and splashes across the floor, the frozen, exultant faces of the men with whom he had arranged this ambush. Then he turned, as much to conceal his shaking hands as for any other reason, and walked to the top of the stairs.

Below, in a welter of gore and splintered wood, Lieutenant-Colonel John Ridgeley, the terror of North Somerset, lay staring up at the rafters with blank, amazed eyes.

"'The rest is silence,'" Nick said, smiling with bitter satisfaction as he sheathed his bloody sword in its scabbard.

CHAPTER

TWENTY-ONE

*The flowery way that leads to the
broad gate and the great fire.*
—ALL'S WELL THAT ENDS WELL

The body of Lieutenant-Colonel Ridgeley was buried, in some haste, in the churchyard at Philip's Norton that afternoon.

By then, the early sun had been covered by cloud, and a light chilly drizzle was falling. The few mourners were composed entirely of the colonel's officers: Captain Hellier and Captain Bull, Lieutenants Byam and Combe, Cornet Wickham, Ensign Parset and sundry lesser men. In the tall elms lining the churchyard, a great gaunt black crow sat and croaked throughout the brief ceremony, while the curious, gloating villagers peered over the wall and commented with great satisfaction on the suitably unsavory end of the man they had all hated so much.

As soon as the first clods of red earth smacked down upon the rough, hastily constructed coffin at the bottom of the grave pit, the crow arose with an evil-sounding "kaark!" and flew away with ponderous wingbeats. It was said by the superstitious, gossiping in the Fleur-de-Lys later, to be the incarnation of the colonel's undoubtedly black and hellbound soul. And for many years after the rebellious children of Philip's Norton, not to mention of Wellow and Hinton, were told threateningly that Black Jack Ridgeley would snatch them away if they did not behave themselves.

No one from the Wintercombe household attended the funeral. As Diggory commented, the sight of them all a-dancing on Ridgeley's grave would probably have sent the parson into a seizure. The prevailing mood in the house was one of overwhelming, delighted relief. Who cared how the evil and ungodly man had met his end, so long as they were now forever free of him?

There were others, in Bath and Bristol, who would care, and Nick Hellier had given much thought to it. That was one reason why he had planned to have the colonel ambushed within the close confines of the tenement, rather than in the highway or the streets of Norton. Only he, and the three men he had enlisted to help him, knew the truth of

Ridgeley's death and who had struck the fatal blows. All three had ample reasons for wishing him dead: Flower Churchhouse's sister had been attacked, Edward Walker's corrupted, and Thomas Coxe's eleven-year-old son Francis had died, and the rest of his family suffered sorely during the winter, after the colonel had ruthlessly appropriated most of their stored food. There had been many in Norton eager to strike a blow against the wicked Cavalier colonel: Nick had been able to pick and choose his accomplices.

Ned Walker had dealt the first blow, but he himself had delivered the coup de grace, and he was well aware that if that fact ever became known to the Governor of Bath, he would face a firing squad, the inevitable penalty for murdering his superior officer. It was an ugly word for a reprehensible, appalling act. And yet he had chosen to do it, and in cold blood, for Silence's sake.

So in the aftermath of that gory deed, he acted with the same cool sense of purpose. There was no hiding the cause of Ridgeley's death from the two troopers left outside the tenement. They had rushed in with drawn swords, to find his bleeding carcass lying on the floor. But it was easy to persuade them to keep their mouths shut. Neither man had approved of the colonel's grosser activities, and Nick was able to exploit their instinctive revulsion over Ridgeley's plans for Rachael's rape and murder. Nor of course would Churchhouse, Walker, and Coxe divulge their part in the colonel's slaughter.

It was Margery Parsons, the sister-in-law of the Fleur-de-Lys's landlord, who came to lay out the body, stripping off the buff coat and doublet, stiff with congealed blood, pierced by three significant holes, and washing the pale flaccid corpse beneath. Thomas Stent, who lived in North Street and was the nearest of the village carpenters, was summoned to measure the body for a hasty coffin. And Cornet Wickham, his pleasant face puzzled and thoughtful, was dispatched to Wick Farm, to bring the St. Barbe children back to Wintercombe.

Their arrival, just before dinnertime, was the first intimation that Silence had of Ridgeley's demise. For hours she had waited in her lonely chamber, hungry and apprehensive. She had passed the time at first by tidying it, restoring order to her world. She dared not ponder the events of the past twenty-four hours and would not speculate on what was to come. Whatever the future held, there was danger: from Ridgeley, or from Nick.

It was no use any longer denying it: She was infatuated by him. The thought of his kiss raised the hair on her flesh and made her shiver with . . . what? Fear? Longing? She had never dreamed it possible to feel for any man like this. Her husband had aroused nothing in her, no more than affection, and she had submitted with wifely duty to his brief, energetic desires. She had expected no more and had not been disappointed. Her children, inevitable result of those perfunctory nighttime couplings, were the light of her life, ample rewards of an activity that she had always found inexplicable and tedious. There was the man's pleasure, that went without saying. But surely only a whore was supposed to enjoy it too?

She was no whore, but if she gave way to this temptation, she would become one. She must not think of it. She must reject all his advances, even the offer of friendship, because that was the primrose path that led to ruin. To avoid blighting her whole life, she must turn as cold a face toward him as a stranger. She was too frightened even to think of the consequences if she did not.

It was a poor return for the help he had given her, for the risks he had taken for her sake. But she had fallen in almost too deep, and now, in panic, she was struggling back to the safety of an ordinary, loyal, dutiful wife.

She sat pensively in the oriel, looking out of the window down to the courtyard. Pye, temporarily deserting her kittens, lay curled in her lap, having her head gently rubbed between the ears. Doubtless she was as hungry as her mistress, neither having eaten since dinner the day before, but at least the kittens had their food supply close to hand. Silence wondered about Lily, whether she was being looked after in the kitchen, and above all about the children. Were they safe at Wick? Had they coped successfully with the two-mile walk across the cold moonlit countryside?

Movement caught her eye. She turned her head and saw a two-wheeled tumbril cart, of the sort usually employed to take dung to the fields, being driven in under the gatehouse. It was crammed with bobbing heads and driven by a man whom she recognized as one of Mistress Baylie's farm workers. Behind it rode a couple of troopers, and the young cornet who was Nick's closest friend among the officers of the garrison.

She needed to see no more. Her heart beating wildly, she set Pye down on the window seat and ran to the door. It took a few precious seconds to turn the key, then she was hurtling down the twisting stone stairs, through the garden room, across the hall, still strewn with the squalid debris of last night's carouse, to the front door. She flung it open and plunged out into the courtyard just as the tumbril drew up outside and spilled out a crying, laughing, jubilant mass of children.

Breathlessly she hugged them all, and Mally, listening to their joyous and confused accounts of escape.

"We walked and walked and walked and walked, and my feet hurt!"

"William fell in a ditch and got soaking wet!"

"We met Captain Hellier in the garden," Tabby said, her face serious. "And he *is* our friend, Mama, you needn't worry any more—he said he had a secret plan to get rid of Colonel Ridgeley, and now he's dead and I'm not sorry, I'm glad!"

"Dead?" Silence stared at her in astonishment. "Who's dead? Ridgeley?"

"Aye, the colonel have got his comeuppance at last, m'lady," Mally said. Even her hair seemed brighter with her delight. "We be quite safe, all on us be safe—and now maybe we can carry on our business without they soldiers a-sticking their noses and swords into what bain't theirs."

The nightmare had gone. It was as if the terrors of this morning and the previous day had never really existed, had achieved instead a curious, remote quality, like the miseries she had endured in childhood. There was much to do, and to ponder, but for the moment all she wanted was to exult in the company of all her children and their freedom from fear.

Eventually, of course, reality must intrude. Eliza peered around the front door as if she thought that Ridgeley would pounce on her, and then emerged hesitant and blinking into the light, evidently hardly able to believe that the terror was finally ended. "Oh, my lady, m'lady, you be free—and the children, oh, thank the dear Lord, you all be safe!"

After her, like frightened deer, crept the other household servants: Doraty, Hester, the three scullions, the Turbers, Bessie Lyteman, and, shepherding them all out of the porch, the massive figure of Darby. Leah was conspicuous by her absence: Silence wondered hopefully if she had already gone from Wintercombe. She did not relish the confrontation and dismissal that must surely follow, if she had not.

Mally spread the news of Ridgeley's death jubilantly, and Silence knelt to welcome small pale Lily, wriggling with delight, her tail wagging her body in her joy. All, it seemed, were safe. And with William, thumb in mouth, clinging to her skirts as if he feared ever to let go of her again, she turned to Wickham, who was obviously about to leave. "Please, Cornet, wait—tell me, is Ridgeley truly dead?"

The boy—he was no older than Sam had been—looked down at her from the back of his rather squat brown gelding. There was a curious expression on his face, composed of apprehension, relief, and the marks of a confused and troubled mind. He hesitated and then said slowly, "Yes, Lady St. Barbe. I did not myself witness his death, but I have seen his corpse. He is undoubtedly dead."

She closed her eyes for a moment, so intense was her relief. Save that the colonel had not been so subtle, she had feared that this might be a ruse to draw the children out of hiding. But Wickham was one of the more decent officers, and Nick liked him. She had seen no trace of deceit on his open, plain and honest face. She looked up at him and said carefully, "Forgive me, Cornet Wickham, but—how did he die?"

The boy's brow creased, as if his conscience troubled him greatly, and he did not answer for a moment. Then, with difficulty, he said, "I—I believe he was killed, madam."

"*Killed?* By whom? Where?"

"I believe—I am not sure—some villagers who bore a grudge against him," said the unhappy Wickham. "Captain Hellier knows more than I do, my lady, but he is likely to be absent for a while, arranging for the burial. Their is a great deal to be done, the men must be informed, and Sir Thomas Bridges—I do not know who will be in command here now. Forgive me, madam, but I must go."

She watched him trot out of the courtyard and felt sorry for him. There was no doubt in her mind, and evidently none in his, that Nick Hellier had played a considerable part in Ridgeley's death. Hence, presumably, Wickham's moral confusion. The boy, like all decent-minded people, must have detested his colonel and often wished him to the devil, but was unable to accept the manner of his death.

Murder. Nick had lured Ridgeley to the tenement behind the Fleur-de-Lys, in the belief that Rachael was hiding there—and the colonel had been struck down, ostensibly by some villagers. But she remembered suddenly, chillingly, Nick standing on the terrace, his smoking pistol in his hand and the dead man lying in the orchard grass. And she knew that, whatever the circumstances of Ridgeley's slaying, it was likely that Nick had borne most of the responsibility, even if he had not actually struck the fatal blow.

He seemed so warm, so friendly, but there were chill depths to him that frightened her, sometimes. She shivered suddenly and turned back toward the house.

As Wickham had said, there was much to be done. She found a coin to give to the driver of the cart, and he set off back to Wick Farm, bearing a hastily scribbled message thanking Mistress Baylie for her stalwart and invaluable help. Then, after a quiet word to the joyous, excited children, she called all the servants into the hall.

It was in a disgusting state. They had to pick their way between the debris littering the floor, and the place stank of stale beer and cider, tobacco, and worse. She watched all the familiar faces gathering. Bessie, obviously apprehensive, was hovering at the back. I shall have to have a word with her in private, Silence thought, not relishing the prospect. And if she really is with child, I shall have no choice but to dismiss her.

With the dairying season just beginning in earnest, despite the ravages of the soldiers, it would be difficult, if not well-nigh impossible, to find a replacement. Perhaps Mistress Flower or Mistress Baylie could help. Silence, once more weighed down by domestic concerns, ran her eye over the assembled household. Mally, staunch and loyal, who had saved her children. Eliza, Doraty, and Hester, good dependable servants. Margery Turber with her strong arm and kind eye, and her ancient, deaf and scrawny husband. Bessie, who to do her justice seemed to be somewhat ashamed of her behavior. Darby, who had yesterday, as soon as Silence's imprisonment became known, taken all the female servants save Leah and Bessie over to Clevinger's cottage and told them to keep the door locked and barred and bolted. The groom, Tom Goodenough, and the two lads, and Diggory the gardener with his boy. And, in a bright-eyed huddle, the three scullions.

She said, "Does anyone know where Leah is?"

The servants looked at each other. It was Eliza who spoke up, her face sour with disapproval. "I can tell ee, my lady. She be up in that wicked fornicating heathen's lair, waiting for him to come back."

"She'll have awhile to wait," Silence said dryly. "I have sure and certain news that Colonel Ridgeley is dead."

There was a brief, delighted pause and then a buzz of comment. They did not quite cheer, but she felt they would have liked to do so. She gestured them quiet with a lift of her hand and went on. "I don't know who'll be in command of the garrison here, or even whether that garrison will continue. But whatever happens, I think that all our lives will be a little easier, and safer."

"I'll drink to that, m'lady," Goodenough said cheerfully. "All I ask now, is that they buggers get out of my stables—begging your pardon, m'lady."

Silence smiled at him, and found her mouth stretching wider with her joy and relief and freedom from fear. She added, "Which of you did not go to the fair yesterday?"

There were a few: one of the scullions, Darby, Eliza, the two stable lads and Jemmy Coxe, and Doraty Locke. She said, "You may all go today, if you have not yet had the chance. I am sorry it is now so late, but I expect there will still be plenty for you to do and to buy."

She paused, looking for signs of pleasure among the faces ranked in front of her. But Eliza was turning around, whispering, and there seemed to be something of a conspiracy in operation. Finally, the chief maid turned back, her expression firm. "Thank ee kindly for your thought, m'lady," she said. "But we all d'be of one mind on this. There be a tarblish lot to do here, and we d'want to stay and order the house for ee. This here hall bain't fitty even for pigs."

There were heartfelt murmurs of assent. Darby spoke up from the back. "I'll speak to Clevinger, m'lady, and see if he haven't got a little sweet tender lamb for supper this even, by way of celebration. 'Tis as if the Lord have lifted the yoke from us, m'lady, and it seem only right that we mark it."

Touched by their concern, Silence found herself blinking away tears. She swallowed and said, her voice surprisingly clear and sure, "Thank you— thank you so much—you have all done so well, and been so kind."

"Well, I don't reckon as how you deserve any less, m'lady," Diggory said, and from all around him there were murmurs and nods of assent. Even the sour Eliza was wagging her prim head in agreement, and Silence brushed the tears from her eyes, overwhelmed with gratitude and happiness. At last it had happened. She was no longer a stranger there, a foreigner, unwelcome and resented. Whatever harm her suffering had wrought, whatever the horror and the fear she had experienced, some good had come of it: for now they were truly her allies, and Wintercombe was at last her home.

She said, trying to stop her voice wavering, "Thank you again—you have been magnificent, all of you."

"Nearly all on us," Eliza said, flashing a pointed glance at Bessie. The girl moved backward a step, obviously uneasy, and sent Silence a look of mute appeal.

It fell upon stony soil. She stared at the dairymaid without sympathy and said, "I wish to see you, Bessie, in the study—now. And as for the rest—Doraty, would you look after the children? And Eliza, this is your task—can you organize everyone else to clean up here in the hall? I will join you in a few minutes. Come with me, Bessie."

Once in the study, she sat down by the empty fire. The sun had disappeared by now, and the day was probably not going to live up to its early promise. The room, though tidy and clean, would never look the same again, after the destruction wrought on Ridgeley's orders, and the damage to the furniture still assaulted her eyes. Perhaps there was a joiner or carpenter in Bath sufficiently skilled to mend the fine work on the inlaid drawers of Sir Samuel's walnut writing desk. Once the soldiers were gone, she would make inquiries.

But of course they were unlikely to go unless forced, and the war was by no means over. It could drag on for months, years more, and every hour, every day of that time she would be faced by Nick Hellier, challenging with every movement he made, every word he spoke, the virtuous tenets that she had been taught to hold all her life long.

She dragged her mind away from temptation and addressed Bessie, who had also been tempted and who had fallen with a vengeance. "What have you to say for yourself?"

The girl's blue eyes, no longer so confident, gazed at her and then dropped. She hesitated, evidently unhappy, and then said, "I've told ee before, m'lady, I can't seem to help myself."

"That is plainly to be seen—especially last night."

The eyes flashed up and down again, hidden by ridiculously long lashes. "Were ee watching I, m'lady?" Bessie asked, her voice low. "I diden know that."

"No, because you were too far gone in drink to think of it," Silence said. "That was never a vice of yours, Bessie—why do you tipple now? Is it because of the baby?"

The girl's face jerked up, her mouth round with astonishment and dismay. "Oh, m'lady—however did ee guess?"

"It's not very difficult," Silence said dryly. "The style of dress you favored last night was not exactly concealing. Mally noticed it too, and I'm sure Eliza knows. And you know what it means, don't you?"

"Yes, m'lady." Bessie's voice was very low. "I bain't fitty to work at Wintercombe no more. You'll send me away."

"You have it aright." Silence paused, torn between pity for the dairymaid's plight and annoyance at the reckless irresponsibility of her behavior. "And really, Bessie, you have only yourself to blame—as I'm sure you realize. Only you and Leah have fallen into temptation, and both of you were more than willing."

"Aye, 'tis true, sure enough," Bessie said with some bitterness. "But I'll wager all I d'have, m'lady, that *she* don't get into no trouble."

"Even if she is not with child," Silence said, wondering if there could possibly be a more repellent parentage for such an unfortunate baby, "I will dismiss her today, as I have dismissed you. But with one difference. I will pay you all your wages owing, until the June quarterday." And as Bessie, incredulous, began to speak, she added, "You will need all the help you can, for the child and yourself. Your father won't be able to do very much for you."

"I d'know that too well." Bessie added, "I expect you don't think I any more than a girt vorus-norus wench with a new fancyman every week—but I bain't such a one really, m'lady. I don't mean no harm by it—I just d'like my pleasures, same as any woman would, saving I don't have no husband to do it with. And if the price I must pay is a child, well, I'll just have to make the best of en, won't I? Even if Parson do have plenty to say about fallen women and all manner of what." She looked Silence straight in the eye. "Don't ee make no mistake, m'lady, I bain't sorry for what I done. I enjoyed myself for certain, and I ain't got no regrets—except I don't like to be leaving here." She smiled, almost wistfully. "And I've allus wanted a babe. My mam ain't had norn for years—our Gartred were the last on us, and she be twelve year old now. A bobbant little lad like yourn, m'lady, that be all I d'ask."

"And I hope you have him," Silence said, smiling back. "Good-bye, Bessie—and thank you. Oh, I know I shouldn't be saying it, I know I should be kicking you out of the house with your tail between your legs." Bessie giggled at this, and hastily straightened her face. "But you've worked as hard as anyone here, and you've never given me cause to dislike you. So—I wish you good luck, and if you should need help, for you or the babe, you can come to me."

She reflected later, ruefully, that her husband would undoubtedly have subjected the recalcitrant dairymaid to a four-hour lecture on the evils of fornication and unbridled lust, before inflicting a beating, the better to remember his words, and ejecting her from the house. He would probably also have tried to persuade Byam to marry the girl—a lost cause if ever there was one—so that the baby would not become a charge on the parish. Silence felt that Bessie's plight was in some part her fault—if she had not been so lax and lenient, surely even Bessie would not have had the opportunity for fornication?—and in the end had been even more generous than her original intention. Bessie, her few possessions tied up in a bundle, walked away from Wintercombe with her head cheerfully high and a fat bag of silver shillings slapping bruisingly against her thigh. Her fear of destitution was assuaged: The money given to her by the lady of Wintercombe would support her, and the babe, in her father's house for a year or more, until she could find other work.

The interview with Leah progressed much less satisfactorily. The girl had settled herself in Ridgeley's chamber, as proud as a queen in her flaunting scarlet gown, while the secretary Harris looked at her sideways, showing the whites of his eyes like a nervous horse. She listened in sneering disbelief to her mistress's news of her lover's fate, and laughed. "You can't fool I with such northering tales, m'lady."

In vain, Silence assured her that it was true. Leah, whether from arrogance or stupidity, refused to believe it, although Harris, wringing his hands, seemed to be in a state of great confusion and distress. "Proper betwattled," as Leah scornfully put it. In the end, Silence left her and went to fetch Tom Goodenough, the only able-bodied man among the servants.

Leah's face, pretty, sullen, spiteful, went pale as she saw the big, sturdy figure of the groom standing in the doorway. "You have a choice," Silence told her quietly. "Either you leave willingly and freely, pausing to gather your belongings on the way, or Tom will put you out as you are."

With a vicious twist to her mouth, the maid accepted the inevitable, and within ten minutes was strolling with defiant jauntiness across the courtyard, still in that blatant scarlet, her bundle in her hand. She cast a considering eye at the few soldiers lounging in the barton and on guard at the gatehouse, but Goodenough was standing threateningly behind her.

With a toss of her dark head, Leah walked out of Wintercombe and down the hill toward her father's house at Lyde Green. Whether she would find service in another household, or ply a whore's trade in Bath or Bristol, Silence did not care: She felt suddenly freer for Leah's leaving, as if the maid had tainted the air with her betrayal.

There was still much to be done, though the hall had been restored to something approaching normality by the endeavors of the servants, directed by Eliza. She thanked them, reminded Darby that dinner would need some small preparation if it was to be served at anything approaching the usual time, and thought wearily of the difficulties involved in engaging at least two more female servants. The village, once they heard of the fates of Bessie Lyteman and Leah Walker, would be reluctant to send daughters into service in a house garrisoned by debauched Cavaliers. And yet poor Eliza could hardly do all the work of cleaning the house on her own, nor could Margery Turber manage unaided in the dairy.

At least pondering these mundane problems kept her mind from dwelling on the events of the past two days, the horror that had brushed them all and then lifted, and the barrier that she must now erect between her yearning heart and Nick Hellier's increasingly open admiration. It was not sufficient to be innocent, she knew. If tongues began to wag and common fame reported her adultery, she was condemned out of hand, and with the more virulence because her supposed lover was an enemy soldier. Her position as gentleman's wife would save her from the indignities of public penance, or the Rough Music of disapproving neighbors. It would not save her from idle and malicious gossip if she gave those addicted to such chackle the opportunity to indulge in it. There was her husband to think of (though a small rebellious voice within demanded why she should show him any consideration, when he had given *her* precious little), and her children. She was a virtuous, Christian, godly wife, and she must be seen to be so.

Thus bolstered with good intentions, she sailed busily through all the duties that the day cast upon her, until she came to visit Dame Ursula.

The old lady's first concern was why Silence had not come to see her earlier. Ruth had informed her of many things, and it was disgraceful that she must rely upon a mere servant for vital information. Was it true that the Man of Blood was dead?

Assuming, correctly, that Ridgeley was meant by this, Silence was able to assure her that indeed he was. Dame Ursula lifted her hands in an attitude of prayer and burst forth into exultant biblical quotation. "'So let all thine enemies perish, oh Lord: but let them that love him be as the sun when he goeth forth in his might.'"

Since this passage commented on the slaying of Sisera by Jael, Silence thought it a trifle inappropriate. Nor, unlike Israel, was there much hope of this land having rest for the next forty years as a consequence. She said nothing, with the wisdom of long experience, and waited.

"And I hear you've sent those two strumpets packing" was her mother-in-law's next observation. "It should have been done months ago, do you hear me, daughter?" The stick jabbed out toward her. "*Months*. Bringing shame and disgrace on a godly household with their lewdness—yes, I was watching last night! Such filthiness, such uncleanliness, I never thought to see under this roof—make no mistake, daughter, my son shall hear of this when he comes home."

It was useless for Silence to protest that she had been locked in her chamber, incapable of any intervention. She compressed her lips, kept her peace, and listened to Dame Ursula's vigorous rantings, heavily sprinkled with apt quotation. But her patience was not on so long a string as it had once been. She said, when the old lady had paused for a much-needed breath, "I have a great deal to do, madam—pray excuse me."

She dropped a brief, correct curtsy and went out with a sense of relief. It seemed that Dame Ursula knew nothing of that midnight escape through her chamber, and Silence did not intend to complicate matters still further by telling her of it.

Rachael was waiting outside the chamber. Silence looked at her a little guiltily. She knew that perhaps she should have spoken to the girl on her return, reassured her, tried to hide the fact that all this nightmare, and Ridgeley's murder, had stemmed inexorably from the moment when Rachael had leveled his own pistol at the colonel and fired.

She smiled as genuinely as she could and said quietly, "Hullo. What do you want?"

"Can I talk to you?" asked her stepdaughter, the child whose rape and murder had been planned in cold blood, whose promised capture had lured a man to his death. And yet, Silence saw suddenly, she was a child no longer. The stern firmness of the mouth, the steady gaze of the narrow blue eyes, spoke of a new, and hard-won, maturity. Rachael was looking at her as if she were sure of a fair hearing, and Silence resolved that she would have it.

They sat in Rachael's chamber, from which she had fled only two days previously. The girl was evidently ill-at-ease: Her thin hands plucked nervously at the laces tying her bodice, but her eyes did not falter. She took a deep breath, and said resolutely, "I wish to apologize, Mother. I have behaved very badly. I was disobedient and foolish, and I put us all in danger—you in particular."

It would insult Rachael's intelligence to deny it. Silence, the memory of that peril still starkly clear in her mind, gave her a rueful smile. "You did—but we all do foolish, impulsive, disobedient things that we bitterly regret later. I expect even your grandmother did, in her youth."

Rachael looked at her in frank disbelief. "No, she can't have done. Grandmother isn't like the rest of us."

This, at least, was patently true. Silence let it pass. "But at any rate, no harm has come to any of us, and thanks to Captain Hellier, we are all safe."

Rachael stared at her. "Captain Hellier? What did he do? Did he kill Colonel Ridgeley?"

"No—at least, I don't know—rumor has it that three village men did, and I hope they'll go unpunished. I should think they were in a sense acting for all of us, when they struck him down."

"But it was my *fault*," Rachael said patiently, as if explaining the obvious truth to a simpleton. "If I hadn't stolen the pistol, and shot him, he wouldn't have tried to find me—and—and threatened all those things."

Silence looked at her strained face, wondering just how much Rachael knew of those threats. She hoped devoutly that her twin would have had the sense not to reveal to her the colonel's detailed plans for her fate. It would certainly be most unlike Nat if he had. She reached out and took the restless hand in hers. "I'm afraid that's true—although probably if he hadn't had that excuse to terrorize us, he would have thought of another.

That kind of man can never rest until he has cowed everyone about him and bent them to his evil will. Thank God that Captain Hellier had the strength to resist him."

"Mally said he was hurt," Rachael said. "She said that when Colonel Ridgeley saw me in West Street, he held his horse's bridle until Ridgeley beat him off."

"He did," Silence said. "But he wasn't badly injured. He was well enough to ride out with Ridgeley this morning."

Rachael shot her a very sharp glance. She said, "Did Captain Hellier *arrange* for the colonel to be killed?"

This was so close to Silence's own suspicions that she was startled. She shook her head. "I don't know—I really don't know. He may have done."

"But that's murder," said Rachael. Her tone was thoughtful rather than condemnatory. "'Thou shalt not kill'—the sixth Commandment."

"And probably the one most frequently broken in the Bible," Silence said dryly. "The Israelites seemed to do little else but slay each other, or the Gentiles, did they not? Yet only a little farther on it says clearly, 'He that smiteth a man, so that he die, shall be surely put to death.'"

"Exactly," Rachael said, her face even paler than usual. "So what will happen to them, and Captain Hellier?"

Silence thought for a moment, and then spoke, choosing her words with care. "Probably, nothing. No one seems to know who the men were or what part Captain Hellier played. There are no judges or justices sitting in Somerset, there have not been any since the war began. Each village must deal with its wrong-doers as it thinks fit—and I do not think, somehow, that Philip's Norton will look unkindly on Ridgeley's killers. The only man who might move against them is the Governor of Bath, Sir Thomas Bridges. And I should imagine that what he does will depend on what Captain Hellier chooses to tell him." She paused, and then added, "What the Scriptures say, about a life for a life—well, Colonel Ridgeley had threatened to kill you, when he found you. And I think that Captain Hellier had him killed to save your life."

There was a long, long moment while Rachael, her eyes suddenly filling with tears, turned her head and stared out of the window. Finally she said, her voice wobbling, "I—I don't deserve it—I've been so wicked—and now he's put himself in danger for me . . ."

With more confidence than she would once have had Silence reached out and put her arms about her. For an instant her stepdaughter's thin, tense body stayed rigid in her grasp. Then, with a sudden intake of breath, the girl turned, sobbing, and collapsed against her shoulder.

It took a long time for her weeping to subside, and with it all the pent-up fury and terror and guilt of the last few months. But at last Rachael was able to sit up, and dry her tears, and give her a wan smile. "Is dinner ready yet?"

This was more like the old Rachael. Silence smiled cheerfully. "I hope so. I'm exceeding hungry—I haven't eaten since yesterday."

"I broke my fast at Wick Farm," Rachael said. "It was very nice, staying there. Mistress Baylie was very kind to me, especially last night when I came back from the fair. Tabby told me about what Nat did to stop the soldiers from chasing me," she added. "Everyone has helped me—and I still don't think I really deserve it. I should have obeyed you and stayed at Wick, and then none of this would have happened."

"But you didn't, and it all did, and there's no altering it now," Silence said. "No use weeping after spilled milk, as my Grandmother Richards always told me. You've made mistakes, and had the honesty to admit it. Now you must have the wisdom to learn from them, so that you don't err again."

Rachael smiled, in rather watery fashion, and wiped a hand across her eyes. "I'll try not to," she said. "But it's so difficult—I have such a temper, and I forget."

"Do your best," said Silence. "After all, it's all any of us can do."

A knock on the door announced Mally, saying that dinner was served in the dining parlor. As Silence rose to go, Rachael put a quick hand on her sleeve. "Please, Mother—can I ask a favor?"

"Of course you can *ask*—what is it?"

"When I was at Wick, I helped in the dairy—just a little, there wasn't time to do much—and Mistress Baylie said I worked quite well. And you've sent Bessie away, so can I help Margery until you get another dairymaid?"

Geroge, who had decided ideas on what household activities were and were not appropriate for his wife and daughters, would not approve. But Silence had almost entirely discarded her old habit of referring mentally to her husband's likely opinion before deciding on a course of action. Rachael's fragile happiness was of far greater importance. She smiled. "Of course you may—and Margery will be grateful and glad of your help."

When Rachael smiled so brilliantly, it was as if the sun had come out after a storm. And Silence went downstairs to dinner, feeling happier than she had done for some time.

The rest of the day passed so quickly that she had barely time to notice that it had gone, so busy was she in setting Wintercombe to rights, playing with the children, Lily, and the kittens, and settling a jubilant Rachael in the dairy with Margery Turber, who was obviously relieved at the prospect of assistance but dubious as to the propriety of a daughter of the house doing so much manual work. Silence ignored her doubts, and certainly Rachael fairly sparkled as she set about the delicate task of skimming the cream from the morning milk, set in wide shallow earthenware dishes about the dairy. A proper dairymaid would have to be employed as soon as possible, for assuredly Rachael could not labor from dawn till dusk, milking, skimming, churning butter, and turning cheeses. But for the moment the girl was kept busy and out of mischief, doing something useful and that she greatly enjoyed.

One of the stable lads, Richard Stent, younger son of the village carpenter, had been sent into Norton after dinner to gather what news he could. He returned with the tidings that Lieutenant-Colonel Ridgeley had been laid to rest in the churchyard. "And Parson, he didn't look tarblish pleased about en." Many of the officers had been present, as were a large group of villagers, leaning over the churchyard wall with expressions of undisguised glee on their faces.

The boy's description was vivid and graphic. Silence gave him a groat for his trouble and sent him back to the stable. Then she walked slowly up to her chamber, Lily at heel, with a bowl of meaty scraps for the dog and another of new milk for Pye.

Mally was helping Eliza. The younger children were in bed, and Nat and Rachael were studying in their chambers. The sun was setting, and although she could not see its light from the southern window, the drizzling clouds had thinned and the sky was azure and dove gray and apricot. Below, Diggory labored still in the garden, tying back recalcitrant branches in the cherry arbor, and Jemmy Coxe was on his hands and knees with a fork and a barrow, weeding the knots. Soon it would be suppertime, the twins would join her for their light meal, the servants would gather in their hall next to the kitchen for bread and cheese and thick meaty broth. The soldiers would eat a similar meal out in the barton, and their officers would sup, as usual, in the dining parlor.

And, perhaps, Nick Hellier would come to her, and she did not know what to do.

She sat down on the window seat that overlooked the garden, pulling damask-covered cushions behind her back and shoulders and head. Lily, with much scrabbling, struggled up to join her, her narrow little head resting on Silence's knee, her small, slightly protuberant dark eyes fixed adoringly on her mistress's face. Absently she stroked the short, fine-textured coat, smiling because Pye, usually so jealous of the puppy's attentions, was lying on her side in the basket in the attitude of a contented sow, suckling her kittens. Lily wriggled closer, luxuriating in what she thought was Silence's undivided attention, and the fingers moved gently, ceaselessly, while the mind that directed them pondered other problems.

Her head told her to keep him at arm's length, if not further. All the sensible arguments pointed unerringly in the same direction. He was an enemy soldier, however much he had helped them. Perhaps her acute perception of her own feelings had led her to exaggerate the danger. Perhaps no one else—apart of course from Mally, who was so close to her—had even remotely considered the chance that Lady St. Barbe was in danger of falling into such wickedness. But the danger was there all the same, ever-present in her mind, tempting her to sin, calling her to virtue. And for the sake of her children, her household, and (somewhat behind the others) her husband, she must take the narrow, thorny path, reject friendship, warmth, companionship, and take refuge on her high and lonely mountain-top, bereft.

She refused to dwell on her plight, to wallow in self-pity for something she should never have countenanced at all. But there was no denying it—his look, his words, his manner that morning had left her in no doubt. He wanted her: She had only to crook her finger to have him for her lover.

And with her heart, she wanted him. Her life had been quiet, humdrum, concerned with matters small and domestic, burdened with trivial cares. Her work, her duty, even her love, all were taken for granted by family and household. And they saw only the shell, the calm, efficient, smiling woman who was housekeeper and mother, wife and lady of the estate, like thousands of other such up and down the land. Yet within lurked quite a different Silence, bowed and battered by her father and, later and more subtly, by her husband, but still defiant: still reckless, rebellious, quick to laughter, too prone to unseemly anger when thwarted. And it was that Silence who saw in Nick Hellier a kindred spirit and reached out to him. And that Silence who must be repressed even more rigorously than her menfolk had done, for the sake of her children.

When the double knock came, she lifted her head, her face resolute. Lily, with a ridiculously shrill bark, leapt over her feet, fell on her nose onto the floor, and bounced up to the door, still announcing her presence in no uncertain terms. Her heart battering her chest, her hands cold with sudden sweat, Silence got to her feet, smoothed the folds of her gown, straightened the cap hiding most of her mouse-brown hair, and called above the dog's barking, "Come in!"

He obeyed, closing the door behind him. She looked at him, wondering what had set this man apart in her mind from any other. He wore still the accoutrements of the soldier: the buff coat, the sword belt slung across his shoulder, the scarlet sash around his waist, the low-crowned beaver with its buoyant plumes carried decorously in his hand, his heavy leather boots pulled up for riding, and the bloom of damp weather on him like a grape. He was not tall or thick-set, but his wiry, lean build had a command and a presence to it that was achieved without the naked brutality of Colonel Ridgeley. His brown hair was silvered with fine raindrops, and he was smiling. "Good evening, my gracious Silence."

"Good evening," she said coolly, though her heart was still pumping fiercely within her bodice and her throat was almost closed with fear. She had hardly felt more terror of him that morning when he had thought he would rape her. Don't be ridiculous, she admonished herself. He is your friend. Surely he will understand.

But he could hardly understand unless she gave him a full explanation of why she was withdrawing her friendship; and that she hardly dared admit to herself, never mind to the man who, given the slightest encouragement, would surely lead her to disaster. She must have a pretext, and she seized the first one to hand. "Tell me," she said, deliberately not using his Christian name. "What exactly did happen to Colonel Ridgeley? All we have had are rumors."

He gave her a swift, keen glance, as if something in her tone had alerted him to danger. Lily had finished her volley of barks as soon as he entered and was now fawning and wriggling around his legs, sniffing the thick mud-splashed leather of his boots with enthusiasm. He bent and stroked her, as if seeking time for his answer, and then straightened. He said, his eyes resting on her face, "He was killed."

"In a tenement behind the Fleur-de-Lys," Silence said. "That was where you told him Rachael was?"

Nick paused for a moment, still looking at her. Then he said ruefully, "You seem to need no news from me—you've heard it already."

"Not all of it," Silence said. Her voice was more hostile than she wanted it to be, but somehow the agony of the last few days was pilling over into anger, most unfairly directed at him. Hating herself, she went on. "But I think I have guessed nearly everything. You lured Ridgeley to the place because he thought Rachael was in hiding there. Instead, there were some villagers, by prearrangement with you, and they killed him in cold blood."

There was a wariness now in Nick's eyes, as if he feared what she would say next. He said slowly, "That is true—but only part of the truth."

She stared at him, her eyes steady. "What is the rest of it, then?"

The silence threatened to drag out forever. Outside, in the soft cool evening, rooks cawed as they went to roost. Nick studied her, then he said suddenly, "The rest of it is that one of the men, I will not tell you which, lost his temper and thrust him through with a pitchfork. And because it did not kill him outright, I myself finished him off with my sword."

She knew it. Involuntarily she closed her eyes and the blood leaked from her face, leaving her even paler than usual. She turned away, ashamed and afraid of the tears that had welled up so suddenly. Then she stubbed her toe against the stone wall by the window, and all but fell. She took several deep breaths in a frantic effort to calm herself and felt a hand fall gently on her shoulder, warm and friendly and supportive. "Silence? I am sorry—that was not a particularly tactful or sympathetic way to tell you."

She found she wanted him to take her in his arms, with a power that shook her soul to its heart and left her dizzy, gasping for breath. Instead, she wrenched herself blindly away from his grip and somehow managed to reach her chair by the hearth. Mally had lit the fire earlier, but the wood was green and damp and it smoked, sending out little heat and tainting the room. Her misery and anguish threatened to overwhelm her. She was alone, utterly alone, for how could she tell him of the true reason for her grief?

She closed her eyes helplessly, determined not to give way entirely. She had been strong up until now, she must continue to be so. Yet the nightmare of the last two days seemed to have sapped her will, her spirit, so subtly that she was only just becoming aware of it.

Make, do, mend, she said to herself fiercely, remembering her fishwife grandmother. You must be strong, you must not yield to weakness or temptation, because if you do, you are lost forever, and the children will suffer the most.

"Silence," he said, very close. She opened her eyes reluctantly. He was kneeling before her, and there was deep concern on his face. "I am sorry—I did not intend to distress you. Do you want me to leave?"

She shook her head. That would only prolong her agony. What she must do had to be done at once, or her determination would evaporate, as it was doing already. He was so close, she had only to reach out and touch him, but her hands clenched the arms of the chair as if she feared they would move of their own accord. She fished a kerchief from her sleeve and wiped her face clean of tears, then forced herself to speak calmly. "No—don't go yet. It was nothing you said—I'd no more grieve for Ridgeley than I would for a buried stone, and his death is a blessed relief." She made herself confront his gaze directly. "I cannot condemn what you and those others did. And you saved Rachael, and all of us—and so we owe you our thanks and gratitude." She essayed a wan smile and added, "Perhaps you are an instrument of the Lord's vengeance. I hope so—in that case, you will surely go unpunished."

"I intend to," Nick said dryly. "The message went to Bath four hours ago. According to what I wrote, Lieutenant-Colonel Ridgeley suffered a relapse of his old wound, due to his intemperate and choleric nature, and unfortunately died of it. How will he learn any different?"

His magic was weaving its spell again, enchanting her, making her smile at his effrontery. She said, "How can you manage to tell the truth and lie at the same time?"

"Oh, it takes years of dedicated practice," he told her, grinning. "I must say, I was rather pleased with my explanation. And Bridges isn't likely to inquire too closely into the circumstances of Ridgeley's death. The man was a thorough nuisance, and he heartily disliked him. He'll be glad to be rid of him."

"A dreadful fate," Silence said slowly. "To die unloved, utterly unmourned. But deserved, I think. And though I may shrink from the method of his dispatch, I should not be such a hypocrite. I wished him dead, and he is, and I should be grateful."

He gave her a quick smile in acknowledgment and glanced down at the basket. Pye was sitting watchfully, looking at Lily, and the kittens were rolling and squeaking on the soft bedding, an old worn skirt of Rachael's. Nick bent and lifted one of them up. It was the black and white one that had so nearly been slain. It nestled in his hand, its new blue eyes blinking, bumping against his fingers with a blunt, questing nose. He ran his other hand along the soft fur, harsh-edged where it had been singed, and said, "Whatever happened to this one?"

She had forgotten that he did not know. She said briefly, "Ridgeley threw it into the fire."

There was a short, appalled silence. Then, without speaking, he laid the kitten very gently back by its mother. At last he said, "Why?"

"He was threatening me," Silence told him, and the raw terror of that moment rose again to haunt her. She paused, struggling for composure, and added, "Pye rescued it while he wasn't looking. Fortunately, it had fallen on an unburnt log—so it escaped only slightly singed."

"And with only eight lives left," said Nick. "You'll have to call it Lucky."

"No—Nat is determined to christen her Fortuna," Silence told him. "Since she's destined for some deserving village family, I doubt she'll keep that name for long."

He laughed and fell to stroking Pye. Lily immediately thrust her nose under his arm and demanded affection, whereupon he employed two hands, one for her and one for the cat. Silence, looking down at his bent head, sighed miserably. Almost he had enchanted her again. How easy, how temptingly easy to forget her fear, to fall into his smiles and draw close to his laughter, and to progress a little further along the fair sweet path of damnation.

She was strong, much stronger than she had ever imagined. The events of the past six months had taught her that. She had survived with her mind and body intact, she had successfully protected her house and her children from the viciousness of a man whose brutality was a byword for miles around. And she knew that she would not have achieved this without the help of the man sitting on the floor beside her, playing with her animals as if that morning's murder had never been.

The contrast chilled her and strengthened her resolve. She said formally, "Captain Hellier, I must ask a favor of you."

His face turned up to hers in surprise. "Of course," he said. Lily, suddenly finding that the stroking hand had stopped, whined and pushed her nose at him, to no effect. Silence snapped her fingers and the puppy, aware that she had transgressed but uncertain how, crept around to the other side of the chair with an anxious expression, her tail cravenly curled beneath her belly.

Nick sat back on his heels, his face quiet, watchful, and she wondered if her longing for him was visible like an aura about her, betraying the depth of her feeling. But she must not admit it: She must act as if it did not matter.

She took a deep, desperate gulp of air and said, "I think it would be best if you did not visit me like this, when neither Mally nor the children are here. If you continue, it will only be a matter of time before tongues wag."

He stared at her, the expression on his face unreadable. Then he said, obviously not believing her, "I did not think you cared a toss for malicious gossip."

"My children do," Silence said. She forced her voice and face to stay cool, unemotional, denying the turmoil within. "I have a position to maintain. I am a virtuous wife, and all must see it."

"Caesar's wife must be above suspicion," he said. "Well, it is your decision, my lady, and I will abide by it. What of Tabby?"

"I will have the virginals moved back to the winter parlor, and you may teach her there, should you still have the wish and the time to do so," Silence said. She rose to her feet. Courtesy demanded that he do so too, and he stood in front of her, their eyes almost equal. His smile was bitter, and a little mocking. "I am sorry you should feel this necessary, my lady. I have enjoyed your conversation and your company, and I hope very much that you have gained similar pleasure from mine. I know that Sir Thomas Bridges will probably put me in charge of this garrison, and my duties will most like be much greater—but they would not have been so arduous, with your cooperation and help."

"I'm not saying that we cannot work together to run Wintercombe," Silence told him. "It is these visits that must stop—I'm sorry, I truly am—but it's the wisest course. Surely you must see that?"

"I see it," he said dryly. "But wisdom is not one of my qualities, my lady Silence. However, as I told you this morning under circumstances entirely different, I will not force you to do anything you do not want." He hesitated, as if he had wished to say something more, and then thought better of it. He bowed to her, very correct and punctilious, and then turned and walked to the door.

It felt as if her heart was being torn from within her. Silence watched him go, her hands holding her lips together, so strong was the urge to call him back, to fall weeping into his arms, to succumb to the forces of Satan impelling her to sin. Lily, sensing her distress as clearly as Pye, stared first at her, then at Nick, with worried brown eyes, and whined. Silence bade her sharply to be quiet.

He opened the door. Rachael was just coming up the stairs at a brisk trot, her skirts bunched in her hand and a book tucked under her arm. She stopped when she saw him, and a crimson blush washed unattractively over her thin face. She said, "Captain Hellier, may I speak with you for a moment?"

Silence had at least expected the momentary luxury of some privacy in which to give way to her grief. Instead, she saw Nick retreat into the chamber, followed by Rachael and, more slowly, Nat. The girl stood squarely in front of the captain, still flushed, and her hands gripping a fold of her skirt. She said, her voice loud with nervousness, "My mother says that you have saved my life, because you had Ridgeley killed before he could find me."

"Quieter, you gawcum," Nat said, digging her in the ribs. "Do you want the whole house to know of it?" He shut the door pointedly.

Rachael glared at him and went on. It was not a task that she relished, but her duty was plain, and somehow she had mustered the courage for it. "I—I must apologize, Captain, for all the trouble I have caused you. I was thoughtless and selfish and disobedient, and I put you in great danger. Thank you for saving me."

His smile, Silence saw with a pang, could be singularly sweet. Rachael's blush deepened, and she cast her eyes down. He said gently, "It was something that had to be done. Think no more of it. Above all, don't feel guilty. He was not worth it."

And Rachael's face, glowing, as she curtsied to him, gave another twist to the knife in her stepmother's heart.

TWENTY-TWO

I humbly do beseech you of your pardon
For too much loving you.
                    —*OTHELLO*

"There is a letter for you, Mama," said Tabby. "I think it's from Uncle Woods. Someone's opened it," she added disapprovingly.

Silence leaned back upon the piled pillows. She felt better today, better than she had done for several days, since the sickness first struck. The morning after Ridgeley's death, she had woken with a terrible headache pulsating virulently behind her eyes. At first she had tried to ignore it, but that proved impossible, and by dinnertime she had admitted defeat and retired to her bed. Then the pains had given way to a fever, sharp and high. It was the first time she had been ill, apart from winter coughs and sneezes, since William's birth more than three years ago, and it worried her. But the consequences of her sickness made her still more anxious. How would the household fare while its mistress and director lay in her bed upstairs, incapacitated by fever?

She lay and fretted until Mally, with brisk kindness, assured her that she and Eliza and Darby had everything in hand between them, and she was to lie still and rest. Silence reflected ruefully that this alternative situation was probably even more upsetting to a housewife who had thought herself indispensable, and decided that, since she obviously could not win, at least to enjoy her enforced inactivity.

The fever was debilitating but not serious, although she was alternatively too hot and too cold, and never seemingly at a happy medium. Mally brought her tempting meals and smiled even when she picked at them. She mixed medicines and stood over Silence as she dutifully swallowed them. Since rigorous nursing was not necessary, she busied herself otherwise in the house, relaying messages, directing the other servants, and keeping people at bay when her mistress was asleep—which was, for the first few days, most of the time. As Silence had feared, once she gave way and stopped struggling, it was so much easier just to lie there, warm and comparatively comfortable and above all idle, satisfied that the world had not stopped simply because she had retired from it for a week or so.

When she had begun to take an interest once more in what was happening outside her chamber, the children were allowed to visit. Deb and William proved exhausting in large amounts, and had to have their time restricted. Fortunately, the kittens were growing fast, beginning to move around with tottering steps, and the two littlest children, entranced, spent hours watching them and playing with them despite Silence's urgings to be gentle and moderate, and Pye's maternal watchfulness.

Tabby came every afternoon, and sat on the bed and sang the new songs she had learned from Captain Hellier, and told long amusing stories about each day's events. But this letter was an unexpected treat, and Silence held her hand out eagerly for it. Tabby gave the thick battered fold of paper into her grasp and bounced onto the bed with an expectant look on her face. Letters were always treasured, read by or to all the family, passed around until their folds grew worn and the writing faded, and then kept in a box in the study as if they were jewels. Since the war had begun, the regular supply from her brother and sisters in London had all but stopped. She had received perhaps two or three a year, instead of the weekly epistles that she had received at Chard, and the last had come in March, in company with the letter from George, telling her so brutally of Sam's dreadful death.

She shuddered at that memory, which she had tried, on the whole successfully, to suppress, and unfolded the letter. Tabby was quite right, the seal had been broken, but apart from that, her brother Joseph's erratic and haphazard hand was unaltered from when he had written it, no doubt hunched over a table in his parlor above the draper's shop in Paternoster Row.

He was married—that was the reason for the letter. Married the day before he had written it, to Grace Hayward, a mercer's daughter undoubtedly possessed of a handsome dowry. Endearingly, however, it was her handsome face that had excited Joseph's interest and lent unwonted wings to his pen. More than half the first page described his beloved wife, the aptness of her name, her pleasing features, her sweet and delightful nature, their hopes of children. Whatever the sex of the first, he wrote, his dearest sister was to stand its godparent.

How her duty in this could be adequately achieved when a hundred miles of war-torn England separated child and sponsor, Silence failed to see, but it was entirely typical of Joseph to forget such practicalities. He did, however, thank her for her welcome letter, so at least she knew that it had reached him safely. He did not mention the ones she had sent to their two sisters, Patience and Prudence. She wondered if her husband had received his, full of empty words and hollow phrases because no pen, no language on earth could do justice to the grief and rage she felt toward him, for Sam's terrible death and the way it had been so callously revealed to her.

She hauled her thoughts away from George, and Sam, and turned again to Joseph's letter. The second paragraph commiserated with her over the soldiers' occupation of Wintercombe, advised her to choose the godly path without antagonizing such dangerous men, and finished with a series of luridly tactless atrocity stories about the activities of Goring's Crew in the south of Somerset, butchering innocent women and children, roasting babies and torturing ministers who dared to question their authority. A year ago such things would have aroused her incredulity. No one, surely, could be so stupid, so cruel and brutal.

But a year ago she had not heard of Lieutenant-Colonel Jack Ridgeley. And now, she knew that they could.

"Yet be of good cheer, dearest sister," Joseph continued at the top of the second page, after this blood-curdlingly gruesome catalogue of outrages. "Your captivity is onerous indeed, but with the Lord's help there will soon be an end to the sufferings of yourself and your dear children. It is said that General Fairfax is to march into the West Country for the relief of Taunton and the miserable people of those parts, who daily groan under the Cavalier yoke, and people who know much of affairs confidently report that your deliverance cannot long be delayed."

There followed a paragraph of family news, usually welcome, but Silence scanned the close-written words so quickly that she barely took in their sense. Prudence continued well, the babe expected in July, but Patience had willfully and foolishly declared that she would not marry the young man to whom, apparently with universal satisfaction, she had been betrothed, and had rejected all other contenders. When her eye had passed Joseph's almost illegible signature at the foot of the page, she handed the two sheets to Tabby without even thinking of those graphic descriptions of the atrocities of Goring's men. Her mind was turning over and over the implications of her brother's more factual information.

This new-modeled army, from Joseph's brief, vague but admiring description, seemed to be something quite different from the other forces on both sides. It was well-organized, equipped, and trained, and evidently a power to be reckoned with, owing its allegiance not to one region or general but to the cause of God and Parliament. And if it marched west, to free the country from the "Cavalier yoke," there was no doubt in Joseph's mind at least that it would succeed.

Silence thought of the warring Royalist generals, the child prince who nominally commanded them, the shortage of men and money, the hostile countryside, the scattered garrisons, large and small, each wrapped up in its own concerns, and there was no doubt in her mind either. In all probability, the fall would come some time this year or next. And then her temptation, her joy, her agony would be removed, and Nick Hellier would be gone from her life.

She knew that it was for the best, but her traitor heart cried out at the prospect. And George would come home, and life would return to normal, and how could she ever go back to that narrow, subservient existence?

She closed her eyes, for a moment almost despairing. How could she bear to have George with her again, at her board and in her bed, organizing her, assuming her emotions, taking her for granted?

Make, do, mend, she told herself severely. You have changed—well, so may he. And if he is in this new-modeled army, he may not come home for some time. And meanwhile you are still free, you have the children—and Nat will have the chance to let his growing catch up with the rest of him, before his father returns to claim him as his second-best heir.

George had described the death of the son he had undoubtedly loved, in a detail others more sensitive might have hesitated to employ for a cow's slaughter. How would he treat Nat, whom he had always derided and considered to be a weakling of no account? The boy's sharp, mature, intelligent mind had meant nothing to George, whose ideal son had been the handsome, confident, healthy, and charming Sam. Nat he despised and ignored where possible, and Silence, with foreboding, knew that the feeling was mutual.

"Mama, are they true?"

She looked up, and saw Tabby's pale, anxious face staring at her. The child waved the letter. "Are they true, those stories? Do they *really* roast babies?"

Oh, no, thought Silence, remembering too late that she had not intended to let Tabby see the first, lurid page. She said hastily, with as much cheerful confidence as she could muster, "Of course not. Why, I don't think even Colonel Ridgeley would do such a dreadful thing."

Kittens, though, had been another matter. Tabby did not know of that, however, and Silence hoped that she never would.

"He was going to do terrible things to Rachael," the girl said. "I heard Nat talking to Mally about it. I'm *glad* he's dead, he *deserved* to die."

And all her mother's reassuring words melted away unuttered before Tabby's fierce hatred. Of all those minds and bodies hurt by this stupid senseless war, she feared most for this child: For sometimes, the greater the damage, the more impossible it was to discern.

There was quiet while Tabby finished the letter, frowning with concentration. At last she put it down and said slowly, "I would like to see all my aunts and uncles in London. When can we go? Will it have to be after the war?"

"I'm afraid it must be, chicken," Silence said sadly. None of her children had ever met her family. The distance had been so great, and George had not been encouraging. She wondered suddenly if he had been ashamed of his second wife's comparatively humble origins. He so evidently thought her inferior to him, but she had assumed that it was because she was female. She herself was proud of her fishwife grandmother. She had certainly been a better and wiser person, in every sense, than the aristocratic and malevolent Dame Ursula.

"And there will be a baby cousin by then," Tabby said. She drew her knees up to her chin and a dreamy, faraway look came over her face. "I wonder if it will be a boy or a girl."

"I don't think your Aunt Prudence would mind very much which. She wants as many as possible, so she's bound to have at least one of each."

"Not very prudent, then," Tabby said, and giggled. "But then you aren't silent, are you, Mama?"

"And nor is your other aunt patient," Silence said, smiling. Tabby in this mood would always cheer her: It was as if they had entered a magic and secret world which only the two of them knew, and shared. "She always wants everything now, as soon as possible."

"Just like Deb." Tabby stared into space, humming softly. Even in this idle moment, the sound was perfectly in tune. She added, "Captain Hellier asked how you were."

Silence was glad that the child was not looking at her as she spoke. The lurch of her emotions must surely have been writ clear on her face. She schooled her expression with an effort, and said casually, "Did he? Did you tell him?"

"Oh, yes . . . I said you were much better, and he asked if Mally was giving you plenty of possets and juleps, and I said yes, and some horrible cordial that you didn't like. And he asked after the kittens too. He sounded sad," Tabby said thoughtfully. "I think he misses the evenings up here, and playing chess with Nat, and talking to us. I think he's lonely. He can't have any friends, can he, if he's in command of the garrison?"

Oh, dear Lord, Silence thought wretchedly, out of the mouths of babes . . . Why did she have to mention it? Aloud she said briskly, "Oh, I'm sure he has. Cornet Wickham is his friend, and there are all the other officers."

"They're either nasty or stupid," Tabby said dismissively. "But *none* of them are as nasty or stupid as Colonel Ridgeley was." Her hazel eyes, huge, haunted, lifted suddenly to her mother's face, awash with tears. "What Uncle Woods said in his letter—about roasting babies—would Colonel Ridgeley have done that to *William* if Captain Hellier hadn't killed him first?"

Silence could not tell her the truth, nor ask how she knew, or guessed, that Nick had done the murder. She took Tabby in her arms, and they both wept for a while, until Pye and Lily, alike in their concern and their jealousy of each other, thrust themselves between them and reduced mother and daughter to rather tearful laughter.

*   *   *

Silence spent four days in her bed and several more keeping quietly to her chamber, regaining her strength. She had wanted to venture forth much earlier, but Mally sensibly forbade it, and Nat, laughing and stalwart, barred the door. Laughing with him, she could not help noticing that he had grown some inches. He was as tall as Mally now, and fast catching up to Rachael. Perhaps, when George at last came home, he would find a young man and not a feeble, undersized boy. She hoped so fervently, for Nat, of all his children, most deserved his father's respect.

She did not see Nick at all. Mally, carefully noncommittal, had told her that he had been appointed commander of the garrison—another officer, of the Bath Foot, had become lieutenant-colonel—and that Sir Thomas Bridges had not queried Ridgeley's death at all. He was obviously much too busy. News had recently reached them of the relief of Taunton, where the Roundhead Colonel Blake had held out first against Goring, and then Hopton, for months at great cost. As Joseph had predicted, Fairfax had marched westward with the might of Parliament's New Model Army, only to be ordered away to Oxford to confront the king and Prince Rupert. But some six thousand men had continued westward and had arrived in Taunton, to the wild cheers of the beleaguered populace, on the eleventh of May.

On the same day, Goring returned to Somerset from his visit to the king in Oxford, with the independent command he had craved for so long and the avowed intention of breaking all Roundhead resistance in the western counties, using the utmost force if necessary. Where this force was to be obtained was unclear, for attempts to raise an army were failing dismally. Recruiting officers had come to Norton, as to most villages in northern Somerset, to enlist men, and had gone away empty-handed. Even their attempts at force had been unsuccessful, despite the presence of a detachment of the Wintercombe garrison. Most of the stalwart young men whom they had seized, Mally had reported gleefully, had been shown to be husbandmen, or married, and therefore officially exempt from impressment. The half dozen who were not had been rescued in Wellow when the inhabitants fell upon the startled soldiers with clubs, pitchforks, and scythes. All over Somerset feelings ran high, and the Royalist armies and garrisons found their commands and extortions increasingly resisted by the abused and indignant population.

Philip's Norton had certainly escaped more lightly than the unfortunate villages within Goring's orbit farther south. After Ridgeley's death, they had found themselves once more under the aegis of Captain Hellier, and it was admitted grudgingly in the George and the Fleur-de-Lys that he was at least fair. There was no longer any pretense about payment for what they took, but no one was asked to pay more than they could afford, threats were few, and no family went hungry. But as May advanced, the garrison had to spread its forage net wider. There was an embarrassing clash with members of the Farleigh regiment in the village of Rode, and another one near Mells in which a member of the force at Nunney Castle was hurt. Both incidents were followed by an exchange of recriminatory letters with the commanders involved, a situation reflecting in little the antagonism, rivalry, and confusion rife within the Royalist leadership in the west.

Once, rather naively, Nick Hellier had wanted his own command, to be beholden to no one, like a miniature king. And now, beset by the multitudinous duties and responsibilities that his post entailed, he remembered that wish with rueful astonishment. Somehow, with Ridgeley ill upstairs, it had seemed different; and then the decay within the Royalist forces had seemed less evident. Before there had still been hope; now he knew there was none and that slowly, inexorably, the Roundhead tide would wash over them all.

The king still had an army in the field, of course, and Prince Rupert was still his fiery self, despite his loss of invincibility at Marston Moor. But in the west, the petty jealousies, feuds, and enmities of the various commanders, all of whom wanted to be superior to the rest, were paramount. Winning the war was a secondary consideration. After news of yet another debacle—Goring's failed attack on Taunton, in which he seemed to have been too drunk to give coherent orders—Nick realized grimly that their struggle was doomed to end in chaotic ignominy and defeat. Nothing had been achieved, save for the alienation of the people of Somerset, who were now so heartily sick of the depredations of the soldiers that they were beginning to band together to resist them. The incident in Wellow, echoed elsewhere, was but an early sign of what must inevitably come.

His men were already on short rations: bread, cheese, beer, supplemented by what they could extract from the villages. He had given up asking Sir Thomas Bridges for money to pay for what they took, and for the soldiers. The Governor of Bath had made it quite clear that he had sufficient problems supplying his own garrison and had ordered that coin be levied from the local people. It had raised the princely sum of six pounds and four shillings, and Nick thought wryly that blood would have been easier to wring from a stone. Some of the foot soldiers, poor pressed men for the most part, had wearied of the hardship and crept away in the middle of the night, gone back to their homes or to take up a more profitable existence as footpads or vagrant beggars. He could not blame them; and at least there were fewer mouths to feed.

His own troop remained loyal. There was sickness among the horses, and several died, or had to be slaughtered. They were not so desperate as to eat them—not yet. Most were hastily turned out into the paddocks near to Wintercombe, and the epidemic dwindled away. The dead beasts were replaced with animals seized from the villages around about, a wretched collection of undersized and underfed farm horses, but the best had long since been commandeered.

And to cap it all, he seemed to have lost Silence.

He had thought that his feelings for her were returned. He had wooed her so gently, so subtly, as if she were a wild deer that he must coax to feed from his hand. It had begun as a diversion and grown into something much more delightful, and dangerous, and he could not abandon the chase now.

But she had. Something had alarmed her, and she had retreated from him. It was not the pretense he had made of betraying Rachael to Ridgeley: She understood his reasons for that, he was sure of it. And she could not, as she had claimed, be repelled by the colonel's killing, when she had wished him dead and knew that only thus could Rachael be saved.

He knew that she had at least a fondness for him; he could not mistake that look in her eyes, the smile, the closeness of their minds, the joy they had taken in each other's company. He had known, the evening after Ridgeley's death, that he had only to touch her to have her fall into his arms. It had shone from her face, however much she tried to hide it. And then she had spurned him.

It could not be the husband, whose stout, self-satisfied painted face, somewhat battered and smoke-blackened over the last months, still gazed smugly down from the small portrait on one side of the hall hearth. He was certain that the only pleasure the man had given her was her children. She had never spoken of him afterward, but her distress and anger at that terrible, thoughtless letter was still sharp in his mind. He would have no scruples in setting horns on Sir George St. Barbe's head.

No, it was her scruples that must be the sticking point. She had been reared in godliness and virtue, he knew, and although she had had the courage and strength of mind, and humor, to rebel against much of what she had been taught, he knew that the crime of adultery would in her eyes probably be the greatest wickedness of all.

He wanted her. He had been celibate for too long. But it was her he wanted beside him, to share love and joy and laughter. And he was as certain as he was of the sun's rising that she wanted him. And, knowing it, she had retreated into the chill formality of their earliest acquaintance.

Lines from an old poem kept haunting him, insistent, beautiful, strangely apt:

> *They flee from me, that sometime did me seek,*
> *With naked foot stalking within my chamber*
> *Once I have seen them gentle, tame and meek,*
> *That now are wild . . .*

Her children had not turned away from him. Nat was friendly, and often they played chess together in the dining parlor, which had become almost the officers' private quarters. William had lost none of his fascination with soldiers, and often towed the nursemaid Hester out to the barton to greet his friends. Deb was always ready to chat, indeed sometimes he had to stop the flood of her self-centered and somewhat incoherent talk in full spate or be delayed for hours.

And Rachael . . . Rachael was an embarrassment. Once she had hung about the barton to make offensive remarks about the soldiers. Now it was to catch a glimpse of Nick Hellier. Every time he passed the windows of the dairy, he saw her looking out. Always she would duck away, and he could imagine her pale face suffused with scarlet as she bent over the cream dishes. He had never had a child in love—or in calf love—with him before, and he did not know whether to laugh or be annoyed, or embarrassed. But he knew how fragile and volatile were the girl's moods. He would not show her that he had so much as noticed her changed attitude toward him. He was pleasant without laboring it, and hoped that she would soon fix her fickle, harmless attentions on that brawny and good-looking young stable lad, instead of an enemy soldier who was almost twice her age.

As for Tabby, she was there at the virginals in the winter parlor every evening for an hour before supper, whether he joined her or not. Often, immersed in paperwork in the chamber above, which had once been Ridgeley's, he would hear the soft sure sounds of her playing drifting through the floor. He had never taught music to anyone before, but he was certain that few indeed, especially at so tender an age, had such a swift and eager grasp of the essentials, such an appetite for learning. Her voice was lovely, though of course still a child's, for she was not yet nine. She could now sight-read a part from Sir Samuel's fat manuscript books of ayres and sounds and madrigals, and she had only to hear a tune sung or played once to remember it perfectly. Often she surprised him by humming some melody that he had played once, weeks before, and forgotten about. And now she was beginning to repeat such transitory memories on the keyboard.

He found it entertaining, and invigorating. He had always loved music, and his command of it was extensive, if not especially deep. He was a jack of many instruments but master of none. And to see this child's joy in the thing he loved was to discover his own wonder at it, all over again.

One evening they had tried something new, a duet for fiddle and virginals. She had played the basic tune, plain with no frills, while he had constructed an elaborate, improvised fantasia around her notes. Even as they were playing, it had sounded delightful. It was a shame, he thought, as their last combined harmony died away into the air, that no one else had been listening. Tabby put her hands on her knees and looked up at him, glowing with achievement, as breathless as if she had just run around the garden. "That was lovely! I wish Mama could have heard it!"

"We must play it for her," he said without thinking. Tabby fixed him with her serious, intense stare for a moment and then said, "But you don't see Mama any more. Why not? I thought you liked each other."

He had forgotten how direct children—especially these children—could be. He did not know what to say. How much did she know, or guess? She was eight years old: Surely she could understand nothing of the desires and temptations that he had shared with Silence?

"We do," he said, deciding to evade the truth. It was much safer. "But since I took over command here, I have been very busy."

"You were in command when Colonel Ridgeley was ill," the child said, and her hazel eyes studied him thoughtfully. "And you weren't too busy to see her then."

"She has been unwell," Nick pointed out. "And it would not be right or fair to visit her while she is sick."

Tabby continued to regard him with that disconcerting, level stare that saw, he felt, far too much, as if his head were made of glass to reveal the thoughts churning within. "I suppose so," she said at last, reluctantly. "But she used to look forward to you coming so much. I think she's lonely."

He forced a laugh. "Lonely? When she has all of you, and Mally, and Pye and Lily for company? If I were in her position, I'd want fewer people around me, not more."

"We don't make her laugh like you do," Tabby said. "When you danced with her, that was nice . . . why don't you bring your fiddle up tonight and play for her and we'll all dance? I liked that and I've never danced, just watched. Grandmother doesn't approve of dancing."

"I don't suppose she would—it's much too enjoyable," Nick said dryly, and made her giggle. It was not difficult, after that, to steer her onto safer ground, and soon they were involved in a new and elaborate version of "Greensleeves." But once or twice he felt or saw her intent, speculative stare and wondered just how much she did know. It had almost seemed, for a wild moment, as if she had been encouraging him to commit adultery with her own mother. And Tabby had a strong mind and, he suspected, her own ideas of right and wrong.

He dismissed the idea as ridiculous, and he did not resume his visits to Silence's chamber.

In contrast to the lovely weather earlier, the rest of May was disappointing. There was much rain, cold winds and little sun. But the vine flowered, a marvel that drew the excited attention of everyone in the household. Old Diggory, his shriveled face cracked with delight, pointed them out to anyone who passed and generally received a disappointed response.

"What? They scrawvlin little green things? Nay, Diggory, you be betwitting I for certain!"

"Just ee wait," Jemmy Coxe would say, his face glowing. "Just ee wait, and come October, that there vine'll be so full of grapes, 'twill be bowing right down to the ground!"

"Aye," they said skeptically. "And cows'll grow wings and fly over the moon."

Jemmy became quite annoyed at all their teasing, but Diggory took it all in good part. This was perhaps the busiest time of year in the garden: seedlings to weed, hedges to be clipped, vegetables and fruit to be nourished and tended in the kitchen garden. Despite the dismal weather, the peas and beans were doing well, and the raspberries and strawberries promised much fruit. The rain had done the apple blossom no good at all, however, and the remaining trees in the orchard bore a few sparse tiny green fruits that foreboded a scant harvest and a thin and meager brew of cider.

On the few fine days, Silence worked in the garden, deriving solace from the eternal growth and rebirth of spring. Bulbs grew, flowered, died back, and would do the same next year, whatever happened. It helped to restore a sense of proportion to her life. There was still the pain of losing Nick—and yet she had not lost him, only turned him away before they could go too far. She could still see him, speak to him, if only with that careful, cool formality, holding their relationship at arm's length. But the pain, the longing, the temptation always rose again to remind her why she must at all costs keep her distance. He had nothing to lose; she had everything.

One evening in the middle of May, she had been gathering sweet-scented wallflowers, the deep crimson ones that Diggory called bleeding hearts, and the tawny-gold flowers that were her own favorite, christened amberglows by Tabby. An armful of them, sufficient to scent her chamber for days, lay on the top terrace in the shade, and Silence, yielding to the warm gentle peace, had gone down to the orchard. The niches in the wall that supported the lowest terrace had always been her favorite place to sit, catching the rays of the setting sun. It was here that she had been resting when Rachael had brought news of the soldiers, more than half a year ago.

Half a year, and another world. She sat down, turning her face smiling to the warmth. Bees buzzed gently nearby. The niches had originally been intended to house Italian statues, but Sir Samuel's father had, perhaps fortunately, died before they could be obtained and his son, much more practical, had put bee skeps in them instead. It was the perfect place, between the flowers of the garden and the blossom of the orchard, south-facing and sheltered, and every year Diggory, well shrouded, raided the straw hives for the sweet fragrant honey, to be stored in earthenware jars in the Wintercombe larder. The insects' contented humming was companionable and soporific. She closed her eyes and wondered how long it would be before her peace was disturbed. It would not be by Tabby, at any rate, for the sounds of her playing trickled softly down through the air, hardly distinguishable from the birdsong, and as sweet.

It's ironic, Silence thought wryly. My eight-year-old daughter has his undivided attention for an hour, perhaps four or five times a week, for his music. And I must make do with a polite word or an exchange of courtesies. And, you ridiculous woman, there is no use lamenting it, for you yourself created this situation!

Distantly, a cuckoo called. She could hear Tabby playing still, the same piece over and over again as if there was something she could not get quite right. Closer, the soldiers, still laboring on the fortifications, in somewhat desultory fashion, were talking among themselves. It was strange, she thought, how they had seemed to be bitter foes that first October day. And now they posed no threat at all. Under Ridgeley's rule, the better troopers had been cowed into acquiescence, the worst allowed to give free reign to their baser instincts. With Nick, discipline was maintained fairly, without the floggings that had distinguished Ridgeley's command, and from all accounts, in Norton at least, the troopers were kept well under control. Silence suspected that it was done out of respect, admiration, and fear. All save the most hardened villain must acknowledge Captain Hellier's qualities of leadership. They were content to follow him, yet knew the penalties should they transgress. Ridgeley's punishments had been arbitrary, dependent on his whim, so that a man might find himself given the lash for an offense that another had committed last week with impunity. And Nick, aware that an unwilling soldier was worse than useless, turned a blind eye to the trickle of deserters, while disguising to the rest his own belief that defeat was now only a matter of time.

And so her daughter was given music lessons by the Royalist commander, and her son rode on their horses, played with their weapons, and called the troopers his friends. And their mother, wracked with the opposing forces of guilt and desire—not that, she told herself sternly, it was simply infatuation—no longer trusted her control sufficiently to keep Nick's friendship.

Beset by ironies and complications, by domestic problems—replacements for Leah and Bessie had still not been engaged, despite her own and Mally's efforts—and worries as mundane as finding suitable deserving homes for Pye's kittens, she tried to empty her mind of all thought and open her senses instead to what lay around her. The sweet smell of the warm grass and the wallflowers in the knots on the terrace above her mingled with the sharper scent of smoke from the kitchen hearth, the music, and the birdsong. One lovely liquid thrush had opened its throat to sing down the sun, and she sat and listened, letting its tune soothe her tangled emotions. Next day, next year, next century, a thrush would still be singing in these trees, or in others near. And thinking of that strangely comforting fact made her problems suddenly smaller and of little consequence beside the permanence of lesser things.

Her spirits restored, she rose to her feet and walked, still dreaming, to the steps. She set her hand on the warm golden stone, feeling the tiny ridges left by the mason's tools, and the moss, the softness of the green and orange lichen. She was part of this place, and it was part of her. And many years in the future, when the rest of her had long gone, her shade would still be wandering among the gardens she loved, lost, dreaming, happy.

It was, perhaps, a blasphemous thought, but a very attractive one. She heard footsteps brisk on the gravel above her and looked up, expecting Nat, or Mally.

But instead Nick Hellier appeared at the top of the steps.

Lily, who was as usual with Silence, uttered a yip of welcome and bounded up to him. From his face, he had not known she was there. He was quite still, staring down at her as she stood on the lowest step, and though his face was carefully emptied of expression after the first moment, his eyes were not. She found she could not meet their intensity. She looked past them and said courteously, "Good evening, Captain. Lily—come here, Lily!"

The puppy's ridiculous ears flickered, but she stayed where she was, sitting in front of him, waiting for an acknowledgment of her presence. Nick bent and patted her, and then gently turned around and followed her down the steps.

There they were out of sight of the house and shielded from the men at the bottom of the orchard by the new-leafed apple and pear trees and the long luscious grass. There was nowhere for Silence to go, and so she stayed where she was as he walked down the steps, to halt on the one above her, so close they could have touched.

So close . . . and yet so remote. She was not used to having to look up to him so far. The westering sun touched his face with a soft, golden light, and his hair seemed almost as fair as William's, though its true nut-brown color showed in shadow. "Hullo," he said, conventionally enough. "I did not know that you were here."

"Nor did I know that *you* were," she said, with a small embarrassed laugh that sounded lamentably false. There was nothing else to say that would not be lies, or dangerous, and so she said nothing, not looking at him, tortured by his closeness and by the constraint between them. If only they could return to the early days of their friendship, before feelings grew too intense, too perilous not to be leashed . . .

"Silence," he said, and his voice lingered over the two syllables of her despised name like a caress. "I will not ask any more of you, I promise . . . but I must know this, if nothing else. Why?"

There was no point in idle evasion, when she knew as well as he what was meant. And she realized suddenly that he deserved the truth, whatever the admission cost her, and him. He had risked his life, and his future, to save Rachael, he had helped her over and over again, and yet it had taken months for her to trust him fully, so cautious was she, so careful of her emotions, so suspicious of the enemy, especially when he came bearing gifts. She had determined to heed actions, not words, and yet only when he had killed his commanding officer had she at last believed in him. And in almost the same moment, she had rejected him and withdrawn her friendship.

And, she knew now, had hurt him, hurt a man who had not seemed so vulnerable. And that fact in itself said much. She took a deep breath and gathered the courage to look him in the face. The concern on it nearly overthrew her composure. She set her jaw, determined, and said in a voice that hardly trembled at all, "Because I feared the consequences if I did not . . . did not keep you away."

"And what consequences were they?" His voice was gentle, inquiring. He had never been angry with her, never treated her with anything other than respect, save on that terrible night when he had been so exasperated at her vain attempts to save Nat. And since his own efforts had succeeded, she had not resented that single lapse of courtesy.

Even now she found it almost impossible to utter the truth, for she was not accustomed to taking her inmost feelings out for examination by others in the cold light of reality. But she had begun this and would finish it. She swallowed and said hesitantly, "Of—of becoming too . . . too attached to you."

The words love and adultery lay between them, heavy with significance, but she did not think that her tongue could physically shape them. A hot, humiliating blush had flooded her face. Her eyes dropped, unable to watch his reaction.

For a long time, he said nothing. Staring down at the steps, she saw a woodlouse, a gladdigoaster Diggory called it, trickling busily along the stone. It came to her skirts, hesitated, and then started to make its way around the wall of fine dark gray wool. I will not weep, she thought. I will *not*.

His hand came up to touch her jaw, and turn her face toward him. "Oh, my most gracious Silence, is that so terrible?"

"Yes!" she cried, with an anguish born of desperation. "Yes—you know it is! I have a husband, and children whom I love dearly, a home that I love almost as much—all I have is here—without them I am *nothing*!" She stared at him, her body shaking with the force of her emotions. "I was safe—I may not have known very much happiness—but I was *secure*. And now—and now it's as if there's a great hole suddenly opened up just at my feet, and if I go any farther along the same road, I shall be dead, drowned, lost—I *must* go back, can't you see, Nick, I *must*! I have too much to lose!"

"Then you love me," he said.

The word was spoken, and the earth did not fall. Nor could she deny it: The truth was written on her face. She looked at him in mute despair, and that was answer enough.

He had never felt such tenderness toward anyone in his life. She had endured tragedies, disasters, dangers, and triumphed over them with a quiet strength that had won his surprised admiration. He was certain that few ladies, and few indeed so gentle and sensitive as Silence, would have survived such hardships with mind and body intact. And even now she was making desperate efforts to deny her right to an emotion that she felt to be sinful.

And yet he could not reassure her; for his feelings, too, were so strong that to give way to them would lead to the consequences she dreaded. He could see the sense of her attitude, and, as she had said so forcefully, she had infinitely more to lose than did he. But every time he saw her, saw her neat, unassuming body clad in the sober colors she almost always wore, the linen cap hiding her hair, her face calm, serene, moving among her people with a smile, graceful, gentle, unhurried, the power of his feelings shook him afresh. He did not know why. He had previously been attracted to bold, vigorous women, full of color and vitality. Why had this quiet, dowdy Puritan housewife, with her secret life of laughter and beauty, turned his emotions upside down and led him unawares into love?

There was no answer. He only knew that he desired her, and wanted her, and needed her, and that to be in the same place and not even have her to talk to was unendurable.

But it would make matters so much easier if he did not tell her. Let her think that what looked out of his eyes was lust, unalloyed and impure, and she would eventually lose interest. What she felt was, surely, no more than an adult version of her stepdaughter's calf love, born of restlessness or boredom with her limited domestic life: a swift, flaring emotion, quick to die down to ashes, leaving her to wonder how she could ever have been so stupid.

He said quietly, "I cannot offer you any comfort, save this—and you may not think it comfort at all. I have only just received the orders—I was going to find Lieutenant Byam and tell him. I am required to join Goring's army about Taunton, with the Horse. We are to leave tomorrow."

Silence stared at him, feeling the tears dribble out of her eyes and down her face. She brushed them away and essayed a smile. It was hollow in the extreme. "Perhaps it is comfort, perhaps not. I don't know—and I won't, until you are gone." She swallowed painfully. "I'm not making much sense, am I? Do you think I can so readily forget you? I don't think I can.

You have taught me happiness—how can I unlearn it, and return to my old, unawakened life?" She paused, struggling for self-control, and then said wryly, "I don't think I would want to. What you have given me cannot be taken away. And what you have done for Tabby, that is a gift beyond price, and she and I will be forever grateful."

"Thank you," he said, still watching her.

Her eyes flashed up at him, an expression astonishingly similar to Tabby's. She said, as if she feared the answer, "Will—will you come back?"

"That is what is planned," he said dryly. "It depends on Goring. He is supposed to be blockading Taunton, and requires all the Horse he can lay his hands on for the task. When it is done, we are supposed to return here—but whether that will happen, and when, is a completely unknown quantity." He smiled rather grimly. "Johnny will be pleased at the prospect. Goring's debauches are legendary—he frequently disappears for three or four days put together. And probably half the army will feel constrained to follow suit. It should make Colonel Ridgeley's excesses look like a parsonage supper."

Almost, but not quite, he had made her laugh. She smiled wanly. "And will you also follow suit?"

"Perhaps. I have swilled enough wine and beer in my time to flood a city—but I find in my old age that I dislike making a fool of myself. And in that crew, someone has to have their wits about them. If I am one of them, so much the better—you'll see me a major, or even a colonel yet!"

Stricken, Silence stared at him. His lighthearted smile did not deceive her. She said urgently, "Take care—please take care. I will pray for you."

"I will—I have never been one to risk my life for a whim or a gallant gesture. Captain Bull is left in command here—I will give him explicit orders, and he should not trouble you. And with the Horse gone, life should be a great deal easier for you all, and for Philip's Norton." He studied her pale, tear-streaked face. "Have I brought you any comfort?"

"Yes," Silence said steadily. She raised her chin and looked him straight in the eye. "I cannot pretend that I will forget you, or fail to think of you with anything other than love, and grief. But your going makes it easier, I think. We are not children, to succumb to every wild desire like a wind-blown weathercock. We are adults, each with our responsibilities, isn't that so? And so we must bow to them, and go our separate ways, and deny what we feel in case it brings us to grief, because others have prior claims upon us."

He said nothing for a moment, and then began to speak. She realized that the words made part of a poem:

Shake hands forever: cancel all our vows,
And when we meet at any time again,
Be it not seen in either of our brows,
That we one jot of former love retain.

"That is by a poet not long dead, called Michael Drayton. I will lend you my books, when I leave, for there is much in them to delight you, or perhaps comfort you—or make you sad." He smiled at her. "Thoughts echoed in verse seem to have a strength and beauty that ordinary words lack—I can't explain it very well, but it is like music. You've already caught a glimpse of the world of words—at least I will give you something to remember me by, while I am gone."

"Even if I do not wish it?" Silence asked. "I'm not sure I want to have my emotions made greater still—this is quite bad enough already." She found that her voice was quite matter-of-fact, and her face seemed calmer. She took a deep breath and added, "But I thank you—yes, leave me your books. If I have time to read them, I will."

"But you mean to make yourself so busy that you have not a single instant in which to think of me?" he said, and there was a teasing note in his voice. "So, my dearest Silence, 'Since there's no help, come let us kiss and part.'"

He bent his head toward her, his hands barely resting on her shoulders, and his lips touched hers. It was the lightest contact, but she shivered with the rush of longing that swept over her. Sensing her reaction, he lingered, exploring, gentle, loving, seeking not to devour or force her but to show her little by little what delight could lie in wait for her.

It was a mistake. Something that neither of them could control took over: Her hands came up to pull him closer, and her body pressed against his, desperate for a pleasure she had never before experienced. Astonished, dazed, bewildered, he lifted his head at last, half expecting, with belated caution, to see a ring of appalled or grinning faces around them. But there was no one: They were still quite alone. Her eyes were closed, her face chalk white, her lips parted, and her weight dragged suddenly on his arms, so that he wondered if she had fainted.

He said softly, "Silence—Silence, I'm sorry—I didn't mean—"

"I'm all right," she said, suddenly restored. Since he seemed to be making no attempt to let her go, she gently removed his hands and stepped aside from his embrace. "Perhaps we should take it as a warning." She smiled ruefully, as shaken as he was. "Play with fire, and it burns. Nick—I love you—and I think you should go now."

He stood looking at her for a moment, and she met his gaze, no longer afraid. Then he said, so quietly that she wondered afterward if she had imagined it, "And I love you. Good-bye, Silence."

He ran down the last step past her and through the orchard. She watched until he was no longer to be seen. She must go back to the house; she must behave as if nothing had happened; and she must never, never, ever give away, by sign or word or deed, the power and joy and pain he had unleashed in her.

"Oh, dear God," she whispered, staring down at the apple trees. "Oh, sweet Lord—what have I done?"

PART FOUR

A SUMMER'S DAY

JUNE–SEPTEMBER 1645

CHAPTER

TWENTY-THREE

This above all: to thine own self be true.
—HAMLET

The forty-odd men of Sir Thomas Bridges' Horse rode out of Wintercombe at first light the next morning and left a hole in the fabric of the lives of the household that surprised them all, and proved very difficult to fill at first.

There were, of course, advantages to their going. Clevinger had his barn back, almost to himself. The company of foot left to man the garrison could now muster only thirty soldiers, and they occupied one corner while the bailiff, helped by Tom Goodenough and the stable lads, cleared out the rest of the debris accumulated during the winter occupation. Haymaking was several weeks off, harvest of course still more distant, but the squalid condition of the barn had long offended Clevinger's fastidious nature, and he wasted no time in setting it, and the barton, to rights. Almost all the horses were gone, those remaining being the riding animals of Captain Bull and his officers, and so the makeshift horselines in the linhay and the barn could be dismantled, and the piles of dung shoveled into one great heap, unfortunately too late to enrich this year's crops, although corners of the kitchen garden benefited.

To all this activity, Captain Bull remained indifferent. He was a dour, silent man, middle-aged and given to chewing on a clay pipe without ever lighting it, and he had no wish to step outside the strict confines of his duty. He and his men were to guard the house and forage for their support. Since they were not cavalry, their range was limited to Norton, and at first the villagers tolerated their demands. After all, the number of Royalist soldiers at Wintercombe had diminished by more than half.

William missed the Horse greatly. He kept asking his mother where they had gone and, when tired of the unsatisfactory answers (Taunton meant nothing to him), started wondering when they would be back. The plumes and buff coats and pistols and swords, the horses and the cheerful air of most of the troopers, contrasted painfully with Captain Bull's rather down-at-heel musketeers, most of whom were poor, landless men who had joined up for the plunder, or to escape punishment for debt or other petty offenses. Nearly half of their number had deserted since they came to Wintercombe, and the residue were a surly, villainous-looking crew, who brushed past William as if he did not exist, or cursed him for being in the way. Hester confided to Doraty that the little master was much easier to handle since the troopers were gone, but she did not like to see him so quiet and biddable.

Rachael moped too. She took refuge in the dairy, neglected her studies, and had to be dragged away to perform them. With some desperation, Silence redoubled her efforts to find a dairymaid. Eventually she discovered Jemmy Coxe's aunt Joan, a large young woman a couple of years younger than herself, who had recently left employment on a Wellow farm to nurse her stepmother through a winter sickness. Joan Coxe had been reluctant to come to Wintercombe, but the offer of three pounds a year, a new gown at Ladyday and Michaelmas, and her keep proved sufficiently enticing. Silence knew that she was not supposed to offer such an inflated wage. In more normal times, this sort of inducement might well bring her to the notice of the justices, who were supposed to regulate such things. But she was desperate, and no justice had sat in North Somerset for some time. And Joan Coxe was a strapping wench of plain appearance, who stood some inches taller than many of the ill-nourished, undersized soldiers and would stand no nonsense from anyone. Rachael, her nose put thoroughly out of joint, sulked.

Tabby reacted in a different way. Deprived of her lessons, but left all her grandfather's music books, and Nick's, to plunder, she rejoiced in her temporary freedom. She had the skills now to take advantage of the resources offered, and told her mother, her eyes glowing, "When Captain Hellier comes back I'll have learned so much—he'll be so pleased!"

Her confidence heartened Silence. At least Tabby seemed sure of his return, and her belief was so complete that it brooked no alternative. And yet the child had no knowledge of the true situation. Goring's qualities as a commander of men were erratic to put it mildly, and from all accounts he seemed to have antagonized most of the population of southern Somerset— those who were not starved, murdered, or fled. Indeed, some of the people were beginning to band against the plundering soldiers, ringing the church bells to warn of their approach and attacking them with makeshift weapons when they attempted to enforce contributions. These Clubmen, as they were called, did not claim to be against the Royalists in particular but against all soldiers who threatened their livelihood.

There was talk, in Philip's Norton, of the movement spreading to all parts of Somerset as well as Wiltshire and Dorsetshire. Looking at the quiet knots of people, heads together around the Market Cross, and the sullen, assessing stares earned by the soldiers as they tramped past, Silence did not think that it would be very long before the people of the village decided that resistance to Bull's men was a viable proposition. The well-armed, well-drilled cavalrymen were much too intimidating for husbandmen and small farmers to challenge with makeshift weapons, but the disreputable musketeers did not pose much of a threat.

And if the villagers did keep them out of Norton, Wintercombe alone would carry the burden of feeding them.

The winter's depredations lay listed in her neat, clear hand on a small stack of paper in the study. The apple trees, a third cut down for firewood or for a makeshift barrier for the fortifications. Timber in the hedgerows around the house, chopped up for the same purpose and to make the horse-lines. Of Sir Samuel's prized herd of Somerset milch kine, only half were left, though mostly the younger animals, good milkers and proven moth-ers. Fortunately the bull, a massive and vicious beast called Russet, had proved more than a match for greedy soldiers, and still inhabited one of the paddocks opposite Clevinger's cottage. But the sheep, not an extensive flock in this dairying country, had dwindled to a poor fraction of their former numbers, the bailiff's pigs were down to two sows and their new litters, and not even the wiliest and quickest hens had survived both the soldiers and the attentions of a local fox. Hay, straw, oats, wheat, flour, peas and beans, barley, cider, wine and beer, hams and bacon, eggs and milk and cheeses and butter—all had had to be bought because the soldiers had taken their stores. Add to this tally the damage caused by disturbances and searches and riots, Silence thought sadly, and the cost to the Winter-combe estate had run into hundreds, if not thousands of pounds. And the destruction of the house at Chard had not come into her reckoning at all . . .

They could afford it; they would not starve. There was still silver and gold under her mattress, and the land itself could not be destroyed. Sir Samuel had died a very wealthy man, his riches well able to absorb such heavy expense and depredation. But it would be some years before Winter-combe returned to the position it had enjoyed before Colonel Ridgeley and his locusts had descended upon it.

If it had not been for Nick, his forbearance and fairness, it could have been very much worse. She did not like to think of the greatness of the debt they owed him. She missed him, in the long lonely evenings, at any moment when she had time to stop and think and remember with an unhappy mixture of joy and guilt their last conversation, and above all the moment when he had kissed her.

Just to recall it made her shiver with longing and caused her bones to melt. And she had spoken of love, at last, and so had he. And then they had parted, perhaps forever. The fortunes of war might well ensure that he never returned: perhaps sent into Cornwall, or to Bristol, or marched off with the rest of Goring's army to attack the Parliament forces. She knew that such a thing was quite likely. She had even convinced herself, in the dark unhappy hours she spent when sleep eluded her, that she could accept such an eventuality. What she refused to face, turning her mind resolutely from the possibility, was the very real chance that he would be killed, perhaps in some small pointless skirmish many miles away, and that she would never know what had happened to him.

Nor, if she were honest with herself, did one kiss, one agonized exchange of emotions, give her the right to know. To the world, she was Lady St. Barbe, wife, mother, housewife. She had duties to do, tasks to perform. The departure of the soldiers was a profound relief, greatly easing the burden on their resources and vastly improving both the daily life of the household, and its moral tone. The misguided children, in their innocence and naïveté, might show distress. For Silence, there was no such luxury.

May turned to June, and shook off the cold weather, the rain and wind. Suddenly there was sunshine and warmth, and the garden, which had hesitated during the bad spell, burst into instant and joyous life. Birds sang, fledglings hopped perilously about the gravel walks, risking the malicious attentions of Pye and the bumbling good-humored pursuit of Lily, swallows and swifts swooped and dived above the orchard, twittering, and fed their offspring in mud nests under the eaves until the light drained from the sky and bats took their place in the insect-laden air. The roses came into bloom all at once, and the higher knots, where they grew, were a mass of color: red flowers, white ones, petals of such a dark crimson they seemed almost black, others the palest sun-washed pink, and the showy stripes of Rosa Mundi and York-and-Lancaster. Every afternoon, when the dew had dried, Silence or Mally would take out a basket and gather the fallen petals and shake those that were about to drop, often helped by Tabby, Deb, and William. Then they were carefully dried, to make pomanders or to scent clothes and chambers, or infused in water or oil as the basis for a vast variety of perfumes, cordials, ointments, and recipes.

It was a busy time. What with work in the stillroom, the dairy, and the rest of the house, Silence found herself with little leisure to brood, and to think of Nick, and was thankful. Tabby's ninth birthday passed with much merriment and laughter, strawberries and new cream, skimmed by Rachael, for her dinner. Pye succumbed to the attentions of the lean iron-gray cat who kept the kitchen and storerooms clear of vermin. There was a new serving maid, Christian Merrifield, the eldest of Mally's half-sisters, somewhat taller but even more brightly capped with hair and scattered with freckles. She annoyed Eliza with her empty chatter, but earned her grudging approval for the unbounded energy and efficiency with which she set about her tasks.

Leah and Bessie were no longer missed. The former, rejected by her disgusted family, had gone to Bristol for a whore, so village rumor asserted, and the latter remained at home, her belly swelling up daily, mark of the shame she should properly feel and evidently did not in the least. Since Bessie was not sorry for herself, Silence would not pity her: That she would reserve for the unfortunate base child, when it was born in the autumn.

If it had not been for Captain Bull and his men, the war would have seemed impossibly distant and remote. And this sorry band, their coats patched and threadbare, their boots down-at-heel, too dispirited to indulge in the lewd, riotous and destructive high spirits that had so frequently distinguished—if that was the right word—the troopers, particularly under Ridgeley's leadership, did not seem somehow to be part of the Royal army, but a collective piece of disreputable flotsam washed up on an isolated beach by a high tide, and left stranded there. Captain Bull, a man of limited resource in every sense, was always courteous to her in a rather preoccupied way, and for the most part used Clevinger and Darby as his intermediaries. The lieutenant, Combe, and Ensign Parset were shadowy figures, glimpsed in the barton, on guard, or in the nether regions of the house. They too were polite but distant, even cold. She wondered if they thought of her as the enemy, and certainly she felt little attraction toward these dour, gloomy men and their tatterdemalion and dwindling company—every week saw more deserters.

And then, in the third week of June, a bright blowy season when poor Jemmy had had to stake all the foxgloves, the news came. The king and his army, against the considered advice of Prince Rupert, had unwisely sought battle with General Fairfax and had comprehensively lost it. The army was broken, dispersed, many good men taken prisoner or slain, and all the king's baggage captured, including his highly incriminating correspondence with the queen, revealing his plans to bring over Papist troops from Ireland. Even the loyal officers at Wintercombe were shocked by this. Ensign Parset, who was so desperate to share the terrible news with someone, anyone, that he told Silence when he encountered her in the courtyard, seemed bewildered and distressed, as if a parent he loved and respected had suddenly betrayed him.

It was said, he added, his round earnest young face crinkled with anguish, that the battle had been lost because of Goring's willful disobedience to the orders bidding him march out of the west and join forces with the king. Goring's excuse had been that he must continue the blockage of Taunton and erase all resistance to his rule. Instead, he had indulged in wild debauches that lasted four or five days together, while supplies to the beleaguered town passed unhindered through his lines, and men, sickened and demoralized, deserted in ever-increasing numbers. And the New Model Army, blooded and confident, was marching westward with all speed, to make an end of this sorry crew, the last force of any size left to the king's side anywhere in England.

The Clubmen of southern Somerset, used to Goring's plunder and rapine, were amazed by this army, the well-clad, well-drilled, well-equipped men, the determination and enthusiasm of the officers, and above all the fact that they committed no rape, stole nothing, and paid good coin for what they took. Goring's men plundered even when contributions were paid to them, and let their baser instincts run riot, unpunished.

For Nick Hellier, it was an experience he wished never to repeat. As he had expected, Goring was a drunken, idle brute, reputedly an excellent commander in times of crisis—and sobriety—but content to lie in his quarters about Taunton, swilling stolen wine and conducting acrimonious feuds with other western commanders such as Grenville and Berkeley, while his men, deprived of positive leadership, plundered and destroyed at will. The countryside was a pitiful sight, fields lying derelict for want of corn to seed them, trees hacked down, houses burnt, hardly a cow or a sheep to be seen, and this in an area once described as the paradise of England because of its greenness and fertility and the beauty of its orchards. By comparison, Wintercombe and Philip's Norton were almost untouched.

There was no money, and the soldiers were paid in plunder. Goring had discovered a convenient method of obtaining coin for essential supplies. A detachment of men would be sent to detain some still-wealthy gentleman, usually of the Roundhead persuasion, who would be released only when his anxious family had paid a substantial ransom. In this way quite large sums were obtained, until the local gentry told the people that the soldiers could legitimately be resisted, with force if need be, for they had shattered the law of the countryside. Already desertion and sickness had reduced the ranks of his men. Less than forty remained to him now, and Byam, always the sot, had degenerated so far into drink that he was not sober even in the morning. At least, however, Nick had managed to halt his attempts on the virtue of a maidservant at the farmhouse where they were quartered. Johnny Byam knew what had happened to Ridgeley, and some deep-buried instinct of self-preservation made him desist. He had turned instead to an obliging widow in the nearby village, who also conveniently kept the alehouse.

Nick had wondered if he should send Byam packing. But men, even in such a condition as this, were a vital and dwindling resource. His own competence would most likely be called into question, if he did. And why make an example of Byam, who had after all once been his friend, when the army's commander was even deeper sunk in drink?

So, reluctantly, he tolerated the man, curbed his excesses, and made sure that he was never put in a position of unrelieved responsibility. Tom Wickham, the unofficial lieutenant, took over Byam's duties with weary resignation, understanding the situation perfectly. Long after their inebriated colleague had collapsed over, or under, the table, the two men, captain and cornet, would sit with a jug of cider, their tobacco smoke writhing up to the low beamed ceiling of the farmhouse parlor, discussing the deteriorating situation in the west.

The writing was plain on every wall, and both knew it. And Nick, at least, was utterly weary of this seemingly never-ending conflict. For the sake of themselves, their families and homes and, perhaps more important, the families and homes of the distressed people on whom they sucked and clung like life-draining leeches, they should quietly split up and go their separate ways tomorrow.

But they would not; he knew they would not. Some, the dregs, the desperate, the faint-hearted, had gone already, but what kept these men together? Was it camaraderie, the spirit of companionship that had been forged in hardship and battle, or the opportunities offered, to men who had never had very much, of free plunder and rape, the chance to throw off all restraint and go unpunished? Or another kind of fear, the fear of going back to a world that did not understand, of return to boredom, poverty, debt, perhaps to a disliked wife, or one who had set horns on her husband's head in his absence?

He thought of Silence, even at moments when she seemed far from his mind. The sight of a slender woman in mulberry or blue might catch his eye and jerk his heart. The foxgloves in the hedges, a black-and-white cat sunning itself in a doorway, a mother smiling at her child, all brought her presence back, painfully and with unbearable vividness before his eyes. He had never loved like this, had never known before this agonizing intensity, sharp as if caused by a dagger, the sleeplessness, the longing. Drink—not in the quantities imbibed by Byam, just a few tankards—helped to dull his senses, but on any fine June morning, all birdsong and fresh green, the hedges frothing with flowers, her presence was so real that he felt her shadow riding beside him, quiet, unassuming, utterly beloved.

He did not know why it should be her, so unlike all other women to whom he had been attracted. He only knew that it was her face, pale, calm, some might say ordinary and insipid were it not for the size and beauty of her eyes, her voice, low, dry, apt to laughter, her smile, her meek and modest bearing so at odds with the recklessness and rebellion still sparking beneath, all combining to make a woman as unusual and lovely as her name.

And one reason for staying in the army was that by doing so he had a chance, small and remote, of seeing her again. No matter that she had turned his love aside, despairing. Only to see her, he said to himself with a desperation that in itself gave him the lie. Only to see her, no more, and then somehow I will be cured of this malady.

Inexorably, Fairfax's army marched unhindered southward, while the king, eternally optimistic, lingered in Wales and looked forward to a new army formed of enthusiastic Welshmen. Reports of the New Model Army's approach reached Goring's quarters daily: They were at Salisbury, Dorchester, Blandford. Goring, working his way through good wine sent from Wyndham, the Governor of Bridgwater, realized abruptly, and somewhat belatedly, that Nemesis was at hand if he did not bestir himself. Bridgwater and Bristol, his remaining sources of men and supplies, must be protected. For the moment, Taunton could wait.

Reinforcements from Wales were expected. Waiting for them, Goring withdrew to the country around Langport, relying on the rivers that crisscrossed the low, marshy countryside to block the New Model's advance. But the rain-swollen streams, their bridges for the most part destroyed, proved no great obstacle to the advancing Roundheads. They crossed the Parret at Petherton Bridge without meeting very much resistance, and the River Yeo with even greater ease, thanks to the inefficiency of the Sherborne garrison, which was supposed to be guarding it. The Cavaliers fell back toward Langport, and Goring, outwitted and outmanned, considered his next move.

The Welsh levies were on their way, and he must if possible wait for them. Meanwhile, there was a desperate chance of splitting Fairfax's army. Goring's brother-in-law, George Porter, his boon companion in debauch, was sent with the better part of the cavalry toward Taunton, to draw a force of Roundheads after him.

Nick's troop did not go with them. They had been attached to Sir John Digby's Horse, one of those left behind at Langport. He was relieved, not trusting Porter's somewhat dubious qualities of leadership. And the next day, when the news came in of their ignominious defeat, he was extremely thankful of this narrow escape. Porter's men had been taking their ease at Ilminister, the men lounging on the banks of the river or bathing in it, the officers drinking in taverns. Most heinous of all, there was no lookout posted, no one on watch to cry a warning when Colonel Massey and his four thousand horse came charging across the river out of a clear day. More than half the Royalist force were slain or captured, and Porter somehow got the remnant back to Langport, and the fury of his brother-in-law and commander. They had had little enough chance before. Now matters were truly desperate.

Goring and his officers discussed their strategy late into the night, while their officers drank their cares away in the Langport taverns, and the New Model Army, only a couple of miles distant, fortified itself with prayer and the unassailable conviction of the righteousness of its cause. The people of

Somerset had hailed them as deliverers from Goring's evil band of plunderers, had greeted them with thrown flowers and cheers and tears of joy. They had God with them, and the wicked men of blood could not prevail.

Early the next morning Nick Hellier sat his horse at the head of his men, on the crest of a low hill just outside Langport. The sky was pale and milky with mist, promising another dry and dusty day, a pleasant contrast to the heavy rain of the previous week. A mile away, to the southeast, lay another low hill, topped by windmills, on which could just be seen an amorphous dark mass: the feared New Model Army. And between the two ran a long narrow lane, dipping down to ford a small but deep, swift-flowing stream, then climbing once more, lined with high hedges, toward Goring's position. To attack, the Roundhead cavalry would have to advance no more than three or four abreast up this constricted highway, and in the blaze of fire from the musketeers whom Goring had ordered to line the hedge on each side and cover the ford. All the cannon had been sent with the baggage back to Bridgwater, bar the two that had been placed at the top of the lane. But Fairfax had artillery, and it was their bombardment that began the battle.

The horses, mostly inured to loud noises, stood resigned, champing at their bits and trying to snatch grass, their ears flickering at the explosions. Nick soothed his chestnut and wondered at the detachment he felt, as if someone else sat there and risked death for a cause he now doubted. No missiles came near them, but soon reports arrived that their own guns had been disabled by a well-aimed shot from the enemy. Then the crackle of musket fire, farther down the hill, announced the advance of the Roundhead infantry. But the enemy cannon kept up the fire, making it impossible for those on the hill to go to the aid of their comrades at the ford. And slowly, inexorably, the superior morale and equipment and efficiency and numbers of Fairfax's men began to tell.

It was almost noon, and swelteringly hot despite the brisk westerly breeze. Clouds, high and blazingly white, divided the sky and provided grateful relief when they happened to obscure the sun. At Wintercombe, it would be dinnertime. He thought of the cool dim dining parlor, the oaken paneling and the white-clothed table at the center, laden with country produce: pork, beef, lamb, fish, fowl, cheeses, tarts and syllabubs and pasties. And Silence, cool and smiling and remote in the tawny gown she had worn for the Prince of Wales, the only clothing she possessed that enhanced her subtle looks rather than shrouded them. He chewed on the stale bread and cheese that was all that Langport had been able to offer them, and Wintercombe filled his mind like a jewel of great price, beautiful, yearned for, and at this moment as unattainable as the moon. So great was his longing for the house, and the lady who ruled it, that it formed a physical pain in his chest, and the bread turned tasteless as dust in his mouth. He swallowed it with some difficulty and peered down the hill, trying to see what was happening.

A shout rose up from around the ford. Through the smoke and dust of conflict, Goring's cavalry saw their Roundhead counterparts, held all this time in reserve, begin to move down their hill from the windmills. The sun, dulled by the intervening smoke and dust, shone dimly on weapons and armor, and Nick drew a deep, not entirely steady breath. This was the climax of the fight, and it was hard to escape the suffocating feeling that it was their doom approaching.

Relentless, the New Model Horse came down the hill at a good trot and splashed across the ford. Their horses were superbly trained, and each man was alike in his devotion to the cause as in his uniform, buff coats, back-and breastplates, pot helmets, red doublets, all clean and new and polished, supplied from the boundless wealth of London and the eastern counties. The musketeers had done their best, but many were dead or wounded, and the withering fire that alone might have mown down the Roundheads did not materialize. Four abreast, the cavalry charged at a gallop up the lane, while their foot began to close with the musketeers and crashed into Goring's horse, waiting for them at the top.

The result was never really in doubt. Nick, almost in the front rank, discharged his pistols into the attacking enemy, with no discernible effect, and drew his sword. All around him men were doing the same. There was a lot of smoke, confusion, the clash of swords and cries of aggression or agony. His chestnut, unused to close-quarter fighting, chose this moment to resist the commands of his hands and heels, and reared up, squealing. A Roundhead's sword slashed close and Nick parried it desperately, fighting his horse as much as the enemy. And then suddenly the men around him were falling back. No way of telling if this were a ruse, or a retreat, or a rout. He disengaged and dragged the chestnut's head around. There were riderless horses wandering loose, aimlessly, and men lying on the ground. He glimpsed Byam, who had drunk deeply from a blackjack that morning, blearily surrendering to a contemptuous trooper. Then they were free of the fight, and galloping farther up the hill, the New Model in hot and jubilant pursuit.

At the top they turned at bay. "Surround them!" someone bellowed, and Nick waved the remains of his troop forward again. Others plunged back into the fray, but the Roundhead leader had seen the danger, and his men were already wheeling around to regroup farther down the hill.

In the breathing space thus briefly offered, there was a chance to catch the breath, to load and span pistols, to find men separated from the rest of the troop. Nick, running his eye over them, saw to his surprise that less than half a dozen were missing, Byam of course among them. That loss, at any rate, would not exactly be tragic.

There was no time for any more. The Roundheads, reinforced and re-grouped, were attacking again from the front and the left. And behind them, like some dour and monstrous mechanism, came the infantry.

The Royalist cavalry in the rear, on the crest of the hill, had the better view, and did not like what they saw. Their own musketeers were broken and fleeing, the New Model advancing, and yet more men coming up in reserve. It was obvious that this was the end, and rather than stand and be slain to no purpose, they turned and fled. The panic was infectious. As the Roundhead Horse plunged into the forward ranks of the Cavaliers, it spread farther.

As Nick had once said to Silence, he was not one to hazard his life when all hope was gone. But when the moment came, he did not want to turn and run with the rest of that rabble. It was the chestnut who decided the issue. Always unruly and hard to control, he saw the other horses galloping away and took the bit between his teeth. So sharply did the animal turn that Nick almost fell off, and his opponent's sword sliced down his sleeve, slashing the leather but leaving the flesh untouched. And then he was fleeing with all the other cowards, northward, while the Royalists still in Langport fired the town to cover their retreat and the New Model with fanatic glee embarked on a joyful pursuit.

On the hill crowned with windmills, Fairfax and his staff exulted in their God-given victory. But Nick, trying to keep the ragged remnants of his troop together, knew that it was their lack of morale and discipline that had defeated them. If they had been even ordinarily competent troops, adequately led, the New Model Horse would never have survived that reck-less, insane charge up the hill lined with musketeers.

He gathered his men together, some two miles north of Langport. All around, similar small bodies of men were galloping, making for the gar-risons at Bridgwater or Burrowbridge. But his heart was not with Goring's Crew. Like a wounded animal seeking home, it turned northeast, across fifty miles of largely unknown, hostile countryside, to Wintercombe, and Silence. He would go there, he told them, and they could come with him, or throw in their lot with Goring, or make their way to their own homes and put the war behind them.

To his astonishment, they were unanimous. "Us'll follow ee, Cap'n!" shouted one man, one of William's especial friends, and was echoed by the rest. He did not understand it. He looked from face to face, counting. There were thirty-two left, enough to garrison Wintercombe along with Bull's men. The Welsh levies were coming. Perhaps something could still be salvaged from this most sorry mess.

And the wild recklessness in him that always surged up at such moments took over him now. He had felt ashamed of their precipitate flight. He had not thought himself such a man of honor, but the memory was unexpectedly humiliating. And maybe at Wintercombe, or Bath, they would be given the chance to regain some self-respect.

The possible consequences of that to the house, and the woman he loved, never once crossed his mind.

"Mama, Mama, MAMA!"

It was Deb's voice, shrieking across the garden from the top terrace. Silence, on her hands and knees on the gravel gathering clove gillyflowers and sops-in-wine for scented waters, looked around and wondered what it could be this time. Deb had much the same reaction to any novel situation, whether it was an argument with William or fire, flood, or pestilence.

Sighing, she dropped the handful of flowers into her basket and stood up. Deb, who had reached the sundial and was looking about her with an air of barely suppressed panic, saw the movement and charged along the arbor toward it. Her cap, Silence was sorry to see, had come off, revealing quantities of wild and honey-gold hair, and her face was scarlet with effort. As she ran, she shouted, "Mama, Mama, they're back, they're back—the soldiers are back!"

Silence felt as if all the blood had drained from her skin, and her heart began to thump erratically. She brushed her hair out of her face, unwittingly leaving a dirty smear across her forehead, and said, "You mean the troopers, Deb? Captain Hellier and the Horse?"

"Yes!" her daughter cried, skittering to a halt in front of her with a crunch of gravel. "And Nat told me to come and find you. They've been in a *battle*!" She said the word as if it were something marvelous, and Silence felt cold.

She asked, trying to sound normal, "Were any of them hurt?"

Deb looked at her in surprise. "I don't know, I didn't see." Her face changed to expectancy, and she pulled urgently on her mother's sleeve. "Oh, come on, Mama, please come quick!"

And Silence, in her old grubby gardening apron, allowed herself to be led up to the house.

Deb was right. The courtyard was filled with horses, exhausted, dust-smothered animals, and soldiers no less weary. Even Silence's unpracticed eye could tell that they were not the numbers that had ridden out two months ago. And her frantic, searching gaze could not find Nick.

She fought her panic and put her basket of gillyflowers down onto the floor of the porch. There was a movement, footsteps behind her. She turned, and he was there.

It took every ounce of strength she possessed not to rush into his arms. For an instant she stood, poised on the edge of action, and then the tension drained abruptly away and she smiled, a little shyly. "Hullo. Deb said that there had been a battle."

Nat had appeared in the gloom at his back. She noticed suddenly how tall he was getting, past Nick's shoulder now. He said, "I've seen Clevinger. The cottage paddock is empty—the horses can be turned in there for now." He grinned at his stepmother. "I see Deb found you, then."

"If I'd been down at the mill, I'd have heard her," Silence said. She drew a shaky breath, hoping that Nat had not discerned too much in the dim light of the porch. "What news do you bring, Captain Hellier?"

He appeared exhausted, his face filmed with dust and his eyes haggard and sore. But they looked at her with that familiar intensity, whose nature she had recognized too late, and there was a half-smile forgotten on his face, as if he could not help himself. He said quietly, "Ill news, I fear—or perhaps not so ill for one of your persuasion, my lady." The ironic tone was back in his voice. He paused, and then added slowly, "There has indeed been a battle—and Goring's crew soundly defeated by General Fairfax and his New Model Army. How many days ago? Three, four? I've lost count. We've been on the move ever since, riding across country." He smiled a little grimly. "And the country wasn't exactly friendly."

"From what I've heard of Goring's Crew, I'm hardly surprised," Silence said dryly. "And where is your general now?"

"The last we heard, fled to Bridgwater. As for Fairfax, I do not know his plans—he may even now be marching to Sherborne Castle, or Bridgwater, or even northward, to these parts. And to be honest with you," Nick said, his quiet charm stripped bare by weariness, "at this precise moment I care not a toss. Now, if you will forgive me, my lady, there is much to do—the men and horses must be fed, watered, and rested."

Nat and Silence were left staring at each other in the porch, while Nick, outside, could be heard issuing a concise stream of orders to his men. The boy shrugged his thin shoulders and grinned wryly. "And to think I'd convinced myself that we'd seen the last of them! But then," he added with a shrewd glance at his stepmother, "one's chickens always do have a habit of coming home to roost, don't they?"

And with that cryptic remark, he followed the captain into the court-yard. Silence, uneasy and disturbed despite her joy at Nick's safe return, picked up the basket of gillyflowers and made her way to the kitchen, leaving Deb hovering in the porch, gazing with fascination at the milling soldiers.

Rachael, studying in her chamber overlooking the barton, was absorbed in a history of England and at first unaware that the cavalry had returned. Normally she would have fretted at being kept indoors on such a de-lightfully warm and sunny July afternoon, but her mind had wandered from the strict path of her allotted task, which was to read about the momentous and instructive events of the reign of King Harry the Eighth, into more distant and fascinating realms. The romance of the Hundred Years' War filled her with excitement: She felt as if she herself had fought at Crecy alongside the Black Prince, winning his spurs when scarcely older than were Rachael and Nat. The tortuous wiles of King Henry's attempts to free himself from the domination of the wicked Bishop of Rome were unbearably tedious. These tales of glory, chivalry, and courage stirred her blood. I wish I had been born a man, and older, Rachael thought fiercely. And if I had, I would be fighting now, instead of sitting in this stuffy chamber reading about it!

Sam had gone away to war—and Sam had died. Ignorant of the true manner of his death, she visualized him riding at full tilt at the enemy, waving his sword, firing the pistols that she remembered so clearly—and then the shot, the slow graceful fall from his horse, to lie pale, beautiful, dead, under the stars of the battlefield.

A tear dropped onto the page, and then another. Ashamed of her weakness, Rachael scrabbled in her sleeve for a kerchief and wiped her eyes. Sam was dead, but he had died gloriously, for a great cause—the cause of ancient rights and freedoms, and the Protestant religion, against that interfering king and his Papist queen and courtiers. And she would be willing to fight for it too, if *only,* she had not been a despised and skirt-burdened female.

The inconvenient reality of war, and the small unpleasant part she had played in it, the shooting of Ridgeley and its consequences, she had relegated to a distant corner of her mind and locked the door on it.

She became aware suddenly of an unusual bustle in the barton below. Horses—many horses! She jumped up from her chair, almost oversetting it, and plunged around the table to the casement window. It was open on this hot day. She pushed it farther, as far as it would go, and hung eagerly over the sill.

The horses were being led into the barton. They were dusty and weary, and had obviously been ridden hard for a considerable distance. She recognized Captain Hellier's tall white-legged chestnut, for once too exhausted to be difficult, and let out a sigh of relief. He was safe, it seemed. As the troopers brought their thirsty mounts to the water trough and began to unsaddle them, she sought through the crowd for Nick. There was Cornet Wickham with the standard, and the middle-aged quartermaster whose name she had forgotten. Byam she failed to see, and was glad. She had hated the way he looked at her when he was drunk, which had seemed to be most of the time. I hope he was killed, she said to herself, frowning. I hated him, though he was not quite as bad as Ridgeley. They are all loathsome, wicked men—save for *him.*

She had thought him evil too, once. But then he had shot the man who had attacked Tabby; he had defended them all against Ridgeley; he had earned Nat's respect, which she had good reason to know was not easily done; and above all, he had saved her life when the colonel had pursued her through the town—once when he had grabbed Ridgeley's bridle, and the second time when he had killed him.

It had been hushed up, of course, but the whole household knew the truth. And Rachael, who at the bottom of her complicated, unhappy soul had never considered herself to be worthy of any such sacrifice, basked in the thought of it. A man had risked his life for her—had killed for her. And though, sometimes, a small rare voice of common sense whispered to her that he would have done the same for Nat, or Deb, or any of them, still the idea grew and took hold. He had done it for her, and her alone. And she loved him.

His voice, deep and calm, cut into her mind. She located him instantly, by that scarlet cloak, its brilliance now dimmed by dust and dirt, draped over his arm. Rachael put her elbows on the sill and her chin in her hands, and gazed down at him. He was not precisely handsome, she must allow, but he had such an air of command. And yet he was not brutal nor insensitive, but brave and true, the pattern of chivalry and the perfect gentleman. Mentally she divested him of the tediously familiar buff coat, the breeches and boots and cloak and beaver, and fitted him into a suit of armor, riding on a white charger, shield and lance in hand. She thought of the tales of King Arthur. He could be Sir Lancelot, perhaps, the matchless knight, fighting evil giants and monstrous dragons, just as he had rescued her from Ridgeley . . .

At that moment, Nick glanced up and saw, as he had expected from the prickling at the back of his neck, Rachael's thin white face looking down. Inwardly he cursed, but he gave her a cheerful wave, exactly as he would have greeted William. Even from here, he could see her sudden and fiery blush. Then she ducked out of sight in confusion. He frowned, staring unseeing at the busy troopers all around him. This childish infatuation must be nipped in the bud if it were not to end in pain and humiliation for the girl, but he could not see how to do it kindly. And his feelings for Silence were an added complication. Once he would have gone to ask her advice, with friendliness and wry good humor. Now, his love was no longer a secret from her, and ironically seemed to have driven out that dear, delightful spirit of kinship they had shared, to be replaced by wariness, shyness, constraint, for any closeness must be shunned . . .

Someone came up asking where the saddles must be put, and two of the scullions had emerged from the kitchen, carrying baskets of bread and a large cheese. He put the matter out of his mind with relief, and lost his greater care in the lesser problems of the troop. But the longing to see her, to speak with her, despite the insurmountable barrier between them, was of a strength that could not long be denied.

As had become their custom during the soldiers' occupation of Wintercombe, Silence and the children ate their supper in her chamber. Only Nat seemed his usual, rather acerbic self, unaffected by the troop's return. Rachael played with her food, eating hardly anything, although the mutton fricassee was one of her favorite dishes, and speaking not at all. At the other end of the table, Deb and William chattered incessantly about the soldiers, horses, and whose turn it was to ride Dumbledore tomorrow, and ate nothing either. Tabby's food found its way to her mouth almost by accident, for her mind was evidently lost in a musical world of her own, and occasionally a muted string of notes escaped her lips.

Silence surveyed her brood with rueful resignation. For a Roundhead family, supposedly groaning under the yoke of their military oppressors, they seemed remarkably animated by the cavalry's return. When—if— George came back, he would not be best pleased.

He would be considerably more unhappy should he ever learn of his wife's feelings about her chief oppressor. But she was an adult, and could school her face, act her part as she had done all her life, lock away her secret heart until it starved and withered from lack of air and light and nourishment. She had faced that prospect stoically, knowing that it was inevitable for the sake of all, save Nick, that she held dear. During his absence, aware that she might never see him again, she had discovered that life without him was endurable, if she kept herself busy with the smaller and greater trivia and crises that always beset any household. It was at night that the ache, the longing rose up in her like a grim gray cloud, to surround her and suck the life and spirit from her, until she wept into Pye's soft fur of Lily's close harsh white coat. And then she would sleep, exhausted, and dream, sometimes of him, and wake to another dawn, another empty day filled with things that had never had much meaning and served only to divert her mind from its endless treadmill.

Yes, she could endure it, as she had endured pain all her life. Her dreary childhood had at least accustomed her to that. But he had taught her happiness, and the present lack of it had torn a ragged hole in her days.

After supper, Christian Merrifield bearing the uncleaned plates away with a disapproving cluck of her tongue, she sent the younger children to bed in Doraty's capable charge. Nat laid out his grandfather's backgammon tables and counters, and continued the task of teaching Rachael to play. He had despaired of imparting to her any more than the basic rules of chess. And Silence, with Pye, round and swelling with her next kittens, snug on her lap, took up one of the books that Nick had lent her before he went away.

There had been at least a dozen of them. One military manual, of no interest, she had not touched, but the rest were works of poetry and prose. She had greatly enjoyed the essays of Sir Francis Bacon, though she had not agreed with all of what he had to say. It had been an unexpected pleasure to discover that a man so learned and renowned had written with such wisdom and understanding about gardens. Holinshed's chronicles she had read avidly, and passed on to Rachael, feeling that the girl's mind could benefit from a little knowledge of her country's history. The book of sermons written by the Dean of St. Paul's she found beautiful, although sometimes obscure, their meaning hard to understand. But she remembered Sir Samuel's maxim, that a man might best be known by the books he possessed, and had wondered anew at the complexity of their owner's mind. Sermons, histories, essays, plays, Hakluyt's Voyages, and a dubious but diverting piece of fiction called *The Unfortunate Traveller* spoke of a wide rage of interests.

But her real delight came as she read the poetry, those rough, urgent, complex and vivid descriptions of carnal love, by that same the Dean of St. Paul's, who had also written lyrical evocations of divine adoration. At first she had been shocked, then curious, then moved almost to tears by the intensity of some of those poems:

They who one another keep
Alive, ne'er parted be.

There were sonnets and plays by Master Shakespeare, and by Master Jonson, verses by Drayton and Carew, and two collections of songs and airs. She devoured them all greedily, and with the facility trained by her father long ago learned many by heart. Some of the songs turned out to have tunes that Tabby could play, and they had spent several happy hours trying to fit words to music, with much laughter. Unlike her daughter, Silence was not the possessor of an accurate or tuneful singing voice.

Tonight she had Shakespeare's sonnets on her lap. Trying to accommodate both the book and the cat was a problem, and Pye soon jumped off in disgust and curled up on the bed. The twins, bent over the tables board, were completely absorbed in their game, but Silence felt a restlessness that could not be stilled. It was dusk, the evening air blowing softly in from the open windows held the scent of hay, and the lavender just beginning to open. She stared down at the close-printed lines, and though the words had not long since enchanted her, she hardly noticed them:

Shall I compare thee to a summer's day?
Thou art more lovely and more temperate . . .

Outside, the lovely summer's day was drawing to a close. She looked at Nat and Rachael, and then at Lily, resting at her feet in heraldic pose.

With the intuition common to dogs, the puppy sensed her mood and sat up, her brown eyes hopeful, the tip of her pale tail, which Nat had unkindly compared to a rat's, just stirring over the floor. Silence smiled at her, and the tail wagged harder. Lily was very sensitive to every nuance of her expression or mood. She rose, and the dog's hope turned to certainty. She jumped up, uttered two or three happy barks, and raced to the door, where she jumped and whined expectantly.

"I'm taking Lily outside," Silence said, somewhat unnecessarily. Nat and Rachael, too intent on the game, hardly seemed to notice as she opened the door and went out, followed by both Lily and Pye, who was not yet so ponderous that she could not enjoy a stroll in the garden.

The terraces were lit by the setting sun, in a warm red-gold light, and they were empty of human life, though the arbor was rustling and chirruping with sparrows and starlings. Down there the air was soft and heavily fragrant. Lily, still full of energy despite a long walk into Norton with the twins earlier in the day, bounced down the steps from the garden room and sprang gracefully between the knots, reveling in the sheer joy of being young, and free, and alive.

Silence looked down at her wistfully, and with a little envy. Her own children ran like that. So did Pye's kittens, and Pye when she was not burdened with motherhood. But the days when she herself could scamper heedlessly among the flowers like a hoyden were long gone—indeed, had never existed. There had been no room, let alone the opportunity, in that dark narrow confined tenement above her father's shop to run wild as she now permitted her children to do on occasion. And her father had forced his three daughters into the mold of quiet, submissive girlhood, out of which they burst at their peril. They had walked everywhere, eyes lowered, speaking only when spoken to, discouraged from any independent thought, word, or deed. And yet there had been, under this repressive fog of disapproval, a lively energy, affection, and camaraderie between the three sisters and their brother Joseph. But their rebellion had been word, and thought, and there had never come the chance to run and play. Only now did she recognize and regret the lack.

She walked slowly along the middle terrace, toward the summerhouse. If she ran to catch Lily up, Diggory would probably appear from behind a bush like a benevolent gnome and her dignity would be shattered. She was Lady St. Barbe, after all.

"But I am Silence too," she said aloud, and laughed suddenly with recklessness that answered her mood. Lily had reached the summerhouse and was looking back, panting and expectant. Silence picked up her skirts and ran along the gravel path to her dog.

As she had feared, there was someone to see her lapse from grace. But it was not the ancient gardener climbing the steps from the lower terrace, but Nick Hellier.

She stopped perhaps five feet away, her breath coming quickly, but not because of effort. From somewhere, she found the wit to produce a slightly shamefaced grin, and received a much more wholehearted one in return. "Hullo," Nick said cheerfully. "I took the liberty of cutting across the garden after I'd seen the men guarding the fortifications. I hope you do not mind, my lady St. Barbe."

"Silence, if you please," she said, drawn irresistibly into his mood despite her good intentions. "My lady St. Barbe does not gallop along her terrace as if she were one of her own children."

"No, she walks in a most demure and seemly fashion—like this," Nick said, and minced toward her with tiny steps, his eyes modestly downcast. She could not help it, she laughed as she had not done for weeks. Her sides and face ached, and her eyes sprang tears of joy. He laughed with her, in a similarly abandoned fashion, and the sound echoed around the terrace.

Belatedly aware that there might after all be someone else in the orchard or on the terraces or at the windows of Wintercombe to hear or see what she did, Silence wiped her eyes and attempted to control her merriment. She succeeded only with great difficulty. All the tension, the uncertainty, the misery and fear of the past months had been released, and it was all but impossible to close the gates against the flood. Nick was watching her, a smile on his face. He could have had no chance to rest since his return, and yet the signs of exhaustion and stress had gone from around his mouth and eyes. He looked fresh and alert, in a clean suit of Taunton blue, the stained buff coat discarded and his sword bright at his side. He indicated Lily, standing looking from one to the other, her curling tail slowly wagging, and said, "She has grown somewhat since last I saw her."

"She must be near her full size now," Silence said, glancing down at the little dog and smiling. Lily lifted her upper lip and smiled back. "And I cannot tell you how dear she is to me—and how jealous is poor Pye."

"Like cat and dog, in fact," Nick said dryly. "Is Pye well?"

"Exceedingly so—she expects more kittens in a week or two. All the others have gone to homes in the village. Mally's mother has the one that Ridgeley threw into the fire, and it is already a great favorite. They have every hope of it catching a mouse before long." She looked at him, a little shyly, not really happy with this restricted small talk. But she must turn the conversation to matters of somewhat greater import. They did not live in limbo, at Wintercombe, what happened in the outer world would sooner or later affect them too, and the more so since the soldiers were with them. She must have some idea of what might befall them now that Goring's Crew had been dispersed. She took thought, and then added slowly, "I have been meaning to speak to you about . . . about other matters. I would like your opinion as to what is going to happen next. You said there had been a battle, and Goring beaten, and Fairfax loose in Somerset. What will it mean to us? And to the war in general? And what will you do?"

"You don't want much," he said, still dryly, and turned to lean on the balustrade, looking down onto the lowest terrace. After a pause, she joined him. The knots were hazy with flowers: the purple-blue of lavender, the soft lacy carnation colors of the gillyflowers, the tall spires of foxgloves. Their fragrance drifted up on the air, and the sun was just setting behind the low shoulder of the hill to their right. The orchard lay in the valley, girded by soldiers and water. Beyond, the farther bank of the stream climbed more steeply to a long ridge, and beyond it, just showing about the hedgerow bushes, the pinnacles of Philip's Norton church. Among the apple trees, blackbirds called, going to roost, and the three family horses left, Dumbledore, Strawberry, and Cobweb, stood under the old mulberry, nose to rump, idly swishing their tails to keep the flies from each other. It was a scene of profound peace and beauty. Battle seemed a thousand miles away, and yet suddenly, irrationally, she gave a shiver of fear.

He noticed it, and glanced at her with concern. "Are you cold?"

"On a day like this? Oh, no, no . . . something walked on my grave, I think."

"I am sorry," he said after a while. "I had forgotten that it would be so important to you—we, after all, have other places to go. You have not." He took a deep breath, staring out at the infinite and glorious blue of the sky, unsullied by cloud. "Goring is finished. He has no army—much of it was taken prisoner after the battle, and the rest killed, or dispersed, or fled with him to Bridgwater. There was talk of more men sailing over from Wales, but I have heard too many false rumors and foolish optimism in this sorry struggle to have much faith in the prospect. And Goring, in his infinite wisdom, has succeeded in turning all the countryside against us. You cannot force men to fight—and he has now no chance of raising another army anywhere in Somerset.

"So, what remains? There are the garrisons. Bridgwater, of course, which should be able to hold out for a while. Wyndham, the governor, is a staunch man, and they can be supplied from the sea. And its fortifications are strong. Even against Fairfax, they should have a good chance. He cannot afford to waste too much time sitting down in front of each and every garrison. While their main army is here, Royalists in other parts of the country may revive. And when—if—he reduces Bridgwater, there is still Sherborne Castle, and Nunney, and Farleigh, and Wintercombe, and Bath. Determined opposition could keep him in this country until winter."

There was a short pause, filled by Lily's hopeful whine. When she received no response, she thrust her muzzle, long and tipped by a cold wet nose, at her mistress's hand. Silence took it out of her reach and clasped her fingers together on the rough honey-colored stone on the top of the balustrade. She said quietly, "What would be the point of it? The king has no army anywhere in England capable of resisting this New Model. He has had his chances and thrown them away. Sooner or later even he must surely acknowledge it. And so must you, and all your kind. You have said as much to me in the past. So why go on, when it can only lead to further bloodshed and grief and loss?"

She thought that he was not going to answer at first. The pause threatened to go on forever. But she waited, and at last he turned to face her. She looked back at him candidly, seeing no certainty in his expression but an unhappiness she had never before noticed in him. He said slowly, "I know. You don't have to tell me—I know. And all the reasoned, sensible argument points in one direction. If I obeyed it, I would call my men together tonight and tell them to take their horses and leave their arms and make their way quietly back home and pretend that this war has never happened. And less than a week ago, I would have been willing, not to say eager, to do it."

"So what has changed your mind?"

Again the pause, as if he were trying to sort out his answer before he spoke. "Langport. Langport did it. There, though we had a good chance, and a strong position, we threw it away. The men were demoralized, and we could not prevail against Fairfax's army like that. And I have never run away from a fight before."

She saw the bitter memory of it, shadowed around his eyes. He added, "Disheartened, undisciplined, and unpaid troops, and bad leadership, have lost the war for us. But . . . call it pride, call it stubbornness or stupidity or what you will . . . I do not *wish* to surrender so tamely and meekly submit to punishment for supporting my anointed king, whatever his failings. I want at least to make them fight for their victory, even if it costs me dear. Oh, I know you think it is a stupid, worthless gesture—I can see it in your face, however you may try to hide it." As if of its own accord, his hand came up and gently touched her cheek. "My dear, wise, gentle Silence—can you understand?"

She did not flinch from his fingers, though all the fires had leapt up again at his touch. She said wryly, "Perhaps. But I understand one thing very well—that your glorious and heroic and foolish gesture will be made at Wintercombe's expense."

Across the glowing sky a heron flew, legs trailing, going home to the heronry in the trees by the mill. In Nick's face, still strongly lit by the sunset, there was love, and anguish, and resolution. "Yes," he said, very low. "Yes, you have the right of it. And so we are your doom after all."

"And I cannot dissuade you?" Silence cried, forgetting caution, decorum, moderation in her sudden and surging anger. "You will risk our *lives,* Nick—innocent lives, the women's and children's, for a *whim?*"

"It is not a whim," he said. "It is a matter of honor."

"*Honor?* You? You had your colonel murdered, and you talk of honor?

It's not my idea of honor," she said, unable to disguise her bitterness, "to fight on when there's no hope left, and innocent people are at risk. That's a man's honor, but it isn't mine, nor any woman's when her children are at stake."

"Then take them away," he said. "The way will be clear to London now—take them to your brother in London, and forget us."

"But I can't!" she cried furiously. "I have stayed at Wintercombe all through the worst that Ridgeley could do to us—do you think I'm so spineless as to flee now?"

There was a pause. Then he said wryly, "But you are stating my own beliefs exactly—can you not see it?"

She could. Her anger drained away abruptly, leaving her shaking. She put her face in her hands for a moment, trying to pull her shredded nerves together, and then turned toward him. "It seems neither of us has much choice. I have been charged with my responsibility and cannot desert it. And nor can you shed yours. Why can't you go off to Bath, or Bristol, and make your show of defiance there?"

"Because Wintercombe is my command, and if I left it empty to run away to another garrison I would be guilty of desertion of my duty, cowardice, disobedience to orders—any one of which is punishable by death." He stared at her intently. "I was ashamed, at Langport. I do not want that on my conscience again. I want the chance to regain some respect for myself."

"At the cost of Wintercombe? And us?"

"You will be safe," he said. "You would not be harmed by either side. If Wintercombe were besieged, you could be sent out to safety. The children can go to the village, if you yourself do not wish to leave. But it may not come to that. The garrison may be withdrawn to Bath or Bristol, if Fairfax comes too close—and then we will all be spared."

"Then I shall pray for it," Silence said bitterly. She thought of the lovely house behind her, serene in the fading light, so dear and now, it seemed, in such peril. She had heard what a determined siege could do. In Taunton, hardly anything had been left standing save the chimneys, rising forlornly from the heaps of ashes. And the house at Chard, though it had never suffered siege, was a blackened, uninhabitable ruin. Was the same fate to befall Wintercombe?

If she stayed, there might be something she could do to prevent it. Besiegers might be less ready to inflict wanton damage if the wife of one of their army's colonels were there to dissuade them. If the children were sent to Wick Farm again, she would not be so afraid. But she still thought he was wrong: pig-headed, stubborn, immovable. She could not see the point to it, when they were already defeated, but then she had always had something of her fishwife grandmother's pragmatic, down-to-earth nature.

"I am sorry," he said again. "I wish I could make you understand, but it seems I cannot. Will you be my friend still, despite it?"

The light was slowly trickling away. The birds had almost lapsed into sleep, and the sunset had grown hot and red and fiery in the west, promising further fine weather. She looked at him unwillingly, afraid of all that had been unsaid between them, all the emotions that lay just below the surface of their speech. "Perhaps," she said at last, and smiled, quoting him a poem from one of his own books. "After all, 'Love is not love, that alters when it alteration finds.' Good evening, Captain Hellier."

He watched her as she turned and walked along the arbor, her stride determined, Lily following dejected close at heel, her lowered ears and drooping tail a sure indication of her lady's mood. And the irony of it made his mouth twist in a rueful smile, for he could understand her anger and bitterness—he felt much the same—and yet for pride and honor and self-respect he could not tamely surrender his command, even for her sake.

Perhaps it would never come to a siege. Looking at the dim, lovely garden, and the tranquil, vine-covered house to which they both were bound by love and duty, he hoped fervently that it never would.

CHAPTER

TWENTY-FOUR

The bubble reputation—
Even in the cannon's mouth.
—AS YOU LIKE IT

The town of Bridgwater held out against Fairfax for almost a week, and fell to storm and flame on the twenty-second of July. At Bristol, governed now by Prince Rupert, the plague had reared its ugly head, Clubmen prevented most of the reinforcements from Wales from landing, and the bad news from the south had had a demoralizing effect. The prince was concerned for the other garrisons in North Somerset, many of which could see the future just as clearly as could Nick but were less anxious about pride and honor. In particular, the Governor of Bath had been displaying worrying signs of faintheartedness. The final straw had come when Rupert, on a brief visit to the city, found Sir Thomas Bridges urging capitulation as the only sensible course. The king's nephew, white with fury, had ridden back to Bristol after a blazing argument, making plans for the governor's immediate replacement.

Fairfax, meanwhile, had decided to turn north, judging the Royalist garrisons there to be a greater danger to him than the broken remnants of Goring's Crew, skulking in Devon. On the twenty-eighth of July, the New Model Army reached Wells. Rupert, hearing the news, dispatched a more stalwart and reliable officer, accompanied by a couple of troops of horse, to hold Bath instead of the wavering Sir Thomas Bridges.

The people of Bath were frightened, and furious. The soldiers were from Bristol, and could well have brought the plague with them, to infect their clean, sweet, and pleasant city, and they did not see why they should risk such a disaster when the Royal cause seemed well and truly lost. When it became apparent that many of the reinforcements were the hated and despised Welsh, their rage was redoubled. Crowds surrounded the governor's house in West Street, throwing rotten eggs and filth and stones, and shouting "No Welsh!"

Tom Wickham, who had ridden into the city with various messages to deliver and errands to perform, reported on his return that Bath was in uproar, Sir Thomas had refused to give way gracefully to his appointed successor, the citizens were on the point of open revolt, and the garrison seemed confused and very despondent.

At Wintercombe, however, matters were somewhat different. Desertion and war had thinned their ranks, but those who were left were the most determined, courageous, and capable fighters. Under Nick's leadership, efficient and cheerful, morale stayed high. A rota for guard and forage duty had been worked out and was strictly and fairly followed. The horses, which would be of little use in a siege, were turned out to graze in closes around Wintercombe, and cattle and sheep were driven into the orchard.

Silence, deeply disturbed by these developments, had wanted to protest, but she knew that Nick had made up his mind. It seemed ridiculous to her, this matter of honor. She did not think any the less of him for running at Langport, for she would rather a live Nick than a dead one, however much honor his fatal courage might have brought him. Her love had not changed, and she did not think that it ever would. As in the poem, it was a star for her to steer by. And if it had not been Wintercombe, her beloved house, that stood in danger, she might have felt some admiration, excitement even, at the preparations going on all around them, the air of purpose that every soldier seemed to have. But she could not forget Bridgwater, and Langport, and Chard, and all the other towns and houses and castles destroyed by the war. Would Wintercombe, too, fall to guns and fire?

She had made arrangements with Christian Baylie, and at the first sign of trouble, the children were to be taken over to Wick Farm with their nurses. Every bucket in the house had been filled with water and put in a strategic place. Extra supplies of ammunition had been obtained from Bristol, although the prince had been very reluctant to let anything go. His command, after all, was the most important garrison left in Royalist hands, and nothing must be allowed to prejudice its survival. Wintercombe, even Bath, was by comparison insignificant, even expendable.

When the news came that Fairfax was at Wells, twenty miles away, she knew that it probably meant that he was intending to move against Bath rather than Bristol. Nick posted scouts all around Wintercombe and Norton to warn of hostile approaches. And Silence, with fear close about her heart like a stone, called her children to her.

They stood wide-eyed and solemn in her chamber. William, the delightful little boy, everyone's friend, with his pale-gold, silky hair in curling fronds around his face, his brown eyes staring at her earnestly. Deb, strong-willed, devious, difficult, neat and tidy for once, her cap straight and her apron clean, William's hand held firmly in her own. Tabby, slender, cloudy-haired and graceful, carrying her music with her like a talisman. Rachael, with her moods, her secret thoughts, the burdens of her fierce, uncompromising nature. And Nat, her twin, as different from her as might be, no longer the undersized child but a young man, his voice deeper, his face sharper, the intelligence behind it even more shrewd, watchful, and balanced than ever. And she wondered again, uneasily, just how much he knew of her feelings for Nick, for those blue, assessing eyes saw altogether too much.

She explained the situation, couching it in simple terms for the benefit of the younger ones. An army was coming to Bath, and there might be danger. She was therefore sending them to Wick Farm for a few days, so that they would be safe—just as they had gone there before, though not now of course in such frantic and secret circumstances.

William was happy. He liked going to Wick, and all the Baylie girls had made a great pet of him last time. Rachael did not object either, for she had greatly enjoyed helping in the dairy, and Mistress Baylie's grand-daughters were her good friends, whom she saw too rarely for her liking. Deb, understanding too much and too little, saw her mother's anxiety and, not really aware of the cause, announced her intention of staying put. It was Nat who managed to soothe her and persuade her that a day or two at Wick would be like a holiday. "And just think," he finished, with a glance at Silence that could only be described as wicked, "you won't have to see Grandmother every morning."

This aspect of the situation had evidently not occurred to Tabby, who had been looking most unhappy. She brightened at once. Dame Ursula, though increasingly frail in body, had not suffered any diminution of her mind, or her personality, and the daily interviews with her grandchildren were a trial to which they succumbed, according to their characters, with fear, resignation, loathing, or sullen and insolent acquiescence. Silence, though she herself heartily disliked the old harridan who had once done her best to poison her marriage and now seemed to bring the same tireless mental energy to disrupting her relations with her children, could not help but admire that indomitable spirit, which even Ridgeley had not quenched. But Dame Ursula was failing, no doubt of it. She tired very quickly now, and slept much of the day, spending the rest of it conning her Bible, or listening to the unattractive Ruth read it for her in her thick, monotonous Somerset voice. But she could still strike terror into the younger children, though Silence, as well as Nat and Rachael, had now grown past that stage.

So, four of them seemed happy to leave Wintercombe: Nat, however, was immovable. And indeed, his argument was reasoned and irrefutable. "I am Father's heir now—I know I wasn't very enthusiastic about it, but that doesn't mean I'll shirk my duties. And that includes staying here to watch over Wintercombe, whatever happens. I'm not a child any more, Mother, I shall be sixteen in November. At my age, Prince Rupert was a seasoned campaigner."

Rachael, who had been quite happy to go to Wick if all the others were coming too, at once changed her mind. Why should Nat have all the excitement while she, who was the same age, was packed off like a baby to Wick? She could fire a musket like any soldier—

"Yes," her twin said dryly. "I think recent events have proved that to everyone's satisfaction."

Rachael had the grace to flush, but she said mutinously, "It's not *fair*. Why should he stay? Either we should both go, or both stay. And I want to be with you, Mother—and Nat."

Silence gazed at her in despair. She could not rant and rave and wave a big stick. Any authority she had over the girl was not based on such crude and brutal methods, but on more subtle means of persuasion, reason, and appeals to her stepdaughter's better nature. And Rachael, obstinate, sullen, her lower lip thrust out in a way distinctly reminiscent of Deb, was in no mood to listen. Moreover, the other children, particularly Tabby, were obviously now having second thoughts themselves.

This then was the test of her relationship with Rachael, so recently and hesitantly improved. She took a deep breath and said quietly, "No. You must go and look after the children. Nat has a right to be here, as he has said—though I would much rather he was safely at Wick with the rest of you. But you, Rachael—I want you away from Wintercombe."

"But why?" Rachael's voice rose to a belligerent shout, and Nat, his patience for once exhausted, turned to her in exasperation.

"I expect Mother's afraid that if Wintercombe is taken, you'd be raped."

"Nat!" Silence said, too late.

Rachael's jaw dropped and her color receded. Remorselessly, her brother went on. "You silly gawcum, can't you see beyond your nose? That was why you were sent to Wick before. And if you go there now, that's something less for Mother to worry about—and believe me, she's got quite enough problems without wondering what mischief you've got up to. You'll leave if I have to tie you to the horse."

"You can't order me—you haven't the right!" Rachael cried, and raised a furious fist.

Silence, at the end of her tether, stepped forward briskly and grabbed it before it could strike. "Rachael, you're behaving like a baby. Nat's duty is to stay with me and look to the house. Yours is to go to Wick with Doraty and Hester, and look after the children. Can I trust you to do that?"

Rachael's hot blue eyes stared into hers and then dropped. Silence let go of her wrist and watched as her stepdaughter rubbed it sulkily, her face averted. At last she said reluctantly, as if the words had been forced from her, "Very well. I'll go."

They set off that afternoon. Deb and William rode Dumbledore, led by Doraty on Strawberry, Hester pillion behind her. Rachael was allowed to have Cobweb, with Tabby at her back, after Nat had graciously given permission, and she did not look at all pleased about it. Silence's quiet words of encouragement had produced no effect on the girl but a vivid glare, as if she hoped her stepmother would turn instantly to stone. She had no idea that Rachael, for some brief, glorious moments, had imagined herself taking a heroic part in the siege, thereby proving to Nick Hellier that she was not a child but a young woman of extraordinary courage and resource, and worthy of his notice. Her fantasies shattered, but too proud to acknowledge their existence, she rode to Wick with an invisible but lowering cloud above her head, blocking out the sun.

"She fancies herself in love with Captain Hellier, you know," Nat said as they walked back into the house after waving good-bye to the children.

Silence's heart altered a beat, and she felt the blood rush to her face. He might just as well have said the same about her. She said casually, "Oh? Does she? How do you know?"

"Well, she didn't tell me—you know how close she can be. But it's obvious, really. She spends a lot of time leaning out of her window, looking at the soldiers. And every time Hellier is in the same room, she follows him with her eyes. And when he speaks to her, she goes red and mumbles—and you have to admit, that isn't like Rachael."

"No, it's not," Silence said. "How very perceptive of you—I hadn't noticed."

"Well, no, I didn't think you had," Nat said. In the dim light of the screens passage, his pale face shone with sudden mischief. "But I thought you ought to know. There might be trouble because of it—you know Rachael."

"I do indeed—and thank you for telling me," Silence said, feeling more than a little shaken. He must be aware of her own feelings for Nick—she was certain of it, knowing that if Nat, so subtle and observant, had seen Rachael's heart so plain, then her own must surely also be visible.

"Think nothing of it," the boy replied, grinning, and went away to consult Clevinger, who was teaching him, little by little without ever really intending to, all he knew of farming. And Silence was left to ponder what he had said, and not said. How many other people had noticed? Was it common knowledge at Wintercombe that their lady was enamored of the enemy captain? Were they the subject of lascivious speculation in the servants' hall or, heaven forbid, in the taproom of the George or the Fleur-de-Lys? She trembled at the thought, and then relaxed. Nat was unusually perceptive. Because he had noticed, it did not mean that anyone else had. She had not been aware of any nudges, whispers, or sidelong glances, nor had she sensed any change in the attitudes of her servants toward her. Surely, if they suspected that she was more than friendly toward Hellier, they would show a lessening of respect?

Only Mally had some inkling of the situation and had initially disapproved. Since Ridgeley's death, however, her hostility toward Nick had been transmuted to a grudging acceptance. But her loyalty was to Silence.

She would never reveal what she knew, or what she thought, to the other servants.

And anyway, Silence decided as she climbed unhappily to her chamber, there will never be anything to hide. If I am certain of anything, I am certain of that.

The children, with Lily as well—Silence had heard terrible tales of what might befall a tasty young dog in a prolonged siege—had gone to Wick on the afternoon of Tuesday, the twenty-ninth of July. On that same day, in the evening, a small party of New Model horse and dragoons rode over the hills from Wells to Bath, to assess the ease with which the city might be taken, for reports of the disturbances there had reached Fairfax the previous day. The city might well be ripe for the plucking, and in any event should be taken before proceeding against Bristol.

In the city, all was turmoil. The people, even those loyally disposed, had refused to bear arms any more for Sir Thomas Bridges, who had made himself heartily disliked during his governorship. The reinforcements sent from Bristol had caused such an uproar that their officers, including the man intended to replace Bridges, had taken most of them back to Rupert in disgust. The troops on guard at the little gate at the end of the bridge watched with alarm as the Roundhead horse and dragoons came down the lane called Holywell, just at sunset, and took up their positions less than a pistol shot from the gate. There was a brief and rather erratic exchange of fire, and Colonel Rich, the Roundhead commander, summoned Bath to surrender. The citizens waited hopefully, but Sir Thomas Bridges, mindful of Prince Rupert's rage, refused.

Colonel Okey, in charge of the two companies of dragoons, then led his men forward. On their bellies in the gathering dusk, they crawled right up to the bridge gate, unseen by the defenders. Above them, the muskets of the Royalist soldiers protruded from holes cut in the wood. Suddenly the dragoons leapt up, seized the ends of the weapons, and yelled for surrender.

Not surprisingly in view of the mood of fear and despondency in the city, the Royalist soldiers panicked. They left their muskets hanging from the gate and ran back along the bridge to the safety of Bath, crying that Fairfax's men were attacking. Behind them, the dragoons fired the bridge gate and took up closer and more threatening positions on the bridge itself.

In Bath that night, all was terror and rumor and uncertainty. Believing that the entire might of the New Model Army was encircling the city, there seemed only one sensible course to take, and Sir Thomas Bridges, harassed, exhausted, and despairing, capitulated at sunrise. Bath, its strong defenses, its copious supplies of arms, and garrison of two hundred men had been taken by two regiments of horse and two companies of dragoons.

The news came to Wintercombe before dinner, brought by a sympathetic countryman. Nick gave him a shilling, and posted lookouts on the roads leading to Bath, at Charterhouse Hinton, and at Wellow, while two men in civilian dress were sent farther, to gather news and find out what they could of Fairfax's intentions.

That day was cool, with a brisk wind and rain threatening, and for Silence it dragged mightily. She found herself unable to concentrate on anything, her ears alert for the slightest change of emphasis in the activity outside. She missed the children terribly. She had been parted from them before, of course, and most recently when they had escaped from Ridgeley; but somehow this was different. She knew that she had done the most sensible thing and that it would have been lunacy to have kept them with her, to suffer the privations and dangers of a siege. But still their absence left a great void in her life, still she worried about them. Were they being good? Were they eating properly? Were they unhappy without her, in a house they hardly knew, in the care of a woman who was not their mother?

But Doraty and Hester had gone too, and at least she had no qualms about their capability. The house seemed empty without the children, though, and her chamber silent, lonely, and oppressive in the long dark evening. Nat kept her company, played tables and chess with her, and together they were reading through Holinshed and discussing Bacon's *Essays.* Nick, of course, had little time for casual visits. In the fever of preparation, he seemed always preoccupied, forever on the move, sought by everyone on matters ranging from the essential to the trivial. And Silence, knowing that she had lost him, continued her own preparations for the siege.

With Nat and Mally, she brought Sir Samuel's precious and battered collection of books up to the comparative safety of her chamber, and other precious items: his desk, a particularly good piece of tapestry, the most important estate documents. There was still coin under her mattress, though not a great deal, and with only her servant and her stepson to see, she hid most of it in the roof space above Mally's closet. The bags, covered in dust and cobwebs and hidden behind a rafter, would be almost impossible to find by chance. The New Model Army did not have the reputation of plunderers, but she did not wish to take any risks at all.

Outside, the guard on the north side was doubled, the gatehouse kept permanently barred, and none was allowed in or out without good reason. No foraging party had set off since news of Bath's surrender had arrived— the danger that they might be caught outside the walls, or cut off by a sudden siege, was too great. With only just over fifty men to man Wintercombe, Nick could not afford to lose any.

The north was well guarded, at any rate, but he was much less happy about the south. Although it was not the obvious place for attack, since the enemy would have to struggle up the valley from the mill and negotiate the stream, hedgerows, ponds, and ditches, he could not risk neglecting any possible weakness in his defenses. The fortifications around the orchard were unfinished and unsatisfactory, and to man them would leave his men strung dangerously thin. There was only one sensible course, and with great reluctance, he took it.

Silence, gazing down from the south window of her chamber, saw the men trampling over her beloved terraces, heedless of the carefully tended flowers or Diggory's indignant protests, and turned away, unable to look any more. Tears of grief rose to her eyes, and she angrily brushed them away. It was only a garden, and gardens could bloom again. Was not the rebirth and renewal of her knots and arbors one of the greatest delights of her days?

But he knew how much her garden meant to her. He had said that he loved her. And then he had wantonly destroyed it.

"Don't ee weep, m'lady," Mally said, dear, stalwart Mally, looking at her with those earnest and practical eyes. "'Tisn't nothing as can't be set to rights. And do ee think on the time you'll have, building en up again."

"You're right, of course," Silence said, after a while. "But I wish he'd warned me—then at least we could have gathered some of the flowers first, to scent this chamber." And she smiled bravely, but it did not deceive her clear-eyed maid.

Sir Thomas Fairfax, general of the New Model Army, was delighted with the ease with which his horse had so unexpectedly taken Bath. Truly, God's hand was shown in this. Now, without the loss of a single man, they were in possession of a well-fortified, well-supplied base for their attack on Bristol. Still more fortunately, it had transpired that Prince Rupert had actually been on the way to Bath with a relief force when he had heard of its capture, and turned back.

There was no doubt. The Lord was with them, inspiring their own men, filling the enemy with fear and foolishness. Bath could have held out for weeks, but it had fallen in a few hours to panic and rumor. Fairfax spent the night following the surrender in the city, inspecting the stout defenses and installing two foot regiments under Colonel Birch for its garrison. Bristol was the most vital objective, but in the meantime, it would do no harm if the new governor wished to move against the two Royalist garrisons closest to the city, at Farleigh Castle and at Wintercombe.

Well pleased, Fairfax returned to his army, still quartered around Wells, and moved south to deal with Sherborne Castle, which was threatening their rear. And Colonel Birch, who did not believe in wasting time, sent his colleague, Colonel Sir Hardress Waller, a cousin of the general, with part of his regiment to invest the two Royalist strongholds.

They came along the Bath Road on the Thursday afternoon, four hundred musketeers, marching with grim precision along the soft red road. It was raining, very lightly, and their stockings were splattered with the russet earth, their shoes squelching in the mud. Unlike the rather disheveled Royalist soldiers that the villagers of Philip's Norton were used to, they were uniformly clad in coats of Venice red, their soft felt hats keeping the rain from their faces. A dozen packhorses carried ammunition and other supplies, and a couple of guides went with them to point out the way.

In the village, the people peered cautiously from their doors. They had heard much of this New Model Army, but for the moment preferred to judge for themselves. It might indeed be that these men did not rape or murder or plunder, and that, miracle of miracles, they paid good coin for what they took. But the war-weary villagers were going to wait and see what these men would do before welcoming them with open arms.

The soldiers halted for a while in a convenient open space between the main village and the church, farther down the hill. After the ease of the taking of Bath, they were buoyant and full of confidence. Morale in these two small garrisons was undoubtedly low. The hostile countryside, the inevitability of defeat, and now the collapse of resistance in Bath would all have combined to drain away their spirits.

Sir Hardress Waller conferred with his chief officers, while the men ate bread and cheese from their snapsacks and were offered ale, somewhat clouded, from a barrel rolled down the hill by order of the landlord of the George. To his astonishment, he was paid for it. Word ran around the village, and soon most of Norton was peering over the fair close wall at these wonderful soldiers, who gave money for what had been intended as a conciliatory gift.

It was easy to find informants among this increasingly friendly crowd. Sir Hardress soon learned that the two garrisons were quite different. One was very small indeed, inhabited by some two and a half score of mixed horse and foot, their numbers diminished by death and desertions. Their commander was said to be a most capable officer, but a mere captain. Moreover, the house belonged to one of Parliament's colonels, at present with Fairfax's army, and a man with whom Sir Hardress was well acquainted. Apparently his wife, mother, and children were still within the house, as hostages, and ill used by the soldiers. Hair-raising stories were bandied about, and their courage and endurance was spoken of with admiration.

Obviously the ladies must be rescued, and preferably with as little damage to the house as possible. Since they had no artillery with them—there had not been time to organize a train, and the road from Bath was hardly suitable for dragging heavy cannon—there was little danger of that, but Sir Hardress was determined not to storm the place with too much ferocity. And the mere appearance of a New Model regiment outside the walls would probably be enough to terrify the defenders into submission.

Curiously enough, Farleigh Castle was also owned by a Roundhead colonel, Sir Edward Hungerford. However, it was altogether a tougher proposition. There was a whole regiment, the Earl of Marlborough's, garrisoned within it, led by Sir Edward's half-brother John, and its stout walls and strong position, perched on the steep south bank of the river Frome, made it almost unassailable without ordnance. However, the success of Colonel Rich's venture against Bath proved that even the most unpromising situation might, with God's help, be turned to advantage.

Accordingly, Sir Hardress split his regiment into two parts. The first, and greater, which he led, was to proceed to Farleigh. The second, a company and a half of musketeers under the command of his lieutenant-colonel, Cottesworth, would summon the pathetic force at Wintercombe to surrender. There was no shortage of willing guides to tell them the way to both garrisons, and the strengths and weaknesses of each. And so, a little past four o'clock, under a clearing sky, the regiment divided and marched singing to its separate objectives.

At Wintercombe, they had had good warning of the troops' arrival. The lookout posted on the Bath Road had come galloping in, shouting his warning, and at once the garrison had sprung to bustling life. Each man filled his powder flask and his bandolier, twelve small containers hanging from a belt slung across his chest, and each containing sufficient for one charge. There was more than enough match, and bullets, to last them in normal use. How long their supplies would hold out in a siege, Nick did not know.

To reach Wintercombe, the enemy must march through the barton of the Manor Farm, to Lyde Green, past the mill, and then turn left, up the track that led to the house. There was a low stone bridge over the stream there, wide enough for a wagon or a carriage. One of his first acts, after the news of Bath's surrender, had been to send men to break it down. It had proved difficult to remove, and in the end only a small, judiciously placed charge of gunpowder had done the job, by loosening the stones so that it could easily be dismantled.

The attackers must now ford the shallow but swift-running Norton Brook and climb the narrow lane to Wintercombe. The situation was remarkably similar to Langport, and Nick, remembering the wasted opportunities of that battle, picked a dozen of his best men to hide behind the hedge. The enemy would have to run the gauntlet of their fire. Perhaps that would convince them that this garrison, at least, did not intend to surrender tamely, without a fight.

The capitulation of Bath, far from disheartening the men at Wintercombe, had served to increase their determination. It was disgraceful that a fortress capable of being held for months had been yielded after such a brief and ignominious struggle. If the New Model wanted to see whether Royalists could still fight, let them come to Wintercombe—they would learn that there were still honest and courageous men in Somerset, capable of resisting the rebels!

Nick's words to his men, along these lines, had had the desired effect. They cheered him with fervor, and there was no shortage of volunteers for the Forlorn Hope. Captain Bull, somewhat against Nick's better judgment, was given the command of it. He could follow orders to the letter, but the man had no imagination, no flair. He would much rather have sent Tom Wickham, who had both qualities, but the offense the appointment of a junior officer would cause outweighed more practical considerations. He watched them deploy themselves along the hedges, each man well supplied with powder, match, and bullet, and then returned to the house to complete the dispositions of the remaining men.

All the entrances to Wintercombe were guarded. A barricade of timber, empty barrels, and brushwood had been erected across the gatehouse, and four men lurked behind it. Similar constructions blocked the three entrances to the barton, with a couple of men to guard each, and Cornet Wickham was the officer in charge there. In the kitchen garden, which contained the only, and vital, well, the quartermaster and three troopers kept watch behind the high wall, their view helped by the holes knocked through the stone. Along the lower terrace, timber and brushwood lined the balustrade, offering some protection to the four men, under Ensign Parset, who guarded the approach from the orchard. On the eastern flank, the wall bordering the gardens, ten soldiers led by Lieutenant Combes, painfully far apart, gazed across the sloping pasture bordering the lane, up which the enemy must come. And the northern wall, enclosing the yew walk and the courtyard, was under the protection of another ten, with Nick to lead them: for this, surely, was where the enemy was most likely to attack.

He had briefly outlined their strategy. The musketeers in the hedgerow were to warn of the Roundheads' approach, to effect casualties, and to give notice that they would not be able to walk straight into Wintercombe. Then, firing at will, selecting their targets, the men guarding the walls would do their best to ward off the enemy. If they were stormed, there were several lines of retreat. If necessary, the lower terrace, the yew walk and the barton could be abandoned, and the defenders concentrated in the immediate vicinity of the house. There was apparently no artillery with the enemy, and if their force was split in two, one to deal with Farleigh and the other to attack Wintercombe, Nick's men would face, at the most, some two hundred Roundheads. They had plenty of ammunition and powder, and food for a month. And above all, they were determined to give a good account of themselves.

Silence heard the cheers with a sinking heart. It seemed they were set on making a fight of it—and the consequences to Wintercombe might well be dire. She had already called all the remaining servants to her, giving them leave to return to their families if they wished.

To her surprise, they all stoutly refused to go. "We won't leave ee, my lady," Darby had said, speaking for all. "And if ee wants it, we'll fall on they Cavaliers from behind, when they be least expecting it." He brandished a meat cleaver threateningly, and she had had to dissuade him gently from his plan. It was true that these soldiers were nominally their enemies and the ones attacking them, their friends. But she had no wish to add further confusion to an already complex situation, or to allow the servants to put themselves in danger. The men were to stay in the kitchen area, which was comparatively safe if attack came from the north, and the women could go either to Dame Ursula's chamber or to her own.

Dame Ursula, of course, was staying where she was. She seemed somewhat revived by the news of imminent attack, and quoted lavishly from the Bible about the righteousness of the just and the overthrow of the wicked. Silence suspected that if she had been twenty years younger and in possession of a firearm, the backs of the defenders in the courtyard would not have been safe. She had Ruth to look after her, a small store of food in case of desperate need, and Eliza elected to keep her company as well, a choice that afforded Silence profound relief. The other female servants—Mally and Christian Merrifield, Joan Coxe and Margery Turber—were much more pleasant company.

They had had perhaps an hour's warning, and were ready in half that time. Silence looked at the anxious faces around her in her chamber, and at Nat, quite at ease in this room full of women. She realized suddenly that the waiting, the uncertainty, would be harder to endure than anything else.

The door had been locked, but someone tapped upon it. Mally opened it, and Nick walked in. He looked tired but elated. He wore the familiar buff coat and a pot helmet, which completely altered his face. The narrowed, shadowed bones and the dark-ringed eyes were those of a stranger, and Silence found it easy to look upon the man who had destroyed her garden with cold, unwelcoming eyes. "Good afternoon, Captain Hellier," she said formally.

"Good afternoon, my lady," he said, and bowed gracefully. She had perforce to make a curtsy in return. The four servants were watching him like fowl eyeing a fox at the gates of the hen run, but Nat, she realized suddenly, was looking at her.

"I see you are all ready," he said, glancing around the chamber. "May I give you a word or two of advice? I am sure that the men who are marching to attack know well that there are women in the house and will moderate their behavior accordingly—but accidents happen frequently in war, and it's best to be cautious. I hope I don't need to warn you of the dangers of looking out of the window, even if you think there's no danger from that direction—you'd be surprised how far a bullet can travel. Keep your door locked, and don't venture forth until you are certain it is safe and the fighting has ended—one way or the other." He smiled wryly, and, despite herself, Silence felt her heart move within her. He had ruined her garden, his defiance would quite possibly destroy the house she loved and put her life in danger. And still she loved him.

"They have no ordnance as yet," he went on, and smiled at her. "So you need not fear for the fabric of your house, my lady. And if it is taken, then you are in the hands of friends, and have no further reason for anxiety."

"If I am still alive," Silence said dryly. "Captain, for the last time, will you not consider surrender? If it is to a greatly superior force, there need surely be no dishonor."

"After Bath, and Langport?" he said, and laughed. The sound had a wild, bitter, reckless note. "No, my lady. We are determined to teach these rebels a lesson. They have had it altogether too easy here in Somerset—we intend now to make them rue their error."

"And die in the attempt?" Silence asked.

Their eyes met, and she could not disguise her anguish. "I hope not, my lady," Nick said, and grinned like a schoolboy. "I have every intention of continuing in this delightful and sinful life. Until we meet again, Lady St. Barbe—and I hope it will be in happier circumstances."

It was the only chance they could have to say good-bye, and yet nothing could be spoken aloud. She wondered, as he left, whether the other women had noticed that brief moment when their minds had reached out to each other wordlessly. And then she realized that she did not care if they had. She cared for nothing, so long as he was safe.

TWENTY-FIVE

> *Hoist with his own petard.*
> *—HAMLET*

The six score New Model soldiers under Lieutenant-Colonel Cottesworth tramped through Philip's Norton, followed at a safe distance by a rabble of children and young people, consumed with curiosity. One of the captains had to turn them back, with forceful warnings about the dangers of becoming enmeshed in conflict. Cottesworth had a good picture in his mind of the lay of the land, the position of Wintercombe and the strength, or otherwise, of its garrison. What he did not know was the disposition of its men and their level of enthusiasm for the fight. He suspected, and hoped, that they would surrender as soon as his infantry approached, and accordingly had taken little care to ensure that his route of march was well covered.

They could see the house on its low ridge as they marched past the mill. It appeared sleepy and unprepared, although the defenders must surely have had warning of their coming. Cottesworth mentally rubbed his hands with gleeful anticipation. It looked as if this would soon be over, and without a drop of blood spilled. The Lord indeed favored their cause, if their enemies were inspired to such terror.

Barely had this thought crossed his mind when the first shots rang out. Captain Bull had been ordered to hold his fire until the first ranks had crossed the bridge and, obedient as ever, had carried out Nick's instructions to the letter. Cottesworth stared in horrified amazement as three of his men fell, while the rest came to a stumbling halt, bewildered, much of their match unlit and therefore unable to return fire. Before their leader could bellow at the drummer to beat a retreat, more bullets flew through the hedge. The colonel felt one whistle past his ear, and just in front of him a musketeer staggered and fell, blood pulsing from his neck. At last the drummer changed his rhythm, and the men of the New Model retired to the shelter of the Wellow Lane, leaving several of their number dead or hurt in the road by the stream.

At Wintercombe, they heard the firing and waited, tense. The musketeers lining the hedge were vulnerable to cavalry and also to a determined charge by sword-wielding foot. It took upward of a minute to reload, and in that time they were all but unprotected. Nick, crouched in the bastion in the center of the front courtyard, listened intently. There had been a burst of fire, soon over, and then a lull. If he were the New Model commander, he would regroup his men and split them, sending some up the lane while others worked their way around behind the hedges to challenge the hidden musketeers. He hoped that Bull had been able to inflict the greatest possible damage to the enemy. They were possibly out-numbered by four to one, and any casualties he could inflict at this stage might prove invaluable later in the struggle.

There was further firing, drawn out and more ragged than before, and distant shouts. He glanced along the wall and saw his men, hunched, intent, their muskets resting on the wall, primed and loaded and ready, the match in each one glowing faintly red. He himself had a fowling piece that had probably belonged to Sir Samuel St. Barbe or his son. It was a new and practical weapon, a firelock, with a rifled barrel that was supposedly more accurate. His experience with such arms was strictly limited, but he was a tolerable shot with a pistol, and hoped that this gun would enable him to pick off his targets at will.

There was more firing from down the hill. He trusted that Bull would have the sense to withdraw once the advantage of shock and surprise had been lost. They could not afford the death or capture of any of those twelve men, with the remainder spread so thin.

But there they came, running up the hedge, clutching their muskets, Captain Bull's stout and sturdy figure among them. Nick ran to the eastern wall as they struggled up to it, panting, and were helped over by the other defenders. Lieutenant Combe yelled to his men to give covering fire, but the pursuers had already seen the danger and had come to a halt well out of effective range. There was time to question Bull as to the number of the enemy, to commend him for following orders so capably—at which the captain swelled out his chest with self-satisfaction—and to ascertain the numbers of casualties on both sides. One of Bull's men had a bullet in his arm and another had twisted his ankle running through the rough pasture, but there were half a dozen enemy dead or wounded, Bull reported with justifiable pride. First blood had unequivocally gone to the defenders.

The two injured men were sent within doors, with a comrade to deal with them. The obvious person to minister to the wounded was Silence, but Nick did not want to ask her. She might be placing herself in danger, and she might also be unhappy at succoring an enemy soldier. Trooper Lobb had been apprenticed to a barber and could bind wounds effectively. That would have to suffice.

But Silence had seen the wounded men crossing the courtyard. It had proved impossible to sit quietly in her chamber, trying to pretend that the sharp cracking sounds were not muskets firing, that men were not fighting, and dying, less than a quarter of a mile from the house. The four maidservants with her were all capable, steady women, unlikely to panic or give way to hysteria, but the atmosphere in the chamber was tense and apprehensive. They all had sewing on their laps, but only Margery Turber, relentlessly cheerful, was making any attempt to work. As the first sounds of gunfire had assaulted their ears, the needles had stopped, poised. Then Christian, Mally, and Joan had turned their eyes to the eastern windows. And Silence, feeling that danger, probably quite small at this moment, was preferable to ignorance and uncertainty, got up and went to look.

The dark pyramids of the yew walk obscured her view of the bottom of the lane. She gazed out for some moments in frustration, her hands clenched on the sill, and then turned and went to the oriel, which gave an excellent view of the courtyard.

"Oh, m'lady," Christian began nervously. She might be sensible and energetic, but she was the youngest of them, and at this moment of crisis it showed. "Do ee be careful—mind what the captain did say!"

"I am minding," Silence said, with a reassuring grin that Christian reflected wanly back at her. She peered cautiously around the stone frame and stared down at the courtyard. As she watched, men began to stumble through the gate that led into the yew walk and took up new positions along with the northern wall. She saw Nick, obviously giving orders. Then two men appeared, one limping heavily and supported by the other, whose left arm dripped red.

There was something to do after all. Silence ran the contents of her linen presses through her mind and came to a decision. She turned back to the four women, who were all looking at her expectantly. "How do you feel about tending the enemy wounded?"

It was a measure of the way the garrison had insinuated themselves into the Wintercombe household over the past nine months that there was some initial confusion in the maids' minds over which of the two sides was meant. When that had been sorted out, however, they were as eager for something to do as was Silence.

The two soldiers were sitting on one of the hall benches, exchanging battle stories, while the barber's former apprentice struggled to bind up the wounded arm with a spare and distinctly grubby stocking. They looked up in amazement and some alarm as the redoubtable Lady St. Barbe bore down on them, considerable quantities of torn linen in her hands, with three maids at her back: Margery Turber had volunteered to stay in the chamber to finish tearing up the rest of the sheet.

"Now," Silence said, standing over the two men with much the same briskness as she approached her children's scraped hands or knees, "I assume that you are in need of assistance?"

They nodded mutely, trying to rise. She pushed them firmly back onto the benches and told the former apprentice that he could return to his post. Mally went to the stillroom to find suitable salves and plasters, Joan was sent for water, and the bemused soldiers had their hurts tended as efficiently and thoroughly as if they had been a great deal more serious.

Outside, all was quiet for some time. Then the beat of a drum was heard, and up the lane, looking somewhat nervous, came the drummer, an officer beside him. Nick smiled to himself. This, obviously, was the demand for surrender.

It was couched in the usual terms. All the men of the garrison were to have quarter for their lives, the officers free to march away with their arms, horses, and baggage, the common soldiers kept prisoner or turned loose on taking an oath never more to fight against the righteous cause of the Parliament. Nick heard them out with patience and then shook his head. "I do not propose to yield so tamely to save my skin, sir, and neither do my men. If you want Wintercombe, by God you'll have to fight us for it!"

There was a pause, filled with a scattered cheer or two from the defenders within earshot. Then the Roundhead officer said, "That is your decision, Captain. But I am asked to say that if you have women and children within the house, you should in charity release them now, before hostilities begin."

"I have already tried to persuade them to leave," Nick said. "They refused. The children have been sent to safety, but Lady St. Barbe and her husband's mother are determined to stay."

The officer looked extremely skeptical. "Are you keeping them prisoner, sir? May you answer to the Lord if you are putting innocent lives at risk!"

"I have told you already," Nick said patiently. "They refuse to go. Lady St. Barbe conceives it her duty to stay in the house, and I cannot tell her any different. Short of tying her up and forcing her out, there is nothing I can do."

The other man seemed less than satisfied with his answer. His face red, he shouted, "At least tell us where she is kept, so that we may avoid causing her unnecessary distress."

"Of course," Nick said, waving a hand. "Her chamber is on the eastern side, marked by that oriel window. I'm sure she'll be most grateful if you can avoid it when your musketeers start firing."

His sarcastic tone was not lost on the Roundhead officer; his only reply was a contemptuous snort. Nick was sorely tempted to send him on his way with a harmlessly aimed bullet, but did not think him worth the waste. He watched, smiling, as the officer and the drummer retreated down the lane, and then settled down to await their next moves.

In fact, nothing else happened that day. The defenders, nervously on edge, itched for the chance to show the Roundheads what they could do, but there was no activity within musket shot. Nick sent a couple of men indoors to keep watch from the upper windows. They reported that there was much movement in the fields around Wintercombe, out of range. The men of the New Model were preparing to storm the house.

It would not be possible for all the defenders to stay awake. The night would be warm and dry, some could sleep at their posts while the others watched. They had plenty of match, and he might as well employ the old ruse. When the enemy looked toward the walls of Wintercombe, they would see the glowing match ends ranked like glow worms along the parapets, with no way of telling whether each marked a soldier or not. If they had counted those pinpricks of red light, they would have thought that the garrison numbered a hundred or more.

Sir Hardress Waller was having second thoughts about the two strongholds. Farleigh Castle had also proved obdurate, and short of a prolonged siege would be almost impossible to take without guns. Colonel Birch had given him two days in which to reduce the Royalists, and no more. There was every chance that the regiment would be needed against Bristol, and ammunition was short. These places were no threat to Bath. They could be safely left until Sherborne and Bristol, much more important targets, had fallen. Then the full might of the New Model Army would be turned against them, and with the Lord's help it would prevail against these stubborn, wicked, and ungodly men.

But, just in case, he was prepared to sit before Farleigh for another day, and sent word to Cottesworth that if the lesser garrison could be stormed without undue loss, to do it without delay.

The self-appointed guardians of Wintercombe had all spent an uncertain and wakeful night. Food and blankets had been taken out to the men on guard but, even as tired as they were, it was not easy to snatch some sleep. At least it was mild and did not rain, although clouds obscured the sky.

The darkness gave Nick an idea or two, and there was a certain amount of activity for some hours, in the barton and around the terraces. A little while later the attackers, camped in the fields around Wintercombe, were roused by their sentries. A sortie was taking place—there was a group of musketeers making straight for them, their matches could be plainly seen!

It took some time of confusion, cursing, and stumbling blindly about in the dark before the truth was realized. An elderly horse, too scrawny and lame to be of any military use, had been festooned with lighted matches and turned loose to cause what havoc it could. Like the deceptive lights along the wall, it was an old trick, but an effective one. Cottesworth wondered uneasily what other ruses this most determined captain had in store for them, and decided on swift and overwhelming action.

Inside the house, they had had rather more rest, though it was not entirely peaceful. Pallets had been brought down to the kitchen, and the three scullions, feverish with excitement, had been persuaded to bed at last. Darby and the other male servants, scornful of danger, had returned to their bedchambers at the end of the north wing and slept there. In Silence's room, the truckle bed had been brought out and was shared by Christian and Joan. Margery Turber had another made up in Mally's closet, and Nat had installed himself cheerfully with the clothes presses on a heap of pillows and blankets in the other tiny chamber.

Silence, exhausted by the task of keeping them all busy and free from fear, since the siege began, found herself unable to sleep. Long after Joan's gentle snores had begun, she lay awake, thinking of the day's events: the cheerfulness of the injured men—the one with the twisted ankle she had dismissed with mutual laughter, as a fraud—the apparently boundless enthusiasm of the defenders for a resistance that would surely leave many of them dead or maimed—and Nick.

His face moved through her thoughts, resolute, reckless, laughing in the face of death. It was yet another facet of a man whom, she now realized, she had never fully understood. He had once claimed, cynically, to be without honor, too careful of his life, a practical soldier who was willing to compromise with God and man. But now it seemed he had changed. Like her, the calm, dispassionate exterior concealed a reckless, wild, and passionate soul. She had recognized in him a kindred spirit, almost from the first.

It could never be. She knew that their love was doomed, could find no expression that her world would accept. She thought that she might find the courage to let him go, but she was not sure if she was brave enough to watch him die.

There was no way out, no happiness waiting for them. She had faced that fact, long ago, but the thought still brought tears to her eyes. She lay listening to the servants' snores and breathing, trying not to sob, while her anguish wrung her heart.

She must have dozed eventually, and was woken, abruptly, by shots.

She lay motionless, wondering if she had heard aright. It was still dark. Even with the bedcurtains drawn, light would filter through, but she could see nothing. She was exhausted. She had slept for perhaps an hour or so, and her body ached as if someone had set about it with a bludgeon.

But she had not dreamed those shots. As she tensed, listening, they came again. They were closer than the firing yesterday, frighteningly close.

Almost before she had thought, she flung off the bedclothes, covering poor Pye, who had been sleeping in her usual place next to her shoulder, and leapt through the curtains. The chamber was dark, and she had forgotten its unusually crowded state. She stubbed her bare toe painfully on the truckle bed. It made her gasp, and the two maids began to stir and mutter as they emerged from slumber, but she felt her way around the obstacle, past the foot of her bed, and thence by feel and memory to the oriel. The heavy green curtains had been pulled across the window. She dragged them aside and stared out.

The night was dense, cloudy, with no sign yet of dawn. She saw the matches first, small glowing red pinholes of light, marking where the defenders crouched behind the courtyard wall. Then more shots cracked the darkness with sound, but no flame. She thought that they came from around the barton, and craned her neck.

At first there was nothing to see. Then she became aware of a dim orange glow, almost imperceptible, but growing stronger by the minute, so that she could no longer delude herself that she was imagining it. Something was on fire.

"What be happening?" came Christian's voice, thick with sleep and fright.

And Joan's slow, sensible response. "I don't know, do I? Do ee let I get up and I'll tell ee soon enough."

Behind her, Silence heard the creak of the truckle bed and Joan's purposeful footfall approaching. Her toe throbbed and from the wet stickiness around it was probably bleeding. But out there, men were fighting for possession of Wintercombe and suffering much worse. And what, oh what, was burning in the barton?

"Dear Lord," Joan said beside her. "What be that there all in flames, m'lady? Can ee see proper?"

"I hope it's not the barn," Silence said. It seemed unlikely. In common with the rest of the farm buildings, it was roofed with stone tiles, and unlikely to catch light from a carelessly placed match or even a deliberate attempt to fire it. The new-gathered hay had been piled in ricks in strategic places around the Wintercombe fields, largely to avoid the unwelcome attentions of plunderers, and save for the soldiers' belongings and supplies, the barn was empty.

"'Tisn't the barn," Mally said from her closet. She was obviously watching out of her window. "'Tis in the wrong place for that. I d'reckon as how they've fired one of they barricades."

Abruptly there was a vivid sudden white flash, against which the gatehouse and courtyard wall were outlined in sharp flat black, and then the thump of an explosion. With an incongruously sweet crash, several panes of glass blew free of their lead mountings and showered Joan and Silence with small sharp shards. From Mally's squawk of surprise, the same thing had happened to her.

Outside, the darkness had instantly returned, even more impenetrable than before, and through the broken panes came the warm rain-promising wind, a great deal of distant shouting, and shots. Silence, ignoring the stinging pains on her face and arms, shook herself free of glass and stared urgently out. But there was nothing to see. The fighting seemed to be taking place beyond the barton, and the bulk of the north wing and the gatehouse blocked her view. The barricade, or whatever it was, seemed to be still alight, and she saw, plain against its reflected glare, the men guarding the gatehouse, their muskets at the ready, peering toward the barton.

"Oh, m'lady, what be ee doing? The glass—oh, m'lady, your face!"

Brought back unwillingly to the reality within her chamber, Silence turned to meet Joan's anxious gaze. Beside her, the Merrifield sisters stood, each holding a candle, and Margery Turber, a large and stout-hearted figure in her chemise, stiff and billowing like a ship's sail, with her mistress's soft indoor shoes in her hand.

"My face?" Silence repeated, bewildered. She lifted her hand to her cheek, which was still stinging. It came away streaked with scarlet. She looked at Joan, who had been standing beside her, and saw that she was almost unmarked, though her arms bore one or two cuts and her thick brown hair had a faint frosting of shattered glass.

"Don't ee move, either of ee," Margery warned. "That there floor be thick with splinters—you'll cut your feet all to ribbons, m'lady. Do ee put these on, and come away from the window afore another bullet do go through it."

"It wasn't a bullet—the explosion blew the glass in," Silence said. She felt curiously numb, detached, and all her fear had left her. She knew that out there, Nick might be lying dead, hideously mangled by the ferocity of that blast. But there was nothing she could do at this moment, no power on earth that she could employ to affect the outcome of the fighting, one way or the other. She looked down at her arms. They too had been cut and grazed by the flying glass, and were bleeding in two or three places.

"It's my own fault," she said to Margery, summoning from somewhere a rueful grin. "Captain Hellier told me to stay away from the window, didn't he—and unfortunately he seems to have been right."

"More fool you," Nat said dryly. He stood in the middle of the chamber in his nightshirt, a candlestick in his hand and his eyes glinting. "Shall I fetch something from the stillroom?"

"No—you stay here, Mally can go—she knows where everything is," Silence told him. Her maid emerged from her closet, her bodice and skirt hastily pulled on over her chemise. There was a small trickle of blood across her freckled nose, but no other sign of injury. "There'll be others in need of help, m'lady, unless I be mistaken," she pointed out. "But I'll bring ee what's needed first."

She ran from the chamber, her bright hair flying loose, her feet thrust stockingless into her shoes. In the brief pause after the door shut behind her, there came another brisk burst of gunfire, and then nothing.

The pause threatened to go on forever. The women stood, still and tense as if, Silence thought, they were all trying to emulate Lot's wife. Then Margery handed her the shoes and she put them on, brushing stray slivers of glass from her feet, and walked away from the window to her chair by the hearth, which of course in this summer season was clean, swept and empty. Nat came to stand in front of her, his bright eyes searching her face. He said quietly, "It's not too bad. There's a cut on your cheek and another on your forehead, but nothing that won't heal—I don't think you'll be scarred for life."

"I didn't think that I would be—and I wouldn't be unduly worried if I was," his stepmother told him. "My face is hardly my fortune, is it?"

"No?" Nat said, and smiled. He looked so exactly like Sir Samuel, wise, quizzical, cynical, that she was jolted out of her unreal calm.

"Oh, Nat . . ." she said, despairing, and found that she could not go on. Her hands, her body, her mind, were suddenly all alike trembling with shock and fear.

"Don't worry," the boy said. He dragged up a chair and sat beside her, setting the candle on the mantelpiece. "Please don't worry, Mother. It'll be all right—I *know* it will—don't worry!"

He held her hand while she fought her tears and her terror for herself, and for him, and Nick, and Wintercombe. She had some success. By the time Mally returned with a copious supply of salves, ointments, and plasters, she had managed to regain some of that earlier detachment. This time, however, it was no reflection of a genuine state of mind, but as of old, a mask to hide the turmoil beneath.

Mally brought some news, scanty indeed, but like crumbs to the starving. She had encountered the male servants milling about in the hall, like a gaggle of betwattled old geese, she said scornfully—however had the lie been put about that men were the superior sex? "'Twouldn't northen get done in this world if 'tweren't done by us women—excepting fighting and killing, naturally."

With some difficulty, Silence managed to steer her back on course. What had the men been able to see from their vantage point overlooking the barton?

"Well, not much, as far as I could discover," Mally said. "But 'twas the barricade burning, not the barn. And old Diggory, he d'reckon that blast of gunpowder were set off by Captain Hellier, to frighten the enemy." And then, realizing what she had just said, she put her hand across her mouth and looked ruefully at her mistress.

"Let's have this settled," Silence said. "The enemy are the people at present occupying the house. Our friends are the ones trying to break in and rescue us. I find it confusing too—but that's what we must remember, or when all this is over our menfolk are going to be somewhat annoyed. Were there any hurt, Mally, did anyone see?"

"Darby reckoned as how he'd seen a dead body lying in the barton," Mally told her. "But Tom Goodenough said *he'd* seed it get up and walk away. All I d'believe now is what I've seed with my own eyes, m'lady. That crew'd tell ee they'd seed parson kiss the pope if they thought you'd want to hear it."

At which comment, and the picture it conjured up, Silence burst into rather painful laughter.

She suffered her maid, a little later, to clean and salve her cuts, after her own and Joan's had been attended. Then, brushing aside all protests, she ordered Mally to help her dress. She did not think that she could stomach much more of this waiting in ignorance and uncertainty. Whatever the risk, she was determined to find out exactly what was happening.

With Nat in shirt and breeches at her side, and Mally still grumbling resignedly behind her, she left the other maids to tidy the chamber and walked down into the hall. Dawn showed now, a thin yellow line in the east, surrounded by gray clouds; the day would not be a fine one. The hall, lit by its six high windows, was cool and dim, and somehow unwelcoming. It was also empty. There had been no shots for some time now. Silence paused a moment, thinking of the geography of the house, and then walked briskly to the kitchen.

It was warm, and full of people—the male servants, catching an early meal. They leapt up guiltily when she came in, and stood with the bread and cheese and beer in front of them, trying not to look as if their mouths were full. She ignored them, though from somewhere deep within had come the unsuitable desire to laugh, and went through into the north wing beyond. In the dairy, at the end, there was a window giving out on to the gatehouse arch. Surely she would be able to obtain some information from the soldiers on duty there?

"You won't thank me for saying so," Nat pointed out as they entered the dairy, cold and clean and smelling of cheese. She wondered suddenly who would milk the cows, on this violent and disrupted day. "But please, Mother, do be careful."

"Of course I will," she said with a quick grin, and obediently approached the gatehouse window with some caution.

There was evidently no immediate emergency. The four men leaning against the opposite wall, on the inside of the barrier, were talking cheerfully, their muskets propped up beside them. One had even lit a pipe. Silence rapped on the window. They looked up, startled, and one approached as she pushed the casement open. "Yes, m'lady?"

"What is happening?" she asked. Beyond his shoulder in the barton, she could see that the barn seemed untouched, and there were no bodies visible, no shots to be heard.

"Happening?" the soldier repeated. He looked tired, unshaven and dirty, but there was a spring in his step, an air of high spirits that indicated that the night's skirmishing had gone well for the garrison. "Well, m'lady, nothing be happening just at this here moment, but you should've seed it whiles afore this. They Roundheads was attacking us, all sudden-like, and Cap'n Hellier, he calls to us to fire up the barricade, and then we fires it and he calls for the mortars we made this last night and just as all they soldiers be rushing up at us with their swords waving in the air, we lights the fuses and throws them and whoof!" The soldier spread his hands, and his pipe knocked and broke against the window. With a curse and an apology, he bent and picked up the pieces, and then resumed his story. "They goes off all at once, and you should've seen all they Roundheads! Them as wasn't knocked flat was running for their lives. Oh, 'twere a sight for sore eyes, m'lady, it truly were!"

"I'm sure it was," Silence said dryly. "Tell me—were any hurt, or killed?"

"None of ours hurt, m'lady, but a good few of theirs. I saw 'em being dragged off when the rest of 'em ran away." He grinned at her. "That Cap'n Hellier, there bain't no flies on *him*—and he've a few more tricks up his sleeve. Spent a good part of last night, he did, making up little gewgaws to tickle the New Model's fan—"

His last words were shattered by an explosion of musket fire. Silence gasped and knocked her hand on the window. The soldier whipped around and plunged to the barrier, as a great yell went up from the barton. "Stand by! Make ready—give fire!" she heard, and at the same instant Nat screamed at her in a voice cracked high with urgency, "Duck!"

Abruptly she found herself lying on the floor of the dairy with the cold flagstones pressed into her cheek, her shoulder, her hip, while above her head the firing went on and on—were there so many musketeers in all the world? A hand touched her arm, and she started involuntarily. "Mother— are you all right?" Nat shouted above the din.

"Ow—yes—I shall be black and blue with bruises, though," Silence said. She struggled into a sitting position. On the other side of the table, also seated on the stones, was Mally, a look of surprise on her small freck-led face.

"Begorz," she said with a gusty exhalation. "That fair gi'ed me the whitemouth."

"It was somewhat alarming," Silence agreed. The shots still continued, more raggedly, and there was an acrid smell in the air that reminded her sharply of the moment when Rachael had aimed the pistol at Ridgeley and fired. She heard much shouting, some close, some more distant, none of it decipherable, and cries that, she realized with sudden sick horror, were those of wounded men. This was no game of honor; this was reality, messy and agonizing and, as Mally had pointed out, created entirely by men.

And who will have the mending of the damage? Silence thought. The women, that's who.

"M'lady! M'lady!" It was the voice of the soldier, frantic. She looked around and saw his broad bristly face under its disreputable cap shoved in at the window, a length of lighted match clenched between his grimy teeth. "Run, m'lady—they be inside the barton—*run!*"

As he withdrew, Silence scrambled to her feet. There was a crash as of glass, distinctly audible even above the shots and shouting that continued unabated, and something like a feather stroked past her hair and buried itself with a thud in the whitewashed stone wall. She stood staring stupidly at the hole, until Nat tugged at her arm. "Mother, get *down!* That was a bullet!"

"Oh, dear Lord," Mally cried, as Silence dropped to her knees again by the table. "You could've been killed, m'lady!"

"Well, I wasn't," Silence said. She took a deep breath, calming herself deliberately, and looked at her maid and her stepson. "I suggest that we crawl out of here with as much haste and dignity as we can muster, and shut the door behind us."

In the barton, the shots had diminished. The defenders, with no time to reload their weapons, were fighting for their lives with swords against greatly superior odds. And Nick Hellier, from his vantage point in the courtyard bastion, could foresee the outcome all too clearly. Unless he acted at once, the little group under Wickham's command in the barton would be overwhelmed, and the attackers free to enter the courtyard.

He had a dozen men with him, and Combes, on the eastern flank, a similar number. He ducked down below the parapet, leapt to the ground, where a young trooper stood waiting, and gave his orders, swift and concise. There was time, as the boy ran off, to load and span his wheellock pistols and to run briefly through his strategy. Then Combes and his men were there, panting, and he told them the plan. Grins broke out on their faces. Some picked up, as indicated, some of the little pots that were piled at the foot of the bastion. He and one or two others had spent a few hours last night carefully packing empty earthenware storage jars with gunpowder and a lethal assortment of scrap metal, finally fitting a short fuse through holes broken in the lids. They were makeshift and unreliable, but the best he could devise in the circumstances. And when they did go off at the right moment, as had happened before dawn, they could do a considerable amount of damage.

After they lit the fuses, they scrambled over the wall. Here it was only four feet high, but there was a drop on the farther side to an overgrown ditch and the track that led up from the Wellow Lane. Keeping to the ditch, running low, Nick led them past the end of the gatehouse wall and around to the barricade at the entrance to the barton.

It was charred and collapsed, and had presented no obstacle to the men of the New Model. Their immaculate red backs were immediately distinguishable from the faded blues and buffs of the Royalists. The barton held twenty or thirty of the attackers, advancing steadily on Tom Wickham and his handful of defenders.

"Now!" Nick cried, and the six favored men rolled their grenadoes like bowls across the stones with a great warning shout and then ducked around behind the barn.

Even if only one went off, it would be enough. And just as Nick put his hands over his ears, there were two explosions, and a great spattering shower of debris erupted from the barton. Something small and pale and bloody landed near him—the shredded remains of a man's finger. He counted to ten, to make sure that there would be no further blasts, and then beckoned to the soldiers and plunged around the side of the bar, his pistols in his hands.

A scene of utter devastation lay before them. Smoke hung, heavy and acrid, over the familiar buildings. Men, dead, dying, wounded, lay strewn about like bundles of rags. Almost all of them, he saw at a glance, were from the New Model. Through the smoke and yells and groans, someone shouted, and he saw Tom Wickham, waving his sword triumphantly in the air, while his men, who had mostly had the wit and the time to shelter in the barn and stables, emerged to herd the enemy survivors into a dazed, deafened, bleeding group in the center of the barton.

"Prisoners!" Tom exclaimed, exultant, as the Roundheads were swiftly divested of their remaining weapons. "Where shall we put 'em? In the barn?"

"Turn them loose," said Nick. As his cornet stared at him in bewilderment, he repeated it. "Let them go. Drive them out. They'll tell their friends what manner of resistance we offer, and with a little luck they'll not come back." He raised his voice to the little huddle of captives. "Go on— go back to your commander and tell him there's no profit here. Go on— go!"

Their haggard, bloodstained, dirty faces stared at him in bewildered shock. He waved his pistols at them threateningly. "Go on—*run!*"

Shambling, they obeyed, weaponless and humiliated, stumbling through the burned remains of the barricade and out into the cool fresh clear air beyond the barton. Nick ran his eyes quickly over the bodies left. Fourteen lying still, dead or comatose, another half dozen showing some signs of life. More for Silence to tend and bandage, he thought wryly. And there were only two blue coats among all of them.

"Captain! Captain Hellier!" It was Hodges's voice, from the gate that led into the kitchen garden. "Looks as if they're coming from this side now, sir! There's men in the orchard!"

Nick swore softly. He glanced at the men surrounding him, all filthy, tired, some hurt, but possessing still a vivid and unquenchable spirit of defiance. Their mood struck sparks from him, and he grinned. "Well,

well—it seems some people never learn! Tom, take a dozen men and guard the gatehouse and the courtyard. Ellis, you're accounted to have a steady aim—take my fowling piece and powder and shot and go up to my chamber within the house. You should be able to pick off a few of the enemy from there. The rest of you, follow me!"

Hodges, a stolid stout man, led him to one of the loopholes punched in the high stone wall and pointed. "There you are, sir—down there, between the trees."

There was indeed some movement. Nick made a quick calculation. The attackers had comprised a single company of men, some hundred and twenty strong. Thirty dead, wounded, or disarmed in the barton, another dozen or so killed or hurt in the earlier skirmishes. There might be eighty or so down there among the apple trees. He had two or three more grenadoes, and they could be thrown into grass without the risk of breakage. The lower terrace would be the ideal place to take up positions. Hodges and half a dozen men were left to man the gateways into the barton and the orchard, and Nick led the rest, a score or so, through the eastern gate into the garden.

Ensign Parset and Captain Bull already guarded the lower balustrade. The air was heavy with the aroma of crushed herbs and bruised flowers. Bull was peering through a gap in the makeshift timber barrier, his beaver pushed low on his head. As Nick, crouching below the level of the stone balustrade, came up to him, he looked around and nodded. "They're in the orchard, Captain."

"What strength?"

"I cannot ascertain that as yet," Bull said rather stiffly. He was some ten years older than Nick and resented the fact that the man in command was younger and in his view much less suited for the task than himself. "Some two score, perhaps. They are using the trees as cover."

From the house there was a sudden crack of gunfire, and a bullet howled over the parapet. A Roundhead soldier, previously invisible to the men on the terrace, suddenly toppled from behind a tree, to sprawl in the grass. A cheer arose from the defenders, and Nick grinned. "Good to see that my faith in Trooper Ellis was justified."

Within the hall, Silence and Nat stood listening. They had been hurrying along the north wing corridor when the grenadoes had exploded in the barton and had therefore been safe from injury, despite the fact that all the glass had been blown out. Nat had defied her pleas and looked out of the brew-house window. He refused to let her do likewise. "It's not pleasant, Mother. Don't even try—you'll only distress yourself."

Silence had fixed him with a determined eye. "Do you think I need protecting, Nathaniel my lad?"

"Of course," Nat had said. He was even paler than usual, but resolute.

And Silence, recognizing his strength, decided to acquiesce. Instead, she found the male servants, still in the kitchen but all peering agog from the window into the now-empty barton, and asked for volunteers to bring in the wounded.

To her surprise, all were eager to help. She told them to carry the men into the hall and then went in search of her women. As she walked into the screens passage, she was almost knocked over by a young soldier, laden with bandoliers, clutching a musket with an extremely long barrel. He ran up the turret stairs, and Silence turned and looked at Mally and Nat.

"Sniper," the boy said immediately. "That was Grandfather's fowling piece, I think—I recognized the shape of the butt. There must be another attack coming—probably from the south."

"Across my garden," Silence said bitterly. She clenched her hands tight together and forced a laugh. "But what do a few plants matter, when far worse is happening? Mally, go fetch Joan and Christian and Margery, and as much linen and salves as you can find."

"May I assist, m'lady?" Eliza asked from beside her, making her jump. Silence had completely forgotten the existence of the chief maid, not to mention her mother-in-law. She said guiltily, "Yes, of course you may, Eliza. There are several hurt—the men are bringing them in now. How does Dame Ursula?"

"Oh, she be pretty fair well at ease, m'lady," Eliza said. "And reading of Holy Writ—it do I good to hear it, m'lady." She sounded quite exhilarated by the struggle. Silence, squashing her annoyance, sent her to the stillroom for more plasters and ointments, and then joined Nat in the hall. The rush matting had long ago been burnt, ruined by the soldiers' drunken feasting, and the cold flagstones would make a chill bed for wounded men. There were plenty of blankets in her linen presses, however, and matting could be brought in from other rooms to ease their discomfort. She forced her mind to work logically, listing all that would be needed, ignoring the struggle outside. But the shot from above, loud and sudden and somehow shocking, shattered her good intentions.

"The fowling piece," said Nat, who had made himself useful by lighting the fire. Logs were always kept piled in the hall hearth, even in summer. He sat back on his heels and surveyed with satisfaction the thin, greedy flames consuming the kindling. "I was right—they must be attacking across the orchard. And no, Mother, you *can't* go and look."

"I wasn't thinking of it," Silence said, although every muscle in her body ached to propel her up those stairs and into one of the south-facing chambers, to see what was happening. But at that moment Darby and Goodenough entered, moving slowly and carefully, with a hurt and bleeding man groaning between them. The first of the wounded had arrived. From now on, she doubted if she would have much time to follow the progress of the attack. She must forget about Nick, and the other men fighting and dying out there, and concentrate her mind on these, who most urgently needed her help.

Out in the garden, trampled and torn and disconcertingly and incongruously fragrant, the defenders waited, their muskets protruding through the loopholes in the boarded balustrade, their eyes fixed on the orchard. Occasionally one of the enemy would show himself unwarily, and then there would be a shot from Ellis's eyrie in the house, with its panoramic view of the trees and the grass. Two or three men at least had fallen to his careful aim. Nick, a grim smile on his face, glanced up at the sky. It was patched with gray, hardly any blue visible at all, and the rising sun had not yet revealed itself. It did not look as if rain were imminent, and he was relieved. A downpour would cause havoc among the musketeers, dampening powder and extinguishing match.

Suddenly a yell came from below him, and the orchard, which just now had seemed all but lifeless, suddenly came alive with running figures. "Give fire!" he shouted, and all along the balustrade the muskets went off in clouds of smoke. As the soldiers hastily began to reload, he peered through the acrid fog. The volley had had little effect; they were still coming on. Nick aimed both pistols at the rushing men and pulled the triggers. He could not tell if the bullets had hit their mark. Still the enemy ran, leaping over the grass and between the trees, their swords gleaming in the pale light, shouting godly watchwords. There was no time to reload, though already a scattering of shots along the line of the terrace indicated that some of the defenders had succeeded.

Nick bent, picked up the earthenware pot lying by his feet, and lit the fuse with the length of glowing match wound around one of the wooden uprights supporting the barricade. His earlier experiments indicated that he had perhaps half a minute before the grenado exploded. Through the loophole, he judged distance and aim; then in one swift movement he stood up, threw it, and ducked back again as a shot wailed above his head. There was no explosion. Cursing, he took another, lit the fuse, and threw. Again it failed to go off, and already the enemy had almost reached the steps, while behind them musketeers gave covering fire. But their way was blocked by brushwood, stones, two felled trees, anything that the defenders had been able to lay their hands on in those few frantic hours of preparation, and sharpened stakes thrust outward as a further deterrent. The attackers were halted by the obstacle. They began hacking their way through, while Nick's men aimed their fire at them, with limited success.

Lieutenant-Colonel Cottesworth, peering through the orchard, was conscious of many things, not least of which was the nagging ache of an old wound in his shoulder. Hunched and scowling, he surveyed the disappointing progress of his men. The house that he had thought would surrender without a blow had so far killed or captured a score of his soldiers, including a good lieutenant whom he could ill afford to lose. They were short of ammunition, and their presence would certainly be required at the storming of Bristol, if not at Sherborne. This place could wait a little longer to be reduced. By the time Bristol had, with the Lord's help, fallen to Fairfax, the morale of Wintercombe's defenders would be lowered to the level of submission, and the house that he had been ordered not to damage could be surrendered without further bloodshed. At present, only cannon seemed likely to induce a proper respect in this most obstinate captain, and Cottesworth had no ordnance with him, nor any prospect of it. And besides, the owner of the house would certainly have something to say if he returned from the wars to find his home demolished by his own side. Colonel St. Barbe was now with Major-General Massey's army, and although his regiment had not been absorbed into the New Model, he had powerful friends.

Thwarted, Cottesworth glowered through the leaves at the house and did not like to think what his colonel was going to say. Men, particularly the trained and experienced soldiers under his command, were not expendable, nor were the weapons, equipment, and ammunition that he had lost. It would not harm morale to withdraw now, before further misfortune befell his company. Those grenadoes were a fiendish invention and had accounted for most of his dead and wounded, although only a few of the things had actually gone off. Who knew what other devilish devices that ungodly captain was plotting?

Nick, crouched behind the palisade, lit the last grenado. This time he blew softly on the fuse, holding the deadly little jar, which had once contained butter or honey or spices, close to his face. The match glowed evilly. Nick smiled, stood, and tossed it casually into the mass of men at the bottom of the steps. Then he yelled to the defenders, who needed no second bidding. Already, as arranged a few minutes earlier, they had left their posts and were pelting back to the steps that led to the upper terrace. Nick, running himself, reached the sundial and glanced back, cursing under his breath. Once more the infernal firepot, as Tom Wickham called them, had failed to go off.

It had not. He saw it rise, thrown back by some more quickwitted soldier at whose feet it had landed. It seemed to hang in the air, trailing its ominous little plume of smoke, and he realized quite suddenly that, ironically, it was this one that would explode.

He ran, though it would not avail him anything. He knew the power of the things, he had spent half the night packing them with powder and pitch and brimstone and broken shards of pottery, metal, and glass. But he had reached the steps, the last of the men to do so, and was halfway up when the grenado exploded with ear-shattering power.

He was lying on earth, his helmet pressed into it, the sweet smell of lavender all around him. He was conscious of a vague surprise. He had been so certain that the blast would kill him outright that to find himself still, for the moment, alive seemed improbable, to say the least. But he doubted that there was lavender in heaven—or, given his past, in hell— and his suspicions were confirmed when Ensign Parset's earnest voice, shocked out of its normal prosy tedium, said just above him, "Sweet Jesus! Is he dead?"

"No," Nick said, as loudly and positively as he could. "No, you great gawcum, I'm not."

He had used Nat's expression, he realized suddenly. And with the thought came a vision of Silence, her mouse-fair hair coiled about her face, white, haunted, grieving. She had been right about this foolhardy defiance, he knew that, but he was damned if, to add to everything else, she would have to watch over his deathbed.

"Captain—are you all right?" It was Parset again, much closer. "Your back—does it hurt? The blood—"

He broke off as Nick swore at him, and added, "What are you talking about, Parset? I can't feel anything—I'm all right. Tell them to keep firing, damn you—keep firing!"

"There's no need, sir," the ensign said with a note of triumph mixed with astonishment in his voice. "I think they're withdrawing."

There was a disbelieving pause. "Are you sure?" Nick asked. He wished he could move from this ridiculous position, facedown in a flower bed, but somehow could not summon the energy. What had the fool meant about his back? He felt no pain, and his head, though ringing from the blast, was otherwise perfectly clear. He added brusquely, "Help me up, will you? I have to see. Do you hear me?"

"Very well, sir, but you're hurt—" Parset began. Nick cut him short with a well-chosen epithet, and in a sulky silence the ensign obeyed. Nick felt his shoulder and arm lifted and pulled, and suddenly a wave of agony swept over him, leaving him dizzy and gasping. He set his jaw and managed to brace himself against the pain as Parset, too clumsy to be gentle, hauled him into a sitting position, unstrapped and removed his helmet, and indicated the scene behind him. "Look, sir, you see—they're going!"

He turned his head, slowly and cautiously, and looked down the steps. The sundial lay in shattered fragments among the devastated arbor. The force of the grenado's explosion had stripped leaves and twigs and unripe cherries from the trees and flung them over the knots as if a hurricane had been at work. Beyond, the orchard was empty. Distant shouts and the drums, beating the retreat, showed that they had already withdrawn to the line of the ditch, and farther.

Captain Bull was suddenly at his side, his ruddy face concerned. "Dear God, man, you took all the force of it—I thought you were dead for certain. Your back—"

"I don't want to hear about my back," Nick said heatedly. "I want to know what the enemy are doing." He turned his head again, painfully, to look up at the window of his chamber. "Ellis! Ellis, are you there?"

There was a pause, and then the young trooper's face appeared at the casement. Nick realized suddenly that it lacked most of its glass, presumably a casualty of the explosion. "Aye, sir?" the young marksman said. His face changed, and he added with concern, "Be ee all right, sir? Thy back—"

"My back be buggered!" Nick shouted, exasperated. "What are the enemy doing? Can you see?"

"I'll tell ee, sir, soon as I've looked," Ellis said, and his head disappeared.

With a wry twist to his mouth, Nick glanced up at the ensign and the captain, standing on either side of him. "Help me up, will you? And if you mention my back again I'll recommend you for a post in the most plague-ridden part of Bristol."

Tom Wickham would have laughed; these men had no sense of humor. In a resentful silence, they bent and pulled him efficiently to his feet. The pain, he discovered, was almost bearable once he was accustomed to it. He supposed that his back was peppered with all the nails and shards he had so lovingly packed into those pots not six hours before. The irony of it made him laugh. It hurt, and he regained control of his wayward emotions with an effort. He had never been seriously wounded before. Was this light-headed feeling a result of it, or merely a continuation of the mood of wild death-defying recklessness that had saved Wintercombe, it seemed, from capture?

They could, of course, just be withdrawing to attack again, and there was only one way to find out. He said to Bull and Parset, "Take me inside. And you—Ellis!"

The trooper reappeared above him. "'Tis true, sir—they be gone! I can't see no sign of them!"

"Well, find a window where you can see, and then report to me in the hall." He glanced around at the defenders, grimy, tired, triumphant, standing about him, their faces showing considerable concern. "Just because they've withdrawn doesn't mean that they're not coming back. Stand to your posts, and keep a keen watch."

"Sir," Parset said doggedly. "For the love of God, sir, come inside—your—"

"Yes, Parset?"

"You're bleeding, sir," the ensign said, after a pause, and was startled to receive the full warmth of his commanding officer's amusement.

"Oh, take me inside," Nick said, trying unsuccessfully not to laugh. "And for Christ's sake be careful about it, both of you."

The last explosion had showered the hall with glass, which Ned Merrifield was sweeping up with all his family's energetic efficiency, and a broom almost as large as himself, around the thirteen men prone on the floor. Silence, after examining them all, had hopes that perhaps half might be saved. But two had lost a hand, three feet or legs, and another had a dreadful wound in his belly that was beyond any power to cure. A barber-surgeon was needed, but the nearest lived in Bath, and Bath was no longer a Royalist garrison. These men would have to take what chance they could, and she doubted her competence to do anything but make their dying more comfortable, with the memory of Sam's horrible death always at the back of her mind.

She had thought she would feel squeamish, if not sick, at the sight of such appalling injuries, but somehow there was no time for that. Joan Coxe, however, proved uncharacteristically fainthearted, and had to retire, gray-faced and retching, when she saw the man with the opened belly. Silence, staunching, bandaging, salving, found herself handling these torn and mutilated men as if their injuries were cuts on a joint of meat, and wondered at her callousness, or detachment. Afterward, she suspected, would come the reckoning, but for now her capable calm kept the horror at bay.

There had been quiet, she realized, for a while. Were they parleying? She finished tying up the ragged, bleeding stump of a boy no older than Sam had been, and stood up. Christian, Mally, Eliza, and Margery were each bent over a soldier, ministering with gentle, bloodstained hands. Her maid called to her, and she went over. The man with the belly wound was dying, his eyes rolled up in his head and the breath rattling in his throat. A final spasm, and he was gone. She uttered a quiet prayer, closed his eyes, and pulled the blanket over his head. Then the outer door to the garden opened, she heard voices, and Nick came through the curtains.

She saw his face first, dirty, flecked with blood, and underneath the grime and the brown skin as white as paper. Then she realized that he was being supported by Captain Bull on one side, Ensign Parset on the other, and that blood was dripping copiously onto the floor.

He was responsible for the carnage around her, his intransigence had caused all this, and yet as she looked at him now her only feelings were of love and an overwhelming and desperate fear for him.

"A chair!" the tubby young ensign was crying.

She saw the flash of Nick's grin, and heard his voice, rasping with pain and yet still capable of humor. "Not a chair, you gawcum—a stool, if you value your life."

"Here is a stool," Silence said. She picked it up and began the walk toward him, between the two rows of wounded men. His eyes followed her. There was a smile still on his mouth, but she saw the agony in his face, which he could not hide, and her heart twisted in answering anguish. But it was easy, so disturbingly easy after the ghastly things she had seen over the past hour, to keep the calm mask on her face, concealing her terror.

It did not deceive Nick. The stark, haunted eyes were exactly as he had imagined a few moments before. He said, seeking to reassure her, "Don't worry, my lady—with luck I'll mend before Christmas."

"What has Christmas to do with it?" asked the literal-minded Parset, who had always been out of his depth in Nick's conversations.

His commander gave an unwise snort of laughter. "Nothing, Parset—nothing at all."

"Dear Lord, will you not sit down?" Silence asked, placing the stool before him. There was blood on the floor, a young lake of it shiny on the flagstones. Then she saw the thick buff coat cut to shreds, blood welling up dark crimson between the tattered ribbons of leather. Suddenly she felt faint, and her head reeled. "Your back," she said, in a horrified whisper. "Your back—"

"Oh, no," said Nick, and the face he turned to her was that of a drowning man, wryly amused at the irony of his fate. "Oh, no, not you as well . . ."

And he slid forward out of Parset's grasp, surrendering at last to the dark.

T
he chamber above the winter parlor, where Ellis had practiced his sharpshooting to such murderous effect, held the stillness of the grave. Dark had come in company with rain, and the drops rattled on the panes like bullets whenever the wind gusted from the south or east. But thick blue damask curtains kept out the drafts, and a fire burned low and glowing in the grate.

Silence, Lady St. Barbe, sat on a chair by the bed, her hands empty, and her eyes fixed on the man who lay there. He had not stirred since Darby and Goodenough had carried him up there, bleeding and unconscious, so that his wounds could be tended in the comparative comfort of his own chamber, the one in which Ridgeley had also once lain injured. It was natural that she should want to take charge of his treatment herself, but the other maids were full occupied with the rest of the wounded, and so, reluctantly, she had turned to Nat for help.

She did not know, now, why she had been doubtful about doing so. He proved to be the perfect assistant, competent, obedient, quick. Together, with care, they had cut the ruined buff coat, and the doublet and shirt beneath, from Nick's body, and had stared in appalled silence at the damage revealed beneath.

"Mother," said Nat. His voice was very gentle. She turned and looked at him, and saw that he knew of her feelings for Nick. "Mother, you don't have to—if you tell me what to do, I will do it."

And she had smiled and shaken her head. "No—it were best done quickly, between the two of us, or he will not survive it. You take the water and the cloth and bathe a little area at each time, and I will try to pick out the pieces of—of whatever they are."

It had taken a very long time, and she had been unspeakably glad that the body beneath her hands, torn and bleeding, had shown no sign of waking. She had begun to realize, after some time, that the damage seemed mostly to be quite shallow. The thickness of the buff coat had saved him from certain death. But, she thought, as she laid the last linen pad in place, ready for the bandages, it would be some time before he was able to lie on his back.

She and Nat wound the long frayed strips of linen about his body, holding the dressings in place. She had already soaked each square of cloth in her sage and honeysuckle water, a sovereign remedy for wounds or cuts. Whether the physic that had healed William's grazed knees would cure this devastation, she did not know. But she thought, with a shuddering sigh of relief, that if the wounds did not fester, he would live.

Mally, her face gaunt, lacking her usual cheerfulness, came up to report that the New Model had indeed withdrawn, had in fact left the village altogether and gone back to Bath, having also failed to reduce Farleigh Castle. The garrison, of course, were elated, but Dame Ursula was working herself into quite a rage, according to Eliza. And, Mally added, three of the wounded men had now died, and what was to become of the corpses?

She left Nick, reluctantly, with Nat to watch over him, and went down to organize it all. There were dead men in the barton and the orchard as well as in the hall. The soldiers were busy carrying them in and laying them under empty sacks in the barn. Silence talked the problem over with Captain Bull, and soon one of the stable lads was riding off to the village on a borrowed cavalry horse, to discuss their burial with Parson Willis. She was able to inform the captain that his commander's hurts were less serious than had at first appeared, and that he might well be recovered enough to resume his duties in a week or so.

Captain Bull looked disappointed, thanked her, and asked about the progress of the wounded. There were many, less badly injured than the Roundheads caught in the barton explosion, who would with care and God's help soon be well, and she was able to reassure him that his garrison would not long be under strength. Then, at last, she went back upstairs to see how Nick did.

He lay as she had left him, his head turned to one side, his eyes closed. She had washed most of the blood and dirt from his face, but the stubble of two days' growth of beard gave him a disreputable, rakish look at odds with the peaceful expression on his face. At some stage, she realized, unconsciousness had changed imperceptibly into sleep. And since he had had none for two days, it could only be to the good.

He slept all day, while the life of Wintercombe gradually returned to normal. Glass was swept up, the barton cleared and tidied, makeshift barriers put up at broken windows until a glazier could be found to replace the shattered panes. The wounded in the hall had been moved to the stables, where they could be tended in greater comfort, and the flagstones scrubbed clean of blood. Silence, looking at the empty, quiet room, the high dim rafters in the gathering dusk, found it hard to believe that only a few hours earlier the place had been filled with the groans and cries of the wounded and the dying.

She thought of Nick, of the bright reckless laughter and defiance that were the other side of that dark coin, and the cause of all the suffering. It was strange that only now, after trying to mend the damage he had caused, did she understand. If she had been a man and in command of a garrison like Wintercombe, she also would have found it hard to surrender to the enemy without a fight. She too might well have given way to the mood of wild, joyous, and inventive defiance that had seized Nick during the siege. He had wanted to regain his own self-respect, and, she thought wryly, he had certainly succeeded in that.

But at horrible cost to those enemy soldiers, and also to himself. He had so nearly died. Any one of those ugly, bloodstained pieces she had so gently and patiently extracted from his back could have gone an inch, two inches deeper, and killed him. And she was also aware that she herself had come close to death in the dairy that morning.

She had seen the direction her thoughts were taking and wrestled with them through the rest of that long, busy, exhausting day. And now she sat alone in his chamber, listening to the soft sound of his breathing and the sharp shrieking of the owls hunting over the fields of Hassage Hill.

A chance, two chances gone astray, and they could both be lying now, cold and stiff and shrouded in the barn. And the narrowness of their escape gave new meaning to the smallest detail around her and lent an urgent poignancy to her feelings. She had thanked God over and over for the great mercy shown to her, and to him, although why He should save someone who appeared to care very little for Him was another matter.

Her life was precious to her, and so was his. How precious, she had not fully realized until now. And because she had so nearly lost him forever, she was acutely conscious of the value of him, of how much and how deeply she loved him. It had come upon her secretly, like a thief, and she had denied it, struggled against it, fought to suppress it for months, causing them both great anguish in the process. And, she thought now ruefully, it had been a particularly futile exercise. She knew that all the reasons she had employed to justify her resistance still applied; but somehow this day had changed the balance of her soul.

She loved him. She loved him enough to cast all her former caution to the winds that beat about the house, because the only gift she could give him, the gift of greatest price, was herself.

The decision made, it was as if a great burden had been lifted from her mind. The meek wife and mother, who had only ever been a facade against the world, must give way now to the Silence she had for so many reasons suppressed for all these years. The rebellious child who had, at the age of five, flashed her bare bottom at a worthy divine in the street for the pleasure of seeing him so shocked, the adolescent who had retreated into a hidden world of laughter and mockery with her sisters, and the mother who had indulged a secret, joyous communication of words and ideas with her children, these were the real Silence. And this, this would be the greatest revolt of all, against her absent, boring, insensitive husband, his domineering, interfering mother, and the narrow little domestic world into which she had been confined and indeed, to be fair, had come to accept as her lot and duty, as a good Puritan wife should.

But Nick had come, with his music and laughter and irony, and nothing could ever be the same again. He had taught her that happiness lay within her and without her, inside her grasp. And now all she had to do was to reach out and take it.

She looked up, smiling softly, and saw him watching her. She drew in her breath sharply, startled. So strongly had she been thinking of him, it was as if she had summoned him from sleep. She went swiftly to crouch by the bed, her love shining from her as transparently as candlelight, all her masks and barriers and defenses forgotten. "How do you feel?"

"Sleepy, and sore," Nick replied. His voice was low but clear, and there was a smile woven into it. "Will I ever move again?"

Silence knelt, her hands laced flat on the mattress and her chin resting on them, and smiled in return. "Perhaps. You might even be up before the week's out, if the wounds heal cleanly. Is this what they mean by 'hoist with your own petard'?"

Nick gave an unwise snort of laughter, followed by a wince of pain. She saw the sweat break out on his forehead. His eyes closed briefly, and opened again, searching her face, so close to his own. "Which play?" he said.

"*Hamlet, Prince of Denmark,*" Silence told him. "What *is* a petard? Is it what you made out of all my empty honey pots?"

"No—they were grenadoes, though I doubt any respectable captain of ordnance would recognize them as such. A petard is shaped like that tall hat that your friend Mistress Baylie wears, and you pack it full of gunpowder and nail it to the door of the fortress you wish to enter."

Silence thought about it and then said dryly, "I presume the man who does the nailing is not expected to live to a ripe old age?"

"Hardly," he said. "That's why they tend to be the stupid ones. I am sorry I was rude to you."

"Rude?" She stared at him in bewilderment. "When were you rude?"

"When you offered me a stool, and all I could find to say was, 'Oh, no, not you as well.' I remember it distinctly."

"I'd forgotten," said Silence. "I was so worried about your back."

"And that was why I was rude. It seemed to be all that anyone was concerned about—and I became somewhat impatient. The whole of the

New Model could have been creeping up the terrace to take us by surprise, while Prosy Parset and Boring Bull were agonizing over the state of my back. I'm glad you can still laugh."

"There hasn't been very much to laugh about, of late," she said wryly. "I'm afraid I find those grenadoes, as you call them, unspeakably evil weapons—and your current state of health no more than justice."

As soon as the words were out, she wished them unsaid, but Nick only smiled at her. "As to that, you are probably right. I shall leave you to hold the high moral ground and tell me what I should or should not have done—I'm just the soldier who uses whatever means are to hand." There was amusement, not bitterness, in his voice. "But I can promise you this— I will never subject you to another siege. The next time Fairfax beats a path to this door, I shall either be long gone, and all the soldiers with me, or I shall wave the white flag as soon as their helmets appear over the hill. I have made my foolish, pointless gesture, and I hope I'm the wiser for it. You were right, as usual."

"I thought I never was."

"In others' eyes perhaps—not in mine." He paused, gingerly trying to move into a more comfortable position, and then said, "Tell me—honestly. How bad is the damage?"

"Not as bad as everyone thought," Silence said. "I think your buff coat saved you. You shouldn't have put all those dreadful things into those pots. Can you see the table?"

He twisted his head a little. "Yes."

"And the heap upon it? That is what Nat and I dug out of your back. You deserved to die," said Silence, her voice suddenly shaky, "and how unutterably glad I am that you did not."

There was a long pause in which their eyes met and held. Painfully, his hand crept up, to brush away the tears that rolled slowly down her face. "Did I ever say how much I love you?" he whispered softly.

Mute, she shook her head, while his finger traced the tracks of her tears and left a trail of fire in their place.

"Well, I know that to say it is difficult—I know it puts you in a position you would rather not be in. Perhaps you would wish it unsaid. But, as you have so rightly pointed out, I nearly died this morning—and it would have been no more than my just deserts. And I find that it has cleared my mind most thoroughly. There are things that once seemed important, which I find now are much less so, and things that I tried to pretend were not and now seem more essential than anything. Do you understand, my dear love?"

"I do," Silence replied. "Since I have been going through much the same process myself . . . this morning a bullet passed me by, closer than you are to me now. And to see you hurt . . ." She stopped, swallowed, and added shakily, "That was the moment when I realized how much I love you."

The rain battered against the window, seeking a way in to their warmth. They stared at each other, wordless, communicating with their eyes. Slowly, as if of its own volition, her hand crept out to touch his, and his fingers, long and scabbed, the nails dirty with earth and powder, twined among hers.

"Your eyes are like water," he said dreamily into the quiet. "The same color as a stream, or a pond—"

"Or a ditch," said Silence, going red. No one had ever complimented her on her physical appearance before.

He smiled and his head moved slightly in negation. "No, assuredly not a ditch. All shades of brown and green, sometimes deep and still, sometimes quick and lively—like your face. Don't blush."

"I can't help it," she said. "And do you mean that my *face* is all shades of brown and green?"

"No, damn it—you know very well what I mean, you're not stupid."

"Thank you," said Silence. "That's one of the nicest things that anyone has ever said to me."

Nick smiled, and the love and warmth in his face made her heart lurch. "My own dear lady Puritan, you have led such a deprived and sheltered life up until now—what could I not teach you, if your tender care had not rendered me immovable!"

"Don't worry," Silence said. She found this casual, mocking banter at once disturbing and invigorating, as if sparks were being struck that could easily burst into a flame that would consume them both. She wanted him to kiss her, but in his present condition, the foot and a half of bedspace that lay between her face and his might just as well be a mile and a half. "There will be time enough for that, when you can move without tearing your back to shreds. Are you hungry?"

He looked at her, and his fingers squeezed hers. "Only for you, my beloved," he said in the sighing voice of a lovesick swain, and made her laugh immoderately. She did not hear the tap on the door that announced Mally. Only when her maid coughed significantly did Silence realize her presence. Guiltily she jerked her hand free of Nick's and scrambled to her feet. Mally stood just inside the door, neat and tidy, her face inscrutable. Beside her, grinning, was Nat.

Another fiery blush washed all over Silence's face and neck, to be followed by a powerful feeling of anger, directed at herself. She had made her decision, and although discretion was obviously vital, she did not see why she must feel shame, or the urge to justify or excuse herself, to these two whom she trusted above all others.

"Next time, m'lady, maybe you'd do best to lock the door," Mally said. Silence looked at her for a long, quiet moment, seeing neither approval nor disapproval but acceptance. Mally would not attempt now to judge or to offer advice. But to the end, she would always be loyal.

And Nat? She suspected that Nat had known all along. He came forward, the candlelight lending his unnaturally pale face some warmth, and said, "How are you, Captain?"

"As well as can be expected," Nick said. "Forgive this somewhat unconventional position—I find movement a trifle difficult."

"I'm not surprised when you think of what we dug out of your back," Nat said cheerfully. "I wonder that you've got any muscles left there." He sat down on the chair by the bed and proceeded to quiz Nick as to the exact recipe for firepots.

Silence turned to Mally, who said, "Do ee want I to watch over en tonight, m'lady?"

Silence glanced at the man in the bed. It was strange how someone could be at once so still and yet so alive. She shook her head. "No, I don't think so. Perhaps if your sister sleeps in the outer chamber, so that the captain can call her if necessary. Unless the wounds become inflamed, I think he will make a complete recovery."

"I be right glad to hear of it, m'lady," Mally said, sounding as if she spoke the truth. "Captain Hellier, do ee want ort for vittles tonight?"

"I thank you, dear Mally, but no," Nick said from the bed. "I shall wait until tomorrow, when your good lady might be tempted to ease her tight bandaging a trifle, so that I may raise my head. Until then I lie like this."

Their moments alone had vanished for now, but she knew, as did he, that they had possessed a significance far beyond their number. For silently, wordlessly, promises had been made and vows spoken, and now it was only a matter of time until their love could come to fruition.

In the wider world outside Wintercombe, Fairfax and the New Model sat down outside the recalcitrant Royalist castle of Sherborne, the cradle of Cavalierism, as one disapproving Roundhead had described it, the nest of the cocktrice's eggs. After miners had breached the walls, its governor, Sir Lewis Dyve, had no choice but to surrender. The demoralized remnants of Goring's forces, in Devon, posed no further threat. At last the way was clear for the most important task of all, the attack on Prince Rupert in Bristol.

Ever since the abortive sieges of Wintercombe and Farleigh, there had been the possibility that the Bath garrison might return to finish what they had earlier begun. But as Fairfax's army moved north toward Bristol, the order went out to Colonel Waller and Colonel Birch. They were to leave a small defense behind, no more than a company or two, and march to the siege of Bristol. Sir George St. Barbe's old friend, Sir John Horner, was ordered to raise the loyal men of North Somerset in support of Parliament. During similar Royalist appeals, they had remained unmoved, but now the weavers and husbandmen and dairy farmers came flocking in to the army around Bristol, eager to join the fight against the hated Rupert.

Contrary to Silence's confident prediction, Nick's back was at first slow to heal, and he spent several uncomfortable days prostrate on the bed, eating with difficulty and unable to move any more than was absolutely necessary, while Captain Bull made full use of his brief days of command. But little by little, the raw wounds closed and scabbed over, the torn muscles began to knit together, and by the time that Pye's second litter was born, six days after the end of the siege, Nick was able to sit, and stand, and even move a few steps.

Silence was delighted with his progress, hugging it to her soul like a small warm ember of joy. And though their moments together alone were brief, and snatched from her multitude of tasks and duties, although in those times their talk never strayed from the trivial, domestic news and idle banter and one memorable flood of quotations, each capping the other until they dissolved into helpless and, in Nick's case, painful laughter, there was always an undercurrent, never mentioned, never openly acknowledged, of their mutual love and desire.

Silence did not worry about the moment waiting, when she would shed her principles and become another man's lover. It was enough, for the moment, that she had admitted it to herself and to him. How she would actually set about the process, how it could be managed in a house full of people, almost all of whom must never know, she could not imagine. But somehow, she did not doubt, a way would be found, the appointed time would come, and she would enter willingly, even joyfully, into the dreadful crime of adultery. The future lay closed and perfect in her mind, like the bud of a rose, needing only the right touch of warmth to burst into flower.

The children had returned, of course, eager with questions about the siege and curious about the unfortunate wounded occupying the stables. Silence had tended their hurts assiduously and took some pride in the fact that, after the first few days, none had died, and none of the wounds showed signs of putrefying. Soon they would be well enough to be packed into a wagon and sent back to Bath, where they could be nursed at the New Model's expense. Meanwhile, Wintercombe could afford to be generous.

The children had been evicted from the stables with some difficulty, and settled with the avid gaze of a flock of vultures in Nick's chamber. He did not mind William, who was allowed to play with an empty powder flask and who asked for stories of the siege with an eager and charming smile. Deb, who had not the sensitivity to know when she was causing pain, he had to discourage from bouncing heavily onto the bed, and hid his smiles when she took umbrage. Tabby, however, was a delight: She sang for him, and on one lovely sunny afternoon opened all his windows, then ran downstairs and into the winter parlor to play her entire repertoire, skilled or

hesitant according to the difficulty of the piece, so that the music floated in
on the warm scented air.

And Rachael . . . Rachael, thin and intense and gawky in her blue
gown, came and sat on a chair, conspicuously silent as the others chattered,
and gazed at him with the hungry, greedy stare of a child who does not
know the price of what it wants. It made him uncomfortable, but he exerted himself to behave to her exactly as he did to the other children. Nat
played chess with him, and tables, but Rachael could never be persuaded to
join in. She sat, and looked, and listened, and would not do anything else,
though Nat teased her and even Deb thought her behavior strange.

Silence, knowing that her stepdaughter's presence made Nick uneasy,
and aware of the reason for it, tried to ensure that the girl was kept as fully
occupied as possible in the dairy and with her studies. And, conveniently,
Dame Ursula began to take an increasing interest in her granddaughter.
She had always favored Nat, the only one who did not fear her, but
Rachael's extraordinary boldness in the shooting of Ridgeley had gone some
way toward softening the old lady's flinty heart. Too frail now even to leave
her bed, though her malevolent spirit was undimmed, Rachael's grandmother spent her days in prayer, in sleep, and in listening to her maid
Ruth reading the Bible to her, for of late her eyesight had faded and the
print was now too blurred. And when Ruth's voice grew faltering and
hoarse, Rachael would be summoned.

Curiously, she came to enjoy these hours. She was still afraid of her
grandmother, but she sensed now an undercurrent of approval in Dame
Ursula's manner toward her, and approval for Rachael was such a rare and
precious commodity—far-vaught and dear-abought, as they said in Somerset—that she flowered in its presence, no matter what its origins.

She did not know that the old lady, in her long periods of dozing, had
looked back nearly seventy years to the child she had once been, just such
an awkward, plain, prickly girl as Rachael. Like her granddaughter, she
had been wicked, forward and difficult. Her sudden recognition of the
powers of the Lord had saved her, and as one of the Elect she was determined that Rachael, too, be brought to a state of grace through long wres-
tlings with the devil within. A thorough knowledge of the Scriptures was
one way to win the girl's soul. And indeed, there was a savagery and a
certainty of faith in Dame Ursula's favorite parts of the Bible that greatly
appealed to the fiercer elements of Rachael's character.

Silence saw only that the time she spent with her grandmother was not
time spent disturbing Nick, and was relieved.

One evening, a fortnight after the siege, she walked in her garden. Pye
was not with her; she lay in her basket up in her chamber, suckling her sole
remaining kitten. Of her litter of four, three had for some reason been

stillborn, leaving only this one, a female of curious color, gray and white so blurred and mixed that Silence suspected that when she was grown, she would flicker like a wraith in and out of the silvery lavender bushes. Indeed, Tabby had already christened her Misty, and Silence had decided that, if the tiny kitten survived, it would stay with its mother at Wintercombe.

Diggory and Jemmy, with the help of some boys gleaned from the village, had done wonders with the garden. Mindful of Nick's promise to her that there should be no more sieges, she had told the old gardener to spare no labors in restoring it to its former glory. The temporary barricades had been taken down and stacked in the barton to provide firewood for the winter. The riven sundial had been taken away, used for mending walls, but she had kept the metal face, still riveted to its circle of broken stone, so that when the war ended a mason could set it on a pedestal once more, in the center of the lowest terrace. The wrecked and trampled flowerbeds had proved harder to set right, and Diggory had cursed the ungodly Cavaliers who had battered down years of hard work in a few hours. But he had nurtured and clipped the torn box, pruned the broken rosebushes, replanted the lavender and marigolds, and set the boys to raking the gravel smooth and anointing the torn bark of the cherries with his own aromatic concoction, to prevent disease.

It *would* be the same; she was sure of it. A garden could forever be made new, and better. When the war was over, she would write to Joseph in London and ask him to seek out rare, precious bulbs and seeds. She could not yet admit it, even to herself, but the garden would be there, to take and absorb and heal her hurt, when Nick was gone.

It was approaching harvest. Nat and Clevinger had walked out into the fields of wheat and barley, spangled blue and yellow and scarlet with cornflowers and marigolds and poppies. They nibbled the grain, comparing, waiting for the perfect day. This year would be no better or worse than most others, but at least the soldiers might not come riding across it, trampling it flat before it could be gathered in. Bristol could prove hard to take. At least let the corn be safely harvested before the New Model came stamping blindly across the fields to Wintercombe.

She leaned on the balustrade and looked down at the orchard. In the fading light there was little sign of the damage done, the raw scars of tree stumps, the hacked branches, the ugly ditch and earthen rampart beyond. The apple harvest would be scanty—the May rain had come at the wrong time, and too many trees had been destroyed—but Diggory was grafting and nurturing more in his special bed in the kitchen garden. There had been no cider for some time, the soldiers had drunk it all, and she missed its sour, sharp, refreshing taste. Beer, which was brewed every fortnight, was much less to her liking, and the supply of wine, shipped through

Bristol, had long since dried up. She had made quantities from cherries and elderflowers, as an unusual but palatable substitute, and the vine might even be persuaded to yield enough for a bottle or two.

The three horses, Dumbledore, Cobweb, and Strawberry, grazed contentedly by the mulberry tree that Sir Samuel had planted when King James had been obsessed by the need for England to produce silk. Unfortunately, the trees had not been the correct type to nourish silkworms, but their berries made excellent jams, preserves, and dyes. Her old and favored gown was mulberry-colored; she wore it now.

A bat swooped and dived above her, heralding night. There were no soldiers on guard here. Two men manned the gatehouse, and another two the entrance to the barton. Already several of the garrison had deserted, going home before their fate could catch up with them. She did not blame them, and neither did Nick. The rest waited, sheltered and fed, idling their time away. Silence wondered if they could be prevailed upon to help with the harvest, and grinned to herself at her presumption.

It was time to go in. The children were abed, supper long eaten, the house settling down for the night. On these late summer evenings, there was little lingering by candlelight, for dawn and the next day's work were too near. She turned and walked up to the highest terrace, where the door to the screens passage lay open. Lily trotted behind her, pausing now and then to sniff at something.

The shrouded house loomed dark above her, the windows lit gently from within. She wondered why, this year of all years, the vine should have flowered and borne fruit. Under every leaf there was a bunch of fat tight green grapes, the size of peas, and Diggory was grumbling, even as he marveled, at the work involved, balanced up a ladder thinning out each bunch, so that what remained could grow to a proper size. Silence and all her children had helped him, for she could not rid herself of the sense that this glorious, unprecedented blossoming and fruitfulness had been called forth in answer to something of the same, within herself.

There was a shadow by the door. Lily, whose eyesight was keen even in this light, stopped and stared, a low growl at the back of her throat. The shadow moved, and Silence relaxed. "Ssh, Lily," she said quietly. "Friend." And then to Nick, whom she had recognized merely from his height and build, "You should be in bed. You only got out of it three days ago."

"It seemed too fine an evening to shut it out so soon," Nick said, his voice soft and warm and dark, so that suddenly her blood began to stir and her breathing quickened. "So I came down, exceedingly carefully, I might add. Believe me, dear lady, I am not going to move in a manner that pains me."

"Then I'm surprised you moved at all," Silence said. She wanted above all else to touch him, to hold him and feel his hands about her. But from fear of hurting him, and perhaps even now a fear of something else, she did not dare. She did not know what to say, for to speak her feelings would reveal too much here, where it was hardly private despite the lateness of the hour. So she said, "Lily has been chasing rabbits in the orchard."

"And did she catch any?"

"No, or we would have had pie tomorrow." Silence could hardly see him in the dark. An owl screamed suddenly, hunting like Lily among the apple trees, and she jumped.

He said, his voice amused, "Are you frightened of the dark, then?"

"Not at all," she told him with some indignation, and then added reflectively, "It's as if I have one skin less tonight, as if I can feel more, hear more, and the flowers seem to smell so much sweeter. Did you hear Tabby play this evening? It was utterly lovely . . . you have given her something that will last her forever."

"I enjoyed it," he said. "I do not like to see gifts wasted . . . she told me that Pye had had her kittens, but that all of them died save one."

"Yes, it was very sad. Do you think you can climb the stairs to my chamber?" said Silence. "Mally will fetch wine for you, and you may see the kitten, and we can talk. This week seems to have been filled with children, and gardening, and why it seems to take all day to churn the butter. Joan thinks a witch is at work, she swears the dairy has been overlooked, as they say."

"I can't think why any witch would trouble herself over something so trivial. And yes, I will avail myself of your offer, although I warn you, I may not be able to leave as soon as you would wish. I was not planning to climb two sets of stairs, you see."

"I'll lend you Sir Samuel's walking stick," Silence offered, and heard his laugh.

She gave him her arm, though, when they came within the hall, lit by sconces, and she saw the stiff, tense way in which he moved, as if the pain could be kept at bay only by holding himself rigid. He looked at her and smiled, and her bones melted; she felt his hand warm on her arm, for she had rolled up the sleeves of her summer gown, a habit of which her husband had always disapproved ("It makes you look like a washerwoman, my dear."). So late, well past dusk, there was no one about, but she was careful to guide him along the right-hand side of the hall, well out of the limited line of sight from Dame Ursula's looking mask behind them. Probably the old lady was long since asleep, but Silence was certain that Ruth spied for her and might even now be lurking behind that incongruously laughing face.

They reached the stairs, and safety, although his fellow officers lay behind the door to their left, in the two chambers beyond. But no one saw, or heard, and they began the long slow climb up to her chamber. There was no room for two to go abreast, so she followed him, hoping that he would not fall. But though he went very carefully, holding on to the wall, taking one step at a time, he did not falter, and turned a triumphant face to her at the top. "Your ministrations are evidently having their effect, my lady. An hour ago I doubted I could do that."

"It's hardly due to me," Silence said. "All I've done is change the dressings and anoint your injuries with various nostrums."

"I don't mean that," he said. There was little space, just a small square of stone, in front of the door. She was standing very close to him, and her heart was behaving strangely. He took her hands in his and smiled. "Your presence has been sufficient to heal me. And now I know what lies in store for us, I have a further and greater incentive to get well."

His face left no doubt of his meaning. He pulled her against him and kissed her. She almost put her arms around him, and remembered just in time. Even as he explored her mouth, gently and passionately, she felt him shake with suppressed laughter. When they were done, she found herself breathing quickly, her senses thoroughly aroused. She stared at him, wide-eyed and trembling very slightly, and he said quietly, "You do not look as though you were used to this."

"I am not," said Silence, thinking of George, who had never kissed her like that in all the years of their marriage, during all those fumbling, undignified, and inelegant couplings in the darkness behind the bedcurtains. She had endured it dutifully, as she had endured everything, but that enjoyment and pleasure could attend such an act had never, until Nick, entered her head. To take delight in such things was for whores and peasants. Women were naturally lascivious, true. It was one of the burdens laid on them since Eve, but it was the mark of a lady to deny such desires in herself. Her husband had gained some satisfaction, of course, but that was a natural consequence of the difference between men and women. Her reward and consolation had been her children.

"Then I will accustom you gradually," said Nick. "Which is just as well, since gradually is probably all my back will allow me." He opened the door, and they walked inside.

Mally was dozing in one of the window seats. She leapt up as they entered, and cushions scattered over the floor. "Oh, m'lady, I be main sorry—must've fell asleep, m'lady."

"Don't worry, it doesn't matter," Silence said, smiling. "Can you fetch us some of my elderflower wine, Mally, and two glasses? And then I think your duties are done for the night."

Mally bobbed a curtsy and left with an efficient whisk of skirts. Nick could have sworn that she winked at him as she went past, but it might only have been his imagination. He walked to the hearth and looked down at the basket. Pye slept there, her fantastic black and white blurring the lines of her body so that it was hard to tell which end was which. The blue-gray kitten was also asleep. Silence, realizing that Nick would find it impossible to bend, knelt and picked it gently up. At once it started squeaking, its tiny paws with their bright fresh pink pads waving violently, and Pye sat up, alarmed. As soon as she saw who had her baby, she uttered a low, warning miaow and watched intently, but without real concern.

"Tabby has called her Misty," Silence said. "Isn't she delightful?"

"How old is she?"

"Oh, a week or so. She'll grow big and fat, this one—all that milk, just for one kitten when it was meant for five. Do you want to hold her?"

The kitten nestled in the warmth of his cupped hands, and the pink nose bumped against his fingers, seeking milk. He stroked the tiny body, conscious of a sense of wonder at this life so new, so recently conceived, and yet so perfect. When he looked up, Silence was watching him, and as before, when he had lain wounded in her bed, all her fortifications were down, and her soul stood there in her eyes. She took the kitten, still mewing, and replaced it in the basket, where it immediately sought out its food supply and began to suckle fiercely, while Pye lay and purred, her green eyes slitted with happiness.

"Do you want to sit?" she asked Nick. "And if you do, on what? A stool?"

"A chair well backed with cushions will be more comfortable, I think," he told her, and watched as she fetched an armful from one of the windowseats and piled them in her own chair, the one with the arms. Carefully he lowered himself down and leaned against the soft feather-filled tapestry and damask. The relief to his back was so intense that he closed his eyes for a moment, almost dazed by the sudden freedom from pain.

"You must be careful," Silence said, drawing up another chair and settling a cushion behind her own back. "You don't want to overdo things and find you've reopened your wounds. Ah. Mally, thank you—can you put it down over there?"

Mally laid the bottle of new elderflower wine, made a month or so before, on the cold hearth, with two pewter cups beside it. She stepped back, eyeing the two of them sitting companionably by the fire, and said politely, "Be ee better, Captain Hellier?"

"I wouldn't be here if I wasn't," Nick said. "Yes, I thank you, Mally, I am much recovered. I shall be able to sit a horse before the next week's out, I expect—due to your lady's care, and your own."

"Thank ee, Captain," the girl said, bobbing a curtsy.

"You may go to bed now, Mally," Silence said.

There was a pause. Her maid did not move, but her eyes flicked from the man to the woman and back again. She said, her voice careful, "Do ee want I to busy myself elsewhere for a while, m'lady?"

Startled, Silence's eyes flew to Nick. He was staring at Mally, a smile on his opened mouth; then he glanced at her. Their gaze met. She saw the reckless look appear again, and almost imperceptibly he nodded. A wild surge of joy flooded through her, and she turned to Mally, her pale oval face glowing as the maid had never seen it, a look almost of mischief as well as delight. "You do that, Mally," she said. "And . . . thank you."

"I'll be back in an hour or so," Mally said, and so transparent was her lady's expression that an answering grin spread across her own freckled face. She bobbed a curtsy and left. They heard her shoes clattering cheerfully down the stairs and die away into the distance.

Silence found that she was trembling. To hide her confusion, the turbulent mix within her of joy and apprehension, she bent and poured the wine. It splashed a little onto the stones as she lifted the two brimming cups, both rather more full than she had intended, and gave one to Nick.

"Your Mally is very surprising," he said. "I thought she didn't like me."

"She didn't, but I think the demise of Ridgeley changed her mind." Silence sipped her wine, which tasted fragrantly of flowers and summer, and wondered whether she was shaking from fear, or from something else. She looked into Nick's face over the top of the cup and added, "She is loyal—I would stake my life on her loyalty. She may not have approved of you once, but I know she can be trusted."

"You are trembling," he said softly. "Why are you trembling?"

Silence finished her wine with a despairing gulp. Despite her earlier resolution, a traitor worm coiled serpentine within, and whispered adultery, and hellfire, and betrayal. She said, her voice low, "Because the moment is on me, and I cannot escape it."

"But you can." He leaned his head back, the wine cup resting in his hand on the arm on the chair, and his smile was very gentle. "The door is not locked, and you have only to give the word and I will leave you. I have said in the past that I will only do to you what *you* want me to."

"But how can I?" she said, despairing. "When I don't know enough to know what I want—except that I love you, and when you sit so close I want you to touch me, and hold me, and kiss me—and yet all my teaching cries out at the evil of it, and my soul says something else entirely." She stopped, and fought successfully for control. Then she added, "I decided, when I saw you hurt, to—to indulge my feelings, because I think—I think the truth of them became too great for me to deny. And now . . . oh, Nick, I am so frightened!"

"Of what? Of the deed itself, or its consequences?"

His calm, quiet voice did much to soothe her. She stared at him, seeing the face she loved, a strong face, changeable and apt to laughter, the lines of it already graven around his mouth and eyes, the cheekbones shadowed by illness and pain, the narrow eyes warm and steady. It was a face that could be cold and hard and ruthless, and she had seen it as such too often. But now the love in it almost stopped her breath. She laced her hands together and said slowly, "Both. I—I've never even dreamed of doing this before—before you. I didn't even think that it was something I'd ever *want* to do—I couldn't imagine *wanting* to have any man in my bed."

Those words told him what he had already suspected. And he wondered at the man who had possessed her, and was too selfish, or ignorant, or thoughtless, or bigoted, to pay any heed to his wife's needs and feelings as well as his own. Certainly he would have no compunction whatsoever in cuckolding Sir George St. Barbe. He said, "But you do now—or you would, if you were not so confused and afraid. My sweet Silence, there is no need to be frightened. Mally will make sure that we are not disturbed— I will lock the door in a minute—and there is no chance that we will be discovered. And as for the other—well, don't you think that I myself have excellent reasons for proceeding with great care and caution?"

He had made her laugh. She got up and walked the few paces to his chair, and stood looking down at him. There were tears on her face, but she was smiling. She said, "Will you teach me? You will have to be very patient."

"I am passing good at that—have I not put up with Deb bouncing on my bed all these days? Ah, lady, my lovely lady Silence, you can trust me—or have you not learned that yet?"

"I have learned," Silence said. She knelt in front of him and took his hands in hers. "Almost all my lessons have been learned, but some better than others. And I love you, and you love me, I do not doubt you for I can see it in your face when you look at me—and if we have that, surely all the rest will follow?"

"You have put my thoughts into words exactly," he said, and his hands came up to unfasten her cap, feeling her skin tremble at his touch. Underneath, most of her hair was pulled back plainly into a knot behind her head, the rest curling loose around her face. "Will you unfasten your hair for me?"

Her eyes on his, she reached up and pulled out the pins that held it in place. She shook her head to free it, and the heavy, waving, light-brown locks fell about her face, giving her a wild look quite unlike the demure Puritan he knew so well. Her gaze was vast, trusting, loving, like a child's, but there was also a note of desire that was entirely unchildlike.

"Come with me," he said, and rose to his feet with an effort that he disguised quite successfully, though not from her. "Apart from anything else, I shall probably require your support."

She gave it as he walked slowly and painfully to the door, and turned the key firmly in the lock. Then, carefully, he set his back to it, avoiding the hinges that studded one side, and pulled her against him. And this time, as he kissed her, she surrendered herself completely to the sensual pleasure of it, letting her desire and delight sweep her along with him, forgetting all scruples and anxieties. When his hands, warm and deft, unbuttoned the modest collar at her neck, letting it drop to the floor, and began to unlace her bodice, she no longer felt any urge to stop him. Ministering to injured soldiers and sick children had made her long familiar with the fastenings of a man's doublet. With a sense of wonder at her own boldness, she unbuttoned it and slid it carefully from his shoulders.

"To the bed, I think," he said very softly, his lips nuzzling her ear and his hands exploring her breasts, making them tingle hotly and sweetly with the force of her desire, and his. And together, entangled, discarding their clothes as they progressed, they made their way to it.

Silence stood there trembling, her eyes enormous, as he pulled the fine holland chemise over her head, further disarranging her hair, and admired her body. Suddenly self-conscious, she turned and dived beneath the bedclothes. Ruthlessly Nick turned them back to expose her nakedness, and Silence, acutely aware that she was nearer to thirty than to twenty-nine, and that she had borne four children, stared up at him, a hot flush mottling her face and neck. Seeing her unease, he said softly, "What is wrong? Surely you are not ashamed?"

"Like Eve," she said, with a reluctant smile. "I—I'm just not used to—to being looked at."

"Not even when it's with considerable appreciation?"

"Oh, no—you flatterer," Silence murmured, shaking her head on the pillow.

"Flatterer? Why should I need to be, when I have you here already? Oh, my love, listen, listen—you are beautiful, all of you, from the top of your head to the end of your toes—and never more so than when you laugh."

"Don't be ridiculous," Silence said, trying not to. "I am a very ordinary housewife, and mother, not some immaculate Court lady."

"I know that, don't I—it's Silence I want, no one else." Nick paused, and then pulled his face into a ludicrous expression of appeal and said timidly, "Please, can you help me off with my shirt?"

This time she gave way to her laughter, and the feeling of joyous mischief bubbling up to defeat her embarrassment. Carefully she knelt on the bed and unlaced the neck, then disentangled his arms from the sleeves and coaxed it over his head. Underneath, the dressings that she and Mally had changed every morning for twelve days were strapped firmly to his back, disguising the fine pale skin and lean muscles of his body. There was a sharp line between his brown tanned face and the rest of him, and the hairs on his chest and belly were darker than those on his head. Silence, who had never seen her husband naked, nor any man save those whose hurts she had tended, kept her eyes on his face and hoped that he would not comment on her woeful lack of experience in love. For being an active, desiring partner seemed so much more difficult than just to lie there, acquiescent, and let George do with her exactly what he wished.

But Nick said nothing, only let his eyes wander up and down her white body, which had once been painfully thin and was now, after four children, pleasantly rounded, her hips plumper and her belly still gratifyingly flat, her breasts firm and full, though a little low. Then, overcome with desire, he reached for her.

In his arms, letting her own hands stray with increasing boldness, she discovered at last her own capacity for taking and giving pleasure, so that when he entered her, it was the natural culmination of what they had already enjoyed rather than the forbidden act that she had resisted for so long. And the dizzying explosion of delight, making her cry out with joy, was followed almost immediately by his own.

It was suddenly very quiet, very peaceful. Silence, coming back to reality by slow degrees, lay with his warm weight on top of her and thought, I am an adulteress.

The idea was so remote that she almost laughed. What had wickedness to do with the marvelous feelings his hands and body had aroused in her?

"It must be forbidden because it's so delightful," she said dreamily, and felt his sudden shake of laughter.

"Undoubtedly," he said, his voice slow and lazy. He moved a little, taking his weight on his elbows, and gazed down at her. To her surprise, there was an echo of her own wonder on his face. He added, "You are superb, my lady, did you know it? Superb. And I have remembered another quotation to add to our collection. 'Silence is the perfectest herald of joy.' And I love you."

"I love you," she said, and the simple beauty and truth of those three words made her want to shout it from the windows. But she was not a fool, though in the relaxed and contented afterglow of lovemaking she cared for nothing at present save his closeness above and around and inside her, and the fact that, miraculously, wonderfully, he loved her as much as she loved him. Already the absolute necessity of secrecy and the complications this would involve were looming menacingly on the horizon.

But that would come later. For now she could surrender to the glories of these moments and luxuriate in her bliss like Pye soaking up the fire's heat. Her arms tightened about him, forgetting, and he gasped. Instantly contrite, she said, "Oh, I didn't mean to—did I hurt you?"

"Nothing that won't mend," he assured her cheerfully. "But I am afraid, lady, that I have opened something. I can feel it bleeding."

Very cautiously he slid from her and lay on his belly, while Silence, her earlier discomfort at her nakedness quite forgotten, gently explored his injuries. There was one small place where the scabs had cracked, letting the blood through to soak the folded lint. She had a good recipe to staunch that, a flour and honey paste, if it did not stop of its own accord.

"You'll do," she said, smiling, thinking of his lovemaking, which had been considerate and gentle and characterized by none of the undignified gaspings and thrashings of her husband. The image of George did not make her feel guilty, though she suspected that might come later. With a sigh of remembered pleasure, she lay down beside Nick, her face turned to his, and her fingers linked with his hand.

For a long, wordless time they gazed at each other, drinking in the small subtle details of face and hair and eye. Then at last Nick said softly, "I hate to bring us back to life, but Mally will probably be back soon, and I should go."

"I know," Silence said. "I've been trying not to think of it." She rolled over and sat up, the bedclothes drawn up around her waist, her arms crossed on her raised knees. Her hair was impossibly and luxuriantly tangled, and her face was subtly altered, softer and with a genuine serenity, the mask discarded and the lines of strain and worry utterly vanished. Suddenly she laughed, the sound throaty and genuinely amused. Nick, watching her intently, thought she looked more beautiful than he had ever seen her, transformed by love. He said softly, "What is it?"

"I was just thinking . . ." Silence said, and turned toward him a face of delighted mischief. "*Now* I understand Bessie Lyteman!"

Amid their laughter, they kissed and rose from the bed. Finding and putting on their scattered clothes was a task accomplished with much merriment, especially since Nick found it well-nigh impossible to bend his back. Eventually, however, each fastening the other's laces and buttons like a pair of children, they achieved a measure of respectability. Only Silence's hair, wild and tangled, betrayed how the last hour had been spent, and Nick offered to brush it, a task that for years only Mally had performed for her.

She sat at the table, looking into the little rosewood mirror, feeling the bristles stroke again and again at her hair, teasing out the tangles with a patience and dexterity that told her that he had done this task before, for someone else. She felt no jealousy. The past was gone, the future far away, only the present mattered for the moment.

The face that looked back at her was her own and yet not her own, the features unchanged but the bruised mouth, the flushed skin, the dreaming, languorous eyes speaking of another, sensual Silence who had lain entirely unsuspected beneath that despised and dowdy exterior. Experimentally she smiled at herself and saw Nick's face reflected, like a Hallow's Eve prophecy, smiling back.

Mally, returning a few minutes later from the stillroom, where she had been making up more salves, was able to view them with the satisfaction of a matchmaker. The doubts she had had about Nick Hellier—and, it had to be admitted, they had been legion—had vanished the night of her escape with the children, when she had known for certain that he would not betray them, and her opinion had swung around to positive approval after the death of Ridgeley. Like many of the villagers, Mally was a person of practical rather than moral persuasion. She did not know Sir George St. Barbe well, but she did not care for the little she had seen of him. Silence she respected and liked as a friend as well as a mistress, and her loyalty to her was unshakable. She deserved better than Sir George, Mally had always thought, and now along had come this personable, amusing, and above all *young* man—a man her own age, not one old enough to be her father—who was obviously head over ears in love with her. Why not take advantage of this opportunity and snatch at happiness? She would do so herself, in the same situation, and so would most of the wives she knew in the village. And so Mally, being no hypocrite, had decided to help her lady, if that was what she wanted, to commit adultery.

And by the look of it, she had succeeded. There were the lovers, smiling at each other, still lost in the circle of delight that surrounded them. She said quietly, "'Tis late, m'lady."

"I know," Silence said, turning her glowing, fulfilled face to her maid. "Thank you, Mally—thank you so much."

"I be main glad to help," the girl said. "And I d'want ee both to know—I'll do the same again, any time that you want, m'lady."

Silence and Nick looked at each other, and again there was that long, wordless moment of communication. Mally thought of the young men she knew, none of whom had ever looked at her like that, and was conscious of a wistful sliver of envy. She sternly suppressed it.

"I think that would be most welcome," Silence said. She glanced again at her lover and then added, "But it must be *very* discreet, Mally—you know how important that is. If anyone should find out . . ."

"I d'know that as well as do any," Mally assured her. "M'lady, you d'know as how I'd never tell, not if they offered to slit my throat. And I'll make sure that none of them find out. Master Nat, though, *he* d'know, I be certain of it."

"I think so too," Silence said ruefully. "He hasn't said anything to me, not in so many words—but I'm sure of it, just the same. But Nat was always very perceptive—he sees things that no one else would. And like you, Mally, he is a dear true friend, and he would never give me away."

"So four people know," Nick said. "We must make sure, Mally, that it goes no further. It matters nothing to me, but for my lady it is of the utmost importance." He smiled at Silence, and Mally noticed that their hands were entwined. "For she has so much more to lose."

"Don't ee fret, Captain," the girl said firmly. "I d'reckon an oyster'd be a blabbermouth aside of me. No one else will know of it."

And Silence, suddenly aware of the depth of the abyss over which she stood and the fragility of the bridge which supported her, hoped devoutly that she was right.

TWENTY-SEVEN

The tempter or the tempted, who sins most?
—MEASURE FOR MEASURE

For Silence and for Nick, those long days as August drew to an end and September began were an idyll, a dream of love and happiness, a fragile bubble protecting from the world outside, from an unhappy past and the uncertain future. Sherborne was taken, Bristol besieged, and men from all over North Somerset were flocking to the army camped around it, eager after years of resentful neutrality or acquiescence to be in at the death of the Royalist cause in the west. Several young men from Norton went, hungry for action and excitement, and were given arms and duties and, hugely swelled with a sense of their own importance, marched and drilled like real soldiers. More men from Wintercombe had slipped away; the garrison now numbered less than two score, most of who were determined to see out the war, though Nick had so far forgotten his duties as to point out to them the advantages of going home now, before the Roundheads could catch up with them. But, as one corporal reminded him, they had stuck with him so long that it was a habit very difficult to break, and he suspected that some of the more bloodthirsty hoped for another chance to slaughter the enemy.

But he had promised Silence: There would not be another siege. And that was one vow he intended to keep. He had seen the injuries his grenadoes had inflicted, and for the first time a sense of his own responsibility in the matter had pricked his conscience. The maimed survivors found themselves well treated, pampered even, and decided that these Cavaliers at least were a decent enough lot, even if they did smoke, drink, swear, and fornicate more than the Lord permitted. They had even been promised a wagon ride back to Bath, once the harvest was in.

The most important season in the farming year was now upon them. All over Norton, farmers great and small consulted wisely with each other about the weather, studied their wheat or barley or oats, and watched everyone else like hawks, waiting for the first sign of action. Clevinger made much of the fact that he was upsides the rest, as he put it, too superior to indulge in such petty practices, but Nat saw him eyeing the Manor Farm fields, assessing their ripeness. For in a village where almost every family, save the very poorest, had their own little plot of arable to harvest, it was impossible for everyone to gather their crops in at the same time, and there was always a certain amount of devious maneuvering by the larger farmers in order to secure the best and biggest workforce without having to resort to employing day laborers from other villages, of dubious or unknown honesty or morality, who were even more liable to get drunk, molest the women, and pilfer the corn than their own servants.

But all the omens were good, and Clevinger, always cautious, at last gritted his teeth, organized a workforce from certain reliable villagers and their families, and made all the preparations for beginning harvest at dawn the next day.

Wintercombe, being principally a dairy farm, did not grow very much itself: wheat to bake its own bread, barley to brew the beer, oats and peas and beans for animal fodder. Money from breeding cattle, horses, and sheep, selling cheese and butter and wool had been so profitable that it had been more convenient to buy what was not grown. It had meant hardship during the winter of the soldiers, and cattle had died, but Clevinger had not been tempted to plow up pasture for a quick crop. In the long run, the cattle were far more profitable.

Almost as a joke, Silence had suggested to Nick that some of the soldiers might help with the harvest. Much to her surprise, many of them had taken up her idea with enthusiasm. They were mostly farmers, or the sons of farmers, and had been away from the land sufficiently long for harvest work to seem like a refreshing novelty. The consequent addition of a dozen burly young troopers to the band of laborers marching out with their sickles, called shekels hereabouts, in their hands, and the small leather containers known as plow bottles, full of Wintercombe beer, hanging from their belts, made an incongruously mixed and faintly comical procession.

Silence, reared in the dirty, noisy confines of London, always loved harvest. Of necessity, it usually took place in warm, fine weather, and was a time at once of hard work and holiday. The men moved methodically in rows from one end of the field to the other, their bodies swaying in rhythm with the swinging of their sickles, laying the long-stalked corn beside them in neat sheaves, ready for binding. Behind came the women and girls, one to every three reapers, whose task this was to free the cut corn of weeds and grass and poppies and to tie each sheaf with a dozen or so stalks of straw before putting it down again, to await the time later in the day when it would be stacked in hiles of the customary ten sheaves, to dry in the sun and wind before a final journey, some days later, to the barn.

The first fields to be harvested lay on the northern slopes of Hassage Hill, several closes adjoining each other below the dark stunted trees of the coppice, and Clevinger split the workforce into groups. Nick Hellier, to his amusement, found himself in command of one, but the sight of Rachael among his allotted binders gave him pause. She was looking at him hungrily, but when she saw that she had attracted his attention, she glanced away, flushing, her eyes cast down in a manner more in keeping with her age. Nick had approved of his lover's policy in expending her step-daughter's energies with hard physical labors in field or dairy, but now, looking at Rachael, he wondered if it was entirely appropriate. Her arms and face had become quite brown, in a most unladylike fashion, and in her plain gray gown, rather patched and shabby, she was almost indistinguish-able from the wives and daughters of village husbandmen and yeomen and laborers all around her.

Silence stood in the corner of the field, her younger children leaping about with the others, talking to Nat and Clevinger. As always when he looked at her, Nick's heart contracted with love, and he was conscious of a wry amusement. If anyone had told him, a year ago, that he would be head-over-heels smitten with some Puritan's plain and dowdy wife, he would have laughed incredulously. And yet there he was, helping to har-vest her fields for her, utterly besotted.

Once he had tried over and over again to analyze the hold she had on his mind, his body, his senses. Why this woman, above all others, with none of the lovely graces that usually attracted him? He had searched for a reason as if the finding of it would somehow cure him, but in vain. And now he no longer wanted to be cured. Why attempt it, when the sickness was so utterly, gloriously delightful?

They had not been able to come together every night: His duties as a soldier, hers as a mother, had seen to that. But seven times in the past ten days they had made love, and each successive union seemed more wonderful than the last. His back was vastly improved, which was just as well, for her early shyness and hesitancy had swiftly given way to a boldness and passion that had surprised, and excited, them both. And he wondered that her mood of utter bliss, the glow of sensual satisfaction that shone in her face, did not seem to betray their secret to all the world at Wintercombe.

He had made her happier than she had ever been in her life before; he knew, because she had told him so. And because he was so closely attuned to her, because there was that feeling of kinship between them that had always been the basis of their friendship, he sensed also that she was drink-ing in this miracle to the full, because it was inevitably doomed to end. And, like her, he preferred not to think of that destined moment when he would be forced to ride away from Wintercombe and leave her behind.

To make that parting easier for both of them, it was his care now, and Mally's to practice the utmost discretion. In public, there would be no speaking glances, no touch of hands, only the continuation of that friendly companionship that they had shared for so long. All Wintercombe, and Norton, knew of the debt she owed him, over the matter of Ridgeley; they accepted with equanimity the once-curious sight of their Puritan lady and the Cavalier captain conversing amicably together, and would have looked surprised if an ignorant outsider had suggested that a hostile relationship would have been more appropriate.

Secrecy, of course, was second nature to Silence, but she could not disguise her mood of joy, her delight in life. It was the cause of it that must forever remain hidden. So she curbed her passion, and the glow in her senses and in her loins whenever she looked at him, knowing now the contours of his body and the sweet fiery touch of his hands, arousing her to still greater delight. She kept her secret warm within her, to unfold in the privacy of her chamber when he came to her at night. Soon the idyll must end. But, like him, the reckless, rebellious part of her soul gloried in this passionate surrender to her fate.

All morning the reapers worked. The early, unblemished blue of the sky was soon dappled with high white cloud, providing brief and welcome shade for those who labored. Rachael was no shirker. She enjoyed the chance to dissipate her tempestuous energies under the warm sun, in the friendly companionship of servants with whom, somehow, she was now on equal terms. Her hands and arms were scratched and bleeding from the sharp straw, her back ached, and from the way her face felt hot and stretched it had fairly caught the sun, but she was as happy as it was possible for such a moody person to be. And Nick Hellier was working in her field—and even if he did treat her in the kindly manner he reserved for the children, she was still under his eye and in his presence, and she would not have admitted her discomfort to him under torture.

One of the other girls shouted to her, and she straightened up, remembering just in time not to put a hand to her back. So absorbed had she been in her thoughts and her work that the morning had flown by, and it was now, obviously, time for the noonday break. Already there were people collapsing gratefully in the shade of the hedgerow and coppice farther up the hill, taking thirsty swigs from their plow bottles and munching on the generous hunks of bread and cheese that the Wintercombe kitchen had provided for every worker. There would be an hour or so, to sleep and rest, before work began again.

Rachael finished tying the sheaf and walked up the hill to join the others. Someone made a jocular comment on her sunburnt nose, to which she answered with a preoccupied grunt. It did not offend, for her ways were well known. But when Nick Hellier told her, casually, that she had worked well and hard, her smile rivaled the sun.

It was only when she sat down beside Christian Merrifield, whose face was a riot of freckles, that she realized how tired she was. She ate her bread and cheese like all the rest, with famished enjoyment, and drank from her bottle. For once it was the adult brew, not the small beer with which the children had to be content. She drained it greedily and then, after a few pleasantries exchanged with Christian and another girl, lay back like them in the stubble under the hedgerow, shaded by a tall and luxuriant ash.

She had not intended to fall asleep, but she must have done so, for something woke her. The sun had shifted, and her legs were no longer in the cool shade. She lay, squinting up through her lashes and the movement of the leaves, the brightness of the light behind them. Then she heard someone walking carefully through the stubble toward the hedge. She turned her head idly to discover who was moving about unnecessarily when, probably, the entire workforce was enjoying well-earned slumber, and saw that it was Nick Hellier.

She immediately closed her eyes, not wishing him to see that she was awake. She heard the quiet rustle of branches, and diminishing, similar sounds, dying away into the muted birdsong of the coppice behind the hedge. Cautiously Rachael opened her eyes and sat up.

As she had thought, everyone else was asleep, and soundly so. Several of the reapers were snoring, and one or two of the women. The loudest rumbling of all came from Dame Ursula's servant, Ruth, who was lying with her mouth open, her unlovely skin turned a glowing scarlet by the sun. Rachael, who did not care for her, grinned. The stupid woman could expect nothing else if she only ever stepped out of doors to go to church and to work on the harvest.

There was no sight nor sound of Nick. He had doubtless gone to relieve himself. From other fields, farther down the hill, came laughter and snatches of song. They can't have worked half so hard as us, Rachael thought scornfully, if they're still awake. She lay down again, waiting for Nick to reappear through the hedge.

Moments passed, and it occurred to her suddenly that he had been gone a considerable time. Perhaps he was taking a cool refreshing walk in the shade, or resting well away from everyone else. He had joined in the reaping, although his back could hardly be healed as yet, and had done as much work as any of them. But Rachael could well understand it if he wished to be alone for a while—perhaps his wounds still pained him.

The thought popped unbidden into her head and stuck like a burr. Why not herself go for a stroll in the coppice? He had thought her asleep. He would not realize that she had seen him. If she were to meet him, casually among the trees and the long dying leaves of the bluebells, it would look like a happy chance. And perhaps he would talk to her as if she were an adult instead of a child.

Rachael got slowly and cautiously to her feet, and glanced around her. Still they all slumbered on, oblivious. Her heart pounding with pleasurable apprehension, she wriggled through the gap in the stout hawthorn hedge and entered the cool dim light of the coppice.

In this part of it, where the soldiers had not penetrated, it was some years since the trees had last been cut, and they were growing tall and straight, shooting out from the gnarled mutilated stumps that had been planted here for this purpose a century or more ago. Despite the warm sunlight outside, there was a smell of damp and decay in the coppice, and something very dead quite close. Rachael wrinkled her nose and moved as quietly as she could, without seeming furtive, between the ash and hazel. She had not been here before and had little idea of how far the wood extended.

Not far, it seemed. Already the light was growing, and the sun shafted between the leaves in great silver spears. Something moved in the undergrowth, and Rachael froze, her heart thumping. But it was not Nick. Whatever it was, it seemed much too small, a rabbit perhaps. Even as she was scolding herself for her foolishness, the leaves parted and a little pale shape trotted out.

It was Lily. Mystified, Rachael stared at her stepmother's dog for a moment and then bent and snapped her fingers. Lily paused and glanced at her, her tongue lolling, her round eyes slit, her formerly immaculate coat covered in leaf mold and burrs, and then ran on in search of her prey.

The little hound never, ever strayed far from Silence. It was a joke at Wintercombe, with much banter from Nick and Nat about her white shadow. Frowning, Rachael stared in the direction the dog had taken, hearing increasingly distant sounds of pursuit. It must be a rabbit. Nothing else would take her so far from her mistress's side.

And then, as her ears strained, Rachael heard something else. A low voice, laughter, another voice. It came from the far side of the wood. Already made uneasy by the unexpected appearance of Lily, Rachael pushed her way through the nettles, stinging herself thoroughly in the process and losing her cap on an overhanging branch, and emerged with blinding suddenness out of the coppice and into the full glare of the sunlight.

Pasture stretched out in front of her, sloping gently up to the long crown of Hassage Hill. Cattle, red-brown and contented, grazed on the skyline. Just to her left was a small natural depression in the ground, hidden by the folds of land from all positions save one, her own. And sitting there in the sun, kissing with a passion and urgency that raised the hairs on her flesh, were Nick Hellier and her stepmother.

All her dreams and her illusions cruelly smashed, Rachael could only stand and stare in horror and disbelief. She must have made some sound, for the lovers in the grass looked up, their faces bemused, and saw her. At once they sprang apart, their guilt more eloquent than any words, and Rachael, her heart breaking, knew beyond doubt that this was not some idle chance encounter but something they had often done before.

"Rachael!" Silence exclaimed, getting to her feet.

The girl's face, blotched red where the sun had touched it, stared at her, the blue eyes distended and aghast. She put out her hands as if to ward off something unspeakably evil, backing away into the coppice. Then, unable to bear any more, she turned and fled.

In the depths of despair herself, Silence heard her blind, crashing progress growing fainter through the wood. She wanted to scream, to sob, to panic, but she could do none of those things. Why, oh, why had it been Rachael, the one person who would not understand, who idolized Nick, who was so terribly vulnerable? If Tabby or Nat had seen them, it would have been unfortunate, but not a disaster. But Rachael . . . She trembled to think of the damage this would do to the girl's tortuous mind.

"Go after her," Nick said, in the quick incisive tones that had ordered the siege. "I'll make my way back to the field, as though nothing has happened. As long as you can catch up with her before she tells someone, or does something stupid, you might be able to talk to her." He gave her a heartening smile that did something to strengthen her and kissed her forehead with much love. Then he turned and ran back into the coppice. And Silence, fighting her terror, sped in the direction that Rachael had taken.

Her ears had told her that the girl had not gone back toward the harvesters, but to the east, toward Wintercombe. Her skirts bunched in her hands, she ran along the edge of the coppice. And there, sure enough, fleeing like a hunted hare across the pasture, was Rachael. She did not look back, but forward, to where the chimneys and trees of Wintercombe showed beyond the long line of the hill.

Silence slowed down, her hand to the sharp pain of a stitch in her side. There was no one at Wintercombe, thank the Lord, save for Darby, who considered himself superior to harvesting and was laboring with the scullions to produce a splendid supper. And Rachael was hardly likely to burst into the kitchen and reveal her stepmother's adultery to that particular audience. It would be safe to follow at a discreet distance.

She had forgotten her mother-in-law, but Rachael had not. Once she had feared her grandmother, but now, in this moment of crisis, she had turned toward her blindly, like a hurt animal seeking sanctuary. Anguish lent wings to her feet. She leapt over grass tussocks, dodged clumps of thistles, and dived through the hedge at the side of the field as if it did not exist. Just one more stretch of pasture now, grazed by a leisurely flock of sheep, and then another hedge, the track up from the Wellow Lane, and the long gray gable outline of Wintercombe.

The house was quiet, save for distant sounds from the kitchen. Rachael burst in through the front door and flew along the screens passage to the stairs, her breath sobbing in her parched throat. But however hard she ran, she knew that she would never escape the nightmare that followed her heels like an evil spirit. Her stepmother, the woman who had tried all these years to befriend her, who had consoled her in the aftermath of Ridgeley's shooting, whom she had been ceasing, hesitantly, to regard as her enemy— that woman, her father's wife, she had seen in adulterous communication with the man for whom Rachael herself felt the overwhelming pangs of first love.

Propelled by her grief and rage and despair, Rachael plunged up the stairs and into her grandmother's chamber without so much as a knock.

Dame Ursula had been dozing, enjoying, for once, the absence of Ruth. The girl had her uses, but there were times when her docile and obedient presence had an extremely irritating effect upon her mistress, and she had been glad to be rid of her for the day.

The crash as Rachael flung back the door startled her from sleep. Her heart leapt and raced painfully, and she peered angrily at the blurred shape standing in the entrance. "Who is it? Who's there? Speak up, I say!"

The shape made no effort to shut the door. Instead, it advanced on the bed. Dame Ursula, furious, struggled to sit upright against the pillows, and then relaxed a trifle as the amorphous figure suddenly resolved itself into her granddaughter, Rachael. But even by the girl's lamentably low standards, she looked disheveled, her cap gone, her hair like wild snakes around her head, her gray dress torn in several places, and her arms and hands scratched. There were tears on her face, and her breath came in great unconrollable sobs.

"Oh, it's you, is it?" Dame Ursula said, surveying the girl with a none too friendly eye. "What do you mean, eh, bursting in here without so much as a by-your-leave?"

Too late, Rachael realized that her grandmother might not, after all, be such a very present help in trouble. She could not, *could* not say anything about her own feelings for Nick, could not lay bare her soul to this venomous old woman's contempt. But her sense of horror and outrage and injustice drove her on, and her desperate urge to strike out, to hurt, to punish the person who had stolen Nick from her. And who better as an instrument of vengeance than Dame Ursula, who would ensure that her son, her relatives, indeed the whole of Somerset know of her daughter-in-law's shame?

She said, gasping, "Oh, Grandmother—I had to see you—I had to tell you—it's terrible!"

"Well, come on, girl, out with it," Dame Ursula said sharply. "I haven't got all day."

Nat would have said something impertinent to that. His twin sister, so very different, stood there like a terrified rabbit, obviously in two minds as to whether or not to scuttle off. The old woman ignored the dizzy feeling she always seemed to have these days when woken too soon and added in slightly softer tones, "Well, Rachael? What has happened?"

At that, the child burst into tears. She bowed her head down on the ancient but beautiful counterpane and sobbed as if her heart was broken. Dame Ursula's wizened, contorted claw crept out toward the bent, tangled head and then retreated as she thought better of it. That foolish woman that her beloved George had so unaccountably married ten years ago had treated the girl too leniently, had not been nearly strict enough. If she had been mine, thought Dame Ursula, whose only daughter was a cowed mouse of a woman married to a parson in Wiltshire, I would have beaten all the nonsense out of her long ago.

"It was Mother!" Rachael said suddenly, lifting her head to stare at her grandmother with those compelling, distraught eyes. "Mother—she—she was *kissing* him!" She gulped for air, appalled all over again at the bitter memory of it.

Dame Ursula wondered if she had heard aright. There was a ringing in her ears. She shook her head impatiently, to no avail, and said, "Who, child? Who was kissing who?"

"*Mother!*" Rachael cried wildly. "Mother, Mother, Mother—*she* was kissing him, Captain Hellier, it was horrible, they'll go to hell!"

"What?" her grandmother exclaimed. Her hand shot out to grip the girl's wrist, painfully. "*What* did you say?"

"I *told* you!" Rachael shouted frantically. She leaned forward, thrusting her face at the old woman's. "My—father's—wife—was—kissing—Captain—Hellier!"

There was no doubt this time that Dame Ursula had understood. As Rachael drew back, frightened, the look on her grandmother's face changed to an extraordinary mixture of fury and triumph.

At last, Dame Ursula was thinking, at last I have her trapped! George will never be able to ignore this dreadful thing, this evil act. All these years I've been waiting for her to make an error, to do something that cannot be passed over. And now she has, and he will be able to put her away. I knew it, I always knew it—she is a wicked and ungodly woman.

Aloud, she said fervently, "'A virtuous woman is a crown to her husband, but she that maketh ashamed is as rottenness in his bones.' Proverbs twelve, verse four. 'Her end is as bitter as wormwood, sharp as a two-edged sword. Her feet go down to death: her steps take hold on Hell.'"

Rachael stared at the old woman's face. There was a gargoyle on the roof of Wintercombe, a ghastly leering mask that spouted water in wet weather. As a small child visiting her grandparents, it had terrified her. And now Dame Ursula's expression had the same look of grotesque glee. For the first time a worm of doubt entered Rachael's mind, as she began to realize what she had unleashed.

Behind her the voice of her adulterous stepmother suddenly spoke. "'He that is without sin, amongst you, first let him cast a stone at her.' Are either of you so spotless?"

Rachael turned. Silence had closed the door behind her and stood in front of it, sunflushed, breathing fast, not quite so disordered as was her stepdaughter. She had followed Rachael at a distance, all the way to the dim cool emptiness of Wintercombe, nursing her aching side and legs, thinking that the desperate harm might yet be undone. And then she had heard Rachael's frantic voice upstairs and knew that it was too late.

And now here was the fearsome old harridan who was George's mother, spouting her pieces of Scripture, judging and condemning her with pleasure. Suddenly Silence felt a great freedom coming over her. Dame Ursula would never believe anything she said, would never think her anything other than an adulteress destined for hell. And so, for the first time in her life, she was able to say to her mother-in-law exactly what she thought.

"You're delighted, aren't you?" she went on, as Rachael gaped at her and the old woman's face creased with disgust. "You've been looking to destroy me for ten years, and now Rachael has put the ideal weapon into your hand. Have you thought of anything else except the hatred that's eaten into your soul? You selfish old crone, you haven't once considered the children."

"Nor have you!" Dame Ursula shouted, enraged beyond all caution. Extremely agitated, she struggled further upright in her bed, her shaking claw thrust at her daughter-in-law. "How many times have you deceived him, eh? I'll lay odds none of those precious brats are his—none of them! He'll cast 'em out with you, if he's any sense."

"And will he relish you telling all Somerset how your precious son has had horns set on his head? Do you want him made a laughing-stock among his friends? Because that's what will happen."

"Adulteress! Fornicator! Whore!" the old woman screeched. "The Lord will see—He will judge you—may you spend eternity in hell for what you've done, you filthy wicked harlot! No doubt of it, George is well rid of you—he will never let this evil pass!"

"And let me tell you, I'm well rid of *him*," Silence said. The other, calmer self stood aside in horrified wonder as she spoke. "I hope, madam, that when my own children grow up, they will not be selfish, thoughtless, callous prigs like their father, so blinded by self-righteousness that they can't see any other point of view but their own!"

Dame Ursula, overwhelmed by fury, screamed abuse at her, a vile string of epithets interspersed with vengeful biblical verses. Her hand, extended, tried to stab at Silence, but her daughter-in-law was well out of reach. Spittle formed at the sides of her lips as she shouted and sprayed over the counterpane in a spluttering shower.

And then, suddenly, dreadfully, a change passed over her face, a spasm that pulled one side of it upward as if tugged on a string. Her body jerked forward and back, and ghastly sounds issued from the distorted mouth. As Silence stared, horrified, there was a terrible, unmistakable rattling in her throat, and she fell back against the pillows.

Rachael backed away from the bed, her eyes staring, and bumped into her stepmother. Silence caught her shoulders, feeling the rigid, shuddering tension beneath her fingers. "Is—is she dead?" The girl's voice came in an appalled whisper, and rose higher with realization. "She is, isn't she—she's dead, she's dead!"

Silence had seen it too often to deny it, but her own sense of horror was constricting her throat. A few seconds before her mother-in-law had been villifying her in terms that were more appropriate in a brothel. And now, with terrifying suddenness, she had been wrenched out of life.

She lay there propped against the pillows in her chemises and night rail and cap, her wrinkled face sagged and twisted, her fierce eyes half open, glinting as if they saw her. A trail of spittle still drooled from her open mouth, and the wizened claw lay on the bed, pointing unerringly and accusingly at Silence and Rachael. Several times her body jerked and twitched in spasm. And then, nothing.

Rachael screamed twice, harshly, like a hurt rabbit, and turned to run. Silence flung her arms around her and clasped her tight, despite her frantic struggles. She knew that now, and only now, would explanation and reconciliation be possible. Rachael held the happiness of everyone at Wintercombe in her hand; and for everyone's sake, she must be persuaded not to speak.

And yet it is I who have done wrong, Silence thought as she clung to the weeping, hysterical girl and grappled with her own profound shock. I committed adultery, not Rachael—and she died blaming me. In a sense, I killed her.

But try as she would, she could feel no remorse, but only relief that the tyranny was over and that the one person George adored, whose word he would accept without question, was dead.

Rachael was calmer, though she was still sobbing, the front of her stepmother's bodice wet with her tears. Silence stared at the body of her tormentor lying in the bed, with that dreadful illusion of life. She found it almost impossible to believe that Dame Ursula's voice was silenced forever, that her malevolent presence no longer loomed over everything done at Wintercombe. It is a trick, her mind cried in bewilderment—a trap she has set, and at any moment she will sit up and accuse me of being a whore.

The thought was so horrible that she let go of Rachael and walked the few steps to the bed. She could not suppress the shudder of revulsion that shook her body as she felt for a pulse on the blue-veined, knotted wrist and at the flabby, wrinkled throat. There was nothing, and already the dead flesh seemed cooler and utterly lifeless.

Convinced, she closed the baleful eyes. With that action, Dame Ursula's corpse seemed to lose much of its power. Silence stepped back, looking down at her, and saw only a shrunken and pathetic old woman, struck down by the hand of fate—or of God.

Keep calm, she told herself urgently. Keep calm, and something might be saved from this. But her emotions were already too tangled and overwrought: guilt, despair, horror, grief, shock all warred within her. Appalled, she felt the helpless tears begin, pouring down her face. She turned blindly, gasping for breath, and saw Rachael, still weeping furiously. The girl's chin came up, and her hostile gaze had the hardness and quality of steel. She took a gulp of air and said, "You killed her—you killed her!"

Since it was what she herself had thought, Silence could not argue with her. She tried to wipe the tears from her own face, without success, and said simply, "Yes, I think I did."

That gave Rachael pause. She looked at her stepmother more narrowly, and then said, "All the things she said—were they true?"

"I suppose by her lights they were," Silence said despairingly. She fumbled in her sleeve for a kerchief and held it out to her stepdaughter. Rachael flinched away as if from a poisonous snake, and her lower lip came out in an expression wearily familiar from her childhood. "I don't want it. You're a whore, like Bessie Lyteman—a whore, a whore, I hate you!"

It was then that Silence realized that passive acceptance of the girl's words would not be enough. She did not know if she could succeed in convincing Rachael of her own point of view. The sharp prickings of her conscience, the knowledge that in the eyes of most godly people she *was* a whore, sapped her confidence. But she must try, for Rachael's sake, and for her own.

She said sharply, "Stop it, Rachael—and listen!"

"I won't!" her stepdaughter cried in exactly the same tones as she had used to defy her new stepmother at the age of five or six. "You killed her, you wicked woman, you *killed* her!" She started to cry again, with huge noisy sobs, and Silence, suddenly angry and afraid, gripped her shoulders and shook her, hard.

"Rachael—*listen* to me! Do you want to be treated as a child, or as an adult?"

Rachael stared at her, surprised, her mouth open on yet another flood of abuse, her face red and blotched and mottled with weeping. She said at last, sulkily, "I'm *not* a child."

"Good," Silence said. "Then behave like an adult. Wipe your eyes with this." She held out the kerchief. Bemused by the unusually authoritative tone of her voice, the girl took it, scrubbed obediently at her wet scarlet face, and blew her nose thoroughly. She then handed the sodden square of lawn back to her stepmother and sniffed, her eyes staring past her shoulder to the dead woman in the bed.

"If you are an adult," Silence said into the quiet, "then you will be able to talk to me as one. And we must talk. Shall we go to your chamber?"

Rachael's eyes were still on her grandmother. She said shakily, "What—what about her?"

"She's dead," Silence pointed out. "We cannot help her now. It's you who must be helped—you, and all of us. There's no one in the house save Darby and the scullions, and Clevinger is desperate to get the harvest in." She turned the girl around and propelled her gently to the door. "When we have talked, we'll send a message to Master Willis, and he will come and give us comfort. And don't you think that your grandmother is now at bliss in heaven, with your grandfather?"

"I don't suppose they'd either of them be happy," Rachael said between sobs. "They never liked each other." She gulped and then added, "I didn't like Grandmother much either—and I don't think she liked me."

Silence, tired of lies, could not summon the energy to deny it. She said dryly, "She didn't like me either."

"I know." Rachael turned, just by the door. She looked terrible, the hesitant signs of prettiness vanished in a flood of tears, but the wild, glaring expression had gone from her eyes. For the first time, Silence felt a dawning hope: Perhaps, after all, she would listen to reason. "She didn't like anyone," the girl went on. "Except Father—and Nat, I think she liked Nat, but I can't see why, she was always scolding him for being impertinent."

"Some dogs only bite those who fear them," Silence said. She opened the door. "Shall we go to your chamber?"

"If you want," Rachael said, the sulky expression reappearing. And with considerable apprehension, Silence walked there at her side.

The chamber was cool, since the sun had not yet moved around far enough to strike in at the window. Silence did not suggest that it be opened. She had no wish for any of Rachael's outbursts to be heard by the handful of soldiers lounging below in the barton, playing dice or cleaning their weapons. She looked around at the untidy room, strewn with discarded clothing, and said thoughtfully, "You know, it's time I engaged a maid for you. You're much too old to rely on Doraty or Hester."

Rachael's head jerked around, and Silence saw with trepidation that her face was once more hostile and suspicious. She said venomously, "Are you trying to bribe me?"

Nothing had been further from her stepmother's mind. Genuinely surprised and upset, she shook her head. "No—*no*, of course not. Oh, Rachael—surely you know me better than that."

"It won't work, anyway," the girl retorted, ignoring her protests. "You can't stop me telling anyone else, can you? Not unless you kill me too."

Silence sat down slowly, wondering how she could keep calm under this sort of onslaught. And the pity of it was, she could understand only too clearly the girl's desperate, grief-stricken enmity. Rachael was hitting out at her most immediate and vulnerable target, not caring if what she said was preposterous, so long as it struck hurtfully home. In her situation, I'd probably be the same, Silence thought unhappily. But how, how to win her over? Especially since her own, still-kicking Puritan conscience seemed to welcome the accusations. She *was* an adulteress, a whore, she had betrayed the trust of her husband and her children, and the shock of discovering this had undoubtedly led directly to Dame Ursula's death.

Oh, yes, she was guilty. But her guilt could not be undone. And her practical side, inherited from that grandmother who had urged her to make, do, mend, was telling her forcefully to salvage what she could from this wreckage. Indeed, she deserved punishment—but unless the secret was kept, more lives than hers would be brought to shame and ruin.

Resolutely she turned to Rachael. The girl stood by the table, one hand resting on it. Silence saw the tears and scratches, the flush of sunburn and the raised red weals from the nettles through which she had run, and felt a sudden rush of pity for this young, fierce, tormented child who was, assuredly, her own worst enemy. She said quietly, "What has happened has happened, and cannot be altered. And I know better than anyone else how it is my fault. I don't want to excuse myself, or justify my crime—all I want is to try and make you understand *why.*"

Rachael glanced at her from under her lashes and said nothing. Silence waited a moment and then went on. "I know you love Nick."

"How?" Rachael cried, and a great scarlet betraying wash of color covered her face. "It was supposed to be a *secret!*"

"Nat told me," said Silence. "He knows you better than anyone else, after all."

Rachael stared down at the table. She said in a low voice, "I didn't want anyone to know, anyone at all. Does Nick—I mean Captain Hellier—does *he* know?"

This was one time, Silence decided, when a lie would be kindest. She shook her head. "No, he doesn't."

There was a long, long pause. Then Rachael said, very quietly, "He loves you, doesn't he?"

No point in denying it. Silence murmured, "Yes."

"But my father doesn't love you. I heard him talking to Grandfather once, before he married you. I thought he was talking about a cow he wanted to breed from. Then he said something about a good mother above all else, and I knew he was speaking of you. I remember it quite clearly," Rachael said. "And he *couldn't* love you and say the things I've heard him say to you." She looked up, her eyes brilliant with yet more tears, unshed. "Do you love Nick? Nick, and not my father?"

"I love Nick," Silence said steadily, meeting her gaze. "But I know, none better, that it does not give me license to—to break my marriage vows. I promised to love, honor, and obey your father, forsaking all others. And for nine years, nearly ten, I kept that promise. And now I have cast it all away for love. It sounds like a stage play, doesn't it? The world well lost for love. But love of that kind isn't everything. I love you, and Nat, and Tabby and Deb and William, and I love this house too. I care for you all, so much. And I know that by loving Nick, I have put it all in jeopardy."

Rachael chewed at her lip. She said at last, "But you couldn't help loving him, could you? I couldn't. After he saved me . . ." She broke off, swallowing tears, and added painfully, "It was a dream I had, a silly child-

ish dream, oh, how Nat would laugh—and when I saw you kissing I felt—
I felt as though *I'd* been the one betrayed. And I wanted to hurt you, so I
told Grandmother. And if I hadn't, she'd be alive now, so *I* killed her, not
you."

"Stop it," Silence said quickly, hearing the rising note of hysteria in her
voice. "That's nonsense. Probably if we hadn't burst in on her today, she'd
have had a seizure berating Ruth, or William, or Deb. And that would
have been as bad, if not worse."

"I suppose so," Rachael admitted after a while. She thought for a moment, and then went on, her voice puzzled. "I don't feel sorry—it was
horrible to see her die like that, so suddenly—but I don't feel sad at all. I
feel . . . relieved. Is that very wicked?"

"I feel it too," Silence told her, wondering if it was wise to admit so
much.

"And I suppose everyone will speak well of her now she's dead, they
always do—but sometimes I hated her," Rachael said. She looked at her
stepmother, as if seeing her properly for the first time, and added on a note
of sudden fear, "What are you going to *do*? You and Nick? Are you going
to go away with him?"

For one wild moment her heart leapt. Away, free, to be with the man
she loved so much, unshackled from her responsibilities and burdens—the
world lay intoxicatingly bright before her. Then reality, grim and gray,
intruded. She shook her head sadly. "No. No, Rachael, I can't. I can't
leave you, or the others—I can't leave Wintercombe. Your father will come
home soon, and he will need my help and support. He has suffered much
in the war—remember, Sam is dead."

"I'd forgotten," said Rachael. "How could I forget Sam?" She stared
down at her battered hands and then up at her stepmother. "I—I'm sorry.
I should not have said those things. And I don't like it that you love Nick,
I don't like it at all—but I know really that he'd never think of me in—in
that way, and if he truly does love you . . . I'll try not to mind, I promise
I will. And I promise, Mother, I promise I'll never say anything about it to
anyone, ever."

Silence looked at her difficult, wayward stepdaughter who so unexpectedly seemed to have listened to reason. She felt her eyes fill with tears and
said slowly, "I don't deserve that, Rachael. But I thank you, with all my
heart."

"Don't cry!" the girl said, jumping up from the chair. "You *mustn't*—
I'm sorry, I'm sorry, please forgive me!" And she flung her arms around
Silence as if she were the child in need of comfort.

For a long time they hugged each other, overcome by shared emotion.
Rachael, for the first time, was thinking more of someone else's problems
than her own. She knew something of the sharpness and the anguish of
love, though she was dimly aware that what she had felt for Nick was but a

shadow of the glorious reality. And she also must acknowledge that in Silence's situation, loving and being loved in return, surely only a saint would have resisted such temptation.

"Let him who is without sin" . . . the words came back to her mind. No one was without sin—and therefore who could judge, save God? If God thought her stepmother worthy of punishment, then He would do it. And because her mind now shied away from the horror, the shame, the scandal and misery and complications that would ensue if she told her father about his wife's adultery, she knew that she would keep her promise.

I do not deserve it, Silence thought, blinking away her tears. I do not deserve her allegiance—not after what I have done to her, and to all of them. I have laid this terrible secret on her, and probably on Nat as well— and Mally. And yet I can't complain, for it was my own decision, and I knew what it might lead to. I went into it with my eyes open, knowing the consequences. And now my chickens are beginning to come back to roost.

But despite her sorrow, and guilt, she knew that nothing yet had the power to diminish, or deny, or destroy her love for Nick.

C H A P T E R

TWENTY-EIGHT

False face must hide what the false heart doth know.
                                        —MACBETH

Dame Ursula St. Barbe was laid to rest, the day after her death, in the vault beneath the aisle of Philip's Norton church. The entire household, and many of the village, attended her funeral, despite the claims of the harvest. There were few tears shed, though, for she had been feared and respected but not loved. And Silence wondered how many felt, as she did, a guilty sense of relief and freedom, as if a tyrant monarch had died.

She had dispatched Ned Merrifield back to the harvesters to tell them about Dame Ursula's death and to ask Ruth and Margery Turber to return. She did not dare send any message to Nick. She hoped desperately that he would take some small comfort from what had happened. Only in private would she be able to reassure him.

But there was no chance of that until very, very late, after the vicar and the carpenter and the sexton and various other interested parties had visited her, after the laying-out and the funeral arrangements had been completed, when the children, bewildered, tired, and shocked, but not in any sense grieving, had been sent to bed.

Silence sat in her chamber, not knowing if he would come to her. In the bustle of the aftermath of death, she had had no chance to speak to him, nor even to give him some sign that all was well—at least, well in comparison with what might have been. Pye's solitary kitten, magnificently plump and healthy, suckled industriously, her mouth clamped on the teat, her front paws kneading rhythmically as she drank. Silence felt suddenly weary, so weary of it all: the secrets, the complications, the lies and the evasions, and then, at the end, as inevitable as nightfall, the moment when he would leave.

Despite her words to Rachael, she was tempted. The devil sat on her shoulder and showed her the kingdoms of the world. For so long she had wished to be rid of her responsibilities, to abandon them all and enjoy the freedom she had never in her life possessed. And now, the chance, un-looked for, miraculous, might be offered to her. Nick would leave when the Roundheads came back, as they were bound to do after Bristol's surrender, which must surely come soon. They would mop up all the remaining Royalist garrisons—Farleigh, Wintercombe, Devizes, Laycock, all were doomed to fall, even she with no military knowledge could see that. Nick would ride away, and she knew that, if she wanted it, he would take her with him.

It had been better when she had thought she had no choice. But now that they were lovers, as passionate and true as any in ballad or play or romance, whatever decision she made would inevitably bring great anguish. To live without Nick, or without her children?

There was a protesting squeak. Pye, exhibiting once again that uncanny ability to sense her distress, got out of her basket, leaving the kitten bereft, and jumped onto her lap. And not just without the children, Silence thought as she stroked the cat while her hot tears fell onto the black and white fur. Without Wintercombe, and my garden; without Pye.

Make, do, mend, said her grandmother's voice, scornful of self-pity. And inside her head Nat, bright-eyed and cynical, commented dryly, "More fool you, to fall in love." Annoyed with her weakness, she pulled a kerchief from her sleeve and resolutely rubbed her eyes with it. Pye purred loudly, but before she could settle down where she liked best to be, Silence, who had discovered a sovereign remedy for the mopes, set the cat on the floor, rose, and went to the table.

A pile of books lay there, both Nick's and Sir Samuel's, in cheerful confusion. The volume she wanted lay on top. She returned to her chair and began to leaf through Nick's battered old copy of one of Shakespeare's plays, called for some reason *Much Ado About Nothing.*

It worked. She was smiling at the barbed banter of Beatrice and Benedict, when his knock came at the door. Instantly, her heart pounding, she leapt up and flew to open it. Mally was already asleep in her closet, behind two inches of stout oak, and would not disturb them. The night lay in front of them, when they could be alone.

He came inside, wearing his tawny doublet, unbuttoned. The better of the blue ones had been ruined in the grenado's explosion, not even fit for polishing pewter. As soon as the door was locked, he took her in his arms and kissed her with lingering delight, and all her fears and doubts and sorrows were swept away in his power. Unlike the first occasion, which had been a hasty slaking of hungers that had consumed them both too long, their lovemaking now was a slow, languorous exploration of each other's pleasure, delaying the moments of consummation and climax for as long as possible, before the final glorious eruption of joy.

This time Pye took it into her head to walk over their entwined bodies at precisely the wrong moment, causing considerable laughter and some writhing because, as Nick remarked, she was too damned inquisitive and her whiskers tickled. But her intervention made no difference to the outcome, though Silence had to smother her giggles. Afterward they lay in a sweaty, entangled embrace, utterly and drowsily at peace until Nick saw, over his beloved's shoulder, a pair of interested black-and-white ears. At his indignant hiss, she leapt off the bed and returned, offended, to her kitten.

"We don't step on her tail when she's up to no good with a tom," Silence said, when they had finished laughing. "So why she feels she must poke her nose into our business, I don't know."

"Curiosity will kill that cat," Nick commented. He leaned on his elbow to look down at her flushed, contented face. "Silence, my dear love—I know this is the wrong time and place to ask, but we won't have another chance. What the devil happened today?"

Slowly, with many pauses to marshal her thoughts, she told him everything. At the end, she was trying not to weep. Not, she hastened to assure him, from overmuch grief at her mother-in-law's death, but from the memory of her talk with Rachael. "And you say she has promised not to tell?" Nick said thoughtfully. "Can we rely on her?"

Silence considered it. She too had had her doubts on that score. At last she said, "I think so. I think that once she had got over her shock at seeing us, once her grandmother was dead, she realized that it was so much better, for all of us, to say nothing. She is very confused, Nick, confused and unhappy and still moonstruck with you, though I think she realizes now just how foolish she has been."

"Thank you," Nick said dryly.

Silence gave him a wry smile. "I didn't mean it in that way, and you know it, Captain Nicholas Hellier. But really, I think Rachael is safe. She knows how much there is to lose. And somehow, in the middle of all this, we are beginning to be friends. You and I will have to be very circumspect with her, and it wouldn't be wise to parade our love before her, even though she knows of it. Rachael prefers to ignore inconvenient truths, and if we give her the chance to pretend that all this never happened, both she and I will be happier."

Nick lay back on the pillows, his hands crossed behind his head. It was only in the last few days that he had been able to lie thus in comfort. His back was still a mass of new scars and half-healed scabs, crisscrossed in ugly purple and red, but there was no inflammation, no putrefaction where a piece of metal might have been overlooked. The great good fortune of his escape struck her all afresh, and she wriggled next to him, put her head on his shoulder and her arm across his chest to hug him even closer. "Wise Silence," he said. "Do you know me as well as you know your children, I wonder?"

"I doubt it," she said dryly. "Since I don't know who your parents are, where you were born, how old you are, how you came to be in the Royalist army—I don't know anything at all about your life before you came to Wintercombe."

"Perhaps you would not wish to know," Nick said. She could see his mouth stretch in that dearly familiar, lazy smile. "Anyway, you don't need that information, do you? You didn't fall in love with my upbringing or my history—you fell in love with *me*."

"The you I love is the result of your upbringing and history," Silence pointed out. "But I'm only expressing idle curiosity. As you say, I am in love with *you*—and I need nothing else to confirm or deny that feeling." She grinned, feeling ridiculously happy considering her earlier misery—but then, he had always had the power to lighten her moods. "Don't worry—you don't have to reveal your doubtless exceedingly checkered past to me. I'm probably better off not knowing about it, as you pointed out. But I do sometimes wonder how you have come by such incongruous talents. Not every Cavalier captain can make a hat from a folded napkin and quote the Scriptures."

"I like to be different," Nick said, quite unworried by her gentle probing. "But I will answer one of your questions. I am twenty-eight years old, and my birthday falls at the end of October. I am of the sign of Scorpio, dear lady, and you if I remember correctly are Aquarius, the bearer of water—a most apt sign for a gardener."

"I don't know anything about astrology," Silence said. "To my father, it was but another branch of sorcery."

"Well, Scorpio people are reckoned to be dark, and secretive, and sullen."

"I'll agree with the middle of those qualities—the rest I would argue with." She snuggled closer. "The twins were born in the second week of November—does that make them Scorpios too?"

"I would think so—and certainly Rachael fits the description to a nicety."

"Poor Rachael," her stepmother said. "She doesn't help herself—but I can understand something of what she feels. I remember much the same when I was her age, save that I had to hide everything, or have my father beat me."

His arm tightened about her. He said, "Is that why you are so good at concealing what you feel?"

"When the strap is the penalty for not doing so, yes," Silence replied dryly. "Oh, don't worry, I am not one to indulge in too much self-pity, especially for what has been long gone—but it is also one reason why I am perhaps more gentle with Rachael than most people would be."

He was quiet for a while, then he said, "What tale have you put about concerning Dame Ursula's death?"

"I said that Rachael had felt unwell, so she and I had returned to Wintercombe. I looked in on Dame Ursula to see if she wanted anything, since her maid was harvesting, and found her dead. It is very close to the truth, and it has been accepted without question. Her mind was so vigorous that most did not notice it, but she had been ailing much these last few months. And, Nick, I know I should not feel like this, I know it is wicked, but I am *glad* she is dead! It's as if the greatest of my burdens has been lifted from me—I feel such a sense of freedom, you can't imagine it. Since Sir Samuel died, she did her best to make my life miserable." She smiled. "And probably would have done so had not a certain troop of soldiers come to my rescue, quite unwittingly, and given her something of greater importance to complain about."

"And is that the only reason you welcomed my presence here, eh?" Nick teased. He rolled over and pinned her arms down, grinning. "Well, I'm very sorry, my lady, but I do not intend to leave just because your *bête noir* is as dead as a doornail in her coffin. Only the full might of the New Model Army can tear me from your arms!"

He kissed her with rising passion, and his words were forgotten in the mutual delight that followed. But later, when he had gone creeping like a thief from her chamber to his, she lay wakeful and alone, her body sated but her mind still very much at work. He knew as well as she that their dream must end, sooner or later. But she wished somehow that he, usually so considerate and perceptive, should not have put the terrible inevitability of it into words.

Dame Ursula was buried, and the harvest went on. The shorn, golden fields lay beneath the sun, lumpy with the hiled sheaves steadily drying in the warmth, and all over Norton, a scene repeated throughout Somerset, people toiled to bring in the grain that, by God's mercy, might not be taken by soldiers this year.

In the south, in Devon, Goring's demoralized remnants plundered or deserted while their commander drank himself into a stupor and ignored the plight of Bristol. That city, key to the fortunes of the king but also to the future of Nick and Silence, lay beleaguered by Fairfax and the New Model without and by the plague within. Parliament's ships blocked any attempt to relieve the garrison by sea, and although it was well fortified and supplied, the inhabitants were depressed and unhappy, uneasily aware that if the town were taken by storm, their goods and even their lives might well be forfeit.

On the last day of harvest, sunshine turned to rain and beat on the backs of the reapers as they worked. Fortunately, many of the hiles, thoroughly dry, had already been taken in cart and wagon to the barn. The rest must sit sodden in the fields until the weather turned fine again, for they could not be stored wet. Nick sent the Wintercombe wagon to Bath with the wounded New Model men. It did not return, and Walker, who had driven it, came stumping back in a foul temper, saying that the Bath garrison had appropriated both cart and horse for the good of Parliament and given him not a penny for them. Silence noted it down with the rest, the first in a new column reserved for the depredations of her own side, and wondered wryly if that list would grow as long as the other.

The rain, which had curtailed the activities of both armies at Bristol, ceased in the first week of September, and the fields sat steaming in the sun while Clevinger and the whole village offered up their thanks. At Bristol Prince Rupert, still hoping for relief, played for time. Eventually Fairfax, exasperated, broke off negotiations, mustered the might of his twelve thousand men, and attacked.

The next morning, on Thursday, the eleventh of September, 1645, the prince, faced with the certainty of annihilation if he continued to resist, sued for surrender.

It was inevitable. Many good men on both sides had already been slain, and many more would be condemned to death if the fighting continued, and all to no avail, for they were outnumbered by nearly five to one, and the defenses had been breached in several places. The garrison marched away with honor, drums beating and colors flying. And Fairfax, after giving thanks for God's help, turned his attention to those Royalist garrisons remaining in Somerset and Wiltshire that must be taken before the sorry but still-dangerous remnants in the west could be disposed of.

At once, two colonels came to him. They were not of the New Model, but part of Massey's army, whose regiments had assisted in the attack on Bristol. By a coincidence, both had houses occupied by the Royalists, within a few miles of each other, and both asked that their own regiments be allowed to take back their homes, to lessen the damage to the fabric and contents of Farleigh Castle, and Wintercombe.

Fairfax readily agreed. His information suggested that there would be little or no resistance, although both of the enemy commanders had only a month or so previously been prepared to fight. Poor Lieutenant-Colonel Cottesworth, who had been killed during the attack on Bristol, had had much to say about the devilish intransigence of the Wintercombe garrison, and Colonel Sir George St. Barbe was plainly most anxious to recapture his house as soon as might be. Fairfax could well understand it, since the colonel's wife, mother, and children seemed, astonishingly, to be still in residence.

At Wintercombe, the news of Bristol's surrender came the next morning, the twelfth, brought by an eager villager, ghoulishly pleased to be first with bad news for the garrison, even if it was good tidings for the household. Silence, her heart like stone within her, gave him sixpence for his trouble and sent him on his way. Then she went in search of Nick.

He was in the barton, inspecting some horses that had been brought back from the paddocks around the house. She waited unobtrusively until he had finished examining the leg of a stocky, feather-footed bay with the troop's farrier, and then moved forward to catch his eye.

He left off at once and came over. She saw that he knew what she would say: It was written clear for her to read in his face.

"May I speak with you apart, Captain?" she asked courteously, and led him into the house. There, in the north wing, were storerooms opening off the corridor that ran its length. She opened the door of one of them, ushered him in, and shut it behind her.

The storeroom was large, stone-floored, with shelves high up, laden with jars, bottled and various other containers. Below, wooden bins contained flour of various kinds, peas and beans, rice and oats and barley, and there were racks of cheeses, and tubs of butter, salt fish, and other essentials. The air was cool, and pungent with food. From a corner, the green eyes of the iron-gray cat, father of Pye's one kitten, on duty because mice had been seen, watched them warily.

"Bristol?" said Nick, and she nodded, pale and mute. They could not embrace, not even here. The window gave onto the barton, and soldiers were constantly passing outside. She had wanted to tell him in private first so that the troopers and servants would not be unduly alarmed, but now there did not seem to be much point. Everyone knew the truth. Why deny the inevitable?

"Then they will be here next," he said, his face gentle and compassionate. "And you know what that must mean. I promised you that there would be no more sieges, and I meant it. Besides, we have scarcely thirty men left, and I don't think we'd have much hope of holding out. And I have had my fill of bloodshed. Silence, my dear love, in a few days I must ride away from here and leave you alone. And I don't know how I can bear it."

"We will both have to," she said bleakly, trying to smile, though her own heart was breaking. She wanted to cry out, Take me with you! but the words died unborn, strangled by the chains that bound her to her family, her duty, and to Wintercombe.

"Yes," he said, and she supposed his smile, brave, wry, no more than a twist of his mouth, was the image of her own. "Yes, I suppose we will have to."

Their eyes met, and held. Then he smiled again, more successfully, and added, "We must make the best of the days we have left, don't you agree? Come on, I must go outside again and tell them gently about Bristol—and probably tonight half of them will desert. Quite honestly, I'm beyond caring." He looked at her with that old, unsettling intensity and then came over to stand close to her, just beyond her touch. He said very softly, "I will see you tonight, and we can try to forget our cares for a while. Thank you, dear lady."

Silence, somehow, managed to struggle through the day as if nothing had happened. And in fact there was a great deal to do in the house, as usual, compounded by William, who had fallen down one of the flights of steps in the garden and grazed his hands and face quite badly. His beauty would be quite spoiled for a day or two, Silence teased him, and Nat asked him if he had left much of himself on the gravel.

Very seriously, William examined his hands, both sides, with great thoroughness, and then said solemnly, "I don't think so."

I cannot leave them, his mother thought in anguish, while her face stayed as calm as ever and her hands busied themselves, mopping bits of dirt and gravel from William's fat and bloodstained cheek. My pain, Nick's pain, is something that we can both endure, if we have to. We are adult, we are strong, we can cope. But these children, five children—how can they bear the loss of their mother? Only Nat, probably, has the firmness of character to survive it.

Her husband, whom she had once vowed to love unto death, she did not think of at all.

She knew, because she had done her best to look at everything logically, that these few days, when a term had been put on her happiness, were the worst. Before she had been able to delude herself that these wonderful nights would have no end. Afterward she would carry on, assuaging her grief and misery in the never-ending round of daily tasks and domestic duties. She knew that she could never go back to that old unawakened Silence. Yet she also knew that now she was stronger, more self-confident, more capable. She would endure his absence, because she must, but her heart would be broken.

William, salved and happy, scampered out of the stillroom. Nat, who had brought him in, bloody and screaming for attention, stood by the shelves, examining her still. He glanced at his stepmother, who was stopping up the jar that held her beeswax and spikenard ointment, especially gentle for face wounds, and said casually, "I hear Bristol has fallen."

Silence was surprised at the way in which her hands continued to move without a break. "Yes," she said, pushing the wooden bung home. "John Lyons came by this morning with the news."

Nat watched her as she put the pot back on its shelf with all the other salves and ointments. Silence was methodical in her stillroom, and everything was arranged according to the sickness it was intended to cure, waters to heal fevers in one place, plasters for sore joints and aching limbs in another. He said quietly, "Mother, you have never been able to fool me, though you might well think you have. You and Nick are lovers, aren't you."

It was a statement, not a question, and Silence knew that it was pointless to deny it. She turned to face him, her hands clasped in front of her, neat and slender and somehow glowing despite her plain black gown and rather grubby apron, upon which a wailing William had wiped his blood and tears. "Yes," she said, and added, "When did you guess?"

"I've known you were sweet on each other for months," Nat said. "But lovers . . . that came only recently, didn't it?" And as she stared at him, he went on, smiling. "Don't look at me like that—who am I to judge? I'm not going to reprove you or go telling Father when—if—he comes home. And I don't think any of the servants have any idea of it—you've been very careful. Mally must know, though."

"Yes, she does." Silence hesitated, and then said, almost shyly, "Do you—you *must* have *some* opinion about it, one way or the other. Do you disapprove of what I have done?"

"My main feeling," Nat said with that sly grin that always reminded her so poignantly of his grandfather, "is more fool you for falling in love with probably the most unsuitable man I could think of. Oh, it's not that I don't like him—I do, very much. To be honest, I greatly prefer him to Father. But a Cavalier captain, cuckolding a Roundhead colonel—you have to admit, if Father ever finds out, you couldn't have chosen someone more calculated to infuriate him."

Silence, hearing his lighthearted, mocking tone, could only gaze at him in disbelief. For months she had agonized over her emotions, tortured herself with thoughts of adultery and hell fire and damnation, and even now that she had at last succumbed, she was still, when Nick was not with her, prone to feelings of guilt and self-doubt. And yet here was her stepson, a boy not yet sixteen, without any experience of the world and strictly reared, treating her dreadful wickedness almost as a joke. She said, her voice hoarse with astonishment, "You mean—you don't *mind?*"

"Of course not," Nat said. "I mind when you're unhappy. And as I said, you can't fool me. You weren't happy with Father. You *are* happy with Nick, he treats you as you deserve, he makes you laugh, he loves you. Father doesn't do any of those things, even though he's your husband. And I think if I'd been in your shoes, I wouldn't have been ruled by my conscience for half so long as you. Handsome young man paying court to me? I wouldn't have believed my luck!"

"Oh, Nat," Silence murmured, her eyes watering. "I don't deserve *you*. You have a knack of putting it all so matter-of-factly—and it's something that I have felt so guilty about."

"Well, don't," Nat said bluntly. "Your trouble is that you're not by nature a Puritan, but you were reared as one—like me, in fact. Rachael, now, she's very much like Grandmother in some ways, I can see *her* terrorizing her grandchildren. Tell me, who was the wisest and most sensible man you've ever known?"

That was easy to answer. "Your grandfather," Silence said without hesitation.

"And I don't think he'd have disapproved," Nat said. "A practical sort was Grandfather. I know exactly what his opinion would have been. 'What you do is your own affair, my dear, I'm not going to censure you or interfere in any way, but do make sure you don't give the servants any cause to gossip.'"

The imitation was so exact that Silence laughed. "Of course I haven't," she said. "Apart from Mally, I don't think any of them have guessed. We've been very careful, Nick and I."

"Not careful enough where Rachael is concerned," Nat pointed out. "She found you together, didn't she—did it have something to do with Grandmother's death?"

"I'm afraid it did," his stepmother said sadly, and told him what had happened.

"Well, I suppose she's happy in heaven now," Nat commented. "Making poor Grandfather's life a misery, I should think, if I know her. I expect you're glad she's dead."

This was uttered totally without malice. Silence could only look at her stepson helplessly. She said after a moment, "Yes, I suppose I am, terrible though it is to admit it."

"Why? It's the truth," Nat said.

"It may be, but the truth is not always welcome—nor is it wise to reveal it, sometimes," Silence pointed out.

Nat laughed. "Oh, don't worry. I have more sense than to blurt out my thoughts to those I don't like and don't trust. And anyway, my honest opinions would probably raise the hair on most people's heads."

"Mine included, I suspect," Silence said, laughing. She found, to her astonishment, that she could almost face the dark future with some hope. Nat, so dear and wise and perceptive, knew her secret and did not mind. He would be her ally, her bulwark, her comfort, when Nick was gone. And she found his cheerful, sensible support enormously encouraging. I can bear it, she thought, because Nat is my true friend.

But still the longing gnawed at her, to go away with Nick. And she knew herself too well, knew the danger in which she stood. The wild, reckless, long-buried Silence, who had taken control and led her into adultery, might dominate her again, overcome her doubts, her fears, even her love for the children and for Wintercombe, and tempt her to follow the man she loved so dearly.

There was another possible reason for flight, which was only just beginning to nag at her mind. It was a hazard so obvious that she should have considered the risk she ran, but somehow, engulfed in the passion and love she felt for Nick, she had forgotten it. Now, however, as their idyll was about to be brought to an abrupt end, she must face at last the fact that she might very well be pregnant. Her courses were four days overdue—not a significant delay, true, but she had always been as regular as the moon, almost able to set her clock by their appearance.

And if she was expecting Nick's child, then her sin would become plain for all to see, and the secrecy and discretion would be set at naught. She shrank from the shame, the humiliation, the pointing fingers, the sidelong pitying glances at her children and, worse, the suspicion that they too might be illicitly got. And George . . . as Dame Ursula had pointed out, this he could not possibly overlook.

There were wise women in the village, the Widow Curle for one, who would rid her of it, but she refused even to consider that. To kill Nick's child before it had even lived seemed an evil greater by far than bearing it in shame. And her choice was suddenly and brutally stark. To stay and endure the inevitable scandal, face George's justifiable wrath, the very real possibility that he would dispatch her to live in disgrace in some mean farmhouse, her child taken away from her and reared by foster parents in ignorance of its origins in love and delight. Or to forsake Wintercombe and her children, which would probably happen even if she stayed to face her husband with the proof of his cuckoldry, and to follow Nick, burdened with their child.

Perhaps, she told herself, quailing at the thought of the terrible decision she must soon make, she was being unduly pessimistic. She might have mistaken the date, or the emotional upheavals of the last few weeks might have upset her body's rhythm; she knew such things happened. Tomorrow, or the day after, the dark blood would flow as it always did, and she would be safe—and bereft.

But it did not. Instead, on the next day the Roundheads came.

CHAPTER
TWENTY-NINE

The bright day is done
And we are for the dark.
—ANTONY AND CLEOPATRA

The sun was sinking into the west when Walker ran up from his cottage at Lyde Green to bring the news. A power of soldiers, he said to the assembled men in the barton, far more than last time, with drums and colors all brave, a forest of pikes and a multitude of musketeers. They were marching along the Bath Road, he had seen them on the ridge and had come straight to Captain Hellier.

Captain Hellier gave him a coin, which Walker privately considered inadequate. He had still not forgiven the Cavaliers for corrupting and debauching his daughter Leah, so that she was forced to seek her living as a whore in Bristol to the shame of his family, and as if that were not enough, poor Tom Lyteman up at White Cross had to watch his daughter Bessie daily swelling with the child got on her by some drunken lieutenant. Still, by the look of that there army, the largest body of soldiers he had ever seen, it would not be long before the wicked Cavaliers were rudely ejected from Wintercombe and Farleigh, and Philip's Norton could at last return to its small, peaceful existence.

With a cheerful smile, Walker went back to his cottage, his belief in natural justice restored. And Nick faced his anxious men. He told them that there was no point in further resistance: Bristol had fallen, so their source of coin and supplies had dried up, and the end for the Royalist cause was now only a matter of time. But he would not tamely surrender to the enemy. Even though he would be negotiating from a position of extreme weakness, he was determined to obtain the best terms he could for his troops. And, finally, he thanked them for their loyalty and courage. "When the king is restored to his rightful place, then you will receive your just reward."

They cheered him for that, and he grinned at them, heartened. These were the core of the men he had commanded, the best, and their appreciation was evident. Somehow, perhaps during the siege, respect had been transmuted to something warmer and stronger. He would do his utmost to persuade the Roundheads to let them march away, to their homes if they so desired, or perhaps to Oxford, where most Royalist officers who still had the heart to fight eventually made their way.

From her chamber window, Silence saw the distant red and brown flood of men, never ending, like some vast snake flowing along the Bath Road on the ridge a mile away. Her doom, and Nick's, was approaching, and she faced the hardest task of her life: to stay serene, gentle, innocent, untouched, when it seemed that her guilt must shine from her and that appalling decision, to lose her lover or her children, must soon be made.

"M'lady?" Mally came to stand at her shoulder, small and shrewd, valiant and loyal.

Silence said, still staring at the soldiers marching so inexorably toward Norton, "They are coming. You see our freedom there, Mally, and if I was skilled in sorcery I would weave a spell to make this place invisible."

"He may not be gone forever," Mally said. From being openly hostile to Nick, she was now as much his partisan as she was to Silence. Her mistress's glowing happiness had had much to do with her change of heart, but also she liked Nick for himself.

"Of course he'll be gone forever," Silence said bleakly. "My husband will return when the wars are ended, and then . . ." Her voice trailed away as she thought of the child who might, months hence, put an end to any remaining comforts she had left.

"M'lady," Mally said, very low. "I can guess your trouble—don't ee worry, I can get a potion from the Widow Curle, I'll say 'tis for I, she won't know any other, and Sir George will never find ee out."

Silence stared out at the September fields, green with grass or yellow with stubble, the trees still heavy with leaf. Soon it would be autumn, and the man who would be forever linked in her mind with that season would be gone. And the child, if there was one, would be born in May or June, child of sun and summer. Boy or girl, it would be Nick's, and hers, the only evidence of their brief consuming passion. And she knew that, whatever the danger to her future and her security as George's wife, she could never, ever bring herself to cause its death.

"Thank you, Mally," she said. "But I don't want any of the Widow Curle's potions. It's very early yet, but if there *is* a child, I will keep it."

There was a startled pause. Then Mally said, forgetting respect, "Be ee ramping mad, m'lady? If you have the babe, everyone will know it bain't your husband's—and then what will he do to ee?"

"Put me away, I expect," Silence said bleakly. "But I *can't* kill it, Mally—I *can't!*"

Her maid hoped devoutly that her mistress would not so far forget herself as to run away with her Cavalier captain, desperate in love though they might be. Mally was essentially a realist, and knew that such a foolish gesture would surely be doomed to disaster, quite apart from its effect on those abandoned thereby. But this probable baby, whose existence she had, like Silence, begun to suspect a few days ago, changed everything. No chance of covering *that* up, she thought despairingly. What in the name of heaven am I to do? I shall have to persuade her to take the widow's cure, or she is utterly undone.

She touched Silence gently on the arm. Her mistress turned, her face pale and shadowed with pain and sorrow, but tearless. "Don't worry, please," she said. "It's so early—I might miscarry, or even not be with child at all. But I will tell you this, Mally—no matter what happens, no matter what odium is heaped on my head, no matter what miseries I must endure, I will never ever repent of what I have done, for it's the most wonderful thing that has ever happened in my life."

And Mally, despite her deep misgivings and dark foreboding, gazed at her suddenly brilliant face and could do nothing but agree.

Sir George St. Barbe bade Sir Edward Hungerford good-bye, wished him good fortune and the help of the Lord in his bid to recapture Farleigh, and led his men down the hill to Lyde Green. At last, after more than three years of warfare, three years of hardship, defeat, victory, and bitter, bitter loss, he was coming home to the house where he had been born and that was now his inheritance.

Sam should have been there by his side, his dark curls stirring in the breeze, eager and glowing. But Sam had been nine months and more in his grave, and now his heir was the puling sickly bookish boy whom George had always despised. He thought briefly of his other children, but since they were all girls save for William, whom he had last seen a babe four months old, they did not occupy his mind for long. His mother would also be at Wintercombe. He wondered if she were well and hoped that the ordeal of losing her husband, followed so closely by the house being over-run by soldiers, had not affected her health. His father he had not overly mourned. Sir Samuel had been almost into his dotage, after all, and he had never, George felt, really liked his son.

The feeling was mutual. George, reared in godliness by his mother, had always deeply distrusted his father's devious, irreligious brain, his learning and broad mind, his sly and wicked sense of humor. He looked forward to the time, once this war was ended, when he would be able to be master of Wintercombe without any question.

He could not understand why his young wife had felt it necessary to remain at the house while it was under occupation by enemy soldiers, instead of making her way to Bath or even to her worthy family in London. He hoped that she had been able to prevent the worst of wanton destruction but had no great opinion of her abilities. However, if she was indeed at Wintercombe, and it was surrendered to him without trouble, he would be able to lie with her tonight. His blood quickened at the thought. He was not a man who pursued women, both by nature and by conviction, and the three years of abstinence had not been especially irksome, but now that he was approaching his property, his loins felt the first anticipatory stirrings of desire.

The sun had almost set when he led his weary men up the track from the Wellow Lane, glancing from side to side at the fields around, which were his. There was little sign of neglect, though the hedgerows looked somewhat battered. He recalled poor Cottesworth's tale of the siege he had vainly conducted here and how his company had been forced to withdraw by the valiant efforts of a most ingenious captain.

Mindful of those stories, Sir George had been careful to send out scouts, but all had come back reporting no sign of the enemy, only a considerable number of villagers watching curiously from a respectful distance. And now they had reached the top of the ridge, and Wintercombe lay ahead and to the left, surrounded by trees and fields, its gardens sloping out of sight to the stream at the bottom of the little valley. His major called to the drummers, and the beat changed and stopped. The regiment halted, footsore after the long hilly march from Bath, and gazed with curious eyes on the house they were to take, which belonged to their colonel.

Still fearing a trap, Sir George sent a detachment of men down into the valley to surround the place. Then he dispatched his major, with a drummer, up to the gate, while the remainder of the regiment, glad of the chance to rest, sat down in the hedgerow, their weapons by their sides, to await events.

Silence had watched them from her vantage point in the oriel, her heart pounding in her throat. She did not even know if she would have the chance to say good-bye to Nick in private: They had not expected the Roundheads to arrive so soon, and last night's lovemaking had not been characterized by any sense of urgency or farewell. Suddenly she could not bear the thought that there would be no more, that she would lose him forever, that in an hour or so he would ride away and leave her behind. If she did not see him again, she would not be able to tell him about the baby. And the choice that she still had not been able to bring herself to make would be made for her.

The thought was almost enough to destroy the quiet and fragile mask that she had so desperately struggled to maintain ever since the first sight of the soldiers on the Bath Road.

Deceptively calm, she watched with Nat and Mally and Rachael as the two Roundheads approached the gatehouse. Many of the remaining men in the garrison were crouched behind the courtyard wall, their muskets at the ready. She was disturbed and puzzled by this. Surely Nick did not mean to offer resistance to a force so overwhelming, and in spite of his promise to her?

"What are they doing?" Rachael asked.

Nat answered, "Parleying, I expect. Nick will want the best terms he can get. It wouldn't do for the cavalry to march away without their horses, now would it?"

Despite her misery, Rachael managed a wan smile. Silence hugged her close, feeling her initial tension collapse into acquiescence. Her step-daughter's grief she could well understand, for it shadowed her own. But she was sure that, with the resilience of youth, Rachael would soon wonder why she had ever felt so miserable. Silence, on the other hand, knew in her soul that until the day she died Nick Hellier would keep company in her heart, always.

He stood at the gatehouse, his head courteously bare, the soft September wind blowing his long, earth-brown hair across his face. Wickham and Captain Bull stood beside him, but he held the command here, and although he would acknowledge their opinions the final decision, the final responsibility was his, and his alone. He looked with a curious sense of detachment at the lean major, who had lank carrot-red hair and a face decidedly lacking in chin, and listened to his quiet West Country voice demanding their unconditional surrender to the lawful authority of king and Parliament, and his colonel, Sir George St. Barbe.

Nick stared at him, wondering if he had heard aright. "Your colonel is Sir George St. Barbe? Is he the gentleman who owns this house?"

"He is indeed," the major answered, stiff with disapproval. "And he is most anxious to occupy his property without further let or hindrance from you and your men, sir."

Nick wondered how he could bargain with this unsympathetic man, when he had nothing to lay in the balance. Then a wild idea came to him, a final flourish of defiance. After all, he did have a counter to bargain with, which would probably ensure that he was granted the conditions he wished. He said, smiling in a way that made Tom Wickham's scalp prickle, "My demands are these. We will leave Wintercombe freely, tomorrow morning at sunrise, with all our horses and weapons and baggage, drums beating, and colors flying, as befits honorable surrender."

"You are in no position to haggle terms, Captain," the major replied, frankly incredulous. "I am instructed by Colonel St. Barbe to request your immediate capitulation, or storm the house. And as one officer to another, sir, I need not remind you of our overwhelming numbers, nor of the usual fate of a garrison when taken by storm."

"You can tell your colonel that if he does not agree to my conditions, it will be the worse for his house," Nick said coldly, and smiled. "We are still well supplied with powder and shot, and I am quite prepared to blow Wintercombe sky-high rather than surrender to you on terms so dishonorable. And perhaps you would also remind Colonel St. Barbe that his wife and her children remain within the house. Up until now they have been well treated, but should this place be stormed, I would not be able to guarantee their safety any further."

The major stared at him and so far forgot himself as to take the name of the Lord in vain. "Dear God, man, do you presume to threaten an innocent lady and her children? Rest assured, sir, you will answer for this before the Almighty, if you are not punished on earth for such vile cruelty!"

"I do not threaten," Nick said mildly. "I merely state an obvious fact. Even in the best-conducted sieges, bullets can go astray. I would not dream of harming a hair of their heads—it is your colonel, sir, who holds the fate of his wife and children in his hands."

Silence, watching, saw the major tramp back down the lane with the forceful stride of a very angry man, and wondered apprehensively what Nick had said to him. Surely he could not have refused to surrender? The garrison now mustered scarcely thirty men, and the regiment that lay outside the walls must be twenty times that number. Oh, Nick, Nick, she prayed, don't do anything rash—for my sake, please keep safe!

Colonel Sir George St. Barbe heard the report of his major in a furious and disbelieving silence, while all about him the soldiers strained their ears. "A most insolent knave," Major Bawden said angrily. "And they are so few, they would be overrun in a moment if you chose to give the word, sir."

"No," said George, chewing his lip beneath the bristling moustache he still cultivated, though for younger men it was out of fashion to wear with a beard. "No, Bawden, he's right, may he soon feel the fires of hell—I must not risk my dear wife and children for the sake of trouncing such a rogue, however much he deserves it." He did not add that he wished to return to a well-ordered house, not a pile of stones. "Have Secretary Creed draw up the terms now, and I will take them to him."

So the regiment's secretary, a thin young man with a hectic flush and a continual barking cough, got pen and ink and paper out of his snapsack, and rested them on a drum while he wrote. Then his colonel, his ruddy face dark with annoyance, took the neatly written paper from him and, with Major Bawden and the drummer, walked past the refurbished walls to his own gatehouse, which was barred to him by some impertinent and ungodly Cavalier.

The insolent villain was a man of middle stature, a little shorter than the colonel, but much more lightly built. He was young, and his lean brown face bore the marks of recent illness, or stress, but a joyous and reckless spirit of defiance overlaid it all and raised George's hackles immediately.

Nick said, "Have I the honor of addressing Colonel Sir George St. Barbe?"

"You have," George said shortly. "And who are you, sir, in unlawful occupation of my property?"

For some reason that seemed to amuse the Cavalier; his long mouth curved up into a decidedly mocking smile. "Captain Nicholas Hellier at your service, Colonel. Have you agreed to my terms, sir?"

For two pins, George would have flung the paper in his face, such was the fury this young man engendered in him. But he thought of Wintercombe, and Silence, and kept a hard rein on his temper. He said shortly, "You give me no choice. My secretary has written them out, from the details my major obtained from you. Kindly peruse them and tell me if they are to your liking."

Nick took the paper ungraciously thrust at him and scanned it quickly. All he had asked for was neatly listed, and at the foot, the scrawled, spluttering, and undoubtedly furious signature of the man standing belligerently before him: Geo. St. Barbe, Bt.

He looked up, studying the man who was Silence's husband. The portrait in the hall had on the whole been fair. The sanguine face before him was supremely self-confident, assured of its own position and the righteousness of its beliefs, and impatient of resistance and argument. He thought with anguish of Silence, whom he loved so much, returned to this man devoid of joy and affection. His skin crawled at the thought of her in his bed. St. Barbe, despite his arrogance, did not have the look of a brutal man; he was not like Ridgeley. Instead, he would be thoughtless, boring, and insensitive.

But if he ever finds out that Silence and I were lovers, Nick thought, his heart chilling at the prospect, his punishment will surely be as cruel and implacable as ever Ridgeley could be.

"All seems to be as I requested, sir," he said. "If your secretary will make up another, we will each be able to have a copy, signed and sealed by both of us. Then, as agreed, you will withdraw all your men save a small patrol until tomorrow at sunrise."

Even now George was tempted to give vent to his spleen and wipe the knowing look of mockery from the captain's face. With a supreme effort, he restrained himself. Only one night, and then the Men of Blood would march away defeated, no doubt to join the sorry remnant of Royalists in Oxford. Fairfax would soon deal with them, and then their humiliated king, misruled by his Papist wife and his corrupt and evil councillors, would have no choice but to sue grovelingly for peace.

"As agreed," he said, his mind already accepting with frustrated fury the inevitability of a comfortable room at the George instead of his own chamber, his own bed, and his own wife to warm it. "But you'll be out of here at sunrise, d'you hear me, sir, you and your draggle-tailed soldiers with you—at sunrise!"

"At sunrise," the captain agreed, and bowed with a most courtly flourish. In contrast, Colonel St. Barbe's was a perfunctory and graceless affair. He grunted something and turned away. And Nick, who had gained everything he wanted, and a last night of love with the colonel's wife into the bargain, smiled joyfully at his retreating back.

Silence and her stepchildren had watched all this from the oriel. The bulk of the gatehouse shielded much of the confrontation from their intense gaze, but it was evident to Silence, merely from the set of Nick's shoulders, that for some reason he was delighted at the outcome. Then he turned to speak to Wickham, and even from here she could see the flashing brilliance of his smile.

"There goes the Roundhead leader," Nat said, pointing. Silence tore her eyes from Nick and saw the officer, resplendent in fine red coat with blue facings, his sword bright by his side and his hat pulled down, stumping along the track on the other side of the wall, followed by another officer, thin and orange-haired, and a drummer. He walks just like George when he's in a rage, she thought, staring down at the distant figure, though he's thinner by far than my husband.

She turned away from the oriel, wondering what had been discussed to make the Parliament man so angry and Nick so elated. Surely, *surely* he was not going to subject Wintercombe to another siege, probably at the cost of much damage to the house and almost certainly a great deal of bloodshed?

No, Silence thought, from the depths of her knowledge of Nick. No, he would not do that.

But she had to know for certain. She glanced around at Nat, Rachael, and Mally, who were still peering avidly out of the window, and said, "I'm going down to see what's happening."

There was no one in the hall, but a great many servants packed in the porch, jostling for a view. Silence, Mally beside her, stood at the back unnoticed for some moments, listening to their interested comments.

"Do ee reckon as how there'll be another siege?"

"Ooh, I do hope not—I couldn't abear they bursty great things a-going off bang."

"Good riddance to 'em all, that's what *I* d'say, pack of ungodly hang-gallize trubagullies *they* be."

"Aye, sooner us d'get our own Sir George back to we, the better 'twill be."

"Nay," said another voice, which she recognized as Darby's. "M'lady have done us proud, and I won't have a word said otherwise, do ee hear?"

Silence was gratified to find that there were a number of assenting voices to this last comment. If I have done nothing else this past year, she thought, at least I have earned their respect. Unwilling to surprise them, she turned as quietly as she could and gestured to Mally to follow her.

The barton, when they reached it, was the center of much activity. The light was already beginning to fade, and the young trumpeter was firing the torches in the sconces on the barn and stable walls. Others were leading in the horses, fat and grass-fed, from the fields, and a little group of men were sitting in the entrance to the barn, cleaning and polishing their swords. No one seemed to notice Silence standing by the kitchen door, her eyes, stricken, watching the preparations for departure. Then Tom Wickham saw her and came over. He had long suspected that something lay between his captain and this quiet, unassuming woman with the wide, beautiful eyes, and one look at her face, stark with sorrow, confirmed it. He said gently, "May I assist you, Lady St. Barbe?"

Silence had found that the effort of maintaining her usual calm facade was far greater than she had expected. Now, seeing the imminence of her loss, all the agony of parting from Nick had returned. And how could she bear to say good-bye to him now when, if she stayed at Wintercombe, her future bore nothing but grief and utter desolation because of the babe she might carry?

She stared up at Tom Wickham, who was some inches taller than Nick, and said quietly, "When do you leave, then? I assume you *are* leaving?"

"We are," he said, and grinned at her. "But not tonight. Nick struck a most advantageous bargain with the Roundheads, and we march away at sunrise, with all our horses and weapons, colors flying, free to go where we will."

So she had one more night with him. The uprush of joy and relief almost overwhelmed her, although it was but a few more hours to postpone the terrible moment of decision. She said, "Will the men require provisions, sir? They will surely go hungry on the march otherwise."

"They will indeed," Tom said, gazing at her. "Are you suggesting, my lady—"

"I am telling you that there will be bread and cheese for their snapsacks if Captain Hellier wishes it," Silence said firmly. "And also I feel this occasion should be marked in some way." She paused for thought, for this idea had only just come to her. "I would like you and Captain Hellier and the other officers to join me in the dining parlor for supper. We have been enemies in the past—surely now the war is all but over we can be friends."

"Of course, my lady," he said, surprised but pleased. "I am sure we will all be most happy to attend. And may I say this, my lady, that whatever our past differences, I am sure every man here is deeply appreciative of your courage and your gracious conduct under very trying circumstances."

Silence found that she wanted to laugh. Her voice sparkling with it, she said dryly, "I have never before heard your late and unlamented lieutenant-colonel described thus, sir."

His face broke into a cheerful grin. "Neither have I. Most people used less mild epithets. If you will forgive me, my lady, there is much to do before we can be free to partake of your generous invitation. What time do you expect our company?"

"At eight," Silence told him and, still buoyed up with that unjustified delight, acknowledged his courteous bow and went indoors to tell Darby of her plans.

The vast man stood in a clean apron at his table and listened to her instructions with an impassive face. Then, quite unexpectedly, he smiled. She did not think she had ever seen such an expression on his face before, and stared at him in amazement. "If 'tis the last meal I cook for them," he said, "I'll be sure and make it a fine one. We'll surely do better without them, m'lady, and I'll be happy to see them on their way with a memory of what good cooking ought to be."

Two hours later Wintercombe vibrated with rich and delicious aromas, as the rose of a lute quivered with sound. Eliza, begrudgingly, had set the table for fourteen, seven officers, six St. Barbes, and Mally. Silence put her head around the door when she had finished and let her eyes linger on the crisp white cloth, the neatly folded napery, the polished spoons and knives, the pewter dishes and wine cups. Bowls of dried rose petals scented the air, and waxen candles burned on table and mantel and court cupboard, flooding the dark-paneled room with soft yellow light. She drew the heavy red damask curtains across the three windows and went to change into a garment more fitting for such an occasion. This, after all, was a celebration— or a wake.

When all was ready in the barton for an early departure, the officers of the sadly diminished company and troop left their men in the charge of the corporals and made their way to the quarters that they had occupied since arriving at Wintercombe, in the east wing below the chamber belonging to Silence. There they donned their finest clothes, rubbed the surplus mud from boots or shoes, made sure that swords and buckles sparkled, and returned to the hall to stand before the fire and await the arrival of the lady of the house.

Nick, in the room that had once been Ridgeley's, dressed with care. He had no servant to assist him, for Harris had fled soon after Ridgeley's death, but he was used to the lack. Deliberately, he put on his tawny suit, slung his sword from its broad embroidered sash, cleaned his boots with a damp cloth, and finally, smiling, laid the vivid scarlet cloak over a chair, ready for the morrow. His books he had left with Silence. He would carry away nothing but his fiddle and a small bag of clothing.

And, of course, a memory.

He wondered if he should tell her that the commander of the forces outside the gate was her husband. He did not wish to leave her to discover it in the morning. Neither, however, did he want to spoil their last evening together with unwelcome thoughts of the bitter future. He had ordered his officers to say nothing of it and decided to choose his moment carefully, if at all.

One more night, and then a lifetime to look back on it. Honestly, he acknowledged that he would not always think of her. Indeed, he planned to assuage his grief and loss in adventure, new countries, even a New World, just as she would lose herself in domestic activities and the humdrum life of Wintercombe. But she would always be with him, as he knew that he would go with her, inside her soul forever.

In the hall, his officers stood waiting. Tom Wickham, tall, friendly, pleasant. Solid and unimaginative Bull, who never saw anything that was not thrust under his nose. Combe, a very quiet young man, originally given a commission because his father, a clothier, had supplied Sir Thomas Bridges with enough cheap material to outfit his entire regiment. Parset, wordy, tedious, and unintentionally amusing. Hodges, the quartermaster, like Bull much older than the rest, a weathered hard-drinking man who by the look of him had once been a farmer. And the young cornet, Hunter, raised from the ranks after Wickham had taken over Byam's duties, an eager boy, one of William's friends, with the makings of a good officer if he ever obtained the experience.

They were none of them bad men in the way that Ridgeley had been evil. They had followed where he led, that was all, but then they had feared his unpredictable and vicious rages. Under Nick's command there was more comradeship and more respect on all sides. At least, he thought wryly, they smile when I approach.

And then there were children's voices, footsteps behind the screens, and Silence entered with her brood around her.

She was wearing the golden-brown silk, the color paler than his own, which she had put on for the Prince of Wales and never since. But this time no lace collar hid the pale smooth lines of her shoulders and the soft full swell of her breasts behind the embroidered, old-fashioned stomacher, and Mally had dressed her hair to fall in loose tawny ringlets about her face. She wore no jewels, but her eyes sparkled in the firelight and candlelight, and he saw the other men look at her in astonishment, as if the dowdy brown Puritan sparrow had suddenly cast off her feathers to reveal the brilliant beauty of a kingfisher.

The children clustered about her, the younger ones hopping with excitement at what they sensed to be a special occasion, the twins standing dark and solemn behind. The mourning worn for their grandmother had been put off in favor of fine silk in muted but glowing colors: yellow for Rachael, dark red for Nat, amber and hyacinth blue and sea green for Tabby, Deb, and William. In a great lord's house, Nick had once seen a family portrait by the master Van Dyke, and only such an artist could do justice to the vivid and delightful children before him, and their mother, whom he loved so much. And he knew that, whatever came after, he would always like to remember her thus, in the colors of earth that suited her best and with her beloved offspring around her like flowers.

"Are we all ready?" she asked, smiling, and as Nick assented, led the way to the dining parlor.

It was indeed a merry evening, considering that one half of the party would be ejected on the morrow to make their way in defeat to Oxford, and the other half were sad, and more than sad, to see them go. But there was wine, though it was made by the lady of the house from elderflowers and cherries, and beer if that did not suit. And Turber, tremulous and bent, entered at the head of a procession of servants—Eliza, Joan, Christian Merrifield, Margery—bearing the dishes that Darby, with the pleasure of a true artist, had spent the past two hours creating. There was a fine pottage of mutton flavored with chicory, spinach, cabbage, and parsley, with country wine in the broth; a carp from the pond, netted by Diggory not an hour since, flapping almost as it went in the pan, boiled and served up with a sauce of lemons and verjuice; a dish of roast chickens, basted with sweet butter and cinnamon and accompanied by a sauce of onions, breadcrumbs, wine, oranges, and lemons; a carbonado of beef; and buttered eggs with anchovies and toasts. Silence, aware of the chaotic state of the storerooms, where some of the rarer and more exotic items had almost run out, gazed at the feast with appreciation. Once more Darby had done his duty magnificently.

No one spoke much during the first course; all were too busy filling hungry stomachs. Soon each platter was almost clean, and Lily, hearing the scrape of knives and spoons, looked up hopefully, expecting scraps or bones. Silence nodded to Turber, who was waiting by the door, and the table was cleared in preparation for the next course. This was simpler, with neat's tongues, a brawn with mustard, a piece of boiled gammon, and cheesecakes, tansies, and pies of quince and plums, with a plate of dark spicy gingerbread for the children.

"And you are not to fight over it," Silence told them, seeing their round greedy eyes. "Darby has cut it into exactly fifteen pieces—so how many each, Tabby?"

Tabitha, surprisingly, was already showing a facility for numbers that equaled her gift for music. "Three," she said, grinning.

The gingerbread was solid, heavy stuff, specifically intended to keep small chattering jaws busy with chewing rather than talking. The end of the table accordingly relapsed into quiet, even Nat, who had claimed to dislike the stuff, being not so far from childhood as to spurn such a sticky and delicious treat.

Silence, at the head of the table, sipped her wine and watched as the men who had once been her enemies demolished the second course with enthusiasm. Memories of the past year came to her, pictures of Ridgeley at Christmas, the man whom Nick had shot in the orchard, Nat running up West Street untying the cattle that would block the colonel's path to Rachael. And Nick, smiling, absorbed, playing carols on his fiddle. He had brought the instrument down from his chamber; she had noticed it lying on the small table. She said softly, "Will you play for us, Captain, when the meal is ended?"

Nick, on her left opposite Mally, raised his cup to her and smiled. "Of course. Shall we dance, on our last night?"

"I don't think that would be appropriate," Silence pointed out dryly. "I know we are celebrating your departure, but that's hardly seemly. What would the New Model say?"

"There's only a dozen of them out there, they'll not disturb us," young Hunter said, gulping down his wine.

But Nick shook his head. "Lady St. Barbe says no dancing, so there will be no dancing. But music, yes, that you shall have."

And they did, laughing and clapping in time as he gave them rounds and catches and jigs, unseasonal carols and drinking songs whose words, sung in a cheerful roar by the other officers, were sometimes hastily muted, with guilty glances at Silence. She found it impossible to keep her fingers still: They beat a tattoo on the cloth, and William and Deb, perhaps remembering that other evening when Tabby had played, and Nick and Silence had danced, leapt down from their stools, seized each other in a fervent embrace, and bounced up and down giggling until they fell in a happy heap at the fiddler's feet. To his credit, he did not falter. But Silence knew, reluctantly, that she must bring this supper to a close.

She got to her feet as the notes of the tune died away and Nick, flexing his fingers, lowered his bow. Immediately the laughter and talk diminished, and they all looked expectantly up at her. It was very difficult, suddenly, to say anything. Her throat felt dry, and somehow the words she wanted seemed inadequate. But she had to speak, she could not just sit down again. She took a deep breath and said, trying to smile, "I think that it is time the children were in bed—it's almost ten. And you all must be up betimes."

They looked up at her, inquiring, polite, as she struggled to find a way of saying what could never be openly expressed. Finally she said quietly, "I feel that you depart as friends, all of you. And I thank you for that, because you could so easily have become my enemies in truth, over the past year. If this sorry war is ever brought to an end, you will always be welcome as guests in this house."

Tom Wickham leapt to his feet. "No, my lady—it is *we* who should thank you. You have kept us alive here for nearly a year, and with small thanks for it. Well, now we can show our appreciation. A toast, gentlemen, to Lady St. Barbe!"

And she stood, deafened by their cheering and the wild hurrahs of the children, as they filled and drained their cups. Outside, the Roundhead guards that George had left to huddle under a hedgerow all night heard the noise and muttered to each other enviously of the Cavaliers' debauch.

With a gesture that touched Silence deeply, they came to her, one by one, to bow over her hand as if she were queen of Wintercombe and they her courtiers: gruff Captain Bull, shy Combes, cheerful Tom Wickham, even stout little Parset, she knew them all now, and bade them farewell, and William was lifted and petted until his face was cracked wide, smiling, and Deb and Tabby clustered around, each begging a last kiss as if these men were cousins, not enemies.

Mally collected them up, clucking at them like a mother hen, as soon as the officers had filed from the room. "I'll take 'em up to bed, m'lady."

"Good night," Silence said to each of her children, and to Nat, who had grown so tall over the last year, and Rachael, whose eyes were filled with the tears that betrayed her first, tentative feelings of womanhood. She watched them leave the room—Nat, impertinently, had winked at her as he closed the door—and then turned to face Nick.

He had stood all the time in the shadows, his bow and fiddle put aside, and she had seen him hug Tabby as if she were his own daughter, with a poignancy that had brought a lump to her throat. Now she held out her hands, and he came into the light smiling, her autumn-colored man, brown and russet and chestnut, the colors of earth in which her soul had flowered. He did not embrace her immediately. Instead he stood by the table, littered with the scraped, gnawed, and sticky debris of the meal, and said quietly, "I want to remember you as you are now—in that gown, with your hair loose. You may be no Court lady, my dear love, but you are surely no Puritan either."

"I know I am not," she said ruefully. "That is another thing you have taught me—that it is not shame to take delight in music, or laughter, or even dancing, because all these things gladden the heart."

"'A man hath no better thing under the sun, than to eat, and to drink, and to be merry,'" Nick said, smiling, and his lover, smiling in answer, supplied chapter and verse.

"Ecclesiastes eight, fifteen. I never could think that the Lord delighted in misery."

She walked around the end of the table toward him, and he watched her approach with desire suddenly plain in his face. "Shall we to bed, my lady?"

And, for the last time, she assented.

While, still unknown to her, George's soldiers watched the dark bulk of Wintercombe, they walked separately through the sleeping house, taking care even now that suspicious eyes would not fall on them. She found her chamber warm, the fire glowing, Pye playing with her five-week-old kitten on the bed. Seven or eight days after its birth, they had become lovers. And now this was the only time left to them, the brief hours till sunrise.

With a tenacity that surprised her, she held fast to this final shred of happiness, wringing what she could from it, not letting thoughts of tomorrow's parting spoil the delicious pleasure that she enjoyed in her lover's arms tonight. With desperate urgency, they clung together, not even undressing in their haste, while the cats scampered and Lily, ears pricked, watched curiously from the bed. But when their first hunger was slaked, amid soft laughter he carefully took off her garments, his hands lingering over each fastening, raising desire in them both until, entwined and giggling like children, they stumbled to the bed.

Silence lay afterward in dreamy contentment, her head on his shoulder and his arms about her. Like this, drowsy and sated, she could almost deceive herself into thinking that the moment would go on forever. Better, surely, to pretend, to sink into sleep, to preserve the illusion for the last few hours, for tomorrow, no, today, he would be gone.

But she could not forget the stark choice she faced. To forsake her children, and her husband, and Wintercombe, and go with him to bear their child, if there was a child, apart from everything else she had ever loved? Or to let him ride away, leaving her to bear her baby in disgrace, the subject of George's justifiable fury, almost certainly separated from her children and from Wintercombe as a punishment for her wickedness?

She had never been one to worry over what might happen tomorrow. Her grim childhood had taught her to cling on to her joys, and by so doing assuage, just a little, the grief that was sure to come. But the choice must be made, and whatever she decided, she was assured of terrible grief.

"Where will you go tomorrow?" she said softly.

Like her, Nick had been on the edge of sleep, but her words roused him. He sat up, looking down at the beloved woman lying beside him, and saw the white edge of tension in her face. He spread his hands, brown and callused from handling sword and reins, yet so light and gentle and subtle when he touched her. "I have no idea. I don't particularly want to fight any more—as you have taught me, there is no point, and certainly no honor, in struggling on. No force the king has left, and probably no force he has ever had, could withstand this New Model Army. They will make their peace soon, and then all the fighting will be among themselves. I think Parliament will discover that they have created a monster, which will turn and rend them when it has disposed of the king's men."

"All the king's horses . . ." Silence whispered. "You haven't answered my question. Where will you go?"

"To the Low Countries, perhaps, or France—experienced soldiers are always useful," Nick said. "Or to the New World, or the Indies. I am not the sort, my love, to settle tamely back into ordinary life. I have tasted too much of adventure."

And she knew now which choice she must make, the kinder decision for the children, all of them, both the living and the unborn. She said, on a sob, "Nick—take me with you."

The silence threatened to stretch out into eternity. She waited rigid, shuddering with tension. She had finally said it, at last she had given voice to the temptation that had tortured her for days. Now, however, it did not seem like foolishness. Better that the children should remember their mother as a woman who, however misguided, had left them for love than one who was sent away amid pointing fingers, the buzz of horrified scandal and gossip, the shame and degradation. Better that she should vanish from their lives.

Nick, too, was in the grip of temptation so strong that it almost overwhelmed him. Despite all the sensible arguments against it, he wanted her, wanted her beside him, to love for all his days. But, like Mally, he was a realist, enough to know that his dream was inevitably doomed to diminish into ashes. He had no money, no resources, no means of living save by selling his sword. And his mind's eye, clear and anguished, saw the certain consequences if he succumbed to that temptation. The poverty, the struggle to survive, the squalid rooms, the cold and the misery and uncertainty of such an existence, would surely destroy the strongest feelings of love and desire. And he wanted desperately to remember their brief affair as something perfect and beautiful, something to illuminate, even with sadness, the rest of his life. What they had shared was too wonderful, too precious and rare, to hazard to the chill winds of fortune and knight-errantry.

But she would not understand, he knew that already. In some ways so wise, she was an innocent in these matters. Despite her stern childhood, she had never wanted for comfort, and she had lived all her life cushioned unthinkingly by a wealth that the vast majority of people never attained. She could have no comprehension of the dreadful tedium and worry, the weariness of grinding poverty, the sadness and waste of it, the impossibility of relief. She would not complain, she would do her best, buoyed up by the belief that love, this unlooked-for, joyous emotion, could solve all her problems. And one day, in a year, or two years, or four, she would wake up beside him and wish, too late, that she had never left her husband and her beloved children, and regret most bitterly her foolishness in following her lover.

And that was something that in truth he would never be able to bear.

Unable to look at her, he clasped his hands and said, in a voice so low that she could hardly hear it, "Oh, my dear love . . . I can't."

She did not believe it. She had been so certain that he would assent with joy, that she would not after all be parted from him, that even if she abandoned her children there would be another, as greatly beloved, to console her for her loss. And now he had taken her gift, her love, and flung it back in her face.

"Why?" she whispered at last. "Why? Why can't you?"

Another woman would have claimed that he did not love her; Silence only stared at him, utterly stricken, her eyes wet with helpless tears, and almost, despite his resolution, he put his arms about her and told her that he did not mean it, that he had changed his mind, yes, she could follow him into exile and penury and death, the death of their love, the most valuable thing that either of them had ever possessed, all their lives long.

He did take her in his arms then, and hugged her and rocked her as if she were one of the children, and his own eyes were wet. She wept on his shoulder, on and on, as if she could not stop, but quietly, no sobs or cries, just the endless tears and the hopeless tremors that shook her body. And at last, when he thought that she had calmed a little, able at least to understand what he was saying, he spoke softly. "You may hate me for this. I have told you very little of myself, and to purpose. What I said just now, about going to foreign parts when I leave Wintercombe, was a lie. I lied to you, because I knew that the truth would hurt you very much. And now that I must tell you, you may be very angry with me for deceiving you. But I tell you this—my love is no lie, and I will love you for the rest of my life."

"And I will love you likewise," she said, her voice muffled in his shoulder. His whole chest was damp with her tears. Suddenly she pulled away from him and stared into his eyes. Her face was red and swollen and ugly with weeping, she had lost any beauty she had ever possessed, but she was still, and always would be, infinitely dear to him. And with the desperate courage that he had always loved in her, she said quietly, "Tell me."

"I have a wife," he said gently. "I have a wife in Worcester, and an apothecary's shop, and two children."

She had not thought that anything he said would have had the power to hurt her further. But this, *this,* struck her heart like a knife, so that she almost felt the blow. Appalled, struck dumb, she stared at him, her tears drying on her cheeks. A wife! He had a wife, and children. And suddenly much of the mystery was explained: his knowledge of medicine, his ease in the company of small children, even the secrecy about his past, all became clear to her. And she thought about his wife, who had the right to that neat, strong, scarred body as George had the right to her own, and said, "What is she like? Does she love you?"

"She is, as they say, a good help-meet," he told her, praying silently that she would believe him. "Her father owned the shop—she is his only daughter. I married her six years ago. I like her, but I do not love her."

"But does she love you?" Silence cried, unable to hide her anguish.

And Nick said softly, "Yes."

"And the children? Tell me about your children," Silence said, thinking with agony of their own child, perhaps curled minute inside her, a means of destruction every bit as devastating as one of Nick's grenadoes.

"John would be five now. He was just beginning to walk when I went away to fight. And the little girl, Sarah, she is William's age. I only remember her as a tiny baby."

It did not occur to Silence to disbelieve him. It explained so much, seemed suddenly so likely that she did not doubt what he said. And Nick, who had described his elder brother's wife, and his brother's shop, and his brother's children, looked at her stricken face and hated himself for this necessary yet heartbreaking deceit.

"So that is why you are so good with my children," Silence said at last. She was shaking, her whole body disturbed by the tremors that ran through her. But in the face of this, the ultimate disaster, the strength that she had always denied in herself, until the soldiers had forced her to call on it, was seeping into her heart. So, she had chosen, and her choice was rejected. Now she must begin to make what she could of the other, the dark path of truth, shame, and loss.

Make, do, mend: The litany pulsed in her head. And because in the end she had no choice, had never had any, she lifted her face, shiny and disfigured with grief, with a ragged and desperate pride. She said softly, "Oh, Nick . . . nothing you could say to me would ever change my love for you. That poem . . . 'love is not love' . . ."

"'That alters when it alteration finds,'" he said with her, his deep voice chiming with hers. "So all the books I lent you were not wasted. Keep them, my dear love, keep them—I know it's a poor substitute for myself, but there may be some comfort there. And you will still have Wintercombe, and the children, and perhaps one day you will find that the pain grows less."

She knew already that she would not tell him about the baby. It would only add to his own pain. Let him ride away thinking that their secret was forever safe and that a small measure of happiness might in the end be waiting for her. She said slowly, "I will survive without you, because I must, but I will never, ever forget you . . . you made me realize that I am alive, Nick. You have given me great grief, but also a happiness I had never even dreamed could exist, least of all for me. And Tabby . . . you have given Tabby her music."

"And William will doubtless grow up to be a soldier," he said, smiling. "And no one's lives will ever be the same—but we are not unique in that."

"At least we have been happy, even if for too brief a time. Think of how many people have lost so much—I *must* think of that," Silence said. She found that she could even essay a smile, for she must not make him feel guilt at his rejection of her. Nor could she give him any indication that her future was so much more bleak than he believed.

Yet, she thought in despair, perhaps it was not so bad. She might be mistaken about the baby. Or perhaps in the end she would weigh her living children in the balance of the unborn and sacrifice the child in her womb for her sake, and theirs. She did not know. She only knew that in a few hours Nick would be gone forever. And suddenly she could not bear to be separate any longer, and flung herself into his arms.

They made love again, with renewed urgency, because they did not have much time left to them, and at last she slept for a little. He sat for a long time looking at her, the closed eyelids still reddened with tears, the mass of golden brown hair spread across the pillow, the face calm and peaceful, like that so very deceptive mask that she showed to most of the world. He hoped that he had not misjudged her, that she would have the strength to endure, and survive, and live without him in, if not happiness, at least not in utter misery. He did not think that she was so fainthearted. She had the courage, the sense of humor, and the greatness of spirit to accept their fate and even, eventually, to see the inevitability of it.

There was something else he must tell her, he remembered suddenly. He touched her gently on her face and saw her eyes open, dreaming, and the sudden change as she mistook his reason for waking her. He shook his head, smiling. "No, you have only slept for a few minutes—we have time yet. But there is something I think you should know."

The serious note in his voice alerted her. Suddenly awake, she sat up and stared at him. "Nick—what is it?"

He said nothing for a moment, not looking at her but into the shadows beyond the bed, still wondering if he ought to tell her, after all the grief of this night. Finally he said, "The Roundhead colonel who will take over the house tomorrow—Silence, he is your husband."

For a moment she did not believe him. She said in astonishment, "*George?* The men outside are *George's?* Why didn't he come marching straight in this afternoon?"

Nick produced a grin that could only be described as wicked. "Because I said I'd blow up his house if he did."

For a long moment she stared at him, and then she suddenly burst into rather helpless laughter. "But—but you wouldn't blow up Wintercombe."

"I know that. You know that. But *he* doesn't. And that is why he agreed to everything I asked, in return for his house, and his children, and his wife, safe and undamaged on the morrow. He didn't have any choice, really. You could see that he was furious, but there was precious little he could do about it."

"I saw him," Silence said thoughtfully. "I saw him from the window, walking away—he walked like George, but he was so much thinner, I didn't recognize him. He must have lost a great deal of weight." She glanced at her lover. "Do you think he suspected anything?"

"He looked the kind of man who wouldn't suspect anything till it hit him on the nose. I'm sure in his self-satisfaction he's never even considered that you might want anyone else but him in your bed."

She thought suddenly of the baby, and hope struck her, flooding her with relief. Tomorrow George would take possession of his house, and his wife, and he would assuredly lie with her. Her flesh quailed at the thought of once more having to endure his unpleasurable lovemaking. But she must, would even invite him into her bed if he seemed unaccountably reluctant. For if she was indeed pregnant with Nick's child, it was so soon since its conception that, with luck, George would never know that it was not his.

And so she and the baby were safe from vilification, and calumny, and pointing fingers. She had deceived her husband in his absence and taken a secret lover. Now she was preparing to foist another man's child on him without his knowledge.

A year ago she would have been horror-struck at the very thought. Now, made devious by the necessity of survival, for the sake of all her children, she contemplated that awesome deception with equanimity. It was wicked and sinful, and no doubt of it, and many would condemn her to hell because of it. But for her baby, and for the other, legitimate children, she would hazard even her salvation.

And suddenly it was all too much for her, the unlooked-for hope and the thought of having to face her husband like the innocent, virtuous wife that he believed her still to be, and above all the imminent and irrevocable loss of her lover. Before she could do anything, she began to sob, and once more he took her in his arms to bring her the comfort that, after this night, it would no longer be possible to give. And somehow, because neither of them could bear that there would be no more, they made love yet again, half laughing, half weeping, and slept almost as soon as they finished, exhausted and yet strengthened by a simultaneous sunburst of pleasure and joy.

She woke to the sound of someone knocking, or rather scratching, on the door. It was still dark. Her heart pounding, she jumped from the bed, pulling her night rail about her, and felt her way to it. Unlocked, it revealed Mally, who had by the look of her rumpled garments been to sleep in them. "M'lady? It d'want a little while till dawn. Will ee wake the captain? His men will be stirring any minute."

So it had come at last. She nodded, and Mally, with a discreet grin, went down the stairs. Silence turned and went to the hearth. Scraping flint and tinder, she lit a candle.

Nick lay sleeping still, his face relaxed, almost boyish, under the light morning stubble. She stood looking at him for a moment and then gently shook him awake. "It's time, Nick—time to go."

With the alertness of the soldier, he sat up at once, pushing his hair out of his eyes. She ached to put her arms around him, to love him just once more, but it was impossible, and they both knew it. Delay now could ruin all their care, all their subterfuge. Instead, bleakly practical, she handed him his clothes before fetching one of her ordinary plain black gowns from the clothes closet. Last night she had been Silence. Today, and forever after, she would be the Puritan wife again.

They helped each other dress, smiling, touching, but speaking little. All the words had been said already and now idle chatter, even the lighthearted banter that they so delighted in, seemed superfluous beside the force of emotion that overwhelmed them both. When he was ready, Silence went to the little inlaid box on her walnut table in which she kept small treasures. She took something out of it and turned toward him. He saw that her eyes were full of tears, though she was trying valiantly to smile. She said, "You have given me so much, Nick, you have changed my life—and I wanted to give you something to remember me by, just as I will have your books, and Lily."

The little dog heard her name and pricked up her ears. Silence held out her hands to him. "Here you are, Nick—I want you to have this."

In her fingers was a thin silver chain, the links worn almost through with age, and attached to it a tiny locket of the same metal. She said, "It was my mother's. She wasn't a Puritan either. I know it isn't suitable, but I couldn't think what else to give you. And . . . look inside the locket."

He took it and opened it. The catch was simple, probably as worn as the chain, and the design of the locket was absolutely plain, no ornament anywhere. And inside there lay a tiny circlet plaited together with infinite love from two strands of hair, one the color of dark earth, the other golden brown. She said, looking at his face, "I remembered that poem, a line in that poem, it was in one of your books."

"'A bracelet of bright hair about the bone,'" he quoted for her. "Oh, my love, I thank you. At least now I'll have something of you that proves it was no dream." And he added softly, "'Since there's no help, come let us kiss, and part.'"

He had spoken that line to her before, in circumstances that were almost as painful. And this time she was giving up far more, in the full knowledge now of what his love meant.

And so they kissed for the last time, his hands in her hair, pressing her mouth against his, while she clung to him desperately. But at last the moment of farewell could not be delayed any longer. Gently he disentangled himself and set his hands on her shoulders. Fiercely, she wiped the tears away and gave him a brave, gallant smile. "I shall be all right," she said. "Another thing you have given me is strength. And perhaps with the effort to behave as though I was still a virtuous wife, I shall become one again. Good-bye, Nick, and God go with you."

"And with you," he said, his eyes on hers, dark with pain. "Oh, my herald of joy, I love you so much."

"And I love you," she said, smiling with more success. "Nick—you must go now, before we are found out."

He kissed her forehead, with love, and turned and walked to the door, her locket and chain still trickled bright between his fingers. She stood and watched, holding every movement, every feature in her mind, for it would have to last her forever. And then he opened the door, gave her one last long, lazy smile and a blown kiss, and was gone.

Bereft, she stood staring at the door for a very long time, willing herself not to weep. He was gone. Soon he would ride out of there, and she would never see him again. And she must adjust her mind, bring herself to welcome George, to encourage him, if he needed it, into her bed—George, who had never lain with her except in darkness, who had never seen her naked, who had never gloried in her body, unashamed and desiring, as Nick had done. And a small ember of comfort flickered into life within her cold heart. Whatever happens, she thought fiercely, I have been very much loved, for myself: I *am* beloved, still. And not even George can take that away from me.

There were sounds from outside. She wondered where Mally was. For the moment, she was glad of her maid's absence. She wanted to gather her strength, and it was so much easier to do it without the girl's sympathy. She went over to the oriel, drawn by compulsion, though she had intended not to look out until he had gone, and drew back the curtain.

The courtyard was filled with soldiers, a score or so on horseback, rather less standing ready with muskets. Their blue coats and generally shabby air contrasted painfully with the neatly serried ranks outside lining the track. She saw Nick, standing by his tall chestnut, instantly recognizable by his scarlet cloak. And with him was her husband.

She could see little of him at this distance, save what she had earlier noted, his loss of weight. She watched as they talked, conscious of a strange feeling, almost of defiance, to see George talking all unawares to his wife's lover. She had failed George, she had been unfaithful once. She did not regret it, and never would, but she knew that she would never again take a lover. It was not in her nature to be promiscuous; and where she loved, she loved for life.

But the man she loved was not her husband.

Nick mounted and called something to his men. The boy trumpeter blew a piercing note on his battered instrument, and Captain Bull's drummer beat out a brisk marching rhythm. Above them, the colors fluttered bravely, if rather ragged, in the gray light of dawn. With all the honors of war, won for them by unscrupulous deception, the rump of Sir Thomas Bridges' Horse, and Foot, tramped for the last time under the gatehouse of Wintercombe and turned right to march along the muddy track toward Philip's Norton, and Oxford, or wherever in the world they wished to go.

She stood at the oriel, watching, her pale face pressed to the glass. Just before he rode out of sight behind the trees, Nick turned and stared up at her chamber. He raised a hand in salute, and farewell. And then he was finally lost to her.

As if in a dream, she saw the courtyard fill with the men of her husband's regiment, well disciplined, well clothed, well equipped, everything that the Cavaliers had not been. She saw George, the carrot-haired major by his side, giving orders. She thought of Wintercombe below her feet, the tasks she must direct, the false welcome she must give to a man she would have been happy never to see again. Like a sleepwalker she turned, ignoring Lily's whines and pleas for attention, and left her chamber.

All the servants were ranked in the hall, from old Turber down to Ned Merrifield and Jemmy Coxe. She saw Mally's bright encouraging smile, and the excited faces of the children beside Doraty and Hester, and Nat grinning at her like a lunatic. He stepped forward, glancing around at the people behind him, and then at the screens. Silence, puzzled, stopped in the middle of the hall and saw her husband push briskly through the curtains.

Nat winked at her, she could have sworn it. Then he turned back to the children and the servants and said, his voice loud and fervent, "Let's raise a cheer for my lady St. Barbe, who has kept us all safe from harm amid great dangers. Hurrah!"

"Hurrah!" they yelled, and the noise crashed up to the rafters. Silence, stunned, her hands flying involuntarily to her ears, gazed at the servants who had never accepted her, who had resented her, who had thought of her as a foreigner and who now, it seemed, had unequivocally and wholeheartedly changed their minds. And she had an extraordinary feeling of kinship with them. Together they had endured so much and were all bound, children, servants, and mistress, by a shared comradeship that excluded anyone, such as her husband, who had not similarly suffered. Now, she realized, the boot was on the other foot. Before she had been the outsider. Now, after three years' absence, it was George.

She saw him, his face bewildered, staring at her as if some kind of monster had been changed for his wife, and knew that Nat had done this deliberately, so that her husband might have some small idea of what they, and she, had surmounted. And indeed, I am changed, she thought, altered for all time, though he does not know it yet. But he will discover soon that the meek little wife, so easily put down, so readily discouraged, no longer exists. And he must make the best of it, for I am no longer content to be thought of so little account.

She walked forward, thinking with love and anguish of Nick, and held out her hands.

"Welcome home, husband," she said coolly, and smiled.

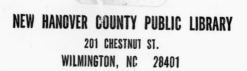